Caesar Ascending – Pandya

By R.W. Peake

Also by R.W Peake

Marching With Caesar® – Birth of the 10th
Marching With Caesar – Conquest of Gaul
Marching With Caesar – Civil War
Marching With Caesar – Antony and Cleopatra, Parts I & II
Marching With Caesar – Rise of Augustus
Marching With Caesar – Last Campaign
Marching With Caesar – Rebellion
Marching With Caesar – A New Era
Marching With Caesar – Pax Romana
Marching With Caesar – Fraternitas
Marching With Caesar – Vengeance
Marching With Caesar – Rise of Germanicus
Marching With Caesar – Revolt of the Legions
Marching With Caesar – Avenging Varus, Part I
Marching With Caesar – Avenging Varus Part II
Caesar Triumphant
Caesar Ascending – Invasion of Parthia
Caesar Ascending – Conquest of Parthia
Caesar Ascending – India

Critical praise for the Marching with Caesar series:

Marching With Caesar-Antony and Cleopatra: Part I-Antony
"Peake has become a master of depicting Roman military life and action, and in this latest novel he proves adept at evoking the subtleties of his characters, often with an understated humour and surprising pathos. Very highly recommended."

Marching With Caesar-Civil War
*"*Fans of the author will be delighted that Peake's writing has gone from strength to strength in this, the second volume...Peake manages to portray Pullus and all his fellow soldiers with a marvelous feeling of reality quite apart from the star historical name... There's history here, and character, and action enough for three novels, and all of it can be enjoyed even if readers haven't seen the first volume yet. Very highly recommended."*
~The Historical Novel Society

"The hinge of history pivoted on the career of Julius Caesar, as Rome's Republic became an Empire, but the muscle to swing that gateway came from soldiers like Titus Pullus. What an amazing story from a student now become the master of historical fiction at its best."
~Professor Frank Holt, University of Houston

Caesar Ascending – Pandya by R.W. Peake

Copyright © 2019 by R.W. Peake

All rights reserved. This book or any portion thereof may not be reproduced or used in any manner whatsoever without the express written permission of the publisher except for the use of brief quotations in a book review.

Cover by Laura Prevost

Cover Artwork Copyright © 2019 R. W. Peake
All Rights Reserved

Foreword

With this next chapter in the saga of *Caesar Ascending*, which has become something much bigger than I ever thought possible, I want to offer something of a warning to my readers. I'm often asked, "How do you write these stories? What's your process?" To which my honest answer has been, "I have no idea," which has been the best explanation I can offer; once I get immersed in a story, during the dark hours of the night while I toss and turn (I'm a very light sleeper, a habit that I picked up more than thirty years ago), my mind is busy at work, although I'm not aware of it. Then, when I get up the next morning, I sit down, and the continuation of the story that I apparently have been composing in my head comes pouring out. That has been the best explanation I can offer, until I read something a few months ago which makes sense to me. A literary critic was offering up his theory of the two types of writers, "planners" and "pantsers," and as I read, I realized that I am the latter, which I'll explain, and why it's germane to *Caesar Ascending-Pandya*.

"Planners" are those writers who, before they write a word of prose, map out their story, creating an outline and plot points. They know where their story is going, the roadblocks their characters are going to encounter, and the dramatic interaction between those characters.

I'm not one of those; I'm a "pantser," although I will say that in the original seven volumes of *Marching With Caesar*, I knew where my character, who I now refer to as Titus the Elder, would end up. However, as most long-time readers know, this alternate history series began as a "mad scientist experiment" on my blog, where I wondered, "If the Legions of Rome faced the samurai of Japan, who would win?"…and I ended up writing what will still be the end of the *Caesar Ascending* series, *Caesar Triumphant*, which means I knew how what would become this series would end. I just had no idea readers would be so interested in "What happened in those ten years before they get to Japan?" So, in that sense, I'm perhaps not a pure "pantser," as in someone who creates a story by the "seat of their pants," where they allow the story to take on a life of its own, and they simply follow where it takes them. In this article, the author mentioned George R.R. Martin as a "pantser," which is one reason why his fans are left waiting as one deadline after another passes by. I only became aware of Mr. Martin's work through the HBO series, and once I took a look at his actual works, my first thought was, "Whew! He's not the only one who writes really long books." Like him, albeit in a different genre, I prefer to allow a story to grow and progress organically, but behind that growth is my own particular method for growing it.

Which leads to my "warning" about *Caesar Ascending-Pandya*. When I return to this alternate world where Caesar lives and is doing his damnedest to outdo Alexander the Great, I do a whole lot of "What do you think might happen?" kind of thinking. And, as I thought about it, I realized that, along with the challenge of taking such a vast swathe of territory and the different cultures that come with it, there's the even greater challenge of holding it. Consequently, it made sense to me that, here in the third and fourth year of this ten-year saga, Caesar and his Legions would be confronted by a number of internal challenges that doesn't result in the kind of fighting my readers have come to expect from my stories, but they are no less of a threat, and in my conception, would be just as difficult, and crucial to overcome.

One struggle that readers might find somewhat surprising, and mundane, is how Caesar's Legions must struggle with acclimating to a radically different environment as they move south towards the Equator, which they didn't know existed. What they *would* know is that, compared to the arid heat of much of Parthia, the sub-tropical climate of India would pose a real challenge, and in this I'm speaking from experience. As most of my readers know, I was born, raised, and essentially spent fifty years in Houston, Texas, and as much as I love my hometown, I'm not stupid; I know that to most visitors from more temperate climes, it's a hellish mixture of heat and humidity, where the ambient temperature can be 72 degrees, but you're still sweating. Growing up in it as I did, it wasn't something I noticed; not once in my childhood do I remember thinking, "Wow, it's *way* too humid to go outside and play today." However, once I removed myself from that environment for a long enough period of time then returned to it, I realized just how harsh this kind of climate can be to the uninitiated. It saps the energy, you basically stay damp all the time, and you have to essentially pick your poison when it comes to strenuous activities outside; mornings the temperature is lower but the humidity significantly higher, while late in the day it's the opposite. Personally, I have more problem coping with damp heat than dry heat, and I have air conditioning and modern fabrics that help alleviate the conditions, neither of which Titus and his comrades would have.

So, I thought, what would it be like for men who had just spent two years in an equally hot environment but one that was significantly less humid? The first thing that came to mind was how I would have responded if the only clothing I had was made of wool, and how I'd be willing to try any other kind of fabric, because I can't think of anything worse than being stuck wearing something that actually traps your body heat and takes a long time to dry out. And, as my ever-alert editor, Beth Lynne pointed out, one reason that people in hotter climes tend to favor spicier food isn't just because they have a fixation on sticking a flamethrower in their mouth, but that it induces sweating, which is our system's way of cooling the body. Trying to imagine how much of a challenge it would be to compensate for this radical change in environment is an example of how I try to immerse myself in this world as I think, "What would I do if I was in command?" These are all of the things that a man like Gaius Julius Caesar, and the men who march for him, would have to confront, and overcome if they're to be successful in achieving their goal, whatever that may be.

In closing, I'd like to thank Beth Lynne; at some point, I know it sounds trite and repetitive, but I can't express what a great job she does putting up with my obsessive behavior on things like what I described above, and how she "gets" me in my role as a teller of stories. And, to Laura Prevost, thanks for another great cover that I think conveys the exotic nature of this new land of India in which Titus and his comrades find themselves.

Semper Fidelis,

R.W. Peake

September, 2019

Historical Notes

As I explained in *Caesar Ascending-India*, while I try to ground all of my work, even this alternate history series, in the historical record as much as I can, this foray by Caesar and his Legions into India has taken me into some uncharted territory. If anything, what this exercise has shown me is how little I know about ancient India, particularly the era of the First Century BCE, and unfortunately, there isn't a whole lot of detailed historical record to go on. As a result, as I did with Abhiraka, King of Bharuch, who was in fact one of those men known as a Western Satrap, I took a real figure from history, Puddapandyan and the first King of Pandya, uprooted him, and moved him about a century earlier. Which, in turn, means that the development of what would become the Pandyan Empire is already well underway in this story. And, as I did in the previous book, for this I ask my readers' forgiveness; since I never imagined that I would be filling in the ten years prior to *Caesar Triumphant*, I freely admit that I was a bit cavalier in using some of the cultures and kingdoms that Caesar and his Legions would encounter as I mapped his imaginary progress across the vastness of Asia.

With that out of the way, the cities and towns that Titus Pullus and his fellow Legionaries will encounter are all real, although in all but one case, the names have changed over the millennia. The city of Muziris existed, although today it's called Kodungallar, which is located at 10.233761°N 76.194634°E, while the ancient city was apparently closer to the shoreline. It was an important trading post, situated on the confluence of the Periyar River and the Arabian Sea, and the Greek name, Pseudostoma, is an apt description even today. Using Google

Earth, one can see the opening that is barely two hundred yards across, while the actual entrance to the river is some eighteen miles south, and is more than a quarter-mile across. When I first examined this area as I was in the process of deciding exactly where a general like Caesar would want to conduct an amphibious assault, I was certain that this had to be a manmade canal that paralleled the coast north for eighteen miles, until I referred to the incomparable Barrington Atlas, and saw the ancient name, which literally means "False Mouth," so despite undoubtedly being improved over the centuries, this unique condition is a natural occurrence.

Of the other towns that play a role, Kalliena and Honnavar, they both exist today, and while the former is now known as Kalyan, the latter Honnavar has been known by that name for more than two thousand years. My description of the conditions at Honnavar, specifically the mouth into what appears to be a natural harbor created by the Sharavati River that's protected by a sandbar is based on Google Earth, but I am working off the assumption that the conditions are essentially unchanged.

The city of Karoura is something of a riddle, not whether it existed, but where it was located. Every online reference I could find to the ancient city places it at modern-day Karur, which is located at 10.95°N 78.08°E; however, the Barrington Atlas places Karoura much closer to the coast, and located on the Periyar/Pseudostoma River, at the base of the Western Ghat Mountains, and I chose to use the Barrington location.

As far as the makeup of the Pandyan army, this proved to be one of the most difficult aspects of trying to keep this story even somewhat authentic. Specifically, there is very little primary source material about the Pandyan "grunt" who would be facing Titus and his Legionaries, but from what I could glean, their "armor" essentially consisted of using leather in the wrapping of their turbans, a spear and a wicker shield. As I mentioned in the Foreword, having grown up in what has the distinction of being the most air-conditioned city in the world in Houston, the idea of wearing heavy chainmail or a cuirass is not appealing in the least. However, I just couldn't bring myself to depict the Pandyans as not wearing any kind of protective armor, so I have them wearing leather lamellar armor. We also know that the northern part of Indian, down to Bharuch, was more heavily under Greek influence, while southern India relied on elephants and missile troops, with their infantry being not much more than fodder. While Bharuch was an amalgam of two cultures, the Pandya I have created is almost purely southern Indian, presenting Caesar and his Legions with a decidedly different tactical problem than the Parthians and the Indo-Greeks.

Finally, this is as much a cultural note as a historical one, and it concerns something that I actually encountered in my previous life working in the software industry, during a time when we began moving our development efforts "offshore" to India. It was during our first meeting with executives from the company we would be contracting with that I noticed something that I considered odd, because they seemed to be having the exact opposite reaction to our conversation than one would expect, at least from a Western perspective. After all, why would someone respond to, "We're very excited to work with your company" by shaking their heads? And, why would they be nodding their heads when we said, "But the rate you're asking for is too high"? Thanks to the patience and understanding of a gentleman named Vimaldeep Singh, with whom I developed a good relationship during this process, I learned a valuable lesson, that not all of our gestures are universal, that in some places, nodding one's head is the exact opposite of what we in the West have come to learn is a signal of acceptance. Now, I have no idea whether those customs were in place back then, but since this is my "world," I decided to use it, as a reminder as much to myself as to my readers that the manner in which we communicate is as widely varied and different as human beings themselves. Sometimes, you have to actually have a conversation to find that common ground.

Table of Contents

Chapter 1 2

Chapter 2 44

Chapter 3 93

Chapter 4 132

Chapter 5 194

Chapter 6 236

Chapter 7 287

Chapter 8 331

Chapter 9 371

Chapter 10 419

Chapter 11 468

Chapter 12 504

Chapter 1

"I never thought I would say this," Quintus Balbus muttered, then paused long enough to wipe the sweat dripping from his face with a rag that was already close to sodden, "but I'd rather be in fucking Parthia than this *ca*hole."

This elicited a humorless laugh from the man sitting across from him, who reminded Balbus, "You said that yesterday."

"And," the third member of the party added, "the day before that."

"So?" Balbus shot back defensively. "It doesn't make it any less true."

This, Titus Pullus understood, was nothing more than the simple truth, and he was every bit as miserable as his Primus Pilus Posterior; he was also aware that Sextus Scribonius, his Secundus Pilus Prior and the man sitting next to the other two at the table, felt the same way.

"Even when there's a breeze, it doesn't really help all that much," Scribonius complained. Then he plucked at his soldier's tunic as he admitted, "Although now that we're wearing cotton instead of wool, it's more bearable."

Despite his general discontent, even Balbus couldn't argue this point, and as miserable as not just weather conditions were here in Bharuch but the overall situation with Caesar's army, switching out the type of fabric worn by the Legions had been a gift from the gods. Otherwise, things, while not quite as dire as they had been, were still somewhat unsettled. On this late afternoon in the month the Romans called December, the three men were sitting on a veranda, open on four sides but with an ornate roof that extended to the building that served as Pullus' quarters, watching the afternoon rain coming down while drinking what had become their beverage of choice, which the natives called *sura*. Not, it should be said, that it was a natural transition for Romans to make, going from wine made from the grape, with perhaps a few spices thrown in, to this concoction of rice, wheat, some grapes, and what the locals referred to as "sugar," a cane-like plant that grew in abundance in the lands on the far side of the Ganges, and was one of the several major imports of Bharuch. However, when the *amphorae* of wine ran out, and given that there was no resupply coming from Parthia for the foreseeable future, it was not long before the conquerors turned to this drink. As they had learned the first few days after the city had fallen, it was incredibly potent, far more so than wine, but that was only partially responsible for what had taken place during the attack on the city. Through a process of trial and error, each of them had discovered what their particular limit with *sura* was, so on this day, they were being judicious with the beverage, especially since Diocles was watching them keenly. Somewhat to the Greek's surprise, it wasn't Balbus who he had to moderate most closely, despite the Centurion's well-deserved reputation for debauchery. Instead, it was his master, which wasn't really the proper term since the relationship between Pullus and Diocles could hardly be described as a master and slave, who had proven to have developed a taste for the beverage, to the point where he had wrought a fair amount of havoc when in its grips.

This afternoon, however, Pullus seemed content to sip as he stared moodily out across the expanse of the palace compound, and while Diocles, as well as Scribonius and Balbus understood why their Primus Pilus' eyes lingered on the large building that was the royal palace, they were all wise enough not to mention it. As they all knew, what held Pullus' interest wasn't the building, but what it contained; actually, Diocles reminded himself, it's *who* it contains that's the key here. Under different circumstances, the Greek would have been thrilled that Pullus had found happiness after suffering the loss of his wife Gisela and their two children in a plague that struck Brundisium during the African campaign of Caesar's civil war against the forces of Gnaeus Pompeius. But this? This was doomed, Diocles was certain of it, and the few times he had held whispered discussions with Scribonius and Balbus, the only other two Romans who were aware of what was happening, they shared his sentiment. Nevertheless, on another level, Diocles thought that there was a deep level of poetic justice in the idea that the Queen of Bharuch had been seduced by a Roman, and his name was not Gaius Julius Caesar.

Unknown to the three Romans and one Greek, Queen Hyppolita was standing just inside the double doors that led out onto the balcony of her chambers, staring in the opposite direction of Titus Pullus. If she had been informed that her thoughts and his were running along identical lines, she wouldn't have been able to decide whether to laugh or cry. Like so many things, she thought, it had begun with, if not noble, then at least intentions that had been in the best interest of her kingdom, and her husband, Abhiraka, first of his name and the King of Bharuch. Once it became obvious that the city would fall, something that Abhiraka, his queen, and every subject of

Bharuch would have sworn was impossible, and even more devastatingly, that Bharuch's corps of armored elephants were not invincible, Hyppolita had devoted herself, first to enabling her husband's escape, then to doing whatever she could to undermine the rule of their new conquerors. Her effort had begun even as the city was falling, amid immense slaughter by this foreign army that she had almost immediately deduced wasn't nearly as under the control of their general as he let on when he strode up to her standing on the portico of the palace. She had never been more frightened in her life, yet even in her fear, she had been intrigued by the Roman named Caesar, if only because his Greek was so flawless, and his manner had been, while firm, still very courteous. At the time, she had certainly noticed the truly huge Roman who accompanied him but had dismissed him as nothing more than a muscular, huge brute who was clearly very fierce, and judging by his scars, an experienced and fearsome warrior. Still, most of her attention had been on Caesar, as she both did her best to delay him as her husband, along with his two most trusted bodyguards, were using a secret passage to escape the city, and to get a better sense of this Roman. She certainly had heard of him; there wasn't anyone in their world who hadn't heard of Gaius Julius Caesar by this point, especially after conquering the entirety of the Parthian kingdom in the space of two years. And, despite the gossip among her ladies, and the fears of the common people of Bharuch, she didn't believe he was the bloodthirsty monster he had been made out to be. That, however, had been before all that transpired within the walls of the city had taken place, when she had been forced to watch helplessly as so many of her husband's subjects were despoiled, savagely beaten, or slaughtered. She had been disbelieving at first, but during the days immediately following the fall of the city, she had become convinced that the sacking and rapine that had taken place had not only not been at Caesar's command, it had been against his express orders.

Before a week had passed, she had determined that Caesar's control of the army was one in name only, that for reasons it took her quite some time to learn, the Legions under Caesar's command were disaffected and, for all intents and purposes, in a state of mutiny. For the next month, Hyppolita and her ladies, along with the skeleton staff of attendants Caesar had allowed her to keep, had been prisoners in everything but name, yet despite this, she had managed to glean more information, which confirmed the tenuous hold Caesar had over his men. Not, she thought with some amusement, that Caesar was present to confirm this; it had taken a few days after the event, but Hyppolita had learned that, just three days after the fall of Bharuch, Caesar had departed, not in pursuit of her husband, but back to Parthia. And, if her information was correct, he had taken just enough of the massive fleet that had carried the Roman army with a speed that was, simply put, astonishing, that even if the men of the Legions had wanted to leave, they were unable to do so. In effect, Caesar had stranded his men in the middle of a foreign and hostile land. He didn't leave without issuing some orders, and one of those had been that the responsibility for both her continuing captivity and security rested on the broad shoulders of the Roman she had learned was the chief Centurion of one of Caesar's Legions, of which there were eleven now present in Bharuch. She had never been told why the Roman she had learned was named Titus Pullus and the men of his Legion were the only ones assigned this duty, but she had deduced that, for whatever reason, Caesar trusted this giant Legionary. Not that she had; now, months later, she could smile at the memory of what had been an extremely tense and trying time for her personally, as she became accustomed to the presence of stone-faced Romans placed at strategic points around the palace, always in pairs, but never speaking, although she certainly felt their eyes on her as she and her ladies went about their daily routine.

In some ways, she thought sadly, being held so closely in the palace was a blessing, especially in the days immediately after the fall of the city, because it largely insulated her from what she knew was a level of suffering and anguish that none of her subjects had ever experienced. Naturally for this time, there had been wars before; her husband was an ambitious man, so that in the twenty years of his reign, he had managed to substantially enlarge the kingdom, and inevitably, there had been households within Bharuch that had suffered losses as a result of those wars. Never before, however, had the city's occupants had to worry about an army outside its walls; the last time that had happened had occurred seventy-five years earlier, with Abhiraka's grandfather, who founded what was now known as the kingdom of Bharuch, and he had been the invader, so any of the original inhabitants of the city, many of them Macedonian stock, who were still alive had been very young and had no memory of that time. Of course, Hyppolita had been aware that both Greeks and Romans called this city Bargosa, and there had been a Greek presence for centuries, even before the Macedonian king Alexander's arrival. She herself was something of an amalgam between the people her new conquerors called the Indo-Scythians and Greek, having been named for the demigoddess who was Queen of the Amazons, and had grown up speaking that tongue. And, while she had learned to speak the native language of her husband's subjects and was fluent in it, she was still more comfortable conversing with her ladies in Greek. Which, she reminded herself, served as an important lesson in never underestimating one's enemy, and despite her seeming acceptance of Roman rule, she never forgot that they were her enemy; with one exception, and her thoughts were on that exception as she stood just out of sight in her palace, staring across the grounds to the buildings near the far wall of the royal enclosure, where she could see three men seated at a table on the attached veranda of one of the buildings, while one she knew was Pullus' servant stood off to the side. He's at least easy to pick out of a group of them, she thought with some amusement, but as quickly as that humorous aspect came, it was swept away by the darker, guiltier sensations that came from the predicament in which she found herself. And it had all started because he had surprised her one day, perhaps twenty days after Caesar's disappearance, suddenly arriving to inspect the Romans who he had posted as guards. By this point, she had learned the futility of fighting the Romans on their heavy-handed attempt to keep her safe from their countrymen who were still rebelling, something that she refused to acknowledge any appreciation for, despite her implicit understanding that it was absolutely necessary. Not a day had gone by after the fall of Bharuch where she didn't hear some sort of major disturbance out in the city, along with columns of smoke occasionally, although it was never as bad as it had been for the five days after the city fell. During that period of time, she could stand outside on the continuous porch that ran along the second floor of the palace on any side and she would have seen signs that buildings were burning. What was most frustrating about her captivity was not the inability to go anywhere she pleased, but in the sense of isolation, and how little she knew of the larger situation. This didn't mean she couldn't surmise certain things, and she had correctly guessed that the Romans of the Legions had, for whatever reason, decided they were done obeying the commands of Gaius Julius Caesar.

That hadn't been the topic of conversation between her and one of her ladies when, as had become his habit, the giant Pullus had suddenly appeared to inspect his men, prompting the lady, Darshwana, to remark, in Greek, as he passed by, "I must say, my Lady, these barbarians don't stink as much as I expected."

"That's true," Hyppolita granted, her eyes on Pullus as he crossed the room in front of her, his face betraying no sign that he understood a word they were saying, something that she and her ladies had assumed to be the case before this moment. "I wonder why? Although," she added in an afterthought, "they do smell a bit like olives."

"Maybe they bathe in olive oil," her lady suggested, jokingly of course, and it did cause Hyppolita to chuckle in a most unqueenly manner.

They stopped talking to watch as the Roman Centurion spoke softly to the pair of guards who were positioned in front of the large double doors that led out onto the southern porch that overlooked the large palace compound that, at this moment in time less than a month after the fall of the city, was still almost filled with the square tents of the conquerors. Since they spoke in Latin, it was impossible for Hyppolita to understand, even if Pullus had been speaking loudly enough for her to hear. She pretended to be interested in the scroll she was holding, a series of satirical epigrams by Meleager that had been a state gift from one of the kingdoms to the north, although she couldn't remember which one. Her eyes, however, kept wandering back to the Roman Pullus, who had just finished and was moving back across the room. She was not wearing her veil; in the beginning, she had made sure to cover herself at all times, but it had proven to be too wearisome and she had given up using it, something that she was regretting right this moment. Just as he was passing in front of her couch, their eyes met when she could no longer keep her eyes on the scroll, and to her horror, she felt her face burn as she flushed, but oddly, she felt a stab of anger when his own expression didn't flicker, nor did he even acknowledge her. *If he knew that I could order a subject of Bharuch executed for daring to look me in the face*, she thought with a level of irritation that surprised her, *I wonder if he'd be so arrogant. Not that she ever had, but she could.*

It was when Pullus reached the door, and actually had his hand on the latch that he turned his head to look over his shoulder, and for the first time, he addressed Hyppolita, although it was ostensibly aimed at her lady, speaking in accented but otherwise perfect Greek, "Actually, we don't bathe in olive oil. We use it for after we've bathed. Maybe," he added, and once she knew Pullus better, she would recognize the humorous glint in his eye, "you should try it yourself."

Then, he was gone, shutting the door to leave an astonished and extremely discomfited queen behind. Thus had begun what, even now these months later, Hyppolita was still struggling to define, and more importantly, what it meant for her, both as a married queen, and as a woman. That Titus Pullus was, at that moment, struggling with the same feelings wouldn't have made her feel any better.

With Caesar's sudden departure, it had fallen to Asinius Pollio and Aulus Hirtius to cope with the turmoil and unrest created by nine very angry Legions. Only the 25th and 30th weren't disaffected, although that was only because they were the latest arrivals to Caesar's army, but both Legates understood that this was likely a temporary condition. Certainly, much of the discontent was based in the fact that the men of Caesar's army had been under the impression that Caesar's goal had been the subjugation of Parthia, which had been accomplished. Regardless, both commanders were in agreement that even more than the fact that they were in their third year, it was where they were that was the substantive issue for the men. And, if either of them had been asked privately, both Pollio and Hirtius would have expressed, if not outright agreement with the men, at least strong sympathy. India had quickly proven to be a miserable place, especially for men who had become somewhat acclimated to the dry heat of Parthia. Their first real conquest in India, of the city and kingdom of Pattala hadn't been a true indicator of what the Romans could expect since, because of its location up the Indus, it was more like Parthia than the vast land mass to the south. It was on the move south, with half the army marching under Pollio's command, while the other half sailed with Caesar, that they were subjected to the brutal conditions that, as they quickly learned, was the climate of India. Between the regular rain showers and the general dampness of the air, it created conditions that few if any of the men who marched under the eagles of Rome had ever encountered, at least to this degree. Nothing ever dried out; the leather *caligae* worn by the men that was so vital to their ability to move rapidly stretched out because they were always wet. Worse, the tunics of the men proved to be completely incompatible with the environment, both because they were made of wool and they absorbed the moisture from sweat and the regular rain to a degree where they remained sodden. If that had been the only challenge facing Pollio and Hirtius' part of the army, it would have been bad enough, but the march south to Bharuch had been across a stretch of completely flat terrain that, to the eye, appeared to be a plain but was in fact a morass, the ground soaking up just enough of the moisture that it gave the appearance of solid ground when it was anything but. And that had been before Pollio's infantry and Hirtius' cavalry had been the first of the Roman army under Caesar to confront the justifiably feared armored elephants.

Only because of the quick thinking on the part of the crusty Primus Pilus of the 5th Alaudae, Vibius Batius, was a crushing defeat averted, when he had broken out the jars of the flammable material naphtha, which the Romans had encountered during the first year of the Parthian campaign, turning what had been the most terrifying weapon the Romans had faced to this point into huge, flaming torches. It had been a victory, but a terribly costly one, and both of the senior Legates understood that it wasn't just the climate and terrain the men hated. Bharuch had been the first of the Indian kingdoms Caesar's Legions had confronted to use these huge beasts, but it was accepted as fact, both by men and officers, that they wouldn't be the last. Caesar's sudden decision to leave the army had only delayed a reckoning, and while the men had settled into a state of semi-obedience, all of the officers, from the Legate level down to the Optios, believed that this was due as much to the recognition that they were stranded as to the idea they owed their allegiance to their commander. It had been a cunning move on Caesar's part; by taking most of the fleet, he had forced the men to confront the reality that, if they truly wanted to return home, their general had taken the means for them to do so. Slowly, over a period of about a month, tensions were reduced to the point that the officers no longer feared moving among their men alone, and it was during this period that Pollio had developed a belief, which he had broached with the Primi Pili of the Legions at a meeting.

"Do you think that the men are just too miserable to stay angry?"

Even as he said it, Pollio understood how absurd it seemed on the face of it; the fact that not one of the senior Centurions even smiled at this gave him a hint that he was not far off the mark.

"I know that they've been waiting for it to cool off," Sextus Spurius, the Primus Pilus of the 3rd Legion commented, "but from what we're being told by the people here, this is how it is all the time."

"I've heard the same thing," Torquatus of the 25th agreed. "All I know is that I'm just as fucking sick of it as my boys are."

"We need to learn from the natives here. We need to find out how they cope with it so much better than we do."

As usually happened, when Pullus spoke, the others all paid attention, but despite his reputation and acknowledged prowess, Primi Pili were competitive men by nature, and there was one in particular who, when he replied, nobody was all that surprised that it would be contentious.

"They cope with it because they were born here, Pullus." Gnaeus Clustuminus of the 8th laughed as he said this. "Unless you're a sorcerer of some sort and can go back in time and move us all here so that we could grow up in this *cac*, I don't see much to learn from these barbarians."

Pullus was very aware of Clustuminus' hostility, and he knew where it came from, but the fact was that he didn't hold much respect for the man to begin with, which was why he countered in a bored voice, "Just like we had nothing to learn from the Parthians about how to use naphtha, Clustuminus?"

Pollio intervened, seeing the 8th's Primus Pilus' face flush and not wanting to indulge in this sort of thing—there was enough of that going around in the ranks—so he asked Pullus, "Is there something specific you're thinking about, Pullus?"

"No," Pullus was forced to admit, unhappy that Pollio, in his attempt to quash this squabble, had inadvertently helped Clustuminus, who snorted in disgust, which Pullus ignored. "Not anything specific. Although," he frowned, "I have noticed that their clothing seems to be lighter than ours. Or," he pointed out, "at least they don't walk around looking like they just stepped out of a river."

As soon as Pullus said it, Pollio realized that it was true; while they had not interacted that closely with the citizens of Bharuch, the minimal contact he had had with the surviving members of the royal administration as they reorganized confirmed that Pullus' statement was true. The men seemed much more comfortable, and while, however barbed, Clustuminus' observation about them having been born and lived their lives in this climate certainly accounted for some of it, he was equally certain there was more to it.

This was what moved him to tell Pullus, "See what you can find out, Pullus."

While he would never admit it, Titus Pullus' suggestion hadn't been without an ulterior motive. Who better to ask than the Queen of Bharuch?

Despite being completely unaware of his meeting with Asinius Pollio, Hyppolita immediately sensed there was something different about Titus Pullus when he made his regular appearance at the palace the next day. By the Roman calendar, it was now the Ides of September, about six weeks after the fall of Bharuch, and somewhat unusually, the day was actually mild, but that didn't mean that Pullus' face didn't shine with sweat. There wasn't anything overtly different in his behavior; he made his usual awkward bow in her direction, yet as always, he didn't actually look at her when he did it, then he strode over to the pair of guards who were within her range of sight, standing just inside the doors to the south porch. Then, as he always did, he left the main room to go to the other stations where he had placed his men before returning to check on the pair of his men who stood in the same spot as their comrades on the northern side, but rather than cross the room and leave by the door through which he entered, he came to an abrupt stop, directly in front of the queen. This day, she had been involved in an embroidery project with three of her ladies, all of whom had followed her example by eschewing the veil and head covering. It was the only change, however; Hyppolita and her ladies were all wearing the voluminous robes that hid their shapes, but it wasn't until much later that she learned it was actually those robes that gave Titus Pullus the opening he needed.

Somewhat ironically, this was one of the few times Hyppolita wasn't pretending to ignore the Roman, because she had become absorbed in a section of stitching that was quite elaborate, and her head was bowed in total concentration. She was also unaware that this gave Pullus the opportunity to really examine her without being observed doing so. It wasn't a terribly long span of time, but it was enough for Pullus to become even more smitten than he had been when he hadn't even glimpsed her face, although he couldn't have explained why this was the case, even if he had been disposed to do so. She had hair the color of a raven's wing, which was long but bound up in what he assumed was the fashion for queens, although Cleopatra was the only other example of such a personage he had ever met, yet while the Egyptian queen had her own allure, it wasn't with her physical appearance. Yet, for a reason he couldn't explain, Pullus sensed a similarity between the two, which reminded him of the extraordinary conversation that he had been a mute witness to between Hyppolita and Caesar, when she had alluded to a kinship between herself and Cleopatra. And, given their shared Macedonian heritage, Pullus thought it was certainly possible. Her features were of a pleasing proportion; an aquiline nose that wasn't quite as prominent as a Roman's, with a wide mouth and full lips, but it was her eyes that Pullus found most arresting; as she concentrated on her work, her brow furrowed and eyes narrowed as she jabbed her needle through the fabric that served as the basis for whatever it was this would become.

Finally, he cleared his throat, which startled her to the point where she accidentally jabbed her finger with her needle, prompting a yelp of pain, followed by Pullus muttering, "Pluto's cock." Fortunately, he had uttered the expletive in Latin, but this didn't seem to matter much as Hyppolita scowled up at him as the lady sitting to her right immediately took the queen's finger and stuck it into her own mouth. The manner in which she did so, and the way that the queen behaved as if this was a perfectly ordinary thing told Pullus that it, in fact, was what passed for normal.

"Yes, Centurion Pullus?" Hyppolita demanded, clearly irritated, making Pullus wonder if she was so delicate that jabbing herself with a needle amounted to a near-mortal wound.

Somehow, he managed to sound respectful, and he actually thought to bow again, albeit just as awkwardly as always as he asked, "Queen Hyppolita, er, Your Highness. I was wondering if I might have a word with you?"

Hyppolita was still irritated, yet she was also intrigued, but she kept her tone cool as she countered, "It depends on what it is you wish to discuss, Centurion."

Pullus blinked in surprise; it had never occurred to him that she might refuse, and while this wasn't an outright rejection, she was making it clear that her agreement was conditional.

"Oh. I see." It was all he could think to say in the moment, and he was obviously so flustered that, despite herself, Hyppolita felt her ire dissolving.

"So," she asked in a softer tone, "what is it you wish to discuss, Centurion?"

Titus Pullus, despite lacking a formal education, was an extremely intelligent man, although he was nowhere near the intellect of Caesar or Scribonius, but what he lacked was any ability to be diplomatic, or even subtle, which was why he blurted out, "How can you and your people survive in such a miserable *cac*hole? Does it ever cool off?"

While Hyppolita had never heard the term for feces in Latin, she shrewdly guessed that, whatever "*cac*" was, it wasn't a compliment.

Nevertheless, she was now more amused than irritated, and she replied lightly, "Why, Centurion, I think that being born here has quite a bit to do with it."

She was completely unprepared for Pullus' reaction, which was to groan and mutter what might have been another Latin curse, and she decided that she would have to learn what "Clustuminus" meant.

"I mean," Pullus managed to continue, trying to regain some of his composure, "aside from that. Yes, I can see that is a large part, maybe the biggest part, but..." Suddenly, he was inspired to ask, "...were *you* born here, Highness?"

Of all the things she had been expecting, this was the last on the list, and she suddenly felt shy, even as a part of her wondered why; it wasn't like he was asking anything truly personal.

"No," she admitted, after a pause. "I was actually born in Sagala, but I have been here in Bharuch for more than twenty years now."

"Was your birthplace like this, as far as the climate?" Pullus asked.

This elicited a small laugh from her, and she now realized why Pullus was asking, so she replied, "Goodness no, Centurion. It was much, much drier than here. And," she thought back to that time, when she had been barely a woman, fourteen years old and frightened out of her mind as her father sent her to the man who would be her husband, "I confess I was miserable for the first several months. Although," she added with a lightness that, despite not knowing her all that well, Pullus could tell hid a deeper emotion, "only part of my discontent was from the climate. But," she allowed, "yes, much of it had to do with the weather, both the heat and the way it always feels wet, even when it's not raining."

"Yes!" For the first time, Pullus showed an emotion, nodding emphatically, and actually smiling slightly. "That's what I'm talking about! We Romans aren't used to this kind of thing at all. And," he continued, "the last two years we spent in Parthia were hard, but we at least never walked around feeling like we were in a *caldarium*, soaked in sweat. It's so dry there that sweat evaporates so quickly, you don't even notice. Although," he said ruefully, "that poses its own problems."

While the queen was interested in everything Pullus was saying, her mind latched on to the unfamiliar Latin word, and she asked, "You said a...*caldarium*? I am unfamiliar with this word. What does it mean?"

It was as Pullus was explaining the Roman system of bathing, and how the *caldarium* was a tiny room where the combination of high temperature and steam served to induce sweating that Hyppolita suddenly felt as if she was being rude, and she signaled to one of the ladies, who hopped up and brought a chair. This clearly embarrassed the Roman, but he did sit down, and Hyppolita heard the distinct cracking sound created by the immense weight.

"Centurion, I do not wish to alarm you, but that chair happens to be over one hundred years old and, as I understand it, was a gift from a descendant of one of Alexander's generals. I hope," she said this with a smile, "that it will be safe from Rome."

While he reddened slightly, Pullus didn't appear offended, and he actually grinned at her as he replied, "It wouldn't be the first chair I've crushed, Your Highness. But if I do, at least you'll have a good story to tell of how a Roman was brought low by a chair."

As he had hoped, this amused her, and she laughed, as did her ladies, which pleased Pullus, but he knew he was lying to himself, that it was only because he wanted her in a pliable mood to give him the information for which he had come.

Once the laughter died, he continued his description of how the Roman baths worked, but when he was finished, Hyppolita asked, "But how do you do this when you are on, what do you call it, campaign? Or," she indicated the area outside the palace with her hand, "someplace that does not have this system that you just described?"

"Then all we do is use oil and scraping, with a strigil," he explained, then gave her another grin. "You know, instead of taking a bath in it."

It was Hyppolita's turn to feel her face flush, but somewhat to her surprise, she wasn't angered, sensing that Pullus was teasing her in a good-natured manner.

"What is a strigil?"

Pullus turned to the lady who asked, and it was only because he'd never really examined her before that he was surprised to see how beautiful she was, but what surprised him more was how she didn't avert her eyes at his gaze, staring back at him with a directness that was unusual in a female, no matter where they were from.

"What is your name, Lady?" he asked, but before she could reply, it was Hyppolita who answered firmly, "Her name is Amodini, and please forgive her, Centurion. She forgets her place sometimes."

Pullus was surprised at the sharpness in the queen's tone, but he instantly saw that it was the same for Amodini, who looked as if she had been slapped, although she immediately averted her eyes. As shocked as the pair was, it was nothing compared to the feeling Hyppolita experienced; she had never spoken to Amodini, or any of her ladies, so sharply before, at least in front of others. And while it was true that Amodini was the most flirtatious of her ladies, particularly with the officers of her husband the king's army, Hyppolita had always indulged her, and in fact encouraged it, albeit as a means to an end, knowing as she did how men loved to show females how important they were, and their normal method of doing that was by divulging all manner of useful information. It had always been a profitable relationship, and of all the men from whom important information could be gleaned, this huge Roman would be a perfect candidate. So, she thought miserably, why did I chastise her like that?

"Your Highness, may I answer Lady Amodini's question?"

With a start, Hyppolita returned her attention to Pullus, but while he didn't say as much, she was certain that this was the second time he had asked the question.

"Yes, of course," she answered hastily.

He proceeded to describe it, then quickly gave up, saying instead, "Tomorrow I'll bring one to show you."

There was an awkward silence then, and more out of a need to fill it than anything, Hyppolita said, "Back to your original question, Centurion. Now that I have thought about it, I do think I have some suggestions. The question I have is," she cocked her head, and her tone turned audibly cooler, "why would I want to make you and your men more comfortable as they're occupying our city and our kingdom?"

It was, Pullus understood, a fair question, and one he had dreaded she would ask, yet despite his discomfort, he felt compelled to give her a direct gaze as he answered without hesitation, "Because we're not going anywhere, Your Highness. At least," he allowed, "not for the next few months."

"You assume that my husband the king will not be marching at the head of an army to remove you from our land," Hyppolita shot back, her cheeks coloring as her anger began to war with her self-control.

For the first time in his life, Titus Pullus responded not as a Centurion of Rome's most victorious army, an army that had never been defeated, snapping that if her husband was foolish enough to do so, he wouldn't escape this time, but as a diplomat.

"If the gods will it, Your Highness," the words sounded foreign to his ears, particularly the calm manner in which he was speaking them, "then that will be our fate. But," he said gently, "until that day comes, you're stuck with us, neh? And miserable men are dangerous men, wouldn't you agree?"

Hyppolita's jaw was clenched so tightly that it took a conscious effort to relax the muscles so that she could say, however tersely, "Yes, I would agree with that."

They stared at each other then, for a long span of time, one in

15

which the other ladies scarcely breathed, none of them wanting to draw attention to themselves and suffer Amodini's fate.

Finally, Pullus broke the silence by asking, "If I agreed to some…concessions regarding your confinement, would you be willing to give me some ideas?"

"What kind of concessions?" she asked warily.

"I can only imagine how it must feel to be cooped up in this palace," Pullus replied. "What if I offered you the ability to leave the palace? Not," he held up a hand to forestall any unrealistic ideas, "outside the compound, but at least the freedom of walking outside?"

It took an effort for Hyppolita to keep her expression impassive, but she was worried that her heart was suddenly beating so rapidly that it might be apparent through the fabric of her robe.

Somehow, she managed to sound almost disinterested when she countered, "When you say the freedom of walking outside, am I correct in assuming that I would be free to do so without being guarded?"

"No," Pullus answered immediately and firmly. "That won't be possible. You'll have an escort, of course."

"Guards," she shot back, the anger returning. "Please do not insult me with calling them an escort."

Pullus was growing desperate; he had sincerely believed she would jump at the chance to get out of this palace. Granted, it was large and spacious, but it was still a building, and there were only so many things one could do within its confines.

"What if," he ventured, "it was only one man? And he'd allow you and your ladies to move about the compound, with the only condition that you stay within his sight?"

Hyppolita considered this, then she impulsively answered, "This is acceptable, but on one condition."

Only Pullus would know how much effort it took to keep him from bellowing in frustration, but he was completely unprepared for her answer when he finally asked, "What is this condition?"

"That you are our escort," she replied immediately. Pullus' mouth dropped open, but before he could say anything, she hurried on, "You are the only Roman with whom I am familiar. And," she hesitated, "while I do not trust you completely, you have behaved honorably to this point." Hyppolita hadn't said this to flatter Pullus, but she saw that this pleased him, although he managed to sound grudging as he accepted her terms. With this settled, Hyppolita said, "Now, I have noticed one thing that I believe might help make you and your men more comfortable." When Pullus said nothing, she added gently, "Did you bring something to write on, Centurion? You are probably going to want to write this down."

"Ah, er...yes. Right," Pullus mumbled, then pulled the leather satchel he had slung over his shoulder around to extract a wax tablet, taking up the stylus that, to Hyppolita, looked almost comically small in his huge hand. Ready, he said, "Please, go ahead, Your Highness. And...thank you for this."

By the time Hyppolita was through, Pullus had been forced to withdraw another tablet, and from his perspective, he was more enamored with the Bharuch queen than he had been; he was blissfully unaware that she was, at the very least, confused about the feelings she was experiencing.

"Why would we do that?" Hirtius asked Pullus. Then, realizing he needed to clarify, he explained, "I'm talking about paying for the fabric and the labor to make the tunics." He shrugged, adding, "We can just make them do it and save the money."

Fortunately, Pullus didn't have to respond, because it was Pollio who answered, "And we'd have a populace that's simmering with more discontent than it already is. It's true that they're calm right now, but that's only because our men ran wild and slaughtered more than a tenth part of the city." Shaking his head, he said, "No, I agree with Pullus. I think he did the right thing to offer this concession. Although," he sighed, "it would make it easier if their treasury hadn't been cleaned out."

This startled Pullus, who exclaimed, "Surely we're not running out of money! Pattala's treasury was stuffed full! Send to Ventidius for more bullion if we need it."

The Primus Pilus, who was the only man of Centurion rank present at this meeting, caught the look that Pollio exchanged with Hirtius, the latter suddenly more interested in his cup than the conversation.

"What?" Pullus asked warily. "What aren't you telling me?"

Pollio shifted uncomfortably, but he didn't hesitate, saying, "Before I tell you, I want your word as a Primus Pilus that you won't share this with anyone." Before Pullus could respond, Pollio pressed, "And I mean *anyone*, Pullus. That includes Balbus and Scribonius." He didn't like it, but Pullus agreed readily enough, and Pollio continued, "We can't do that, because Caesar has already claimed most of that money, Pullus."

"Claimed it?" Pullus echoed. "Claimed it for who?"

"Himself," Pollio said shortly, then he pointed out, "which is perfectly within his rights, both as Dictator for Life, and for the commander of this army."

This Pullus couldn't argue, so he didn't even try, yet he was troubled by it, and judging from the Legate sitting across from him, Pollio was as well; a glance at Hirtius assured Pullus that the two friends were of a like mind.

"Any idea why?" Pullus asked quietly.

"No, not a clue," Pollio sighed. "He hasn't exactly been…communicative since he left."

That, Pullus knew, was certainly the truth, and it was a source of growing concern among his fellow Centurions, of all grades. While it was true that, in some ways, Caesar's departure decreased the tensions that had flared up and resulted in what every officer understood was nothing short of an outright mutiny, although none of them ever used that word, even in private, they were unanimous in their belief that this was a temporary condition. Sooner or later, their general would have to return to face his army, and either acquiesce in their demands to return back to, at the very least, Parthia, or somehow convince them that it was in their best interests to stay here, in India. At this moment in time, Pullus was as certain as he had ever been that not even Caesar would be able to sway the men of the Legions to remain in India. Months later, he would have cause to remember this moment, and although it was only to himself, he acknowledged that, once again, he had underestimated Caesar.

The distribution of the new soldiers' tunics began six weeks later, and Pullus felt absolutely no qualms about claiming head-of-the-line privileges for his Equestrians.

"If it wasn't for me, you bastards would be sweating your balls off for the rest of the time we're here," he had declared at a meeting of the Primi Pili.

Certainly, there was complaining, but it was muted, and if it was less because Pullus had a point and the fact that he chose to pin each one with a challenging stare meant that this was all that occurred. Although the tunics themselves were cut to the identical pattern of the soldier's tunics, the instant Pullus picked one up, he noticed how much lighter it was, and it definitely had a different feel to it. The other change was that, unlike the woolen tunics that had been dyed with madder root to make them red, these tunics were the natural color of the material, which Pullus would have described as a dirty white, and he did wonder if their fastidious general would have an objection to this when he returned. As soon as the thought came,

Pullus dismissed it, thinking with grim amusement, if he'd wanted us to look tidy with dyed tunics, he should have been here. Despite Pullus' trust in Pollio, who he held in high regard, he couldn't deny that there was a niggling worry in the back of his mind that, if Caesar made an issue of this upon his return, Pollio might succumb to the pressure and point directly at Pullus as the originator of this idea.

Each Legionary was issued two tunics, and there was almost a small riot when the men, who as usual, had been summoned to the palace enclosure since that was the only space in their area large enough to accommodate them, began taking off their woolen tunics and donning the new cotton ones. Even in the moment, Pullus knew that it wasn't meant with any kind of malicious intent, but he was acutely aware that it was a virtual certainty that the Bharuch queen and her ladies were all watching from the palace, and the idea of hundreds of men stripping naked mortified him. Making matters worse, as far as he was concerned, anyway, was that early on those men who had worn the *subligaculum* under their tunics had discarded them, which included Pullus after he developed a rash because the cloth was always soaked with his sweat.

"Get your men in hand!" Pullus roared at his Centurions. "They can wait to change their tunics when they return to their quarters!"

While Balbus and his counterparts in the First Cohort all looked startled by this, they didn't hesitate, wading in and swinging their *viti* as they stopped those men who were about to disrobe, forcing them to snatch their two tunics from the long tables that had been set up. Once the men were in hand, the process went smoothly, although in this first batch, there were enough tunics for only two full Legions and part of a third. And, to Pullus' pleasure, his fellow Primi Pili had assiduously courted him, since Pollio had entrusted the entire project to him, and the large Primus Pilus had cheerfully announced that he could be bribed. In exchange for the last three amphorae of Falernian wine he possessed, Spurius' 3rd Legion was the second Legion; the fact that his friend's Legion would have been the second no matter what was something that Pullus had no intention of divulging to his fellow Primus Pilus. It was the part of the third Legion that was a bit more problematic; his natural inclination would have been to reward Balbinus and his 12th, but it was actually Atartinus' 11th, five Cohorts of which received the new uniform, which was accomplished when the Primus Pilus offered to take a guard shift for the 10th, since the size of the city was such that an entire Cohort was required to stand guard. The process took the better part of the morning, and while the change wasn't miraculous, almost immediately, men could be heard commenting that they felt more comfortable.

"That," Pullus commented to Scribonius as they stood watching the men admiring themselves and chattering to each other about this reduction of their misery, "was the easy part. There are a couple of other things that the queen suggested that are going to be harder to enforce."

"Such as?" Scribonius asked, although he was certain he had a suspicion what it might be.

"Stop drinking wine and *sura*," Pullus answered, confirming his friend's guess, and despite not being a heavy drinker himself, this elicited a groan from Scribonius at the thought of how this would go over with their men, officers included.

"Why?" he asked, but Pullus shrugged as he replied, "I don't know exactly, but Queen Hyppolita says that the intoxicants in them make it harder to cope with the heat. So," he said glumly, "we're going to be drinking more water."

"This isn't going to go over well," Scribonius agreed.

"What isn't going to go over well?"

The pair exchanged a grin, but Scribonius shook his head firmly, saying, "You're the Primus Pilus. You tell him." Suddenly, he took a wide step away from his friend as he added, "And let me stand over here when you do."

Balbus scowled suspiciously, first at Scribonius, then to Pullus as he demanded, "Tell me what? Why are the two of you looking at me like that?"

"Quintus," Pullus used a tone that men adopt with skittish animals, "these new tunics aren't going to be the only change we're going to need to make."

Scribonius was trying his best to hide his amusement as he watched Balbus' face, which those who didn't know him well would insist was carved from stone because his features had been immobilized by the sword slash that had severed the nerves and one ear. It had left him horribly scarred and with the inability to move one side of his face, but Scribonius, Pullus, and the men of his Century had learned to read him, and as Pullus explained that intoxicating beverages would no longer be consumed, he saw the look of utter horror and despair cross his friend's battered features.

Finally, Balbus managed to gasp, "Wha...What? But *why*?"

Pullus was having a hard time maintaining his composure, reading Balbus' expression the same as Scribonius, but he patiently repeated what he had been told by the Queen of Bharuch.

When Pullus finished, Balbus shook his head and muttered,

"Fuck that. I'll just sweat my balls off."

Both of his friends chuckled at this, but Pullus' tone was firm as he reminded his second in command, "You know that I expect my officers to set the example, Quintus. So if they can't drink, neither can you."

"Fine," Balbus muttered, knowing an order when he heard it, but he still was moved to add, "but I'm not going to pretend I like it!"

"I wouldn't expect you to," Pullus agreed, then knowing how it would make his friend react, he grinned as he added, "Besides, that will show how much you care about the men, that you're just as upset about it as they are."

"That's not why I'm doing it!" Balbus almost shouted this before he realized that Pullus had been goading him, and he glared at his Primus Pilus but said nothing else, turning and pointedly looking at the last of the men filing past the tables.

Scribonius and Pullus exchanged a grin, but Pullus wasn't quite through tormenting others, and this time, he knew it would be Scribonius who would be most affected as he said, "There's more."

Balbus spun around to stare at Pullus suspiciously, but Scribonius only looked wary, and it was the latter man that Pullus addressed.

"We need to change our diet as well."

"How?" both of his friends asked in unison.

"We're going to be switching to rice," Pullus answered. "And we're going to be eating more foods that don't need to be cooked."

This time, it was Scribonius' turn to look horrified; of the three of them, he was the most concerned with his diet, while Pullus was notoriously indifferent to anything but quantity, while Balbus was somewhere in the middle.

"*Gerrae!*" Scribonius exclaimed. "You can't be serious! The men are going to want their bread, Titus. You know that!"

"Yes," Pullus answered dryly. "This is just about the men and not about how much you love a good loaf."

Scribonius flushed, but neither did he deny it, simply pointing out, "And I'm not the only one in this army."

For the first time, Pullus' air of good humor vanished, and he took a quick glance around to make sure there weren't any prying ears nearby, but he still made sure that he kept his voice down. "Sextus, this was going to be coming anyway. You know we haven't gotten any shipments of wheat since Caesar left, and Pollio has sent at least three requests, but he hasn't gotten any kind of answer one way or another from Parthia."

"Are you certain about that, Titus?" Scribonius asked, equally quiet now. "If Caesar has communicated with Pollio but told him to keep his mouth shut about it, you know that Pollio will do that very thing."

"I thought about that," Pullus admitted. "But that's why I've had Diocles spending time at the *Praetorium*, and while he can't be certain, he's almost positive that Pollio is in the dark as much as we are. And," he returned to the original topic, "we're about to run out of wheat in the next month or maybe two. If we switch now, it will get the men accustomed to it."

"And it will tell them we're not going anywhere any time soon," Balbus pointed out, but Pullus didn't even try to deny this.

Looking Balbus in the eye, Pullus said, "Which we've known for weeks now, Quintus. And we both know the men have figured this out as well. We're stuck here, probably until spring."

That, the pair knew, was something they couldn't argue, so neither tried.

Instead, Scribonius sighed and said wistfully, "Well, we can start eating that *cac* tomorrow. Tonight, I'm having a nice loaf of *castra paneris*."

"And I'm going to get drunk!" Balbus declared, glaring up at Pullus as he said it, but the Primus Pilus just rolled his eyes, shook his head and said, "You're an idiot."

As the men of Caesar's stranded army slowly became more acclimated to their surroundings, very gradually, the people of Bharuch adjusted to this new reality of their lives. And, as had happened in Ctesiphon and Seleucia, Susa, and even before that in faraway Merv with the *Crassoi*, the interaction between the citizens of Bharuch and the Legions began with the most basic transaction that could take place, between men and women. Hyppolita was no prude; she was aware that, long before Rome showed up outside the walls, there were several brothels inside the city. Naturally, her husband the king never deigned to darken their doors, but that was only because there were pliant, willing women who were more than happy to come to the palace. Frankly, it didn't bother Hyppolita all that much, although this wasn't always the case, and it was early in their marriage, when her husband seduced one of her ladies in waiting that, after a period of growing tension, matters came to a head between them. The result was that, somewhat to her surprise, Hyppolita had extracted one concession, that the king viewed her ladies as off-limits for his amusement. Otherwise, Hyppolita was acutely aware that her husband wasn't unique, that it was in the nature of men, married and otherwise, to avail themselves of other women in order to relieve their urges, so she wasn't at all surprised when she heard that Romans had started showing up at the various brothels around the city. What *was* surprising, and in fact shocked her, was how she learned about it, or more specifically, from whom she learned about it.

"I wanted to let you know something," was how Titus Pullus broached the subject as they walked together around the compound on what had become their daily stroll.

This was the third week since they had reached their agreement, and Pullus had turned out to be a man of his word, appearing either early in the morning or shortly before dusk to escort the queen, with all of her ladies, of course, around the enclosure. It had been another of Hyppolita's suggestions, although in this case, it wasn't really necessary, that the Romans suspend their activities during the noon hour, dividing the day into two, something that Pullus and the rest of the army had learned during the Parthian campaign. Mornings were cooler, but the air was damper, while in the late afternoon, it was hotter, but not quite as damp, and without any discussion, they began alternating, Pullus showing up in the morning one day, and the late afternoon the next. Today, they were walking in the dusk, and Hyppolita glanced up at him with an amused expression when he broached whatever he wanted to talk about.

"Oh?" she asked with an arched eyebrow. "Are you going to tell me that you have decided to leave and return home?"

As she hoped, this made him laugh, although it was as much about the fact that this wasn't the first time she had made this joke as it was the tone she used. After a somewhat uncomfortable beginning, where Pullus insisted on walking behind the women, over the days, the reserve between Queen and Centurion had dwindled bit by bit. It was at the end of the second week that, with an exasperation that was only partially feigned, she commanded that Pullus walk by her side; it was his sheepish obedience that she found particularly disarming.

"No, Highness," Pullus gave an exaggerated sigh, "the answer is still the same. But," he suddenly seemed interested in the small shrubs that lined this part of the walkway that they used most frequently, "there's probably going to be some…additions coming." Seeing that she didn't understand, he groaned inwardly, then said awkwardly, "To your population."

It took another few paces before the look of dawning recognition crossed her features, and now it was her turn to appear flustered, but he admired how quickly she recovered herself as she answered, "Ah, yes. I see. Although," she added in an offhand manner, "I'm certain that the...women who your men are...seeing are quite experienced in taking precautions against that."

When he didn't reply immediately, it forced her to turn to look up at him, but he refused to meet her gaze as he said in a gentle tone, "Yes, I know they do. But those aren't the women I'm referring to."

As his meaning became clearer, she suddenly turned angry, "If you're talking about your men raping the women of this city, then we have nothing more to speak about!" Stopping abruptly, she lifted the hem of her gown in preparation to spin and stalk away, and Pullus could see that she was not only angry, she also truly didn't understand.

"Your Highness," he held up a placating hand, "I'm not talking about the victims of rape." He paused, trying to determine the best way forward, finally settling on, as usual, blunt honesty, "It's just that this isn't the first city we've conquered. In fact, it's not the third, or fourth city we've taken. And, while I know that from your viewpoint it's not true, the fact is that Caesar is a different general from anyone who's come before him except for Alexander. He's always taken great care that we don't mistreat the people. At least," he added hastily, seeing her features darken and knowing what was coming, "under normal circumstances. What happened here was...unusual for us."

"Unusual?" she shot back, her lips twisted into a scornful expression. "That's what you call what you and your men did to my people?" Without warning, she actually took a step closer to Pullus so that she was within arm's reach, but she stared directly up into his eyes as she thrust a finger into his face as she stormed, "I watched this city burn from right over there!" She twisted her head in the direction of the palace. "And I heard the screams, the *women's* screams, and the screams of little children!" Hyppolita's anger was on clear display, but what disturbed Pullus was the sudden shine of tears in her eyes as the thought leapt into his mind that he would rather face another horde of armored elephants than see this woman cry.

"I know!" he protested, holding his hands up in a supplicating gesture. "Your Highness, remember, I was out there, in those streets, and I know what happened. And, all I can tell you is that the men of my Legion weren't part of the worst that was happening!"

It would have surprised Pullus to know that Hyppolita was actually aware of this, having heard from one of her ladies, who had learned that the group of Romans led by the giant had seemed content to sit in the streets on the northern side of the city, while the rest of Caesar's army ran rampant.

She shocked herself when she heard her voice say, in a softer tone, "I am aware of that, Centurion Pullus. Which is why you are the only Roman I wish to have anything to do with, because I know that this is true." There was a silence between them, as both Pullus and Hyppolita had completely forgotten the presence of the ladies who were standing around them, until one of them coughed softly. This clearly startled the pair, and they shared a sheepish look, but it was Hyppolita who said, "So, what were you saying?"

They resumed walking, and Pullus did his best to forewarn Hyppolita of something that he had witnessed, going all the way back to when he was a Gregarius, and the Legions commanded by Caesar during the Gallic campaign spent winters in ostensibly hostile territory, then marching away with dozens, if not hundreds of pregnant women behind them. He did his best not to be too graphic, and actually tried to make it as humorous as possible, and he was encouraged that, while she didn't laugh, she did smile a few times, but it was the tittering of her ladies that told him he was on the right path. By the time they had returned to the palace, tensions between the pair had eased, and Hyppolita, while still skeptical, was aware that there was a possibility that her subjects, at least the females, may not have viewed the Romans with as much hatred and hostility that her husband would expect. It was this thought that spurred her to, without thinking, reach out and place her hand on Pullus' arm, stopping him as he was turning away to return to his duties, and she realized that this was the first time they had physically touched. The effect was immediate, alarming her to the point where she had to stop herself from yanking her hand away as if she had touched a hot oven; if she had known that Pullus was similarly affected, it would have made matters even worse.

As it was, she realized that, while she knew what she wanted to ask him, she had no idea how to go about it; finally, she began, "May I ask you a question, Centurion Pullus? And that you will give me an honest answer? And," she swallowed, "that you will not try to spare my feelings?"

Pullus knew that he could make no such promise, yet what came out of his mouth was, "Yes, and I promise to be honest. And," he grinned, "to treat you like a man."

"I'm sure you do not need to go *that* far," she answered immediately, smiling up at him as she did so. Then, the smile faded. "What I want to know is, why are you so sure that my husband's subjects will stop hating you Romans? I mean," she added, "to the point where you are so certain there will be Roman babies born in the coming months?"

Pullus considered for a long moment, realizing that he hadn't ever really put much thought into what was behind what he understood was the most likely outcome, so when he began talking, it was slowly as he developed the thought. "I think that not as much of it has to do with Rome as you might think. Yes," he felt compelled to add, "we're part of it, because there are things that we bring, and have brought to people through our form of government, and the idea that even men of my class have certain rights that nobody above us can take away." He paused, and he saw the skeptical expression, which made him realize that this wasn't the time or place to try and educate the queen on Rome's Republic and how it worked. Instead, he went on, "But also, once we take a city, and things…settle down," was how he put it, "I think that the common people see that their lives aren't really any different, and certainly not any worse. Caesar always takes pains to keep as much of the government in place as possible, and he not only doesn't raise taxes, in most cases, he adjusts the tax rate so that it doesn't fall as heavily on the common people as it usually does." Once more, he paused, trying to decide how far down what he was certain would be a perilous path he would go, then plunged on, "And, forgive me, Your Highness, but I've been marching with Caesar now for more than twenty-five years, and we've conquered more people and taken more territory than anyone, even Alexander. What I've seen is that monarchies tend to be the places where the people are more likely to appreciate what Rome has to offer than what they're experiencing under a king. Or queen," he thought to add, thinking of Cleopatra.

For a moment, he was certain that he had enraged the queen, and that she would finish storming off, but while she glared up at him, her mouth compressed into a thin line, he saw also her breasts rise as she took a deep breath, before saying tersely, "Go on."

Heaving an inward sigh of relief, Pullus continued, "What I've seen is that the only people who care about who's above them are the nobles. And," he allowed, feeling that it was a politic thing to say, "our patricians are some of the most uppity bast…people you're ever likely to meet. So, yes, they care, and they care deeply about their status and are always looking to other men of their class who will help them maintain, or even elevate their position. The rest of us?" He shrugged. "We care about feeding our children, that we can live in safety and without the fear that someone above us can just show up on our door and take everything from us, without any way to stop it. Now," he asked gently, "is that how things work in your kingdom? Is there anything in place that your subjects know will protect them from the whims of their king?"

As Pullus talked, Hyppolita's emotions ebbed and surged, almost with every word. Yes, she was angry, but she was fair enough to recognize that, not only was it not Pullus' fault, she had told him to be honest. But it was more than that; at her core, there was a growing unease as she recognized that what Pullus was telling her was the case. While she knew that her husband tried to be fair, she also wasn't blind to his faults, and the truth was that he had been harsh in his dealings with his subjects in the past. And, she thought, there's nothing that our subjects can do about it. They rely completely on Abhiraka's justice, without any protection from his decisions. If he decided to wage war on one of the neighboring kingdoms and demanded that the men of Bharuch who weren't part of the regular army drop whatever they were doing to march with him, they did so, under penalty of death. And, he *had* dealt out death on multiple occasions when men had balked at serving. She had never been present for these punishments, but she knew what they were; being crushed to death by one of the armored elephants, slowly and quite painfully. Now, here she was, feeling nauseous as Pullus essentially informed her that, unless Abhiraka acted, and did so sooner rather than later, his subjects might not welcome him as a liberator. As unlikely as this seemed to part of her, there was something deep within her where Pullus' words resonated, and while she only dimly realized it in the moment, as she thought about it more later, she understood that this was something that had nagged at her since childhood. Thanking Pullus, who recognized that she had been shaken by what he said, she made her way up the steps of the palace, trailed by her ladies, in a daze.

Far to the south, and at roughly the same moment, her husband, King Abhiraka, first of his name, was standing with his son-in-law Crown Prince Nedunj, and Nedunj's father Puddapandyan, the King of the nascent Pandyan Kingdom, the three of them staring north as they were engaged in an intense discussion. A few feet away, Ranjeet Aristandros, Abhiraka's Commander of his royal bodyguard, deputy commander of what remained of Bharuch's army, and the king's closest friend, was watching with unfeigned interest, and a fair amount of concern. A short distance away from him, almost directly behind the Pandyan king and prince, was Nedunj's advisor, a younger man named Alangudi, but his title wasn't martial. In fact, Ranjeet wasn't really sure what role Alangudi played, although he had his suspicions. The topic of conversation was, Ranjeet sighed inwardly, the same that it had been for weeks now, and that was what Abhiraka intended to do in order to reclaim his kingdom, and more pressing to the Pandyans, when he intended to do it. As steadfastly loyal as Ranjeet was to Abhiraka, he also couldn't deny that their hosts had cause for concern, and he had wondered the same thing himself. It was understandable that Abhiraka's pride had been battered beyond recognition; of his vaunted corps of armored elephants that had numbered two hundred, less than fifty had survived what had been a horrific slaughter, and of those, almost twenty had suffered burns and other wounds that rendered them ineffective, although they could be used for breeding stock. Losing them had been a massive blow for Abhiraka, Ranjeet knew and understood, but he also shared his king and friend's revulsion for the method the demon Romans had used to slaughter the animals, using flaming jars of naphtha. Or, as Abhiraka had been forced to witness as he stood on the northern rampart of the city that he had been certain would never fall, they used the pernicious substance to coat the missiles that they sent from devices that, while he was familiar with artillery, Abhiraka had never seen before but were like large, mounted bows that hurled their large arrows with a blinding speed. Indeed, so much of what Rome brought as they assaulted his kingdom was unfamiliar to the king, and he realized now that he had been woefully unprepared to face the demon Caesar and his army of savages. Nevertheless, he was as aware as Ranjeet that both Puddapandyan and Nedunj had cause for concern, yet he still didn't feel ready to return. Not, he thought, until I have more men, and I know more about this Roman Caesar and his army.

"Abhiraka," Puddapandyan's patience finally broke, but he was aware that he was speaking to a fellow king, and he couched his words carefully. "Please forgive me for my blunt language. Know that I mean no disrespect, but your men are now fully healed. Every man of your army that escaped from Bharuch who wished to rejoin you has done so; those that have not have undoubtedly returned to their homes in your kingdom. You," he said gently, "have as many elephants as you will have." Raising his arms with his palms turned upward, he asked, "What more do you need?"

"Tell us, Father Abhiraka," Nedunj interjected, his voice eager, "tell us what you require from us to retake Bharuch, and my father and I will do everything in our power to make it so!"

It took a massive effort for Ranjeet to maintain his impassive demeanor, and he had to fight the urge to laugh at the expression that crossed Nedunj's father's face. He looks, Ranjeet thought, with a combination of amusement and a bit of alarm, as if he might keel over dead on the spot, and Ranjeet guessed that it was the eagerness of the son to offer a rival king aid that was the cause.

Abhiraka didn't hesitate, pouncing so quickly that Ranjeet suddenly realized that at least part of his king's seeming hesitance had been by design, as he waited for the right moment.

"I would need at least ten thousand more men, and a hundred more elephants," he replied immediately.

"That's half of our army!" Nedunj gasped, but while his father didn't have a similar outburst, Ranjeet saw he was equally disturbed.

"You asked me what I needed," Abhiraka countered calmly. "That's what I will need."

Father and son exchanged a long glance, yet surprisingly, it wasn't either of them, but the younger Alangudi who spoke next.

"Your Highness, forgive me, but given what happened to your men and animals the first time, what would make us believe that we aren't just throwing our own men and animals away?"

Before he had conscious thought to do so, Ranjeet hissed a curse and had taken a step towards the younger man, instinctively reaching for a sword that wasn't there, but Abhiraka held up a hand, stopping him in his tracks. If he was as angered as Ranjeet, it was impossible to tell, but while his tone was controlled, his old friend heard the rage there.

"Because, Alagudi," Abhiraka said coolly, the deliberate mispronunciation of the courtier's name causing him to flush, while Ranjeet unsuccessfully smothered a laugh with a cough, "I'm not encumbered by walls and a city to protect this time. This time, I am on the offense, and I will be choosing ground that I know better than these Romans ever will. And," he went on, his voice becoming stronger to Ranjeet's ears, "Caesar will be forced to divide his forces. He cannot afford to leave Bharuch undefended, but neither can he afford to have my army roaming the countryside destroying the farms and crops they produce that will go to feed his army."

Suddenly, Ranjeet's emotions shifted once again, and while his expression remained impassive, he felt disquieted about his king's terse description of his intentions.

"That," Nedunj interjected, "will mean great suffering for your own subjects, though, Father Abhiraka."

"It will," Abhiraka agreed. "And it will be a terrible thing I do, but what choice do I have?" He paused, clearly inviting a response as he looked from his fellow king, to his son-in-law, then in a clear insult, didn't even glance at Alangudi, finishing with Ranjeet, whereupon he repeated quietly, "What choice do I have, Ranjeet?"

Ranjeet's hesitation was barely a flicker, his mind having adjusted to what he now understood was indeed his king's only alternative. Between their weapons of war, their numbers, and their training and discipline, fighting a set-piece battle against the invader's entire army would undoubtedly end with the same result, a resounding defeat. Only by luring part of the Roman army out into the countryside surrounding Bharuch and facing them in this piecemeal fashion was there any hope for success. And, as Ranjeet scanned the faces of the others, he saw that, with the exception of Alangudi, the others had understood and accepted this as well; and, Ranjeet thought with amusement, this young pup may share the prince's bed, but he has no voice here.

Seeing the same thing as Ranjeet, Abhiraka asked bluntly, "Now, what will this cost? What is it that you will require in payment for what I've requested?"

While the change in attire was welcomed by the men of the Legions, the shift in diet was met with a decidedly different reaction. From Pullus' perspective, it was hard to determine what was more unpopular, the idea that bread was about to become a thing of the past, or the sudden restriction on wine and what had become the most popular beverage of not just the rankers but Pullus, Balbus, and many of his fellow officers, the sweet but potent *sura*. Fairly quickly, Pullus and his fellow Primi Pili recognized that they had made the mistake in introducing both of these changes at the same time, and when it became clear that, within three days of the announcement, matters with the men had degraded back to the point close to the mutinous period immediately after the fall of the city, it was quickly decided to rescind the restriction on wine and *sura*. This did reduce tensions, but the men were still disgruntled about their change in diet; all Pullus was concerned about was that he could walk through the streets of the neighborhood adjacent to the palace complex that now housed the 10th Legion without straining to listen to his men, worried that they were plotting another insurrection. Not yet, anyway, he thought dismally as he was making his way to the palace for the morning walk, which had become something that he looked forward to a great deal, although he tried to hide this fact from Diocles and his friends, none of whom were fooled in the slightest. And, as had become the custom, Hyppolita was standing on the broad portico waiting, but Pullus instantly saw that today she only had one lady with her, and that it was the young woman Amodini.

Seeing his face, Hyppolita had to suppress a smile, but she said briskly, "I decided to give my ladies the option of participating on our walk. And," she gestured to Amodini, "Lady Amodini is the only one brave enough to protect her queen. Although," she added teasingly, "I think that the Lady might have other things on her mind than me."

"That's not true, Your Highness!" Amodini protested, not terribly convincingly, but it was Pullus' reaction that made Hyppolita laugh, as he suddenly became interested in his feet.

Descending the stairs, Hyppolita chided, "Surely, Centurion Pullus, you must know that you have this effect on women!"

Not for the first time in her company, Titus Pullus suddenly wished he was anywhere other than where he was, although he also knew he was lying to himself, yet he honestly didn't know what he was supposed to say.

Finally, he mumbled, "It's just my size, Your Highness. I'm very tall, especially for a Roman."

Deciding to take some pity on him, Hyppolita used that as a way to guide the conversation to safer waters, observing, "Yes, I have noticed that. You're easily the largest of your people, at least of those I've seen. In fact," her tone turned thoughtful, "I confess I was surprised to see you Romans for the first time. Apart from you, and Caesar of course, your men seem to be..."

Her voice trailed off, but Pullus, both amused and relieved, supplied, "...short, Your Highness. Roman men tend to be shorter than the men of other nations."

"Why is that?" she asked, genuinely curious, but before Pullus could reply, she added, "And why do you think you're so different?"

"Honestly," he admitted, "I've wondered that myself. Both about why Romans tend to be shorter and why I'm so large." He paused as he thought about it, then continued, "One thing I *have* noticed is that the tribes and nations where the men tend to be more my size than my comrades have a diet that's quite different from ours. Gauls and the German tribes in particular barely know what bread is. They eat a lot more meat than Romans do."

Hyppolita considered this, then pointed out, "But you're a

Roman, and you're big, and as you say, you don't eat meat to that degree."

"Actually," he surprised her, "that's not true. At least," he allowed, "when I was a boy, I ate a lot more meat than anyone else I knew. Now I don't eat as much, but I still eat more than most of my comrades."

"Oh?" she asked with a raised eyebrow. "Why is that?"

"Because," he answered bluntly, "my father Lucius was a drunkard, and he was a horrible farmer." They walked a few steps in silence before Pullus continued, clearly reluctant. "I grew up in the province of Baetica, which is part of Hispania, and the land there isn't suited to grow wheat. It's best for olives, or even grapes. But Lucius thought he was clever enough to figure out a way to grow wheat, thinking that he would be able to make more money that way. And," he finished bitterly, "he wasn't."

Hyppolita was torn; she could see that this was a topic that Pullus didn't want to discuss, but she was almost overcome with curiosity, given this sudden and unexpected chance to learn more about the large Roman beside her. Somehow, she managed to refrain, steering the conversation with a deftness that, under other circumstances, her husband valued a great deal.

"Speaking of diets," she said, "how have your men handled the change?"

"Not well," Pullus answered immediately. Now it was his turn to hesitate, but then he admitted, "In fact, we've lifted the restriction on drink."

"Oh? Why?" Hyppolita tried to keep her tone as it had been, interested but not suddenly consumed with curiosity as she wondered if she was about to learn something that would be helpful to her cause.

"Because we found out that making them eat rice sober was going to cause a riot," he answered glumly, yet it was the way that he said it that, before she could stop herself, Hyppolita burst out laughing, while Amodini giggled from her spot just behind them. Giving the queen a glare, Pullus tried to sound angry as he grumbled, "I'm pleased you find that so amusing, Your Highness. Although," his weathered features changed as he grinned, "I suppose it *is* funny now that I think about it."

They walked a few more paces in silence, while Hyppolita struggled with competing emotions; on one hand, having the occupiers of her city unsettled and at each other's throats wasn't a bad thing, yet neither could she deny the simple truth, that her subjects were just as likely to bear the brunt of Roman discontent as each other.

Making her decision, she said casually, "You know, Centurion, there are ways to make this food you're eating more palatable."

"Oh? How? Do you know a magic spell to turn it into bread?" Pullus joked, but while she smiled, she shook her head.

"We have many different spices here in India," she explained. "And we use them in our cooking to quite an extent, and some of those spices also help us cope with the heat that you find so troublesome. Although," she allowed, "I also know that it is not always palatable for those who are unaccustomed to it."

She was pleased to see that Pullus was genuinely curious, and he asked her, "What do you mean?"

"Actually," she answered, "it is quite hard to describe. But," she added, as if this had just occurred to her, "it is probably more effective to show you. If you are interested, you can come tonight for our evening meal, and I will have my cooks prepare several dishes that use these spices so that you can judge for yourself."

Pullus hesitated, but it wasn't for the reason Hyppolita thought, so that she was caught completely off guard when he asked, "May I bring a guest, Your Highness?"

Hyppolita's first instinct was to flatly refuse, but she stopped herself from an outright rejection, asking, "Who did you have in mind?"

"My nephew," Pullus answered. "He serves in my Second Cohort."

"So," she spoke cautiously, "not another Centurion? Or a…what do you call them?"

"A Legate? Like Legate Pollio or Hirtius?" He shook his head. "No, he's a Gregarius." Understanding the term was unfamiliar, he added, "A common soldier."

"Very well," she agreed. "Although," she added mischievously, "I find it hard to believe that anyone related to you would be common."

She liked that this pleased him, and they finished their walk, chatting about other matters, while Amodini trailed behind the pair. It was a good thing that Hyppolita never bothered to glance over her shoulder; she might have caught Amodini glaring at her queen's back.

"But why? Why me?"

"Because," Pullus snapped, his patience gone, "your Primus

Pilus told you to." His tone softened fractionally. "Not your uncle, Gaius."

Gaius Porcinus knew that he had reached the point where further argument would only arouse his uncle's temper, and he understandably had no desire to do that, so he merely asked, "Should I be in full uniform?"

Pullus considered, then shook his head.

"No, just tunic and *baltea*. But," he warned his nephew unnecessarily, "those leathers better gleam!"

Porcinus assured him that they would, then after rendering a salute, he left his uncle's quarters, leaving Diocles to sit at his desk regarding his master with undisguised amusement.

Pullus, seated at his own desk, tried to ignore the Greek, then finally threw his stylus down in disgust, demanding, "What is it? Why are you sitting there looking so smug?"

"Smug?" Diocles echoed innocently, arching an eyebrow at Pullus. "Why do you think I look smug? I'm just happy for you."

"Happy for me? Why?" Pullus asked warily, certain he had a good idea.

Which was confirmed when Diocles answered, "Because you're having dinner with a queen…again!" Before Pullus could reply, the Greek added, "How many Roman Centurions in history can say that they've had a private dinner with not just one, but two queens?"

"That…" Pullus had been about to protest that this wasn't the case, but then he realized that indeed it was, so he tried to shrug it off. "…isn't important."

"Somehow, I have a feeling that Caesar wouldn't agree," Diocles replied dryly, but within a heartbeat regretted his words, seeing that Pullus was now deeply disturbed.

"Pluto's cock," the Centurion gasped. "You're right! Cleopatra picking my brain was bad enough, but she's his…" He realized he had almost used the word "wife," but having seen how Caesar reacted to that characterization, and despite the fact that his general was thousands of miles away, he used, "…woman. And she's an ally." Shaking his head, Pullus stood abruptly, saying, "You're right. This is a bad idea. I'm going to go tell her that I can't come."

Diocles wasn't panicked, but he was alarmed nonetheless, and he scrambled to his feet, saying quickly, "Master, I didn't mean to imply that this was a bad idea, truly! In fact," his mind was working furiously, "I think that spurning her invitation this late would cause more problems than it solves."

Pullus looked unconvinced, but he had also learned never to ignore his scribe's advice, and he asked cautiously, "Why do you say that?"

"Because you are the only Roman with whom she has any interaction," Diocles replied immediately. "And we both know that Legate Pollio has used you on more than one occasion to relay messages to the queen that he otherwise would have been forced to come to the palace and create some sort of scene, given how she feels about him." This, Pullus knew, was certainly true, which he indicated with a thoughtful nod that encouraged Diocles to continue, "The more she trusts you, the better for us. And," he finished with a shrug and a grin, "who knows? Maybe she'll fall in love with you."

Pullus felt his face grow warm, and he growled, "All right, funny man. Enough of that. But," he agreed, somewhat grudgingly, "you make a good point. Fine," he sighed, "I'll go."

Diocles rose, wisely not reveling in his small victory, if only because his motives in convincing Pullus to change his mind were mixed; while he had been sincere enough, more than anything, he had become aware that, for the first time in many years, Titus Pullus seemed happy, and he was certain that it had almost everything to do with the Queen of Bharuch. Even then, however, it never occurred to him that matters would evolve and have such a dramatic impact on his master and friend as they would. More than once afterward, he wondered if he had done the right thing by convincing his master to show up for that meal.

As far as Gaius Porcinus was concerned, the evening turned out to be one of the greatest nights of his life, despite his early misgivings. Both he and his uncle wore their soldier's tunics, and as always, Porcinus was acutely aware of the contrast between his uncle and himself, especially when standing side by side. Although Porcinus was much taller than the average Roman like his uncle, and in fact only stood about an inch shorter than Titus Pullus, where they differed dramatically was in their respective breadth and musculature. Even now when he could afford to have his soldier's tunics tailored, the fabric stretched tightly across Pullus' chest, while his arms almost filled the sleeves that were deliberately made larger than a civilian's version. Porcinus was of a much slenderer build, although he was tightly muscled, and as his uncle would have been quick to tell anyone, was deceptively strong, although he never said it in front of Porcinus.

That evening, as they ascended the steps of the southern portico,

Porcinus reveled in the envious glances of the pair of Legionaries who stood on either side of the main doors, and he did wonder if it was a coincidence that the men were from his Second Cohort, although not from his Century. Waiting for the two Romans was the wizened man of an indeterminate age who was one of only three males that were still part of the palace staff; the fact that this man was mute was why he was one of them. Clearly accustomed to Pullus' appearance, he didn't wait to see if the two followed him, but for the first time since Pullus began coming to the palace, the man didn't head directly for the staircase that led to the second floor. Instead, he led them down a long hallway that ended with a double doorway, which was open, and Porcinus could see that it was a room that was naturally lit. Reaching the doorway, the man stopped, beckoning the pair into the room, which was one of the largest that Porcinus had ever seen. He immediately saw that this was the dining room, and two of its sides were outer walls, with large windows that were open, although there were long curtains of a sheer, translucent fabric that, as he would learn, did an excellent job of screening out the bugs, but also allowed the gentle breeze to circulate. It was the table, however, that arrested his attention; more specifically, the fact that there were by his count almost a dozen women seated around it. Most astonishing of all was when the woman who was seated at one end stood, and his uncle immediately bowed, which Porcinus quickly copied.

"Your Highness," to Porcinus, his uncle sounded as if he was experienced in such things as he said, "thank you again for this gracious invitation. May I present Gregarius Ordinarius Gaius Porcinus, who serves in the First Century of the Second Cohort of the 10th Legion. Which," he added and, for the first time to Porcinus, sounded self-conscious, "as you know, I command." Turning to Porcinus, Pullus continued, "Gaius, this is Her Highness Hyppolita, the Queen of Bharuch."

It was then that both Romans suddenly realized something that was equally mortifying to them; Pullus hadn't instructed Porcinus on how he was to respond, and for the span of what was a couple of heartbeats but seemed much longer, the young Roman was in an agony of indecision. Do I come to *intente* and salute? he thought desperately. Or should I bow again? Hyppolita was wearing her veil, as were the other women, but even with the fine mesh covering her eyes, Porcinus was certain he could see that she was amused by his quandary, and perhaps she felt sorry for him, because she took a step forward from her spot.

"Thank you for accepting our invitation, Gregarius..." Suddenly, she stopped, and Porcinus could only tell by the way her head moved that she was looking to Pullus, who supplied, "Gregarius Ordinarius, Your Highness."

"Yes." The veil bobbed, and she repeated, "Gregarius Ordinarius Porcinus. I hope that you enjoy yourself this evening."

Porcinus would never know that Hyppolita hadn't actually forgotten his rank, but Pullus hadn't been fooled, understanding that she had done this to put his nephew at ease by making her own error, and he felt a surge of gratitude for her kindness.

"Thank you for inviting me, Your Highness," Porcinus managed, but while he had never seen it done, somehow Porcinus understood that he wasn't supposed to grasp the hand the queen had just extended, but to kiss it.

He felt slightly ridiculous doing so, yet despite his youth, he experienced a moment of insight that would cause him to recall this moment years later as he wondered if this was just the first of many strange customs that he and his comrades would have to learn. With the introductions done, Hyppolita indicated the two empty seats on either side of her, but when Pullus took his seat, he grinned at her as he sat with an exaggerated care that recalled their first real conversation. Because of her veil, he couldn't see her expression, but he clearly heard the soft chuckle, although she didn't say anything, at least about that.

"I thought we would begin with some of the fresh fruits and vegetables that we enjoy here in Bharuch," Hyppolita announced, and as if by magic, two attendants carrying silver platters appeared through the single door on the opposite side of the room from the entrance. "I'm sure that you will be familiar with some of them, especially now that you have..." She hesitated, and there was no mistaking the coolness that suddenly colored her tone. "...been here for a few months."

Pullus wisely did not respond one way or another to her words, while Porcinus was determined that, for the rest of the night, he would only speak when spoken to. He was already acutely uncomfortable, with the queen seated to his right and one of her ladies seated to his left. Between the shapeless robes that Porcinus recognized were made of silk and the veils that obscured their faces, the young Legionary realized that at this moment he was relying on his sense of smell, taking in the scent of what he assumed was some sort of perfume. And, he was certain, he had never smelled anything as wonderful in his life, a heady mixture of some sort of flowery scent, but with a hint of what he believed was cinnamon, to which he had only recently been introduced.

Despite his vow, Porcinus was moved to murmur, "What is your name, Mistress?"

That he did so in Latin meant that the only reaction from the woman was a slight tilting of her head, and he realized that she didn't understand him.

Before he could say anything, Hyppolita told him, "Her name is Amodini, Gregarius Porcinus, and she is one of my ladies who attend to my needs. And," she added this in a slightly teasing tone, "she is one of my escorts to protect me from your Centurion when we walk around the palace grounds."

Porcinus glanced over at his uncle, wondering how Pullus would respond to what could be construed as some sort of slur on his honor, but he instantly saw that he wasn't offended in the least, and was actually grinning at the queen, then turned to Porcinus to mockingly warn, "You need to be careful, Gaius. Don't let those robes and veil fool you. Mistress Amodini is a fierce protector."

Before Porcinus could say anything, Hyppolita translated the exchange, not in Greek but in what both Romans knew was the tongue spoken by the common people of Bharuch that, they had been told, was called Sanskrit. Even before she was finished, the table erupted in laughter, and Porcinus was struck by the contrast between the coarse, raucous mirth of his comrades and the feminine version, which sounded almost like music.

"What did you tell them?" Pullus asked Hyppolita warily. "What I said wasn't *that* funny."

"I may have...embellished your words a bit, Centurion," Hyppolita replied, but despite having never met the woman before this, Porcinus was certain that she was teasing his uncle. "Just a bit."

The prospect of seeing his uncle uncomfortable made Porcinus even happier, but he was also wondering when the actual eating would begin. He got his answer when the pair of attendants returned again with trays, but this time, each one held a jug.

"If I recall correctly, Centurion," Hyppolita spoke as the pair placed the two jugs roughly equidistant from each other, "you have developed a taste for our *sura*." Before he could reply, she pointed at the jug nearest to the three of them and explained, "That is what this jug holds. That one," she pointed to the other, "is simply water, drawn from the well here on the palace grounds. And I would suggest that you drink both."

"Oh?" Pullus regarded her quizzically. "Why?"

"You will find out soon enough," she answered, then before Pullus could reply, she said, "Please, try these fruits."

Both Romans were familiar with most of the items arrayed on the large tray, although only by sight in the case of one. Once Bharuch had returned to a semblance of normalcy, every Roman had seen the citizens carrying these in bunches, but while some of his comrades had tried them, Porcinus wasn't particularly adventurous in this regard, and neither was his uncle. They eyed each other, silently urging the other to be the first to pick up the fruit that, Porcinus suddenly realized, resembled an erect cock, the thought making him flush a deep red. If Pullus had the same thought, it was impossible to tell, and with a muttered curse, he picked up one of the fruits, examining it closely. Then, with a fatalistic shrug, he started to bite into it, but he was stopped by Hyppolita, who placed a hand on Pullus' arm; even as preoccupied as Porcinus was by all that was happening around him, he didn't miss the way that Pullus reacted, and he felt perversely happy that he wasn't the only one blushing.

"Centurion, may I show you how to eat this?" she asked, and naturally, he nodded.

Grabbing the stem, she deftly pulled down on it, revealing that this was an outer covering, exposing a white flesh. Holding it out to him, Pullus leaned over and hesitantly took a bite, and once again, Porcinus noticed that there was...something there, between this queen, who he had yet to actually see, and his uncle.

Swallowing, Pullus said with some surprise, "That's very tasty, Your Highness. And it's sweet. What's it called?"

"Banana," Hyppolita supplied the name. "It grows wild here, especially to the south and east. My husband's father was responsible for planting several orchards of banana plants, and this is only one variety, but it is the sweetest."

Seeing Pullus' reaction, Porcinus understood what was expected of him, and he reached for one of the newly named bananas, but to his surprise, when he was about to imitate the queen to remove the skin, Amodini reached over and took the fruit from him, saying something as she did so.

"Amodini said that since you are our guest, you should not be expected to have to work so hard," Hyppolita informed him. "She is happy to help you."

Just as Hyppolita had done, Amodini peeled back the outer covering, and like the queen had, offered it to Porcinus, who behaved as his uncle, leaning over and taking a bite. And, like Pullus, he nodded approvingly.

"It *is* good," he mumbled, then without warning, leaned over and snapped up the rest of the exposed fruit, which unleashed more laughter from the women.

Porcinus glanced over at Pullus, who was grinning at him, but he also noticed his uncle reaching over to refill his cup, and he was certain that it was not water. One thing he had been intensely curious about once he saw that his dining companions were all veiled was how they managed to do things like eat and drink. He got his answer, watching as with an ease that obviously came from much practice, the women leaned forward slightly so that the veil hung away from their face, whereupon the cup disappeared as they sipped from it, then returned to view when they set it back on the table. Whether or not this had to do with what happened next, neither Pullus nor Porcinus would ever know, but Hyppolita spoke again in her native tongue. Her ladies reacted with small gasps that to Porcinus sounded like a combination of astonishment and unease, but they obeyed what he quickly understood had been a command, because one by one, the ladies reached up and unfastened their veils, allowing them to fall away from their faces. Naturally, Porcinus immediately turned to Amodini, and before he could stop himself, he was the one gasping in astonishment, his reaction needing no translation at the sight of her beauty. Pullus, who had seen all of the women in this state by this point in time, was watching his nephew with a mixture of amusement and a bit of disquiet, knowing his own reaction the first time he was able to view these ladies. Hyppolita was the only one still wearing her veil, but only because she had been whispering instructions to one of the attendants; once she was finished, she turned back to the table and unfastened hers as well. Porcinus, sensing the movement, somehow tore his gaze away from Amodini, who was demurely looking down at her hands, folded and in her lap, and once more lost his breath. While her skin was of a lighter hue, the queen was every bit as beautiful as Amodini, who Porcinus had judged to be the most attractive of all of the ladies; none of whom, he noted happily, could be considered homely. But the queen, Porcinus thought to himself, is in a class by herself, and he was surprised at the strength of the stab of envy he felt for his uncle, realizing that Pullus was in her presence on a daily basis.

"We are about to try a series of dishes, and while they all are made with rice, I think you will find them quite different from each other," the queen explained. Then, she added something that only made sense later. "You may want to keep your cups filled."

A few moments later, both Pullus and Porcinus understood

why.

As her lady Darshwana brushed out her hair later that night, Hyppolita felt quite pleased with herself. Her invitation to Pullus hadn't been as spontaneous as she made it seem to the Roman; in fact, she had been planning it for more than a week and had been looking for an opening that would enable her to extend the invitation without it rousing Pullus' suspicions that she had an ulterior motive. Unknown to Pullus, Hyppolita had experienced reservations just like he had when Diocles made his comment about Caesar, but in her case, it was because Pullus brought a guest, and she worried that the presence of another Roman might disrupt her plans. Once she learned his identity, not only were her fears assuaged, it gave her an unexpected opportunity. Her original plan had been to have Amodini use her considerable charms to turn Centurion Pullus' head; after all, she had done it before, although the youngest lady in her court had initially balked.

"Your Highness, I am not comfortable with this," she had cried out when Hyppolita informed her of what was expected of her, but the queen was unmoved.

"You were comfortable enough having an affair with that idiot Bhadran," she had snapped.

And, as she had known it would, this was enough to convince Amodini that, at the very least, it was a futile attempt to change her queen's mind. The man who had been charged with command of the northern wall, including the newly constructed canal that her husband had ordered built, had failed abysmally, and in the feverish watches when the surviving defenders had fallen back to the palace enclosure, Hyppolita had learned that Bhadran hadn't just failed, he had proven to be a coward, and where he was now was anyone's guess. Amodini had been hopelessly in love with the nobleman, and now Hyppolita was behaving like a queen, using the shame caused by her lady's misjudgment to achieve her own ends. But then, the nephew had shown up, and while Hyppolita wasn't a bit surprised to see young Porcinus gazing at her lady like a moonstruck calf, she had quickly seen that Amodini was no less stricken, which forced her to adjust on the fly. The fact that she had relayed her instructions for Amodini to turn her attentions to Porcinus instead of Pullus right in front of the pair, with neither of them having any idea, made Hyppolita smile. She was no fool; the longer these Romans stayed in Bharuch, the higher the probability that they would pick up enough of the commoners' tongue that such conversations in front of them would be next to impossible. The fact that Amodini didn't speak a word of Latin—neither did Hyppolita for that matter—was certainly a challenge, but it had been during the course of the dinner, after the *sura* had flowed for a sufficient length of time to loosen her guests' tongues, that she had learned Porcinus spoke and understood Greek. So did Amodini, although she had ordered all of her ladies to keep their personal fluency, which varied quite a bit, in the one language with which they could communicate with their conquerors a secret until she deemed otherwise. It wasn't ideal, she admitted to herself; if it wasn't going to be Titus Pullus, then she would have preferred another man of Centurion rank, but the other thing she observed over the course of the dinner was the relationship between the pair, and how it was even closer than one might expect between uncle and nephew. Still, she felt optimistic that she would at least have a better idea of what was going on outside the palace walls, aside from what Pullus was willing to tell her. She was certainly pleased that it had been quiet for several weeks, but the more she thought about it, the more disturbed she became because of the conversation she and Pullus had had about what her subjects could expect from their conquerors.

Hyppolita, like her husband, was a product of her environment, and she lived in an age and a region where countries were ruled almost exclusively by kings, although the title varied, and whose authority was absolute, including the administration of justice. What little she had learned from Pullus, that Roman citizens of all classes were endowed with a set of rights and protections, however minimal they may have been, that had never been part of the makeup of any kingdom of the East of which she was aware. She knew a great deal about the monarchy of the Seleucids, because they were her ancestors, and she had been born to a royal house. Hearing Pullus talk, she immediately understood how this could be attractive to her husband's subjects, but more than that, it also helped explain how Parthia was conquered in two years. If the commoners were treated better by their overlords, would they really care that it wasn't those of their own people? Although she had never discussed this with her husband, she felt confident that she knew what his position would be, that the people of Bharuch would be loyal to their king, no matter what blandishments a foreign invader could provide. She was equally confident that this was a ridiculous belief; no, she hadn't been particularly close to her subjects, but she was an astute observer, a keen listener, and she understood the danger Abhiraka was in grew with every passing day. As the fear, pain, and outrage of what had taken place after the fall of the city began to fade, and people began seeing tangible benefits to living under the rule of these strange people, it would be more difficult for him to retake Bharuch. Time, she understood, was of the essence, and she hoped that her instinct about the closeness between Titus Pullus and his nephew was sound. Darshwana finished, and Hyppolita shook her hair out, something that privately peeved Darshwana, but the queen loved the feeling of her hair unbound, and it was as she was shaking her head that, without any warning, she was struck by a thought that, in its way, was every bit as troubling as what she had just been contemplating. Was she relieved that Amodini was turning her attentions on Gaius Porcinus and not Titus Pullus? The instant it came to her, she felt deep in herself that this was true; what was even more troubling was why she felt this way. She had been quite tired and was looking forward to a good night's sleep, but it was long in coming as she tossed and turned.

Chapter 2

Thousands of miles away to the northeast, Gaius Julius Caesar was sitting in what Octavian had begun to think of as his chair, behind the desk that had been placed on the raised dais where the Parthian throne had once stood. Certainly, it had irritated Caesar somewhat that his nephew had rearranged the furniture after the Dictator for Life had returned to Seleucia, but of all the concerns pressing him, this was the least worrisome.

"How is it possible that now that you have two Legions, along with your cavalry, that you've been unable to bring Valash to heel?"

While Octavian had certainly been present when his uncle had behaved in this manner with a subordinate, it had never been aimed directly at him, and there was nothing even remotely familial in the ice-blue eyes of Caesar as he pinned his nephew with a cold stare. Even worse, Octavian understood, was that he had no real excuse. Trying to pin the Parthian dog down in the vast expanse north of Susa and south of Ecbatana had proven to be a challenge along the lines of tying a knot in a column of smoke. Oh, there had been two skirmishes, and they had managed to inflict some casualties, but had also suffered some in the process.

"He is...slippery, Caesar," Octavian spoke carefully, and added frankly, "and he's a better general than I gave him credit for being as well."

"Well," Caesar allowed, somewhat grudgingly, but he had to be fair, "your cause wasn't helped by Cleopatra's terrible advice about reprisals." Before Octavian could pounce on this, anticipating that he would do that very thing, Caesar added pointedly, "Which is why I personally escorted her and Caesarion back to Seleucia. She's under strict instructions to remain there and not to involve herself in this matter anymore."

Too little, too late, Uncle, Octavian thought bitterly, but he knew what was expected of him, and he said with as much sincerity as he thought he could muster without it appearing completely false, "I'm still the commander here in Susa, so the responsibility and the failure are mine, Caesar."

While it was certainly true that Caesar was miffed at Octavian, he was even angrier with Cleopatra, and he had seriously considered banishing her all the way back to Alexandria, under guard if necessary. The reason he didn't was because of Caesarion; despite his limited contact with his son, he was utterly captivated in a way that he hadn't been with the only other child of his who had survived into adulthood, Julia. He was a remarkable child, extremely intelligent, and he seemed wise beyond his years, all six of them now. Consequently, the idea that he would be even further removed than he already was in the twin cities was unacceptable to Caesar; somewhere, in the recesses of his mind where there were so many ideas and partially formed plans for the future, the Dictator for Life anticipated a time when his son would be old enough to travel with him personally, where he could continue the boy's education and make him worthy of carrying the name Caesar. The fact that, in the eyes of Rome, that would never happen, was particularly galling to Caesar, but as he had learned the hard way, almost to the point of his death, there were some customs and traditions that, going against them, was a threat to a man's life. And, as of this moment, nobody who was born of a non-Roman parent, even if it was the mother, could ever be considered Roman, but when that mother was the Pharaoh of Egypt and there were Roman patricians who believed that Caesar secretly harbored dreams of making himself king, the idea that they would ever accept Caesarion simply wasn't realistic.

In other ways, however, he had taken steps to break some of Rome's traditions that he considered wasteful or counterproductive, starting with his decision to never send for men of his own class to come from Rome to help govern, for the simple reason that the patricians of Rome were notoriously greedy and had long viewed a Praetorship as a means of enriching themselves. For what Caesar had planned, this type of governance would be disastrous to his plans, and while he had never uttered it publicly, the truth was that every high-ranking Roman he ever intended to have serve with him and his army were already on this side of Our Sea. That, however, wasn't of utmost importance now, and Caesar turned his attention to more pressing matters. While it was true that this last spark of resistance with Valash was important, and he was certainly frustrated with his nephew's handling of it, it wasn't at the top of Caesar's list of concerns. In fact, depending on developments in Merv, the Parthian nobleman and his small force might only be third on the list.

Although his departure from Bharuch had been abrupt, Caesar hadn't shared his real reason for doing so with Pollio or Hirtius, nor did he confide in Ventidius, who had descended the forty miles down the Indus from Pattala to meet his general at Barbaricum as Caesar was making his way back to Parthia. Not even Octavian knew that, in the tumultuous days after the fall of Bharuch, when Caesar's army essentially rebelled, a lone Liburnian had sailed up the Narmada, carrying an urgent message from Caesar's other nephew, Quintus Pedius, who was serving as Marcus Lepidus' Quaestor in Merv. That Octavian was unaware that his cousin had, if Caesar was judging it correctly, circumvented the normal process that was still in development, of messages being routed through Susa, where Octavian was located and coordinating everything, could be meaningful, but the contents of the message were disturbing enough on their own that Caesar didn't even consider it as an issue. If Caesar had been asked on the day after the fall of Bharuch, and he was coming to grips with the reality that he had finally asked too much from the men of his army, whether it would be possible for there to be a worse crisis, even his prodigious mind couldn't have conjured up what had been contained in that dispatch. Oh, he had always known Marcus Lepidus was a fool, of a type of Roman patrician that Caesar despised, those men who thought that the illustriousness of their names and the achievements of their ancestors was somehow passed down through the blood of their fathers, and very quickly in the campaign, Caesar realized that he had made an egregious error in Lepidus. And, Caesar was honest with himself, part of his antipathy towards these men was due to the fact that, for whatever reason, even the lower classes put their faith in their betters who carried the proper bloodlines that hearkened back to the days of Hannibal. It was utter nonsense, and for a man like Caesar who had become accustomed to bending anyone and anything to his will, it was a particularly bitter concoction to swallow. Now, if Pedius was to be believed, Marcus Lepidus had decided to take advantage of the challenges posed by the vast distances between Parthia Superior and Inferior to claim Merv as his own, although as of the dispatch that Pedius wrote, now two months earlier, everything was still in the planning stages. When forced to choose between assuaging his army and nipping what might have already developed into a plot to overthrow his rule, Caesar chose the latter, but in doing so, he instinctively understood that at that moment removing himself from these men, of whom he had asked so much, was perhaps the wiser course than attempting to confront them when tempers were still running so high. Not that he was foolish enough to leave the means by which the men could essentially follow him back to Parthia, and the fleet was now anchored at the newly constructed port of Caesarea at the mouth of the Euphrates River. Some things, he thought with bitter amusement, one shouldn't leave to chance. The fleet would be there, waiting; first, he had to decide what to do about Marcus

Lepidus.

The events that triggered Caesar's abrupt departure from Bharuch occurred at roughly the same time that Caesar's army assaulted Pattala, when Numerius Pompilius, who still sometimes thought of himself as Caspar, let out a groan before he even read the contents of the wax tablet that had been brought to him as he stood on the ramparts of Merv, watching a large cloud of dust, recognizing as he did the cramped, slanted letters as belonging to the Praetor Marcus Aemilius Lepidus. That the man was inept at military matters was, he supposed, something that Lepidus couldn't help; the fact that he refused to recognize that ineptitude meant that, within a month of their departure from Susa, Pompilius was regretting taking Caesar's offer for his *Crassoi* to return to their duty of guarding the trade route that passed through Merv, doing it in the name of Rome instead of their old Parthian masters. Throughout the march, on an almost daily basis, Lepidus had inserted himself into the daily routine of a Legion on the march, fussing about the order of the Cohorts that Pompilius had ordered for the day, or even about the length of each rest stop. It had taken a serious crisis, when Lepidus' refusal to stop at a waterhole simply because it was only a third of a watch into the day's march ended up with more than a dozen pack animals and almost as many draft animals dead of thirst because the next day's march didn't have any water, before Lepidus lapsed into a sulk that at least allowed Pompilius to handle the business of the march.

Once they arrived in Merv, more than three months after departing Susa since their families were accompanying them back home, very quickly, Lepidus resumed his meddling, carping about matters like the duty roster for the guard Cohorts. If that had been all, it would have been a minor nuisance that Pompilius and the other Centurions could have dealt with, but it wasn't more than a week after their arrival that Lepidus announced that he would be holding a full inspection of what was now officially called the *Legio Crassoi* and was considered part of the Army of the Dictator For Life Caesar. This was certainly within his authority, but it was less the inspection itself than the punishments he levied for various infractions that caused a near-mutiny. Violations like an improperly applied coat of varnish to the *baltea,* for example, was worthy of a flogging in Lepidus' view, although he magnanimously announced that it wouldn't be with the scourge. Use of the scourge was reserved for more egregious violations, like a spot of rust on a *gladius,* and it took a visit by a delegation of Centurions and Optios to the newly designated *Praetorium* to dissuade Lepidus from trying to see the punishments were carried out. The fact that this was accomplished by a barely disguised threat, in the form of a reminder that Lepidus was now two thousand miles away from Caesar, and even farther away from Rome, meant that relations between the Praetor and his Legion were very strained. Now Lepidus confined himself to moments such as this, in the form of a command to make sure that the honor guard, who he demanded be present for a banquet that night, hosting the prominent merchants of Merv, be up to his standards.

Pompilius understood that, without a doubt, one or more of his men would be found wanting, although the Praetor had given up on doing anything other than carping to Pompilius about it whenever they met. The only bright spot for Pompilius lay in a member of Lepidus' staff, the Tribune Pedius, who much to Pompilius' surprise, turned out to be another nephew of Caesar. Unassuming, and perhaps modest to a fault, at times Pedius could be almost unbearably earnest in his desire to do his best at whatever duty Lepidus assigned him, but the *Crassoi* Primus Pilus had determined that the man was far from dull of mind, and that he actually had a very good grasp on not just his duties, but the inner workings of Roman politics. Specifically, Pedius was serving as Lepidus' Quaestor in the administration of what was being referred to as the Roman province of Merv, part of the larger Parthia Superior, although the inhabitants of this province still had some ways to go as far as recognizing the change in their overlords. All that meant at the moment was that whatever resistance there was could be classified more as mischief than any serious attempt to regain control, but Pompilius had been hearing disquieting rumors from some of the caravans traveling through the Bactrian wastelands that the petty princelings, who were little better than bandit chiefs, were setting aside their differences with an eye towards trying to take Merv.

Because of its strategic location on what was called the northern route of the Silk Road, the city was probably the wealthiest of the former Parthian Empire, stuffed full of all manner of goods from the East and the land of the people called the Han, waiting for their turn on one of the regular caravans south. It would make whoever captured it an instantly wealthy, and more importantly, powerful man, but nobody had tried for several years. Not lost on Pompilius, any man of the *Crassoi,* or the people of the city and its environs for that matter, was the reason for the period of peace, and that was the

Crassoi themselves. It had been hard fighting, certainly; the ten thousand original survivors had been whittled down to the point that they now numbered less than a Cohort more than a full Legion, and that was using the traditional system of eighty-man Centuries, instead of the Legions under Caesar's command with their hundred-man Centuries. That Caesar hadn't insisted on Pompilius reorganizing to meet Caesar's standard was his recognition that by doing so, there would be a significant amount of retraining and shuffling of men from one Century to another, and just by virtue of their service, starting with Crassus, they had been in this configuration for well more than a decade.

Turning to Pedius, who had delivered the message and was standing on the rampart with him, Pompilius kept his eyes on the dust cloud that he could see was following the road to Merv but was still a few miles away as he said to the Tribune, "You can assure the Praetor that the men I send tonight will meet his approval, and will bring honor to him...and Rome," the Primus Pilus finished with heavy humor.

Pedius shifted uncomfortably; while he secretly agreed with Pompilius' scorn for his superior, he was in a ticklish situation, but his presence on the parapet with Pompilius was merely a pretext. He had asked to be the courier of this message because he had something important to relate to the Primus Pilus, but he was suddenly reluctant to do so, which Pompilius must have sensed, because he turned to eye the Tribune.

"What is it, Pedius?" he asked, but the younger man didn't reply immediately, choosing instead to cast a quick glance to either side where the men of Pompilius' Century were standing their guard duty on the wall.

Seeing that they were out of earshot, he still whispered to the Primus Pilus, "On that other matter we talked about? The one you asked me to look into?"

Immediately, Pompilius understood Pedius' hesitance, and like the other man, he took a quick peek over his shoulder; seeing that the nearest ranker was walking away, he turned back and said urgently, "And? What did you find out?"

"That," Pedius' voice dropped to even more of a whisper, so Pompilius barely made out him answering, "you were right. Lepidus is skimming from the tax revenues."

Pompilius swore softly; he had hoped he was wrong, but because Lepidus had seen fit to leave a handful of clerks in their positions, Pompilius had long before cultivated them as sources of information back when Teispes was the man in true command of the *Crassoi*. This kind of corruption had been a matter of course with the Parthians; the King of Kings was thousands of miles away, and as long as it wasn't too egregious, it was relatively safe, especially if the *satrap* made sure to grease the palms of those who were in a position to know about the movement of funds because of their duties.

"How bad is it?" Pompilius asked, but to his frustration, Pedius could only shrug as he replied, "I don't know yet." He paused, then added soberly, "But I'm guessing that it's quite a bit of money."

"Stupid bastard," Pompilius spat over the parapet to emphasize his point. "I know he's already as rich as Croesus, so what does he want more money for?"

Something in Pedius' demeanor changed suddenly, and noticeably enough that the Centurion turned to regard him sharply, but his tone was coaxing as he commented, "Judging by the look of you, I'd say you have an idea what it is."

"Not really," Pedius answered, but if he hoped this would be sufficient, he could tell by Pompilius' expression that it wasn't, and the truth was that not only was he disturbed by Lepidus' actions, he had come to trust the older Centurion quite a bit. Consequently, he went on, albeit reluctantly, "But, if I had to guess, I would say that Marcus Lepidus fancies himself as being worthy of challenging Caesar, and to do that, he needs money."

Pompilius considered this, but he was clearly unconvinced, saying, "He'd need a lot more money than what he could skim out of our tax revenues."

"Yes, he would," Pedius agreed, "but what if this was just the first step? What if," Pedius suddenly turned to indicate the city behind them, "his first step is to hire an army that would secure Merv itself? Would that give him the money he needs?"

Even before Pedius was finished, Pompilius realized the Tribune was correct, at least as far as any man who controlled Merv immediately becoming wealthy. Suddenly, he was struck by a thought; what if those Bactrians who were supposedly organizing to come try and take Merv weren't acting on their own, but were coming by the invitation of Marcus Lepidus? It would be a horrifically stupid thing for Lepidus to do; Pompilius had enough experience with those barbarians to know that they couldn't be trusted, but on the other hand, Lepidus had demonstrated his stupidity on more occasions than Pompilius could count. It was a staggering thing to consider, yet, somehow, Pompilius was certain that Pedius had guessed correctly. Before he could say anything else, however, one of his men who was actually doing their job of watching the road shouted for attention.

Turning in the man's direction, he saw the Gregarius pointing, with his javelin, out from the wall. Pompilius shifted his attention and saw that, while it was indeed a caravan, there was clearly something wrong. First, they were moving much more quickly than seemed necessary for this last mile to the gates, where they would be greeted by men of the *Crassoi* and a clerk attached to the Praetor's office, but it was missing some of the subordinate parts of what constituted a normal trade caravan; namely, there were no outriders visible, and several of the carts only had one man attending them instead of the normal two. Finally, there were no camels, which usually constituted the bulk of a caravan, the carts only serving to haul goods that could not be borne by a camel.

"Come with me," Pompilius said abruptly, forgetting that Pedius technically outranked him, although the Tribune certainly didn't take it amiss.

Trotting over to the stone steps, the pair descended to the street and arrived at the heavy iron-bound gates in time to meet the leading cart.

"What happened?" Pompilius shouted, speaking in the dialect he knew the lead driver spoke, recognizing the man.

"Ambush." The driver's face was spattered with blood, but it was the large, dark stain on his upper chest, along with the drawn, tight expression of pain that wounded men have that told Pompilius that the man was likely in his final moments. "We were ambushed," he repeated wearily, although the cart continued rolling through the gateway, the wheels echoing off the paving stones.

"Where?" Pompilius asked, making sure to walk with the cart, but only after issuing a snapped order to the clerk that the normal procedure of checking the carts wouldn't be followed. "Where did it happen?"

"About five miles from here," the driver managed, just before he slumped over to one side, which prompted Pedius to help brace the man, even as Pompilius exclaimed, "Five *miles*? What are bandits doing this close to Merv?"

The driver's eyes were closed as he half-leaned against Pedius, who was trying unsuccessfully to keep the man's blood from staining his own tunic, but this caused him to open them to look down at Pompilius, shaking his head as he said flatly, "It wasn't bandits."

"What do you mean it wasn't bandits?" Pompilius asked, but

even as he did, he felt a twisting in his stomach. "Who else would it be?"

The driver's strength was clearly failing, and Pompilius did feel a pang about prolonging the man's agony; he had seen very quickly that the wound he had suffered was mortal, the wooden seat of the cart puddled with the man's congealed blood, but this was too important.

With a weak shake of his head, the driver answered, "It was a band of *Tokharoi* raiders, I'm certain of it."

Pompilius froze in his spot, ignoring the remaining wagons that were being maneuvered around the one he had stopped, but his mind was racing as he tried to determine what this meant. Maybe, he thought, the driver was mistaken and just thought his attackers were the fierce warriors from Bactria, or maybe, because of his condition, he was confused, and the attack had happened much farther away. Yet, even as this entered his mind, he dismissed it; just the fact that the blood on the driver's seat of the cart wasn't completely dry proved that the driver was probably accurate in his assessment of the distance. A sudden movement from Pedius caught his eye, and he glanced up to see the Tribune, his tunic smeared with blood, lay the driver on his side on the seat, then stepped down to stand next to Pompilius, giving the Primus Pilus a brief shake of the head. Pompilius barely noticed, still grappling with this unexpected development.

Finally, he told Pedius, "We need to go to the *Praetorium* and tell Lepidus that it's possible that the *Tokharoi* have crossed the border."

He was already turning to walk away when the Tribune called his name, and in a way that caused the Centurion to look at Pedius with a raised eyebrow.

"What if," Pedius asked him softly, "Lepidus already knows that they've crossed the border?"

At first, Pompilius didn't grasp what Pedius was trying to tell him, and he asked skeptically, "How could he possibly know that if we just found out?"

"Because," Pedius replied immediately, his tone grave, "maybe he invited them."

For a moment, Pompilius could only stare incredulously at the Tribune, but as the idea settled into his mind, he experienced a queer, turning sensation in his stomach, and somehow, he was instantly certain that Pedius was right.

Two weeks later, Quintus Pedius was in a state of keen anxiety, and more than a little fear, which had begun within the watch of him handing the scroll to the man that Pompilius had brought to him, with the assurance that the man could be completely trusted to reach Caesar. It was only when Pompilius informed Pedius that, contrary to his appearance, the man was a Roman, albeit one who had seemingly wholeheartedly adopted the Parthian style, before Pedius relented and reluctantly handed the scroll to the man.

He did feel a little better when the man opened his mouth to speak with an Umbrian accent to assure Pedius, "It will never leave my person, Tribune. And I trust the men with me completely. We will get this to Caesar, I swear it, wherever he may be."

There was a regular courier service between Merv and Susa; in fact, there had been one before Rome invaded, but even under the best conditions, there was currently almost a month's delay between sending a message and receiving an answer, and as Pedius was acutely aware, much could change in that time, not just for him, but for what was now referred to as Parthia Superior. Pedius had no unique insight into why, in his estimation, Marcus Lepidus had lost his mind, of which there was precious little to lose, but if he had to hazard a guess, the young Roman believed that it was that very distance between himself and Caesar's authority that had convinced Lepidus he was fit to rule. Not govern, but rule; this was what Pedius' message contained, the results of what had begun a few weeks earlier, when Pompilius and Pedius had stood on the rampart of Merv and the Tribune had confided his suspicions. To Pedius' growing alarm, it hadn't been that difficult to unravel Lepidus' plans, such as they were, and that fact alone had convinced Pedius that Lepidus had gone mad. How else could defying the Dictator for Life, the most powerful man, not just in Rome but in the known world be explained?

Pompilius took a different view, which he expressed succinctly one night in Pompilius' private office, when the Primus Pilus had said flatly, "Marcus Lepidus is a stupid man who doesn't know that he's stupid. He thinks that along with his ancestry came the wits of whoever it was up his line that got his family into the patrician class." Pompilius had paused then, and he looked over the rim of his cup with a mischievous gleam in his eye as he added, "You know that the upper classes think their *cac* doesn't smell like ours."

As he knew it would, this only elicited a grin from Pedius, who raised his cup in a mocking salute. It, reflected Pompilius as he eyed the young Roman fondly, was something I never expected, both liking and respecting this noble Roman as much as I do. Just as his more ambitious cousin, who Pompilius distrusted, had observed, all Quintus Pedius wanted was to do his duty to Rome, to the best of his ability. His own ambitions, such as they were, revolved around his faith in Caesar and the belief that, should he acquit himself in an exemplary manner, Caesar would reward him. Of that, Pompilius wasn't so sure, if only because he didn't know Caesar very well, although it was well enough to convince this *Crassoi* to eschew a comfortable retirement and return to Merv to essentially resume his duties guarding the city and trade route. And, at first, he thought ruefully, it looked like it would be easy duty for the next ten years until I really do retire, but now Lepidus has fouled that up. Pedius and Pompilius had begun to make it a habit of meeting; at first, it was as much to allay any suspicions that Lepidus might have about why his Quaestor and "his" Primus Pilus, which was how Lepidus termed it, were meeting so frequently, which Pedius had explained to Lepidus as simply his attempt to help relieve the Praetor of his many duties. Fairly quickly, it became clear that Lepidus harbored no such suspicions, simply because, in his view, neither man was important enough to matter. As unambitious, for a Roman, as Pedius may have been, being seen in this light angered him, and gave him extra incentive to try and find out exactly what Lepidus had in mind. And, as such plans went, it was fairly straightforward; just as Pedius had suspected, Lepidus had sent envoys in secret to meet with representatives of the *Tokharoi,* offering them a quarter of the tax revenues coming from the lucrative trade along the Silk Road. That this wasn't Lepidus' to give was no impediment to the Praetor; oddly enough, this had been the sticking point between Pompilius and Pedius when it came to agreeing about what Lepidus was up to. From Pedius' perspective, it was inconceivable that Lepidus would think he could act with such impunity and not expect to suffer consequences. Finally, during one of their meetings, Pompilius had altered his tactics in attempting to persuade Pedius, as well as to pass along some information he had just acquired; acutely uncomfortable information at that.

"What will happen when Caesar learns about Lepidus' plans?" Pompilius had posed the question as if he was really interested in Pedius' answer, and while he was, he was also certain he knew it would force the Tribune to actually confront the reality of the situation.

"Why, he'll..." Pedius began confidently, but very quickly, his countenance clouded, he fell silent, then after a moment, finished lamely, "...I'm not sure what. But," he insisted, though Pompilius felt certain this was more from loyalty to Caesar than real conviction, "he'll think of something."

"He very well may," Pompilius agreed, then when Pedius clearly was about to argue the point, he added hurriedly, "in fact, I think he will. But the question is, how long will that take?"

And that, both knew, was the crux of the problem.

Seeing that he had made the first of his points, Pompilius pressed on, "I think that what Lepidus is banking on is the fact that by the time Caesar can do anything about it, he'll be so firmly entrenched here that the effort to retake Merv and drive him out will be too much trouble for Caesar to seriously consider."

"Then he doesn't know my uncle," Pedius scoffed. He took a swallow from his cup, but there was a hesitance in his manner that gave Pompilius some forewarning of what was coming. Careful to keep his eyes on the cup, Pedius asked quietly, "And what about the *Crassoi?*"

Despite sensing that this was going to be the topic, Pompilius had to stop himself from flinching; instead, he heaved a sigh.

"That," he admitted, "is a question that I don't know the answer to. At least," he added at Pedius' alarmed expression, "to the extent that will ease both of our minds." Turning his attention to the matter, the Primus Pilus began ticking off his internal list, extending a finger as he said, "I know Asina is with us. I trust him more than anyone else. Although," he felt compelled to add, "I don't want you to take it that I'm saying I don't trust anyone else. It's just that I know Asina and trust him with my life." *That's fine, but what about mine?* Pedius thought, but he wisely kept this to himself as Pompilius continued, bringing up his Secundus Pilus Prior, "Artabanus might be a problem. Of all the Centurions, he's the one who went native the most." He allowed himself a smile of morbid amusement. "He liked the idea of having more than one wife. Now he's up to his eyeballs in debt because he picked women with expensive tastes. But," he allowed, "if he turns it will only be for money, not for any other reason."

"In some ways," Pedius observed, "that's worse."

Pompilius nodded his agreement but extended another finger as he continued, "Glabrio is solid, but he's got a Princeps Prior who's in a similar situation to Artabanus. Perperna," he named his Quartus Pilus Prior, "might be shaky, but not Macrinus, the Quintus Pilus Prior. He's a horrible gambler, but he's never squeezed his men or run any kind game out in the city to make extra money."

Continuing down the list, by the time Pompilius was finished, Pedius was in a glum mood.

"That sounds like almost a third of your Centurions might throw in with Lepidus."

"They might," Pompilius conceded, yet he wasn't nearly as worried as his Tribune, and he reminded Pedius, "but that doesn't mean their men will follow them."

"Why do you say that?" Pedius asked, curious but somewhat skeptical.

"Because for ten years, these men thought they'd been abandoned by Rome," Pompilius answered quietly. "None of us wanted to fight for Parthia in the first place, but we had no choice. Then, when we started having families, it's true we had more to fight for, but once we learned *why* we had been forgotten, well…" He shrugged, not having the right words, so he simply finished, "…That changed things. So I don't think the men are going to be willing to risk betraying Rome now that we're back to being Romans."

"What about what happened with Pompeius? Weren't some of your men originally from the *dilectus* held by Pompeius?" Pedius asked, and Pompilius ruefully reminded himself that, behind his placid, somewhat plodding exterior, Quintus Pedius was not like Lepidus.

"That," Pompilius agreed, "might be the one thing that would cause some of the men to hold resentment towards Caesar. But," he argued, with some conviction, "none of them can fault how he's treated us. And," his expression turned grim as he remembered the night and day spent fighting outside Susa, and despite himself, he remembered the huge Primus Pilus who, with a simple turn of his wrist, spared his life when he had no reason to do so, "we all saw what Caesar's capable of, and I know *I* don't want to go through that again."

There was a silence then, both of them taking the time to drink, then Pedius asked, "So what do we do now?"

"Now," Pompilius counseled, "we're going to have to wait for Lepidus to do something stupid enough that it gives us the reason we'll need to take him prisoner."

Pedius considered for a moment, then surprisingly, he grinned at the Primus Pilus and said cheerfully, "Then we shouldn't be waiting long."

Both men erupted in laughter, but underneath, it was the knowledge that, as inept as Lepidus was, because of his status alone, he was a dangerous man. Fortunately, Rome was far, far away.

Pollio had come up with the idea more as a way to keep the men occupied than with any thought that Caesar's army would be staying in Bharuch for any length of time. It had taken some weeks for the men to settle down enough that their collective reason returned, and they realized that it was actually in their best interests to obey their nominal commander. The men liked Pollio well enough, Pullus knew, particularly the men of the 5th, 8th, 11th, and the 12th, their bond with the Legate strengthened by the ordeal of their march south from Pattala. Nevertheless, he hadn't been sanguine that the men would be as receptive to the idea of marching out into the countryside as Pollio seemed to be. Pollio's reasoning was certainly sound; Caesar's army may have entered a period of inactivity, but as he and the other Roman officers were acutely aware, the deposed King Abhiraka had escaped, and while he only had a fraction of his armored elephants remaining, he still commanded a respectably sized force, and there were persistent rumors that he had fled to a friendly kingdom to the south. That, at least, was the belief; in this area, Titus Pullus had been singularly unsuccessful with Hyppolita, who had refused to even mention her husband's name. In fact, she had been most informative during her moment with Caesar the day the city fell, when she had cheerfully confessed that her husband had escaped. And, despite their best attempts to control any access to the queen, Pullus was all but certain that she had somehow received word that he had been successful, both in evading capture, which Pullus would have known about, but that he had reached whatever destination he had decided on when he fled. How he was certain, Pullus couldn't articulate, but as he had gotten to know Hyppolita better, his surmises about her and her thought processes became more accurate, and he had learned to trust his instinct in such things. When Pollio had broached the topic, to Pullus, it appeared that his fellow Primi Pili were evenly divided on whether it was a good idea or a bad one, although he understood that the Primi Pili who objected weren't against the idea in itself, just that they didn't feel the timing was right. And, Pullus admitted to himself, it was a risk. Yes, the army had settled down, and men were obeying their officers, but to this point, every order they had been given concerned routine matters that were necessary to maintain an army that was ostensibly in the field, like the construction of permanent quarters right outside the city wall. This, however, was different; marching out into the countryside with a potentially hostile populace, and with the whereabouts of whatever forces the Bharuch king still commanded unknown was another matter altogether, and was the cause for the split.

"How many Legions are you talking about?" Balbinus asked Pollio.

"Two," the Legate answered immediately, telling Pullus that Pollio had given this some thought, which he explained by saying, "because three or more Legions will mean a baggage train that has to be guarded by at least a Cohort. And," he added, "I'm proposing that the men march in light order, and there only be two wagons per Legion in the field."

"That won't be enough to transport our wounded if something happens," Atartinus objected, and in this Pullus agreed with him, and he saw that most of the other Primi Pili did as well.

"That's not the only problem with just two wagons."

The others turned their attention to where Batius, the Primus Pilus of the 5th Alaudae was seated, next to Felix of the 6th, who was the oldest Centurion's closest friend, or what passed for it.

"Why is that, Batius?" Pollio asked politely enough, although Pullus sensed some irritation there.

"Because you're not going to get any Legion in this army to set foot outside this fucking city without a supply of that naphtha handy, and that *cac* has to be transported by itself. At least," he turned to glare at his counterparts as if daring them to gainsay him, "my boys won't. I won't speak for the other Primi Pili, but if you're expecting us to go out there, we need to be prepared for those fucking elephants."

Batius hadn't even finished before Pullus knew two things; that the other Primi Pili agreed with Batius, and that Pullus was one of them.

Pollio didn't hesitate, nodding as he agreed, "That's very true, Batius, and thank you for making that point."

Batius clearly wasn't expecting this, and it caused him to blink rapidly several times before he managed, "Yes, thank you, sir. Just doing my bit."

"So," Pollio continued, scanning the faces seated across from him, "each Legion will march with four wagons instead, but one of them will contain just the jars of naphtha, and three will be available for the wounded if it's necessary." Suddenly, his expression changed, and the Centurions learned why as he continued, "And while we're on this subject, I'm afraid that the news isn't good. I had Volusenus perform a full inventory of our remaining stocks of supplies, and while we've managed to at least partially solve the rations issue by substituting rice for wheat, I'm afraid that most of our remaining stock of wheat has spoiled."

As Pullus was certain Pollio expected, this was met by a chorus of dismay and a bit of anger. When the decision had been made to transition to rice as the staple, after some vigorous debate, Pollio had decided that the remaining stock of wheat would be used for special occasions, allowing the men to make their *castra paneris* on festival days and religious holidays. That had been the plan, at least; hearing this bit of news instantly ruined even that, and Pullus was with the others in not underestimating how serious it was.

"Any idea how it happened?" Spurius asked Pollio, reminding Pullus that, in this, he and the 3rd's Primus Pilus were very similar in outlook, preferring to focus on causes that could be rectified rather than bemoan the result.

"The damp," Pollio answered simply, which confirmed their suspicions. "The sacks we use weren't designed with this kind of climate in mind. I had the physicians examine every sack, and they assure me that the type of mold that has infected it will not only make us sick, it could kill us."

Naturally, they had all heard of such things happening, although it had never been on such a wide scale; more commonly, it was one corrupt sack of a Century's or even Cohort's supply, so it was confined to just those men. That it was every sack, and even after Pollio, who was aware that there was a risk of this contamination, had ordered the grain to be transferred to a warehouse in the city well away from the river, hoping that even a slight reduction in the dampness would save it. Obviously, this was bad news, but Pullus made sure to keep his eyes on Pollio as his comrades muttered to each other about the prospect of letting their men know that, now, there wouldn't even be a loaf on a festival day, and he was certain that this was the least bad of the bad news.

Which Pollio confirmed by continuing, "But, back to the overall supply situation. Our stocks of shafts, iron ingots, leather, and such can be replenished here, and the *Immunes* for each Legion have been doing that, as you all know." He paused then swallowed hard before he said, "But there's one vital material that we can't replenish here, and unless Caesar suddenly returns with a new stock, we're dangerously low. Especially if the king Abhiraka is lurking out there somewhere with his beasts."

There was no need for him to expand on this, every Centurion instantly understanding that it was the naphtha to which Pollio was referring, yet somehow, Pullus sensed there was something more to the story.

"Sir," he asked bluntly, "what is it that you're not telling us?"

Pullus was rewarded with a glare from Pollio, but the Legate wasn't the type to hold a grudge, and his irritation at being forced to fully divulge the state of affairs passed quickly enough.

Still, he did feel compelled to snap, "Well, Pullus, if you had waited a moment for me to catch my breath, you'd know already." Before Pullus could reply, he went on, "But while I agree that the Legions we send out will have a wagon devoted to just carrying the jars, I'm afraid that it won't be one wagon for each Legion. And," he hurried on, determined to get it all out, "that wagon is going to be the same one for every foray we send out."

In an eyeblink, the rustling and murmuring stopped, the silence becoming total as they each processed the meaning of Pollio's words at their own speed, and it was Pullus who spoke first, gasping, "Are you saying that we only have one wagonload of naphtha left for the entire *army*?"

"Essentially," Pollio replied grimly, "yes, Pullus. Oh," he waved a hand, "there will be a couple of crates left over, but we don't have enough to fill two wagons."

"The men can't know about this." Balbinus was the next to speak, his tone flat. "If they do, we'll never get them outside the walls of this fucking city."

"But we've proven that we can defeat those creatures," Pollio protested, but Pullus sensed that his heart wasn't really in it, knowing what was coming.

Which was supplied by Batius, who shot back, "And the only way we did it was using that *cac*." As he shook his head, his tone was every bit as firm as Balbinus'. "As long as the men know that we have enough of the stuff, I know my boys will march. But if they know this?" He shook his head again. "There's no way that they'll leave here. And, the gods know they hate this fucking place."

There was really nothing that Pullus could think to add, so he didn't try, and apparently, his counterparts felt the same way, because they all turned to Pollio, who nodded grimly.

"I agree," he addressed Batius. "So only those of us in this room, along with Volusenus, know the state of our naphtha supply, and we're going to keep it that way."

May Fortuna make it so, Pullus thought to himself with grim amusement.

"I'm not going to be able to make our walks for the next few days," Pullus told Hyppolita, waiting until the end of their evening circuit of the palace grounds.

"Oh?" Hyppolita had been ascending the stairs, and she stopped to look down at Pullus. "May I ask why, Centurion?"

"Of course you can," Pullus answered, then before she could say anything, he grinned and added, "but that doesn't mean I'll give you an answer."

"Why not?" she demanded, but in a playful manner. "I've told you all of my secrets, Centurion!"

This caused Pullus to laugh, replying, "Somehow, I doubt that, Your Highness. Although," he added, "I was quite shocked when you told me that you kissed one of your father's stable boys."

As he had hoped, this made her flush, quite prettily in his opinion, but she surprised him by laughing. "I never should have had that second cup of *sura*, but you talked me into it, Centurion, so you only have yourself to blame. Besides," now it was her turn to make him color, "I suppose it was worth it watching you trying to use your napkin to wipe your tongue."

Pullus glared up at her, but in the same playful manner. "You should have warned me that your people have found a way to start a fire in a man's mouth!"

"It did make the rice taste better, didn't it?"

"I don't know about better," he shook his head, "but it certainly was different."

They stopped speaking for a moment, and the silence stretched out until, unable to stand it any longer, the queen said quietly, "The fact that you will not tell me where you are going tells me what I need to know, Centurion. And I hope you will forgive me if I do not wish you success in your endeavor."

"I'd be disappointed in you if you did," Pullus answered without thinking. "And I wouldn't be surprised if you offered a prayer to your gods that we never came back, Your Highness, nor would I blame you."

"I cannot wish for your success," Hyppolita repeated softly. "But I confess that, if I never saw you again, Centurion, it would make me quite sad."

Then, before he could say anything, Hyppolita spun about and ran up the last couple of steps, rushing across the portico, so she didn't hear him say, "And me as well."

By the time he had gone a half-dozen steps, Pullus had almost convinced himself that he had imagined the whole conversation. You, he thought miserably, are one of the gods' biggest fools, Titus.

Truly you are.

Before he made his decision, Caesar summoned Teispes, and as he waited for him, he reflected on the irony at play here. First, Teispes was a Parthian, and if anyone had told Caesar a bit more than a year before he would come to trust a Parthian to the degree with which he was about to, he would have simply assumed that person to be mad. Yet, for Caesar, it was a simple proposition; Gundomir, the commander of his bodyguard, trusted his former enemy with his life, and nothing in anything the one-eyed Parthian who was close to Titus Pullus' size had said or done had given Caesar cause to distrust the man. The second irony was concerned more with the role the Parthian had played, and most importantly, where he played it. His thoughts in this direction were interrupted by the knock on the door to Caesar's private quarters, the only place where he felt confident to hold this conversation without fears of prying ears. At his permission to enter, the door opened and Teispes walked in, trailed by the German who had become his close friend.

"You wished to see me, Caesar?" Teispes had learned to not use the appellation "lord" or "master" with his commander, yet he couldn't seem to stop himself from bowing, although it would have displeased the King of Kings to see it performed at such a shallow angle.

"Yes, Teispes," Caesar was standing behind the small desk in his room, and he indicated the two chairs. "Please, both of you sit. I have some questions for Teispes, but I want to hear what you have to say about it, Gundomir."

Despite his scarred visage and his taciturn manner, Teispes was extremely intelligent, although it was something he rarely showed, and if he noticed that Apollodorus, Caesar's senior scribe who was almost always at his side was missing, as were any other occupants beside the three of them, his expression and manner didn't indicate it.

"Anything I can do to help you, Caesar," the Parthian said simply, "I will do."

"Given the time of year, how quickly do you think we can get to Merv?"

As he intended, this shocked both Teispes and Gundomir, and now it was Caesar who observed the two men exchange a glance with each other, although they didn't say anything.

Turning back to face Caesar, Teispes replied cautiously, "That depends, Caesar."

"On what?"

"The size and makeup of the party going there, for one thing," Teispes replied frankly. "The quality of the animals that they would be riding. And," he hesitated, "the quality of the men doing the riding."

Caesar's expression didn't perceptibly alter, but Gundomir recognized the amused gleam in the Dictator's eye.

"Let's just say," Caesar said equably, "that the men will be mounted on the best horseflesh that's available, and that the men are of..." his voice trailed off, as if he was trying to think, "...my quality. What would you say then?"

This got Gundomir on his feet as he stared at Caesar in astonishment, and while it was harder to tell with Teispes, Caesar could see he was similarly affected.

"Are you saying what I think you're saying, Caesar?" Teispes asked quietly. "That you're thinking of going to Merv?"

Now all hint of amusement was gone from Caesar's face, and he answered tersely, "It appears that I may have no choice, Teispes. But," he held up a hand, his voice hardening, "before I tell you why, I need you both to swear to me to your gods and your households that you won't divulge a word of what I'm about to tell you." Their hesitance was barely noticeable, although Caesar did, but decided to ignore it, thinking that it was not unwarranted, and most importantly, they both offered their oaths. Nodding, Caesar said, "Actually, before I burden you both with this, I have another question for Teispes." Leaning forward, Caesar's obvious interest was a bit unsettling as he asked, "What can you tell me about the *Tokharoi*, Teispes?"

Teispes frowned, not immediately understanding, but then quickly, his good eye widened noticeably.

"Are you saying that those dogs are causing Caspar and the *Crassoi* trouble?" he asked Caesar.

"Yes," Caesar admitted, "and no. It's a bit more complicated than that. But before I tell you what that complication is, I need to know about these people."

"They're scum." Teispes spat the word out, but quickly realized that this wasn't the kind of thing Caesar wanted to know, and he hurried to add, "But yes, they can be dangerous, if only because of their numbers. And," he allowed grudgingly, "they are our equals in using the land to their advantage. They are able to move quickly, and they do have a...talent for showing up when and where they are least expected." Frowning, he thought for a heartbeat, then shook his head as he continued, "But they won't pose a threat to the city, or to the *Crassoi* defending the walls if only because they do not possess the kind of artillery that would be needed. Their infantry, however," his tone turned thoughtful, and to Caesar, a little worried, "is superior to our own, because they do wear armor, and they fight using the same method as Alexander's Macedonians. Still," he shook his head, "as long as the *Crassoi* are on the walls, the city will be safe."

"What about the Silk Road?" Caesar asked, but he expected the reluctant shake of the head Teispes offered him.

"They certainly have the capability to sever that trade route," Teispes replied flatly. "Which is why our King of Kings always found it easier to bribe them."

Finally, Caesar realized that he couldn't put it off any longer, and he began by saying, "It appears that the *Tokharoi* may have found a higher bidder for their services."

He stopped, studying the faces of the other two men, somewhat surprised at himself that he was so reluctant to utter aloud what the message from his nephew Pedius had contained, and he silently willed them to work through the possibilities on their own.

And, somewhat to his surprise, it was Teispes whose expression changed to one of dawning recognition, only because Gundomir had expressed his opinion of the culprit.

"You don't mean Marcus Lepidus," Teispes gasped, but Caesar confirmed this with a grim nod.

"Yes, I am afraid I do, Teispes," Caesar answered, while Gundomir unleashed a string of oaths but managed to stop himself from spitting on the floor, a habit that it had taken Caesar a great deal of time to break with his German bodyguards when they were indoors. Taking a deep breath, the general continued, "I've received a message from Pedius that Marcus Lepidus has been skimming the tax revenues from Merv, and his purpose in doing so is to bribe the *Tokharoi* to aid him in his cause. And, while Pedius doesn't know with any certainty, he says that Pompilius thinks that it's possible that some of the *Crassoi* Centurions and their men may be involved with the plot."

"But what is the plot?" Gundomir asked, clearly somewhat bewildered, and it reminded Caesar that this kind of duplicity wasn't part of the German's makeup.

"To seize Merv and rule it as a king, and not in the name of Rome," Caesar answered tersely.

"Caesar," Teispes interjected, his tone almost gentle, "unless you are going to march with one of the Legions here, we will be unable to bring enough men to tip the balance back in our favor."

"That is true," Gundomir nodded emphatically. "And there is no guarantee that what your nephew is warning about has not already happened by now. We could be riding into a trap, Caesar." Shaking his head, the German said, "I know that it is your decision, but I must urge you to not make this journey."

Rather than confront the issue directly, Caesar turned to Teispes and asked, "How long would it take us to reach Merv? With," he paused, certain that the commander of his bodyguard was about to be even unhappier, "the three of us, and one hundred of my bodyguards?"

While Teispes shared Gundomir's reservations, he also could tell that Caesar's mind was made up, and he considered for a moment before answering, albeit reluctantly, "If you want to arrive on animals that are close to death, three of your weeks. Otherwise," he shrugged, "it would be a month. And," he warned, "we will probably lose some men on the journey, and we will definitely have less horses."

While Caesar expected the dire prediction about the animals, he was slightly unsettled by the Parthian's words about their riders, and he asked, "Why do you say we will lose men, Teispes?"

"Because, Caesar," the Parthian answered quietly, "I have never made that journey in either direction where we did not lose some men." Sensing that Caesar needed more, he explained with the Parthian version of a shrug, holding both hands palm up as he said, "Sometimes a man suddenly falls ill because the water is bad, and for whatever reason, the gods decide that he not recover. Other times, it is because a horse stumbles and it catches the rider unaware, and he lands badly. The cause may be different, but the result has always been the same. We will lose men."

"And then, we may lose our heads if that coward has managed to take control of the city," Gundomir put in.

Caesar couldn't deny there was truth in this, yet there was something in him that refused to consider, let alone accept, the idea that Marcus Aemilius Lepidus could ever best him in anything.

Whether or not this was the deciding factor, the pair would never know; what they did see was that Caesar didn't hesitate, ordering them, "Make the necessary preparations. Pick the best men you think will hold up the best on this journey, and I want one," suddenly, he paused, then amended, "make that two spare horses per man. And," he smiled slightly, "judge the horseflesh with the same care you use to choose the men, since we'll be relying on them. How many days will you need?"

"Three," Teispes and Gundomir answered, in unison, which made Caesar smile slightly.

"You have two," he told them, and he instantly saw that neither of them were surprised in the least.

The day after Pullus' conversation with Hyppolita, Pullus and his 10th, with Felix of the 6th, were finally south of the Narmada River, which had posed the first logistical challenge. Far too wide and deep to ford, the nearest fordable spot being more than twenty miles east, the Legions and their baggage, as minimal as it was, had to be ferried across the river, which took the better part of the morning. Accompanying the pair of Legions were two full *alae* of cavalry, under the command of Decimus Silva, who had been promoted to the rank of Prefect, an astonishing rise through the ranks that in many ways was similar to the meteoric ascent of Titus Pullus, who trusted Silva implicitly, more than any other cavalry commander with whom he had ever served. While the Roman cavalry had become more diverse in its makeup, missing completely were the *cataphractoi* from this march, for the simple reason that heavily armored horses laboring in this climate would have been more of a detriment than any kind of asset. Representing the Parthians was a complement of horse archers, led by Darius, who had been summoned from Pattala by Pollio in anticipation of this new venture out into the countryside. His inclusion in the force was met with some resistance, namely from Pullus, who didn't trust the young Parthian, although it had nothing to do with his abilities in the field. Despite his ignominious beginnings as the bastard son of the dead former commander of the garrison at Susa, Gobryas, Darius had proven to be quite capable of leading men in the field, and while Pullus wasn't happy about it, he hadn't done more than grumble. Because of the time it took to cross the river, the march didn't begin immediately, as the Romans had begun taking the advice given by Hyppolita to avoid strenuous activity during the hottest part of the day, which meant the men had been given permission to leave their packs in their spots to head to a grove of trees, mostly banyan, that were still standing.

"I'm happy these savages think these things are sacred," Balbus commented as he stood with Pullus and Scribonius, just under the shade of the overarching trees. "Otherwise, we'd be fucked. Even," he plucked at the sleeve of his tunic, "with these."

Pullus was only partially listening; he was focusing most of his attention on what had transpired since sunrise, which was what prompted him to muse aloud, "We're going to have to come up with a better way to get across the river so that we don't end up spending a watch just lying around." Scribonius shot Pullus an amused look, certain that his concern was more about the idea of men not engaged in some sort of activity the Primus Pilus thought was productive, but discovered this was only partly the cause, when Pullus continued, "You know that we're being watched, and now whoever's south of us is going to have more warning that we're coming. And," he finished worriedly, "the chance to prepare for us."

It was, Scribonius immediately understood, a valid concern, but it also served as yet another ramification of all that had transpired immediately after the fall of Bharuch, because by this point in time, Caesar would have had the region to the south thoroughly scouted. Not that Scribonius, or any officer for that matter, faulted Pollio for his caution in sending forays out, ordering that any mounted scouting party not exceed a distance of twenty-five miles in every direction from the city. Nevertheless, the end result was the same; the Romans were woefully ignorant of what lay in their direction of travel, although they had gleaned that there wasn't much variation in the terrain, nor any prominent land features. Felix hadn't been particularly happy about it, but neither was he surprised when Pollio designated Pullus as the overall commander, and while a Prefect technically outranked a Primus Pilus, it didn't even occur to Silva to argue for the leadership. Understandably, Pollio didn't feel confident in leaving Bharuch, but the only reason Aulus Hirtius wasn't in command was that he had been sent on his own task, leading the rest of the cavalry, north of the river, but farther east than the Romans had gone previously. It was a calculated risk, certainly, but not a large one in Pollio's estimation, and with every passing week and no word from Caesar, he had begun to feel the strain of being in complete command of this massive army, which had prompted his decision to explore more of this kingdom.

Finally, the time passed sufficiently that Pullus nodded to his *Cornicen*, and the men went streaming from the banyan forest, resuming their spot in the formation. Very quickly, the march resumed, taking them farther away from the city, meaning that there was a corresponding rise in the tension. Pullus deliberately set a slower pace than normal, but as the column moved south, Silva's men were ranging several miles ahead, searching for one of the few landmarks that the Romans knew lay to the south, another river. As frustrating as it was to have such limited information, the difficulty was compounded because, to this point in time, there was only one man in the entirety of Caesar's army who was able to communicate with the common people of Bharuch. That he was next to Pullus, albeit on his horse, was a signal of his importance, and it was something that the Primus Pilus actually worried about, thinking about what conclusion he would draw if he observed a lone horseman marching alongside a column of men entirely on foot, since it clearly marked Achaemenes as an important figure of some sort. Fortunately, early on in the march, there was an expanse of open ground that, while there were belts of forest lining either side of this area, they were far enough away from any kind of missile. Before they had traveled five miles from the river, Pullus had determined two things: they wouldn't be making even ten miles on this first day, and every single inhabitant of the two small villages they had passed through had fled, presumably into those forests. He had done his best to enforce Caesar's orders against looting any habitation where there had been no resistance, which was now widely known by the army as their general's policy, but he also knew it was a forlorn hope to think that a total of twenty Cohorts of hardened Legionaries hadn't thoroughly searched every dwelling and every outbuilding for anything remotely valuable. The fact that he had quietly ordered his Centurions to look the other way and had suggested the same to Felix was something that, as far as he was concerned, Caesar never needed to know about. If he was so worried about it, he thought sourly after he had led his men down the single track that bisected what passed for a village, he should be here. It did not rain that day, at least, something that every Roman had learned to appreciate, although only once had it gone an entire week without some sort of rainfall.

"I wish we could find someone for you to talk to," Pullus commented to the young Parthian, who, aside from his natural talent for languages, was normally diffident in his habits, and it wouldn't have surprised Pullus to learn that Achaemenes was thoroughly intimidated by the Roman whose head came up almost to his waist, even on horseback.

Still, he understood a response was expected, and he admitted, "It would be good. Although," he ventured timidly, "I'm not sure what help these villagers would offer, Primus Pilus."

"Why?" Pullus asked curiously, mainly because it was so rare for Achaemenes to speak so many words at one time, but he thought to expand, "Because they don't know, or because they're not willing?"

The Parthian glanced down at the Roman, somewhat surprised

that this giant had made that kind of distinction, and he reminded himself not to underestimate anyone associated with Caesar's army.

"Both," he answered honestly. "Although," he added quickly, "not so much out of any loyalty to the king, but because you," he gestured to indicate the entire column and not just Pullus, "are so foreign to them. Still, it is more because they do not know anything. If the King of Bharuch is anything like our King of Kings, Primus Pilus, sharing information with the peasants was never a priority."

Pullus nodded thoughtfully, then felt compelled to point out, "That's not altogether different from we Romans, Achaemenes, but I suppose it's just a matter of degree. We know more, but not because our patrician class wants to share information with us." Shaking his head, Pullus added, "And it took a lot of turmoil and strife before we got to where we are now. We had kings at one point, just like here and Parthia, but those days are gone."

"But," Achaemenes interjected, clearly puzzled, "surely you consider Caesar your king."

The look Pullus gave the Parthian was one mixed with equal parts amusement and alarm, and he warned, "You need to be *very* careful who you say that to, Achaemenes, and never say that to another Roman."

This startled Achaemenes, and he shook his head in bafflement.

"But that's what he is, Primus Pilus! He has unlimited power, does he not?"

"Yes," Pullus agreed readily enough, but he was unmoved, repeating, "but don't refer to him as a king, Achaemenes. Not," he thought to add, "if you value Caesar's life. And," Pullus made sure to look the Parthian directly in the eye, "if you value yours. I know you mean no harm, and I can see why someone like you would think of him in that way, but words like 'king' matter to us, and it could endanger Caesar's life. Do you understand me?"

Even if he had been disposed to argue, Achaemenes' throat had gone so dry that he would have been unable to, and all he could manage was a nod. This wasn't enough for Pullus, but before he could press the issue further, there was a shout from the section of men who were two hundred paces ahead of the rest of the column.

It took a moment, but Pullus finally caught movement beyond them, which Achaemenes was able to identify given his higher vantage point, and he informed Pullus, "There is a party of riders approaching, Primus Pilus."

Pullus didn't hesitate, turning to Valerius, his *Cornicen*, ordering him to sound the halt, then began trotting towards the approaching riders, but he thought to call over his shoulder, "Don't forget what I said, Achaemenes."

Who assured him that he would do no such thing, drawing up to watch as Pullus hurried to meet the returning scouts, trying to imagine all the things that Titus Pullus could do to him, and not liking anything that came to mind. Such was his concentration that he didn't notice that one of the riders had another person sitting behind him, and it took Pullus two times to bellow his name before he understood he was needed. Moving at a trot, the Parthian finally saw that there had been a passenger, although the person was now on the ground, a man wearing what was not much more than a loincloth and whose exposed skin was a much darker brown than even the commoners of Bharuch, betraying that this man spent every waking moment under the broiling sun.

Without any preamble, Pullus said, "They found this man tilling his fields, along with a couple dozen others. Everyone else got away. This one," he added with grim amusement, "was a bit too slow."

Achaemenes hadn't received any real training in the art of interrogating people, but he instinctively understood that he needed to put this man, who was clearly terrified, as much at ease as was possible given the circumstances. To that end, he dismounted, then approached the man, whose age was impossible to determine, and was visibly shaking with fear, offering him a smile.

Speaking slowly, the Parthian bowed to the man, an incongruous gesture, and his tone was as polite as he could manage. "Greetings to you, friend. My name is Achaemenes. While I am originally from Parthia, my father moved us to Bharuch when I was young, which is how I know your tongue." This was a lie, but Achaemenes believed it was in a good cause, and he was rewarded by seeing the man relax, not much, but enough to notice. "May I ask your name?"

"My name is Javas, lord," the man replied, and Achaemenes immediately discerned there was a slightly different accent to the man's words.

"We will not hurt you, Javas," Achaemenes assured him, although at the same time, he wondered if that was actually true. "We just have some questions."

"What kind of questions, lord?" Javas asked, his suspicion replacing fear as his predominant emotion.

Achaemenes thought quickly, and he realized that it was better to start with a topic that was less dangerous than asking about Abhiraka and his whereabouts.

"What lies that way?" He pointed south.

"The river," Javas answered immediately. "The Nanagounas (Tapti) River, lord."

"And how far is it from here?" Achaemenes asked.

Javas considered for a moment, then answered, "A half-day's walk, lord."

"And what is on the other side of that river, Javas? What is the land like?"

The look the farmer gave Achaemenes was an answer in itself, and would serve as both a reminder and a warning that, for the common people of this land, their world could be measured by their ability to reach it on their feet.

"I do not know, lord," Javas admitted. "I have never been across the river. Although," he added thoughtfully, "a *Vaidya* came to my village a few months ago, and he said he had come from far, far away, to the south."

"And what did he tell you? Are there mountains? Or," Achaemenes gestured to their surroundings, "is it like this?"

"He said that there are high hills to the east," Javas pointed in the general direction to the southeast, "but that they curve west." He thought for another moment, then said, "He also said there is a very powerful king, with many men and many elephants. But," he shook his head, "that is all I know of this." Then, before Achaemenes could respond, Javas added, "I know that the daughter of the King of Bharuch is married to one of that king's sons, but I do not know which one."

Pullus, who had been standing listening but not understanding anything, did pick up the use of "Bharuch," but it was the manner in which Achaemenes reacted that caused him to look sharply over to the translator to demand, "Well? What did he say? I heard him say Bharuch."

Without thinking, Achaemenes held up a cautioning hand, his attention fixed on the native farmer, and realizing this was the opportunity for which he was looking, asked, "And have you seen the king, Javas? Has he been anywhere near here?"

Somewhat surprisingly, Javas didn't hesitate, shaking his head and answering, "I have not seen King Abhiraka for many months now." He shrugged and added in an offhanded manner, "I had not even seen men on horseback until this morning, but we saw them first, and ran and hid in the forest."

Achaemenes was about to move on, thinking that the farmer meant the men who had captured him, until his mind caught up with the meaning, the real meaning of the farmer's words.

Still, he wasn't unduly alarmed, but just to make sure, he gestured to the mounted party who had brought him in, saying, "You mean these men, Javas?"

"No, lord," Javas answered firmly, shaking his head. "I mean the ones who rode south just after the sun came up." He turned and indicated the cavalrymen. "These are the men who caught me." Javas made a face that, under other circumstances, might have been humorous. "This time, I was too slow."

Pullus had been watching this with growing irritation, thinking that the Parthian was wasting time, but as the interrogation progressed, he began feeling a sense of alarm. When Achaemenes finished with the farmer, who still looked frightened but wasn't quaking in terror anymore, one glance at the Parthian's face gave Pullus a presentiment that the news was bad.

"We were spotted, and this farmer says that he saw a group of horsemen riding south very early today."

"So," Pullus said grimly, "whoever is south of here will be waiting for us."

It had been an extremely trying time for Bolon, forced as he had been to lurk south of the Narmada, ordered by his king to never risk getting closer than a point where he could safely observe the city walls from hiding. At first, it had seemed to be a blessing from the gods that, for reasons he was able to put together from bits and pieces of information provided by the few inhabitants of the city who were allowed to venture away from Bharuch, the Romans had been far too occupied with their own problems to send any kind of force south of the river. He learned in general terms that there had been some sort of mutiny by the men he still thought of as demons, these Romans who had brought fire and sword to his kingdom and his King, and it had been of such a severe nature that it had completely curtailed any activities of an offensive nature on the part of the invaders. Certainly, this was good news, yet as the days turned into weeks, Bolon and the four men remaining with him, all volunteers from Abhiraka's royal bodyguard, couldn't stop themselves from dwelling on what they didn't know, specifically the status of their families. The fate of their surviving comrades who had been left behind when Abhiraka fled, using a secret passage that had been created for just such an emergency, was largely unknown. From one person, they heard that they had all been slaughtered; from another, they had all been spared but were being held prisoner, while a third version went that the rank and file soldiers had been spared, while men of high rank or the royal bodyguard had all been executed. Bolon had no way of knowing, but for reasons he couldn't articulate, he leaned towards the last alternative.

Aside from this relatively rare contact, which was always done with extreme caution and never by more than one of them, what Bolon found the most wearing was the isolation, and the lack of knowledge of the larger situation. It had surprised him that he had adjusted relatively well to living rough, using the thick forests that were still abundant throughout the expanse of the territory that had been controlled by Bharuch. Initially, they decided that the best way to avoid capture was to not spend more than one night in the same place, fully expecting that upon their return to Bharuch, the enemy would have established firm control of at least a portion of the southern bank of the river. However, within a couple of days after their return, which was a week more than a month after the fall of the city, they had been shocked to learn this wasn't the case. Consequently, they established a series of semi-permanent encampments, which they used for a period of time before moving to the next, all while waiting for what they had believed was inevitable. Originally, their scouting force had been composed of five men, but once Bolon determined that there was indeed a situation that had forced the Romans to remain north of the river, he had deemed this noteworthy enough to dispatch one man south to the Pandyan kingdom, where Abhiraka had been received by their king friendlily enough, although Bolon was certain there were limits to his hospitality. And now, these months later, Bolon and his comrades' patience had finally been rewarded, in the form of what he estimated to be at least eight thousand men who had been ferried across the river. There had been some argument between Bolon and his comrades about whether they should stay to observe longer to get a better idea of what the Romans were up to, but Bolon was adamant.

"Our king told us to alert him the moment those demons set foot south of the Narmada," he said firmly, "and that is what we are going to do."

They had saddled their mounts and were moving within a third of a Roman watch, heading south at as rapid a pace as they could manage without killing their horses. Abhiraka would be warned, and then it was up to the king to decide what to do.

In a manner eerily similar to what had taken place in Bharuch, Octavian had awoken to learn that Caesar had departed Susa. This was troubling enough, but after some questioning of a number of men that grew increasingly heated, by the time he was satisfied that he at least knew as much as he was going to, he wasn't much better informed, but he was far more alarmed.

"How could he just vanish like that?" he cried out, not for the first time as he paced back and forth in front of his desk.

"Because," Agrippa replied calmly, "he's Caesar."

"I know who he is," Octavian snapped, showing a rare flash of temper at his subordinate and friend. "But that doesn't mean he can just…leave!" He took a deep breath, then asked plaintively, "And what am I supposed to do about Valash?"

This prompted Maecenas to interject, "I think that you might want to look at this as a chance to show Caesar that, despite some setbacks, you're the man for the job."

Octavian stopped pacing then, his manner suddenly turning thoughtful, and it was a trait that Marcus Agrippa admired, how quickly his friend could regain his self-control of matters, and when he spoke again, it was back to his normal, slightly dispassionate tone.

"And now that I have the 14th here, and with the 21st supposed to arrive before the beginning of the next campaign season, I need to take advantage of this while I can. Because," at this, he turned to Agrippa, his voice inflected in a manner that Agrippa knew was his way of seeking advice. "I can't expect Caesar to keep both of those Legions here in Parthia. He clearly has plans for them."

"That," Agrippa agreed, "is my assessment as well, Gaius."

Octavian actually smiled then, seeing another side to this matter, "And with Caesar disappearing, without leaving specific instructions, the 14th is mine to command as I see fit, wouldn't you agree?"

This elicited an exchange of glances between Maecenas and Agrippa that, as usual, confirmed their thoughts were running along the same lines, that while this was true on its face, there was a vast difference between talking about it and actually doing it.

Finally, Maecenas offered, "I would agree…provided that you win, Gaius."

"I will," Octavian declared flatly, not in a boastful manner, but with the determined tone that they had both heard before.

Teispes had been telling the truth, Caesar thought grimly; this is going to be a brutally hard ride. Surprisingly, what bothered him the most was the itch from his growing beard, although he did wake from the watches of sleep he and the rest of them snatched during their rest intervals with a growing deep ache in his body that reminded him that not only was he mortal, he was older than the oldest man with him by more than fifteen years. The Parthian pointing out that at least this wasn't at the height of summer didn't help much, because at night, it got brutally cold, but Caesar took quiet pride that he was holding up better than most of the other men of his party. Another thing that had surprised Caesar was how the utter barrenness of their surroundings was affecting him, and he saw that he wasn't alone. Only Teispes seemed impervious to both the elements and the seemingly unending lack of variety in the terrain, and Caesar had the strong sense that the Parthian finally felt truly in his element. He set a quick pace but insisted that they swap mounts every watch, stopping only long enough to unsaddle their current horse and switch it to the fresh horse, although he also insisted that the animals be watered, even if they were spares. While it was true that the spare animals were spared a rider, they weren't completely unencumbered, each of them with a pair of water skins slung over them. Nevertheless, even with these precautions, it was inevitable that of the three hundred animals, a handful would go lame, and it was here that Teispes truly showed his worth, the Parthian aware of every village, minor *satrapy*, and way station that had been created decades earlier by one of the King of Kings for those traveling under royal authority to the farthest reaches of the far-flung empire that was now the largest Roman province. It required some deviation from the most direct route, but in a sign of his trust in the Parthian, Caesar accepted Teispes' assurance that it would make up for itself in the long run by keeping them supplied with fresh, sound mounts.

Mile by mile, and day by day, they made their way across some of the most desolate terrain imaginable, and it deepened Caesar's appreciation and admiration of those men of the *Crassoi* who had endured this dreadful march, under much worse conditions. Understanding that the survivors of Crassus' ill-fated campaign suffered more than Caesar and his party were helped somewhat, but it was ten days into the journey that Teispes' grim assessment of losing men was fulfilled, when the horse of one of Gundomir's men lost its footing on the shifting sandy expanse they were crossing. It was something that wasn't unusual, even for experienced horsemen, but before the German could throw himself clear, his left leg was crushed underneath the massive weight of his animal, breaking his thigh bone. Even a simple fracture would have been devastating, but in the bodyguard's case, when the horse, who was ironically unharmed, regained its feet and went trotting off, the first thing that

Caesar saw was the dull white of bone poking through the man's *bracae*, the leg of which was already soaked in blood. Writhing in agony, the doomed man instantly understood that his fate had been sealed, and it was left to Gundomir, his commander and comrade to kneel behind his trooper, allow the man to gasp out a prayer to their gods, then draw his dagger across the man's throat. The fact that Caesar, unbidden, had dismounted to kneel at the man's side and hold the German's hand as he was sent to the afterlife was a memory that every man who witnessed it would remember.

Naturally, once they remounted and resumed the day's ride, the mood was somber, and it was several miles before Caesar suddenly turned to Teispes to ask, "How many more times do you think something like this will happen, Teispes?"

As was his habit, Teispes thought carefully before he replied, "Four, perhaps five more times, Caesar." Before Caesar could respond, he added, "Although we are about to enter a stretch where water is very scarce, and what little there is can be close to undrinkable." Shrugging, he finished flatly, "So it is likely that we will lose one or two men to that."

Caesar considered Teispes' words, then finally replied, "As long as we get to Merv to stop whatever it is that Lepidus is up to, then it will be worth it."

"To you, perhaps, Caesar," Teispes countered, although there was no censure in his tone; to Caesar's ears, it seemed that the Parthian was simply stating a fact when he finished, "but I suspect the men we lose will disagree with you."

That, Caesar understood immediately, wasn't something even he could argue, so he didn't try.

Eleven days after their departure, Titus Pullus led the two Legions back to Bharuch, both of which were intact for the most part, while those who had ended up in the wagons hadn't suffered from a blade or missile, but from the foreign and harsh climate. There had been one death, in the Fifth of the 6th, but that had been from the bite of a serpent, the likes of which none of the men had ever seen before, with what seemed like a hood and a symbol on the back of its head resembling the Greek character Omega, which they learned the locals called a *Naja*. Neither Pullus nor any of the men of the 10th, and most of the 6th, hadn't witnessed it, but a clearly shaken Felix had arrived at Pullus' tent one night, describing in gruesome detail the last watch of his Legionary's life. Completely unsurprisingly, this created issues with the Centurions and Optios, as men who could look over the top of their shield at a screaming enemy rushing to kill them without blinking were literally quaking in fear at the thought of death at the hands of some scaly beast. What made it worse were the circumstances, which despite the grim topic, forced Pullus to maintain his solemn demeanor as Felix described what would ultimately be the cause of the man's demise.

"Postumus stepped out of the march to take a piss," Felix had explained to Pullus, staring down into his cup, "and he only took a few steps away from the column. That fucking...thing bit him right on the end of his cock!"

It was, Pullus thought, anything but funny, yet he also knew that, before long, men would turn this into a source of humor, and he also knew that he would be one of them, not out of cruelty towards a comrade, but because, really, what else could one do but laugh?

Aside from the demise of the Gregarius Postumus, the result of the extended march out into the southern portion of the kingdom of Bharuch had been informative, although it was mixed with equal parts good and bad. Within a third part of a watch after Pullus was in the first boat back across the Narmada, leaving Balbus to supervise the 10th's crossing, he was standing in front of Pollio in the large building that was on the eastern edge of the large square that was used for gatherings and a monthly market with merchants and vendors from outside the city, a practice that was currently halted, but Pollio was considering reinstituting. He had never learned exactly what purpose this building served, since it seemed to be for some sort of governmental function, although there was a spacious private apartment on the second floor, but Pullus had never gotten around to asking Hyppolita about it. Now, sitting in front of the desk that he was beginning to think of as Pollio's and not Caesar's, the Primus Pilus consulted the tablet containing the notes he felt were important to relay in this first meeting.

"The southern boundary of what is considered Bharuch is more than a hundred miles south of here," Pullus began. "There is a fair-sized town on the northern bank of a river that the natives call the Goaris (Ulhas) River. It's about the same width as the Narmada, again according to the natives."

"Did you enter the town? Was there a garrison?" Pollio asked, also taking notes.

"No." Pullus shook his head. "Only Silva and his boys got close enough, and that was only close enough to see that there was a wooden wall."

"What's the ground like?"

"That," Pullus frowned, "is where the news isn't particularly good. For the first fifty miles south, the ground is as flat as it is here, but there are more forests. Just on the other side of the first river to the south, which is twenty-five miles, that's when you can see some low hills off to the east. We were told by the first native we could question that the line of hills ran parallel to our direction of march before they curve west, but he didn't know how far it was since he's never been on the other side of the river." Pullus paused, taking a sip from the cup of water Pollio had offered, then grimaced as he explained, "Honestly, at first I was skeptical that these barbarians know as little as they seem to and they were just being sly, but they almost always had the same story."

"Story?" Pollio frowned. "What kind of story?"

"That their world is measured by how far they can walk in one, maybe two days," Pullus explained. "As I said, I didn't believe them at first, but their stories were too similar not to be at least partially true." Realizing that this wasn't of utmost importance, Pullus returned to his notes. "As it turns out, those hills curve west starting about twenty miles south of that second river, and while it's not terrible, it did force us to march closer to the coast. The last day before we turned back, Silva told us that we were only five miles from the coast, and that it narrows down even more a few more miles south."

"So," Pollio mused, "it sounds like there is a natural choke point, which is probably where this Abhiraka is likely to meet us when we move south."

"That," Pullus agreed, "was my thinking." Returning to his notes, Pullus went on, "Aside from the handful of villages and their inhabitants, we didn't see any signs of anything that would indicate there is a presence of whatever is left of Bharuch's army. Now," he added, "there are elephants, but no war elephants. Every animal that we saw was being used for some form of labor."

"That's good news," Pollio agreed, but then he saw something in Pullus' face that caused him to ask cautiously, "What is it? What aren't you telling me?"

"The day we crossed the river," Pullus answered immediately, "we learned that a mounted party went riding south, very quickly. I put Silva on their trail, but," he shook his head, "it went cold two days later."

Pollio instantly understood the meaning.

"So we were being watched, and now it's likely that Abhiraka has been warned. Although," Pollio added, not terribly concerned, "he can't have much of his army left."

Again, Pollio got an instant's warning before Pullus said, "There's more."

Pollio listened as Pullus explained what they had learned from Javas, and had subsequently been confirmed; even worse, enough details had been added that Pullus could inform Pollio that, with a relative degree of certainty, the Primus Pilus could let Pollio know why they had been unsuccessful in finding the contents of the royal treasury of Bharuch.

By the time Pullus was through, Pollio was barely able to remember any of the positive news, and he rubbed his face as he thought aloud. "So Abhiraka may not have an army left, but it probably doesn't matter since he's got only the gods know how much gold and silver to buy another one." Before Pullus could respond, he added, "I wonder how much there is."

"Judging from the overall wealth of this city," Pullus observed, not particularly liking what he was saying, "I imagine it's a fair amount."

Pollio nodded, then his expression hardened, and he pointed a finger at Pullus. "You need to talk to that fucking queen of yours, Pullus. We need to know not only how much money her husband has, we need to know how cozy a relationship he has with this king of...what do they call themselves?"

"The Pandya," Pullus responded, although his mind was only partially on this part of the conversation.

"Right. Them." Pollio nodded. "In fact, I think you need to make your way to that palace immediately, before she knows that you're back. Better to catch her by surprise."

Recognizing that he was being dismissed, Pullus stood, saluted, but in a breach of protocol, didn't repeat Pollio's last order. While he understood that the Legate was correct to be concerned and had a right to be angry, neither could Pullus deny that his words about Hyppolita had stirred his own sense of anger, but while some of it was directed at her, most of it was at Pollio. It was, he thought miserably as he made his way down the street to the palace, very confusing.

"Why didn't you tell me that you have a daughter who is married to the crown prince of the largest kingdom to your south?"

As he hoped, Pullus saw that this caught Hyppolita by surprise, and if he had been confused before, it was even worse now, because he had recognized the look of pure happiness she had given him when he had been shown into her chambers on the second floor, if only because he had instantly felt the same way.

However, Hyppolita was a queen, and while she wished she had worn her veil, it was too late for that, so the shock she had displayed, as much at Pullus' abrupt tone as the words themselves, was only there for a flicker, and when she replied, her tone was cool. "And why, may I ask, should I have told you that, Centurion?"

Suddenly, Pullus realized that, when put this way, it was not only a pertinent question, it was one without a good answer, yet he was still sufficiently irritated with her that he snapped, "Because, Your Highness, in case you haven't noticed, this city is under the control of Rome!"

"For now," she shot back, now equally angry, her cheeks flushing with color as she glared at the large Centurion.

"For now," Pullus seemingly agreed, but his voice grew cold as he added, "and for as long as Caesar wants, and the sooner you accept that, the better it will be for you and your people."

No sooner were the words out of his mouth did Pullus wish he could recall them, because he was certain that if he had slapped her, the effect wouldn't have been as dramatic. The color that had rushed to her face instantly left it, her eyes going wide; as if, Pullus thought miserably, she was seeing me for the first time.

"So," she said softly, confirming Pullus' fear, "the true face of the conqueror presents itself, Centurion Pullus." He could see that her shock and hurt were quickly turning to anger. "I am afraid that I cannot comply with your...request. I am the Queen of Bharuch, and I am faithful not only to my husband, but to the people he rules, which means that I will *never* accept the idea that you Romans are here to stay."

How could I blame her for that? Pullus wondered. She is doing what would be expected of any Roman woman, declaring her loyalty to her husband and her people. So why does it bother me so much?

Pullus took a deep breath before he spoke, and as much as he hated to do it, he acknowledged, "I...apologize, Your Highness. I spoke intemperately, and you're right, I was foolish to expect you to behave in any manner other than what you're doing now." He swallowed the bitter lump in his throat before he finished, "I humbly beg your forgiveness."

Hyppolita said nothing, choosing to continue glaring at him, but Pullus refused to look away from her, giving her a steady gaze as he waited for what came next.

Finally, her lip twitched in the shadow of a smile as she replied,

"That must have been painful, Centurion."

Before Pullus could stop himself, he blurted, "You have no idea."

He hadn't said this with the idea of making her laugh, but he was intensely relieved that she did. They were silent then, while Pullus struggled with how to broach the subject, but Hyppolita spoke first.

"I will confess, Centurion, that I have missed..." suddenly, she stopped, and a look flashed across her face that Pullus couldn't immediately identify, not until later when he thought about it, "...our walks," was what came out of her mouth.

"Is that your way of saying that I'm forgiven?" Pullus asked lightly.

"Partially," Hyppolita answered, but with a smile.

"Then I will see you in the morning, Your Highness," Pullus assured her.

It was only as he was descending the steps of the portico that Pullus realized two things; this had been the first time he was completely alone with Hyppolita, which he had assumed was simply because he had shown up without warning. The second wasn't as pleasant; he hadn't learned a thing that Pollio demanded he find out about.

When Octavian led his army consisting of the newly arrived 14th, along with his specially trained force of cavalry, the column was a fully equipped force with a full complement of artillery. It wasn't because Octavian intended to march directly to Ecbatana and besiege it, but after many watches of discussion with Agrippa, who would serve as his second in command, and the Decurions Cornuficius and the Galatian Arctosages, it was agreed that it would be better to be prepared for such an eventuality.

"Hopefully, Valash will see reason, but in the event that he doesn't, we'll take Ecbatana," Octavian had announced to his assembled officers on the eve of his departure, when he was issuing his final orders. "That should bring him to heel."

Every man present understood that this was the ultimate goal, but only Agrippa knew just how big a risk Octavian was taking, although Primus Pilus Crispus of the 22nd had begun to suspect there was more going on and had begun asking Agrippa questions before their departure that were growing more pointed. The Primus Pilus of the newest addition to the massive army that was under the command of Caesar, Gnaeus Figulus, was in an almost identical position to his counterparts Torquatus and Flaminius of the 25th and 30th respectively, who were who knew where; his men weren't fully recovered from the ordeal of the march from Syria, but he didn't feel it politic to venture an opinion one way or another. The Decurions were acutely aware of their commander's dilemma, but because they both felt a shared responsibility for his predicament, they had privately sworn to each other that they would do whatever was necessary to finish this thing that, while not quite a rebellion, was more than simple banditry. Other members of the command group were something of a surprise; the Parthian Artaxerxes, who had sworn his allegiance to Rome and had been the commander of the force of *cataphractoi* who had been trained to fight in the Roman manner on foot known as The Thousand, had sufficiently earned Octavian's trust. However, it was Octavian's decision to refuse the request of Bodroges, who had arrived with Caesar from India, to come along that had caused the commander and his second to quarrel, Agrippa flatly declaring that he couldn't be trusted.

"He turned on his superior, which was bad enough, but he slit the man's throat in the bargain!"

Octavian had seemed to take a more pragmatic view, pointing out, "Which spared us the cost of an assault on Susa and effectively won Parthia for Rome."

Agrippa knew that he couldn't argue this, so he didn't try, saying instead, "Leaving him behind will put him in a position where he might be tempted to try and raise a rebellion, just like Valash is doing."

"Marcus, you need to trust me on this," Octavian replied calmly, although Agrippa was certain that he was trying to fight a smile. "You're going to be giving the orders in the field, while I'm just along for the ride, but right now, I am making the decisions about who will accompany us, and Bodroges will stay."

Marcus Agrippa had heard this before from Octavian, and he knew in his bones that, when the moment came, his superior would want to exercise his authority in tactical matters, just as he had done before. Fortunately, while Octavian wasn't the natural born general his uncle already was, and Agrippa himself was becoming, Caesar's nephew's instincts were essentially sound; where he faltered was in the execution of those orders, if only because he didn't possess the thirst for martial glory expected of a Roman. And, Agrippa thought to himself, in the killing, which he views as wasteful, while war was only a last resort. It was a distinctly non-Roman view of the world, yet despite his own martial instincts, it was one of the reasons

Agrippa had chosen to serve his friend, with a long view of what lay ahead for Rome and for Octavian. Simply put, there wasn't a mind that Agrippa had ever encountered that was in the same class with Caesar, except for his nephew, this wheezy, somewhat delicate-looking Roman who was sitting at his desk, looking up at him with an intent stare.

Agrippa realized that he wasn't changing Octavian's mind, and he tried not to sound surly when he said, "It's your decision, of course, Gaius. Know that I'll support you no matter what. Not," he added, unnecessarily in the view of Octavian, "just about Bodroges, but in anything. And everything."

It was unlike Agrippa to be so open in declaring his allegiance, and while it was unintended, his candor had an effect on Octavian that, in a rather ironic manner, both assuaged Agrippa's concerns about the Parthian, and proved to him that Octavian wasn't just being blindly loyal to what he thought Caesar would want.

"Marcus," Octavian smiled at Agrippa, "why do you think I want Bodroges to stay here? I happen to know that Caesar has given him a task that will keep him far too busy to have any time to make mischief, and that it's probably the most important of the things that need to be done before Caesar returns to India."

"Maecenas will be here," Agrippa pointed out, feeling a glimmer of hope. "We can make sure that if Bodroges does try something, Maecenas can command delegate Crispus and the 22nd to stop him."

"Yes," Octavian agreed, "he will. But as lacking in martial ardor as I am, I'm Achilles compared to Maecenas. And let's be honest; he doesn't exactly inspire men to follow him, at least not like that."

This elicited a chuckle from Agrippa, who agreed with Octavian's assessment of the third member of this group of young Romans.

Going on, Octavian explained, "Bodroges may not fear me, or you for that matter, but he fears Caesar." Seeing Agrippa nodding, Octavian said, "And, I do know that he bears a fair amount of ill will towards this Valash, because he had convinced Caesar that the man could be trusted, and that might have been something that could have proven useful, but Caesar was very clear"

Agrippa was convinced, which was why Bodroges was standing next to Maecenas and Crispus watching as Octavian led his army north, to crush Valash's insurgency, and prove to Caesar he had the necessary makeup to be considered worthy of the mantle of Caesar's heir. At this moment in time, it was a secret ambition, one that he had never revealed even to Agrippa and Maecenas, but it was the guiding ambition of his life, and this would be a first step.

"Are you certain?" Pompilius stared down at Quintus Pedius, who was seated behind his small desk, which was stuck in what had clearly been a room used for storage, yet another calculated and petty insult by the Praetor. As tended to happen with Lepidus' vindictive schemes, it had rebounded in a material way; it was a private space where nobody came, and the two could speak freely as long as they didn't raise their voices above a certain level.

Which was why Pedius didn't hesitate to respond, "Yes, I'm certain. My uncle is on his way to Merv." He paused before delivering the even more important news, taking a deep breath before he added, "In fact, he's less than a week's ride away. If," he waved what looked to Pompilius like barely more than a scrap of parchment, "what this says is true."

"May I?" Pompilius asked, but when Pedius shook his head, it wasn't in a rebuff.

"It wouldn't do any good," Pedius replied. "This is a code that my uncle made me memorize before I left for here. And," he admitted, "I'm not altogether certain I deciphered it correctly."

This seemed to Pompilius to be a major problem, and he couldn't stop his voice from becoming a bit louder than necessary when he exclaimed in alarm, "What? What do you mean? Does that mean he might not be coming at all?"

Pedius winced, signaling Pompilius, and they both immediately paused to listen for any sound beyond the closed door.

Finally satisfied, Pedius returned the volume of the conversation to its previous low pitch, "Oh, he's coming, that much I'm certain of. It's the amount of time that I'm not sure about. See," he held up the scrap and pointed to what Pompilius could see was a smudge on a pair of symbols that made them virtually illegible, "I *think* that these characters represent a week, but I can't be certain."

Although Pompilius' initial reaction was one of relief, he quickly realized it was misplaced, since the time of Caesar's arrival had no bearing on the actual problem at hand. Or, he wondered, did it?

Aloud, he asked Pedius, "Have you been able to find out what came out of Lepidus' meeting with that *Tokharoi* bastard? What's his name?"

"Kujula," Pedius supplied, but that was all the information he could provide, saying in frustration, "That's the only thing Lepidus has ever been tight-lipped about. I haven't heard anything."

The meeting had been arranged between Marcus Lepidus and the *satrap* who, according to some of the more influential merchants in Merv, was the most powerful among several sub-chieftains, and through whose territory the Silk Road ran. When the delegation of Merv's citizens had beseeched an audience with the new Praetor, Lepidus had been expecting the worst; savages whose distinction was only that they were greedier than the other savages and had managed to accrue some wealth. Culture, on the other hand, he was certain would be one thing with which he would be doing without for the foreseeable future, thanks to Caesar's effective banishment to this place. It was true, he admitted only to himself, he had been surprised at not only the size but the prosperity of the city, situated so it not only sat astride the Silk Road, but the only reliable river within hundreds of miles. That was a shade compared to the shock he experienced when a quartet of richly dressed men, attired in silk robes that, to his greedy eyes, had real gemstones sewn into the seams, entered the room. While it was true they wore their hair in the long, oiled curls that was the fashion among the people of this land, their Greek was almost flawless, and by the end of the first conversation, Lepidus was certain that he had at least found men with whom he could converse as civilized people, despite their barbarian blood.

Pedius' observation of this meeting, one of the few in which he was allowed to participate, was that the four merchants had almost immediately taken the measure of Marcus Lepidus, understanding that the key to his pliancy was through flattery. And, Pedius thought disgustedly, money, of course. It was an observation that was more usual from men like Titus Pullus, but Quintus Pedius was as acutely aware of the greed of Rome's upper class, where there was no such thing as too much money. The seduction of Lepidus that was begun during that first meeting had progressed with a rapidity that Pedius hadn't expected, so that within a matter of three months after their arrival, Pedius harbored serious concerns that Lepidus had, to put it plainly, gone mad. Oh, outwardly he was the same insufferable snob and petty martinet that had made him the most despised Legate of Caesar's command, but there was an added element to it, and sometimes Pedius imagined he could see Lepidus' mind working as he began to formulate, with the aid and abetting of those merchants, a plan that was so audacious in its scale that it actually helped Lepidus' cause, for the simple reason Pedius refused to believe the man would be so stupid. Yes, Caesar was almost two thousand miles away in India; at least, that had been the case when Pedius finally became convinced that Lepidus was up to something, but to the young Tribune, the fact that less than a month before this meeting with Pompilius, Lepidus had been informed that Caesar had returned to Parthia should have put an end to the Praetor's madness. It had actually been Pompilius who had correctly predicted the opposite would happen.

"He's going to speed things up." He had said this confidently to Pedius, but while the Tribune had grown to deeply respect Pompilius, who he knew some of his men still referred to as Caspar, he had been certain that the Primus Pilus of the *Crassoi* had been wrong.

Then Pedius had discovered that a meeting had been arranged between Kujula and Lepidus, and by this point, through Pompilius' contacts in the city, most of whom received the return of the *Crassoi* with unabashed joy, the pair had learned more about the makeup and possible motivations of the merchants who were seemingly conspiring to overthrow the city by inviting a people who had been their enemy for generations.

"The worst of the bunch is Dotarzes," Pompilius had informed Pedius, back when the Tribune was trying to get a grasp on the social and political landscape. "He's as greedy and ambitious as our Praetor, but he's also very clever."

"Well, at least we don't have to worry about that last part with Lepidus," Pedius had commented without thinking, prompting an appreciative chuckle from Pompilius.

Returning to the topic, the Primus Pilus went on, "There have been rumors about Dotarzes playing both sides for years, and I know that when Teispes was here, he spent a lot of his time and effort trying to prove that he was secretly aiding the *Tokharoi*. But then," Pompilius made a waving gesture, "everything else happened, and we left Merv." He paused, but in a meaningful manner, which he explained when he said, "Before we left Susa, Teispes asked me to check on two men who worked for Dotarzes. They had been helping him gather proof so that Dotarzes could be brought before Orodes on charges of treason. Naturally, I did. And," his face turned grim, "both of them had vanished, without a trace." This was certainly disturbing, but neither did it have a material impact on the current situation, and Pompilius moved to the next of the four, giving Pedius as much information as he knew on each of them. "But it all revolves around Dotarzes," he concluded. "And he marked Marcus Lepidus very quickly. Make no mistake, Tribune," the Centurion leaned forward to offer Pedius an intense stare, "Dotarzes is the most dangerous man in Merv. His wealth is such that he could essentially buy the loyalty of whoever he wants."

Pedius hated that he had to ask, but he did so anyway.

"Does that include the *Crassoi*?"

Although this was a topic they had discussed before, back then, it had been more of an abstract conversation; now that the moment of decision was approaching, and now that they knew Caesar was coming, more quickly than either of them had anticipated, Pompilius was forced to acknowledge, "I think that I have three Pili Priores who would be inclined to at least entertain anything Dotarzes had to offer, and they have sufficient control over their Cohorts that it's in the realm of possibility."

"Can't you replace them?" Pedius asked, which caused Pompilius to offer the Tribune a smile that held no real humor.

"Would that it were that easy," Pompilius allowed, "but it's not. First, I don't have anything more than my suspicions, and these men are all very competent Pili Priores, but it runs more deeply than that. Their Centurions and Optios are all hand-picked men, by them. Which," Pompilius felt compelled to add, "is the custom and has been for as long as anyone can remember. The Primus Pilus certainly has a certain amount of influence, but not even I can know everything about my officers." When he saw Pedius nod his acceptance, he concluded glumly, "All we can really do is wait and see if my guesses are correct."

Pedius shook his head, dismayed at the level of helplessness he was feeling, but it was in his nature to try and find the bright side of things, which was what prompted him to offer, "At least we're going to know sooner rather than later."

That, Pompilius had to acknowledge, was certainly true, not that it made him feel any better, and the pair sat in glum silence, wondering what the future held.

"Amodini is quite taken with your nephew, Centurion."

This served to stop Pullus in his tracks to stare at Hyppolita, his expression seemingly an equal mixture of amazement and concern, but as unexpected as this was, it did explain one thing.

"Is that why Lady Amodini isn't with us today?" he asked, just as much to stall for time as he tried to determine what this meant.

"Partially," Hyppolita admitted. "I didn't want her to feel embarrassed."

A partial reason isn't the entire reason, Pullus thought, but he kept that to himself, asking instead, "Is there a particular reason you are bringing this up, Your Highness?"

She flushed slightly, but she kept her eyes on Pullus as she answered, "Yes, there is, Centurion." Before she said anything else, she resumed walking; if Pullus noticed she had chosen her spot where they were screened by the high shrubs of the small garden that, at his queen's insistence, Abhiraka had ordered created, he gave no sign of it. "While I appreciate the gesture that you made in allowing us these walks. Which," she added quickly, "I have come to treasure, it does not change the fact that we are essentially prisoners here."

This, Pullus knew, was something that he couldn't argue, and he had wondered on more than one occasion what Caesar would have ordered if he had stayed in Bharuch. But, he hadn't, so there wasn't much point in dwelling on it.

When Pullus made no reply, she continued, "And, as pleasant as the company of my ladies may be, it can still be a trial keeping them from quarreling. This," she sighed, "is one way to do it."

"But how will that help?" Pullus asked, genuinely puzzled; given what he knew about women, it seemed to him this would have the opposite effect, by arousing jealousy on the part of the other ladies who didn't have the diversion of his nephew's company.

"Because Amodini is the youngest of my ladies," Hyppolita explained, "and as you've seen, she is quite beautiful, which has already created some friction. Between her youth and the manner in which she is being treated by the others, I am concerned for her."

"In what way?"

"She has stopped eating, for one thing," Hyppolita answered. "But it is more than that. She is so young that she is not equipped to deal with the kind of...viciousness that my ladies are capable of, I am afraid."

"Just tell them to stop," Pullus countered, slightly incredulous that this woman he had discerned was very intelligent was unable to see the simple solution. "Tell them that you will have them punished."

Hyppolita shot Pullus a look of scornful amusement that, although she had no way of knowing it, ignited a searing pain inside Pullus that it took all of his self-control to hide from the queen, reminding him of Gisela, his woman and mother of his two children, all three of them dead by plague in Brundisium when, as he usually was, Pullus was off fighting for Caesar. The look he was the recipient of from Hyppolita was, at least in his mind, identical to those that Gisela had given him when she thought he was being obtuse, or more often, mystified by how the feminine mind worked.

"Centurion," Hyppolita spoke patiently, oblivious to the effect she had just had on Pullus, "this is not your Legion. I cannot simply demand that my ladies stop their treating Amodini in this manner. For one thing, there are more of them than there are of me, and I can only be in one place at a time. Besides," her tone altered slightly, and her lips curved in a smile, "I have sympathy for Amodini's plight, but I have something more...subtle in mind."

Pullus was now completely bewildered, still unable to see how Gaius had any role to play in what he was, with some justification, viewing as little more than a spat between a group of women. Seeing this, and interpreting it correctly, Hyppolita realized that she should be straightforward about her idea, except that, for reasons she couldn't articulate, she decided to prolong Pullus' mystification a bit longer.

"Centurion," she said, seemingly out of nowhere, "tell me what you see right now."

She was rewarded by Pullus' reaction, although he did take the time to make a complete revolution, but when he faced her again, he still had the same expression of utter bafflement.

"Can you see the palace from here?" she asked, and for the first time, his weathered features showed a glimmer of understanding, which he confirmed by answering, "Only the roof of the palace."

"Which means," Hyppolita explained, "that this would be a perfect spot for a...meeting." She decided this was the best word. "One that would not be seen by prying eyes."

This, Pullus could see, was true, and now that he was looking at it differently, he immediately saw that whoever had created this garden had designed it in such a way that there was only one way into it. Granted, it wasn't a huge space, but as he had learned the first day, there was room for a bench, placed immediately beneath a tree that provided the kind of shade that was almost a necessity. One side of the garden was bounded by the outer wall of the compound, although there was also a line of dense shrubbery that, because of the current circumstances, were no longer trimmed, so that the tops of the plants now extended above the wall. Pullus had of course examined the garden within a couple of days after the city fell and the 10th occupied the compound, and he recalled that at the time he had noticed that this was a carefully maintained area, with all of the shrubbery, plants and two trees within it being carefully maintained.

Although Pullus saw that Hyppolita was correct, he still wasn't convinced, reminding her, "That would work for Amodini, Your Highness. She can walk from the palace and enter the garden. Although," Pullus amended, "I would have to alter the rules to allow her to leave without an escort. But, even *if* I was inclined to allow my nephew to see her, the only way I could do that is by giving him a special pass to enter the palace compound, and it would have to be when he was not on duty. And," he acknowledged, "while it's good that none of my men who are guarding the palace can see in the garden itself, there's no way he can get across the grounds without being seen."

For the first time, Hyppolita looked doubtful, and Pullus thought that perhaps he had pointed out the obvious flaw in her plan, however well-intended it may have been.

But, as he was about to learn, her hesitance had nothing to do with that, and she began by asking, "What if there was a way where your nephew could reach this spot without being observed?"

Pullus' response was a laugh, although he did ask, "How? Do you have a way to make a man be invisible?"

Her eyes narrowed, which Pullus was learning was a sign that she was irritated, but she simply asked, "May I show you something, Centurion?"

"Of course," Pullus agreed, but felt a slight fluttering that he interpreted as a sign that he wouldn't like whatever it was.

Hyppolita turned, except rather than go to the entrance into the garden, she crossed the few paces towards the outer wall and the thick line of shrubbery in front of it. When Pullus had examined it a few months earlier, he had seen that the trunks of these shrubs had been planted at even intervals along the wall; at least, that was what he had thought. It was only when Hyppolita walked up to a seemingly impenetrable wall of foliage, then promptly disappeared into it that he realized that this had been an illusion. Not surprisingly, he went rushing after her, thrusting himself into the barely visible gap, only to find that she was standing next to the wall, but had turned so that it was to her right. His shock at what he found behind these shrubs was so profound that he didn't even realize that he and the queen were now standing more closely than they ever had, which under other circumstances would have flustered him and shattered his composure; the presence of what he instantly saw was a cunningly hidden door in the outer wall meant he barely noticed her, at least in this moment.

"Pluto's *cock*," he gasped, and again he didn't see Hyppolita flush, or that her face was turned up to his, her eyes never leaving his face as she studied him intently. "Has this been here the whole time?" The instant the words were out of his mouth he realized his error, muttering, "Of course it has, you idiot."

"I hope that you are not angry with me, Centurion," Hyppolita said softly.

The words served to yank his attention away from the door, but not before he had mentally placed where this garden was in relation to the other side, while at the same time he was reminded of the secret door at Sostrate. Then, he returned his attention to her, inches away from him, and he was acutely aware that his heart was beating so rapidly that he was certain she could hear it, or see his tunic moving because of it.

"Angry?" He heard the word, in his voice, which sounded strange to him. "I wouldn't say I was angry." Shaking his head to clear it from the swirling of feelings that he was experiencing, before he could stop himself, he said with a note of incredulity, "You could have left any time you wanted, Hyppolita! You knew this was here the whole time, and you could have escaped!"

"To where?" she asked, outwardly calm but, completely unknown to Pullus, struggling with emotions that were decidedly similar to his, and she was just as confused as he was. "Every citizen in Bharuch knows me, and while not all of them have seen me without my veil, there are many who know my face when they did work here. How long before one of them would have betrayed me? Not," she hurried to add, "out of any malice, but because people are terrible at keeping secrets." For the first time, she broke her gaze from his face, dropping her head and shaking it as she said bitterly, "And you Romans would have punished my ladies for my actions."

Pullus instantly understood she was speaking the truth; what he didn't know was that it was only a partial one, because it wasn't just her ladies and their possible fate that had convinced Hyppolita to not attempt escape. While she had no way of truly knowing, given how limited her contact with Rome had been, she had thought about what Abhiraka would have done to one of his officers who allowed a high-ranking captive like a queen to escape, and it made her shudder whenever she thought about it. This, more than anything else, created an inner turmoil that tormented her more than any other, because she knew that her duty required her to do whatever she could to inflict damage on her husband's enemy. She had spent many watches agonizing about it; what better way to do that by using that hidden door, which would initiate a series of repercussions, not just on herself, but on those who were supposed to be her mortal enemy, the men who had conquered her city and forced her husband to flee like a dog in the night caught stealing scraps? She was honest enough with herself to know that, if she could have been certain that whatever kind of punishment the Romans meted out for men who failed in their duty fell on those largely faceless, anonymous men who were her constant guardians, she wouldn't have hesitated, and let the consequences come. But, her honesty with herself extended to the recognition of how unlikely it would be that this huge, scarred Roman now standing inches away from her would escape unharmed, and the very thought unleashed a torrent of powerful but conflicting emotions, and ultimately, what she had concluded was that she couldn't live with the idea of causing this man, her enemy, that kind of harm. They stood there, in silence, neither aware that there was an internal struggle going on inside the other that was remarkably identical, made up of guilt, regret, and a desire to simply reach out across that short but infinitely vast few inches.

It was Pullus who broke the silence, and she noticed that his voice suddenly sounded as if he had been bellowing at the top of his lungs as he asked, "What do you want me to do, Your Highness?"

Chapter 3

While it wasn't all that uncommon for Gaius Porcinus to be summoned to the quarters of the Primus Pilus, given his familial relationship, the fact that it was midnight, and it was none other than Diocles who appeared at the dwelling that housed, in quite cramped conditions, three sections of his Century, was quite unusual. It also aroused a small riot of complaint when the knock on the door came, but when Porcinus came stumbling out, bleary-eyed and more puzzled than alarmed, he was completely unprepared for Diocles' first question.

"Have you bathed today?"

Porcinus had to think for a moment, then said, "Not a full bath, no. That was yesterday. But I got a scraping earlier."

"That will have to do." Diocles sighed, but then turned and began walking away, saying only, "Your uncle needs you."

"Let me get my *baltea*," Porcinus called out, but Diocles said over his shoulder, "You won't need it."

Once he caught up to the Greek, Porcinus did his best to learn the reason for this mysterious summons, but all that Diocles would say was, "You'll find out soon enough, Gaius."

Porcinus was expecting Diocles to lead him into the palace compound and to the building that had once housed the men of the royal bodyguard, and was now the barracks for the First Cohort, while the smaller attached building was his uncle's quarters and the Legion office. When Diocles walked past the gate that was the most direct route, Porcinus was somewhat curious; when the Greek led him past the second gate, he came to a stop.

"Diocles, what is this about?"

Diocles stopped, letting out a sigh when he turned to see that Porcinus had stopped, so he walked over to Pullus' nephew, then asked quietly, "Gaius, do you trust your uncle?"

"Of course!" Porcinus responded indignantly.

"Then you need to follow me," was all the Greek said, then turned and resumed walking, Porcinus following behind.

Because of the dark, it wasn't until they were within fifty paces that Porcinus realized that the slightly darker shape that he had thought was some sort of shadow on the outer wall was actually his uncle. Who, it appeared to Porcinus, was just standing there, motionless, but he continued walking until he finally saw that Pullus was facing in their direction.

"Uncle Titus?" Gaius did think to whisper once he and Diocles were standing in front of him. "What is this about?"

Like Diocles, Pullus' response was to ask, "Gaius, do you trust me?"

"Why do you two keep asking me that?" Gaius' voice rose, not much, but enough for Pullus to hiss at him, and he lowered his voice to say, "But yes, I trust you."

For the first time, he could see Pullus' face split into a grin, but he wasn't any more enlightening when he told Gaius, "Then you need to just go along with this, because I suspect that you're going to be very happy."

Before Porcinus could respond, Pullus turned, and without any warning, suddenly rapped, twice, on the wall, which to Porcinus' eyes, didn't appear any different than the rest of this expanse, which was several stadia in length.

At first, nothing happened, and Porcinus was beginning to think that perhaps the pressure had gotten to his Primus Pilus, but then he heard some sort of rustling sound on the other side, followed by a barely audible clinking sound. It was the sudden transformation, as a section of the wall seemed to detach itself, swinging outward, and while there was no light, Porcinus got the sense of a shape standing in what he now understood was a doorway.

He was completely unprepared to hear Pullus whisper, "Your Highness, I've brought Gregarius Porcinus, as requested."

"Thank you, Centurion," Hyppolita whispered back. "He will be back in his quarters before dawn, just as we agreed."

Porcinus stood there, unable to move, so it fell to Diocles to gently nudge him forward, towards the doorway, and he moved willingly enough, albeit in a daze. Just as he was about to step into the doorway, seeing that Hyppolita had moved back into the compound, he felt Pullus' hand on his shoulder, his uncle leaning over to put his mouth close to his ear.

"Gaius, before you go in there, you need to swear to me, on the black stone, and on the eagle, that you will *never* breathe a word about this to anyone, not even to Pilus Prior Scribonius. If you need to talk, you come to me, and to me only. Is that understood?" Gaius nodded, but he felt his uncle tighten his grip, causing him to wince. "That's not good enough, Gaius. I want to hear you swear it."

"I swear it," Gaius whispered, then even more softly, "I just wish I knew what I was swearing to."

Again, he saw his uncle's teeth as Pullus smiled at him,

repeating, "Trust me. You'll have no cause for complaint. And," he warned, "remember. You must be back to your quarters before the *bucina*. Understood?" This time, when Gaius nodded, it was sufficient for Pullus, then with a firmer push, he guided his nephew through the hidden doorway. As he did, he added with a chuckle, "Although I suspect that you're going to be tired tomorrow."

Before Porcinus could respond, he felt the slight push of air as Pullus shoved the door shut, and he heard the slight click of the lock, but by this moment, he was more concerned with his disorientation. It was even darker than it had been on the other side of the wall, and there were…things tickling his face and touching his arms that, after blindly reaching out, he determined were branches of some sort of plant.

Hyppolita's voice called out, "This way, Gregarius. Come towards my voice."

Porcinus moved in that direction, pushing through the vegetation that he could tell was a bit denser than right next to the wall. Then he was standing in a cleared area, and as his eyes adjusted, he sensed as much as saw a figure standing a few paces away, next to a dark shape that he determined was another person, although that one was seated.

"Thank you for coming, Gregarius," Hyppolita said, but before he could respond, she turned away, and moving quickly, especially in the gloom, seemed to vanish.

Porcinus stood for a long moment, completely at a loss at what to do, particularly since the remaining person was sitting there silently. Finally, he took a tentative step, and within a couple paces, he saw that whoever it was, they were sitting on a bench, but it was in the next pace he caught a scent of…something, and he suddenly remembered that he had been certain it was the most wonderful thing he had ever smelled.

"Amodini?" he gasped, which prompted the figure to move, actually standing erect.

"Yes," came the timid reply, Porcinus instantly noticing that she was speaking in Greek.

"You…you speak Greek?"

"Yes," she answered again, but when she didn't say anything else, he protested, "But you didn't tell me that you could speak Greek!"

"You," for the first time, Porcinus heard more than timidity, and he was certain that she was smiling, "did not ask."

That was the last moment of conversation they had for a fair amount of time.

"There is a problem, Caesar."

Caesar rolled out of his bedroll, coming awake immediately; it was something that the Parthian had noticed early into the journey, and it impressed him deeply that Caesar seemed to need less sleep than any man he had ever met, and that when he awakened, he was instantly alert.

"What is it, Teispes?" Caesar did rub his eyes, but otherwise was completely attentive, his face just barely visible from the coals of the fire they had used only for cooking before letting it die down.

"The scouting party I sent ahead of us has returned. And," Teispes' tone turned grim, "there is a sizable armed force between us and Merv."

Caesar responded immediately, "If it was a friendly force, you wouldn't have awakened me." When Teispes nodded, he asked, "Are they Parthian? A minor *satrap* who Lepidus hasn't brought to heel yet?"

Now the Parthian's head went in the opposite direction.

"No, I do not believe they are, Caesar. My men did not get a truly good or long look because it was getting dark, and they did not want to risk detection by getting closer. But they saw enough. Caesar," Teispes said flatly, "they were *Tokharoi*."

Despite preparing himself, Caesar felt a sudden shiver that had nothing to do with the biting cold. It hadn't been that he doubted his nephew, especially since Pompilius had added his own report to the message that had prompted Caesar to take this drastic action, but he realized in the moment that he hadn't truly thought Lepidus would be such a fool. No, he immediately remonstrated with himself, while outwardly he appeared to be in thought, you knew he was a fool, but you thought he was sufficiently scared of you not to act on his own stupidity.

Aloud, he asked, "What do you suggest, Teispes?"

"We stay here tomorrow," the Parthian answered immediately, then corrected himself. "I mean, *you* should stay here, with most of your bodyguards. However, I request that I be allowed to take some of the other Parthians with me and give me tomorrow to learn more. They are more accustomed to using this kind of ground without being detected." He hesitated for a moment, and Caesar understood why when he asked, "And may Gundomir accompany us as well?"

Caesar regarded him with a raised eyebrow as he pointed out, "The last time I looked, Teispes, Gundomir isn't Parthian."

While Teispes had learned that Caesar liked to tease his subordinates on occasion and, unlike most noblemen, enjoyed when they bantered back with him, to that moment he hadn't engaged in any such thing.

Now he got his revenge by allowing, "Yes, Caesar, he *is* a bit fat for a Parthian. And he rides a horse about as well as our children do, but I trust him."

His reward was Caesar roaring with laughter, at a level that awakened several of the other men, some of whom shouted a curse since they couldn't tell who it was disturbing their rest.

Wiping his eyes, Caesar chuckled. "Very well, Teispes. You make a compelling argument. I think I can survive without Gundomir, especially since Barvistus is with us as well."

"Thank you, Caesar." Teispes stood. "I will go let those men know."

Settling back down onto his cloak, Caesar wrapped it around him, trying to pretend that the chill he was feeling in his bones wasn't nearly as deep as it felt. What, he mused, could Lepidus possibly offer these *Tokharoi* that is more lucrative than what the King of Kings had already been paying them, an amount that Caesar had immediately ordered Lepidus to match as one of his first duties when he reached Merv? Surely, he thought, Lepidus wouldn't offer them something like…Roman citizenship, which would of course include right of entry into the city? Even as the thought came to him, his stomach twisted, a sign that this was in all likelihood exactly what Lepidus was offering. As he would be learning soon, it was even worse than he imagined.

It was difficult for Caesar the next day; waiting was never something he did well, and very quickly, the rest of the men of the party learned to avoid a patch of ground near the remains of the fire, where the Dictator was pacing back and forth. What compounded matters was that, even when he was waiting, Caesar was always working, which was why he was always surrounded by a small army of clerks and scribes, none of whom were present now, not even Apollodorus, and it was early into the journey that Caesar suddenly realized this was the first time his personal secretary had not been by his side, or at least within easy reach, in several years. Pacing back and forth like a caged lion, Caesar alternated between staring at the ground and glancing at the sun, willing it to move more quickly through the sky. The day was clear, which meant that it was bitterly cold, but Teispes' choice for a camping spot was one he had used on every one of his trips, a sizable depression in the ground that formed what could be described as a bowl that was mostly protected from the unrelenting wind, where a small seep bubbled up from the ground at the base of some rocks, where over the gods only knew how many centuries, the water had created a small pool. It wasn't enough to satisfy the thirst of every man and horse at one time, but it did refill over about a third part of a watch, and in anticipation of the need to depart suddenly, the pool had been emptied twice. Despite Caesar's impatience, the sun moved through the sky at the same speed it always did, so that by the time the sentry on watch called down from his spot that riders were approaching, Caesar had worn a path that would last for several days in this spot, there for anyone who wandered past to see and wonder what it meant. Teispes, Gundomir, and all but two of the Parthians that had been part of the scouting party filed into the bowl, leading their horses, where the sight of the pool essentially empty prompted curses from the German.

Caesar had deemed the normal courtesies of rank superfluous during this journey, so Teispes simply approached Caesar, dropped onto his haunches, and began, "They are definitely *Tokharoi*, but it is even worse than that. I got close enough to see that this is the tribe of Kujula."

He glanced over at Caesar, who had squatted as well, and he saw that the name meant something, which Caesar confirmed by saying, "I remember that name. Lepidus mentioned in his first report that he was the most powerful chieftain of those people." He thought a moment longer, then said, "As I recall, Lepidus said that his army isn't just cavalry, that he had a fair number of spearmen." Caesar lifted his head to look at Teispes as he asked, "Did you see any spearmen?"

"No." Teispes shook his head. "This is a force of about two thousand mounted men."

"How many *cataphractoi*?" Caesar asked, but again, Teispes shook his head.

"They do not use *cataphractoi*, Caesar. But," he held up a cautioning hand, "neither are they as lightly armed as our archers. They are," the Parthian stopped, trying to think of the best way to describe them, coming up with, "similar to your Galatians. Most of them carry bows, but they also have both spears and swords. They do wear some armor, but it is bronze."

"This either means that this Kujula has only part of his army with him, or the rest is somewhere nearby," Caesar mused.

"That," Teispes agreed, "is my belief as well, Caesar." Before the Roman could continue, Teispes said, "Also, I need to warn you about their spearmen. They are not like ours. They are more like the troops of Alexander."

Caesar nodded as he agreed, "That makes sense." Then, he asked Teispes, "So, what do you recommend, Teispes? How do we get past them?"

"We do not," the Parthian answered, but before Caesar could object, he added, "Not all of us, Caesar." Teispes paused, and even with his normally impassive demeanor, Caesar could see the Parthian was troubled; he understood why when Teispes continued, "The only way that we can get past them is if we use the men here as bait."

Caesar's eyes narrowed in thought; as usually happened, he immediately discerned what Teispes was proposing, and had thought it through in the amount of time it takes for a man to take a breath.

"And," Caesar spoke slowly, "there has to be enough bait to lure all, or almost all of those *Tokharoi* out of position." While he had a suspicion that he knew the answer, he respected Teispes enough to ask him, "How many do you think it will take?"

Without hesitation, Teispes replied flatly, "All of them."

Despite suspecting this was the answer, Caesar was still dismayed. Although this complement of men wasn't exclusively drawn from the Germans who had served as his bodyguard for more than a decade now, there were enough that losing a substantial number of them now would be a bitter blow. And, Caesar thought bitterly, this is just to get me into Merv. Depending on how things develop from there, I may need their protection to get back to Susa.

Aloud, he said only, "Bring Gundomir to me, Teispes. I should be the one to give him his orders."

The fact that Teispes didn't respond immediately confirmed Caesar's suspicion, and the Parthian opened his mouth to say something, then abruptly shut it, stood, and walked over to where Gundomir was lying on his stomach, lapping at the water that was slowly filling the pool. Caesar watched the pair impassively, his face betraying nothing because he understood that every eye was on him, and at this moment, he had to be Caesar and not just another member of this traveling party. The pair strode over, but when Teispes turned away, Caesar stopped him.

"Stay, Teispes. I want you to hear this as well." Turning to Gundomir, Caesar explained the situation and what needed to be done; the complete lack of surprise on Gundomir's part told Caesar what he needed to know. Well, he thought even as he was speaking, that is about to change, as Caesar finished by saying, "You and

Teispes are coming with me, and I am placing Barvistus in command of the rest of our party."

As he expected, the German's eyes opened wide with shock, his fair features, which in this land were always in a state of perpetual sunburn turning an even deeper red, but Gundomir did retain enough of his self-possession to keep his voice down as he protested, "Caesar, no! You should take Barvistus and leave me in command!" Suddenly, the German's composure cracked, and Caesar saw the tremor in the man's jaw even through the thick beard. Dropping his tone to a whisper, Gundomir pleaded, "Please, Caesar. I have never asked anything of you before, you know this. I am now. Please take Barvistus with you. Let me lead the men and do what must be done."

Although his demeanor didn't betray it, Caesar was truly torn, partially because he had never seen his stalwart bodyguard commander so affected. It's not like Barvistus isn't a veteran himself, he thought, but he also saw that Gundomir understood the likelihood that, outnumbered almost twenty to one, on terrain with which all but a handful of the Parthians in the group were unfamiliar, the odds of evading death or capture and escaping to Merv were very low. Regardless of this, Caesar was always a general first, which required him to decide which man under his command was more valuable, and the brutal truth was that Caesar valued Gundomir more highly than his younger brother.

Nevertheless, it didn't make it any easier when he shook his head and said firmly, "My decision is final, Gundomir. Your brother will be in command."

Seeing the despair on the face of his friend, despite knowing the answer, Teispes offered, "Caesar, allow me to command the men. I do know the ground and this enemy better than Barvistus," he pointed out.

Caesar didn't hesitate, shaking his head, "No, I need you with me, Teispes. And," he added this, not loudly or emphatically, but with the kind of chilling finality that anyone who knew Caesar understood, "please don't ask me again." Turning back to Gundomir, he asked, "Do you want me to tell your brother, or would you prefer to do that?"

"I will do it," Gundomir answered flatly, and spun about to stalk away without being given leave by his general, something that Caesar wisely ignored.

"When do you think we should make our presence known?" he asked Teispes.

The Parthian had already thought this through, so there was no hesitation in his reply. "One of your watches before sunset, Caesar. We need enough daylight for the *Tokharoi* to see our men, and for them to believe there is enough time to run them down." Before Caesar could respond, Teispes asked, "May I be excused, Caesar? I want to talk to Barvistus and tell him about the ground in the direction I think they should go."

Caesar nodded, although he said nothing; he would never say it aloud, but he was worried that Gundomir would bear him a personal grudge about his decision, although he didn't worry that it would affect the German's ability to do his duties in what was to come. He stood watching the Parthian and Germans conversing in low tones, but their body language communicated their feelings quite eloquently, and Caesar could see that it was actually Barvistus who was getting angry. *He probably is angry that his older brother doesn't have faith in him*, Caesar mused, *but he wouldn't ask about it later.* While Teispes and the two Germans began moving among the others, informing them of what was coming, Caesar saw the range of emotions playing on the faces of the men. Some looked apprehensive, but there was no sign of hesitation as they nodded their understanding; others reacted without surprise, as if they had expected this, but Caesar felt his heart swell with pride that there was no sign of hesitation or argument, each man walking to where his small bundle of belongings was lying on the ground, gathering them up before moving to their mounts. *They know*, he realized, *how important this is*, and he swore to himself that any man of this group who survived to reach Merv would be rewarded to a level beyond their dreams. *It's the least I owe these men*, he thought, but following immediately on the heels of this, and unbidden, another, much, much larger group of men leapt into his mind, causing him to silently curse himself. *Did I have to think of them now?* He shook his head in a physical attempt to drive the subject of his Legions in Bharuch out of his mind, but as always, he had very little success. Every passing day, no matter what he was doing, Caesar understood that at some point he had to return to face whatever it was that awaited him. When he had left Bharuch, the dispatch from Parthia had been a convenient pretext, and it had certainly played a role, but ultimately, the impetus for Caesar's departure stemmed from a situation that he had never encountered before; he simply didn't know what to do about his Legions. Their demand to return to at least Parthia was impossible to ignore, so he decided that the best alternative was to delay the decision. *Although*, he thought wryly, *not exactly by finding myself trying to sneak past a force of barbarians in order to reach Merv so* that I can save Lepidus from his own stupidity. The instant the word "save" passed through his mind, he stopped himself. *No, Gaius, don't lie to yourself. There is no saving Marcus Lepidus. He must die for this*, provided that it's true, although any doubt Caesar had held had been erased with the announcement that the *Tokharoi* were here, less than a full day's ride from Merv, and clearly unmolested.

"The men are ready, Caesar. The last of the horses are being watered."

Surprised, Caesar turned to see Teispes and Gundomir standing side by side, and he unusually avoided the German's gaze, addressing Teispes. "Will the pool fill up enough to water our mounts before we leave?"

"Yes," Teispes replied, then added, "but it will be close."

Nodding, Caesar turned and, without a word to either man, made his way over to where the nearest of his bodyguards were standing, waiting for the order to mount. One by one, Caesar circulated among them, not as their commander but as their comrade, offering his arm in the manner of Rome, which all of these men had adopted as their own. Naturally, they all accepted the gesture, most of them moved at this sign of regard from their general, and all of them aware why he was making it. By the time he was finished, Gaius Julius Caesar's composure was close to cracking, and the ire Gundomir had felt towards his commander had transformed into something else entirely. Then, there was no more time for delay, and Barvistus gave the command to mount in a loud, ringing tone, doing so last before turning his horse's head and leading the men up and out of the bowl.

Teispes handed the reins of his own horse to Gundomir and asked him to water the animal, then told Caesar, "I am going to our observation spot. As soon as I see that they have spotted our men and taken the bait, I will signal you, and we can begin."

Caesar nodded his approval, and the Parthian turned and climbed the slope up to a rocky outcropping that gave a view of the ground to the north. When the Parthian left, Caesar opened his mouth to speak, but Gundomir stopped him with shake of his head.

"You were right," the German said quietly. "It is not only your decision…" he took a deep breath then finished, "…it was the correct decision, Caesar. I ap…"

It was Caesar's turn to cut Gundomir's apology off, "Stop. There is no need for that, Gundomir. He is your brother. I would feel the same way."

There was nothing left to say after that, and Caesar turned his attention to where Teispes was, although he wasn't visible, while Gundomir led their horses to the pool. The German was just finishing when the Parthian suddenly appeared, looking down into the bowl and waving his arm, signaling that it was time to leave. Now, Caesar thought as he leapt into the saddle, it's up to the gods.

It had become increasingly annoying to Quintus Pilus Prior Gnaeus Macrinus that his Primus Pilus seemed excessively interested in what should be a standard guard shift on the walls of Merv, but more than that, it was starting to worry him as well. Surely, he thought as, for what he had counted was the fifth time he watched Pompilius ascending the steps, he hasn't discovered the truth. The cause for his belief that he hadn't was straightforward; if the Primus Pilus did, Macrinus wouldn't be standing here, he would be in chains...or worse. His decision to cooperate with the Praetor in whatever his scheme was hadn't been based in any kind of idealism; simply put, Macrinus was broke. Pompilius had been correct in his description of Gnaeus Macrinus as a horrible gambler; where he had erred was in his underestimation of the size of that debt, and worst of all, to whom he owed the money. Dotarzes, he thought bitterly, had done a really good job of hooking me, just like a fish. Only after the fact did Macrinus realize that this had been part of a larger conspiracy, that the merchant was in league with Lepidus, and Macrinus was now a part of it.

"Anything?" Pompilius asked, puffing slightly after reaching the rampart and tearing Macrinus from his thoughts.

"No, Primus Pilus," Macrinus replied evenly, but couldn't resist adding, "just like the last time you asked."

Pompilius shot him an amused look but said nothing, at least in response, and the pair stood, staring south into the vast expanse of nothingness, with the exception of the ribbon of the river and the fringe of green that lined both banks that vanished off into the distance.

Suddenly, Macrinus turned and asked abruptly, "Primus Pilus, is there something I don't know?"

Pompilius stiffened slightly, but then after a long silence, finally leaned closer to Macrinus, speaking in a whisper, "Caesar is coming, and we think he should be here today."

"*Caesar?*" Macrinus gasped this, far too loudly for Pompilius' comfort, and he saw the heads of the rankers a few paces down the rampart swivel in their direction, although he couldn't tell if they heard the name of their general.

"Keep your voice down," Pompilius hissed. Calming, he lowered his voice even more, explaining, "Macrinus, we discovered that the Praetor is working with Kujula and his *Tokharoi*, and that he's been skimming tax revenues almost since he got here." Macrinus' mouth dropped open, his eyes going wide in shock, but he was about to learn matters were far worse when Pompilius concluded, "And we know that Dotarzes is in on it. But," he spat on the stones of the rampart before finishing, "what's worse than that, I'm almost certain that he's got some of the Centurions in his coin purse."

"That," Macrinus' voice went hoarse, his mouth suddenly going so dry that it took an effort not to cough, "is...disturbing to hear, Primus Pilus."

Pompilius gave his Pilus Prior a scornful smile, although he agreed sarcastically, "Yes, it's disturbing. Quite disturbing. But," he turned to look back to the south, shading his eyes as he said, "hopefully, Caesar will be here and he can clean this mess up." He turned to look at Macrinus as he finished, "And with our help."

Macrinus stood silently, but while he had copied Pompilius by facing south, he wasn't seeing anything, all of his attention turned inward, and his first immediate thought was whether or not he should simply hurl himself off the rampart and drop the twenty feet to the rock-hard ground below. How, he thought miserably, had he gotten himself into this? If Pompilius sensed the turmoil of his Quintus Pilus Prior, he gave no sign, keeping his attention on the landscape.

Finally, Macrinus spoke, his voice a whisper, "Primus Pilus, I need to tell you something."

Pompilius' dash through the streets of Merv seemed to take forever to the *Crassoi* Primus Pilus, but it was even worse because, when he burst into Pedius' small office, he was so out of breath that it took a span of perhaps fifteen heartbeats before he had enough breath to blurt out, "We need to send a cavalry patrol out, right now!"

Pedius had leapt to his feet when Pompilius flung the door open, his nerves as raw as Macrinus', albeit for different reasons, but while he could see that Pompilius was alarmed, and he trusted the man implicitly, it was more out of force of habit that his first response was to ask, "Why? What's wrong?"

"Kujula," Pompilius replied, still needing an extra heartbeat. "Kujula moved south with his horsemen, and he's between here and..." he waved a hand, "wherever Caesar is."

Pedius was about to ask how Pompilius knew, but immediately

understood that this wasn't as important as the fact itself, and he moved from behind his desk, thinking furiously.

"Right now, there are only three *turmae* left here," the Tribune informed Pompilius. "Lepidus sent the rest of them out on patrol."

This was something Pompilius didn't know, and he demanded, "When was this?"

"Yesterday," prompting Pompilius to curse bitterly.

"Of course he did," the Primus Pilus muttered. "Who are the Decurions left?"

When Pedius named the three men, Pompilius relaxed slightly.

"That actually makes sense," he admitted. "They wouldn't be involved in anything like this. Where is Lepidus now?"

"He's dining with Dotarzes," Pedius answered, which they both knew was meaningful as well, but that could wait.

Pompilius turned and walked out the door, calling over his shoulder, "Come with me. You're going to have to issue the order to get them mounted up."

This caused a flutter in Pedius' stomach, but he was right behind the Centurion, hurrying to catch up with him. Pompilius was moving too quickly for Pedius to ask what had caused his reaction, at least not until they reached the barracks where the complement of cavalry was housed, next to the blocks of buildings that were the home of those *Crassoi* without families. It was still daylight, but getting close to dark, which turned out to be a good thing because most of the men were about to settle down for their evening meal. In as few words as possible, and trying to sound as if he knew why, Pedius ordered the ranking Decurion, Septimus Gallo, to prepare to leave immediately.

"Yes, sir," Gallo saluted, but then asked, "But...where to?"

For that, Pedius turned to Pompilius, and the Primus Pilus realized that the circle of men who would know the truth, that Caesar was nearby, and in jeopardy, was about to widen beyond a level with which he was comfortable.

"Follow me," he ordered as he went walking to the door. Gallo did so and when they were outside, Pompilius wasted no time, explaining the situation, and Pedius noticed that when the Centurion mentioned Kujula, something flickered across the man's expression that he was certain was meaningful.

When Pompilius didn't comment, Pedius held up a hand, watching Gallo's face carefully as he asked, "Decurion, when the Primus Pilus mentioned the *Tokharoi*, I noticed you had a...reaction to that. Can you explain why?"

Gallo shifted uncomfortably, but he didn't hesitate, "It's just that I'd heard some…whispers that that bastard Kujula was nearby, but that he'd been invited."

"Invited by who?" Pedius demanded, and Gallo looked surprised at the question.

"By the Praetor, of course," the Decurion answered.

"Who did you hear this from?" Pompilius interjected, even as he understood that this was a subject for later.

"From Decurion Atilius," Gallo replied, naming the most senior officer in the cavalry and the *de facto* commander of the contingent that was located in Merv.

To Pompilius, that meant in all likelihood, Atilius was in on whatever Lepidus had planned, and he recalled seeing the cavalryman and the Praetor talking together one day, which was not at all unusual. What was, Pompilius recalled, was the manner in which they were talking, remembering that at the time he witnessed the pair, standing off in a corner shortly before a routine meeting, his initial thought had been they were up to something. At the time, however, it had never occurred to Pompilius that Lepidus' activities were going beyond squeezing some merchants for money that wouldn't be part of the tax revenues. Again, while this was important in the larger picture, at this moment, it was a minor matter.

"You need to prepare yourself and your men to ride south," Pedius instructed, then hesitated for a breath before he added, "and you're to find Caesar and escort him safely to the city."

Gallo's eyes went wide, gasping, "With less than a hundred men?" Turning to Pompilius, he asked, "Do you know how many of Kujula's bunch is out there?"

"No," Pompilius admitted. "Just that it's going to be more than a hundred men."

This elicited a humorless laugh from the Decurion.

"Yes, I'm certain of that much." Turning to regard Pedius, Gallo asked, "And you're sure that it's really Caesar out there, sir?"

"I am," Pedius affirmed, trying to sound as positive as he could, understanding that his relative youth and his status as a Tribune actually worked against him with men from the ranks.

Nevertheless, the regulations that governed Rome's military hierarchy were clear and unambiguous, so Gallo simply nodded, then saluted as he said, "We'll be ready as quick as Pan, Tribune. And," he added this even as he was opening the door back into the barracks, "we'll make sure Caesar makes it here."

"We'll be waiting at the south gate," Pompilius called to him, but the door was already shutting, and the pair of officers began moving as well, again at a brisk trot. This prompted the *Crassoi* Primus Pilus to grumble, "I'm too fucking old to be running around like a street urchin stealing a loaf."

Even under the circumstances, this prompted a laugh from Pedius, but within a span of heartbeats, he didn't have enough breath to do it again.

The sun was bisected by the horizon, bathing the landscape in an orange-gold glow as Caesar followed Teispes, with Gundomir immediately behind him, the trio moving their horses at a trot. Even in the failing light, it was impossible to miss the towering clouds of dust, one significantly smaller than the other, the sign that the *Tokharoi* had at least partially taken the bait. As his bodyguards galloped in a westerly direction, Teispes was leading them north towards Merv, but not by using the most direct route, the wide track that passed for a road in this part of the world that paralleled the river. Instead, he was using every fold and crease in the ground to avoid detection, and despite the circumstances, Caesar's admiration and respect for the one-eyed Parthian deepened with every mile. They were more than thirty miles away from the city, at least by using the road; although Teispes hadn't mentioned it, Caesar's guess was that moving in this manner would add at least ten miles, and he did wonder if, once it was completely dark, the Parthian would lead them back to the road. It was a unique and not very comfortable feeling for Caesar, being so helpless and at the mercy of a man who, just two years earlier, would have been more than happy to part Caesar's head from his shoulders, yet at the same time, he also appreciated the delicious irony, and he found himself smiling as he guided his mount in Teispes' path.

"I hope they have split up by now."

Gundomir's comment elicited a nod from Caesar, and while he turned his head, it was only so he could be heard as he assured the German, "Barvistus knows what he's about, Gundomir. He should," he wasn't sure if the bodyguard could see his grin, "since you're the one who taught him everything he knows."

"That's true," Gundomir agreed, understanding what Caesar was trying to do and appreciating it. "But sometimes, little brothers do not listen to big brothers. Sometimes, they do the exact opposite of what their big brother tells them."

"Somehow," Caesar replied dryly. "I don't think this will be one of those times."

They fell silent then, forced to concentrate more of their

attention on the footing as, very rapidly, the darkness grew until Caesar could only make out Teispes and his horse's shape, although without any kind of detail. With every step, despite drawing closer to Merv, it also exacerbated the tension and turmoil Caesar and his two companions were feeling. And, Caesar realized with some dismay, that tension was incredibly wearing, so that by the time it was about a third of a watch after sunset, he felt as if he had been in the saddle for much, much longer. As quietly as they moved, it was impossible for them to make no noise, and as surefooted and adept at seeing in the dark as all experienced riders knew horses were, there would come a sudden cracking sound when a hoof dislodged a rock, causing Caesar to start in surprise every time it happened, that feeling transmitted to his own animal. More than his eyes, he used his ears, and he was aided by the relatively slow pace Teispes was setting, both to reduce the chances of detection and to save their horses in the event they had to go to the gallop. Suddenly, for no reason that Caesar could discern, Teispes drew up, and it was Caesar's horse that reacted first, coming to a stop before its rider could draw on the reins. For a span of agonizing moments, they sat there motionless as Caesar strained to listen for a possible cause for Teispes' abrupt halt; it was too early for a rest stop, and his instinct warned him that the Parthian had sensed some sort of danger. Using his ears, Caesar also turned to slowly scan the countryside around them, and he realized with a certain amount of discomfort that his perception they had been riding down in one of the endless dry watercourses was no longer the case, that instead they were now essentially on open ground. Their cause was aided by less than a quarter moon, although the sky was clear, so that between its wan light and the amount of illumination by the countless stars, which Caesar had learned long before provided more light than seemed possible, he could at least make out his companions. As was always the case whenever there was any moon visible, the landscape around them had a silver tint, but even after a complete revolution, Caesar didn't see anything that could be considered a danger. This area had the kind of vegetation that was a feature of such arid climates; scrubby plants that stood at most knee high, seemingly scattered in a completely random pattern but which Caesar had deduced was based in the amount of ground water each of these plants could draw to remain alive. Other than this, there were no shapes higher than the vegetation, either singly or in a group of them, nor did Caesar hear anything but the low moaning wind, which had been a constant for the entire journey. Just as he was about to nudge his horse to ride alongside Teispes to determine what had alerted the Parthian, the relative quiet was shattered by a sound that Caesar instantly identified, although it was the sudden appearance of what, to the ignorant, might have been dark demons summoned from the underworld that seemed to come boiling up out of the ground that was most alarming.

Teispes reacted immediately, and even over the sudden assault on his senses with the thundering sound of hooves and shrill cries of their riders, Caesar clearly heard Teispes shout, "*Tokharoi*! Run!"

That was the last coherent moment Caesar and the other two men would experience for some time to come, yet none of them hesitated, slapping their mounts viciously to get them to the gallop immediately. Caesar pointed his horse's head at the hindquarters of Teispes' mount, counting on the Parthian to guide them, and very quickly the roaring of the wind as his horse went to the full gallop almost drowned out the noise created by a party of horsemen, of whose numbers Caesar had no idea other than there were well more than three. Nevertheless, the high-pitched, undulating sound that he supposed was the *Tokharoi* war cry was audible over the shrieking wind, and it helped the fleeing men locate their pursuers, but even an experienced rider like Caesar couldn't dare risk a glance towards his left rear quarter from where the noise was coming. Everything became a blur, his eyes watering from the wind of his motion and dust churned up by Teispes' mount, requiring Caesar to ride by feel as much or more than by his sight, as well as relying on his horse and its superior night vision to avoid the holes, rocks, and anything else that could end their ride, and his life, in the span of a heartbeat by sending its rider flying. When he suddenly sensed a presence drawing closer, and on his left, Caesar risked keeping his reins with just one hand as the other reached down for the *spatha*, but he learned there was no need when he heard Gundomir shout his name.

"They are getting closer, but they will come from this side! I will protect you by drawing them off!"

As Gundomir knew he would, Caesar instantly understood that the German was offering his life to buy Caesar precious heartbeats of time, but this time, Caesar wasn't a general; he was a man unwilling to allow someone else to sacrifice themselves for him. However, before Caesar could respond one way or another, his attention was drawn by an alarmed shout from Teispes, looking back just in time to see the Parthian suddenly veer to the right, in a manner that reminded Caesar of times when his horse had been spooked by something in its path. Usually, it was a serpent or some other creature that crawled on the ground, but in this case, what Caesar saw was another mass of dark shapes that had seemingly materialized from the ground, just like their pursuers. They drove us into a trap; this was the thought that flashed through Caesar's mind, although the rush of despair was almost instantly washed away by the rage. Well, he thought, even as he guided his horse to follow Teispes, I'll show these savages that it's going to take a lot of them to strike Caesar down.

Lepidus was well on his way to being drunk, reclining on the pillows arranged on the floor in the Parthian fashion, which he had initially refused to do, but as his relationship with Dotarzes had developed, he had, albeit grudgingly, acceded to the custom. Now, he would admit this only to himself, he actually preferred this to lying on a couch, especially when the entertainment provided by his host was so…supple. He chuckled to himself as he allowed the woman to demonstrate an amazing level of flexibility, but as he had learned in the past, it wouldn't do to be hasty in his choice.

Dotarzes, seated across from him and reclining in a similar fashion, smiled at his dinner guest, correctly guessing, "You have learned your lesson, I see, Marcus Aemilius. It never pays to make a hasty decision!"

It had taken the Parthian merchant some time to determine that what Lepidus thought of as his smile was a simple baring of the teeth, which the Praetor did now, but it was his tone that was always more instructive than his expressions.

"You taught me well, Dotarzes," Lepidus acknowledged, showing those teeth as he did so. Suddenly, he shifted slightly, and Dotarzes heard the interest, despite how casual the Roman tried to sound when he asked, "Is she here tonight, by any chance? What was her name?"

"Ah," Dotarzes chuckled again, "if you are referring to Ying, I am afraid she had other…obligations."

"That's disappointing." Lepidus tried to sound as if it didn't bother him, but he had been considering for the last several days demanding the girl as a sign of good faith in their relationship. Still, he did try to sound cheerful as he bared his teeth again and said, "I suppose you need to bring some others out to entertain us to take my mind off her."

Dotarzes obliged instantly, clapping his hands sharply two times, and the response was as immediate, the girl turning and hurrying out of the room, but while the Parthian merchant wanted to be a thoughtful host, he hadn't summoned Lepidus to his home for the purposes of satisfying the Roman's fleshly needs.

"While we wait, Marcus Aemilius," Dotarzes spoke casually, leaning over to pick up a date from one of the bowls arranged in front of him, "perhaps we should discuss what comes next, now that you have met with Kujula." Suddenly, his hand holding the date froze, and there was a subtle but unmistakable shift in his tone as he said, "Provided that the talks went as you say they did."

Rather than be offended, Lepidus actually chuckled again, assuring the Parthian expansively, "Dotarzes, as I said, my agreement with Kujula means that you will become the most powerful man in Merv." He paused for just a heartbeat, then added, "Except for myself, of course."

This time, he didn't offer his version of a smile, and Dotarzes was far too experienced in handling men like this Roman to do anything but offer a grave bow of his head as he replied, "Thank you for your assurance, Marcus Aemilius, and I thank you for your generosity. It never occurred to me to think otherwise, and I have no doubt that you will elevate our humble city to levels of greatness that the world has never seen before."

His ego stroked sufficiently, Lepidus decided a bit of magnanimity was in order, telling the merchant, "And that will only be possible because of such steadfast and able friends like yourself, Dotarzes. Now," he looked towards the entryway leading from another part of Dotarzes' large house and from where the women who were the sole entertainment for the evening had been emerging, "while I liked that last one, I know you," he wagged a finger at the Parthian, "I know you have someone even better."

"As always, it is impossible to outwit you." Dotarzes heaved a sigh that was so overdone that he struggled to maintain this air of sincerity. Suddenly, he frowned, "Actually, I must apologize, Marcus Aemilius. I signaled for the next girl before we had our conversation." He struggled to his feet; Dotarzes wasn't obese, but he was certainly stout, and he assured Lepidus, "Let me go see why there is a delay. Perhaps," Dotarzes gave a leering grin, "she is having trouble getting into the costume I selected for her."

Lepidus actually laughed at this, making a dismissive gesture that, if he had been paying attention, he would have seen caused a ripple of anger to cross the Parthian's face, although he covered it so quickly that even if Lepidus had spotted it, he would have thought it was probably his imagination. Dotarzes disappeared through the doorway, closing but not latching the door, while Lepidus leaned back on his pillows and took another long drink of wine, feeling happier than he had in some time. Everything was coming together nicely, and he was so close to success that he could almost taste it. Not, he acknowledged to himself as he stared up at the ceiling, that there wasn't cause for concern; he had been quite disappointed that he could only turn three Pili Priores of the *Crassoi*, and of the three, only one seemed to doing it for reasons other than the exorbitant sum he had offered for their loyalty. The cavalry had been easier, but he had always known he would need help from an outside force, and the few *satraps* of this region of Parthia who hadn't ridden to the banner of the King of Kings and were the only survivors had proven to be sufficiently cowed by Caesar's reputation to spurn his advances. Caesar! The very name made his stomach twist, and his good mood evaporated in the span of time it took for the image of the Dictator for Life to enter his mind, causing him to sit up, his face twisted with the rage and hatred he felt. He thinks I'm a fool, he thought savagely; he thinks that he's the only Roman who can accomplish great things. Well, he's about to learn a hard lesson that he's not, and this thought actually cheered Lepidus back up as he daydreamed about how Caesar would react when he learned that the most prosperous city in Parthia was no longer under his control. And that was just the beginning; he was still relatively young, and he had already begun thinking about what came next. This Kujula might speak Greek, but he was a savage, and there wasn't a savage born who could outwit a Roman with his bloodlines.

He was so deep in this train of thought that he didn't notice the sounds emanating from the other room; it was only when the door was kicked open that it yanked him from his pleasant reverie, and with a yelp of fear that was completely unbecoming a Roman Praetor, he scrambled to his feet, eyes wide in shock. Dotarzes was in the doorway, but it was the fact that he had one hand clutched to his face that Lepidus noticed first; the blood streaming from his nose was the second, and the fact that there was a figure behind the merchant was the third. However, even when the man behind Dotarzes shoved him into the room by applying a foot to the Parthian's backside, sending him reeling with such force that he lost his balance and hit the mosaiced floor with a thud that Lepidus actually felt through his feet, the Roman was still mystified. Between the shock and the wine, it took him a heartbeat for him to recognize the one-eyed Parthian, which only deepened his confusion. What, he thought, is Teispes doing here? Even as he was struggling with this, the Parthian had entered the room, enabling Lepidus to see that immediately behind the Parthian was the German commander of Caesar's bodyguard, Gundomir, who stepped in and took up a position like Teispes, with his back to the wall but on the opposite side of the door from his counterpart. Only then did Lepidus feel the first stirring of something other than bewilderment, when the third figure entered the room, followed immediately by another, and these two faces *did* belong here.

"Pedius! Pompilius!" Lepidus tried to sound severe. "There better be a good explanation for this intrusion! I," he pointed at Pedius, "gave strict instructions that I wasn't to be disturbed tonight unless it was an emergency! I've been working very hard the last few days, and I deserve a peaceful evening!"

The Quintus Pedius who replied to his Praetor was at once familiar, yet completely unknown to Marcus Lepidus, starting with the smile the Tribune offered him, because there was a quality to it that he'd never seen before. However, it was the complete lack of respect in his voice that both baffled and enraged Lepidus.

"Oh," the Tribune said, sounding almost cheerful, "I think that you'll agree this qualifies as an emergency, Lepidus."

"Lepidus? Have you lost your wits? How *dare* you speak..."

"Shut your mouth. Now."

As much as the words, it was the voice that arrested the torrent of abuse Lepidus was about to aim at the Tribune, because it didn't belong to Pedius. It was a voice he recognized immediately, and for a horrible instant, Marcus Lepidus was certain that he would soil himself as, in utter disbelief, he watched Gaius Julius Caesar step into the room.

It wasn't a dream; nightmare would have been more accurate, and Lepidus' eyes hadn't deceived. Somehow, in some way that Lepidus couldn't even fathom, Caesar was here, in Merv. However, it was a very different Caesar than the last time the two men had been in the same room. This Caesar had lost weight to the point that his already spare frame looked emaciated, but more than anything, it was the shaggy hair, full beard, and the filth that coated his clothing and skin that Lepidus found both confusing and disturbing. One look into his eyes confirmed that it was the real Caesar and not some previously unknown twin conjured up from somewhere, and it was the look in those eyes that informed Marcus Lepidus about his fate more than anything the Dictator could say.

"You," Caesar at least sounded like Caesar; cool, dispassionate, and implacable, "have been conspiring with the *Tokharoi* chieftain known as Kujula to seize control of the city of Merv, and to sit on its throne as some petty king. That," for the first time, his voice showed some emotion, "is treason, and I know that I don't have to remind you of the penalty for that. Although," he did offer a slight smile, "we don't have the Gemonian Steps here, I'm certain we can find a suitable alternative."

Marcus Lepidus wasn't as intelligent as he thought; in fact, he wasn't intelligent in any sense of the word, but he was smart enough to understand that his one and only chance to live past the next few watches, or days at most, was to appear as composed and under control as possible.

"Dictator," he thought using Caesar's title was a nice touch, "I'm not sure where you are getting your information, but I can assure you that you have been misinformed."

"He's lying."

Lepidus turned and gave Quintus Pedius a furious stare, but for the first time in his memory, the Tribune didn't seem the least bit intimidated by his Praetor, yet somehow, Lepidus managed to keep his head, not that it would help much.

"How *dare* you?" Lepidus hissed, his anger only partially feigned. Pointing a finger at the Tribune, he saw that it was shaking, which he thought added to his show of outrage. "By what right do you accuse your superior, *Tribune*? And," before he could stop himself, he was shouting, "who do you think you are, you...*pleb,* to accuse someone who is of the Aemilii and whose father was Consul? Who in your bloodline has earned that kind of distinction?" The instant the words flew out of his mouth, Lepidus knew that he had committed a blunder, but it was Pedius' reaction, turning to gaze directly at Caesar without saying a word that, to the rest of the men present save Dotarzes, was eloquent in itself.

Caesar took the cue by taking a step closer to Lepidus, who had to fight the urge to take a step backward, and he worried that the others could see his knees shaking.

When Caesar spoke, it was in an almost conversational tone, "Marcus, I've always known that you were a fool." Lepidus felt the rush of blood to his face as Caesar went on, "But you were a useful fool. More than that, though, Marcus, you were always reliably loyal to me. And," it was difficult for Lepidus to read the emotions on this bearded, shaggy version of Caesar, but he clearly heard the anger, "I needed that loyalty four years ago, when men I trusted turned on me. They," Caesar's voice rose, "were fools as well." He paused for a heartbeat, then continued, "And all but one of them is dead, and he can't show his face anywhere near Rome for the rest of his days. Now," he folded his arms, "I need to know exactly what you offered this Kujula, and what the next step in this…plan," there was no missing the lacerating scorn when Caesar mouthed the word, "of yours is, and when it's supposed to happen."

There was certainly a part of Lepidus who was screaming at the rest of him to end it now, to admit everything, but this was a moment where Marcus Lepidus' mortal enemy took control, in the form of a man who had spent most of his life lying to himself about his abilities.

"I'm afraid I still don't know what you're talking about, Caesar." Even as he said the words, he heard the tremor there, but he couldn't help it. "I've made no such plans, with anyone."

He expected this to anger Caesar; instead, the Dictator simply turned to Teispes and gave a nod in the direction of the Parthian merchant, who had pulled himself up to a sitting position, using the sleeve of his expensive gown to stanch the blood. Lepidus spun to face Dotarzes, his mind racing as he wondered how he could signal the Parthian that both of their lives depended on the man's ability to withstand whatever it was Caesar had in mind. Certainly, Lepidus thought, with the kind of hopeful desperation that's unique to the condemned, he knows that he can't talk. Yes, he assured himself, Dotarzes is no fool, and he'll hold out as long as it takes because he knows the stakes.

As it turned out, it took far less than a third of a watch before Dotarzes, whose face was now battered beyond recognition, his black beard soaked with blood and bits of teeth, sealed the fate of Marcus Lepidus, and of course, himself. That Lepidus knew this was true was when, at the end of the brutal interrogation administered by Teispes, his scarred features never registering a flicker of emotion as he rained blow after blow down on the merchant, with a simple nod, Caesar passed sentence, which was carried out by Teispes, who grabbed a handful of Dotarzes' hair, and with a skill that made Lepidus shudder, drew the blade of his Parthian dagger across the man's throat. Since they had tied Dotarzes to a chair, his body remained there, slumped over, in a pool of blood that slowly crept across the mosaiced floor, heading right where Lepidus was now seated, the symbolism of that not lost on the Roman.

"I need to know the signal you arranged for Kujula to enter the city," Caesar instructed Lepidus, "and what happens next."

When Lepidus opened his mouth, it was with every intention to continue denying any knowledge, having decided to implicate the senior Decurion Atilius by saying that since he wasn't involved, Atilius was the highest ranking Roman left who could conceivably be considered a suspect. Naturally, both Pedius, who he had instantly grown to hate with a passion that was hard to control, and his lickspittle of a Primus Pilus were above suspicion. Or were they? Consequently, Marcus Lepidus made one last desperate and ultimately futile gamble.

"Someone in this room certainly knows what you want know, Caesar," he tried to imbue his tone with the kind of coolness that he believed Caesar would employ if the situation was reversed; the fact that there were no circumstances where that would happen never occurred to him, "but it's not me."

He turned his head slowly to pin his gaze on Pompilius, who had been a silent observer, leaning against the wall with his arms crossed, and it took the Primus Pilus a moment to realize what Lepidus was trying to do.

However, when he stood erect and opened his mouth to protest, Caesar held up a hand, his eyes never leaving Lepidus, saying only, "Let him speak, Pompilius. I owe him that much."

Despite knowing he shouldn't read anything into this, Lepidus' heart leapt in his chest, a sudden rush of what he knew was hope flooding his mind, which made it difficult for the rational part to maintain control. You *must* control yourself, Marcus, or you're a dead man. Caesar has thrown you a branch; let's see if you can use it to get to safety. In a tone as controlled as he could make it, Marcus Lepidus spoke for several moments, and with every heartbeat, his confidence grew, mainly because both times Pompilius tried to interrupt him early on, Caesar behaved in the same manner, stopping the Primus Pilus. So absorbed was he in his tale, which was essentially the truth of all that had happened, but with Pompilius as the instigator instead of himself, that he didn't notice something. Yes, early on, Pompilius had been outraged, and it took a sharp rebuke from Caesar before he gave up trying, but it was less from Caesar's words and the fact that Pompilius was watching the Dictator's face that he began to relax, and before much longer, he was fighting the urge to grin. Pompilius could see that even Teispes, whose face seemed to be carved from rock in terms of expressing emotions, was deeply amused, as was Pedius and Gundomir. The only man oblivious to the fact he was wasting his breath was Marcus Lepidus, but he learned this was the case when, in mid-sentence, Caesar abruptly began roaring with laughter, and if the other men exchanged looks of slight alarm, it wasn't long before they were joining in. For his part, Lepidus wasn't angry or terrified; he was simply bewildered by Caesar's sudden reaction, and he wondered if the Dictator had lost his wits, and what that might mean for him. Before his mind could soar on this flight of fancy, where he himself was miraculously spared and, because of Caesar's obvious madness, returned from Merv to resume his rightful place in the hierarchy the Dictator had created, Caesar finally spoke.

"Oh, Marcus," he was still chuckling as he wiped a tear from his eye, "I must thank you. That was *quite* entertaining, it truly was. I haven't laughed that hard since the last mummers' show I saw." Then, as if it had never happened, all signs of humor vanished, so quickly that Lepidus could have been forgiven for thinking it was a figment of his imagination, and the cold, hard Dictator of Rome who had seen all of his enemies vanquished returned, "But I'm afraid that this is all the time I can devote to entertainment. Now, I am going to ask you one last time, before I," he lifted an arm to gesture at Teispes, "allow Teispes to take over the questioning."

Finally, Lepidus understood it was over, and all that remained was how much pain he would have to endure in the final watches of his life. Being the coward that he was, when he spoke again, it was the truth.

As all of the parties involved quickly learned, trying to keep Caesar's presence in Merv a secret was a waste of energy, yet it did have one salutary effect; the participants in the plot hatched by Marcus Lepidus exposed their identities through their respective reactions to the news, with one exception, the senior Decurion Atilius.

"I highly doubt that we'll ever see him again, Caesar," was Pompilius' judgment. "Now," he offered a shrug, "how many of his men will come back, that remains to be seen." He paused for a moment, then asked quietly, "And what do you want done with them if they do?"

"Nothing," Caesar replied immediately. "They were following their commander, and I'm not going to punish those troopers for obeying orders."

"Does that extend to the men of the three Cohorts?" Pompilius asked, and again Caesar nodded.

"But Pompilius," Caesar turned to face the Primus Pilus, "I'm afraid that my clemency won't extend to their Pili Priores or to the Centurions under them who were in on it."

"What about Macrinus?" Pompilius asked, afraid he knew the answer. "He's the one who told me, after all."

Caesar considered for a long moment, then said flatly, "He can't be a Pilus Prior any longer. That's not acceptable. Beyond that?" He looked Pompilius in the eye as he continued, "I will leave that up to you."

They both returned their attention to the south from their spot on the southern rampart, scanning the horizon for movement. Pompilius understood why Gundomir was with them, as was Teispes, at least once he heard that the German's younger brother had accompanied them and had led the bulk of the bodyguard on what was essentially a suicide mission, but while he didn't hold out much hope for whatever remained of Caesar's party, he was wise enough not to say it.

Instead, he decided to stay on safer topics, asking Caesar, "Do you think Kujula suspects anything?"

Caesar shook his head, but it wasn't indicative of anything but his state of mind, admitting, "I have no idea, Pompilius." Taking a breath, he thought for a moment. "But if he does, I suspect that he'll understand that Lepidus' plan has failed for one reason or another, and he'll return to his own lands, which we'll know soon enough." Leaning over slightly, Caesar addressed Pedius, who was standing on the other side of the Primus Pilus. "The messenger's party left at dawn, correct, Pedius?"

"Yes, Caesar," Pedius answered, then admitted, "and Lepidus says that we'll have an answer by nightfall. At least, that's how it's supposed to go since they're so nearby."

At the mention of the former Praetor's name, Pompilius felt a stab of anger, along with puzzlement, wondering why the man was still alive, but when he had asked Caesar what fate awaited the man, Caesar had refused to divulge his plans. Suddenly, the notes of a horn came drifting across the rooftops of the city, but from the opposite direction, which meant that it had to be relayed, and all of them turned to stare across the mile of space to the northern wall, despite knowing they wouldn't be able to see anything, at least to a degree that might give them an idea.

"It's Artabanus' Cohort's day for guard," Pompilius commented, shading his eyes, "and I think he's probably there."

"Would Kujula's messenger be approaching from the north?" Caesar asked, but neither Pompilius nor Pedius could supply a solid answer.

It took a fair amount of time for them to learn the cause, but when they did, it was reason for celebration, the first moment of true happiness that Caesar could remember experiencing in many months. Because of their position on the rampart, Caesar and his party were essentially standing over the north/south road that bisected Merv which, while not laid out with the same symmetry as the cities that had been created by the Macedonian king Alexander, still had two major streets, and what was now the *Praetorium* was located where the streets intersected. This kept anyone standing on any of the streets from being able to see the far side of the city on the other side of the building, so that it wasn't until a party of riders made their way around the *Praetorium* that Caesar actually had a chance to see them.

"There's too many to be from Kujula," Pedius commented, frowning as he strained his eyes, trying to identify the party. "Artabanus would never let that many men enter the city."

"Maybe Atilius didn't hear the news, and he thinks he's coming back to do whatever Lepidus wants him to do next," Pompilius suggested, but before anyone else could respond, it was Gundomir who spoke, pointing at the oncoming riders, saying excitedly, "No! They are not *Tokharoi* and they are not Atilius' men. That," his voice choked with the emotion that came from his recognition, "is Barvistus! There's only one man I know who sits his horse that way!"

This was the last normal moment, as the party went rushing down the stone steps from the rampart, their vigil no longer necessary, and it was only because Gundomir moved so quickly that Caesar wasn't the first down to the street.

Kujula was in his forties, and his rise to the leadership of what the Romans, and Parthians, had believed to be one tribe but was actually an amalgam of two branches of the *Tokharoi* had been rapid and brutal. As with any warlike people, Kujula first made his mark in battle, but it was his shrewd ruthlessness that put him where he was now, as the most powerful chieftain among the half-dozen branches of these people who were similar to the Indo-Greek people of Pattala. When he had been approached by the Parthian dog Dotarzes, he had suspected some sort of trap, but ironically enough, meeting the Roman governor Lepidus had actually erased the last vestiges of his suspicion, because just as Dotarzes had, he assessed the character and intelligence of Marcus Lepidus with a level of accuracy that would have dismayed the Roman if he had known of it. The secret message from Lepidus advancing the next part of the plan had come a bit earlier than expected, but neither that nor the fact that it wasn't delivered by the normal method, through a man in Dotarzes' employ, had unduly alarmed him. This Parthian, who was responsible for supervising the trains of camels, carts, and some wagons that moved back and forth between West and East, would leave communications from Lepidus by placing rocks in a very unique pattern at a specific point on the Silk Road to alert the *Tokharoi*. However, now Kujula was much, much closer to Merv than he had been in many years, at least with an army at his back, and he had been waiting for the next phase of the plan, which was ostensibly an official diplomatic visit to the city, under the protection of the Praetor.

Lepidus would announce a new treaty had been signed between the *Tokharoi* chieftain, whereby they would go from simply refraining from preying on the merchant trains that were the lifeblood for Merv to being active protectors against the other tribes of the *Tokharoi*. This was the public part of the plan; the private part was that, with the aid of some troops loyal to Lepidus, who would throw open the eastern gate at midnight after Kujula's arrival in the city, his men would pour in and slaughter those Romans who chose to fight. Then, at least in Lepidus' conception of this plan, Kujula would swear loyalty to the new King of Merv, something that Kujula actually intended to do, except that it would be an oath to himself. Thanks to Dotarzes, the *Tokharoi* chieftain knew exactly how many Romans of the *Crassoi* would be left, and even if the three of what they called Cohorts that Lepidus insisted were loyal to him weren't, he had brought enough of the right kind of troops to overwhelm even the full Legion. It would be bloody, no matter what, and normally, Kujula would have been loath to risk almost his entire strength, leaving behind just enough men to discourage any of the other tribes from raiding his domain, but the prize of Merv was worth the risk. First, however, he must endure the slight indignity of appearing to humble himself before Lepidus, who had been more than happy to go to great detail describing the elaborate ceremony he intended to put on in the large plaza in front of what was once the *satrap's* palace. The messenger brought word that the next phase of the Roman's plan was ready, and of all the parts of it, this was the one that made Kujula the most nervous, not that any of his men knew it. He would be allowed to bring only ten men with him as his escort, so he naturally chose his most formidable warriors from his personal bodyguard, and they began preparing immediately to depart. It was as they were doing this that, led by his younger brother Sadashkana, the men of his cavalry contingent arrived, riding into the well-hidden camp. Kujula had dispatched him to make a scouting trip to the south, wanting to know more about this land that, if all went to plan, he would be ruling very soon. One look at his face told Kujula that something potentially disturbing had happened, and he listened as Sadashkana described the sudden appearance of a band of horsemen who, to his brother's eyes, appeared to be equally mixed between men he immediately recognized as Parthian, but also with fair-skinned, bearded men with red and yellow hair. Neither of the brothers, nor any of the men marching for Kujula had ever seen men with this kind of coloring, which was one cause for his brother's disturbed state.

Once Sadashkana paused, Kujula asked bluntly, "And did you run them down?" Before his brother could reply, he grinned and added, "Surely you brought some heads of these men so I could see them!"

The younger brother looked uncomfortable, but he replied readily enough, "We killed a good number of them, brother, but no, I didn't think to take their heads. Not," he suddenly frowned, "that I recall we cut many of those pale-skinned men down."

Just by the manner in which Sadashkana had said it warned Kujula, yet his face didn't betray the sudden turmoil, asking only, "How many do you think got away?"

"More than half," Sadashkana answered unhappily, and Kujula uttered an oath common to the *Tokharoi*, but after thinking a moment, he shrugged and said, "No matter, really, as long as none of them was the Roman Caesar." Smiling at his brother, he clapped Sadashkana on his shoulder. "By this time tomorrow, I should be King of Merv!" Just as quickly as it had come, it vanished, and he fixed his brother with a hard stare as he added, "As long as you and your men don't fail me again."

"They won't, brother," Sadashkana ignored the flutter in his stomach, trying not to think about the fact that there had once been a brother in between himself and Kujula in age. While it was true that Kujula and Vima, the other brother, had never gotten along, it was still a sobering reminder, and was why Sadashkana spoke so strongly when he vowed, "I swear it, brother. You can count on us."

"I knew I could." Kujula's smile returned, reminding Sadashkana that his brother also could change moods with the rapidity of a lightning bolt, and as Kujula strode off to check on his escort, Sadashkana felt the sweat running down his back, despite the frigid temperature, hoping that Kujula never learned of the part that

Sadashkana hadn't told him.

While Kujula and Marcus Lepidus didn't have much in common, the one thing they did was the belief that Merv's remote location would be the key factor in keeping the Roman general Caesar from making an attempt to retake the city. Kujula didn't fear Caesar, but neither was he a fool; any man who had the will, the ability, and the army to subdue all of Parthia in two years was one with whom he had no wish to war against if he could help it. The very idea that Caesar was anywhere within a thousand miles of Merv was so preposterous that it never entered Kujula's mind, certainly not when he led his ten men towards the eastern gate of the city, as agreed. He was certainly wary, and even a bit apprehensive, his eyes constantly scanning his surroundings, as aware as anyone for whom this desolate region was home that what appeared to be an expanse of flat, open ground was anything but and provided more than enough cover for an ambush. As they drew closer, he began to distinguish that the tiny bumps arrayed along the top of the eastern wall were men, who he knew were watching him and his party with the same intensity he was watching them. His mouth was dry, not surprisingly, yet he refused to move at more than a walk, guiding his horse with his knees so he could keep his hands in clear view; even with the man behind him lofting the large square of white cloth on the end of his spear, he didn't want to give any of these dogs an excuse. He was *so* close, and despite himself, his mind took flight as he thought of all that would come to him, which was nothing more than his due, and it all was beginning on this day. So absorbed was he in his imaginings of a life of wealth and power that, when the voice sounded from above him, he jerked in surprise. Naturally, the man who shouted did so in Greek, and Kujula saw that he was wearing a crested helmet that ran side to side.

"That is far enough! Identify yourself!"

Bristling at the peremptory tone, it was a struggle for Kujula to keep it from showing as he spoke as loudly as he could without shouting, "I am Kujula Kadphises, the King of the Kushan, of the tribe you call the *Tokharoi*! And I am here at the direct invitation of the governor of Merv, Marcus Aemilius Lepidus," this next, despite knowing that it was part of the ruse, was still difficult for Kujula to say, "so that I can swear my obedience and loyalty to Rome, as part of the treaty that was signed between myself and your governor!"

There was no reply from the man Kujula knew was called a *Crassoi*; in fact, there was only a slight turn of his head, but it was obviously an order, because there was immediately a deep, rumbling noise, along with a sudden shower of dust in the gateway. Screaming with what sounded almost a human agony from the giant hinges by which the two heavy doors were suspended and required a pair of men apiece to move, slowly, Kujula saw through the opening crack the city of Merv. And, as he had anticipated, he could see that both sides of the street were lined with people, undoubtedly drawn by the spectacle and the news of an important event that, while it would have an enormous impact on their lives, they had no idea the scale of it. Riding at the same stately pace, he led his men, arranged in a column of two's, through the gateway, noting its thickness and automatically gauging the difficulty of assaulting it, although his face gave nothing away. Nor did he acknowledge the mostly silent crowd, feeling their gaze as he rode deeper into the city, yet he sensed that the populace seemed divided between open hostility and curiosity.

Ahead of him, he saw the large, two-story building, the wide covered portico with steps leading up to it lined with men, one of whom was sitting. Naturally, his first assumption was that it was Lepidus, except that there was a nagging thought in the back of his mind, that there was something different in the man than what he remembered of Lepidus. For one thing, he was sitting more erectly, but Kujula dismissed that as his imagination, or maybe the Roman's back was just stiff. Just as the streets were lined on either side, this crowd continued into the plaza, except that instead of civilians he could see the neatly aligned rows of uniformed and armored men, their shields grounded in front of them, undoubtedly the *Crassoi*. They were probably the troops loyal to Lepidus, although if it had been Kujula, he would have placed some of them on the eastern gate, since that would be where his men were going to be streaming in after dark. One thing at a time, he admonished himself; first, he had to go through this sham ceremony, where he pretended to swear his loyalty to the fool Lepidus. It was the thought of the man himself that, just as he entered the plaza from between the last buildings on the eastern side, it made him realize something, and he almost came to a stop, his heart thudding rapidly in his chest. His initial instinct had been the right one; the man sitting in that chair wasn't Marcus Lepidus. Oh, he was clean shaven in the Roman fashion, but while Lepidus was short and somewhat stocky, this Roman was lean, and clearly taller, which was confirmed when, without any haste, he stood from his chair. It wouldn't be until later, when Kujula actually bothered to look at the freshly minted coins from one of the bags that

Marcus Lepidus had handed him when they had sealed their bargain before he realized that he would have been able to identify this Roman. What difference it would make was something that he would agonize over for the rest of his life, but in the moment, he immediately realized that he had come too far, both in an abstract and a literal sense; by the time he understood that this Roman wasn't Lepidus, he and his party had already entered the large plaza. Even if he had wanted to flee, the fact that those *Crassoi* who had been lining either side had quickly moved into a position blocking the eastern street meant that escape was impossible.

Nevertheless, he drew to a halt, hearing the alarmed muttering of his men but keeping his eyes on the Roman, who seemed content to stand at the top of the stairs, flanked by a number of men who Kujula assumed to be the senior officers. Despite his distraction, he did notice the two large bearded men whose hair was the color of copper, the thought crossing his mind that these were probably the men who Sadashkana had encountered and failed to capture, wondering what this meant. The moment stretched out, Kujula sitting there motionless, about halfway to the base of the stairs, the silence so total that it was unnerving to not just the men, but the animals they were astride as Kujula's mount began tossing its head, forcing him to curb it. Now that he was closer, Kujula noticed the Roman was not just slender, his cheeks were hollowed in a manner that he sensed wasn't natural to the man. It's as if, he thought to himself, he's endured some sort of hardship, and it was this moment that the first blooming of the idea he might know who this Roman was occurred to him. Somewhat strangely, it was Kujula's curiosity that broke the deadlock, and he nudged his horse forward, although he had to kick twice to get it moving. The last fifty paces were the worst, because now he could look the Roman in the eyes, and he saw in them a piercing quality that was quite disquieting, so that he actually welcomed the brief respite that came when he had to swing off his mount, dropping to the paving stones. Then, he was mounting the steps until he was just two steps lower, while the Roman had walked the few paces to stand at the very top of the stairs. Not knowing exactly how to start, Kujula essentially repeated what he had said to gain entry, while the Roman looked down on him impassively, waiting until he finished.

Then, also speaking in Greek, the Roman said, "Greetings, King Kujula, I am Gaius Julius Caesar." He paused, and then he added with what sounded to the *Tokharoi* like humor, "And I believe we have some matters to discuss about your…ambitions."

When Kujula was allowed to leave, he was riven with so many emotions, but the overwhelming one was his relief that he was still alive. It wasn't just that this Caesar was so remarkably well-informed, and he was still having trouble grasping exactly how a Roman who was supposed to be so far away suddenly appeared here, in this city that just a matter of watches before he had been confident he would be ruling. No, more than anything was that, while Kujula was endowed with a high degree of confidence in his abilities, and the qualities that he believed were required for a great ruler, within a matter of moments in Caesar's presence, he realized that he wasn't in Caesar's class. Just the fact that the Roman was confident enough to have a private audience with Kujula, without requiring the *Tokharoi* to surrender his weapons was remarkable, although he wasn't foolish enough to believe that, even if he had struck Caesar down, he would have made it out of the palace alive. But that was only part of it; it was as if, he thought uncomfortably, Caesar had measured him and decided that he wasn't that much of a fool, which was preferable to the alternative, that Caesar didn't think Kujula was a threat to defeat him. Whatever the reason, it had been a most unsettling but illuminating audience, and it had a profound effect on the *Tokharoi* chieftain. No, he wasn't going to be King of Merv, but he could have ended up like Lepidus, whose end he had witnessed, although he hadn't been surprised that the man had died badly, crying and begging for his life up until the moment the one-eyed Parthian giant had decapitated him. In fact, he tried to remind himself, there would be even more money in his coffers, yet despite this, the specifics of the agreement rankled him, if only because it demonstrated Caesar's shrewdness. Not only would Kujula profit, the amount by which he did depended largely on him and his ability to prevent the other branches of the *Tokharoi* from preying on the merchant caravans. In exchange, Kujula would receive five percent of the value of every caravan that arrived in Merv unharmed on its final leg of the journey. In order to seal this bargain, however, Caesar had required some form of surety, which was why Kujula's brother Sadashkana, along with five of his highest-ranking officers were remaining behind in Merv. More than the tangible results, it was the intangible aspect that had the biggest impression on Kujula, because in the span of one day, he had gone from dreaming of greatness, with Merv as the crown jewel of a kingdom that would one day dwarf any of its neighbors, to recognizing that whatever qualities he possessed to achieve that end, they weren't equal to Caesar. Yes, and as Caesar had freely admitted, he had erred in trusting Marcus Lepidus, but when he assured Kujula that he always learned from his mistakes, and never repeated them, Kujula had believed him. Perhaps the strangest aspect of all had been the feast that had been arranged by Lepidus that night, which Caesar had deemed would still go on.

"He put a lot of time and effort into it," was how the Roman had put it to Kujula, "so it is a shame to put it to waste."

Kujula had naturally accepted the invitation, knowing that he had no choice in the matter, and he had been certain that it would be an ordeal, a chance for Caesar to rub what could only be called a defeat in his face. And, at first, it had certainly seemed that way, but as the wine flowed, and after the initial hard stares from Caesar's officers, the atmosphere became more relaxed, which was what encouraged Kujula to finally blurt out the thing that had been eating at him since the first instant he realized that he had been outwitted by Caesar.

"How did you get here so quickly?"

Caesar actually smiled at this, and despite his gaunt appearance, it transformed his face and made him seem much younger, but in answer, he pointed to the three men sitting, quite uncomfortably, on the couch to his left.

"Because of these men," Caesar answered, and when Kujula looked over at them, he could see that the two red-haired men and the one-eyed Parthian seemed to share the same emotion, which was acute embarrassment.

The wine had helped loosen his tongue, and his inhibitions, to a sufficient degree that before he thought about it, he pointed at the man who had been introduced to him as Gundomir and demanded, "Are you the man who evaded my brother?"

"No," Gundomir answered, but while the beard helped obscure his features, Kujula saw the smile and the pride when he turned to indicate the man next to him that the *Tokharoi* had already assumed was his brother, "that was Barvistus here."

"I commend you on your skill in evading Sadashkana." Kujula nodded to him, as he hoped that the fact his jaw was clenched would go unnoticed. Then, more to be polite, he asked, "Were you coming to meet Caesar when you ran into our men?"

The three men across from him exchanged glances, but it was Caesar's clear amusement that gave Kujula the hint that there was more to the story, and that he wouldn't care for it. After listening to the story about how his brother had been successfully lured away, thereby enabling Caesar, the Parthian he had realized was Teispes and whose name he had been familiar with when he was the commander of the *Crassoi* back when Merv had been under Parthian control, and the older brother Gundomir to slip past in the darkness, it took an effort on his part to maintain his composure. The thought that he had been so close, but because his brother had fallen for the ruse, meant that he was actually thankful that Sadashkana would be remaining in Merv, because he knew himself well enough that, at some point on their journey home he would lash out, and he would be less another brother. Vima had deserved his fate; Kujula had uncovered the plot his brother had been hatching to murder him, but he had always been close to Sadashkana, who had shown nothing but loyalty. Regardless, it was still difficult hearing not just the bare bones of the story, but the understandable relish with which it was being told to him, and it took a great deal of his self-control; fortunately before long, the conversation had moved on. By the time the sun was rising, the new bargain had been struck, Kujula had sent one of his bodyguards back to retrieve Sadashkana and the other men he was willing to surrender as hostage, and Caesar had assured him that they would be well treated.

"Provided you uphold your end of the bargain," he said, using the same tone as he had just a moment before when ordering the slave girl to bring another pitcher of wine. "However, if you do not, I will be forced to execute your hostages, starting with your brother. And," he concluded as he leaned over and picked up an olive, "I won't use the same method I used on Marcus Lepidus. It will be much more…painful."

Caesar made sure to look Kujula in the eye as he finished, then popped the olive into his mouth, chewing it while he regarded the *Tokharoi* with an unwavering gaze that was more impactful than the words. Aside from this revelation and Caesar's stark reminder, it was otherwise a pleasant evening, one where the Roman didn't seem to feel the need to constantly reinforce what was ultimately a defeat for Kujula. Something, he felt certain, the dog Lepidus would have done if he had somehow prevailed, although the irony wasn't lost on him that both Caesar's plan and his own ultimately ended with the same result in one respect; the sodden thud of Lepidus' head striking the paving stones of the plaza. Either way, Lepidus' fate had been sealed by his belief that he could match wits with Gaius Julius Caesar, and it was a lesson that Kujula would never forget; underestimating Caesar generally proved fatal to one's plans, and in the case of men like Lepidus, their life.

Caesar spent less than a week in Merv, just long enough for the men of his bodyguard to recover, while only the personal mounts of Caesar's bodyguards were selected for the grueling ride back, which Teispes had warned Caesar about.

"We do not have to move as quickly, which is a good thing," he had informed his general. "But we are now in the dead of winter, so the conditions will be even worse as far as the weather."

That Caesar didn't argue, or even question Teispes about what it would take to move more quickly, was the most potent sign to the Parthian, and to the Germans of his bodyguard who knew him well, that he was still fatigued. It was true that he looked more like himself once he had shed his beard and cut his hair, and he had filled out some, yet there was still a gaunt quality to him that Teispes secretly worried about. A private conversation with Gundomir proved that his friend felt the same way, but he also was resigned.

"We are not going to convince him to stay longer," the German had declared flatly. "Not with what is happening in India."

Although it had certainly been a topic of conversation, because of their constant proximity to Caesar, whenever they did discuss it, it was in snatches, usually in whispers, and always with an eye on Caesar. Who, almost from the moment the ship had sailed down the river from Bharuch, had forbidden the subject to be brought up within his earshot. Only Gundomir had been with Caesar long enough to remember Pharsalus, and the reaction he was seeing with his general now was very similar to that. In fact, just like Pharsalus, Caesar's reaction had been to leave abruptly, that time taking the two Cohorts of the 6th Legion who had surrendered to Marcus Antonius, and led by the giant Roman Titus Pullus, who Caesar had temporarily appointed Primus Pilus of what he referred to as the 6th Legion.

Since they had the luxury of privacy from Caesar's ears, Teispes asked Gundomir bluntly, "What do you think he is going to do about the army, Gundomir?"

"I wish I knew, my friend," the German replied soberly, running his hands through his beard, which Teispes had learned was a sign of his friend's distraction. "Of course," he shrugged, "I will follow Caesar anywhere he chooses to lead. But I cannot say I blame the Legions for their anger. They were told this was a campaign to subdue Parthia," suddenly, Gundomir remembered to whom he was speaking, looking embarrassed; however, Teispes had reconciled himself to this as being not only a fact, but ordained by the gods. Seeing that his friend wasn't visibly upset at this reminder,

Gundomir continued, "But then they find themselves in a place that is unlike anywhere they have ever been, and that certainly holds true for me. I," he shuddered, "hate that place. It's…sticky, and wet. And hot."

"Parthia is hot," Teispes pointed out, although it was more to goad his friend, because he not only understood what Gundomir meant, he felt the same way.

"It is," Gundomir agreed, but then he added, "but Parthia is hot like an oven, and India is like one of those steam baths the Romans love so much, and they are *horrible*."

Somewhat curious, Teispes asked, "Have you ever gone into one of them?"

"One time," the German grimaced, "because Caesar said I stank too much to be in his company, and he made me take a full Roman bath." Still clearly shaken by the memory, Gundomir shuddered, confiding, "It is the closest I have ever come to quitting Caesar."

"But surely he was not happy with you just taking one bath?" Teispes' normally immobile features cracked slightly, as he asked teasingly, "How long ago was that?"

Gundomir thought, then answered, "Seven years."

"Are you telling me you have not bathed in seven *years*?" Teispes gasped, truly shocked for the first time in their association.

"Of course not!" Gundomir countered, indignant. "I just have not had one of those stupid baths where you sit and sweat like a whore, then sit in a tub of water that is the temperature of spit, then jump in a tub of water that turns your balls into raisins. Now," he shrugged, "I do the oiling and scraping part, and once a month, I will use water. That," he admitted, "was the least amount Caesar would stand for."

As diverting and amusing as this was, Teispes quickly went back to the larger subject, saying the thing aloud that was always on their minds. "I wonder if Pollio and Hirtius managed to keep the Legions under control."

While Gundomir agreed that it was a concern, he was also not overly worried, pointing out the one obvious fact. "And where would they go if they did run wild? March all the way back to Parthia?" Shaking his head, he did acknowledge, "I would not be surprised if that city was no longer standing and all its people killed, but otherwise…" he held both hands out, palms up, "…what are they going to do?" Before Teispes could interject, he concluded, "I worry more about what they will be like when Caesar does return."

These concerns aside, when Caesar did depart from Merv, he

had made one substantial change, informing Quintus Pedius that he was, until further notice, the permanent Praetor of Parthia Superior. Just a year before, Pedius would have insisted that he was neither qualified nor ready for such an appointment and would have done his best to change Caesar's mind. However, now that he had Numerius Pompilius' trust and belief in his abilities, it was a different Pedius who solemnly accepted the news from Caesar. The Dictator had also performed a quick but thorough review of the administration of the city, and acceding to Teispes' suggestions, had made some changes among the midlevel officials, relying on the Parthian's knowledge that he had accrued during the period before being summoned with the *Crassoi*. Dotarzes' business was no more, and while Caesar was originally going to confiscate it in the name of Rome, Teispes convinced him that by not doing anything, he would occupy the other merchants of the city, the best way to keep them from mischief.

"They will be so busy squabbling over who gets what piece of Dotarzes' business, they will not have time to plot," was how the Parthian put it, and when he thought about it, Caesar realized that this was a good solution.

When the party gathered before dawn on the day of their departure, Caesar embraced his nephew rather than offer his arm or accept Pedius' salute.

"You saved this city and the people in it from much hardship, Quintus," Caesar had said gravely. "And I apologize to you for putting you in the position in which you found yourself. I thought," he admitted, "I was saving myself some headaches by sending Lepidus up here, but I truly didn't think he would be that foolish."

"Will his death cause you any problems?" Pedius asked, surprised that this was the first time he had thought about it.

"With who?" Caesar asked with a raised eyebrow. "The only men likely to complain are back in Rome. And," he laughed, "if they want to come all this way to conduct an investigation, I'm sure that you can handle them."

Pedius had to laugh at this as well, but he realized with a certain amount of surprise in himself that, if that were to happen? Well, it was a long way from Rome, and he now knew he had Caesar's support in anything that he did; all that Caesar required was loyalty and competence, and he would give the former and strive to be the latter. He and Pompilius stood, watching as Caesar led the party across the plaza, their hooves clattering and undoubtedly waking the people of the city who lived nearby, and neither man had much to say. Finally, when he could no longer hear them, Pedius turned and ascended the stairs into the *Praetorium*; there was work to do.

Chapter 4

Since there were eleven Legions in and around Bharuch, Pullus knew that it would be a fair amount of time before his Legion went out again, meaning that he was left to come up with ways to occupy his men, both to keep them out of trouble and to maintain a level of control and discipline within the Legion. He was far from alone; it was a topic of almost constant conversation among the Primi Pili, but in Pullus' case, his men were in a unique situation. They were the only Legion who were quartered completely within the city, in the buildings ringing the palace compound, and while it caused some friction with his counterparts, Pullus could simply point out that only the 10th was allowed to guard the queen. The consequence of this was that the other Legions had begun constructing their own housing, in three camps ringing the city, but the first time Pullus had tried to get his men to participate in this project, they had flatly refused. In retrospect, he realized that he had done this too soon after the fall of the city, and it was another couple of weeks before his Centurions approached him on behalf of their men, singing quite a different tune.

"They're bored out of their fucking minds," was how Balbus had put it. "They're almost willing to clean latrines at this point...almost."

However, when Pullus approached Pollio, the Legate actually had another project in mind.

"That canal that they built," he began. "I've been talking to Volusenus, and we need to prepare for the day Caesar returns with the fleet. There wasn't nearly enough space for it on the river side, and it would be a perfect spot to add several docks."

"But is it wide enough?" Pullus asked doubtfully, and at this, Pollio did at least look somewhat uncomfortable.

"Not as it is," he admitted. "But," he opened a tablet on his desk and beckoned to Pullus, "Volusenus came up with a way to widen it by using the pilings they lined each side with, and we can remove the dirt rampart."

Pullus immediately remembered this was the case, recalling hopping up onto the wooden pilings that had been driven down, side by side, when he had led his men on the assault of the northern side. He hadn't been back to the canal since; there had been no need, but he did recall that the defenders had inadvertently made their job easier by orienting the sloped part that was required for a dirt wall on the canal side.

"That," he rubbed his chin, "is going to be a lot more work than just building some huts, sir."

"It is," Pollio agreed, "but you won't be doing it by yourself."

"Another Legion? Or Legions?" Pullus asked, but Pollio shook his head.

"No," Pollio replied. "We're going to be calling for volunteers from the civilians."

Before Pullus could stop himself, he let out a barking laugh, asking, "Why would they do that?"

"Because," Pollio didn't seem surprised, and when he leaned back, there was something in his expression that gave Pullus an idea he wasn't going to like what he heard, which was confirmed when he said, "you are going to go to the queen and ask for her help."

"And if she doesn't?" Pullus asked pointedly.

"Her subjects are going to be involved one way or another, Pullus," Pollio told him flatly. "Whether it's under guard or willingly, they're going to be involved. There is," the Legate shifted in his chair, looking down at the tablet, "an element of danger in Volusenus' plan. And I'm not about to risk our own men's lives to get this done."

Something that you're only doing to impress Caesar and show him that we haven't been mutinous bastards the whole time he was away, Pullus thought bitterly, but for once, the thought stayed inside his skull. And, he admitted, it was a smart thing to do.

"Of course," Pollio spoke casually, but there was a feigned quality to it that Pullus had detected before, which meant he was forewarned when the Legate said, "if you could convince your queen to deal with me, you wouldn't have to bother."

As had been happening for some time, Pullus felt a flare of what he had still not identified for what it was, but as he always did when Pollio broached the subject, he lied, "I'll ask her again, sir."

"Well, even if she doesn't," Pollio stood up, signaling the end of the meeting, "you need to get across to her that her cooperation is essential if she doesn't want her people to suffer. Because," he finished grimly, "either way, they are going to be doing the part of the job that is the most hazardous."

Pullus was about to ask what the hazard was but realized that not only did he not care, it didn't really matter, because in this, Pollio was right, and Pullus was of the same mind; if there was a hazard to this project, it wouldn't be borne by his men.

"And why should I do that?"

Despite anticipating this question even before his arrival at the palace, he still hadn't thought of a way to answer it that would sound something like what Caesar or one of the upper classes would say by reminding her of the reality of their situation but not being brutal about it.

What came out of his mouth was, as always, the truth delivered bluntly. "Because they're going to be doing the work one way or another, Your Highness. If they know that you're asking them to do it," he shrugged, "it might make things easier."

"Easier for you," she pointed out, though not with rancor, and he didn't receive it with any because it was the simple truth. After a silence, she asked him, "What will you do? I mean," she hurried on, seeing Pullus didn't understand, "by what means will you force my subjects to do as you want?"

"Your Highness," Pullus answered quietly, albeit with a question of his own, "what would your husband do?"

"Whatever was necessary," she said without thinking, but while a part of her wanted to recall the words, neither could she deny the essential truth that Pullus' question had uncovered, just as he hadn't tried when it had been her turn an instant before. Finally, she said bitterly, "So you will beat them, and if they still refuse, you will execute a few of them until they do."

"That," Pullus acknowledged, "is usually how it's done, yes."

She sat with her hands in lap, her head bowed, oblivious to Pullus' scrutiny, and she stayed this way for the span of several heartbeats before, at last, she raised her head to look him in the eye and asked, "What if there was another way?"

"She wants us to do *what*?" Pollio sat back, flabbergasted, and both Hirtius and Volusenus, the latter having been summoned to this meeting since it was his project, were similarly nonplussed.

"She wants us to pay them," Pullus repeated patiently.

"First," Pollio countered, "why would we do that? Does she think it matters to us how we treat these people?"

"Yes," Pullus interjected, "she does."

It was Hirtius who offered a snorting laugh, and while his words were supposedly addressed to Pollio, Pullus was acutely aware he was the real target. "I think someone has gone soft in the head when it comes this…queen, Asinius."

Pollio gave something of a laugh, though not with much humor.

"Even if he has, Aulus, it wouldn't matter, since her husband took their fucking treasury with him."

Shaking his head, Pollio was about to tell Pullus to go back to the palace with a flat rejection of what he considered a ridiculous and feminine idea, but before he could, Pullus countered, "What if that wasn't entirely true?"

Even if he had shouted the words, the effect would have been the same, as Pollio shot to his feet to lean on the desk.

"What does that mean, Pullus?"

In as few words as he could, Titus Pullus informed his Legate that, while the King of Bharuch had the bulk of the royal treasury, which, just judging from the size of the huge room in the basement of the palace, had to have been immense, an amount had been left behind and buried someplace where Hyppolita insisted the Romans would never find it.

"We'll see about that," Hirtius snapped at this last bit. "Caesar didn't take the torture detachment…"

"Are you fucking *mad*? Or just stupid?"

As shocking as the words, it was from whom they came that caused all three senior officers to gape in sheer astonishment.

"What did you say, Pullus?" Hirtius' face darkened, yet at the same time, Pullus saw him shift ever so slightly to move just out of his easy reach. "Did you really address one of your Legates that way?" Emboldened by the extra distance, Hirtius pointed a finger in Pullus' face. "What the senior Legate and I decide to do with *our* captive is none of your business, Primus Pilus! And I suggest that in the future, you watch your tongue!"

"Or what?" Pullus responded, outwardly every bit as calm as Hirtius was worked up. "What do you intend to do, Legate? Seize me and place me under arrest?"

As he had been certain, hearing it put so plainly instantly deflated Hirtius, understanding that any such attempt on the part of anyone save Caesar himself would ignite a conflagration that, while it was at least smoldering, wasn't completely extinguished by any stretch of the imagination. And, given the circumstances, it wasn't a guarantee that the men of the army would allow it, even if it was Caesar. The look Aulus Hirtius gave Pullus was even more furious because of his impotence, while Pollio was looking thoughtfully at the Primus Pilus. Because of his friend's outburst, Pollio had been able to think through his initial reaction, which had been aligned with Aulus Hirtius'; the very idea of being put in this position, and by a woman at that, stuck in his throat.

Nevertheless, he also demonstrated why Caesar had chosen wisely, and he began by addressing Hirtius. "Despite the manner in which Pullus put it, Aulus, he's right." He turned and gave the Primus Pilus a glare as if to emphasize his disapproval, which he confirmed by adding, "And he owes you an apology for speaking so intemperately. That being said, however," he sighed, and the fact that he dropped back into his chair served as a signal to the other two, leaving only Pullus standing, but he hadn't been offered a seat in the first place, "not only would it be a…harsh measure to take with the queen, it also would violate the policy Caesar set for the people we conquer. All we ask of them is that they abide by the laws we set for them and make no mischief, and for that they can go on living their lives as they see fit. If we were to do anything to Queen Hyppolita, it's not only against what we've done in the past, there's no way to keep it secret."

"She isn't seen by the people now as it is," Hirtius argued, although there didn't seem to be a lot of heat to his words. "They wouldn't know."

"I wasn't talking about the people of this city." Pollio turned and looked Hirtius directly in the eye as he finished, "I was talking about Caesar."

Hirtius didn't reply, slumping in his chair, and while he didn't say anything, Pullus saw the faint nod of his acquiescence.

Pollio returned his attention to Pullus, and there was not a hint of warmth in his gaze as he said, "Tell the queen that we will agree to use whatever money she has hidden away to *appear* to pay the workforce for the improvements we're making to the canal."

"How do I know that your Legate will keep his word?"

"You don't," Pullus answered Hyppolita frankly, but before she could say anything, he hurried on, "but I know Legate Pollio well. He won't go back on his word."

To his surprise, this didn't seem to convince Hyppolita, who had remained sitting on the couch in the room where they met while Pullus had walked to the *Praetorium*. It wasn't terribly far up the street from the compound, but it had seemed an eternity for her. Now he was standing in front of her, and she didn't experience the feeling of satisfaction she thought she would, that in trying circumstances, she had helped her people.

Finally, she gave a slight nod, sighing, "Very well. I will tell you where what remains of the treasury is located. In fact," she said suddenly, "while it is not our normal time for a walk, I will be happy to show you where it is located."

She was correct that it was about the worst time to go outside, close to noon, yet she also knew that Pullus wouldn't be able to resist, and he descended to the first floor to wait for her as she prepared herself, while he did wonder if she would don her headscarf and veil, if only because at this time of day, there would be men inside the compound, mostly Roman but not all. Normally, Pullus had complete control of who had access, and it was easy for him to arrange for privacy within the walls in the early mornings and late evenings, but this was unusual. He did think of postponing for a moment but almost immediately dismissed it, knowing how Pollio and Hirtius would react if he informed them that he didn't want the queen to walk in the heat of the day. By this point in time, Pullus knew he felt protective of her, but had long before given up trying to understand why it was so important to him. Therefore, he stood in what little shade was available at midday, perspiring heavily and wondering if he would ever become accustomed to living in a place like this while refusing to think about why he was considering it at all. He heard movement inside, turning to see that, for this occasion, Hyppolita had her full complement of ladies, all of whom were wearing their veils, but with headscarves that were slightly smaller, and he suspected cooler than what he normally saw them wearing.

"We are ready, Centurion," Hyppolita spoke, and it startled Pullus because the woman he had been certain was the queen because of her attire in fact turned out not to be her, which in turn caused a ripple of feminine laughter.

Moving past him, she descended the stairs and began walking, leaving Pullus to stretch his legs to catch up with her.

"That wasn't funny," he grumbled.

"My ladies seem to think it was," she countered, and he heard the amusement in her voice.

Fighting his own smile, he asked her in mock seriousness, "How do I know that you're not going to try and trick me so that you can escape?"

"You do not," Hyppolita answered, but it was her turn to laugh at Pullus' expression.

They were heading in the direction of the permanent building that now housed the First Cohort of the 10th, and for the first time, it occurred to Pullus that the possibility of the location of the hidden treasury had almost literally been under their very noses.

This must have shown on his face, because Hyppolita assured him, "No, Centurion. That is not where it is. Although," she added teasingly, "I do think you will be surprised to know how close it has been."

She was absolutely correct about that. He learned the truth when, after passing the quarters of the First Cohort, she stopped at the large covered structure that he had begun smelling long before they were within a hundred paces. Normally, the prevailing winds blew the stench away, and he had discovered early on that the only natives of Bharuch who were allowed in the compound were especially devoted to the remaining animals contained within. There had been vigorous debate among the Primi Pili, the Legates, and within the entire command structure about the fate of these animals. Understandably, there was a great deal of support for destroying them, and even less of a surprise, it had been Batius of the 5th who had been the most adamant, but Pullus had been surprised to see that it was almost evenly divided.

"If we can train some men, or convince the handlers to fight for us, we'd have the one weapon that caused us so much damage," Hirtius had argued.

In the end, none of them were willing to take responsibility for making a decision without Caesar, so to that end, the surviving men of Bharuch who handled the animals were found, and they had been maintaining the animals to the best of their ability, although all but three of the animals who had suffered burns had succumbed. Now, according to Hirtius, upon whose shoulders the responsibility had devolved since he was the acting Prefect of cavalry, there were twenty-one fully grown animals, while two of the females were pregnant.

Now Pullus came to a sudden stop, looking down at Hyppolita in consternation. "You must be joking. You didn't bury the treasury in there!"

"No, not exactly," Hyppolita, and Pullus sagged in relief.

It was short-lived, because she continued to walk around the corner of the building, and Pullus did notice that the stench increased tremendously. Turning the corner, he found Hyppolita standing there, but she had one hand under her veil, and he heard her sniffing something, and he correctly assumed that it was a perfumed handkerchief.

"You," Pullus wasn't sure whether to laugh or to be angry, "had it buried under a mountain of elephant *cac?*"

"*Cac?*" While he couldn't see her face, Pullus saw the tilt of her head as she tried the unfamiliar Latin word, but rather than give the Greek term, he merely pointed and said, "That's *cac.*"

"Ah!" The headdress bobbed up and down, but it was the amused recognition in her voice that, despite the circumstances, Pullus still found disarming, making it impossible for him not to smile. "Then, yes, Centurion. The money is buried under *cac*."

It was sometimes difficult for Barhinder to truly grasp the dizzying changes in his life that had taken place from the moment that he and his friend Agathocles had sounded the alarm when they were standing guard on the dirt rampart overlooking the northern canal and the men they thought of as demons slid up in their ships. That night was still the worst of his young life, when he had first witnessed so much death, and worst of all the slaying of his friend; that it had been at the hands of the giant Roman he now knew was called a Primus Pilus and whose name was Titus Pullus, was one of the more confusing aspects of his existence. However, the fact that he was standing, along with twenty other men who, while part of the 10th Legion, weren't Legionaries, holding a shovel as they moved a mountain of shit from one spot to another was eerily reminiscent of his time as a member of Bharuch's army. As many young soldiers discover, and his older brother Sagara had tried to tell him, what he thought life in the army was like and what it was actually like were so far apart as to be unrecognizable, and this wasn't the first time he had been behind the elephants' enclosure with a shovel in his hand. Still, he wasn't complaining, and he knew that he was much luckier than many of his comrades who had survived that night when Titus Pullus had led his 10th Legion up the dirt wall on the northern side of the city. Most of them were dead, many of them maimed with horrible burns when the Romans had unleashed their terrible weapon that had annihilated what even he had believed were the invincible armored elephants of his kingdom. Those who, like Barhinder, had managed to survive without debilitating wounds were still languishing in captivity, albeit of a different sort as they joined the captives from Pattala who now rowed the ships of the Roman fleet, but unlike them, Barhinder wasn't a prisoner. Actually, to be fair, he wasn't sure what his status was, although he was certainly better off than his former comrades. And, in some ways more confusingly for the youth, he was treated better as a captive of some sort than he had ever been treated by his former commander, Bhadran, whose ineptitude and cowardice had helped the Roman cause.

There was only one thing that Barhinder was clear about, and that was his gratitude and loyalty to Diocles, the Greek who had been responsible for determining that in the pile of corpses that had been hastily created by the victorious Romans, one of them had in fact been alive. Now Barhinder and his comrades seemed to be doing nothing more than moving the huge pile of manure from one spot to another that, at least to his eyes, wasn't any different. It wasn't far enough away to make a difference in the stench, but that wasn't the most unusual aspect; he wasn't positive, since she was wearing her veil and head covering, but just from the manner in which she held herself, and how the other similarly attired women were clustered around her in a protective manner, he felt certain that this was the Queen of Bharuch. She made him nervous; the giant Roman standing next to her still terrified him, although Pullus had treated him relatively well, in the sense that he mostly ignored him as he followed Diocles around, eager to help the Greek in anything and everything. Still, what was never far from Barhinder's mind, even when Pullus was standing next to the queen, laughing at something she said, was the memory of this Roman he had first met on the dirt rampart, a giant demon whose eyes still caused Barhinder to jerk awake from his sleep as he relived watching Pullus slay his friend with a combination of ferocity and ease that he would never forget, wearing an expression of a powerful but contained rage. For a span of weeks, Barhinder had actually convinced himself that, when the opportunity presented itself, he would slay Titus Pullus and accept the consequences. He was disabused of this idea when one of his fellow captives, who held a similar post with one of the other units that Barhinder now knew were Legions, had attempted that very thing, trying to stab the Primus Pilus named Felix, but only succeeding in inflicting a minor wound before one of the Primus Pilus' men subdued him. It wasn't that the man was executed that convinced Barhinder to desist from what was, ultimately, a fantasy; it was the fact that the Romans went out into the city to the man's family home and executed his entire family, out in the street for all to see that convinced him. Barhinder had no idea whether Sagara lived or died, because he had been part of the elite corps of heavily armored hoplites that had been King Abhiraka's first line of defense, north of the city. The rest of his family, however, his parents and two younger sisters, were very much alive, and he wanted to keep it that way.

Gradually, his hatred for the Romans diminished, and while he was only dimly aware of it, he knew that his treatment by first Diocles, then over time, by Pullus and the men of the First Century, had much to do with this. Not that it made it any different shoveling manure for Rome as opposed to Bharuch, but despite his nervousness being in the presence of the queen and Pullus, Barhinder was intensely curious. Sweating profusely despite having spent their entire lives in this climate that Pullus and his comrades found so oppressive, he and his fellow workers transferred the pile, until Barhinder could make out an outline of something in the paving stones underneath, and he realized that it had been created when a number of stones had been pried up, then replaced but without any mortar in between them, forming a recognizable rectangle roughly two by three paces. However, once the original group of workers had cleared the manure away to the extent that the loosened stones could be seen, Diocles appeared, and speaking to Barhinder and two of the other men who understood Greek, instructed them to tell their comrades they were no longer needed. However, Barhinder was an exception, which the queen noticed, and while he was too far away to make out what she was saying, the way Pullus looked at him sent his heart racing. Barhinder stood, afraid to move but also unwilling to look away from the pair, and he saw Pullus turn back to the queen, say something that, judging by the manner in which her body seemed to stiffen under the shapeless gown, he guessed she didn't like. He was correct that Pullus and Hyppolita were having a disagreement, but it wasn't specifically about his presence, although it did concern him as a symbol of the problem Pullus was confronting.

"Why would you not trust your slaves to keep quiet about the presence of this money more than you would these workers?" Hyppolita asked. "Does it not defeat our purpose if it is known by my people of Bharuch that the money the workers will be earning actually is coming from me and not Rome?"

"Yes," Pullus admitted, "but I don't know that it will be any different with our section slaves, Your Highness."

"Why?" she asked, not in a challenging manner but because she was genuinely curious.

How do I explain this to her? he wondered, and not have it sound coarse, or confirm what I know she suspects, that our control over our men isn't what it should be right now?

"Because," he began carefully, "any of those slaves that I choose are likely to tell their fellow slaves, some of whom will undoubtedly tell the men of the section they serve, and before the end of the day, both the army and the people in the city will likely know."

He hoped that she would be satisfied with the answer, or at the least focus on the first part of his explanation; it was a hope that lasted the span of a heartbeat.

"While I suppose I understand that you would not want all of your fellow Romans know that there is money here in the city, why are you so certain that my people will learn as well?"

Realizing there was no evading the issue, Pullus sighed. "Because when my boys are through with their duties, they go into the city for…entertainment."

"Entertainment?" Hyppolita echoed, cocking her head in another gesture that Pullus found quite charming. "What do you mean entertainment…" Suddenly, her head straightened, and she said softly, "Ah. Yes, I see." The hardening of her tone was slight, but Pullus had been in her presence enough to know when she was disturbed by something. "I confess that I forgot your men are using the brothels of the city for their own enjoyment. Is that what you mean?"

Actually, there was more to it than that; as Pullus and his comrades in Caesar's army had learned long before, going back to the Gallic campaigns, wherever the Legions spent a certain amount of time, there were unions that weren't based in the exchange of silver, at least not in an overt sense. Certainly, many of the women who entered into some sort of relationship with their ostensible conquerors did so for reasons that were entirely pragmatic, but they weren't measured by a watch candle. Regardless of this reality, Pullus also realized that it was politic of him to simply agree with her characterization that any congress between his men and her subjects was a business transaction.

"Yes, Your Highness."

"I understand, Centurion Pullus." She nodded. "And," she did hesitate slightly, "I confess, while I had not thought of it in this way, I can see why things would be as you describe them."

Hiding his astonishment, Pullus managed to mumble, "Yes, well, thank you for understanding, and that's why I don't want to use my slaves. And," he turned and pointed to where Barhinder and his comrades were standing, "I'm more confident that we can keep these men quiet."

"Do I want to know how you intend to ensure their silence, Centurion?" Hyppolita asked, then he saw her body go stiff, and she whispered, "Are you going to execute these men after they retrieve this money?"

"No, Your Highness," he replied, startled at her question. "Nothing like that!" Sensing she was disbelieving, he lowered his voice, and for the first time in their acquaintance, used her name instead of title as he said, "Hyppolita, no matter what you may think of me, I swear to you that I wouldn't do something like that."

Whether Hyppolita truly believed him or she chose to do so, Pullus would never know, but while she said nothing, he took her faint nod as her acceptance, which prompted him to turn and summon Diocles, who had been standing with the group of workers, all of whom were trying to pretend they weren't watching intently.

"I want you to talk to Barhinder," Pullus said quietly. "Have him pick four men out of this group that he trusts to keep their mouths shut. We should have more men to move this, but I don't want to risk it. And," he finished grimly, "make sure that they all know that it won't just be them who are punished if they talk, but their families."

Diocles acknowledged his master, then walked quickly back to the workmen, signaling Barhinder, whereupon they walked a short distance away.

"Barhinder," Diocles said calmly, "the Primus Pilus is entrusting you with a very important task. Can he depend on you to carry it out? And," he held up a hand to stop the youth before he could speak, "to pick four men that you can depend on with this task, who you know will not run and tell their other friends and family what we are doing?"

Barhinder's jaw dropped, and his eyes went over to where Pullus was standing, watching them, which only made him more nervous. However, overriding his nerves was the sudden sense of pride he felt that the Primus Pilus would be willing to entrust him with something that was clearly important enough to draw the presence of the queen. More important than this was his loyalty to Diocles, knowing that this Greek who was just an inch taller than him was the only reason he was still alive; he had been looking for a way to repay him, and he decided that this was that moment.

Consequently, he hoped the quaver in his voice was audible only to himself, nor that he hesitated much when he said solemnly, "Yes, Diocles. You and the Primus Pilus can count on me. And," he turned then to look at his comrades, scanning their faces before facing Diocles again, "yes, I know four men who I trust to do whatever needs to be done."

Much later, and far from Bharuch, Barhinder Gotra would think back on this day as the moment when he transferred his full allegiance, not to Rome as much as to a giant Roman and diminutive Greek who treated him not as a youth, but a grown man.

It took a third of a watch and two trips with a heavily laden two-wheeled cart out of the enclosure and to the *Praetorium*, the cargo carefully concealed with a tarp. Not until the last ingot was unloaded did Pullus breathe easier, although he also understood that the risk wasn't completely past, but he was totally unprepared for the crisis that was about to explode, once again because of Aulus Hirtius.

Once Pullus had reported to Pollio that the money had been recovered and was now locked in what had been one of the cells used to hold prisoners by the former occupants, it was Hirtius who asked, "Who did you use to move it?" When Pullus explained, the Legate said offhandedly, as if it was a foregone answer, "And I suppose you disposed of those men."

Pullus wasn't completely caught by surprise, but he did realize that he hadn't actually thought it likely, because he didn't have an answer ready, mainly because the first thought that crossed his mind was how he should have realized Hyppolita had forewarned him, a reminder to him how royalty and the upper classes all thought alike.

"No, I didn't," he answered after a pause. "I don't think it's necessary."

"Oh?" Hirtius' tone turned scornful. "And what makes you draw that conclusion, Pullus?" Before Pullus could answer, Hirtius leaned forward to point at the Centurion. "I'll wager that they went scurrying out into the city and right this very moment are telling anyone who will listen that we dug up a massive treasure!"

"If that happens," Pullus countered, remaining calm in stark contrast to Hirtius, while Pollio was studiously avoiding eye contact with either man by pretending to study a scroll, "then there are only five possibilities who actually saw what it was we dug up because I sent fifteen of them away after they moved the pile and the ones who actually moved the money were warned what would happen to not only them but to their families."

"After it's too late!" Hirtius shot back.

"Well," Pullus commented dryly, refusing to allow his temper to slip his tight lead, "if that's true, it's already happened, so I don't see much point in killing five men without knowing whether they deserve it. Besides," he added what he was certain would be the clinching argument, "even if we used our own slaves, do you *really* believe they wouldn't talk to each other or to the boys they serve? Would you expect me to 'deal with' them the same way?"

Hirtius didn't reply, although he maintained his glare at Pullus before, muttering something under his breath, he dropped back onto his chair. Pullus pointedly turned his attention to Pollio and asked if there was any more need for him, and the Legate gave a dismissive wave. Saluting, Pullus executed his about-turn and walked out of the room, fully aware that Aulus Hirtius was glaring at him in a manner that, if looks could have killed, he would be a dead man.

Once he closed the door, Pollio suddenly wheeled on Hirtius, pointing directly at him as he snapped, "I don't know what is going on with you and Pullus, Aulus, but it needs to stop immediately!"

"The man doesn't know his place," Hirtius protested, not in the least bit cowed by the fact that Caesar had placed Pollio in command, each of them confident in their own relationship with the Dictator. "I know he's Caesar's favorite Centurion, but what he's doing with the queen is inexcusable!"

Pollio's mouth dropped open in shock, and he asked cautiously, "What are you implying, Aulus? That he and Queen Hyppolita are having an *affair*?"

"Isn't it obvious?" Hirtius retorted. "Look how he moons over her! The man is besotted by the woman, and who knows what ideas she's putting in his head?" Now Pollio began to laugh, long and hard, doubling over at the waist, prompting Hirtius to snap, "I'm glad you find it humorous! We'll see who's laughing when Caesar returns."

This did serve to dampen Pollio's mirth, but not entirely, and he shook his head as he said, "Seriously, Aulus, I think you're worrying about nothing. She's royalty, and Pullus is of what she would call her peasant class. What could they possibly have in common? And," he finished, "why would she take that kind of risk, eh?"

When put that way, Hirtius subsided, although he still wasn't convinced, and they soon moved on to other topics, mainly when the work on the canal would begin.

The army at Abhiraka's back might have been largely foreign, but just being on the march again had done much to restore his confidence; having Ranjeet, Bolon, and Nahapana by his side was also a help, although being back with his elephant Darpashata had proven to be the best balm for his battered pride. Not so pleasant was having his fellow king as a constant companion, not only because the man served as a reminder that, for all intents and purposes, he was now bankrupt, but Puddapandyan wasn't cut from the same cloth as Abhiraka. He had grown accustomed to his comforts, insisting on traveling with as many of them as deemed suitable, and since those comforts were invariably female, their progress was much slower than it should have been, even for an army with elephants. Nedunj had stayed behind, something that had displeased

Abhiraka, if only because he was certain that he would have had more influence over his son-in-law, but his ire wasn't only with the crown prince but his daughter, who had made it abundantly clear she preferred that her husband stay safely out of harm's way. As irksome as it was, this wasn't anywhere near the top of Abhiraka's concerns. Most worrying to him was the composition of the Pandyan infantry who, to his eyes, looked more like his light skirmishing troops, despite the fact that they carried spears, eschewing any armor other than boiled leather vests, some of them with iron rings or rectangles sewn on, and small wicker shields. It was a striking example of the difference between a culture that had been heavily influenced by the Macedonians and Greeks in his own Bharuch, and one that had never experienced the armored might of the hoplite formations of heavily armored, closely aligned spearmen. More than that, however, was the implicit recognition by the Pandyans that, even for people acclimated to the intense heat, the climate grew more oppressive and stultifying the farther south one went, and the domains of Puddapandyan extended all the way to the southern tip of India. Consequently, the rank and file Pandyans eschewed armor, in exchange for less issues with the heat, more mobility, and a reliance on their missile troops, who actually outnumbered the infantry and were evenly split between archers on foot and mounted on horseback. However, where Bharuch and Pandya were similar was in their reliance on armored elephants. If it had been a year earlier, Abhiraka would have been supremely confident, because Pandya's army relied even more heavily on armored elephants than Bharuch, but that was before the arrival of Rome, and the introduction of their horrible weapon. He had been understandably reluctant to go into the details of the cause for his horrible defeat with his fellow king, and Ranjeet in particular had urged him to offer as little detail as possible to either his son-in-law or to Puddapandyan.

"If they know that they're likely to lose a substantial number of their elephants because of the demon's fire," Ranjeet had steadfastly refused to accept that the naphtha that had proven so devastating was a naturally occurring substance, "you'll be lucky if you get a single animal."

Abhiraka had attempted to heed Ranjeet's advice, but his fellow king was far too shrewd to be put off by a vague story about how so many of Bharuch's elephants had met their demise. He had done his best to minimize how horrifically effective the Romans' weapon had been, but in the end, he was forced to accept the terms set by Puddapandyan, which was in essence every *drachmae* that his queen had smuggled south with their remaining children shortly before the Romans arrived outside the gates of the city. Under other circumstances, Abhiraka thought bitterly, I could have purchased an army twice this size, with twice as many elephants with the money I paid; however, he was also a pragmatist who had long before learned that the cost of anything was measured by how much that thing was needed. Regardless of his understanding of the realities, it was still something that gnawed at the king, particularly as he was forced to listen to Puddapandyan nattering about his favorite concubine of the moment. Perhaps the only thing of a positive nature that could be attributed to their slow march north was that, whenever it happened that they clash with the Romans, the army would be rested, but this was small consolation in the moment.

Now that they were within two days march of Kalliena, the southernmost settlement that was considered part of Abhiraka's domains on the Goaris River, the king spent every spare moment with his commanders as they worked out the details of their plan. In its conception, the strategy hadn't changed; Abhiraka would use his newly reinforced army to reclaim enough territory that it would begin to impinge on the ability for the Romans to feed not only themselves, but the citizens of Bharuch. It was a grim calculation, yet it was one where Abhiraka felt, and his commanders agreed, that this was not only the best way to force the Romans into the field, but the only way. Where the king felt more certain was in his belief that the Roman general Caesar wouldn't be willing to send his entire army out into the field and leave Bharuch undefended. While he couldn't know with any real certainty, Abhiraka was operating on the assumption that the Romans had learned more about the other kingdoms in the western part of India, including Bharuch's most potent and hated rival, the Kanva, who were ruled by Narayana from their capital, the city of Ujjain, which was some two hundred miles east and fifty miles north of Bharuch. Their wealth was substantial, but it was the ambition of Narayana that kept Abhiraka awake at night, at least until the cursed Romans had arrived. Now, however, the Kanva might serve a useful purpose by keeping a substantial portion of Caesar's army penned in Bharuch, because of one thing Abhiraka was certain; Narayana had learned of Bharuch's downfall. As he would learn, his reasoning was sound, and he had anticipated the likelihood that the Romans would be forced to send a smaller portion of their army out into the field. What he wasn't prepared for was when, towards the end of the day's march that put them within two days of Kalliena, there would be a call from the leading elements of his army that riders were approaching. Moving Darpashata into a lumbering trot, Abhiraka hurried to meet the riders, recognizing one of the men as Sagara, a young member of his phalanx corps who had shown such promise that he had been promoted into the bodyguard to replace the losses the king had suffered during the battle for the city.

"Your Highness, we have been to Kalliena, and they informed us that there are Romans nearby!"

The fact that in his excitement Sagara had forgotten to perform the expected obeisance was something that Abhiraka normally would chastise a man for, but between the young soldier's excitement and his own rush of the same emotion, it meant that he barely noticed.

"Did they tell you how large a force it is?"

"Yes," Sagara answered, feeling an understandable surge of pride that he had actually thought to ask the traveling merchant who had been his source of information that very thing. "There are two of the eagle standards they carry," he informed the king. "I made sure to question the man who saw them very closely, and he is certain that he saw two, and only two."

Unlike Barhinder, and those who remained in Bharuch, Abhiraka hadn't learned much about the organization of the Roman army, but from the survivors of Ranjeet's last-gasp attempt to break through to the city defenders, he did know that the presence of the eagle standards represented what the Romans called a Legion. Therefore, there were two Legions within striking distance. This, he thought, was the chance to strike the first blow.

Tiberius Atartinus, the Primus Pilus of the 11th Legion, was indulging himself in what had become a daily habit of cursing the Fates that had ordained that it was his Legion's turn to perform what he thought of as a pointless exercise in wandering around the countryside. If it weren't so hot and wet, it wouldn't have been so bad, but since Legate Pollio had issued a standing order that the men wore their armor at all times, it introduced another level of hardship. Not a single day passed without easily a dozen men stricken down, not by an enemy blade or arrow, nor even because of something like the bite of a serpent, but by the sun. These were the only men who were allowed to shed their armor, and they were slung on the back of one of the mules from the pool of spares, allowed to ride until they recovered. Which, as Atartinus had heard from his predecessors on these long-range forays, didn't always happen. He and his fellow

Primus Pilus, Aulus Mus of the 7th, had been fortunate in that respect, at least to this point, but it didn't mean that his Legion was unscathed. To this point, seven days into the march, he had lost two section slaves who, while it had occurred on two separate occasions, was from the same cause, one that had thrown the hard-bitten veterans of two Roman Legions into a state of near panic. Prior to this, the returning Legions had reported signs that tigers were lurking in the dense forests that, whenever possible, the Romans bypassed, but it wasn't until it was Atartinus' turn that men had actually been attacked, and even worse, eaten. The animal had been driven off by a hail of javelins with the last death, but the half-eaten remains had thoroughly terrified the men to the point that no man who wanted to relieve themselves left the relative security of the column alone. It did have one salutary effect; the men had stopped complaining about building a marching camp at the end of every day, although it wasn't ever to the dimensions normally demanded by Caesar.

Now that they were a day's march to the east of the town that had been identified as Kalliena, Atartinus was looking forward to the prospect of returning by a route that was at least thoroughly scouted, following the coast northward back to Bharuch. The 7th and 11th had been tasked by Pollio to push farther to the east than ever before, and the two Legions had reached the base of the line of mountains that Titus Pullus had learned about from the first villager questioned by Achaemenes. As they had been told, these peaks thrust up from relatively flat ground, making them the most visible landmark in the area, and the two Legions had located the source of the river upon which Kalliena was located. They had been following the river for the previous two days, stopping at every village along the route, where Achaemenes worked tirelessly to learn more about the land in which they found themselves. As absorbed in his own worries as he was, Atartinus still felt enormous sympathy for the young Parthian, the only man currently able to communicate with the native people. Because of this, Achaemenes had been the only man in the entire Roman army who had accompanied the pair of Legions on every march, yet he had done so without complaint, and as his predecessors had, Atartinus quickly learned to not only rely on the translator, but to trust him implicitly. Consequently, it was only reluctantly that he had allowed Achaemenes to leave the security of the two Legions, but that was the case at this moment, the young Parthian off with one of the scouting parties. It was through Achaemenes, for example, that Atartinus and Mus learned that it was a likelihood bordering on certainty that the two slaves had been killed by the same animal, as it was a habit of tigers to stalk the same herd of animals as they moved. Bit by bit, the Romans were learning more about this strange world, but rather than making them more comfortable, Atartinus could see that his men were repelled by the absolute foreignness of their surroundings, and when he made his circuit around the fires at night, he heard them speaking of returning to Bharuch in the same manner they had spoken of returning to Susa, viewing these cities as more of a home. Like every Primus Pilus, Atartinus was aware that several of his men had formed some sort of union with one of the women of the city, reminding him of their time in Parthia, where they had done the same. And, he was certain, there was more than one man in his Legion who had a *de facto* wife back in Susa who was involved with a woman of Bharuch.

None of which mattered in the moment, and since his 11th was the vanguard on the day's march, it fell to Atartinus to receive the report of the half-dozen cavalrymen who had been sent downriver to scout.

"There's only one more village between here and the large town," the trooper in command, Manius Glabius, reported. "But there's a thick band of forest about five miles east of the town. And," he glanced down at the sketch he had drawn in his wax tablet, "there's another river that meets this one just a mile beyond the forest."

"We know about that one." Atartinus pointed to their right. "It's coming down from the north."

"No, Primus Pilus." The scout shook his head, but he turned the tablet so that Atartinus could see. "That was already marked. This is coming from the south."

Atartinus understood immediately.

"Which means," he spat to show his disgust, "that we can't bypass that fucking forest if we go north around it because of that first river, and we can't bypass it to the south because of the river to the south."

"Yes, Primus Pilus." Glabius nodded. "That's what it means. Also," he pointed to a double line he had incised across the snaking line that Atartinus knew represented the Goaris, "less than a mile up ahead, right before the forest, there's a fordable spot on the river that shouldn't come up past the waist of the men. But," the scout assured him, "there's no sign of more than normal activity, just a few cart tracks and the like."

He hesitated then, but in such a way that Atartinus noticed, prompting the Centurion to ask, "What else?"

"It's probably nothing," the scout answered, "but one of the boys swears he saw a group of horsemen on the other side of the river."

"You didn't see them yourself?"

"No, sir." He shook his head. "By the time Vologases called out, they were gone." Pausing to think, he admitted, "He said he saw them just on this side of that forest that's south of the river."

Atartinus understood that the trooper was referring to the line of trees that ran roughly parallel to the river, but about a mile south, and from where they were standing, he could see the eastern edge of it, where it gave way to the scrub vegetation that passed for open country. However, since no Romans had ventured south of the Goaris, and they hadn't come across a villager who had any knowledge of what lay beyond, they had no idea how wide the stretch of forest was, or what lay beyond it.

Rubbing his chin, Atartinus thought for a moment, then shook his head as he decided, "I'm not going to send you across the river just based on what one man says he saw."

"Vologases is a good man, Primus Pilus," Glabius argued, but Atartinus was unmoved, although he did modify his tone a bit as he replied, "I'm not saying that he isn't, Glabius. But I'm not going to risk losing you and the rest of your boys because of only the gods know what may be lurking in those trees. And," he added grimly, "I'm not just talking about any barbarians. That," he pointed across to the treeline, "is the kind of thing those fucking tigers and the hooded serpents live in." Turning his attention back to the more immediate moment, he sighed and said, "So we have no choice but to go through the forest on this side of the river. Once we do that, I'll think about sending you across."

Glabius saluted, remounted, and rejoined his comrades, while Atartinus turned to his *Cornicen*, the preliminary step in relaying his decision, one that would have lasting ramifications, both for him, and for the rest of Caesar's army, which would be compounded by his temporarily forgetting about the presence of a ford that would be behind them as they continued towards Kalliena.

"We cannot reach Kalliena before the Romans," Abhiraka informed his officers. They were seated under a canopy, the sides of which could be rolled up as they were at this moment to allow the slight breeze to cool them. Since they didn't use wax tablets, Abhiraka had smoothed a patch of dirt, around which they were sitting, where he had sketched out a map of the area. Using a stick, he drew an arrow that pointed in the direction of the X that marked his southernmost town. "They are about to enter the strip of *jangla* that is west of where the Kalu meets the Goaris. Depending on what Sagara reports to me when he returns, we are going to turn northwest." His stick moved from the circle he had drawn below the line of the Goaris, and he etched an arrow in the opposite direction of the first one, with the river in between. "They will be unable to see us because of the forest, and we will take advantage of that by marching to the ford that they will pass by just before they enter it once they're out of sight."

"Your Highness," Ranjeet interrupted, confident in his relationship with Abhiraka to do so, "what if they post a guard on the ford?"

"That," Abhiraka replied with a satisfied smile, "is why I said, 'depending on what our scouts report to me,' my friend. If they do that," he moved the pointer, "we will have to make a decision whether to continue directly north to Kalliena. We can still use the forest for cover while we observe what these dogs intend to do to my subjects in the town." All signs of humor vanished as Abhiraka looked at each of his officers. "If they attack the town or make any attempt to harm my subjects, we will stop them from doing so. They will not harm any more of my people without paying a heavy price for it. Is that understood?"

Bolon, sitting next to Ranjeet, shifted uncomfortably but said nothing, so it fell to Nahapana to clear his throat nervously, then ask, "Your Highness, wouldn't attacking the Romans while they are in the town damage both the town and the people in it? And," he pointed out, "that is not the best kind of ground for our elephants. There are too many places to hide, and with the…" suddenly, he realized that he was on dangerous ground, glancing over at Puddapandyan who, despite looking as if he were half-asleep, Nahapana was certain was listening with keen interest. Consequently, he settled on, "…ways these demons have in combating our elephants."

For a moment, Nahapana thought he had grievously erred, as Abhiraka pinned him with an angry stare, the silence dragging out until suddenly, the king relaxed slightly, and he agreed, "You are correct, Nahapana. We would undoubtedly do damage to the town. Which," he said grimly, "is why this is a last resort, and I will order it only if the Romans make any kind of threatening move. However," he didn't like admitting as much, but he did so, "we do know that this is not the first time some Romans have ventured this far south, and they have actually been in the town before, although it was just a scouting party. If they have not attacked it by now, I do not think they will do so today."

"Provided they don't learn of our presence, Your Highness," Ranjeet interjected bluntly.

"Yes, that is true as well," Abhiraka agreed, then stroked his black beard, which had grayed noticeably just in the few months since he had been forced to flee Bharuch, considering for a moment before he said, "We will need to keep a series of outposts all along the northern edge of the forest on this side of the river. If the Romans do venture across the river, we will have to stop them from spotting our own army in order to maintain the element of surprise."

"Who do you want to command the scouts, Your Highness?" Ranjeet asked, certain that it wouldn't be him.

"Gotra," Abhiraka answered immediately, which created surprise bordering on shock on the parts of both Bolon and Nahapana, each of them assuming it would be one of them.

"Gotra?" Ranjeet exclaimed, no less startled than the other two men, both of them subordinate to him but were the most senior commanders left of Bharuch's army. "Isn't he a bit young for such an important task?"

"He is," Abhiraka seemingly agreed, "but he's distinguished himself. Besides," now he favored the three men with a smile, "I am going to need help from the three of you for what I have in mind."

The passage through the belt of forest had been slow, more so than the pace to which they had become accustomed when pioneering a track in this country capable of accommodating a Roman army column, even when it was with as few wagons as these two-Legion armies brought. On this, the fourth foray by Rome into this part of the countryside, Pollio had reluctantly agreed to add one more wagon per Legion, along with expanding the pool of spare animals who, like their human counterparts, were struggling with the heat. Compounding matters was the fact that, as they moved further south, they had encountered what Achaemenes had learned the locals called a *jangla*, which was essentially a forest that was noticeably thicker than what they were accustomed to, with creeping vines, broad-leafed plants, and exposed roots that entwined with anything and everything, connecting every living thing into an almost impenetrable wall of green that the more superstitious of the men claimed was done intentionally by the gods who ruled over this accursed land. This was what confronted Atartinus and the 11th now, and very quickly, men exhausted themselves trying to clear a swathe less than ten paces wide, which was the minimum width that would enable the army to pass through. This required the Centurions of the vanguard Cohort to switch men out more rapidly than they had ever done before, and Atartinus had been forced to relieve the leading Cohort several times as their progress was measured in feet.

The only blessing was that the overhead canopy provided by trees of all sizes at least provided shade, but it also meant that the air was stifling, with the dense vegetation that provided the shade also blocking any breeze, and what air there was stank of rotting vegetation and damp earth. Consequently, it took almost two full watches for the army to emerge out into the broiling sunshine, although it just was a hand's width above the horizon, when the air was slightly dryer and the breeze was no longer blocked. Now Atartinus and Mus were faced with making a choice that neither relished; they were barely two miles from the town, with only a tributary of the Goaris in between them. But, as late in the day as it was, and depending on what awaited them in the town, the two Primi Pili faced the prospect of being occupied with the inhabitants long past dark. Their orders were clear, and in keeping with the policy that had been set forth by Caesar from the very first day of the Parthian campaign; civilians were to be left unmolested unless they offered resistance, and even then, they were to be dealt with in a manner that many of his men, particularly the veterans of Gaul, found surprising. Atartinus had actually been with Caesar, although he had been an Optio then, when Caesar had besieged Uxellodonum, and in frustration at the intransigence of the townspeople, once the town fell, he ordered the hands of every defender chopped off and thrown into a huge pile in the middle of the town. While he hadn't given it much thought, Atartinus supposed that, perhaps, Caesar regretted what he had done then, and had ultimately decided that it was in the long-term interests of Rome, and Caesar of course, to be more temperate in his policy. Whatever the cause, this posed a set of challenges to the two Primi Pili, and they had moved a short distance away as the army paused, waiting for their decision.

"If they plan on putting up a fight, giving them extra time doesn't help," Mus pointed out, but Atartinus shook his head.

"How?" he asked. "We know they don't have any soldiers there, and while they have a wall, it won't take long to take it down."

"What are you suggesting?" Mus asked, which made Atartinus pause, just for a moment, before he answered, "I think we make camp outside the town, then enter in the morning."

"Marching camp, then," Mus replied, already dreading giving the order, knowing that it would fall to his 7th, since the 11th had borne the brunt of the day's work, but he was surprised when Atartinus shook his head.

"Not tonight," he said flatly. "I don't want two exhausted Legions." He considered for a moment then decided, "Fifty percent alert."

Mus' initial instinct was to argue this, thinking of what the reaction back in Bharuch would be if, the gods forbid, something happened, but neither could he deny that even without turning a spade of dirt, his boys were already tired. Not, he understood, as tired as the men of the 11th, but making the men get less than the normal rest wasn't appealing because they would be standing watch. Still, he thought, it's better than the alternative; while he didn't realize it, his own fatigue was a factor in his acquiescence.

Shading his eyes, he turned slowly, surveying the surrounding ground, then pointed at an expanse of open ground that, from this distance, he thought were probably fields used by the people of the town, which was now about two miles distant.

"We can shake out there," Mus suggested, but Atartinus had already seen the same thing and come to the same conclusion, although he did admit, "It's a bit close to the edge of this fucking forest for comfort, but I'd suggest you put more men on that side. And," he thought to add, "deploy the scorpions at least."

"Should we break out the naphtha?" Mus asked, but after a pause, Atartinus shook his head.

"If we had any signs that there were any of those beasts nearby, I'd say yes, but you know as well as I do how little of the stuff we've got, Aulus." He turned to look Mus in the eye as he said soberly, "We can't afford to waste one jar of the stuff because one of our boys gets nervous and starts seeing things." Before Mus could respond, he finished, "But since we keep that wagon separate anyway, we'll put it nearer to you and your boys who are standing watch closest to that forest."

Mus didn't particularly like how Atartinus had put it, but neither could he deny the possibility that this would happen, although in his opinion, it wasn't due to the thought of an enemy army and their elephants that would be the most likely to cause that kind of mishap, but one of those striped beasts that had already snatched men, almost from the midst of their comrades. Nevertheless, Mus agreed, thinking to himself, it's only for one night.

155

Sagara Gotra watched from his spot south of the river as the tail end of the Roman column emerged out into the open, a group of soldiers just behind five wagons, which in turn were following what he guessed were hundreds of mules, each of them with a man not dressed in any kind of uniform that from his earlier observations he had deduced were slaves. One of the five other men was standing next to him, both of them dismounted and standing just within the edge of the *jangla*, while each of the two other pairs were on either side of him but separated by several hundred paces. The light was fading fast, but Sagara had lived his entire life in this place, so he knew that once the sun's lower rim touched the horizon, darkness would be descending with a rapidity that could be counted in a span of perhaps two hundred heartbeats, without the longer twilight of northern climes. It was far from ideal, but he decided it was worth the risk, and he turned to his companion.

"We're going to the ford and cross." He tried to sound confident in his decision. "I need to get closer to these demons before I report to the King."

"Are you sure that's wise, Sagara?" his companion asked, older but accepting that his younger counterpart was ultimately in command, so not in a challenging manner.

Sagara recognized this, which was why he admitted, "No, I'm not sure, Udai, but I know what His Highness is expecting from us." Thinking for a moment, he said, "We won't ride across the open ground. We'll walk our horses, since that will make us harder to spot. Once we get across, we have the *jangla*, but," he grinned at his companion, "the demons were polite enough to chop us a path, so we can move quickly."

Udai returned the grin despite the fact that he didn't share in Sagara's optimism, but this was due to Udai possessing a more pessimistic nature. Nor did he hesitate to follow Sagara, who led his horse by the reins out into the open, then when he was at a point he knew he could be seen by the other two pairs of men, signaled to them to remain in place. The pair moved slowly, although fairly quickly they realized that, with the Romans suddenly changing the direction of their march from heading directly west to a more northerly progress, stealth was no longer necessary because the *jangla* the Romans had just passed through blocked any view. Mounting, they moved at a swift trot back to the east, reaching the ford but pausing only briefly to observe the opposite bank before splashing across, then turning back west. Just as Sagara had predicted, using the Romans' rough track enabled them to move quickly, passing through the *jangla* to reach the western edge, but rather than continue using the track all the way to where the open ground lay, Sagara suddenly veered off, using the bulk of his mount to push a way through the dense undergrowth. Finally reaching a point about four hundred paces north of the track, just as they had done on the other side of the river, both men dismounted well within the protection of the *jangla*, then walked slowly to a point where they had a largely unobstructed view of the open expanse.

"They're making camp," Udai observed, but whereas he hadn't been in any scouting party before this, Sagara had, which meant the young scout instantly understood the significance of what he was seeing, making it impossible to hide his excitement.

"But they're not digging a ditch and building a wall!" he exclaimed, then turned to Udai with a smile. "This is the chance we have been waiting for, Udai! We must get back to the King to let him know!"

Perhaps it was because of Udai's more cautious nature; afterward, Sagara would believe that it was a matter of divine intervention that prompted his companion to point out, "They still have the demon's fire, Sagara. And," he pointed to where small groups of men were carrying what appeared to be pieces of wood, "look at that. They look like the things that Bolon talked about, don't they? The ones they used to slay our elephants with the demon fire?"

Because he had been with the phalanx corps that had been part of the first line of defense when the overland portion of the Roman army had marched south from Pattala, Sagara had only witnessed the demons hurling the flaming jars at the elephants that he and every man of Bharuch had been confident would destroy the invaders. It was only when Abhiraka, protected by Bolon and Nahapana, had escaped from the city that he and the others had learned that the Romans had also used a different method of slaughtering Bharuch's most potent weapon. Thanks to Bolon's description, while neither Udai nor Sagara had ever seen the weapons before, once they watched the Romans assemble them and arrayed them facing the very *jangla* in which they were standing, they both recognized that these machines were those weapons. Which, Sagara immediately concluded, also meant that it was a virtual certainty that the flaming substance that coated the missiles Bolon had described would be present, evaporating his elation.

"Let's stay here a bit longer," he decided. "We can at least count how many men they have."

Even as they were speaking, tents were being erected, yet

without a ditch and wall, both men could see the precision and symmetry of the layout as the Romans arranged themselves in the same manner they always did. However, it was a seemingly random act that caught Sagara's attention, when one of the five wagons were driven away from the other four but heading in their general direction.

"I wonder what that means?" Udai mused. "What makes that wagon special?"

Sagara considered, yet nothing immediately came to mind, prompting him to shrug and speculate, "Maybe it contains statues of their gods and it has to be separated from the others for some reason."

This caused Udai to laugh, and he teased Sagara, "Why would they drag their gods over to this edge, Sagara? If that's what it was," he pointed to the obvious center of the camp where the largest tent was pitched, although neither of them knew that it was in fact just the tent of a Primus Pilus, and not the full-sized tent of the *praetorium*, "they would put it in the center."

Sagara scowled at his companion and shot back, "What's your explanation, then?"

Udai's grin faded, and he rubbed his chin as he squinted, both of them realizing that the light was about to fade, studying the wagon that had just been halted for a few heartbeats. Watching as the team was unhitched and the animals led away, he admitted, "I don't know. The only thing I see different is that this one has a big red circle painted on the side."

It was something Sagara hadn't noticed, and he shifted his gaze from Udai back to the conveyance, seeing that Udai was correct. Suddenly, the meaning dawned on Sagara, so abruptly that he let out a surprised yelp that, despite knowing it was impossible, he worried the Romans would hear.

Rather than explain, he turned to Udai and commanded him urgently, "Go back to the army. Tell His Highness to bring the army across the ford as soon as it's dark enough. Tell him what you saw. And," he gave his companion a grim smile, "tell him that he will know the right moment to attack."

Sagara waited until it was fully dark, and while he waited, he did everything he could think of to ensure that he was as close to invisible as it was possible to make himself. Stripping down to his loincloth, he debated whether his dark skin provided enough cover itself, finally deciding that as dark as it was, the quarter moon would probably make his skin shine. Using his canteen, Sagara moistened the already damp earth into a paste, which he smeared over every part of his body, including his loincloth. He experienced a pang of regret that he hadn't thought to do so before he had sent Udai off, thinking that his companion would have been able to better tell if he was as effective in this camouflage as he hoped. Using leather thongs by wrapping them around both arms, both legs, and around his waist, he stuck the largest leaves from the trees and undergrowth, knowing that he probably looked ridiculous, but hoping that the foliage would blend in with the scrub growth in between his position and where the wagon was located. Even after he had done everything he could think of, it still took him several moments to work up his nerve, but finally, he stepped out from the cover of the *jangla*, moving slowly in a crouch towards the line of fires, each one surrounded by Romans who were more concerned with preparing their meal than a lone enemy. When he was within about three hundred paces, Sagara dropped from his crouch to all fours and began moving even more slowly, relying on his ears as much as his eyes, thanking his foes for the manner in which their fires behind the line of sentries outlined them as they stood there watching for someone to do exactly what he was doing now.

After another hundred paces, he dropped onto his belly, crawling in much the same manner as the *Naja*, slithering over the ground while trying to ignore the pain that came from dragging his bare skin across the rough ground. He would move a pace or two, then stop, always watching and listening for any sign that one of the demons standing guard had detected movement. Sagara wasn't worried about being heard; the rubbing noise of his loincloth against the ground was barely audible to his own ears, although he did have to concentrate to control his breathing, not wanting to be betrayed by panting like a dog in the heat. As he drew closer, he was able to pick a path, using the scattered handful of bushy plants that were about knee-high, moving from one to the other, always pausing after each movement. Once he reached the point where he could hear voices, he froze, straining his ears, understanding that, despite being unable to comprehend the words, he would undoubtedly know if the alarm was being raised. After a span of perhaps fifty heartbeats, Sagara determined that the humming sound wasn't coming from the line of men who were now less than fifty paces away, but from those men behind them seated outside the tents on this side of the camp. When he was within twenty paces, he had maneuvered himself into the space between two of the weapons, which he could now see looked much like a bow, but one that had been turned so that it was parallel to the ground, while there was a piece of wood perpendicular to the arms that was supporting the bow, right where a man's arm would be. This all rested on three wooden legs, two in the rear and one in front, but as interesting as this was, it was the presence of the three men standing behind each one that was of most immediate concern. Not surprisingly, this was the moment when Sagara experienced a doubt so intense, it almost crippled his ability to do anything. What, he thought bitterly, was I thinking? That I was going to become a *Naja*, and wriggle in between *six* men? All of them, from what he could tell, were paying attention to their surroundings, although he was now close enough to hear that, like their comrades outside their tents, they were conversing, albeit in whispers. Fortunately for Bharuch's cause, Sagara retained the presence of mind to recognize that he was fully committed; there was no practical way he could retreat at this point, making his decision for him. Taking a deep breath, he resumed his progress.

"This," Lucius Strabo whispered to his two comrades, "is a fucking waste of time."

The three of them were standing behind their scorpion, which the chief *immune* in charge of this artillery piece had named Diana, and it was left to that chief, standing next to Strabo, to whisper back, "That's as may be, Lucius, but here we are, *neh*? Now," Decimus Seius whispered in a genial enough tone, but Strabo understood it was a command, "shut your mouth."

The third man, Numerius Pictor, chuckled softly, earning a glare from Seius, to which Pictor replied with a grin that, even in the gloom, caused Seius to smile and shake his head.

Sighing, he admitted, "I just want this shift over. I want to get some sleep."

There was a whispered agreement, then the trio subsided, having missed the fact that, barely a dozen paces to their right front, something was moving in their direction.

"Oy! What the fuck do you think you're doing, you *cunnus*?"

The shout shattered the quiet, but more importantly, it tore the attention of Seius' crew, along with the crew of the scorpion to their right, away from what was in front of them, all six men naturally turning back into the camp. Where, much to their amusement, they were treated to the sight of the Optio of the Third Century of the Fifth Cohort, which was the Cohort that would be relieving them within the next third of a watch, using his *vitus* to thrash a hapless ranker.

"I wonder what that poor bastard did?" Strabo whispered, to which Seius snorted and countered, "Who said he had to do anything? That's Optio Sacrovir from the sound of it. When does he ever need a reason to thrash a man?"

This was greeted by appreciative chuckles from the other two, the three of them sharing in the pleasure that comes from not being the man receiving the thrashing. It was an understandable lapse, but a lapse nonetheless, and what mattered was that all six Romans missed the figure that moved more rapidly than it had heartbeats earlier to reach the relative safety of the largest bush in the immediate area. Only Pictor paused as he was turning back around, his eye caught by the slight rustling of the large bush, but he stared at it for perhaps three heartbeats, then shrugged and joined his comrades in staring into nothing but black emptiness.

Abhiraka's decision to rely on Gotra's message, relayed by Udai, who came galloping into their version of a marching camp, had been met with resistance, not just from Ranjeet, but Bolon and Nahapana. Only Puddapandyan seemed to support his fellow king's decision, if by support they meant the Pandyan king was completely silent.

"No, if there is an opportunity, we aren't going to waste it because there is risk," Abhiraka finally said in a tone his commanders knew meant that his mind was made up.

Standing up from his stool, he ordered, "Give the orders for the men to prepare to march, but do *not* use the horns to give the command."

His directive sent his three commanders scrambling, while Puddapandyan remained seated, scratching his iron-gray beard in a seemingly idle fashion, but when he spoke, there was nothing idle in his tone.

"I do not agree with this, Abhiraka."

Abhiraka had turned to walk away, and he spun to face the Pandyan king, asking stiffly, "Why is that?"

"Because it is rash," the Pandyan replied calmly. "And you are basing your decision on incomplete information, provided by a man you admit has little experience in such matters."

The Bharuch king knew he needed to be politic with his counterpart, yet he couldn't keep the hint of scorn from his voice as he asked pointedly, "Is this based in your vast experience in war, Puddapandyan?"

This did cause the Pandyan king to shift uncomfortably on his stool as he countered defensively, "I prefer to grow my kingdom in other ways, Abhiraka. And," he pointed out, "that is why I am in the position to help you now. Don't," he warned, "forget that."

Abhiraka felt the rage stirring, but he managed to keep it partially contained as he snapped, "That's only because you haven't faced Caesar yet. And," he pointed directly at the other king, "unless we substantially weaken him now, you will be facing him in the next few months. In fact," he added something that had been nagging at him for some time, "I don't know why he hasn't moved from Bharuch yet."

"If you lose a substantial part of my army, then he most definitely will defeat me," Puddapandyan retorted, showing more animation in this moment than at any time previously. "You seem to forget that in order to do as you plan tonight, it will be with *my* elephants, and *my* men."

"Given how much I paid you," Abhiraka sneered, "you won't have any problem not only replacing any losses but doubling the size of your army in the bargain!"

"From who and where would I get replacements?" Puddapandyan countered, spreading his hands out in a vague gesture. "I have enemies just like you, Abhiraka. Which is why," he reminded his fellow king, "we are in an alliance through the marriage of our children." Finally, he stood up, and even in his anger, Abhiraka noticed that there was nothing of the detached, slightly bumbling man who was only interested in which of the women who accompanied them would share his bed that night. Standing in his place was someone with an implacable will, with the same kind of clear-eyed ruthlessness that Abhiraka recognized in himself. "Speaking as your ally and as a fellow king, I do not believe this to be a wise decision. And," he finished quietly, "I am going to accompany you. If I believe that the battle is going against us, I will order my men and my elephants to withdraw back across the river."

For a span of a few heartbeats, Abhiraka seriously considered striding across the distance and striking Puddapandyan down; that he didn't act on that impulse was based in two reasons. The first was that, while solving the problem of the moment, it would only lead to inevitable consequences and even more bloodshed, but the second, and perhaps more powerful reason, was that this version of the Pandyan king was one with whom Abhiraka was completely unfamiliar.

Finally, Abhiraka gave a curt nod, saying only, "Very well."

So absorbed were the two kings in their confrontation that, when Ranjeet appeared out of the gloom to report that the first units of their army were assembled and ready to march, both were equally surprised.

"Is Darpashata ready?" Abhiraka asked. Then, in an attempt to mollify his fellow king, added, "And have King Puddapandyan's animal prepared as well."

This obviously surprised Ranjeet, but when he opened his mouth, Abhiraka correctly guessed what his senior commander would say, giving him a slight shake of the head and a warning gaze. Like his king knew Ranjeet, so too did Ranjeet understand Abhiraka, so there was a barely noticeable pause.

"Yes, Your Highness, Darpashata is ready. And," Ranjeet turned and bowed in the direction of the Pandyan king, "I will go inform your handler immediately." He hesitated, then asked, "Should we delay the march until His Highness' elephant is ready?"

"No," Abhiraka answered, and he was somewhat surprised that Puddapandyan didn't object. "Begin the march to the ford. Let our mounted troops cross first, then wait for the rest of us. The sooner we move, the better."

Ranjeet bowed, then hurried off to do his king's bidding, while Abhiraka walked the short distance to his own tent, where his attendants were waiting to help him into his armor. Watching him go, only when Abhiraka disappeared into the tent did Puddapandyan do the same, moving in the opposite direction.

The fact that the wagon was sitting by itself, more than fifty paces away from the nearest line of tents and about twice that distance from the line of scorpions, was a mixture of equal parts good and bad as far as Sagara was concerned. He had paused at the base of the large bush that the Roman Pictor had given a cursory glance, wrapping his body around the base so that he was made invisible by the leaves from the lowest branches. Fairly quickly, he realized he was stalling, but he used the time to plan his route to the wagon, checking to make sure the leather bag was still suspended from his neck. While he was carrying his dagger strapped to his waist, the contents of that bag were his most potent weapon, but it would all be for nothing if he wasn't careful. Even harder for Sagara was estimating how long it would take for Abhiraka to lead the army out of their camp two miles west of the ford to cross the river, then cover the three miles back to the west from the ford, using the newly constructed track through the *jangla*. It was at this moment he realized that he had, in fact, been quite rash in his actions, yet he felt certain in his gut that he had done the right thing. Normally, as he and the other scouts had observed, the Romans guarded what he was now positive was the wagon containing the demon fire that had been so devastating because it was always with the other wagons in the center of the camp. While this one was within the boundaries of the Roman camp, its isolated position wasn't likely to happen again, nor did he believe the Romans would do the same thing they had done here in not digging a ditch and using the dirt for a wall. He had observed the Romans for several days in total by this point, and not once had they ever done what they were doing on this night, which meant this was the best chance to strike a blow for his king and for Bharuch.

Thoughts of his city led inevitably to his family, particularly his younger brother Barhinder, who Sagara knew had worshiped him almost as soon as Barhinder was able to walk. And—he felt the dried mud on his face crack slightly at the involuntary smile that came to his face—Sagara had reveled in every moment of it. However, when Barhinder had announced that he had joined Bharuch's army and he was in the equivalent of the Roman version of the auxiliaries, compared to the Macedonian-inspired phalanx of which Sagara was a part, Sagara had been anything but pleased. By the time of Barhinder's enlistment, Sagara was a veteran of several battles, one of them with the Pattalans, who had been a constant threat from their north, so that he no longer held illusions about the glory that could supposedly be earned on the battlefield. In fact, their last conversation had resulted in Sagara uttering harsh words towards his younger brother, but in the manner of siblings, he hadn't bothered to try and make it clear that those words came from a place of concern. He had been about to march off with Abhiraka, heading north to stop the oncoming Roman army, which in that moment he, his king, and all of Bharuch believed was in its entirety, only to have that illusion shattered by the sight of hundreds of ships sailing up the Narmada. As far as Sagara was concerned, the worst part was knowing that it had been Barhinder and his comrades who had borne the brunt of the Roman shipborne assault, and the fact that he had no idea whether Barhinder had survived or not, and it took an effort for him to shake these thoughts from his mind and return his attention to what came next. There were clouds, but enough of the night sky was visible for him to spot the stars his people used to track time at night, realizing that it was almost midnight. It had been just before dusk when he had dispatched Udai, and his best guess was that Abhiraka was probably crossing the river at that moment, given how long it would take to rouse the army, organize it, and march to the ford. This was what prompted him to take a deep breath, then slowly roll out from under the bush to resume his stealthy crawl…to glory.

If Abhiraka weren't there to witness it himself, he would have been loath to believe that an army such as this conglomerated force, along with the notorious unpredictability of elephants, could move in darkness with the ease that they did this night. Reaching the ford, the mounted troops crossed the river, the splashing sound they made minimized by Abhiraka's orders that they move at the walk across the ford. Following them were the elephants, trailed by the infantry, who were commanded by Bolon, but with a Pandyan named Vimal as his co-commander, while Nahapana had been given command of all the mounted troops, also with a Pandyan second in command. Once across the ford, in a slightly different arrangement, the elephants led the way into the *jangla*; normally, they would have been the third and heaviest line, but this night attack would be different because of the circumstances. If the Romans were prepared and waiting, Abhiraka would have arrayed his troops in the traditional manner, but he was gambling everything on his young scout Gotra's report that the cursed Romans were offering him an opportunity that could be the key to changing everything by giving him the momentum. What nagged at him the most was Gotra's cryptic message that Abhiraka would know the moment to attack, but there was nothing he could do about it, and he led the way as Udai guided them unerringly to the track that had been chopped through the *jangla* just a matter of watches earlier. While the path the Romans created was wide enough for their purposes, it could only accommodate two elephants side by side, thereby lengthening the column significantly, and in consequence, increasing the amount of time it would take to get his army into position. This didn't change his plan, although it did intensify the tension, but he also had absolute trust in Ranjeet, who was leading the column with his Pandyan counterpart next to him. He and Puddapandyan brought up the rear of the column of elephants, which he blamed the Pandyan king for because of what he was certain was the man's last moment decision to take part in this endeavor. Why Puddapandyan had decided to do so was a mystery to Abhiraka, and normally, this would be the most pressing thought on his mind, trying to unravel the real reason why the man he had considered not long before to be barely worthy of being called king as Abhiraka defined it, but in this moment, it ranked among the least of his concerns. Suddenly, the column halted, and Abhiraka was forced to wait for the time it took one of the men who were part of the three-man crew who rode with Ranjeet to come dashing down the column. Because of the darkness, Abhiraka didn't see the man coming until he was less than fifty paces away, so that by the time he could determine the meaning, the man was already there, dropping to his knees.

"Your Highness," Abhiraka recognized the man's voice immediately as the horn player who rode with Ranjeet, "Lord Ranjeet has reached the western edge of the *jangla*. He asks what he should do now."

It was, Abhiraka immediately realized with consternation, a good question, since they hadn't really discussed what they would do next, just another consequence of acting on such a hastily contrived plan. He felt Puddapandyan's eyes on him, which he tried to ignore as he thought furiously.

Finally, more out of desperation and a desire to be away from the Pandyan king's presence, he forced himself to sound confident as he ordered, "Go back to Lord Ranjeet and tell him that his king is coming to take command."

The man did remember to make his obeisance, but he quickly vanished, leaving Puddapandyan to ask pointedly, "And how do you propose to make your way up to the front, Abhiraka? This track isn't wide enough to accommodate three animals side by side. You're going to be making a lot of noise."

Abhiraka knew Puddapandyan was correct; even without the inevitable noise that would come from forcing the elephants ahead of him to move into the dense undergrowth, it was practically an inevitability that the animals would protest by using their massive trunks to trumpet that displeasure at being shoved aside. Nevertheless, the King of Bharuch was determined to lead this attack, not because he didn't trust Ranjeet, but for a much simpler, and deeper reason; he wanted to be the one to avenge the defeat they had suffered.

Consequently, Abhiraka only said, "That is a risk I'm willing to take." Then, before the Pandyan could respond, he ordered the handler to switch places with him, dropping down into the special saddle. Patting his animal on the head, he murmured, "Now, my champion, it's time to let you do what you do best."

As Abhiraka expected, the elephant, the largest bull not only of Bharuch's elephants, but those of the Pandya as well, curled his trunk against his forehead in the animal's signal that he had heard and understood, then making a deep-throated chuffing sound, lumbered forward, shoving his massive head in between the two elephants ahead of him. Their handlers had been forewarned, hearing the exchange, and the animals moved aside without much protest, but before Darpashata had moved more than ten rows up, several elephants had trumpeted in protest, which Abhiraka was certain would be heard, forcing him to slow his progress. Before he moved Darpashata in between the next pair, Abhiraka called out a warning, pausing long enough to allow both handlers to move their animals on their own. It took longer, which made Abhiraka's stomach twist into even more knots than were already there, but he forced himself to be patient. Slowly, Abhiraka guided his elephant forward, forced to rely on the bond between man and beast that had formed over more than twenty years as he fretted that he would miss whatever moment Gotra had warned would be coming. Only later was he able to determine that this delay was fortuitous, because as slow as Darpashata's progress was, it was still quicker than that of Sagara, who was inching forward on his stomach, foot by agonizing foot, heading for the object that would be serve as the signal.

"What was that?" Pictor asked, all signs of his normal cheerfulness wiped away as he frowned in concentration, staring out into the darkness back in the direction of the *jangla*.

"What?" Seius asked, concerned because he knew Pictor wasn't the type to hear things. "I didn't hear anything."

The third member of the crew was standing a short distance away, but like Seius, Strabo knew his comrade well, so he actually untied his helmet and lifted the flap as he turned that ear towards the thick forest. They were all silent, straining to listen, but after several heartbeats with nothing but the normal night sounds from all manner of creeping, crawling and flying things that they had been forced to become accustomed to, Seius turned to Pictor.

"What did you hear?"

Pictor answered readily enough, "I thought I heard a couple of those fucking elephants."

"A couple?" Seius' tone immediately sharpened. "Not just one?"

Among the many things that the Romans had been forced to learn about this strange land was the fact that it wasn't uncommon to hear the high-pitched, screeching noise that elephants made to signal each other, but it was almost always a single elephant calling, and a single elephant responding. More than one elephant, at the same time, Seius and his comrades had learned, was a sign of trouble, especially when it wasn't coming from a place like the town barely two miles away where elephants were used as a primary source of labor and kept in large pens.

For the first time, Pictor's voice relayed some doubt. "I *thought* so."

"Maybe," Strabo suggested, "it was an echo."

Pictor opened his mouth to scoff at his comrade's suggestion, then realized, unless it happened again, there was no way to prove that it wasn't.

Sighing, instead, he said, "Maybe, or maybe I was just hearing things."

"As long as it's not one of those fucking tigers," Strabo shuddered. "Every time I hear one of those beasts out there, my balls shrivel up and crawl back up inside me."

As he hoped, this elicited muted laughter, including Seius, but he finally hissed at them to be quiet, and before long, they subsided and went back to enduring what would be the last third of a watch of their shift before they could return to their own tents to get some rest. Once more, the dominant sounds of the night became the chirping, trilling, and croaking of the creatures for whom night was day, and once again, their momentary inattention aided their enemy's cause as Sagara finally reached the wagon.

The quickest movement Sagara made was when he scrambled the last couple of paces to the wagon, whereupon he rolled under it, trying to control his panting so that it wasn't audible. Once more, he was confronted with the fact that he hadn't actually thought about what he would do once he reached the wagon. Nor was he certain that his king had arrived with the army to be in a position to take advantage of what he was about to do, and the uncertainty was almost paralyzing. His decision was made for him when, from the direction of the nearest line of tents, where the fires had been allowed to die down to coals, he heard a disturbance that, while he didn't know the cause, he understood couldn't have been made by just man. Rolling over, he stared at the tents, and despite the dim lighting, he could see the movement caused by men emerging from the tents within his line of vision. Several men were shouting, but despite not being able to understand the words, Sagara knew the tone when he heard it, that of officers bellowing commands to their men. This was disturbing in itself, but as he watched in dull horror, he saw the shadowy shapes converge into a group that, even in the darkness, had the same regular form to it that he recognized as the type of formation the Romans used when they were moving somewhere. When they began to move, it took a couple of heartbeats to determine that they were actually heading in his direction, which got him moving.

Scrambling backward, still under the wagon, Sagara reached the end of the wagon facing the line of sentries, getting to his feet for the first time in what seemed like a full day, and the sudden stretching of his muscles caused an immediate reaction as his body responded to the change. Stifling a groan from the cramps that seized the back of his legs, for the first time he actually got a good look at the back doors of the wagon; this time, what escaped his lips was a gasp of dismay as he saw the chain draped through the two handles and a large iron device that could only be a lock. Why, he thought with despair, would they lock something that they may need quickly? It was this thought that caused him to reach out and tentatively touch the lock, his breath leaving in an explosive gasp of relief when he felt the hasp hanging free, telling him that, while the lock was in place, it wasn't secured. Moving as rapidly as he could, he lifted the lock free of the chain, dropping it on the ground as he divided his attention between what he was doing and the sounds that, while muffled by the bulk of the wagon, were of men marching in his direction. While he had been under the wagon, thinking what to do, Sagara had come up with a plan of sort, which began with his pulling off his loincloth. His intention was to use it in the same manner he had witnessed during the night action next to the city, stuffing one end of it into a jar that he would retrieve from the wagon, then backing a short distance away before hurling it. In simple terms, Sagara Gotra had every intention of surviving this night, but as he swung one door open, the hinges squealed, although he hoped that the noise just sounded louder to him than it actually was. It was a hope destined to last less than a heartbeat as, from behind him back in the direction of the sentries he had managed to avoid, he heard a shout. Suddenly, it became clear to him what he had to do and more importantly what it meant for him, but he wasted no time, hopping up into the back of the wagon, where a series of small crates were stacked, with what appeared to be some sort of sheets of what felt like clay in between each layer. Although he had no way of knowing the specifics, he immediately intuited that it signified the danger of this demon's fire, and even if the air wasn't filled with the shouting, both from the direction of the sentries and the group of soldiers who had been marching in his direction, his hands would have been shaking. Nevertheless, he was able to use the point of his dagger to pry loose the top of one of the crates on top, and he felt as much as saw the lone jar, nestled in the straw, determining that the mouth of the jar was covered by a piece of leather that served as the lid. Now, not only was the shouting drawing nearer, he could hear the pounding footsteps of men who were undoubtedly rushing to stop him, but even through his fear, he felt a grim sense of satisfaction, recognizing the tone of what could only be described as panic. While his initial plan had been to stuff his loincloth into the jar, he knew this would take time he didn't have, and he noticed with some surprise that, as he deftly sliced through the leather lid, his hand was barely shaking. He was committed to this, and somewhere within him, he had accepted his fate. Maybe, he thought as his hands were moving as of their own volition, the left pulling open the pouch around his neck, while his right fumbled briefly for the flint and piece of iron, they'll write a poem about me and what I did this night. He sensed as much as saw the sudden appearance of a figure immediately behind him, but when a pair of hands reached out to grab him around the waist, they slipped off of his sweaty skin, just for an eyeblink, but it was enough for Sagara to strike the flint hard against the steel. In the last instant of his life, it seemed to Sagara Gotra that it took forever for the first of those sparks to drift lazily down into the substance that he had just begun to smell. Then, his world disappeared in a roaring fireball of pain...then nothing.

When the hinges squealed, neither Seius and his crew, nor the crews on either side of them, thought what they had heard was their imagination, but while they all spun around in the direction of the sound, it was Strabo who reacted first. With a shout of alarm, he went sprinting for the wagon, followed by Seius, but while Pictor didn't follow, it wasn't out of cowardice, it was because of the three of them, he was the man who understood more quickly that the sound he thought he had heard earlier, and this noise he and his comrades definitely heard had to be related. Consequently, he spun back around towards the darker line of the forest, moving behind the scorpion to begin cranking the mechanism to draw the string taut, the necessary step before dropping a bolt into the groove. It was a blessing, albeit a minor one, because he was not instantly blinded by the brutal and brilliant explosion of light from the fireball that resulted from a loyal man of Bharuch sacrificing himself, but barely an eyeblink after the area in front of him was suddenly illuminated as if it was midday instead of midnight to the point where he distinctly saw his shadow, Pictor received what felt like a mighty shove from an invisible giant that hurled him into the back end of the scorpion with enough force that he was knocked senseless. It meant that he was barely cognizant of the sudden blast of heat that made him feel as if he had been thrust into an oven, if the fire in that oven was a piece of the sun, but the pain from the instant blistering of his exposed flesh brought him back to his senses, causing him to utter a shrill scream of agony. Such was his condition that he barely heard the screams of dozens of other men, yet somehow he managed to get to his feet, swaying as if he had just drained a jug of wine in one go, forcing himself to turn towards what appeared to be a blazing pyre, but one that was surrounded by literally dozens of smaller ones, and while most of them were motionless on the ground, he was just in time to see perhaps ten human torches who had still not succumbed to the inevitable, each of them staggering away from the larger pyre in a last mindless attempt to outrun their deaths. By the lurid light, Pictor glanced down to see that his left arm looked like a joint of meat that had fallen into the fire and gotten charred. Despite his own condition, Pictor's first thought was to go to the aid of his comrades, and he began a stumbling trot towards the blazing wagon, but before he had gone a half-dozen paces, his benumbed mind registered that two of the smaller pyres were in the spots Pictor last recalled seeing Seius and Strabo. Stopping, he dropped to his knees before toppling over on the ground, not quite dead, yet not truly alive, and he lay there listening to the cacophony of noise; screams of a pain that only another man like himself could truly appreciate as to the cause, cries of alarm and fear, and the bellowed orders of officers desperately trying to restore some sort of order from what Pictor was certain was a scene identical the lowest bowels of Hades. Just before he drifted away, and from the direction of the forest, he heard the same trumpeting cries that he thought he had imagined, his last conscious thought one of satisfaction that he hadn't actually heard things, but by the time he could have felt the shuddering vibration caused by hundreds of huge feet carrying thousands of tons, Pictor was dead.

Abhiraka was only slightly more prepared for the result of Sagara's sacrifice than the Romans, where, sitting on his elephant like all of the men around him staring in dumbfounded amazement at the sudden eruption of fire that suddenly illuminated everything around it, although unlike a lightning bolt, this didn't vanish. If anything, it seemed to grow in intensity, while the sound of the ignition of the naphtha contained in the wagon took a bit less than a full heartbeat to reach his ears, not as much a sharp report as a rumbling noise.

It was the sound that spurred the king into action, turning to the horn player behind him in the box strapped to Darpashata's back, snapping, "Sound the call to advance at the trot!"

Then, before the man could react, Abhiraka used his goad, jabbing it into the spot behind Darpashata's right ear twice, the signal that told the elephant what to do. The animal reacted immediately, although it took a few strides longer for it to reach the commanded pace than it would a horse. Once they had advanced a hundred paces, Abhiraka used the goad to change Darpashata's direction slightly, moving to the right in order to give the other elephants behind him room to array on the left flank, while aligning himself with the center of the camp by using the large tent that was now clearly illuminated as his guide. Abhiraka desperately wanted to release his elephant to the full gallop to go smashing into the Roman camp, but he retained enough of his self-control to do the opposite by halting Darpashata, while ordering his horn player to sound the command that would bring the elephants into two long lines, the second separated from the first by fifty paces. While he waited, albeit impatiently, he actually had to squint against the glare of the huge blaze, although unlike Pictor, he immediately understood the meaning of the smaller fires around what had just moments before been a wagon. Outlined against the flames, he saw men scrambling in seemingly every direction, and he took a savage pleasure in the sight, thinking, You're not as organized and disciplined as you were the night you forced me to flee from my kingdom.

"My King!" Abhiraka jerked in surprise, turning to see Ranjeet to his left, the grin as plain to see as if it had been at noon. "We are ready at your command!"

Such had been his absorption in the sight before him, Abhiraka hadn't noticed that he was now roughly in the middle of the first line as he intended, but he didn't hesitate now, ordering the player to sound the command.

"Straight to the run!" Abhiraka shouted, although the first part was drowned out as he held his long his sword aloft. "For our families! For Bharuch! *Advance!*"

Going to the elephant's version of a gallop took even longer, but Abhiraka was experienced in such matters, and he had timed it perfectly, the line of animals moving at top speed just as they reached the edge of the range of the scorpions. Since Abhiraka had positioned himself so that the blazing wagon that he understood had contained the pernicious substance was slightly to his left, he was acutely aware that the spacing between Ranjeet and the animal to Ranjeet's immediate left would be drastically reduced since there was no handler alive or dead who possessed a command over his animal to run them straight at a roaring blaze. He also had utmost faith in his friend, enabling him to keep his attention on more urgent matters, like the Romans manning the scorpion off to his right who were frantically working the mechanism that drew the cord that would send the iron-tipped bolt at tremendous speed taut. Fortunately for him, Darpashata, and the four men clinging to the box behind him, the device almost directly to his front appeared abandoned, but despite the lumbering nature of an elephant running, their speed was deceptive, so that the recognition that there were no enemies behind the artillery piece was made superfluous because Darpashata ran right over it even as this registered in Abhiraka's mind, snapping the seasoned wood into several pieces like kindling. His animal was the first to deliver what Abhiraka knew was Darpashata's own war cry, but he was quickly joined by both the other animals, and the men who were both crew and protectors. More rapidly than he would have thought possible, Abhiraka and his crew were carried past the blazing wagon, and despite being more than fifty paces away, the heat was so intense that it made the king wince. Darpashata, however, barely seemed to notice, and very quickly, the king realized that, in the curious manner of these creatures, Darpashata understood who these men were, that they had been responsible for the horrible slaughter of his fellow creatures, and he was there, along with his other four-legged comrades, to exact revenge. The slaughter was commencing.

Because they only used one of their tents, Mus and Atartinus shared the quarters of the Primus Pilus, meaning that they both were alerted at the same instant by the screams of the men who had been near enough to the naphtha wagon to be immolated. For Atartinus, it wasn't the screams that were the most startling, it was when he jerked awake to sit upright in his cot and there was a light outside his tent that was bright enough to penetrate the leather, bathing the interior in light of a quality that he had never seen before, nor would he ever see again.

"The naphtha!" Mus shouted, the first to grasp the basic scope of the emergency, although this was only the bare bones of it.

Both men came to their feet at the same time, and with the speed that bespoke of long practice, quickly donned their armor, although Mus eschewed the greaves, meaning that he was the first to rush out of the tent and be confronted with the true horror that awaited the men of two of Caesar's Legions. So shocking was the sight that this battle-hardened veteran stood, open-mouthed, with no idea what to do; this was how Atartinus found him, and while his reaction was almost the same, standing there gaping as they faced east, watching as the roiling blaze seemed to spit out globules of smaller flames that arced out from the wagon in an indiscriminate circle. Even in the span of four or five heartbeats where the Centurions commanding the two Legions were paralyzed by shock, several of the tents nearest to the wagon caught fire as the sticky, viscous flaming substance clung to the leather. It wasn't until one of the men who had been marching in the small formation to relieve the men at the scorpions came sprinting directly towards them, his features and entire body obscured by flames as the naphtha did the same thing to the ranker's skin and armor that it did with the tents that both Centurions were yanked from their state.

"Rally your men!" Atartinus shouted, even as the man afire came to a tottering stop, then toppled face down not more than a dozen paces away. "I don't know what's happening, but we need to be ready!"

Mus didn't acknowledge his counterpart other than to run in the general direction of the fire since his Legion occupied the eastern half of the camp. *Cornu* calls began sounding, the Centurions and Optios, some of them not taking the time to don their own armor, standing in their respective Cohort streets, bellowing the order to assemble on the standard. It was a chaotic scene that none of them had ever witnessed, and there were men who, inevitably, panicked and instantly forgot their discipline to become just a man out of his mind with fear. There weren't many of these men, at least in the beginning, but a handful of them, rather than obey the orders of their officers, simply fled in the opposite direction, heading west. The tents that caught fire intensified both the heat and the light, although every man escaped the confines before their shelters became fully involved, but almost all of them were forced to choose between escaping with their lives or snatching up their armor. Most of them understandably chose the former, although a fair number did manage to grab their swords, while their shields were lined up on either side of their tents. The only men of the 7th Legion who would have been able to spare the time to don their armor were the men outside the radius of the farthest reach of the exploding naphtha, but even these

Legionaries were prevented from doing so because of a long line of rampaging armored elephants, each of them carrying at least one archer among its complement of men who were drawing and loosing at close range as quickly as their arms could move.

Going from sleep to the raging, fiery chaos that surrounded them further served to disorient the Romans, and more than one man died still unsure exactly what was happening, standing just outside their shelter when they were either struck down by a missile, or worse, crushed under the immense weight of an armored beast weighing several tons. Next to the men who had been immolated, the most unfortunate were those who were impaled on the tusk of one of these rampaging beasts, and several animals had more than one man skewered and hanging from their tusks before they would fling them off with a shake of their massive heads, sending limp bodies flying. It wasn't until Abhiraka's leading line of elephants had penetrated into the third row of tents that there was any sort of organized resistance, when the Centurions of the First and Second Cohorts managed to get their men into a semblance of a Century formation, but as the Romans were reminded, not even the most disciplined and best trained men could stand up to the massive force of armored elephants when they were under the control of their handlers. And, as their comrades could only watch helplessly, standing in neatly packed rows made the damage even more devastating. In fact, the greatest impediment to the animals were the tents themselves, as more than one became entangled in the mass of leather and flailing guy ropes, but this proved to be only a temporary respite from the onslaught. Because of their location, Atartinus was able to rally the 11th, but the only open ground available to them was the western side of the camp beyond the last row of tents, the enemy having reached the forum area. To his credit, Atartinus didn't hesitate, having his *cornu* sound the command to move at the double quick in that direction. More out of habit than from any real plan, the Primus Pilus had his Cohorts take up their normal spots in the *acies triplex*, facing east, where they could only watch helplessly as their comrades in the 7th were slaughtered. Atartinus was standing next to his *Aquilifer*, his mind racing as he tried to think what to do when he and his Legion learned that there was more to this attack than what he now saw was a double line of armored elephants. It began with a new sound, off to their left, quickly becoming audible, and identifiable as thundering hooves, not of more elephants but the more familiar sound of galloping horses, but it was the sudden shower of missiles that materialized out of the darkness that was the most potent message, raining down on his completely unprepared Fourth Cohort, prompting the sudden cries and screams of stricken men.

Atartinus reacted instantly, and under other circumstances, he would have been correct when he bellowed, both to his men and to his *Cornicen*, "*Form testudo!*"

And, like the well-disciplined Legion they were, the men of the 11th immediately obeyed, and in doing so, sealed their fate, joining their doomed comrades in the 7th.

The sky was pinkening before Abhiraka gave the command to his elephant to come to a halt, and it was a sign of Darpashata's exhaustion that, with a groan that was eerily human, the animal dropped to its front knees, the signal that he wanted the men he had been carrying off his back immediately. Abhiraka, as well as the others, quickly complied, although he stepped down onto the animal's knee, while the rest of the men simply hopped out of the box to the ground, each of them instantly collapsing to the ground. Abhiraka paused to murmur his appreciation to his animal, leaning his forehead against Darpashata's in a gesture that communicated the bond between the two more than any words.

"Thank you, my champion." Abhiraka said this for only Darpashata's ears. "You have outdone yourself this day, and I will never forget it."

Darpashata's trunk curled up and around Abhiraka's neck in what could only be described as a caress, while making a low-pitched sound that might have been another groan, but Abhiraka knew was not. Then, the King of Bharuch stepped away from his animal to survey what he hoped was the first of many victories to come. What met his eyes was a scene of utter destruction, with not one of the hundreds of neatly arranged tents remaining standing, although the outermost rows on the eastern side were now nothing more than charred remains, around which were strewn the corpses of their occupants, some as charred as the tents. Even the largest tent in the center of the camp was no longer standing, although one pole still propped up the far corner. This was what greeted Abhiraka as he made a slow revolution, although he had done this once already, but he was frankly still in something of a daze. Yes, he had *hoped* for a resounding victory, but this was beyond his wildest imaginings, and he was having a hard time coping with the scale of the destruction. Thousands of bodies were strewn about, some of them in heaps that, from the height offered by Darpashata, Abhiraka had seen mimicked the kind of formation that he had seen his enemy use on the night of the assault on Bharuch. These Romans had died where they stood, futilely attempting to stand up to the most powerful weapon in the known world, and it restored Abhiraka's belief that, were it not for that evil substance, these Romans were every bit as vulnerable to armored elephants as any of the enemies that had fallen before him.

"Your Highness!"

Abhiraka turned to see Ranjeet, a broad smile on his battered features as he guided his own animal up to Darpashata's side, and the king waited as his commander dismounted in the same manner as he had just done. Then, in a most unusual, and some would say unseemly display for a king, Abhiraka strode to meet his friend, both of them wrapping their arms around each other while laughing, crying, and talking at the same time.

"Can you believe it, Abhiraka? Can you truly believe what we are seeing?"

"No, my friend." Abhiraka shook his head, his tone emphatic. "I am still trying to believe my eyes."

Together, they turned, and by silent consent, began walking down what they didn't know was the *Via Praetoria*, in the direction of what would have been the *Porta Praetoria* had Atartinus deemed the ditch and wall for this camp was necessary. It was beyond the ruins of the last line of tents on the western side that there was even more carnage, although in this case, the killing wasn't quite done, as members of Abhiraka's infantry moved from one pile of bodies to another, first dispatching any of the Romans who still lived, then searching their corpses, although they quickly discovered that what wealth and valuables these men had were in the ruins of the camp. The quicker of Abhiraka's men were already rummaging through the collapsed tents, prompting cries of triumph and the inevitable arguments, which both men ignored for the moment, content to let the men savor this victory as well.

"Bolon is out with the cavalry now running down the survivors," Ranjeet informed his king. "They won't get far."

Abhiraka nodded, but his eyes were roaming over the piles of bodies, and it became clear he was searching for something specific when, suddenly, he moved at a quick walk towards a cluster of his men, one of whom was thrusting a pole in the air, atop which was affixed a carved eagle covered in silver, while his comrades cheered lustily. However, it wasn't the standard that had caught his eye, it was the sight of a Roman lying facedown, wearing a helmet atop which was a crest that, rather than front to back, ran ear to ear, and unlike the others, which were mostly black, with a few red scattered among them, was white. Still vivid in his memory was the sight of the Roman who had led his men in the assault on the northern side of the city, sailing up the new canal that Abhiraka had ordered built to serve as another line of defense, and he fervently hoped this was the same man. He was still several paces away when he realized, with a stab of bitter disappointment, that this Roman was much smaller than the man he had seen from the ramparts. Nevertheless, he closed the distance, whereupon his men immediately dropped to their knees, although one man still held the standard upright with one hand.

"Rise, all of you," Abhiraka commanded, forcing himself to smile at them despite his momentary disappointment. "You and your comrades have performed bravely today, and we all share in this great victory."

Done with this, the king turned his attention back to the dead Roman wearing the white crest, ordering one of the men to turn him over. The Roman's eyes were open, but the most striking sight was the concave nature of his chest, which every man present knew would be an almost perfect match to the circumference of an elephant's foot. Despite seeing that this enemy was too small to be the man he had seen from the rampart, Abhiraka still felt a stab of disappointment, but he consoled himself with the thought that this meant the giant Roman was still alive, waiting to be slain, and if there was any justice, it would be Abhiraka or even his friend Ranjeet who would be the ones to avenge their defeat.

For reasons that he couldn't articulate, Abhiraka had transferred his hatred and desire for revenge not on Caesar, but on the large Roman, although he was certain that the fact that he had been forced to watch as his Commander of the Elephant Corps Memmon, who next to Ranjeet was one of his closest friends, and Memmon's elephant Anala were slaughtered by the men under the command of the giant Roman had more to do with it than anything else. That Roman, Abhiraka had seen, wore the same type of white crest as the dead man he was staring down at, the Roman's eyes open and staring sightlessly up into the growing dawn that he would never see.

"There are only two of these dogs who wear white crests," Ranjeet commented, and Abhiraka glanced up at his friend, asking sharply, "Where is the other one? Is he alive?"

Ranjeet shook his head, turning to point back towards the western side of the destroyed camp, telling Abhiraka, "No, his body is over there. He took an arrow through one eye, but he's the only other one."

"There are two of these," Abhiraka gestured towards the eagle standard, "so that means that we just destroyed two of their Legions." He thought, trying to remember, but he was too tired, so he asked Ranjeet, "How many of these Legions do we think they have?"

"Ten," Ranjeet replied, although after a pause as he forced his equally fatigued mind to think, he added, "Maybe eleven."

"I wish we knew more about these savages," Abhiraka muttered. Then he suddenly stiffened, slapping his forehead as he groaned, "I didn't think to tell Bolon and his men that we want some prisoners!"

Ranjeet's reaction, while not quite as dramatic, was similar, but in an attempt to appease Abhiraka, he pointed out, "We don't have anyone who speaks their tongue, my King."

"No," Abhiraka agreed, "but I know that Caesar and his officers speak Greek, so perhaps some of his men do as well."

This seemed to be a remote possibility to Ranjeet, although he wasn't about to say that at this moment, not wanting to put any kind of damper on his king's happiness at this great victory. And, he thought with a deep sense of satisfaction, it *is* a great victory, given how soundly the Romans had defeated Abhiraka's army in both of the battles they had fought. As disturbing and devastating as both losses had been, what had troubled Ranjeet in the months since was the relative ease with which the Romans seemed to do it. In his more pessimistic moments during his exile with Abhiraka, Ranjeet had wondered whether it was even possible to defeat such a seemingly invincible foe, although he had wisely never mentioned this to Abhiraka. As close as they were, and as much as Abhiraka trusted his oldest friend, he was still the King of Bharuch, and Ranjeet wasn't a blood relative. Now, however, everything had changed, and what had seemed impossible before this night was no longer so, and Ranjeet felt a surge of what he realized was a savage anticipation at the thought that they could actually duplicate this success.

"Your Highness! Our cavalry is returning!"

Understandably, this caused Abhiraka, Ranjeet, and those rankers around them to turn to face north, but it took a span of heartbeats before Abhiraka sagged in relief because Bolon and his men were surrounding what appeared to be several hundred prisoners.

R.W. Peake

Until it happened, it never occurred to Abhiraka or to any of his high-born officers that the most valuable information would come from the lowliest members of Caesar's army. As the king had suspected, none of the rankers possessed more than a smattering of Greek, but among the fleeing Romans were dozens of slaves and freedmen who had, by circumstances beyond their control, found themselves as a member of the smaller army who supported the Legions of Caesar's army. Even so, it had only been because one of the newest additions to the ranks of the small army that supported the Legions of Rome was spotted by one of his junior officers as the man attempted to make himself invisible among the huddled prisoners who had been allowed to sit on the ground, surrounded by the men of the infantry.

"I recognize that man, Lord Bolon!"

Truthfully, at first, Bolon was slightly irritated at being interrupted while telling his tale to Nahapana; he had already given his report to his king, and now was with his friend as they both reveled in their decisive victory, but by the time he spun about, the words and their possible import had registered.

"Which man?" Bolon demanded, and the junior infantry officer, a former comrade of Sagara Gotra, pointed to a man who had his head between his knees, almost directly in the middle of the mass of the noncombatant prisoners who had been separated from those Legionaries who had been captured.

"That one, Lord," the officer said. "His family lives on the same street as mine in Bharuch. His name is Chatur."

"Bring him to me," Bolon commanded, and the man immediately moved to do so, kicking at the prisoners who were too slow to scramble out of his path.

When he reached his former neighbor, Chatur put up a brief struggle, but subsided when the infantry officer drew his sword and used the pommel, striking him in the back of his head, which displeased Bolon when he saw the man's knees sag, but while dazed, he was still able to move more or less under his own power.

"Go get our King, Nahapana," Bolon said, but when there was no answer, he glanced over to see his friend's back as he hurried away, already heading for where Abhiraka was standing with Ranjeet, although they had now been joined by the Pandyan king.

Bolon stifled a curse, understanding that there was no way that Puddapandyan wouldn't want to be present for what was about to take place, but his attention was drawn back to the prisoner, who was shoved forward and down onto his knees in front of him.

Staring down at him, Bolon's tone was cold as he began, "Your name is Chatur?" The man, still not looking up, nodded, and Bolon continued, "You are a traitor to your people, Chatur. You are serving these Roman dogs against your King, and your fellow subjects of Bharuch." His voice hardened even more as he demanded, "Do you know the punishment for treason, Chatur?" This elicited another nod, which didn't satisfy Bolon, who snapped, "Answer me, you vermin!"

"Yes, Lord," Chatur at last spoke, and the quaver in his voice was impossible to miss, "I do know the punishment."

Before Bolon could say anything else, he was alerted that his king was approaching when the officer dropped to one knee, which prompted Bolon to turn and offer his own obeisance, but Abhiraka barely noticed.

"Who is this?" he asked, staring with the same cold hostility as his commander. When Bolon supplied the man's name, and that he had been identified as a citizen of the capital from which Abhiraka had been deposed, for a moment, he was concerned that his king would lose control, especially when Abhiraka reached down and withdrew his sword.

The metallic hissing sound made Chatur flinch, but while he didn't realize it, that reaction actually saved him, for the moment, because Abhiraka was indeed about to strike him down. That simple and understandable response served to jerk the king back from the precipice of his rage at the thought that one of his subjects would serve the dogs who had forced him to flee. No, he told himself, not yet; this serpent is going to tell us everything he knows first. *Then* he will die, horribly and painfully.

"What is his name?" he asked Bolon, who supplied it. Then, with a curt gesture, he ordered, "Stand him up. I want to look him in the eye as I ask him these questions."

It actually took both the officer and Bolon to haul the man to his feet, as Chatur was shaking so violently that it made him hard to control, but finally, he at least resembled a standing man. Whether it was his own small show of defiance or just abject fear, none of the other men knew, but finally, Bolon was forced to grab him by the hair on the back of his head to force his face to turn upward so that Abhiraka could look him in the eyes.

Despite his rage and his deep desire to hurt this piece of filth, Abhiraka realized that there was nothing to be gained by allowing this to show, so he gave a signal to Bolon to release his grip, and his tone was as gentle as he could make it as he asked, "Tell me, Chatur, why are you working for the Romans? Do you not remember what they did to our city? That they made your king flee in the night?"

For the first time, Chatur did look at his king directly, but he had to try twice to form the words before he finally answered in a tone barely above a whisper, "Yes, Your Highness. I know what the Romans did." Suddenly, his face transformed, twisting into an expression of grief and bitterness. "They raped my sister, Your Highness. And they beat my father almost to death."

Although Abhiraka wasn't really interested, he also saw an opening, so he kept his tone gentle as he replied, "I am sorry to hear that happened to your family, Chatur. As your king, it was my duty to protect you. And," now it was his expression that transformed, "I failed you and your family. And the rest of my subjects." He paused, then he made a sweeping gesture as he continued, "But as you can see, I am taking steps to atone for that failure, and to avenge not just your family, but the families of all of my subjects who suffered at the hands of these Roman dogs." His words seemed to unleash a rush of bile up from his depths, and he was honest with himself, knowing that not only were they true, that his self-excoriation was deserved. Consequently, the patience he was exhibiting was starting to fade as he asked, "So, knowing this…why are you working for the Romans?"

For the first time, Chatur didn't hesitate, and while the fear was there, Abhiraka was certain there was a rebuke as well as the man did look him in the eye as he answered quietly, "To feed my family, Your Highness."

"Feed your family?" Abhiraka echoed, confused. Then, he nodded, thinking he understood, "So the Romans took your family as slaves as well, then. They feed them in exchange for you helping them, is that it?"

"No, Your Highness," Chatur answered, unconsciously glancing over at Bolon, who was nearest to him, which Bolon noticed.

It's as if, Bolon thought, *he knows that what he's about to say is likely to provoke our king to the point where he orders me to strike the dog down.*

Bolon was correct, at least in the first part of his thought, but somehow, despite the revelation that was about to come, Abhiraka didn't fulfill Bolon's prediction. From his perspective, Bolon thought it was due more to the state of shock that immediately consumed his king than for any other reason, and the truth was Bolon, Nahapana, and the Pandyan king were every bit as shaken.

"They're *paying* my subjects to work for them?"

While Bolon and the others present had lost track of the number of times Abhiraka had repeated this, it was only because their dismay mirrored that of their king. This hadn't been the only thing they had learned from Chatur, whose dismembered remains were now part of the huge pile of corpses that were already beginning to decay in the hot, moist climate. It was why, instead of moving their camp across the river nearer to the battlefield they remained in place, which was where they were now, in Abhiraka's tent. The mood should have been celebratory, but while there were certainly smiles, the traditional feast for the entire army had been postponed, although the king had sent to Kalliena for their stores of *sura*, which the men were guzzling down outside, the resulting raucous atmosphere forcing the men inside the tent to raise their voices to be heard.

Abhiraka finally stopped pacing, then with a definitive shake of his head, he finally turned his mind to practical matters, asking instead, "What does this mean?" Then, before anyone could respond, another thought occurred to him. "And, how are they paying them?"

"Probably from the gold they took from Parthia," Ranjeet offered, and Abhiraka nodded thoughtfully, seeming to accept this as the most likely explanation.

Then Puddapandyan interjected, "While that may be the case, Abhiraka, I would not count on it."

Spinning to stare at the Pandyan king, Abhiraka asked suspiciously, "What do you mean by that?"

Puddapandyan didn't reply immediately, reverting back to stroking his beard as he seemed to frame his thoughts. Just when Abhiraka was about to repeat his demand, he said, "I want to ask you a…delicate question, Abhiraka. And," he held up a hand, "I understand how it could be construed, but it is not meant in an insulting way, nor is there any other motive than to better understand what we're facing." Pausing, he looked Abhiraka in the eye, who finally gave a curt nod that, while not exactly what Puddapandyan was looking for, he understood would have to do. "Am I correct in assuming," he began, "that when your queen sent the contents of your treasury to us for safekeeping, that wasn't all of it?"

For a brief span, the Pandyan king was certain that he had erred, because Abhiraka's reaction was a sharp intake of breath, although it was the sudden step towards the Pandyan king, his hand dropping to his sword that in turn elicited the response from Puddapandyan's two bodyguards who were always at his side, as they stepped forward. Whether it was that, or that Abhiraka needed a heartbeat's worth of time to regain his self-control, what mattered to Puddapandyan, and to the other men in the tent, was that he did so.

Finally, Abhiraka answered tersely, "Yes, you are correct. My queen directed that a portion of the Bharuch treasury remain behind. She had it buried before the Romans entered the city."

While he was willing, however reluctantly, to impart this much knowledge, there was no way that he would divulge how much of his treasury had been left behind, and he was rewarded in his decision by the flicker of disappointment he was sure he saw in his counterpart's eyes.

Nevertheless, Puddapandyan pressed onward, asking, "How many people know of its location?"

"Two," Abhiraka answered firmly and without hesitation.

"Two?" Puddapandyan echoed, clearly skeptical. "How is that possible? It would certainly take more than two people to move…" his voice trailed off, but Abhiraka refused to rise to the bait, forcing the Pandyan to hurry on, "…however much was moved."

"It did," Abhiraka seemingly confirmed, but before the other man could speak, he added, "and my queen took…steps to ensure that the men who performed the work would never speak of its location."

While he didn't know it, this actually aided Puddapandyan in his effort to sow doubt in the other king's mind. Yes, Abhiraka had been extremely lucky, thanks to one of his men who obviously sacrificed himself to eliminate the most potent weapon these Romans possessed against elephants, but the Pandyan had no confidence that Abhiraka would be able to achieve his larger aim of liberating his kingdom. And, with that in mind, it behooved Puddapandyan to do what he could to weaken Abhiraka, and the Bharuch king had just given him the opening he needed.

He began by saying, "I assume that, of the two, you are one of them, and the queen is the other?"

Abhiraka nodded, but Puddapandyan said nothing, preferring to allow the other king's mind to work its way to the conclusion he wanted Abhiraka to draw. His reward came within a span of heartbeats, as he studied Abhiraka's expression intently, seeing first the look of dawning understanding, followed an eyeblink later by despair, although he managed to smother that fairly quickly, just not quickly enough that Puddapandyan didn't see it.

Aloud, Abhiraka said stiffly, "I can assure you, Puddapandyan, Hyppolita would *never* betray me!"

Holding up a placating hand, Puddapandyan lied smoothly, "I assure you, Abhiraka, that thought never crossed my mind! It's true that I have met your queen only once, but I could immediately see how utterly devoted she is to you! No," he shook his head, altering his tone to convey a sadness, "I am afraid I am thinking of...other ways for these Roman dogs to find out about your treasury."

It was Ranjeet who, suspecting what Puddapandyan was up to, intervened, "While this is certainly something to think about, Your Highness, it's also something that can be dealt with later, can it not?"

"Yes, Ranjeet," Abhiraka answered immediately, and his friend saw the flash of relief and gratitude for his rescue, and the king returned to the larger moment. "So, we should assume that, however it's happening, the Romans aren't forcing my subjects to help them. Now," he gave them a smile, "let us concentrate on the positive aspects of what we've learned from the traitor." Before he did, he turned to Bolon to ask, "Have you begun questioning the other traitors that we captured? And any of the other prisoners who speak Greek?"

"I have men doing that now, Your Highness," Bolon confirmed.

Abhiraka nodded, then continued, "We now know that Caesar isn't in Bharuch. Or," he hurried to add, seeing Ranjeet open his mouth, "he wasn't when these two Legions," he glanced down at the scrap of parchment containing what he considered the pertinent information that had been gleaned from Chatur, "the 7th and 11th, departed from Bharuch nine days ago now. What," he asked them all, "does that mean? Especially now that we know the reason the Romans haven't marched in this direction in force is because Caesar's men refused to obey him?"

"Maybe he fled," Nahapana suggested. "Maybe he feared for his life from his own men."

On its face, this seemed to be a reasonable alternative, yet Abhiraka immediately dismissed it with a shake of his head.

"No, Nahapana, I don't believe that. Caesar is many things, but no coward would be able to control such a massive army long enough to conquer Parthia, and," he had to swallow the bitter lump, "us in less than three full years. No," he repeated, "something else happened."

"As long as he took that fleet with him," Ranjeet pointed out, "the only way that they can move is overland. And," he offered his king a grim smile, "now that they will be missing two Legions, I think we can expect that they *will* come, with or without Caesar, because they'll know what it takes to destroy two of their Legions.

They'll know this isn't a raid, but a real threat, and they will have to respond, even if Caesar isn't there."

While it ultimately didn't matter, the fact that the heads of the other men involved in the conversation were nodding confirmed Abhiraka's own agreement with Ranjeet.

"So," he offered them the same kind of smile as his friend, "we need to find an appropriate spot to be waiting for them, and I think I know the exact place."

When the 7th and 11th didn't return on the scheduled day, it was barely noticed; when it became two days, there was some desultory talk among the Legions, but it was idle in nature. By the fourth day, the possible causes for the delay was the sole topic of conversation with the men of all ranks. A week to the day later, Pollio summoned the Primi Pili for an emergency meeting, and when Pullus entered the Legate's office with Spurius and Balbinus, they all stopped short, seeing in the deathly pallor and demeanor of the Legate a presentiment of a real disaster. They weren't the only ones who interpreted what they saw in the same manner, meaning that the only sounds as the Centurions settled into their chairs were the scraping sounds and creaks as they did so. That silence extended for an agonizing stretch of time until, finally, Pollio broke it by clearing his throat.

"There," his voice was almost unrecognizable as his own, "is no easy way to say this. But, three days ago, I sent Decurion Silva south, searching for the whereabouts of the 7th and 11th. He just returned a third of a watch ago, but I ordered him and his *ala* back out immediately, even before they could switch out their mounts." For the first time, he looked up from where he had been staring at his desk, and Pullus saw the haunted look, causing his stomach to seemingly flip over itself. "My reason for doing so was twofold. First, the enemy that we've been searching for may be *much* closer than we thought. And," he stopped to swallow and closed his eyes as he continued, "the second reason was because it appears that the 7th and 11th Legions have been annihilated."

It would be a moment Titus Pullus and his fellow Primi Pili would remember for the rest of their lives. None of them could think of anything to say, and the silence stretched out for one, two, three heartbeats before, finally, Pullus broke it.

"How do we know this, Legate?"

Pollio glanced down, and for the first time, Pullus noticed the tablet on the desk, which he seemed to be consulting, although he answered readily enough, "Silva's patrol ran into one of the *turmae* that had been attached to the 7th and 11th." Pollio stopped again, overcome with emotion. Taking a deep breath, he collected himself enough to continue, "Atartinus had sent them out as precautionary measure to ensure that there wasn't a force blocking them from returning, and had gotten about halfway back here when the Decurion in command decided they had seen enough. They were returning back to the Legions when they ran into a group of merchants who had been in Kalliena and were fleeing north because of what happened. According to them, there was an attack of some sort." He glanced down at the tablet. "Silva said they didn't know any details about how it happened, just that some survivors made it to the walls of the town, but they were hunted down and slaughtered." Pollio stopped again, but this was to let the Centurions absorb the horrific news, mainly because he knew the worst was to come. Finally, he resumed, beginning, "There's more. A member of that group claimed that he went to the site of the battle, and from what he described and if he's telling the truth, it appears that Atartinus and Mus were surprised in their camp."

For the first time, someone other than Pullus spoke up, as Clustuminus snorted, "That's how we know they're lying, sir. If they were protected by ditch and wall, and with the naphtha, there's no way they could have been wiped out."

On its face, this was a sensible statement, but while the others had turned towards Clustuminus while he was speaking, Pullus had not, and he watched Pollio as the Primus Pilus made his statement.

"They didn't have a ditch and wall…did they?"

Pollio's first reaction was to glare at Pullus, but he immediately realized that his anger was misplaced, although he only said flatly, "No, Pullus, they didn't."

This proved too much for the self-control of the assembled men, some leaping to their feet, but all of them talking at once, or that was how it started. Naturally, each of them began raising their voices to be heard over the others, while Pollio sat dumbly, staring at them as if he had no idea what to do. Which, Pullus quickly decided, was probably the case.

"*Tacete*!... *Tacete*!...*BY THE GODS, SHUT YOUR FUCKING MOUTHS AND STOP ACTING LIKE A BUNCH OF FUCKING WOMEN!*"

While this served to silence all but one of the Primi Pili, the fact that it was Clustuminus who, his face contorted with rage, actually raised his *vitus* to strike Pullus was something that, as the rest of these men understood, had been building for some time. Despite their collective attention riveted to the pair, afterward, none of them could say they actually saw what happened, just the result, which was what served to inform them that Titus Pullus aimed one single blow that struck Clustuminus with enough force that his feet left the floor, and the only reason he didn't land flat on his back was because he caromed into Flaminius of the 30th, who just managed to keep his own feet. Clustuminus was unconscious, yet when Pollio opened his mouth, thinking that he should say *something*, nothing came out, but it was when he glanced over at Hirtius, who had had his own problems with the giant Primus Pilus, his fellow Legate gave a slight shake of his head.

Pullus seemed somewhat surprised, standing motionless while Flaminius shoved some chairs out of the way enough to lay the Primus Pilus of the 8th onto the floor, and in the silence, they heard Pullus mutter, "I'm not sure why I did that."

"I am." Spurius spoke up, immediately and in a tone that, as he intended, sent a signal to the others. "He was about to strike you, Pullus. We all saw him raise his *vitus* as he came at you." Then, turning to the others, he added, "Didn't we, boys? We all saw the same thing."

Spurius was almost diminutive compared to Pullus, but of the Primi Pili, he was not only the closest friend to Pullus, he was almost as respected, so there was only the briefest of hesitation from the others, even Batius, as they murmured their agreement.

Turning to Pollio, Spurius altered his tone to sound more respectful, but his question was as pointed as he asked, "Is that what you saw as well, sir? And," he turned to look directly at Hirtius, "you, sir?"

"Yes," Pollio replied immediately, but Hirtius agreed almost as quickly, while the senior Legate took the opportunity to return back to the original subject, as unpleasant as it was, saying briskly, "Back to the current situation." Pausing long enough to see the men turn their attention back to him, he went on, "We need to decide what to do about it."

This served to get the men settled back in their seats, with the exception of Clustuminus, who was only slowly regaining consciousness, and had been dragged to the other side of the room that served as the Legate's office by Flaminius and a grumbling Batius.

"The question before us," Pollio began, "is how we respond to this…event," was the word he settled on, not wanting to call it what it was. "Should we march south immediately, and leave just one Legion behind? Or," he scanned the room, "are we better served to let this army, however large it may be, make its way here?"

It immediately became clear that the Primi Pili were almost equally divided, while Pullus himself was torn. By his nature, his instinctive answer was that, of *course* they would march immediately and confront the enemy wherever they were found; however, there were merits to the idea of acting defensively, relying on the very walls that they had successfully captured. As the others talked, Pullus mulled the two alternatives, but he decided that he would let the others make their respective arguments to see if he hadn't missed anything.

He quickly learned that he had, when Spurius pointed out, "If we march, it will be with even less of the naphtha than Atartinus and Mus' boys had."

This immediately registered with the others, and there was a deflation of a mood that was already dangerously low, which Pollio correctly sensed.

"That's a very good point, Spurius," Pollio agreed, but when he did cast a glance over at Hirtius, he saw that his counterpart was similarly glum. Turning back to address the others, he said, "I think that we've answered the question. Without restocking our supplies of the naphtha, while we could conceivably maneuver to ground that suits us, or somehow manage to surprise the enemy," he almost added "like they surprised Atartinus and Mus", but decided against it, "those would be the only two advantages we have that might counter their use of elephants. But," he concluded, "since we don't, I'm not willing to risk the rest of this army." Trying to salvage something positive, he offered them a grim smile. "Let them come to us and try to take this city back. That will be the best way to defeat them."

It wasn't a huge victory, but the fact that, for the first time, the scratch cavalry force raised by Gaius Octavian and the 14th Legion, which was led in the field by Marcus Agrippa, had managed to catch the forces of Valash by surprise and inflicted a defeat did more to elevate the morale of the men than any promise of a bounty. More importantly, it sent Valash's army fleeing north, with Octavian in close pursuit, forcing the reluctant leader of this rebellion to fight a running battle, with Octavian following Marcus Agrippa's advice to adopt tactics that were normally those used by the Parthians themselves. Rather than try and force the *drafsh* under Valash's command to stop and fight a decisive battle, it served Octavian's interests to apply a constant pressure sufficient to force Valash to fall all the way back to Ecbatana, the last major city of the Parthian empire that wasn't under direct Roman control. It was a risk, Octavian privately acknowledged only to Agrippa, but he felt it worth taking, and his reasoning was sound. Essentially, campaigning in the bitterest months of the Parthian winter was something to be avoided, but Octavian had been forced to do that very thing. As trying an ordeal as it was just to move a large body of men for any distance in this barren land, dragging them around the wastes as they tried to eliminate this last threat to Roman control, then march all the way back to Susa, simply wasn't feasible.

The plan concocted by Octavian, driven by his desperation to instill some sort of order to restore Caesar's previous confidence in him, was deceptively simple. If all went as he intended, Octavian, or at least the Legion that he now commanded, along with his *de facto* cavalry arm, would winter in Ecbatana once they crushed Valash and seized the city. Nevertheless, he knew he was taking an enormous risk, his kinship with Caesar notwithstanding. Marching out of Susa without Caesar's explicit orders to do so would have been something he wouldn't have even entertained a few months earlier, but the situation had deteriorated to the point that he overrode his inherent sense of caution to issue orders to begin a campaign at the worst time of year. Now, almost exactly a month after their departure, for the first time, Octavian felt somewhat optimistic that his plan would come to fruition. If, he thought, I could only convince that idiot Figulus and his Centurions that this will work, and they will be back under a roof in a matter of a couple more weeks. It had actually been Agrippa who convinced him to take the newly arrived 14th and not the more veteran and better rested 22nd under Sextus Crispus.

"Figulus and his men are too new here to put up a fight about being forced to march so soon after they arrived," Agrippa had argued. However, it was the second point that Octavian felt most compelling. "And they're already conditioned from the march here. They've gotten a taste of what a campaign in Parthia will be like, at least with the weather."

There were moments where Octavian found himself half-angrily and half-humorously wishing that someone would have told Gnaeus Figulus that, because of his recent arrival, he wasn't in a position to offer resistance to Octavian's plans. It was only through Agrippa's mediation and, Octavian admitted only to himself, that

Figulus clearly respected his friend despite his youth that Octavian hadn't been forced to either turn around and march back to Susa or replace the Primus Pilus. Somehow, the young Praetor acting as senior Legate managed to avoid venting his frustration with Figulus with an act that, as satisfying as it might have been, would have been rash, and something that Caesar was unlikely to forgive. Fortunately, despite the tension, he and Figulus came to a certain level of acceptance of the other, and it still made him smile to recall Agrippa's succinct summation of matters.

"Essentially, Figulus is a blister that is rubbing you raw, but is slowly becoming a callous."

And that, Octavian thought wryly, was about as apt a description as anything he could think of. Such were his thoughts as he watched Figulus' men stripping anything of value from the Parthian dead, engaging in the same banter and arguments that occurred after every battle in which Rome was victorious, and he could tell just by their demeanors that, at least for the moment, the men of the 14th had forgotten how cold it was, and how far away they were from any shelter that wasn't constructed of leather. Even Figulus, whose normal expression seemed to be a permanent scowl, offered his version of a smile at Octavian as he walked past him and Agrippa, which Octavian made sure to return; if his teeth were gritted as he did so, there was no need for Figulus to know that. No, he thought, there will be time to deal with Figulus later. At this moment, I need him, and his men, to prove to my uncle that I am the only man truly worthy of being his successor. His train of thought immediately led him to Caesar, which prompted him to turn to Agrippa.

"What do you think Caesar will do when he returns from Merv and finds us gone? Do you think he'll come after us?"

It was Agrippa's turn to hide his feelings, because this wasn't the first or second time Octavian had asked him this same question. Not, he reminded himself, that it wasn't an important question; it most certainly was, but while they were receiving an occasional dispatch rider from Susa, none had arrived for the previous three days, and with every mile north, it was growing increasingly unlikely that they would receive another one, if only because this vast expanse of nothingness tended to swallow up even the most experienced men when they were riding alone.

Aloud, he pretended to muse as he offered the same answer that he had given every previous time, "I think it depends on what happens in Merv and what kind of condition your uncle is in. I've never made that journey myself, but nobody I've talked to has ever said that it was easy, and that was in better weather." Shaking his head, he went on, "And we can't forget that the bulk of the army is in India, and he's been away from them for a long time." Glancing up at a sky with a hue that matched the color of lead sling bullets, he asked wistfully, "I wonder what the weather is like in India? It has to be better than this."

Octavian was acutely aware that he had asked Marcus Agrippa this question more than once, but he couldn't seem to help it, and he also told himself that the moment that Agrippa's answer changed was one that marked a likely turning point. Hopefully, if the gods were kind, his answer would stay the same all the way to Ecbatana.

Rather than respond to the first part of Agrippa's statement, he laughingly agreed, "Marcus, *anything* is better than this."

While it was made honestly, this was a statement with which every man of Caesar's army in India would vehemently disagree, something that neither man would ever know.

Only Caesar knew the real cost of his journey in tapping his reserves of strength and vitality. Outwardly, he strove to be the same Caesar as always, and in his private moments, he acknowledged that just doing this took an enormous amount of his energy. Yet, like Titus Pullus, Caesar's pride always gave him the extra amount of…whatever one called it, to present to those around them the same man they had been following, some for years, some for decades. He only had one lapse when, far off in the distance, he saw what to an uninformed eye would appear to be nothing more than a straight dark line on the horizon, and he was forced to bring his horse to a halt, so overcome with emotion that he worried he would shame himself. As always, Gundomir and his younger brother were riding on either side of him, but it was the older German who, having been with Caesar for more than ten years, understood the need of the moment by continuing to ride. Through no fault of his own, Teispes drew up alongside Caesar, curious as to the reason, although he immediately discerned that this Roman to whom he had transferred his allegiance was affected.

Despite himself, Teispes heard what sounded like his own voice say, "It has been a hard journey, Caesar. But," he turned to face the Roman as he gave the highest accolade he could think of, "you rode like a man born in Parthia." Suddenly aware of an upsurge of his own emotion, the normally taciturn Teispes offered a clumsy but heartfelt tribute. "I am proud to have ridden with you, my Lord."

Caesar's eyes were moist, but while there were no tears, he was visibly moved, although his acknowledgment was a grave bow of his head and replying, "And I am honored that you rode at my side, Teispes. I hope that you, and," he turned and indicated the pair of Germans with his head, "Gundomir and Barvistus will always be my side for however long the gods decide."

"I will be, Caesar," Teispes assured him, and Caesar gently nudged his horse to resume moving.

"Oh, and Teispes?" Caesar gave the Parthian a smile. "Don't call me 'lord.' I," he turned to look back towards Susa, "am Caesar. And Caesar is enough."

Chapter 5

Naturally, it took longer to reach Susa than one unaccustomed to traveling in this land would have thought, as that black line only grudgingly turned into something distinguishable. Before he reached the city gates, Gaius Maecenas had been alerted that the party of horsemen was approaching, not needing to be told that it was Caesar because of the direction from which they approached. For a brief span of time, Octavian's third in command worried whether or not he should ride out to greet the Dictator, not relishing the thought of moving on horseback, since he normally was conveyed by litter whenever possible. His quandary didn't last long; snapping an order, he paused long enough to collect his thoughts before striding from the large throne room, happy that he had been wise enough not to shift the belongings on his desk to the one that Octavian preferred to use on the raised platform in the center of the room. As far as Maecenas was concerned, it was rather silly, this insistence by his friend to defy Caesar, who every time he spent any length of time in Susa, had moved the desk from the platform to a spot nearer to the door. But, he supposed, it was just Octavian's way of showing his independence, an independence that Maecenas suddenly realized put him in a potentially awkward and perhaps dangerous position since he would be forced to explain Octavian's absence. This didn't do much to settle his stomach, but he still hurried out of the *Praetorium*, where his mount was waiting, along with the mixed group of horsemen who had, for one reason or another, been left behind by Octavian. It wasn't much of a bodyguard, he thought, but since there was nothing that he could do about it, he refused to dwell on the indignity. By his own admission, Gaius Maecenas' talents didn't extend to martial matters, and under normal circumstances, he was perfectly happy for this to be known, yet for some reason he couldn't articulate, the thought that Caesar would find him lacking in this area disturbed him deeply. It was probably because, he thought, Caesar is so good at everything, even the things in which I excel as well, it makes me uncomfortable. Not that it mattered in the moment, but he did try to vault onto his horse with the same flair that his friend Agrippa displayed. He instantly understood that it was unsuccessful, but he ignored the snickers from his escort, and quickly enough, they were trotting down the street that led to the gate that would lead them to Caesar. They moved at the canter, which Maecenas endured, trying to remember all the things his riding instructor had tried to instill in him back when he was a boy, the son of an immensely wealthy provincial and one who hadn't yet come to terms with his singular lack of talent in martial matters, of which horsemanship was an integral part. How else, he recalled his instructor saying more than once, can you expect to lead a cavalry charge if you can't stay on your horse? Certainly, it was a valid question, but a young Gaius Maecenas wasn't sufficiently self-aware to understand himself, so he had merely grit his teeth and tried harder to impress the man, to no avail. Now he was simply enduring the jarring that came from the pace, praying to every god he could think of that Caesar, seeing the approaching party, would do the same and thereby reduce this period of agony. It was a wish that would go unfulfilled, as the Dictator apparently deemed that it would be unseemly to match the pace set by the oncoming party, and to make matters even worse for Maecenas, Caesar obviously ordered his group to come to a halt.

Finally, the first part of the ordeal was over for Maecenas, signaled by his drawing his mount up, then saluting in as close to a proper manner as he could manage, but before he could say anything, Caesar asked, "Where is Octavian? Where is my nephew?"

It was a struggle for him to maintain his composure, but Maecenas somehow did it, answering smoothly, "Gaius Octavian and Marcus Agrippa were required to march from Susa with the 14th Legion and the cavalry force that Octavian raised to bring the Parthian rebel Valash to heel, Dictator."

That this didn't seem to be unexpected to Caesar was Maecenas' first surprise, but it was only strengthened when Caesar commented, "So he actually did it, eh?" He nodded. "Good. I was hoping he would do as much. Although," Caesar added, "I was intending to take the 14th with me back to India."

"The 21st is supposed to be arriving any day now, Caesar," Maecenas informed him. "A dispatch arrived a few days ago that they had left Ctesiphon."

Caesar considered for a moment, then shook his head.

"I'm not going to wait for the 21st, so I'll take Crispus' Legion with me. Now," he nudged his horse forward, "tell me everything you know as we ride."

Pullus was in a quandary that, while he understood it was of his own making, didn't make it any easier. He had avoided telling Hyppolita about the news concerning the 7th and 11th, although he was certain that she knew something had happened that had disturbed the few Romans with whom she had contact, namely the men of the 10th who Pullus assigned as guards. There was, he thought to himself with a stab of bitter amusement, another way she might learn of the disaster, yet while he had lectured his nephew on the need for discretion whenever he spent time with Amodini, he didn't hold out much hope that Porcinus would remember that post-coital talk could be dangerous. For perhaps the hundredth time, Titus Pullus wished Caesar was present, certain that the man he had been following since he was sixteen would know how to respond, but there was nothing to be done about it, because he wasn't here, and only the gods knew if he would ever return. The fact that Pullus had reached the moment where he considered the word "if" instead of "when" marked a major turning point for the large Roman, and it was perilously close to the feeling he held for their general in the immediate aftermath of Pharsalus, one of anger and a fair amount of disgust at Caesar's inability to understand the shared sentiment of the men who marched for him. For two days after the meeting with Pollio, Pullus agonized over what to say, if anything, to the Queen of Bharuch, but finally, he found himself standing in front of her, in her reception room on the second floor, a place he could now describe with his eyes closed.

"I need you to dismiss your ladies, Your Highness," Pullus began peremptorily. "What I need to talk to you about is for your ears only."

As always, Hyppolita wasn't easily intimidated, and she regarded the Roman with a level gaze as she replied coolly, "Seeing that it's highly likely that I will be discussing whatever it is that you tell me with my ladies after you leave, is that really necessary?"

Pullus felt his face grow hot, understanding that, as she tended to do, Hyppolita had turned him neatly and seemingly easily.

"That, of course, is up to you," he answered stiffly. "But I'm afraid I must insist that what I am about to tell you is for your ears only, Your Highness. After that?" He tried to offer a nonchalant shrug, but he saw she wasn't fooled. "What you choose to do with the information is out of my hands."

This was enough for Hyppolita, who simply gave a nod that got her women on their feet and, because of their floor-length gowns, appear to glide out of the room. Pullus had dismissed the pair of guards days earlier when the news of the disaster had arrived, and they were now alone. And, Pullus realized as he sat down on the chair that had become his own, he didn't really know where to start.

"There's something that I need to tell you," he began. "Although I suspect that you might have an idea that there has been..." unable to decide on the proper term, he settled on, "...news that we received a couple of days ago."

Hyppolita had decided from the outset that she would force Pullus to fully articulate whatever this news he was delivering was, having deduced that it was something that the Centurion considered bad, yet sitting there watching him struggle, before she could stop herself, she said softly, "And I suspect that the news of which you speak has to do with some sort of defeat or setback. Is that correct, Centurion?"

Pullus was torn between relief and irritation, but he answered readily enough, "Yes, Your Highness. That is correct."

Taking a deep breath, he went on to divulge to the queen that two of Rome's Legions had, if their information was correct, been destroyed, and that it had been at the hands of an as-yet unidentified army that had been south of Kalliena. He studied Hyppolita's expression as he talked, but despite preparing himself, when he saw her eyes widen, then come alight with what was unmistakable happiness, the stab of disappointed anger was so powerful that he stopped abruptly. Hyppolita instantly understood, reading his expression as perfectly as he had hers an instant before.

"Do you really expect me to receive this news with unhappiness, Centurion?" she asked, though not with any defensiveness or asperity. "We both know that it is my husband who is leading this army." She paused, then, choosing her words carefully, she continued, "Whatever...feelings I may have towards you personally, Centurion, now that I have gotten to know you, are of no matter. I am still the Queen of Bharuch, and you still represent a foreign invader who brought death and destruction to my subjects."

There was absolutely nothing Pullus could say to counter this, nor did he attempt to do so, but neither could he deny that he was still disappointed at her display of happiness, however muted.

"Yes," he finally said awkwardly, standing up, "well, I just wanted to let you know what has happened. And," his tone sharpened, "I would suggest that we curtail the walks around the compound for a time. My men are...upset," was the word he chose. "Right now, I don't want them to get any ideas of exacting revenge."

This disturbed Hyppolita, yet it also angered her, and she also came to her feet as she retorted, "Are you telling me that you cannot control your soldiers, Centurion Pullus?" Suddenly, her look of anger transformed into one of acute concern as she gasped, "They would not behave in the manner in which they did after they took Bharuch, surely! Would they?"

Her tone turned plaintive with this last query, which caused Pullus to shift uncomfortably, because this was precisely what he and the other Primi Pili were worried about, despite the fact that, so far, they had managed to keep their men under control. Yes, there had been some attacks by Legionaries on citizens of the city, but nothing on a wide scale, and Pullus had no intention of sharing that with the queen.

Nevertheless, he was still sufficiently nettled that, rather than assuage her fears, he answered simply, "I hope not, Your Highness. Now," he bowed, "I will show myself out."

Hyppolita opened her mouth to respond, but Pullus had already turned and was stalking out of the room. As she stared at his back, wondering what to say, neither she nor he were aware that their state of confusion was shared by the other. Yes, she was certainly happy to know that Abhiraka had obviously prevailed upon the sly old king Puddapandyan, her daughter's father-in-law, and that her husband had begun to fight back in his attempt to reclaim Bharuch. So, she wondered, why was she so worried about the fate of this large Roman? He was the enemy, she reminded herself, yet for some reason, she didn't believe herself even as the thought ran through her mind.

"You did a superb job," Caesar told the small group of men he had summoned to the throne room, "and under difficult conditions. But I commend each of you for doing your part."

It had certainly been a daunting task, Bodroges thought, particularly for himself, a Parthian Tribune who many of his fellow officers, all Roman, still suspected. Yet, he had succeeded in his specific duty of replenishing the stocks of naphtha and shipping them to Caesarea, where the fleet was still moored, waiting for Caesar. In his usual manner, he had arrived in Susa just the day before, and was already preparing to move, but while his manner was as vigorous as always, to the young Parthian, physically, Caesar was a shadow of the man who had left for Merv, leaving himself and the rest of Caesar's staff with a seemingly unending list of tasks that, to none of their surprise, the Dictator expected to be completed, or well on the way to completion by his return. Of them, only Kamnaskires, the Elymais prince, appeared unhappy, but Bodroges didn't know whether that was due to the fact that, of all the subordinate officers who had been assigned a role, he had been the least successful in his endeavors, or his discontent was caused by something else, like the rumor that Caesar wasn't willing to let the prince return to his lands of Elymais. As far as Bodroges was concerned, Caesar's suspicion was warranted; Bodroges was still distrustful of the prince, who was only a couple years older than himself, seeing in the other nobleman an ambition that he recognized because he possessed the same quality. Where they differed was that, in the intervening time since he had surrendered the garrison of Susa after slaying Gobryas, Bodroges had adopted the Roman cause as his own. That certainly hadn't been the case for the first few months, but through his constant exposure to not just the Legions of Rome, but to Caesar, the former courtier had reached a simple conclusion; Rome couldn't be defeated. They were too organized, too disciplined, and in their own way, were every bit as tough as his fellow Parthian warriors, perhaps even more so given how they had adapted to their surroundings. More than once, Bodroges had wondered how the *cataphractoi* and mounted archers of the Parthian army would cope in the frigid lands of Germania or Gaul, and he simply couldn't fathom the idea.

With the accolades aside, it wouldn't have been a meeting with the Dictator if he didn't double check, and he began by yanking Bodroges from his thoughts by asking, "Were you able to add to our supplies of naphtha, Bodroges? Over and above what we took to India?"

"Yes, Caesar," Bodroges replied with what he felt was justifiable pride. "Two hundred more crates, with four jars to a crate to go with the thousand we originally had, over and above what you ordered to be shipped as soon as we arrived."

Caesar instantly deflated the young Parthian by pursing his lips, then saying, "I suppose that will have to do." Before Bodroges could offer a defense by informing Caesar of the immense challenges of locating more sources for this substance that bubbled up out of the ground, the Dictator turned to the man standing next to Bodroges. "Artaxerxes, your *dilectus* was successful?"

"It was, Caesar," Artaxerxes confirmed. "Two Cohorts of infantry, all Parthian, and four *washt*...I mean, *turmae* of horse archers."

"Where are they now?" Caesar asked, and Artaxerxes didn't answer immediately, but it was because he was trying to calculate before replying, "Provided there were no unforeseen delays, they should be within one, or perhaps two days march of Caesarea, Caesar."

Caesar nodded, then it was Kamnaskires' turn, and here the

news was not as good.

"Kamnaskires, were you successful in the task I assigned you?" To Bodroges, there was something in the way that Caesar asked the question that indicated he already knew the answer, which was confirmed when he registered no surprise when Kamnaskires answered reluctantly, "Not as successful as I hoped, Caesar."

"How many men?" Caesar asked, and he got a partial answer by Kamnaskires' reaction, which was to lick his lips.

"Five hundred, Caesar," the prince answered reluctantly.

"So," Caesar's tone hardened, not much, but enough for them all to notice, "half of what you promised to deliver to me." He paused, pinning the Elymais prince with the kind of stare that more experienced men like Titus Pullus knew represented the Dictator at his most dangerous. "Are they at least trained in the same manner as those of your men who scaled the walls of Pattala?"

"Yes, Caesar," Kamnaskires replied immediately, nodding his head in emphasis. "They are every bit the equal of those men."

Caesar held his gaze on the Elymais prince for another pair of heartbeats, then turned his attention to other matters, announcing, "While it was my intention to bring the 14th with us back to India, as you know, Praetor Octavian took them north to crush Valash once and for all. And," he added, "if I'm correct in my guess, he and the Legion won't be back to Susa until the spring."

This prompted some murmurs from the officers, but as the only other Roman in the room, it was Salvidienus Rufus who asked, "Are you saying that Octavian intends to stay in the field for an entire winter, Caesar?" The Tribune shook his head. "That doesn't sound like something Gaius Octavian would do."

Caesar, well aware of the antipathy between his nephew and Rufus, offered him a cold stare.

"No, Rufus," his tone as frigid as his gaze, "I believe that Octavian marched with the intention of quelling this last bit of resistance in a manner that will finish this business. And, to that end, I believe that he is going to besiege and take Ecbatana and will spend the winter there. That," he finished, making it clear to anyone that the matter was closed, "is what I would do, and I trust Octavian to do the same." Rufus wisely held his tongue, dropping his eyes to the floor, as Caesar continued, "Since I can't take the 14th, I've ordered Crispus to prepare the 22nd to march, but I'm not willing to delay my own return, nor am I willing to leave Susa undefended. I have been informed that the 21st departed Ctesiphon and should be in Susa within the next five days, which should be enough time for the 22nd to make the necessary preparations. Once the 21st arrives, Crispus will march to Caesarea, where I will leave just enough of the fleet to transport him to Bharuch." He paused, and seeing that there were no further questions, he said simply, "We will be departing Susa in two days' time to return to Bharuch."

With that, he turned to where Apollodorus was seated at one of the desks along the wall, sending the signal that the meeting was over, and Bodroges filed out with the others, certain that, like himself, they were wondering what awaited them in India.

Abhiraka led his triumphant army north after spending five days in Kalliena, and despite the celebratory mood of his army, particularly the core of it in his fellow men of Bharuch, the king was disquieted by what he learned in the town. He had expected to hear tales of the depredations by the Romans, but they had never actually entered the town in force, despite being sighted several times. Naturally, the civilians had no way of knowing that the identities of the two Legions changed, just that they began appearing at semi-regular intervals, yet their interaction with the foreign invaders had been restricted to nervously watching from the town walls; at least, that was their claim. It was not just unusual, it was unheard of, and even after discussing it at length with Puddapandyan, who was not only older but because of his southern location had contact with other kingdoms that Abhiraka only knew of by name, neither of them could ever recall when a victorious army didn't pillage the towns and villages of their vanquished enemies. What was more understandable was that the Romans hadn't despoiled the fields around not just Kalliena, but every village that they encountered on their northward progress from there. While Abhiraka knew of several routes that could be taken north to reach Bharuch, his guess that the Romans would use the flatter route that was close to the coast was a good one, and it was confirmed by the presence of what was now a well-worn track that was even more pronounced than it had been the last time he had traveled the region. If there was anything positive, it did give Abhiraka something to think about as he rode at the head of his army, although he rode a horse and not Darpashata. One reason for tarrying was because of the difficulty in procuring enough wagons and carts to transport the armor, shields, and weapons that the king had ordered stripped from the corpses of the Roman dead. As he and the part of his army who had faced the Romans for the first time north of the city had learned, the bronze armor; muscled cuirasses for his phalanx troops, and scale armor for his lighter sword-wielding infantry, was insufficient protection against the weapons of these new foes. Abhiraka had outfitted his Royal Bodyguard, along with his officers, with iron armor, but even for a kingdom with the wealth of Bharuch, the prospect of outfitting his entire army had been daunting enough that he had never gotten around to doing so, and it was a lapse that he was bitterly aware cost the slain men of his army their lives. Like the canal, it had always been something that could be done later, and that illusion had been shattered by the appearance of Rome. The only reason that he hadn't immediately distributed the mail shirts was riding next to him, because there was no way for him to outfit only his men without offering the remainder to the Pandyan king. Certainly, he was grateful for the force of men and animals who dwarfed what remained of his army, but Abhiraka's suspicions about Puddapandyan and his larger aims had never waned, although he was surprised that his fellow king had remained silent about his parsimony. Probably, he thought sourly, he's just waiting for the right moment, when I won't have any choice, like when those dogs finally come south. Like his suspicions about Puddapandyan, Abhiraka's certainty that the Romans would be forced to leave Bharuch to come confront him had yet to waver, but with every mile north, when the scouts who were scouring the countryside returned to the army, that confidence was slowly eroding, and with it the recognition that he would be forced to do what he had been certain the Romans had already done was growing. What was difficult for him to assess was how much time he should give his enemy to move before he began laying waste to his own kingdom. And, as always, lurking there in the back of his mind was the one nagging question that, while it could be ignored for a short period of time, kept shoving its way to the forefront of his consciousness; where was Caesar?

By the Roman calendar, Caesar boarded his flagship in Caesarea on the Kalends of Februarius, which in this part of the world, was one of the most dangerous times of year for a sea voyage, something that didn't faze Caesar in the slightest. His sailing companions, however, weren't nearly as sanguine, although it was impossible to discern who was more nervous; Romans, Germans, or Parthians. As for the newly recruited auxiliary Cohorts, the mounted archers, and the men of Elymais who had been specially trained to scale the rugged terrain of their tiny kingdom, and in whom Caesar had found use during the attack on Pattala, they weren't consulted; they were just expected to obey. Because the newly finished port of

Caesarea was two miles upriver, the men were spared the discomfort of seasickness immediately after boarding, which was always a laborious process. For men who had never been to sea, or even seen anything other than the Tigris and Euphrates and were already disoriented by the sudden change in their circumstances by being thrust into the world of Roman discipline, it was a tense time. Despite the difficulties, the boarding process only took a day longer than Caesar had hoped, and the portion of the fleet carrying him and these men drifted downriver in the predawn to begin a journey that, in its own way, was almost as arduous as the overland trip to Merv. Fortunately, those hardships had been lessened with Caesar's foresight in the resurrection of the ports that once were a crucial part of the Macedonian supply chain, along with his commissioning of new outposts that were located either on or near supplies of fresh water, which was the most precious resource along this curving barren coastline. Once the fleet reached the ocean, only then did Caesar disappear from the deck of his huge vessel, retiring to his cabin, and the other officers who were onboard with him would only catch occasional glimpses of him for the next several days. Only Apollodorus was allowed unfettered access to the Dictator, and he quickly became the most popular man aboard ship. After a few days of the constant harassment, Caesar's personal secretary finally had endured enough, announcing that he would offer updates on their general twice a day, once in the morning, and shortly before sunset.

"He needs to rest, and the less interruptions the better," he explained on the day his patience was exhausted. "Right now, he is spending most of his time sleeping, and that's a good thing." When he got no argument from the assembly of men who surrounded him on the open deck, he continued, "He has instructed me that he's not to be disturbed unless it is a dire emergency."

This was accepted, albeit reluctantly, by Caesar's bodyguards and officers, and Apollodorus could see that they were worried; what he didn't share with them was that he was as worried as they were, because for as long as he had served Caesar, he had never seen his master so exhausted nor as emaciated, although he had put on some weight since returning to Susa. In one respect, there was a common bond among Caesar's subordinates, no matter how lowly their status or different their respective backgrounds; none of them could imagine a world where Caesar wasn't there, so when faced with that as a real possibility, it meant that Gundomir and the others scrupulously adhered to Apollodorus' directive. The weather held for the first few days of the voyage, until a raging storm forced the fleet to find a sheltered cove along the coast, and several of the ships were damaged. This was the only time they saw Caesar, when he came on deck after the storm abated, summoned by Tiberius Claudius Nero who, while he was unhappy about it, had proven to be competent in nautical matters for a Roman, and had been appointed as the chief *Navarch*, although it was essentially a ceremonial post since none of the experienced *navarchae* would allow him to actually serve as master of their respective vessel. Most of the stricken craft sustained the damage when their anchors slipped and were driven up onto the beach, although none of the crews had sustained losses. Only Apollodorus had been with Caesar for his two expeditions to Britannia, where both times weather had threatened the army because of damage done to the fleet. Thankfully, the losses were minor, comparatively speaking, and Caesar listened as each of the *navarchae* of the damaged ships told him the extent of the damage, what was needed for repairs, and whether those repairs could be effected onshore. The other men who were fellow passengers stood nearby, pretending that they were interested more in what the *navarchae* were saying than in surreptitiously examining their general, who was studiously ignoring them staring at him.

Once they were through, Caesar considered for a moment, then announced, "We aren't going to wait. I will have the other *navarchae* give you whatever materials they can spare. You will wait until every ship has been repaired, then you will follow us. However, we need to transfer the cargo from your ship," he indicated one of the *navarchae,* then turned to a second, "and your ship, because we may need it immediately after we arrive in Bharuch."

On its surface, this was a simple enough order, but what Teispes, who was one of the interested observers, noticed was how Caesar knew immediately what cargo was on each of the damaged ships, without consulting Apollodorus, who was standing there with several tablets in his hand, and more in his bag slung over his shoulder which, Teispes assumed, contained that information. And, the Parthian silently agreed, Caesar was right to be concerned, and how that cargo was so valuable that it couldn't be allowed to lag behind, given how they were returning to the unknown. While straightforward, the transfer of that cargo between the ships being repaired and those taking that cargo aboard required another full day of delay. Finally, the fleet resumed its voyage, slowly but inexorably returning Caesar to Bharuch and whatever waited for him there.

By the time a month had elapsed after the slaughter of the two

Roman Legions, Abhiraka could no longer postpone his decision, nor could he deny that, for reasons he couldn't fathom, the Romans hadn't sortied from Bharuch in search of vengeance. Although he acknowledged the possibility that the loss of two of their vaunted Legions had shaken the Romans, he refused to accept the idea that it was sufficient to keep them behind the walls of his city. Regardless of the cause, he finally gave in to the increasingly vigorous importuning from his subordinate officers, Ranjeet in particular, who had been agitating for the previous two weeks that Abhiraka and his army had to take steps to force the Romans out into the countryside. As necessary as it was, giving the order to send groups of men out into the surrounding area to begin laying waste to the fields that, in other times, had provided all of his subjects with the food they put on their tables had put the king into a horrible temper. Oddly enough, only Puddapandyan had seemed to understand Abhiraka's torment, and despite warning himself not to be taken in by the older king, Abhiraka had been grateful for the support.

"Who else but another king can understand the agony that comes from ordering the destruction of the very things that feed all of your people?" Puddapandyan had asked, the night Abhiraka had given the order.

The Pandyan king had foregone the pleasure of one of his women, who were still accompanying the army, despite Abhiraka's strong suggestion that they should remain in Kalliena, and the two men were alone in Abhiraka's tent. Also going against his normal inclinations, Abhiraka was sipping *sura* from a cup, and he was on his third by this point.

Sighing, he answered Puddapandyan honestly, "I confess that I am surprised at how much this bothers me. Oh," he waved his hand, forgetting that it was the one holding the cup, sending the sweet but potent liquid sloshing out onto the carpets that served as the floor, "I know that it is necessary, and I know that I should have ordered it earlier." He paused, frowning down into the cup. "Still, it is much harder than I thought it would be."

Puddapandyan said nothing to this, nodding understandingly, but while he was genuinely sympathetic to Abhiraka's plight, his mind was consumed more by the setback he had personally suffered. It was, he reflected, even as he pretended to listen, such an absurd thing, yet it posed a very real problem, one that he had been thinking about every waking moment but still had no idea how to overcome. He hadn't been surprised when Abhiraka had balked at sharing the thousands of iron chain mail shirts stripped from the dead Romans, but neither had he accepted Abhiraka's initially curt refusal. Like a slow drip of water on soft rock, Puddapandyan had persisted, taking every opportunity to work into their exchanges that, as allies, and since Abhiraka was relying on his men and animals, it was only just that the King of Bharuch share in the largesse provided by their surprising but total victory. He held no illusions that, when Abhiraka had finally acquiesced, it wasn't more out of exasperation and being tired of hearing about it, but that didn't matter to the wily Pandyan. And, at first, he was certain that he had won a great victory, one that would perhaps be recognized later as the most important first step towards achieving his own ambitions, although he was aware that he wouldn't live to see them all come to fruition. No, that would fall to Nedunj or perhaps even Nedunj's heir, but this might have been the first, crucial step, except for the one thing that had never occurred to him might happen. The day after Abhiraka had agreed to share the mail shirts, Puddapandyan ordered his officers to begin distribution immediately, and the Pandyans had eagerly crowded around the wagons, excited at the prospect that they would be protected to a degree that had never seemed possible before, exchanging their hardened leather vests that only had either pieces or rings of iron sewn onto them with actual chain mail shirts. That sense of anticipation had lasted only as long as the first men, with help, had the shirts dropped onto their shoulders, whereupon several of them instantly collapsed to the ground from the weight. If that had been all that happened, it would have made for an amusing tale later, but it quickly became apparent that the men of the Pandyan infantry were completely unsuited to be attired in this manner. It was true that, after some struggles, men had climbed back to their feet, and some of them even began moving about, making stabbing motions while holding their spear, but fairly quickly, another problem became apparent.

Puddapandyan's soldiers went into battle carrying a wicker shield and a spear, while their heads were covered by several layers of cloth wound around their skulls, although some men used thin layers of leather in between as well to provide a modicum of protection. What they didn't wear were tunics, or any kind of covering over their torsos aside from these vests, a consequence of the oppressive heat of their kingdom, and as they quickly learned, wearing a chain mail vest on bare skin was a practical guarantee that, before they had marched a mile, blood was dripping down from their upper bodies, staining the cotton trousers they wore. Several men attempted to solve the problem by wearing both their leather vests and the mail, but the combination of the two was not only heavier than mail alone, it also robbed them of the flexibility and freedom of movement that just mail provided. Even this could have been dealt with, although not when they were in the middle of the kingdom of Bharuch, far away from any merchant with the capability and capacity to supply cotton tunics. What proved to Puddapandyan that, for the foreseeable future and definitely for this campaign, his men couldn't make use of the Roman armor was how, one after another, those men who did persevere through the pain of having layers of skin rubbed off collapsed because they had become overheated. Even for men who had lived their entire lives in this climate, they were so unaccustomed to the extra heat created by iron soaking up the rays of the sun, with no protective barrier between their flesh and their protection, that it had taken less than three miles on the march for Puddapandyan to accept defeat. Consequently, if and when these Romans sortied out from Bharuch, while Abhiraka's troops, who had been accustomed to wearing armor even if it was made of bronze, adapted to the heavier but more supple chain mail and would therefore be protected, Puddapandyan's troops would have to rely on speed and agility to prevail against the Legions.

For his part, Abhiraka had immediately seen his fellow king's error in thinking that his men could simply don iron chain mail, with not even a layer of cloth in between bare flesh and metal, but despite knowing that it was in his best interests to point this out to the Pandyan, he had remained silent. However, he was also as ignorant as Puddapandyan about one important point; because of the heavier weight of iron mail, long before Caesar and his army had made their presence known in India, Romans had determined that, by wearing a waist belt, then bunching the mail above the belt, it dramatically reduced the perceived weight for the man wearing it. It was certainly a small detail, but it was an important one, and when Abhiraka, his officers, and his fellow king had surveyed the carnage after their victory, while they had all seen the combination belt and harness that every Legionary wore, they had all thought the same thing; that belt was simply there as a convenient method to attach a sheath for their swords, along with a dagger, and to provide a spot from which to hang things like a coin purse. It never occurred to any of them that there might be another purpose, and the end result was that, whenever the men of Bharuch and Pandya finally did go into battle against Rome, only those of Bharuch would have the same kind of protection as the Legions they were facing.

R.W. Peake

The first columns of smoke that were visible from the walls of Bharuch appeared six weeks after the Romans learned of the loss of the 7th and 11th Legions. By the end of the first day they were spotted, the sentries on the walls, belonging to the 6th Legion on this day, counted more than a dozen of them, extending across their right front quarter. By the end of the second day, those columns had been replaced by even more of them, but now they encompassed the expanse across their direct front, although on this day, it was the turn of the men of the 28th to stand watch on the walls. It wasn't until late afternoon of that day that Pollio called for a meeting of the Primi Pili. When they arrived, the more astute among them noticed that Pullus and Spurius were already present, but they were wise enough not to make mention of it.

"No doubt," Pollio began once they were all assembled, "you've all either seen for yourself, or you've heard about the smoke to the south. And," he added, "I won't insult you by telling you what you undoubtedly already know, that this can only mean one thing. King Abhiraka is on the march, and he's getting close to the city." He paused long enough to ensure that there were no dissenters, then he continued, "And he is undoubtedly doing what we would do when we wanted to force a defending army to face us, razing the countryside and destroying our food supply." Again, he didn't wait for a response, indicating Volusenus as he asked, "What's our situation as far as our food supply? How badly hurt will we be if they destroy most of the crops?"

Volusenus looked unhappy, but he didn't hesitate to reply as he consulted a tablet in front of him, "As it stands, we have enough in stores to feed the army for three months before we need to replenish our supplies, either from Parthia or from the farms here in Bharuch."

This came as no surprise, since this had been Caesar's standard cushion, but that was for the army alone, and Pollio asked, "And if we're forced to share those supplies with the people in the city?"

"No more than two weeks," Volusenus responded flatly, clearly expecting the question, although he did allow, "unless we put both us and them on half rations, then we can probably squeeze another week. But," the quartermaster held up a hand, "there may be some good news. Apparently, along with constructing the canal, King Abhiraka managed to gather more rice than the royal warehouses normally carry." Just by the manner in which he said this, Pullus and his counterparts understood that, while this would appear to be good news on its face, there was something about it that caused Volusenus to look grim. They learned why when he continued, "The problem is that we don't know exactly where that extra food is. We've searched in all the likely places, in the warehouses and storage rooms of the various merchants. We even searched those merchants whose normal business isn't with food of any kind, like the cloth businesses, the tanneries, that sort of thing. But," he concluded with a shake of his head, "we haven't been able to find where it's hidden."

The words were barely out of Volusenus' mouth before Pullus understood what would be happening, and as he expected, all heads turned towards him, although it was left to Pollio to speak the words. "You need to talk to the queen, Pullus. See if you can find out what she knows about this. And," his voice hardened, "tell her that if we're forced to go house to house to search for any hidden stores, it's inevitable that there will be…incidents with her subjects."

Pullus knew he had no choice, so his only response was a curt nod, which Hirtius seemed inclined to take exception to, but as he was opening his mouth, it was Balbinus who intervened, mainly because he didn't want to hear what was likely to transpire between the two. "So, while we're trying to find this extra food, if," he added, "it actually exists, what are our orders? Are we still supposed to stay here and just watch as those bastards lay waste to everything?"

"Do you want to march out of this city with only a few crates of naphtha?" Pollio countered immediately, and while Balbinus didn't respond verbally, his expression was such that the Legate nodded and said, "Neither do I, Balbinus."

The meeting ended a few moments later, and once more, Titus Pullus felt the burden of the expectations of not just his superiors, but all of the men who marched under the standards, and he wondered if this would prove to be one demand too many for the Queen of Bharuch.

"Even if I knew, I would not tell you, Centurion. Surely that does not surprise you."

It took an effort on Pullus' part not to handle this situation in the manner to which he was accustomed, by bellowing at the recalcitrant queen while using his size to physically intimidate her, and as exasperated as he was, there was a part of him that also recognized the joy that this would bring Scribonius and Balbus if they were present, watching this tiny woman thwart the will of Titus Pullus.

Biting down on the inside of his cheek, hard, was a habit that Pullus had developed as a warning to himself that he needed to curb his temper, but despite his best attempts to hide it, Hyppolita knew

Pullus well enough by this point to hear his barely concealed frustration and the anger that was just beneath it.

"Your Highness, you know by now how this will go. Without your help and information, we're going to be forced to take steps that, frankly, neither of us want," he began; he was unprepared for the derisive snort from Hyppolita.

"Surely you do not expect me to believe that you are worried about the well-being of *my* subjects, Centurion."

Pullus didn't reply immediately, staring down at her for a long moment before he finally answered, "Honestly, Your Highness, whether you believe me or not doesn't concern me. What *does* concern me is not putting my men in a position where their dreams are haunted by what they might be forced to do because of your lack of cooperation. So please stop acting like a petulant child."

All the color drained from Hyppolita's face, her mouth dropping open, while Pullus' thought was that if he had slapped her that she probably would have reacted the same way, but he shoved down the stab of guilt he felt, reminding himself that, whether she believed him or not wasn't what mattered, what did was the result. Pullus was more right than he knew, because Hyppolita's immediate thought was, this must be what it feels like to be struck by someone. That the virtual blow came from someone about whom her feelings had become hopelessly tangled made it even worse, yet also like Pullus, she forced herself to maintain her composure, and more than that, acknowledge that the Roman was speaking the truth, however harsh and unpleasant to hear.

"Centurion, where did you hear about this extra food?" she asked, seemingly out of nothing more than idle curiosity, but she was rewarded by Pullus' sudden frown.

"That I don't know," he admitted.

"Would you like me to tell you?" she queried, meeting Pullus' suspicious gaze with a level one of her own.

"Of course I would," he snapped.

Hyppolita proceeded to give Pullus a half-dozen names, then said, "Go and speak to these merchants. They will confirm what I am about to tell you now." She paused for a breath before saying, "There is no extra supply of foodstuffs, Centurion, and there never were. That is a…" She cocked her head as she tried to use another word than "lie." "…deception that my husband engaged in, in order to bolster the morale of the people of the city. And he paid those men whose names I just gave you to spread this deception among our subjects."

Naturally, Pullus was listening and watching Hyppolita intently as she spoke, but despite his desire that she was being deceitful, deep within himself, he was certain she was speaking the truth.

Once she was finished, Pullus said tersely, "I'm going to go and have these men questioned."

Ignoring what had become their normal routine, Pullus didn't bow and wait for Hyppolita to respond, instead spinning about and stalking out of the room, leaving an equally angry and baffled queen in his wake. What she had no way of knowing was that, while Pullus was certainly irritated with her for her delay tactics, he was more concerned with the larger meaning if she was telling the truth, although she might have felt better knowing that he believed her.

"She was telling the truth," Pollio muttered the next day at another meeting, a couple heartbeats after finishing the last of the four tablets he had read. Tossing it on the desk in disgust, he said, "Two of the men she mentioned are dead, but the stories of the other four are all essentially the same. Abhiraka paid them to spread tales of a hidden supply of food that would sustain the city for an extra three months."

While Pullus wasn't surprised, it was only because he had been forewarned by his conversation with the queen, but he shared the disappointment of his fellow Primi Pili.

"We may not have any choice, then," Batius of the Alaudae had to speak up over the muttering from the other Primi Pili. "We can't allow that *cunnus* to roam the countryside like this."

"I know," Pollio sighed.

A heavy silence descended on the room, but it wasn't because there was any disagreement. It was thanks to that quiet that they all heard the pounding footsteps slapping the tiled floor outside of the office, all of them turning in time to see the door burst open, without the customary knock. Standing in the doorway was one of the *Praetorium* clerks who worked in the office on the first floor, although he couldn't speak immediately because he was panting for breath, prompting Pollio to snap at the man to speak.

"The Centurion of the guard Cohort on the southern wall sent a runner, Master! There are ships sailing up the Narmada!"

Pollio's first reaction was one of irritation, and it was shared by the others; it was now a daily occurrence that ships were arriving in Bharuch, as it had been for the previous three months became once it became clear that Rome wasn't interested in interrupting the commerce that had made Bharuch as wealthy a kingdom as it was.

However, the clerk clearly saw by their reaction that they had misunderstood.

"No, sir, it's not a merchant fleet. It's a Roman *quinquereme*, and there are *hundreds* of ships..."

If he said anything else, it was drowned out by the sudden uproar, and he was forced to leap aside as a room full of hard-bitten Centurions behaved as if they were youngsters who had just been told their father had returned from a long trip. Not surprisingly, Pullus was the first to actually exit into the larger room, using his size and bulk to do so, whereupon he led the rush out of the *Praetorium*, heading for the docks.

Caesar was acutely aware that, as they rounded the bend and the walls of Bharuch came into view for the first time, it was the Ides of March, now four years after that day that he always tried, unsuccessfully, to avoid thinking about. Now, as he made his way to the prow of his flagship, draped in his *paludamentum*, garland of ivy, and holding the ceremonial baton that pronounced his office as Dictator for Life, he was as nervous as he could ever remember being. He had been gone from his army for almost seven months, and his last dispatch from Pollio had been more than two months earlier, just before he had departed for Merv. That he had not sent a reply was unusual, especially for Caesar, but it wasn't until after he returned from dealing with Lepidus that he realized that, for the first time in his life, he hadn't been certain that he would be successful, or if he would even return. For all his talents, like all men, Gaius Julius Caesar had a blind spot, and in his case, it came from a lack of introspection, but he was dimly aware that this pessimistic view of his situation would have been unthinkable before the attempt on his life. Now, despite the string of successes he had achieved in Parthia, and his initial victories at Pattala and Bharuch, Caesar never forgot that the reason he departed so abruptly was because he had overestimated his control over his Legions, and their spontaneous uprising had shaken him almost as badly as the assassination attempt by men he thought of as friends, or in the case of Marcus Junius Brutus, something deeper. Now, despite his outward calm, surrounded by bodyguards and the officers who had left with him, as the walls loomed larger with every sweep of the oars, he tried to discern what kind of reception he would receive, staring intently at the ramparts, where he could make out the figures of men standing, presumably doing the same thing he was doing. By the time he could make out individual figures, he saw the southern gates open and a party of men emerge from inside the city, and despite his nervousness, his lips curved upward at the sight of one man who towered over the others.

"You can see Pullus from a half-mile off."

Caesar didn't need to turn to see who spoke, recognizing Gundomir's heavily accented Latin.

"Yes, you can," he agreed; what he didn't mention were the emotions that seeing the large Centurion stirred in him, his mind immediately going back to Hispania, and a raw, immensely strong *tiro* who was credited by none other than Gaius Crastinus, future Primus Pilus of the Equestrians, for saving two Centuries of the Second Cohort, back when Crastinus had been the Secundus Pilus Prior.

From that moment, Caesar had taken a special interest in Pullus, seeing in him more than just a brutally strong youth with a natural talent for killing the enemies of Rome, and that attention had been rewarded by a devotion to Caesar that had caused Pullus to demonstrate that loyalty in a most dramatic fashion at Pharsalus, when he almost struck down his close comrade and childhood friend Vibius Domitius, one of the most vocal men when the 10th had finally had enough and refused to march another step in pursuit of Pompeius Magnus. While he never had uttered a word about this event publicly, Caesar understood he had erred by asking too much of his men, a mistake that he had undoubtedly repeated in Bharuch. However, just seeing Pullus, along with the other Primi Pili, all of them now gathered on the dock, ignited in him a flare of hope. At least, he thought wryly, there's not a mob of angry rankers holding staves waiting for me. In one way, the last furlong was agonizingly slow, as the *navarch* of Caesar's flagship called out the orders to maneuver alongside, expertly guiding the huge ship so that it simply glided to a stop alongside the dock, where men were waiting to accept the ropes tossed by the crew. Within a matter of heartbeats, the vessel was secured, and a half-dozen heartbeats later, the gangplank was in place, which Caesar unhesitatingly strode down to reach the dock, where Pollio, Hirtius, and Volusenus were standing side by side, with the Primi Pili arranged behind them, and it was impossible for Caesar not to look Pullus in the eyes first as he towered over Pollio immediately in front of him. He looks tired, Caesar thought, wondering what Pullus was seeing in his own countenance and demeanor and whether he would like the Primus Pilus' answer if he asked. Naturally, he did not, if only because he was required to return the salute offered by Pollio, other men copying with a precision with which Caesar could find no fault, not that he would have mentioned it given the circumstances. He returned the salute as crisply as it was offered, but then before Pollio could speak, Caesar stepped closer to offer his arm, along with Caesar's Smile, Pollio accepting the arm and returning the smile, although the latter was shared by the others as well.

"*Salve,* Asinius," Caesar said, then added lightly, "I suppose we have some matters to discuss."

As he intended, the manner in which he said this caused everyone who heard him erupt in laughter at what was, by any measure, a massive understatement.

"Yes, Caesar," Pollio laughingly agreed, then stood aside in a signal for the men behind him to step to either side of the dock, "you could say that."

And with that, Caesar returned to Bharuch. As Pullus and his comrades followed behind, there were only muttered snatches of talk, mainly because they all were straining to overhear Caesar and Pollio chatting, but they were quickly disappointed when nothing of consequence was mentioned.

"Who cares about the fucking voyage?" Spurius murmured so that only Pullus could hear. "What's his plan? What are we going to be doing?"

Pullus implicitly understood that what Spurius was really asking was, "Are we leaving India?", yet he felt reasonably certain that they wouldn't be doing that. However, if Spurius had known that Pullus also believed that the men of the army would not only not resist this if it turned out to be true, they would actually welcome it, the Primus Pilus of the 3rd probably would have thought that Pullus had gone mad from the heat.

All Pullus offered, though, was a vague, "I suspect we'll be finding out soon enough one way or another."

If Caesar had been concerned about the reception he would receive, it was nothing compared to his dismayed shock when Pollio, in the presence of the other officers, informed their general of the fate of the 7th and 11th Legions. In fact, afterward, Caesar was thankful that he had heeded Pollio's suggestion to take a seat, albeit behind the desk that Pollio had been occupying for months, or he would have staggered and probably collapsed. Dropping his head, he covered his face with his hands so that his officers couldn't see, but they clearly heard the muffled sounds that told them Caesar was deeply affected, causing them to shift uncomfortably as they glanced at each other, wondering if someone should say something. Fortunately, this only lasted a span of a handful of heartbeats, but while his cheeks shined from the tears he had just shed, in every other respect, when he lifted his head, Caesar was Caesar.

"What do we know about how it happened?" he asked Pollio, and the Legate, who had been dreading the moment, fumbled for the wax tablet that was half-full.

"Not that much, unfortunately," he admitted, but before Caesar could comment, he consulted the tablet. "From what we've gathered, the enemy somehow managed to destroy the wagon carrying the naphtha."

"Wagon?" Caesar interrupted, his eyes narrowing. "Why were two Legions traveling with only one wagon of naphtha? Each Legion should have two wagons at least!"

Caesar instantly saw by the reaction, not just of Pollio and Hirtius, who was seated next to the senior Legate, but by the Primi Pili, that he had missed something.

It took another heartbeat for him to realize that they had as well, and before Pollio could respond, he asked, "Did you not get the shipment of naphtha that I ordered sent as soon as I arrived in Parthia?"

He got his answer from their reaction, and once more, Caesar felt like covering his face with his hands, but he didn't; one emotional display in front of others was all that he would indulge in, and the next one would take place in private.

"No, Caesar, we didn't," Pollio confirmed. "In fact, this was the fourth time we sent two Legions out into the kingdom, and they've all had to share the same wagon."

As devastating as this was to hear, Caesar also understood that dwelling on what occurred without offering any positive news was counterproductive, so he began with, "The good news is that those days are over. I brought enough stocks to not only replenish the supply that we sailed here with, but half that again. So," he offered them a grim smile, "when we march again, that won't be a worry."

Pollio decided that informing Caesar of their suspicions that, for reasons they would likely never know, Atartinus, Mus, or both of the Primi Pili had deemed that it was unnecessary to construct a normal marching camp could wait for them to speak in private. Of all the issues arising from the loss of the 7th and 11th, this had proven to be the most inflammatory, not just with the other Primi Pili, but in the ranks, evenly dividing the army, one half of them refusing to believe that two experienced Primi Pili would make such an egregious error, the other arguing that it was the only explanation for such a resounding defeat.

To forestall this, Pollio got up and walked over the wall where a map of the region had been hung and, with every successive foray, had been filled in. Because of the sensitive nature of the information, and the presence of citizens of Bharuch who sought an audience with the Praetor concerning some civil matter, it was covered with a cloth. Pollio took it off, picking up the stick that was used as a pointer, and Caesar stood and walked to stand beside him, immediately impressed by what he saw.

"As you can see, we know quite a bit more than we did when…" Suddenly, Pollio was unsure how to characterize it, which Caesar recognized and said softly, "When I left, Asinius. You can say it."

"Yes, sir," Pollio nodded, relieved that he didn't have to watch his words. "As I was saying, while it's certainly not complete," he indicated a blank area in the eastern part of the map that marked the interior of Bharuch, "we do know that there are two main routes south. This," he moved the pointer to indicate a round dot, next to which was writing, "is a town called Kalliena, which marks the southernmost extent of this kingdom. It sits on the Goaris River, as it's called by the locals. It is a decent-sized town; we estimate a population of between seven and ten thousand inhabitants." He paused, trying to determine the best way to continue, settling on resuming with a flat recitation of facts. "Primi Pili Atartinus and Mus were actually marching to Kalliena, under my orders to enter the town for the first time."

"First time?" Caesar echoed, frowning down at Pollio as he asked, "How many of these forays had gone out into the kingdom?"

"This was the fourth," Pollio answered, preparing himself for what came next, which was Caesar asking, "And why didn't the Legions that were there earlier enter the town?"

"This was actually only the second patrol that reached all the way to Kalliena," Pollio explained. "The first was with Primi Pili Pullus and Felix, which was the first we sent out, and we wanted more information before we did anything with the town." Before Caesar could say anything, he moved the pointer to the series of hatch marks that the Romans used to represent hills and mountains, then swept the point down from top to bottom as he went on, "There is a line that are more than hills but not quite mountains that separates the coast from the interior. We found two routes that originate here," he pointed to a small circle on the coast, then moved it to one lower down, "and here that are suitable for the army to march inland.

However," Pollio lowered the pointer, and offered Caesar an apologetic look, "we haven't been as fortunate in learning anything from the people of this kingdom who live out in the countryside."

"Are they refusing to cooperate?" Caesar asked, but Pollio shook his head.

"No, it's not that," he replied. "It's two things, really. The first problem is that we still only have one man who can communicate to any degree of fluency with the lowborn natives, none of whom speak a word of Greek. The second," he sighed, "is that even when we do communicate with them, these people know astonishingly little about anything more than a day's walk from where they're living."

The mention of communication did remind Caesar of something, but first he asked, "What about Achaemenes?" Before Pollio could offer a reply, Caesar's mind immediately worked the problem out, saying slowly as he thought through it, "If Achaemenes is the only man who can communicate with the natives, that must mean he had to go out with all four patrols. Which means..."

Pollio quickly caught on, and he stopped Caesar with a shake of his head, "No, Caesar. We didn't lose Achaemenes. You're right that he was going out with every patrol, but he wasn't with the 7th and 11th in their camp because he was with the one *turmae* of cavalry that were out scouting when the attack came." While this was good news, it also seemed to Pollio an appropriate time to mention, "Speaking of being stretched thin Caesar, we have more men on the sick list than we ever had in Parthia. There's something about the climate that seems to cause men to come down with agues more often than we're used to. Although," he added, feeling it necessary to inject some optimism every opportunity, "thanks to Pullus, we've learned some things we can do to at least partially alleviate the effects of the heat. Which," before he could stop himself, Pollio found himself chiding Caesar, "you've missed, Caesar. There are no real seasons here, so it didn't cool down during the winter. It only rained more."

Under other circumstances, Caesar wouldn't have tolerated a rebuke like this from a subordinate, however veiled it was, and he did feel a surge of irritation, but, unlike Pollio, he did manage to stop himself from reminding Pollio that, even with his absence, he still was in command.

Instead, he accepted Pollio's words, but pointedly returned his attention to the map as he said, "We can discuss these matters later, Asinius. First, I need to know more about Bharuch."

Pollio's briefing continued for the next third of a watch, with each of the Centurions present offering an answer to one of Caesar's questions, although the six Primi Pili who had led their Legions out of the city were called on more frequently. Once Caesar decided he had learned everything possible from his officers, he was supremely unsatisfied; there was still far more he didn't know than he did. Not surprisingly, of the Centurions, Pullus was called on more by Caesar than any other, yet with every call of his name by the Dictator, Pullus' anxiety grew, certain that he knew what was coming.

Despite this, he still felt his stomach flip when Caesar concluded the meeting, but as the Centurions were filing out, called out, "Stay here and attend to me, Pullus. There are things we need to talk about."

Of course, Pullus obeyed, trying to maintain a demeanor that didn't betray his feelings about what he was certain was about to happen, that Caesar would be paying a visit to the Queen of Bharuch. The fact that Caesar had told him more times than he could count how easy it was for others to read Pullus' thoughts through his expression and demeanor didn't help, and it only made Pullus more certain that Caesar would discern that Titus Pullus was in love with a foreign queen.

"Your Highness, I am happy to see that you are well and comfortable, and I apologize for my absence. There were pressing matters that I had to attend to in Parthia."

"Yes," Hyppolita responded dryly, "I can only imagine the difficulties that come from conquering so many other nations. It must be very hard for you."

Caesar took the jibe equably enough, although he did wish that the woman wasn't wearing that full veil that obscured even her eyes; it was quite frustrating trying to gauge an opponent when their features weren't visible, yet he also knew that this was exactly why the queen had chosen to wear it. During their walk to the palace, Caesar had pressed Pullus for a number of details, among which was the revelation that Pullus was the only Roman who had seen Hyppolita's features, something that he intended to learn more about later.

"Am I correct in understanding that you will only deal with Primus Pilus Pullus? Has he seen to your needs?" Caesar asked this with a smile, but Hyppolita wasn't fooled.

"I have chosen to communicate through the Centurion for a number of reasons, some of them I will not divulge. But," her head moved slightly, and Pullus knew she was looking at him, causing him to shift uncomfortably, "what I will tell you, Dictator, is that Centurion Pullus has behaved honorably. And," she modified her tone in a way that sent an unmistakable message, "he has proven to be the most trustworthy of all of you Romans with whom I have had contact from the moment you...arrived."

This, as she intended, pierced Caesar's equanimity, clearly interpreting her words to include him as well.

"While I am happy to hear how well you've been treated by one of my officers," he snapped, "I can assure you that every other officer of Rome would have behaved in the same manner."

"Perhaps," Hyppolita replied indifferently, and despite his own discomfort, Pullus had to smother a grin at the sight of Caesar who, exactly like the last time the two had spoken, was clearly put on the back foot.

Caesar was as acutely aware that this impertinent woman was essentially resuming where she had left off the day the city fell, but back then, Caesar had been certain that his awkwardness had been due to the larger situation, with an army essentially mutinying even as the two were speaking. Yet, here he was, in the same position he had been, trying to regain his equilibrium and assert a level of control of at least this conversation.

"Your Highness," Caesar resumed, "now that I am back, I am afraid that your insistence on working only through the Primus Pilus here is not acceptable. When I request an audience, I expect it to be granted."

"Then do not call it a request, Dictator," Hyppolita replied, and while it was subtle, Pullus was experienced enough with her to hear the anger. "Call it what it is, a demand, since a request implies that I have a choice in the matter."

"Very well," Caesar answered her with the same indifferent tone she had used a moment earlier. "When I call on you," he repeated, "you will see me."

"Or what?" Hyppolita rose from her seat, and one didn't need to know the queen to hear the anger there now. "You will force yourself on me, Dictator? Is that it?" Before Caesar could reply, she said icily, "You will find that I am not as pliable as your...consort, Cleopatra, Caesar. Whether we may be related or not, I am no Ptolemy. I am Hyppolita, Queen of Bharuch, and while you may force your way into my presence, you may rest assured that *if* I choose to converse with you, you also may rest assured that any assistance or information I may offer is my choice as well, but that is *all* you will receive from me."

It hadn't occurred to Caesar that Hyppolita might have misconstrued his reason for being in her presence, and he felt the flush rising up his neck as he held out a hand in a placating gesture.

"Your Highness, I assure you that I have no intention of forcing myself upon you in a physical manner," Caesar said earnestly. "And while I will respect your wishes for as little contact with us as possible, all I am saying is that, if I come to the palace, it will be for a matter of utmost importance."

There was a silence where, even from where he was standing, Pullus could hear that Hyppolita's breathing was harsh and uneven, while Caesar stood there looking directly at her, understanding that she needed to be the next one to speak.

"Very well," she finally spoke, and Pullus realized he had been holding his breath in anticipation for what might be coming. "I understand and I will of course agree to see you knowing that it will be important." She hesitated for a heartbeat, then added, "And I apologize for insulting you, Dictator. I am afraid that being restrained as I have been these last few weeks has been trying on me. And," she indicated the line of women lining the wall behind her who, like Pullus had been silent witnesses, although like their queen, they were also veiled, "for my ladies as well."

Caesar's expression became puzzled, and he glanced over at Pullus with a frown as he said, "I'm not sure I understand, Your Highness, when you say that you have been confined recently?"

Pullus stifled a groan, made more difficult when Hyppolita clearly turned to look at him, and like Caesar, although for different reasons, he cursed himself for not explaining to Caesar what had been taking place up until the news of Abhiraka's victory.

Aloud, he said only, "I'll explain later, sir."

Caesar's eyes narrowed, and Pullus braced himself for the Dictator to press the issue, but after a heartbeat, he turned back to Hyppolita.

"Your Highness, since I have just arrived here, there are still several things that require my attention. However, may I call on you tomorrow?"

Hyppolita would never admit it, but she did appreciate Caesar's pretense that she had a choice, and she gave a grave bow of her head and played along.

"Of course, Dictator. Until then."

Without waiting, Hyppolita turned and, because of her floor-length gown, glided out of the room, followed by her ladies, some of whom did turn in Caesar's direction. Pullus was certain he knew which of the queen's ladies would be glaring at his general right now, and before he could stop himself, he chuckled, although he immediately covered it with a cough, which didn't fool Caesar in the slightest, giving the Primus Pilus a glare of his own. Once the room was empty, he turned and stalked out the door, but it wasn't until they were outside that he turned on Pullus.

"Pullus, I think you'd better explain to me what's been going on while I was gone."

"If," Abhiraka asked his officers, "we were to retake Bharuch, how would we go about doing it?"

Ranjeet stopped chewing the spoonful of saffron rice he had just shoved into his mouth, thinking for a moment.

Finally, he said, "Since we had to abandon our artillery when we left the city, and," he glanced over at Puddapandyan, trying to hide his irritation, "since His Highness wouldn't allow us to bring any of his, we can't try to breach the walls."

"As I explained before," the Pandyan king interjected with barely suppressed impatience, "since I have given your king the bulk of my elephants, I could not afford to strip my defenses any further. After all," he turned to look directly at Abhiraka, "I have more than my subjects to think about, do I not, Abhiraka? Now that my daughter-in-law has been joined by your other children, I have a responsibility not just to my people, but to your family. And there are threats to my kingdom other than Rome."

Abhiraka knew that he couldn't argue, even if he was disposed to do so, and he gestured to Ranjeet to desist, saying tiredly, "Since we're not going to have artillery, there's no point in talking about not having it. So," his tone sharpened slightly in a warning, "how can we retake our city, Ranjeet?"

"Ladders," Ranjeet answered immediately. "That is really the only way. King Puddapandyan's archers," he nodded at the Pandyan, which Abhiraka understood would be the closest to an apology he was willing to give, "would have to shower the ramparts with missiles while we advance." Turning to Puddapandyan, Ranjeet asked him directly, "How many arrows does each man marching with us carry?"

"One hundred," Puddapandyan answered.

"That's not enough," Ranjeet said flatly. "You would need double that." Puddapandyan opened his mouth to object, but Ranjeet went on, "And the only men capable of carrying out the assault are ours, my King. The Pandyan infantry does not have the skill, and we saw what happened when we gave them armor."

This made the Pandyan king furious, but this time, he didn't try to argue the point, because it was a truth he had witnessed with his own eyes, so he had to settle for glaring at Ranjeet, which didn't impress Abhiraka's lieutenant in the slightest.

"To have any hope," Ranjeet continued, "we'll have to attack all four walls. If we concentrate on just one side of the city, they can just feed troops into the battle and whittle us down. Naturally, the elephants will be useless for that phase; the only chance we have is if we can fight our way to one of the gates and open it so that the elephants can enter the city. But," he finished grimly, "I know I don't have to tell you that unleashing elephants inside the city walls will slaughter the defenders...and our own people."

"I know," Abhiraka answered grimly. He stared at the fire for a long moment, then added quietly, "I think of little else, my friend." Quite oddly, Ranjeet's demeanor didn't match either his king's, or that of Bolon and Nahapana, whose own expressions mirrored that of their king as they all envisioned a scene of slaughter and destruction that would inevitably ensue if they were successful in entering their home city astride elephants. The Bharuch king noticed this and snapped, "I'm not sure why you think this is a cause for amusement, Ranjeet!"

This did serve to wipe the grin off his subordinate's face, but there was still something there that didn't match his comrades.

"I can assure you, my King, I'm not amused. But I *do* believe that there is another way."

This, unsurprisingly, instantly changed the atmosphere inside the tent, everyone present, including the bodyguards giving Ranjeet their undivided attention; suddenly, Ranjeet seemed hesitant to speak, and the glance he gave at not only the bodyguards but the three slaves who were always hovering there, waiting for their masters to snap their fingers to demand more food or a refill.

Abhiraka, thinking he understood, commanded, "All of you, leave us. You will be summoned if you are needed."

It wasn't lost on any man sitting in this circle that both bodyguards looked directly to Puddapandyan, but their king gave a slight nod, and they were the last out of the tent, although Abhiraka saw that Ranjeet still wasn't comfortable. In the manner of people who have had a long association, the king and his commander communicated with their eyes and expressions, and Abhiraka saw that Ranjeet's concern was centered on the Pandyan king, and it was a concern that Abhiraka shared. Nevertheless, he could only offer a subtle shrug to Ranjeet, who offered his acknowledgement with an almost imperceptible nod.

He began by saying, "I know that I don't have to remind you of the circumstances of your escape from the city, Your Highness."

"No," Abhiraka answered tersely, feeling the same upsurge of anger that came every time he thought about it, although it wasn't aimed at Ranjeet. "I recall it very well. As do you two," he turned and acknowledged Bolon and Nahapana, the two men who had been his companions during that shameful episode.

"You escaped using that secret passage," Ranjeet continued. "But while it served as an exit, it can also be used as an entrance, can it not?"

This caused Abhiraka to straighten up, a range of emotions flashing across his face, but smothered so quickly that only a man like Ranjeet, or his absent wife, would have seen and interpreted. The silence stretched out for several heartbeats, but finally, the king shook his head.

"I suspect that the Romans have discovered that passageway, Ranjeet. They would have been interested in how I managed to disappear, and I can only imagine what they did to discover how it happened."

Ranjeet had anticipated this, and he countered, "Which is why we send no more than two men, Your Highness. They'll swim the river at night, then take as much time as they need to reach the outer entrance, then use the passageway to enter the city." Before Abhiraka could interject, Ranjeet hurriedly added, "And by entering the city, I mean that their only task will be to ascertain whether the entrance inside the walls has been discovered, because if it has, it will undoubtedly be under guard. If it's not?" He offered his king a smile that held nothing but the anticipation of vengeance and the infliction of pain on an enemy. "Then we have our way into the city. It's close to the southern gate, as I recall, although I haven't used it."

"It's less than two hundred paces," Abhiraka said thoughtfully, stroking his beard, which he had stopped oiling and dying its original black. He offered his tacit acceptance by asking Ranjeet, "And when would you consider doing this, Ranjeet?"

"It would have to be when there's little or no moon," his commander answered immediately, which was what Abhiraka had suspected.

"So we have to wait a bit more than two weeks," the king mused. He sighed. "Which means that during that time, we must continue laying waste to the kingdom."

"Why is that, Your Highness?" Bolon spoke for the first time, but Abhiraka turned to Ranjeet in a silent command that was understood.

"Because, Bolon, if we suddenly stop behaving as we have been behaving, it would alert the Romans that something is coming," Ranjeet explained patiently, adding grimly, "It's not pleasant, I know, and it will mean that there will be much suffering in the kingdom for the foreseeable future. But," he finished, "if it rids us of these Roman demons, then it will be worth it."

Bolon didn't like it, yet he also saw that his king was of the same mind, as were Ranjeet and Nahapana. Only Puddapandyan didn't seem distressed, but Bolon didn't trust that serpent, certain that the Pandyan king was acting purely out of self-interest; in this, he knew, his king also felt the same way.

"And, if this fails?" Abhiraka asked Ranjeet, although he was certain he knew the answer. "If the Romans are aware of that entrance? What then?"

"Then," Ranjeet answered with a shrug, "we're back to what we discussed earlier."

Suddenly turning to Puddapandyan, Abhiraka asked, "Have you received any word about the supply train?"

"No," the Pandyan king replied, while Ranjeet exchanged a surprised glance with Bolon, who was sitting across from him, which Abhiraka saw.

"I didn't tell you this, but King Puddapandyan graciously arranged for a resupply train, which will go to Kalliena, where they'll wait to be summoned." Abhiraka bowed from the waist to Puddapandyan, genuinely sincere in this gesture. "And while I don't know with any certainty, I would assume that the train will be bringing more arrows?"

"Yes," the Pandyan assured him. "Another hundred arrows per man at the very least."

Abhiraka considered for a moment, then finally decided, "I'm going to dispatch a courier to Kalliena with the order that the train is to not stop there." For the first time during the conversation, Abhiraka offered the other men a smile that could be considered optimistic. "But if all goes well, they will have come for nothing."

The King of Bharuch wasn't the only one busily engaged in an ambitious plan, and to observers, it appeared as if Caesar was his normal, energetic self, beginning the day after his arrival when, pointedly alone, he made the promised visit to Hyppolita. Who, after his departure, was both mystified and troubled, because the Roman hadn't asked her one question about her husband, or the kingdom and people of Bharuch. He seemed more interested in the neighboring kingdoms, yet although he didn't appear to be more concerned with one than another, his questions had been most pointed about the Pandyan kingdom. Almost despite herself, Hyppolita answered his questions honestly, despite suspecting that, if she did know Caesar's purpose, she wouldn't like it. Yet, in the moment, she couldn't find an obvious reason why she shouldn't do so, and it was only after he left that her disquiet grew. And, if she had known what Caesar did immediately on returning to the building that was the new *Praetorium*, that disquiet would have intensified into alarm and a fair amount of self-recrimination. Caesar began by summoning Volusenus, who, despite being a Legate like Pollio and Hirtius, had never been offered a command of an arm of the Roman army, only because he had never coveted it. Volusenus' talents lay in other areas; he was the best cartographer, not just on Caesar's staff, but in the known world, possessing a keen eye and an ability to gauge distances with a precision that even Caesar marveled at, and while he was also a superb quartermaster, it was the former talent that Caesar needed now.

"Take a Liburnian and five *triremes*," Caesar began, using the large map Pollio had unveiled the day before, running his finger down the large piece of tanned leather, "and map this area. Also, I want you to find something specific that I just learned about."

Caesar talked for the next sixth part of a watch as Volusenus struggled to keep up, relearning how nothing was ever fast enough or good enough for Caesar as he filled three wax tablets. Once Caesar was through, rather than being enlightened, Volusenus was more baffled than he could remember being in some time, another reminder of what it was often like when in Caesar's company.

"May I ask why you want this information, Caesar?" he asked cautiously, but rather than admonish him, Caesar favored him with a grin, saying only, "Of course you can, Volusenus. But that doesn't mean I'm going to tell you."

Understanding what was expected, Gaius Volusenus Quadratus saluted and said only that he would begin preparations immediately.

"I want you underway by tomorrow, Volusenus," was the last thing Caesar said to him, and fortunately, the Legate was walking out of the office so that only Pollio, who had just been summoned, saw the expression on his face.

The door barely closed when Caesar began talking to Pollio,

and sometime later, he walked—perhaps "staggered" was a better term—out of Caesar's office wearing an expression that, had he thought about it, was identical to the one Volusenus had been wearing. He, Pollio thought wryly as he descended the stairs to the ground floor, is definitely back. Despite what seemed to be an overwhelming number of tasks he had been assigned, Pollio was relieved to know that Caesar intended to address the army later that day, but at the same time, he was apprehensive at the reception he would receive. While it was certainly true that tempers had cooled, and the grumbling among the ranks was almost back to what passed for normal, Pollio was certain that there was an underlying anger there that, depending on what Caesar had to say, might make it boil back up again. And, considering the tasks that he had been given, the only thing that Asinius Pollio knew with any certainty was that they were most definitely not returning to Parthia.

Caesar's final meeting of the morning was with the Primi Pili, and as he had suspected would be the case, as he stood in front of his desk watching them file into the room, he saw that their shock at his sudden and unexpected appearance had worn off. Now, he thought, comes the difficult part, but in this, Caesar was almost certain he had a secret ally, and for once it was not in the form of Titus Pullus, or any of the Primi Pili. Seeing Pullus' face launched another line of thought, one that was more troubling, but in its own way, particularly given what he had in mind, could prove to be crucial to his plans. That, he told himself as the Centurions settled into what had become their spots, can wait; it would be one of the few things that, immediately afterward, Caesar would tell himself had slipped his mind.

Once he had their attention, Caesar began, "I'll be speaking to the men today at the beginning of third watch. Which," at this, he glanced over at Pullus, "I've learned is the only time when the heat is bearable, and they'll only be required to be in their tunics…their *new* tunics." Although Caesar wasn't looking directly at Pullus with this, the Centurion still felt uncomfortable, certain that his words were still aimed in his direction, but Caesar was continuing, "What I am about to tell you is not to leave this room. And," his voice turned hard and unyielding, "if that happens, I swear on Jupiter's stone that I won't stop until I find out who among you talked. Is this understood?" While some of them, like Pullus, gave him their promise verbally, some only nodded, and this wasn't good enough for Caesar, who demanded that they all articulate their vow. Only then did he continue, "This army is going to be moving soon. Not," he held up a hand to forestall any possible misunderstanding, "back to Parthia. While it's true that there was some...unrest in Parthia, that has been dealt with. Order has been restored, and the threats to stability of the province have been removed. Or," he acknowledged, "I'm confident they have been by now."

Not surprisingly, every man present had their eyes on Caesar, and he could read the avid curiosity, but while he knew it was inevitable, and in fact did want the rankers to learn part of what transpired, particularly with Lepidus and his attempt to seize power for himself, he wasn't ready for that to happen.

Instead, he continued, "You will begin preparing your men for departure immediately after I speak with them, but until then, remember what I said."

He dismissed them then, ignoring their obvious surprise and disgruntlement at such a summary end to this meeting, and as they left, Caesar did look at Pullus thoughtfully, considering whether it was better to confront what he suspected was going on now rather than put him off. Suddenly, he realized he had forgotten something that was more pressing, so he didn't call Pullus to remain behind.

"They stopped unloading the ships," Diocles informed Pullus immediately upon his return from the quest his master had sent him on. "But it's more than that. They're actually transferring some of the cargo they had already unloaded back aboard."

Pullus immediately looked over to Scribonius, who was seated next to him at the table on the open-aired veranda where they took most of their meals, taking advantage of whatever breeze there might be, but the Pilus Prior was clearly as mystified as he was. Despite Caesar's warning, it had never occurred to Pullus not to tell Scribonius, Balbus, or Diocles what was happening, however little it was, and he was equally certain that every Primus Pilus was doing the same with his most trusted comrades.

"But we're not going back to Parthia," Scribonius spoke in a musing tone, which Pullus confirmed with a shake of his head.

"Maybe," Balbus spoke up, "he's taking us back to Pattala."

"That was my thought," Pullus agreed. "But why? And why by ship?"

"Remember what the boys who were with Pollio said about that march," Balbus reminded Pullus. "It was a nightmare, and that was before they ran into those fucking elephants."

"That's true," Pullus acknowledged, somewhat abashed he'd

forgotten, yet when he glanced at Scribonius and saw his friend's frown that was as potent a sign that Scribonius was considering another alternative, it prompted Pullus to ask, "What is it, Sextus? Why doesn't that make sense to you?"

"Oh, it makes sense," Scribonius assured him, "and I can't tell you why, but I think there's something else going on here." Suddenly, he looked at Pullus as he asked, "What did he say again? Prepare the army to march?"

"No," Pullus answered immediately, proud that he had instantly picked up the slightly different wording than Caesar normally used. "He said prepare the army to *move*, not march."

"So it's definitely by ship, then," Scribonius nodded.

They lapsed into silence, all three sipping from their cups that, instead of *sura*, contained water, which did elicit a comment from Scribonius.

"I wonder if he brought wine with him." His wistful tone caused Pullus to chuckle, but Balbus snorted.

"Why would anyone drink wine when they can have *sura*?" he asked without expecting an answer. "That is nectar of the gods! Bacchus is a weakling compared to…"

Before he could finish, the sound of a horn cut him off, coming from the direction of the *Praetorium*. It was the *bucina*, the horn used to signal the change of watch, and it prompted the trio to stand up.

"Let's get the boys," Pullus stated needlessly, "so we can find out what Caesar's up to."

As they would learn in the very near future, nothing any man, of any Legion, had come up with as a possibility for what was coming next was even close to the reality.

It was only when they were actually assembled that any man in the Roman army realized that this was the first time when the army in its entirety had been gathered together in one place since before their capture of Bharuch. The only place that could accommodate the entire army within the walls was the palace compound, but only because the men were crammed together in a much more compact formation than normal. Instead of an arm's width between men in the ranks, the distance was half that, while the space between Centuries, Cohorts, and Legions was practically nonexistent. It did make for quite a striking visual display, especially from the second floor of the palace, where Hyppolita was peering through the slight crack between the horizontal wooden panels that served as shutters. She made sure to stand a step away from the window, and she did have to move from one window to another to find the view where she could see Caesar; that she was able to see Caesar from her first vantage point but not Pullus was something that none of her ladies, who were crowded behind her, commented about, although there were several glances between them.

The men were in their cotton tunics, which they hadn't bothered to dye red, but Caesar was attired in what Hyppolita recalled he was wearing when he had stridden up the steps of her palace, accompanied by a huge Roman who had been the most intimidating man she had ever seen. Since she wasn't wearing her veil, her ladies saw her smile, not knowing that it was at her memory of that moment, and how she had assumed that Titus Pullus was nothing more than a brute whose obvious size and strength was responsible for being allowed in the company of a man like Caesar. How wrong she had been, yet even as this recognition caused her some rueful amusement, there was a strong stab of something else as her eyes easily found Pullus, standing next to what she had learned was the standard of his Legion. I wonder if he knows I'm watching? she wondered, but almost immediately realized that this was a virtual certainty, given that Caesar was standing on the porch that he had first stood on a bit more than seven months earlier. Has it really been that long? Her thoughts were interrupted when Caesar began speaking, and within a couple of heartbeats, it took a physical effort, specifically, biting her lip, to keep her from shouting in frustration.

"He is speaking in Latin, his own tongue," she managed to say quietly, although she stamped her foot in frustration.

"Your Highness, I may be able to help." Hyppolita spun about to stare at Amodini, chagrined that she hadn't thought of her youngest, and to the consternation of the other ladies, her favorite among her attendants, who admitted, "I do not know much, but Gaius has taught me enough I might be able to give you an idea."

Nodding, Hyppolita extended her arm, beckoning to Amodini, who stepped next to her, but when she got closer to the shutters than Hyppolita, the queen restrained her.

"If you get too close, someone is likely to see us, Amodini," she explained, then gave the lady a smile, "and we wouldn't want that, would we?"

"No, Your Highness," Amodini agreed, but that was all as she began listening intently to what Caesar was saying.

A silence descended on the room, so that every one of them could clearly hear the Roman general speaking, while Hyppolita was intently studying just one man facing Caesar, having learned during their time together that Pullus was almost incapable of disguising his feelings. He, she thought with amusement, would make a horrible king, because everyone would know what he was thinking.

Finally, Amodini broke the silence by whispering, "He is saying something about why he left Bharuch those months ago. But," she shook her head, "I do not know exactly why, just that it had something to do with Parthia." Returning her attention to Caesar, she spoke haltingly, realizing that this was a more difficult endeavor than she had imagined. Suddenly, and before Amodini could say anything, Hyppolita saw Pullus stiffen even more than he already was from his position in front of his Legion, but it was his expression of concern, followed by a quick glance over his shoulder at the men behind him that gave Hyppolita a forewarning, presaged by Amodini's soft gasp. "He is speaking of what happened here, at Bharuch, when they attacked the city."

She paused, and for the first time, there was noise from outside that wasn't Caesar's voice, but the listening women didn't need to speak Latin to hear the angry muttering. This caused Hyppolita to tear her eyes from Pullus to watch how Caesar responded to the reaction of his army, and she was fascinated to see that he didn't look the least bit nervous, or even disturbed. Indeed, he didn't even raise or alter his tone, although when he extended both arms, she didn't know if he had done this earlier.

"He is saying that he…" Amodini struggled to find the right word, settling on, "…made a mistake."

"Is he apologizing?" Hyppolita asked, assuming this would be the appropriate response, but Amodini shook her head.

"No, he is speaking about something else now," she replied, frowning in concentration. Hyppolita had returned her attention to Pullus, but Amodini's sudden gasp alerted her, and she turned to see the young attendant a noticeable shade paler; it was the manner in which she avoided looking Hyppolita in the eyes that was more concerning, although she said readily enough, "He is speaking of what happened with their fellow Romans who were…" She didn't finish, but Hyppolita nodded in understanding, and Amodini continued, "He is asking them if…" Before she got another word out, there was a deafening roar from thousands of male voices, and while Hyppolita watched in a combination of fear and a dreadful fascination, she saw Titus Pullus raise both huge arms in the air, fists clenched and mouth open, adding his voice to that of the other Romans. Finally, Caesar prevailed on them to quieten down, patting the air with both hands, and resumed speaking, but he had only said a few words when he said something that Hyppolita understood.

"What is he saying about Pandya, Amodini?" She demanded.

Amodini shook her head, but it was more out of confusion, which she explained, "I...I am not certain, Your Highness. But it sounds like whatever he is planning has to do with...Pandya?"

Hyppolita froze, and it took all of her self-control not to cry out in despair, remembering her conversation with Caesar earlier. She had tried very hard to guard her tongue, yet when he began asking about Pandya, she hadn't been able to think of any reason why she should not share what she knew, thinking that it was better than giving up anything about Bharuch, her husband, or his army.

"If I hadn't heard it myself, I wouldn't have believed the old man could have done what he just did."

Pullus shook his head at Scribonius' statement, not in disagreement but with a sense of bemused wonder, because he agreed with his close friend.

"Where the fuck *is* Pandya?" Balbus grumbled, but he was slurring his words by this point, and this wasn't the first, or second time he had asked.

"We told you," Scribonius sighed. "It's the kingdom to the south, and it's obviously where the elephants that did in the 7th and 11th came from."

"How do you suppose he knew that, though?" Pullus wondered.

"I can't say that he *knows* with any certainty, but where else would they come from?" Scribonius pointed out.

It was then that Pullus recalled something that Hyppolita had mentioned during one of their walks, after they had slowly developed an awkward but unmistakable rapport, about how she worried about her children. And, he recalled, what she had been most concerned about wasn't the normal things a mother would focus on, at least one of Pullus' class. She had mentioned the Pandyan king; what was his name?

"Puddapandyan," Pullus actually said the name aloud, instantly regretting it, since Scribonius immediately sat upright.

"Puddapandyan?" Scribonius repeated, and now even Balbus was interested, although his gaze was bleary, and Pullus wondered how many cups of *sura* his second in command had consumed. "What is *that*?"

"Not what," Pullus answered. "Who. He's the King of the Pandya, but from what the queen says, he's about as trustworthy as a viper." He hesitated, wondering if he should add another detail, but immediately determined that he owed his friends everything he had learned, then added, "Hyppolita sent their two youngest children to Pandya for protection once we showed up, to join their sister there. She's married to their crown prince." Scribonius, and even Balbus, despite his state of inebriation, noticed the use of her name, but when Balbus opened his mouth to offer some jibe, Scribonius gave him a warning glare and a shake of his head, which Pullus didn't see, since he was staring into his cup. Balbus obeyed, although he returned Scribonius' look with one of his own that signaled he wasn't happy about it, while Pullus continued, "She also said that, if this Puddapandyan character offered her husband any help, it would be at a steep price. And," he went on, "it would only be because he saw an opportunity to strike at Bharuch in some way."

"So why would he want us to go after this Pudderpanda," even sober, Balbus would have butchered the name, but his drunken pronunciation caused the other two men to grin at each other, "bastard if he's an enemy of Bharuch? What is it that the Parthians say?"

"The enemy of my enemy is my friend," Scribonius supplied, but despite Balbus' inebriation, the scarred Centurion's point was a good one, and he frowned in thought before admitting, "That's a good question, Quintus."

"Ha!" Balbus hooted, slamming his hardened hand on the table with enough force to make the liquid in his friends' cups slosh out. "I have my moments!"

"Few and far between," Scribonius said dryly while lifting his cup and moving it away from the sticky puddle.

"Maybe," Pullus offered, "it's exactly what Caesar told us. Maybe we're going after the Pandya because, whether or not it was to help Abhiraka, it was that Pandyan bastard's elephants who slaughtered two of our Legions."

"I'm certain that's part of it," Scribonius agreed. They fell silent, absorbed in their own thoughts, then Scribonius suddenly sat straighter, causing both of his friends to glance at him. Pullus, seeing his friend's expression, felt a surge of anticipation, knowing what that look meant. Scribonius addressed Pullus, asking, "Didn't you say that the queen admitted that what we dug up was only a small part of the Bharuch treasury?"

"Yes," Pullus said, his excitement growing, understanding where Scribonius was heading, "and the rest of it was sent to Pandya, along with their children!"

"And we both know that the Bharuch king wouldn't drag that much money up here when he marched, nor would this Puddapandyan allow it."

"We're going to be attacking Pandya not only because they're weaker right now than Abhiraka, but they're also richer than Abhiraka. And, when all is said and done, I think as much as the men want to go at least back to Parthia, they also want revenge more."

Like Pullus, Balbus' head was nodding as Scribonius talked, but he surprised the others when he pointed out, "This is the first time we've ever lost. At least since Gergovia."

Ultimately, they came to the realization at the same time, this was probably the most potent reason why thousands of men who had been agitating for months to leave this gods forsaken place suddenly were clamoring to board ships, not to sail back to Parthia, but to yet another foreign kingdom and risk their lives again.

The change in the activity level was stunning for the inhabitants of Bharuch, and while Hyppolita was certainly somewhat insulated from all of it, it did impact her and her ladies.

"I'm afraid that I won't be able to escort you every day, Your Highness," Pullus had informed her, and as she looked up at him, she felt certain that his regret was real. "But now that Caesar has returned, he put us to work. This will probably be the last time for the next few days."

He told her this while they were actually walking on the palace grounds, passing by the garden that, whenever they did, caused them to exchange a conspiratorial smile.

"So I have gathered, Centurion," she replied. Then, in a teasing tone, she asked, "I do not suppose that you would care to tell me why?"

He glanced down at her with a grin.

"If I did, where would the surprise be in that?"

Hyppolita stopped suddenly, all traces of amusement gone. Before she said anything, she glanced over at the other ladies, and Pullus realized that this must have been prearranged, judging by the way they kept walking, their eyes down in a manner that suggested they were trying to avoid Pullus' glance. The queen watched them pass until they were a few paces away before she turned back to him.

"You are going to attack the Pandyan kingdom, are you not, Centurion? That is what Caesar intends to do?"

Before he could stifle it, Pullus uttered something between a groan and a curse, but this only served to agitate him further as he understood that his reaction was making things worse, not better.

"Why are you asking me this?" he questioned in a plaintive tone that, despite the seriousness, forced Hyppolita to fight her own urge to smile. "You know that I can't tell you, Hyppolita."

"You realize," Hyppolita replied softly, "you already did, though, do you not?"

Pullus glared down at her, exasperated as much at himself as at her. "I'm not saying another word, Your Highness."

His hope was that by using her title, she would realize that he was now speaking as a Roman Centurion, and not as…whatever he had become, a thought that she found distracting as she tried to focus on her purpose for surprising him as she had.

"Very well, Centurion." She bowed her head. "I will not ask again about your plans. However," now, she hesitated, and the anxiety she had been trying to keep within herself was impossible to miss for Pullus, "I do have a…request."

"Oh?" He looked understandably wary. "What is that?"

"Will you do whatever is in your power to protect my children, Titus?"

Just as she had, Pullus had grown to treasure these moments spent together, although they never spoke of it, but this was the first time he regretted showing her any kind of kindness, because he was acutely aware that Hyppolita was using that intimacy at this moment, and it ignited a flare of anger. Perhaps if he had looked away from her, he might have managed to treat her with the coldness that he was certain Caesar would expect from him, especially since he was aware that Caesar already had suspicions about them, but instead, he looked down and saw an anxious mother, staring up at him with imploring eyes that destroyed any chance of behaving in a manner that Caesar would approve, and even worse, the sudden memory of a sturdy boy, a face smeared with a combination of honey and snot and clutching the toy Legionary his Tata had brought him, thrust itself into his mind.

"I don't even know their names," he protested. "And how do you expect me to be able to do anything for them?"

"Because," she replied calmly, her eyes never leaving his face, "I have come to know you, Titus Pullus. And you are a remarkable man. It is easy to see why Caesar trusts a man of your…" Suddenly, she stopped, seeing his eyes narrow, understanding that she had inadvertently angered him; what was worse, she saw, was that she had hurt him.

"…A man of my lowly station?" Pullus finished for her, his

voice harsh. "Is that what you were about to say?"

She surprised him then, by admitting, "Yes, something like that. But, Titus," she reached out and for only the second time, placed her hand on his arm, "I did not mean it as any kind of insult, or in a demeaning manner, please believe that! And I am speaking the truth, Titus Pullus; you are a truly remarkable man, and that is why you are the only Roman I would even consider asking." He didn't pull his arm away, which she took as a signal, pressing, "All I am asking is that you do whatever is in your power to keep my children from coming to any harm, Titus. That is all."

Pullus stared down, not at Hyppolita, but at her hand, noticing again how white it was in contrast to his arm, and how small it looked resting on his massive forearm, frowning in thought, or so Hyppolita assumed. Finally, he gave a barely perceptible nod.

"All right, Your Highness. If there's anything I can do, I'll try to make sure that your children are kept safe."

She made no attempt to hide her relief, but the mood had been spoiled, and neither spoke as he escorted her back to the palace, standing at the bottom of the steps instead of entering the palace. He watched her as she ascended the stairs, but turned away as she reached the door, striding back towards his own quarters as he tried to think of how he could possibly honor her request, completely missing that she had stopped and stood watching him.

Chapter 6

Before the dawn of the second week after Caesar managed to win the army back over to his cause, the Primi Pili were informed that Caesar had no intention of leaving Bharuch undefended.

"I know how the men feel about giving up anything that we've taken," he had assured the Centurions. "So I'm leaving three Legions here, but while I've decided which one of them will be, I'm still thinking about the other two. Which is why I want all of you to prepare for departure."

"Can you at least tell us which one you've already decided on?" Felix asked, but Caesar shook his head, saying only, "You'll find out soon enough."

And, two days later, they learned the identity of the mystery Legion, and more importantly, that it didn't involve any of the Legions present, including the 22nd, who had come with Caesar after catching up with him when Caesar's part of the fleet had been delayed by the storm, when the *Bucinator* of the guard Cohort sounded the call that a party of some sort was approaching the city. Because the signal originated from the southern rampart, most of the Romans who heard it immediately understood that it meant that a large party of ships was approaching, and those who were near the wall and either unengaged or able to sneak away from their working party, rushed to the southern rampart. Standing in the prow of the lead ship were two figures, but it was the man holding the eagle standard who the watching men were able to discern first, which immediately unleashed a torrent of wagering about the identity of the Legion. It took much longer for those Legionaries with a stake in the identity to learn whether they were winners or losers because the northern canal was still under construction and unavailable for use, and there simply wasn't room on the northern docks. Consequently, it wasn't until it was almost dark before the southern gates were thrown open, and the men of the 21st Legion, commanded by Aulus Papernus marched through them, where they were greeted by a crowd composed of raucous Legionaries, and curious, and somewhat apprehensive, citizens of the city drawn to the spectacle. As the Legion marched directly up the main street towards the center of the city, the cheers and groans from their comrades seemed to be equal in strength, as men either shouted their exultation that they had guessed correctly, while others turned away in disgust. For Papernus and his men, it was something of a homecoming as they joined Caesar's army at last, and for the older veterans, they spied familiar faces lining the street, comrades from their time in Gaul, or during the civil war against Pompeius Magnus; there were even family reunions, as cousins, and in one case, brothers who had been separated by time and distance finally reunited. Despite all the activity, and Caesar's incessant driving of the men, he allowed this display, and there was a festival atmosphere that only ended when the Legion came to a halt outside the *Praetorium*, where Caesar was standing, along with his staff, waiting for their arrival. Then, the Centurions of the rest of the army were given the orders to get their men back to their preparations, and the frenzied activity resumed, along with swipes of the *viti* for encouragement. Later that evening, the Primi Pili were summoned to the *Praetorium* by their general, and as most of them expected, Caesar wasted no time.

"Now that the 21st is here, I am ready to announce the other two Legions that will be staying behind."

Caesar turned first to Lucius Aquilinus of the 15th, who, Pullus noticed, didn't look surprised. Batius of the Alaudae, however, was another matter, and within a heartbeat of Caesar mouthing the words, he had leapt to his feet.

"Caesar! I protest!" Batius had normally swarthy features, but his face was so flushed now that, to Pullus, he could almost pass for a Parthian. "This is an insult to the 5th! You know that it was my boys who beat those bastards with their elephants during that first battle when we were with Pollio!"

Batius didn't realize it, but he had given Caesar the exact opening he needed, although Pullus was a bit surprised that, when the general lifted an admonishing hand, Batius actually subsided, since he was renowned for his argumentative nature.

"Batius," he said equably enough, "that's precisely why I want you to stay here." Before the 5th's Primus Pilus could respond, Caesar picked up a tablet, which he waved at the assembled officers, telling them, "I just received this today, from Prefect Silva." As he expected, this served to arrest their attention, since they had all known that Caesar had sent the cavalry out into the countryside, under strict orders not to engage but observe. "Right now, Abhiraka and the Pandyan king and their combined army is twenty-five miles southeast of here. As you've all seen, they have been systematically destroying their own people's crops, and while I can't say with any certainty, I feel confident that Abhiraka is attempting to draw us out away from the walls. But," he offered a smile that held no warmth, "he'll be wasting his time. And, day after tomorrow, we'll be sailing down the Narmada. Which," Caesar turned to Batius, "is why I want you here, Batius, because along with the location, what Silva's report contains is that they have well more than two hundred elephants. And," he continued, "we all know that at most, Abhiraka had twenty, perhaps twenty-five of the animals left, which means these are Pandyan." He paused, just long enough to see that most heads were nodding up and down, but Batius, who was still standing, wasn't one of them, although he was no longer shaking his, and Caesar addressed him directly, "That's why I want the 5th here, Batius. Your men have the most experience, and they've proven themselves to a degree that makes me confident you are the best choice in the event that Abhiraka decides to try and storm the city."

Batius didn't accept this outright; that simply wasn't in his nature.

Instead, he asked, "How much naphtha do you intend on leaving us?"

"Two-thirds," Caesar answered, and the previous quiet was shattered, now by the other Primi Pili, all of whom began voicing their dismay, although when Caesar signaled for silence, they fell quiet quickly enough. "The reason I'm leaving that much behind is because, not only did we bring enough to replace our original stores but half again as much, the other reason is that Pandya has sent most of its elephants north. They," he extended an army in a general southerly direction, "are out there now, twenty-five miles away, and there's no way they will be able to march back south in time to have any impact on what's going to happen."

"How do you know they don't have just as many elephants left behind?" Carfulenus of the 28th asked, sounding somewhat skeptical, to Pullus at least.

Caesar offered them a smile, saying only, "I have my sources, and they're very reliable, Carfulenus. There will at most be a hundred elephants, and even leaving that much behind, we'll have more than enough to destroy many times that number."

Hyppolita; that was Pullus' immediate thought. Somehow, Caesar managed to get Hyppolita to talk. The rush of anger he experienced surprised him, which he struggled to keep to himself, but for a heartbeat, when Caesar suddenly turned to look directly at him, his eyes narrowing slightly, Pullus was certain that he had betrayed himself. Fortunately, the moment passed, and Caesar returned his attention back to Batius.

"Not only will you have enough naphtha, Batius, along with the

21st and 15th, you're going to be behind these walls, and I have already given the orders to modify the artillery that's on the walls to switch to the iron baskets that can fling the jars."

"Will we be receiving more artillery as well?" Aquilinus asked.

"Only your normal Legion complement," Caesar replied, and once again, there was some resistance to this, but Caesar was unmoved. Instead, he offered a suggestion. "Once we leave, perhaps you should put your *immunes* to work finding what type of wood that is native to this place could be used to create more artillery pieces."

The expressions of chagrin and embarrassment were shared by every Centurion who had been in Bharuch, and it wasn't confined to them, as Pollio and Hirtius exchanged a guilty glance, all of them realizing this should have been thought of long before. And, from everything Pullus and his comrades had seen, there were trees that yielded exceptionally hard and resilient timber that, once it was cured, would probably make for excellent artillery pieces.

Caesar covered a few other items, then finally told them what they had really been waiting to hear.

"The army will begin loading day after tomorrow at daybreak. I expect it to take a full day, but once a ship is loaded, they'll move downstream and gather in the mouth of the bay to wait for the rest of the fleet." Turning, Caesar indicated Apollodorus as he finished, "You'll receive your boarding orders, and when you'll be embarking in the morning from Apollodorus."

This signaled the end of the meeting, and as always happened, men gravitated towards those with whom they had the closest relationship, so Pullus, Spurius, and Balbinus exited the building together, and like their men, they wagered who would be loading when.

"You'll go last, Pullus," Balbinus said unhappily. "Your boys are always the last to load."

Pullus didn't try to deny it, not only because it was true, but he enjoyed reminding his counterparts, "That's because Caesar always saves his best for last, Balbinus. You should know that by now."

"I just don't want to be first," Spurius put in sourly. "I *hate* bobbing around at anchor."

"You'd think that you'd have found your sea legs by now." Pullus nudged him as he said this. "Gods know we've spent enough time aboard ships by now."

"I'm a fucking Roman, Pullus," Spurius shot back. "A *real* Roman hates the sea, everyone knows that."

The truth was that Pullus hated being aboard ship as much as the others, but he would never let them know that; it just wasn't in his nature to betray any kind of weakness, and it was hard to be dignified as a Primus Pilus when you were draped over the side of the ship, puking your guts out.

Instead, he offered, "We're going to be sailing along the coast again, so it shouldn't be too bad."

Spurius looked supremely unconvinced, but he switched subjects, taking a quick glance about before he asked Pullus, "So did Diocles find out anything more about where exactly we're going to be landing?"

"No," Pullus replied, then hissed in frustration. "All I know is that Volusenus is still gone, so he must be the one Caesar sent to scout for a spot."

"We probably won't find out until we're already at sea," Balbinus mused, which turned out to be the case.

Finishing their conversation, they headed towards their respective Legions, meaning that Pullus walked towards the palace compound, but he stopped at each of the buildings outside the compound that served as the barracks for the 10th, checking with the Pili Priores and informing them of their impending departure. By the time he was finished, the sun had finally vanished, and while it was not by much, Pullus and the other men of the army had learned to appreciate even a slight drop in temperature. More importantly, he and a good number of the men had become more acclimated to the climate; how much of this acclimation was due to the change in clothing, diet, and habit, or just by virtue of their having been there for so long, he had no idea. He did worry that as they moved south, the heat would become even more severe, but Hyppolita had assured him that while it was hotter, it wasn't a significant difference that would require acclimating to all over again. So absorbed in his thoughts was he that he didn't notice that he was being watched as he crossed in front of the palace, and he entered his quarters and the Legion office, where Diocles had already prepared his meal. Pullus stared at the bowl, filled with cooked rice, but it was without his normal appetite. Like his fellow Romans, he had found the transition from wheat and bread to be difficult, but because of Hyppolita, he had adjusted by adding spices that, prior to this, only the wealthiest of Romans, men like Caesar, could afford, yet here they were freely available. In fact, some of the Primi Pili had begun to discuss the idea of buying massive quantities of the spices, particularly a variety of something called a pepper that made it feel as if your mouth was on fire. At first, Pullus was like most of the men, thinking it was a distinctly unpleasant, feeling as if you had picked up a coal from the fire and popped it into your mouth, yet over time, he had not only become accustomed to it, he found that he craved it. And, he was far from alone in becoming fond of spicy food, but even seeing the presence of the hottest variety of pepper that Diocles had chopped up and mixed into his bowl, he didn't have much appetite. Still, the demands of his body took precedence, and within a heartbeat after sitting down, he was shoveling a spoonful of rice into his mouth, while Diocles handed him a tablet containing the tasks accomplished by the First Century that day. Because they were within the compound, the walls muffled the noise on the opposite side, but whenever they stopped speaking, the sounds of the kind of debauchery that was typical for the army just before it was about to return to campaigning drifted across the sultry night air.

"Sounds like the boys are getting every *drachma*'s worth out of their last night," Diocles commented, but Pullus only grunted, still absorbed in reading the contents of the tablet.

It was shortly after this that Pullus, rising from his desk, moved across the room and entered his private quarters, which were more spacious than the normal accommodations for a Primus Pilus, but most importantly, was well ventilated with several large windows along three walls, with the same kind of louvered shutters used in the palace. Depending on the breeze, by manipulating the shutters, Pullus had learned he could create a cross breeze that made it actually quite comfortable. However, he also learned fairly quickly that leaving the shutters open too much guaranteed being drenched if one of the many rain showers passed through during the night. Through a process of trial and error, he had learned how to position the slats at an angle that allowed the breeze, but provided a partial protection in the event of a shower.

After he stripped down, Diocles came in with a small flask, towel, and strigil, and within a span of a hundred heartbeats, quickly but expertly rubbed the oil into Pullus' skin and muscles, causing Pullus to slowly relax, his breathing becoming even. With deft swipes with the strigil, Diocles flicked the oil from Pullus' skin, taking the dirt and sweat with it, whereupon he handed his master a towel, and, with a minimum of words, the Greek disappeared as Pullus walked over and settled on his cot. Even when he was exhausted, Pullus was a light sleeper, but he had learned which sounds were common to every night, as Diocles attended to his own needs before blowing out the lamp in the outer office. Consequently, when perhaps a third of a watch later there was a light rap on the outer door, he came immediately awake, his heart pounding as his hand, without any thought to do so, reached out for the hilt of his *gladius*, which he always hung over the back of a chair and within reach from his cot. He sat on the edge, listening to Diocles' footsteps, then the door opening, but while he heard a voice that sounded familiar, it was too muffled to make out, and he wondered whether this was a summons from the *Praetorium* to attend to Caesar, or perhaps it was one of his Pili Priores with an emergency. As it turned out, it was neither; there was another rap, but on his inner door, and when he bade Diocles to open it, while Pullus immediately recognized who was with him, it didn't make sense to him.

"Gaius? What are you doing here?" He was instantly struck by a thought that sent a stab of fear through him, bringing him to his feet as he asked, "What is it? Is something wrong with Scribonius?"

"No." Gaius held out both hands as he stepped around Diocles. "It's not that, Uncle Titus!"

"What is it, then?" Pullus' tone reminded his nephew that his uncle wasn't in the best frame of mind when he was suddenly awakened, and this wasn't like anything he had done before, because he was about to lie to Pullus.

"It's...Amodini, Uncle Titus," Gaius began, but Pullus cut him off.

"Amodini?" He frowned. "Why would she need to see me?" His expression suddenly changed, and he groaned, "Oh, Pluto's *cock*, Gaius! Don't tell me that you got her pregnant!"

"No!" It was how startled Gaius was that told Pullus his nephew was telling the truth; or, he was a better liar than Pullus thought. "It's nothing like that, I swear it!" He did pause, but that was because for a brief instant, he forgot what he had been told to say. Fortunately, he remembered before Pullus could become suspicious, "No, it's about Queen Hyppolita. Amodini has some information that you should know, and she needs to tell you tonight."

"What information?" Pullus asked, but Porcinus shook his head.

"She wouldn't tell me," he replied. "She said she can only tell you."

Pullus was silent for a moment, and while he did consider sending Diocles to alert Caesar, it was only a fleeting thought.

"When," he finally asked, "does she want to meet me? And where?"

He suspected that he knew the location, which was confirmed when Gaius told him, "In the garden. And, she said she will be there immediately after the midnight call is sounded."

"And you don't have any idea what this is about?"

Gaius turned to Diocles, but he was sincere when he assured the Greek, "No. She wouldn't tell me anything about what she needed to tell Uncle Titus. Just that it was important, and it couldn't wait."

A thought occurred to Pullus, and he made sure to look his nephew in the eye as he said, "Did you tell her that we were leaving day after tomorrow?"

"No," he answered immediately. "We haven't seen each other since last night, and when I went to see her tonight, she was already there and told me I needed to tell you. I came here right away before we had a chance to talk."

Pullus turned now to Diocles, because the Greek had the most uncanny ability to measure time, asking, "How long before midnight call?"

"Less than a third of a watch," Diocles assured him, which elicited a muttered curse.

"No point in laying back down, then," Pullus grumbled, then stood and walked over to Gaius. He put a hand on his shoulder, telling him, "You have done your duty, young Gregarius. Now go get some rest." Porcinus nodded, yet he didn't move, but just as Pullus was about to ask him why, the reason came to him. Feeling an impish urge, he asked, "Is there something else, Gaius?"

"Well, no," Gaius stumbled, then shook his head and said, "Actually, yes. Depending on how long it takes Amodini to tell you whatever she needs to tell you, I was thinking that perhaps you could ask her to stay in the garden a bit longer…"

His voice trailed off, but the void was filled with Pullus' laughter, and he clapped his nephew on the shoulder as he agreed, "Of course. How could I deny two young lovers of their last few watches together? I'll come and get you when I'm done talking to her."

Once Gaius left, Pullus actually did think about lying down but decided against it, knowing how likely it was that he would fall asleep, and his corresponding mood when he was jerked awake a second time. Instead, he returned to his desk, and with Diocles' help, they worked through some outstanding items, becoming so absorbed that, when the *bucina* sounded the change of watch at midnight, it startled both of them.

"Well," Pullus stood, then walked over to pick up his *vitus* leaning next to the door, "let me go see what Lady Amodini wants."

"Hopefully, it's not anything bad," Diocles said, prompting

Pullus to shoot him a sour look.

"Thanks for bringing that up," he grumbled, but before Diocles could respond, he was out the door.

Moving quickly, because of the location of his quarters, he didn't have to use the secret entrance into the garden, and he strode across the grounds, wondering for what he was certain was the fiftieth time since Gaius' appearance what this could be about. As he approached the main, and except for a handful of people who knew, what was the only entrance into the garden, Pullus slowed, although he was unsure why he did so. He certainly wasn't worried about Amodini hurting him, nor was there any way for any enemy to infiltrate this deeply into the city, yet he still paused for a moment. Get hold of yourself, Titus, he thought. There's nothing to fear from Amodini. Taking a breath, he resumed walking and entered into the garden, where he saw a dark shape seated on the bench, but as usual, was facing away from him.

"Amodini?" Pullus thought to whisper, and the figure stood while he walked closer. Once he got within a couple paces, he saw that, while obviously a woman, she was wearing the full veil and head covering, yet there was something slightly different from Pullus' memory of what Amodini looked like when she was attired in this manner. Still, he continued to whisper, "Gaius came and told me you needed to see me."

For the first time, the other figure spoke, "Yes. And no."

Pullus froze, instantly recognizing the voice, but until she undid the veil and removed the head covering, he refused to believe his ears.

"Hyppolita?"

When he looked back on the ensuing day and a few watches before he led his Legion onto the ships, Titus Pullus could barely remember any of it. Obviously, he had performed his duties in an acceptable manner, yet for the life of him, whenever he tried to think of anything specific from that period, nothing came to mind. What made things more difficult was that Pullus had been forced to break his promise, never showing up at Gaius' quarters or sending Diocles to fetch him, but while he had a good reason, he still did what he could to avoid the Second Cohort. As scheduled, the boarding process began at dawn two days later, but for once, both Balbinus and Spurius had been wrong, because the 10th was one of the first to load, which led to speculation that for some reason, the Equestrians had fallen out of favor with Caesar. Pullus barely noticed, although he was acutely aware of Gaius' angry gaze on one occasion when he was forced to talk with Scribonius about when his friend's Cohort would load. Otherwise, everything was what passed for normal, with a frenzy of activity, men standing alongside each ship with the long pole with an iron loop attached to the end, the device that had been developed for that inevitable moment when one of the rankers put a foot wrong and went plunging into the water, weighed down by their equipment. By this point in time, Caesar's army had refined the process of boarding so that it went as quickly as possible, at least as far as the men were concerned, although as they all knew, Caesar was never satisfied, certain that there could always be time gained from some further refinement of the process. Century by Century, Cohort by Cohort, the 10th boarded their assigned vessels, and as soon as each ship tied to the dock was loaded, the crew shoved off and the ship was rowed out into the river, where it used the current to drift downstream. The First Cohort was loaded last, and the First Century last of all, although this wasn't appreciated all that much by the rankers, who had become accustomed to being the last aboard of the entire army, thereby reducing their time actually on the water.

Seemingly within a matter of moments after Pullus' ship, a *quadrireme* that carried both the First and Second Century, was safely out into the current, the Primus Pilus disappeared, heading to his cabin, which was the *navarch's* whenever he wasn't aboard. Diocles was still in the process of stowing Pullus' baggage, but he instantly understood that his master wanted to be alone, so he left the work undone, simply leaving the cabin to Pullus. What, he thought dully, have I done? This had to be the twentieth time this ran through his mind, yet he was no closer to an answer now, almost two days later, than he had been in the predawn when he had returned to his quarters. The worst part was that, no matter how much he tried, he couldn't banish the memory to the back part of his mind. While this might have been understandable for most men, it wasn't for Titus Pullus, at least as far as he was concerned, simply because he had always been able to do so before this. Yet, every time he stopped moving, or talking, the images from his time with Hyppolita came thrusting into his consciousness. Troubling enough in itself, but it was the fact that, for the first time, he had actually been torn about leaving with his Legion, and while it wasn't long, he had entertained the thought of simply staying put. Naturally, almost immediately, the rational part of his mind took over, although his reason for not doing so had as much to do with Hyppolita and what she would be facing if he remained behind. There was another part of him that was still struggling to fathom and accept that this woman, a queen, had come to him in the most fundamental manner between a man and a woman, without the trappings of royalty. And, frankly, he was slightly amazed that a woman as beautiful as the Queen of Bharuch would look at him in this manner.

"We will never speak of this, and it will never happen again, Titus Pullus," she had said this quietly, but with the kind of authority that he recognized from hearing Cleopatra use the same tone. "But, tonight, before you leave," she had walked up to him so that they were in closer physical proximity than they had ever been, and even in the darkness, with her face turned up to his, her beauty made him ache, "I am not a queen, and you are not my enemy." She paused for what Pullus was certain was a full watch, before she asked, "Do you accept these terms? Can you live with this?"

What had shocked him to his core was that his initial instinct was to tell her no, not because he didn't desire her, but because, to him, this simply wasn't good enough, that he wanted much more than this. It had been a moment that, over the ensuing years, Titus Pullus would long remember, when he realized that, despite what he had told himself in the aftermath of the death of Gisela and his two children, he longed for a union that lasted longer than something that could be measured by a handful of silver and a watch candle. And, as he looked down at her, this was the woman he wanted.

What came out of his mouth, however, was, "Yes, I accept these terms. I can live with this."

Now, as he dropped onto the narrow cot, listening to the thudding footsteps of the crew abovedeck, and the sound of the beater calling out the count that took him farther away with every single stroke, he wondered if he actually *could* live without Hyppolita.

She had known it was a mistake; no, she chided herself, it was much, much graver and more dangerous than a mistake. And, in the light of day, there was a sense of wonderment that there seemed to be a part of her that was beyond her immediate control. From her earliest days, growing up in the royal house of Sagala, where she had been told as long as she could remember that she was destined to bring honor and glory to her line because she would be marrying a king like her father, she had accepted this as her destiny. No, she certainly hadn't loved Abhiraka, not at first, yet she had not once uttered an objection to her father's announcement that he had arranged a marriage with a young and relatively poor man from the kingdom of Bharuch, farther south of their own kingdom, but one that was substantially influenced by the Macedonians. Thankfully, she had not been repulsed by Abhiraka, and as they got to know each other, her feelings of warmth towards him had deepened. Not surprisingly, it had been the birth of her first child Aarunya, who was now the wife of the crown prince Nedunj, that had done more to solidify her affection towards her husband. It was an affection that she was quite happy to feel returned by him, yet there was nothing resembling love between them; it wasn't until she came into contact with the large, scarred Roman Titus Pullus that she experienced physical desire, which understandably shook her to her core. Abhiraka had his concubines, yet he was not cruel like some kings in parading these women in her sight, and he did share her bed to a degree that, at least according to her mother, was uncommon for a king. But there was something about Pullus that stirred in her feelings that she had never really experienced before, and they not only confused her, they frightened her.

It was when, as she spent that day watching out her window and saw the flurry of activity from the Romans she knew Pullus commanded, coupled with Caesar's sudden visit, that she realized it meant the Romans were leaving, and she was stricken with an emotion close to panic. The thought that Titus Pullus might be leaving Bharuch, and she would never see him again, sent her into a state completely foreign to her, where her mind couldn't seem to override her emotions. Although it had been an impulsive act enlisting Amodini, not once had she questioned herself as to why she was doing as much, or why she had chosen her youngest lady. It had seemed right somehow, to a degree that she had rarely experienced, yet at the same time, she understood that nobody, especially Abhiraka, would view it in the same light. For a brief span of moments, she tried to tell herself that her purpose was to extract more information from Pullus, but it was a fiction she couldn't maintain with herself for long, although she saved this thought for a time she hoped would never happen, when Abhiraka discovered the truth. Nevertheless, when the moment came for her to leave the palace and cross the compound to enter the garden, she was surprised that she did so; in fact, there was an element of disembodiment that made what she was doing seem as if someone else was doing this, not her. Then, when he had arrived, and she had sensed his presence even before he stepped into the garden entrance, what mattered most was that he was there. The entrance, as Pullus had informed her once, was similar to the type Romans used for their marching camps except that, instead of piles of dirt that required anyone entering to take a serpentine path, there were the thick shrubs that screened anyone from view on either side that allowed her to hear him coming, although she refused to react as if she had. There was a part of her screaming that she could stop, that nothing had happened that would stain her honor, and more importantly, the honor of her husband, yet she sat on the bench, unable to rise. Then he was there, standing in front of her; when he had called out Amodini's name, despite herself, she felt a stab of jealousy, a completely irrational reaction, not only because she knew Pullus thought that was who he was addressing, but all of this had been by her design.

The sound of his voice telling her that Gaius had informed him that the woman he thought was Amodini needed to see him gave her the strength to answer, "Yes. And no."

Her voice had sounded foreign to her, which enhanced her sense that, somehow, she wasn't completely there, that perhaps her essence was floating outside her body, allowing the body to do what it wished for this span of time. And, she would think afterwards, perhaps that was exactly what happened, because she was certainly unaccustomed to this feeling of physical desire that coursed through her, and had been doing so whenever she was in Pullus' company for some months now. Thus had begun the strangest, most wonderful, but most unsettling moments of her life to that point, where there was no such thing as Bharuch or Rome. Caesar was a figment of the imagination, and she had never married a man she didn't love; most importantly, Bharuch and Rome weren't at war, and he wasn't her enemy, nor she his. Now, on the day of the departure of Caesar and his army, Hyppolita was reduced to standing on the second-story porch, staring north towards the wall and what lay beyond, despite being unable to see anything. Because of the intervening buildings on the opposite side of the square, she couldn't even see the gate, thereby missing the ordered lines of Romans marching through them on their short trip to the docks. It was supremely unsatisfying, but what she did know was that a substantial portion of the Roman army was leaving, and the Legion she knew Pullus commanded, also knowing it was called the 10th, had already departed, leaving the building that had once housed all of the royal bodyguard and the elephant attendants standing empty.

It actually helped that Amodini had been inconsolable, not only because it gave her a distraction, but her grief was sufficiently on display to a degree that drew the attention of her other ladies away from Hyppolita's own state of mind. She also expected a final visit from Caesar, and she had prepared the questions that she intended to ask, most of them concerning the status of her and her ladies, and who would be replacing Pullus as the Roman with whom she would interact. Hyppolita was under no illusions that she would have any say in the matter this time; the circumstances were substantially different, and most importantly, Caesar had returned. Although, she was certain, he would be leaving with however many Romans there were boarding ships out on the river, which deepened her belief that the general would show up. However, as the sun sank lower and Caesar didn't come, she was beset with doubts, along with a fair amount of fear. She knew that Pullus and the men of his Legion, or at least of what he had informed her was called a Cohort and the one under his direct command, had been her protector, and she was acutely aware that the vast majority of Caesar's army viewed her and her ladies with undisguised hostility. Once Pullus and his men were gone, would Caesar take measures to ensure her safety from whatever Romans were left behind? It was shortly before dark that, finally, she turned away from the window, trying to conceal her anxiety, but her ladies had been in her presence for far too long to be fooled; fortunately, they all believed that it had everything to do with Caesar and nothing else. The fact that they shared her worry about their immediate future actually aided Hyppolita, since this was the sole topic of conversation for the rest of the night until it was time to retire, and she assumed her role as the voice of calm assurance that they were perfectly safe. After spending a sleepless night that was only partly caused by her anxiety about what the day would bring in a larger sense, Hyppolita rose, and after breaking her fast and attending to her needs, resumed her station at the window. As the sun rose higher, only gradually did she become aware of something; the noise level had reduced substantially, and by noon, it was almost preternaturally quiet. It's as if, she thought, everyone in the city is in a daze and wondering what comes next for them.

"I think," she finally said, "they've gone. Caesar and his army are sailing to Pandya."

The reason Caesar hadn't divulged their objective before departure wasn't due to his normal concern about secrecy, but because Volusenus hadn't returned by the time the army was ready to depart. It was on the second full day of their voyage that one of the small *biremes* leading the larger fleet raised the signal flag informing Caesar and the rest of the fleet that other ships had been sighted. This created some tension, as the crews and the passengers aboard who had a rank high enough to be allowed on deck, prepared to receive the next signal about whether the approaching ships were friendly or not. Thankfully, this didn't last long, as the scout ship then added the green pennant that signaled the spotted vessels were friendly, although it would take a bit of time for them to learn that this was actually Volusenus.

On Pullus' *quadrireme*, which was located about a furlong behind and to the right side of Caesar's flagship, it was actually Balbus who correctly guessed, "I bet that's Volusenus."

Even as they watched, a small boat was lowered from Caesar's flagship, and the small crew of four men, all of them freedmen, rowed quickly south, the direction they were traveling. While the fleet continued sailing, it was at a severely reduced pace, yet it still didn't take long for the small boat to reappear, but with a passenger.

"I told you!" Balbus elbowed Pullus.

"I didn't say you were wrong when you said it," Pullus protested.

"No," Balbus retorted, "but I know you thought it!"

Giving his friend an amused glance, Pullus' only response was a shake of his head, then he returned his attention in time to see Volusenus scrambling up the ladder, where they could see Caesar was standing on the deck a short distance away. The Legate saluted, which Caesar returned, but then clasped arms as Caesar led Volusenus towards the stern, where his combination quarters and office were located.

"How long do you think it's going to take before Caesar calls you and the others to the ship?" Balbus asked, but in such a way that Pullus immediately knew his friend was offering a wager.

Rubbing his chin, Pullus glanced at the sky, noted the position of the sun, then answered, "Before the end of third watch."

As he intended, this made Balbus snort with derision, and Pullus had to smother his smile, knowing that he had hooked his fish.

"That soon?" Balbus shook his head. "Not even Caesar can draw up plans that quickly." He paused for a moment, then asked, "So, how much?"

"A hundred *drachmae*," Pullus answered immediately, like the rest of the army having become accustomed to the different currency used in India, and they sealed their wager in the normal fashion.

Pullus knew that Balbus was right, and under normal circumstances, he hated to lose at anything, but he had decided that, in this case, it would help improve the mood aboard the ship, as the men of Balbus' Century would celebrate their Centurion's victory over the Primus Pilus, while the men of Pullus' Century, although they might pretend to be disappointed, would be happy to see Pullus lose at *something*, even if it was to another Century. Such were the small ways that a Primus Pilus kept the men under his command as content as it was possible to be, cooped up aboard a plunging, rolling ship for only the gods knew how long.

As Pullus expected, he lost his bet, because the signal summoning the Primi Pili wasn't sent until shortly before sundown, and even as many times as he had done it, Pullus still grumbled about the prospect of having to clamber down a rope ladder into the small boat that was crewed by just two men instead of four. He arrived alongside Caesar's flagship, clambering aboard as he cursed the rolling of the larger ship, then crossed the deck to Caesar's quarters at the rear of the vessel, meeting Balbinus and Felix at the door leading inside. It would be cramped and stifling, although Caesar had ordered that the wooden shutters that covered the holes serving as windows be raised and secured, but within moments, every face glistened in the light from the heat put out by the several lamps hanging from the beams that supported the upper deck. What greeted the Centurions was a large piece of vellum; actually, it was several pieces sewn together, which was hanging on one wall of Caesar's stateroom. While they had all seen this map before, they immediately saw that far more detail had been filled in. It was still incomplete, Pullus noticed, particularly the lower portion of the map, which was the direction they were heading, ending with the line he knew representing the coast curling back upwards, much like a peninsula would, but he understood that wasn't what it was. Partially, it was the presence of another outline, separated from the point where the line made a fairly sharp line back upward, and Pullus knew the outline represented the island of Taprobane, which had long been the site of the farthermost Greek trading post, at least in the world known to Rome. So, he thought, we now know where India ends; hard on the heels of that came another idea that, despite himself, sent a surge of what could only be called excitement as he wondered, What's on the other side of India? Before his mind could run away with thoughts of the mysteries that awaited Caesar and his army, the general began speaking.

"As you can all see, Legate Volusenus has done an outstanding job of filling in much of what lays south of here." He paused but seemed content that men were simply nodding at this point. Using his customary pointer, Caesar continued, "And, as you no doubt know, this," he pointed to the outline of the large island, "is

Taprobane, which we know is located at the southernmost tip of India." He shifted the pointer to a spot that was farther up from Taprobane, placing the tip on a large dot. "And this," his voice changed enough to warn the men, "is where we are heading. This is the city of Muziris, and it is not only one of the largest and most important cities in the kingdom of Pandya, it is where, according to our information, the treasury that King Abhiraka was taken…" Suddenly, he stopped, and when he corrected himself, Pullus understood that it was no accident that Caesar had shifted his attention from the map directly on the large Centurion. "…Actually, it was his Queen Hyppolita who managed to send it south, shortly before our arrival outside Bharuch." Pullus felt the burning in his face, conscious that none of his counterparts had missed Caesar's behavior, but he refused to make any sign that he was aware of it, particularly to Caesar, who he stared at, stone-faced and immobile, feeling a small satisfaction that it was the general who broke eye contact first.

Before Caesar could continue, it was Clustuminus who interjected, asking, "Why would this woman do that, Caesar? Why would she trust these Pandyan bastards with most of her kingdom's money?"

"I was about to explain that, Clustuminus," Caesar replied acidly, and by doing so, shifted the others' attention away from Pullus, who was both relieved and happy that it was Clustuminus who had been his unwitting salvation. Satisfying himself with just that rebuke, Caesar continued, "The reason that Queen Hyppolita viewed this as a possible alternative has to do with the alliance that was formed between Bharuch and Pandya, because of the marriage of the oldest daughter of Abhiraka with the crown prince of the Pandya."

This created a slight stir, though not much; like Pullus, the Centurions were long accustomed to the arranged marriages that took place between royal houses, knowing that the patrician families of Rome did the same thing, as did the upper classes of every other nation in the known world.

"How did we get this information, Caesar? That the treasury is in this city…?"

"Muziris, Spurius," Caesar repeated, but he shook his head as he replied, "But as far as how we know this, it doesn't matter, does it? And," he allowed, which Pullus was certain was behind his real reluctance to reveal that, somehow, Caesar had managed to convince Hyppolita to provide him with this information, "it's possible that this information is incorrect. But," Caesar's voice hardened slightly, "even if it is, it doesn't matter, because in order to get to their capital in the interior, we have to land somewhere. And," he turned back to the map, stabbing the spot with his pointer, "Muziris offers the best possibility, if only because their capital Karoura is upriver."

Rather than continue, Caesar turned to Volusenus, his meaning made clear when he extended the pointer to the Legate. Accepting it, Volusenus waited until Caesar took his seat, then turned to the map.

"The reason Muziris is the only viable landing spot has to do with this." He swept the pointer upward from the dot marking the city. Less than two finger's width above the dot, a series of marks that resembled an upside down "V" began, then extended up the map for more than a foot, although near Muziris, there was some space between the line denoting the coast and those marks, before they curved until they were directly next to the coastline. "As you can see, while there are spots to land north of Muziris where the ground is flat enough for us to assemble and march, most of it is like that stretch that the part of the army that marched south from Pattala had to cover." Understandably, this drew the strongest reaction from the Primi Pili who had been with Pollio and Hirtius on that march, but Pullus had heard enough about it to have an idea that it was something neither he nor those who had been with Caesar wanted to experience. Continuing, Volusenus indicated the first of the hatch marks. "But even when the ground firms up, it's because this range of hills that runs along the coast comes down to just a couple of furlongs from the beach in some cases. And, even when there would be enough space to land the army, it would be right underneath those heights, and there is enough cover on the slopes to hide a force of some size."

"Wait," Sextus Crispus, the Primus Pilus of the 22nd who had arrived with Caesar raised a hand. "I thought you said that most of these Pandyans are back north somewhere outside Bharuch."

Volusenus glanced over at Caesar, who nodded and stood, answering, "That's our information, Crispus. But," he lifted both hands, palms up, "do we know exactly what portion of the Pandyan army is with Abhiraka?" Caesar held his tongue less than a heartbeat before he shook his head and continued, "No, Crispus. We don't. And, given what happened to the 7th and the 11th, I'm not willing to risk that, rather than three hundred elephants, the Pandyans actually possess five hundred. Besides," Caesar's tone suddenly changed, and Pullus recognized it as one where their general was thinking through something unexpected; they got an idea what it was when he said, "we haven't ever attempted to launch naphtha from our ships, and if we're surprised while we're unloading, that would be our only protection against elephants."

Although Caesar didn't say as much, Pullus was certain that, probably as soon as the Primi Pili were dismissed, Caesar would turn his attention to the problem of how to launch the highly volatile flaming jars of naphtha from the deck of a ship without it resulting in a catastrophic failure that might end up sending the ship launching it down in flames.

Caesar turned the meeting back to Volusenus, who resumed the briefing by pointing once again to Muziris, "The other reason that this is the best spot is that it's like Pattala and Bharuch, located on a river, but it's another one known by the Greeks, who call it the Pseudostoma (Periyar). And," Volusenus moved his pointer inland, "as Caesar mentioned, Muziris is directly downstream from what the Greeks call Karoura, which is the actual capital of the Pandyan kingdom." He paused as there was a low buzz from the Centurions, taking the opportunity to unroll and pin a smaller map that showed a detail that Pullus was certain was Muziris and the surrounding area, then gave a cough that indicated he wanted to continue, pointing to the appropriate spot. "The problem for us, however, is that the mouth of the Pseudostoma is *very* narrow, hence the name, barely two hundred paces across, while widening out to perhaps two furlongs at high tide. And," his voice turned grim, "the walls protecting Muziris on that side overlook the mouth, which is well within artillery range."

"Did you see any artillery?" Spurius interrupted, but Volusenus wasn't Caesar, and therefore not irritated at the interruption, completely understanding the Primus Pilus' concern, particularly since he had firsthand experience.

"We not only saw it," Volusenus answered grimly, "we were forced to scuttle one of the *triremes* when their *navarch* got too close. Thank Fortuna," he went on before any of them could raise the concern, "the *navarch* managed to get well away from the river mouth before he had to so we were able to rescue the crew. Most of them," he finished with a shrug, "anyway."

"That sounds like we won't be able to assault from the river side," Balbinus spoke up. "Not without risking losing men and ships."

"And if one of our fleet goes down in the narrowest part of the mouth," Clustuminus observed sourly, "then we're going to be forced to assault just from the seaward side."

"How far is the shoreline from the western wall?" Pullus asked, trying to transform the series of straight black lines into the walls they represented, imagining what it would look like when he was standing knee deep in the surf that was represented by the second parallel line.

"As you can see, the wall along the beach essentially runs parallel to the surf line, which means that while we're unloading, we'll be just barely out of their artillery range." He moved the pointer to a different spot on the map. "We looked at the idea of landing even farther north, then marching inland a few *stadia* so that we could assault the northern wall. The problem is what I mentioned before, the ground north of the city is marsh. While it's theoretically possible that we could approach from due north, our advance would be slowed because of the boggy ground."

Volusenus stopped speaking, the Primi Pili absorbing the situation, although this time, it wasn't left to Pullus to summarize but Spurius, who said glumly, "Which means that we can really only attack from one side, and they'll know that."

Since it wasn't Pullus speaking, he was watching Caesar, so he saw the slight smile, although it was what Pullus thought of as the smug expression his general liked to wear when he possessed a piece of information the others didn't, or had already thought of a solution to a problem. I *hate* it when he does this, Pullus thought, although he was happy that he hadn't managed to speak before Spurius.

"That," Caesar interjected, still wearing the smile, "would normally be true, but there is something that Volusenus hasn't mentioned. Now, I know that while most of you speak at least some Greek, it's not your native tongue. Still, what does *pseudo stoma* mean?"

"Fake mouth." Pullus decided to speak first, just beating out Balbinus, who glared at him while Pullus gave him a grin.

"Exactly so." Caesar nodded, though that was his only acknowledgement to his favored Primus Pilus. "Fake, or false mouth." Now he turned back to the map, took the pointer back from Volusenus, and returned to the larger map, moving the tip to a spot about three inches below the dot representing Muziris. For the first time, Pullus noticed that there was a slight gap in the vertical line representing the coastline, but along with that, as he squinted at it, he saw that there were actually *two* lines in this area, side by side that extended upward until it ran into the basically horizontal line that marked the river that led to Karoura, and he also saw for the first time that this second line didn't actually intersect, it was the line curving to move inland.

"As you can see, there's a reason that the Pseudostoma is named as such," Caesar explained, "because that narrow opening that's near Muziris isn't the actual river mouth. From what Volusenus could ascertain, it may even be a manmade gap, but what matters is that the *real* mouth is almost twenty miles south. The river runs northward from there, separated from the ocean by a strip of land that's no more than a half mile across at its widest. So," he turned from the map to smile at his Primi Pili, "contrary to appearances, we will be attacking Muziris along more than just the western wall."

As Caesar anticipated, this cheered his Centurions a great deal, each of them smiling broadly, while turning to their comrade on either side to murmur their approval at this new piece of information. I have to hand it to him, Pullus thought, his eyes never leaving Caesar even as he exchanged a word with Spurius next to him. Once again, he has managed to surprise us, and in a good way.

Unfortunately, this air of satisfaction wasn't destined to last long, but it wasn't the intent of Flaminius to dampen the mood when he asked, "So exactly how far away is Muziris, Caesar?"

Pullus, and the other more observant Centurions, saw the instant change in their general's demeanor, which was made more manifest by the manner in which Caesar glanced over at Volusenus, which the Legate correctly took as a silent order to be the bearer of the bad news.

Clearing his throat, Volusenus answered, "As I measured it, Bharuch is a bit more than eight hundred miles north of Muziris. Although," he put in quickly, "the fleet has already covered almost a hundred miles of that."

"Eight *hundred* miles?"

That was actually the last distinguishable thing Pullus heard, as his counterparts erupted in a chorus of protests, and his voice was just as loud as anyone else's.

When the Roman appeared on the portico of the palace, Hyppolita didn't recognize the man, certain that she had never seen him before. While she had never spoken with Pollio, or any of the other Roman officers who outranked Pullus aside from Caesar, she had at least seen them, and this man wasn't one of them. However, she was somehow soothed by his appearance, and later, she realized it was because the man was old enough to be her father, perhaps even a little older. Nevertheless, when she descended the stairs to the reception area, she was wearing her veil and head covering, but she didn't hesitate to nod to one of the only male attendants to open the door, whereupon she glided across the space between them, exiting the palace and stopping a couple paces away from the older Roman. He was dressed in the same kind of attire as Caesar, although his armor wasn't of the same quality, and had a careworn look about it that, oddly enough, Hyppolita found somewhat disarming. More than that, Hyppolita sensed that this was a man who wasn't completely comfortable wearing the trappings of rank, her impression strengthened by the awkward bow he offered her, which she returned with a bow of her head.

His Greek, however, was very good as he introduced himself. "My name is Publius Ventidius, Your Highness. I have recently arrived here in Bharuch under orders from the Dictator Gaius Julius Caesar, and I am now the Praetor of Bharuch…"

Although Hyppolita had heard these terms the Romans used to describe the various offices they held before, she suddenly realized she had never asked Titus Pullus a question, and while it was certainly a breach of protocol in meetings of introduction, she suddenly asked, "What is a Dictator, Publius Ventidius?" Seeing his obvious and understandable surprise, she hurried to add, "I apologize, but I realized that none of you Romans have ever explained to me what all your titles mean, although some of them I have managed to determine for myself. Such as Praetor," for once she regretted wearing her veil, because this was a moment where she would have used her smile to go along with the flattery, "is a very important post, is it not? It means that you are now the governor of my kingdom? Caesar must think very highly of you, Publius Ventidius."

Ventidius, who had arrived in Bharuch just two days earlier from Pattala, had been warned by Caesar not to underestimate the Queen of Bharuch, and the oldest of the Legates under Caesar was certain that he heard an undertone in his general's words that was even more meaningful, although he hadn't asked Pollio or Hirtius if his suspicion that Caesar wanted to bed the queen but had been thwarted somehow was true. Nevertheless, despite reminding himself as he mounted the steps, Ventidius immediately felt put on the back foot, yet for his life, he couldn't have said why he felt that way. Maybe, he thought wryly, it's her perfume, which he could just barely smell a couple paces away from her, although he also felt flattered by her words.

"Er," he fumbled, "yes, Your Highness. A Praetor in our system acts as governor. Although," he added, wondering why he was doing so since he didn't usually feel the need to make himself seem even more important, "I am also the military commander of the garrison here since I also hold the rank of Legate."

"Ah, I see," Hyppolita had long before learned how to use her voice because of the custom that she normally despised that required women of high rank to be veiled and covered, but there were moments it held advantages, and this was one of them as she sounded quite impressed. "So you are even more important than a normal Praetor! I can see why Caesar trusts you, then." Before Ventidius could respond, she repeated, "But what is a Dictator, Publius Ventidius?"

Why does she keep saying my name? Ventidius thought, yet for some reason, something that he would have normally found irritating and would have put him on his guard, he found quite charming with this woman.

"Yes, right. Dictator. Let's see…" Ventidius tried to think of an appropriate way to describe it, then finally decided to give a brief explanation of how the office developed during the early days of the Roman Republic, how it was introduced because of the fear of Romans of another monarchy when a man needed power even greater than the powers conferred on the two Consuls by the Senate, usually during a period of emergency.

Hyppolita listened, occasionally nodding her head, again because she was experienced in how to convey interest without using her facial expressions, until Ventidius was finished.

"Thank you so much, Publius Ventidius," she said sincerely, although she thought she saw an opportunity for some mischief, which she immediately took. "That was a very thorough explanation, but it does make me ask, how is a Dictator different than a king that you Romans say you hate?"

"Why," Ventidius replied, offering her a smile, both because he was certain he had the answer, and he was flattered by her obvious interest, "because the term of office for Dictator is finite, although over the centuries, the term has varied. But once the term is over," he finished with a shrug, "the Dictator steps down."

"That is a very wise policy," Hyppolita seemingly agreed. Then she paused just long enough to give Ventidius the impression she was satisfied, waiting until she saw him open his mouth to say whatever he had come to say, saying humbly, "Forgive me again, Publius Ventidius, but while I am queen, I am also a woman, and we find it difficult sometimes to understand the inner workings of politics." Even as she said it, Hyppolita had to force herself to keep the edge of angry bitterness from her voice, but like using her voice as a tool and weapon, she had long practice at self-denigration. "So I am somewhat confused by something, and I am certain that you can provide an explanation that I can understand."

Normally, Ventidius would have grown impatient by this point, but he was sufficiently disarmed that he actually welcomed a chance to prolong what had turned out to be quite a pleasant meeting.

"Of course, Your Highness," he said, trying to not sound too eager. "I am happy to explain whatever you need explained."

"Thank you so much," Hyppolita replied. "It is just that I distinctly remember when I met Caesar the first time. In fact," she lifted a hand to indicate the portico upon which they were standing, "it was almost on this very spot." Despite knowing that referring to that time when her city had fallen and chaos reigned would invoke emotions, she still struggled to keep them from being revealed by her voice. "And when he introduced himself, he gave his title, which was Dictator for Life." Again, she hesitated just long enough to see the sudden flash of what she suspected was a bit of discomfort on the weather-beaten features of the Praetor before she finished, "Am I correct in assuming that the title means what it sounds like it means? That Caesar is a Dictator for however long your gods deem that he should live?"

"Er," Ventidius actually caught himself shifting from one foot to another, suddenly not quite as charmed and happy to continue this topic as he had been a heartbeat earlier, "essentially, yes, Your Highness. Our Senate has conferred that title on Caesar. And," he admitted, "all the powers that come with it."

"So he has supreme power, for the rest of his life," Hyppolita tilted her head slightly, something she had learned some men found alluring for some reason. "How," she asked in a quieter tone, "is that different than a king?"

"It...it...just *is* different, Your Highness," Ventidius spluttered, Caesar's warning about not underestimating this woman suddenly making sense in a tangible way. His good mood had evaporated, and he heard the irritable tone as he said, "I regret it, Your Highness, but that is really all the time I have for explaining our politics."

"Of course, and I apologize," Hyppolita lied, deeply amused and satisfied at seeing the man she didn't know was called The Old Muleteer by the men of Caesar's army so flustered. "As I said, being a woman, and being unfamiliar with your system of government means that I often test the patience of men. It is," she said ruefully and honestly, "a habit for which my husband the king often admonished me."

Despite warning himself not to be taken in, Ventidius couldn't seem to help himself, and he offered another smile as he replied, "No apology is necessary, Your Highness." Still, before she could possibly resurrect what was a deeply uncomfortable topic to discuss with a foreigner of any rank, he went on, "Now, as I said, I wanted to introduce myself, and to let you know what you can expect from me as the Praetor." He hesitated, then decided it was time to be blunt, "Hopefully, you are aware that the prior…arrangement you had with Primus Pilus Pullus where he was the only contact you had with us is no longer possible."

"Yes." Now it was Hyppolita's turn to be uncomfortable, yet it was for reasons that had nothing to do with matters of state and caused by the mention of Pullus' name, and she heard the bitterness that she had reminded herself to conceal as she left the palace to greet this Roman. "I am well aware that things have changed, Publius Ventidius. Very well aware."

Abhiraka had learned of Caesar's arrival with his fleet and the reinforcements they carried within a day of the event, which had created a deep sense of despondency with the king, his officers, and the part of his army that were of Bharuch, although it wasn't long before that depression spread to the Pandyans. What went unspoken was the certainty that, along with fresh men, whatever foodstuffs they transported, and replacement equipment, the Roman general had returned with a new supply of the substance that, as far as Abhiraka and his men were concerned, was the only reason why they had been driven from their homes and were forced to endure life on the march. Morale was a constant problem, but at least the men from Bharuch had the motivation for both vengeance and for the chance to return home, but the Pandyans were another story, and from Abhiraka's perspective, Puddapandyan didn't seem particularly interested in addressing it. Why this was the case was a subject about which the Bharuch king had conferred with Ranjeet, Bolon, and Nahapana at length, yet he wasn't soothed by their counsel; on the contrary, his lieutenants confirmed his darker suspicions about his ally.

"He's up to something," Ranjeet said flatly during their most recent discussion, which had been held after the Pandyan king had retired from their presence to enjoy his comforts.

"Yes," as always, Abhiraka would agree, but as always, would invariably cry out, "but *what*? He can't possibly think that he can take the city."

"Not while you're alive." This came from Bolon.

Not surprisingly, this arrested Abhiraka's attention, especially since this was the first any of them had broached the topic.

"You don't think he's going to try and assassinate me, do you, Bolon?"

"No, Your Highness," Bolon answered immediately and emphatically. "I don't think he's that stupid to try and have you killed, hundreds of miles from his own kingdom." Shaking his head, he continued, "No, what I believe he's counting on is Caesar doing it for him."

This caused Abhiraka to come to a sudden stop in his pacing, frowning in thought, then with a shake of his head, said dismissively, "But that still doesn't put him at an advantage, because of Bhumaka." Invoking the name of the crown prince, who had been sent to join his sister, along with his younger sister, down in Karoura, Abhiraka went on, "Even if Caesar is successful, I have already named Bhumaka as my heir."

Bolon was reluctant to continue, and his glance at Ranjeet served as the signal to the oldest and closest to the king to say quietly, "Who is only twelve, my friend. And," he hated to have to broach this subject with his king, but he and Bolon and Nahapana had talked of little else for some time, "Bhumaka is in Karoura, which makes him essentially a hostage."

The three of them watched the dawning understanding cross their king's expression, and even in the firelight, he grew noticeably pale.

"Are you suggesting that Puddapandyan would execute my son?" Abhiraka gasped. "With Bhumaka's sister married to Puddapandyan's own son?"

"I think," Ranjeet replied grimly, and without hesitation, "that we have to consider that a possibility."

It took quite a bit of effort on Abhiraka's part not to turn, stride over to the Pandyan king's tent, and force a confrontation that would reveal the truth of the wily man's plans. However, Abhiraka hadn't maintained his grip on power and expanded his kingdom by giving in to his emotions. Taking a seat, he adopted a pose, crossing his legs over each other and placing his hands on his thighs that his subordinates knew signaled that Abhiraka was deep in thought, and they watched in silence, having long before learned that interrupting their king while he was in this state never ended well.

Finally, after a period of time that was impossible to measure,

Abhiraka broke the quiet by saying, "That means it's even more important that we expel those dogs from our kingdom." With this seemingly settled, he turned to the more pressing matter, asking the three men, "In the meantime, do you have suggestions about how to improve the morale? There's not much I can do about the Pandyans if Puddapandyan doesn't cooperate."

This was also something the men had discussed, but this time, it was Nahapana who spoke for them. "Actually, Your Highness, we do have one suggestion." When Abhiraka nodded at him to continue, he said, "While the idea behind it was sound. And," he hurried to add, knowing that even under the best of conditions, his king didn't react well to criticism, whether it was real or not, "it was the only thing that made any sense at the time, trying to force the Romans out from behind the walls hasn't worked."

He paused, eyeing Abhiraka nervously, but the king's only reaction, aside from folding his arms, always a dangerous sign, was to say tersely, "Go on, Nahapana. Finish what you're saying."

"I, or rather we," Nahapana indicated the other two, neither of whom looked happy to be included, "do not believe that continuing to lay waste to the kingdom is necessary any longer. And," he hurried on, "it's one reason why we're having the morale problems with the Bharuch men."

Whether it was out of pity for Nahapana, or he felt it necessary to drive the point home, Ranjeet put in, "There are men marching for us who came from some of the villages and farms we've been forced to despoil, Your Highness. I don't have to tell you what that does to a man. And," now he did hesitate, but Ranjeet could see that his king was unconvinced, so he made the decision to divulge an incident that he and the other two commanders had decided to keep from him, "something occurred last week, when we were outside Naghdara." He named the village southwest of the city, not far from the coast. "In the detachment of men we sent, there were two men who come from Naghdara, and the father of one of them resisted when our men began firing the fields. The commander of the detachment didn't know of the connection, and he ordered the son to strike down the father for his disobedience."

Ranjeet paused then, mainly to gauge how Abhiraka was receiving this information, and he could see how shaken his king and friend was, but then Abhiraka said hoarsely, "Go on, Ranjeet. Tell me the rest. Did this man obey his commander?"

"No, Your Highness," Ranjeet said with a sigh. "He did not." Ranjeet stopped again, but this time it was because he didn't really want to finish describing what had been a sordid, depressing, and frankly, sad affair.

Abhiraka stared at Ranjeet, then took pity on the other man by finishing, "So now there is a house in Naghdara who lost only a father, but a son, is that what you're saying?"

"Yes, Your Highness," Ranjeet answered softly. "The commander was certainly acting in the proper manner," he continued carefully, but Abhiraka waved at him to stop.

"He was a fool," Abhiraka said impatiently. "Who was the commander? Send for him, I want to speak to him." He instantly saw by their reaction that Abhiraka still didn't have the entire story, and he couldn't stifle a groan before he demanded, "What else haven't you told me?"

"It's not that we haven't told you, Your Highness," Ranjeet replied calmly. "It's because we don't actually know what happened to him. He's...vanished."

For the first time, Abhiraka was moved to ask, "Who is it?"

"Rudra Gautama."

"Gautama?" Abhiraka frowned. "I know him. He would never desert us."

"That," Ranjeet agreed, "is my belief as well, Your Highness."

"Which means," Abhiraka continued coldly, "that someone took matters into their own hands." He looked directly at Ranjeet, pinning his commander with a gaze that told the man that this was King Abhiraka and not Ranjeet's friend, asking, "Have you taken steps to resolve this matter, Ranjeet? Has whoever done this been brought to justice?"

"No, Your Highness," Ranjeet was forced to admit, "but that's because the man we suspect of the crime has been vouched for by his comrades."

"And is that man the other villager from Naghdara?" Abhiraka asked, despite being certain he knew the answer.

"Yes, Your Highness," Ranjeet confirmed. "But as I said, the other men in his tent all claim that he was with them at the time Gautama disappeared."

Abhiraka opened his mouth with the intention of ordering that those men be taken into custody and put to torture; to Ranjeet's intense relief, he learned that his king's mind worked through the problem and realized, "And if we take these men and put them to torture to learn the truth, it will only harm morale more than it already has been."

"That," Ranjeet nodded, "was our assessment as well, Your

Highness."

To a man like Abhiraka, who was accustomed to complete and immediate obedience to his every order, the previous months had been a real test of his patience and ability to accept what was a drastic change in his circumstances. However, while he would never accept this as the reality of his life for the rest of his days, he had surprised himself with his ability to adapt, so he didn't dwell more than a span of heartbeats on the frustrating fact that he couldn't simply snatch these men from their tent and have them tortured to find out what he was certain was the truth, that the second man of Naghdara, who was in all likelihood related to the dead soldier and his father, had murdered Gautama in revenge. Instead, he turned his mind to the original topic of the conversation, Bolon's suggestion, but he quickly realized that, even as he was listening to Ranjeet talk about the Gautama business, he had made up his mind.

"We," he announced, "will cease laying waste to our own kingdom." Turning to Bolon, he said, "You are correct, Bolon, that since it didn't serve our purposes in drawing the Romans out, it doesn't make sense to continue the practice." He stood and said, "Relay my orders tonight. That should at least cheer up part of the army somewhat." Turning towards his tent, he added in a clear afterthought, "Now, if we can just get Caesar to do something that gets him from behind our walls, that will do more to help morale than anything else."

Certainly, it was a sentiment that made sense, and the others nodded in agreement, all of them of a like mind as they retired for the night. It would be the coming of the next day that, although they would get their wish, it didn't improve their circumstances in the slightest, and in fact, made their situation infinitely more difficult.

With Abhiraka's decision to suspend their activities, it was decided to remain in their current encampment for at least the next day, while the two kings and their respective subordinates discussed what to do next, and they were in fact engaged in these discussions, which had begun early that morning and were now dragging into the early evening with no clear strategy, when their version of the *bucina* sounded from the outer edge of the camp, playing the signal that a party was approaching.

"Are we expecting any of the scouting parties to report today?" Abhiraka asked Ranjeet, who shook his head as he rose from his stool.

"Not that I'm aware of, Your Highness," he said, already

moving towards the flap of the tent. "I will go see what's happening."

Abhiraka resumed the original conversation, although it was really better described as a long-running disagreement that was gradually becoming more heated, but within a matter of moments, everything that they were discussing previously was forgotten.

They were forewarned by the running footsteps, followed by Ranjeet pushing through the flaps of the tent, entering and sliding to a stop in front of Abhiraka, panting so hard that it made it difficult to understand him as he gasped, "Caesar has left Bharuch again!" As might be expected, this brought everyone to their feet, but Ranjeet wasn't through. "He took the entire fleet with him, and it appears that most of his army went with him!"

Before Ranjeet could continue, he had to pause to catch his breath, but even if he had no need, he would have been interrupted by the shouts of surprise and happiness at this news. Like the others, Abhiraka had come to his feet, but between the somber conversation of the night before and the tenor of the discussions during the day, he wasn't one of the celebrants, his eyes still on Ranjeet, who clearly didn't share the mood.

Holding up a hand, Abhiraka barked, "Silence!" Ignoring the look of outrage on the face of Puddapandyan at what was the kind of rebuke that had been known to start wars, Abhiraka kept his attention on Ranjeet as he said, "Judging from Ranjeet's expression, there's more."

If Puddapandyan was disposed to make an issue of Abhiraka's rudeness, it only lasted as long as it took Ranjeet to answer his king. "As usual, you're correct, Your Highness. There *is* more." This time when he took a breath, it wasn't because he needed the extra wind, but an extra moment to decide how to proceed. "As I said," he continued, "Caesar was seen boarding a ship, along with a substantial portion of his army. However, while we knew that when Caesar returned, there was one of their Legions with him, another one arrived more than a week later, so he has replaced the two Legions we destroyed." This was sobering news, but by now, with their collective attention on Ranjeet, they all also could see there was even more. "Our scouts learned of all this from some of our subjects who have been our eyes and ears, so the information is reliable, but they didn't know where the Romans were heading. Because of that, the commander of the party decided that he would come to inform you of what he had learned, while he left the rest of his men at their spot on the southern bank of the river, trying to gather more information." Again, Ranjeet paused, except this time, he wasn't looking at Abhiraka; instead, he turned his attention to Puddapandyan as he went on, "Since the commander didn't know our exact location, he headed to the last place he had heard the army was anywhere near, which was Naghdara, and it was as he was on his way, and was within sight of the sea that he saw what could only be Caesar's fleet. He said that he counted five hundred ships before he decided he had seen enough, and his guess is that he only counted half of them."

Of the men listening, Abhiraka, Bolon, and Nahapana had the strongest reactions, but while Puddapandyan understood that, while Ranjeet addressing him directly for this piece of information was important, he wasn't sure why, and he looked back at Ranjeet in open puzzlement, making this clear by asking, "This is important, no doubt, but why are you looking at me in this manner, Ranjeet?"

Shooting a glance at his king, Ranjeet saw that Abhiraka wanted to be the man to enlighten his fellow king, and he remained silent so that it was Abhiraka who informed him, "Naghdara is about twenty miles south of Bharuch, Puddapandyan. The Roman fleet is heading south." Although Abhiraka definitely felt a surge of satisfaction, it was more because now at least Puddapandyan was in the same predicament as he was, which he explained, "I seriously doubt that Caesar would take most of his army just to take Kalliena and the other towns in the southern part of my kingdom. If we hadn't been nearby, the Romans wouldn't have needed one Legion to take Kalliena, let alone two, and that is the same for the other towns in that region."

For a span of several heartbeats, Abhiraka wondered if he needed to be more explicit, as the Pandyan king just gave him a blank stare, but just as he opened his mouth, he saw the dawning understanding, confirmed when, with a combination gasp and moan, Puddapandyan took a staggering step backward to collapse back down onto his chair.

"They...they are going to attack my kingdom?" He was silent for a span of heartbeats, then finally, before anyone could respond, he repeated himself, but as a statement. "They're going to attack my kingdom! And," suddenly, the Pandyan became as animated as Abhiraka had ever seen him, leaping to his feet, "we're hundreds of miles away!" Pointing a shaking finger at Abhiraka, he snarled, "All because of you, Abhiraka! All because you couldn't keep these filthy animals from taking *your* kingdom, now I'm at risk of losing mine!"

He whirled about, presumably to give orders to his subordinates to begin preparations to immediately march south, making him the last to see that his reign was about to come to an end. Abhiraka hadn't given any kind of signal to Ranjeet, Bolon, and Nahapana, but he hadn't needed to; they were already moving, as was Abhiraka, and despite Puddapandyan's bodyguards reacting quickly, it wasn't quickly enough. Abhiraka was approaching the Pandyan king from behind, who turned just in time to receive the dagger thrust that Abhiraka had aimed for his back, but ended up striking him just below the ribcage, the point driving up and into Puddapandyan's heart. Abhiraka's face was inches away from the older man, and he was blasted with the last breath of his fellow king who, thankfully for Abhiraka, collapsed immediately without uttering more than a breathy moan. The men of Bharuch weren't quite so fortunate with the other Pandyans, as one of Puddapandyan's lieutenants managed to shout an alarm while Ranjeet and Bolon were slaughtering the two bodyguards and Nahapana was busy with the second of the three Pandyan officers; although the third man didn't shout, he instead darted for the flap of the tent. Bolon was nearest, yet despite grabbing a piece of the man's robe, he was left holding a scrap of fabric, but reacted instantly, charging out of the tent hard on the man's heels. Nahapana had already spun about to lunge at the Pandyan who had shouted, but the man hopped a step backward, just out of the reach of Nahapana's weapon; thankfully, that put him immediately within range of Abhiraka, who plunged his dagger into the man's back. For the span of a couple heartbeats, the only sound within the tent was the harsh panting of the three men left alive, which allowed them to hear a muffled scream. Alarmed, they turned and made for the exit, to which Nahapana was closest, but just as he reached out, the flap was shoved aside and inward by Bolon, who used one arm to do that while his other was wrapped under the arms of the Pandyan.

With the others' help, the last Pandyan who could have raised the alarm was dragged inside and dumped on top of the bodies of the two bodyguards, and Ranjeet asked Bolon in a low voice, "Did anyone see you?"

"See? No." Bolon shook his head. "Hear?"

He turned and cocked an ear in a way that caused the others to calm their breathing, and they all stood listening for more than a dozen heartbeats, but there wasn't any kind of noise that indicated alarm. Random shouts, and sometimes screams, were an integral part of life with a large army, and Bolon had been aided from being seen during his short pursuit by the nature in which the king's tent was surrounded by those of his immediate commanders and the tent containing his royal bodyguards.

It was Ranjeet who remembered the latter, and he spoke quietly, "We're going to have to take care of the rest of Puddapandyan's bodyguards."

Abhiraka nodded absently, but while he heard and agreed, most of his concentration was on the body lying at his feet, as Puddapandyan stared up at him with a mouth open in the last surprise he would ever experience, his sightless eyes wide open and seeming to stare directly at him. It wasn't that he felt the slightest bit of remorse or grief; what the dead Pandyan king posed was a practical problem, and he was having difficulty focusing on what to do about it.

"Your Highness," Ranjeet's tone was almost gentle, "what do we do now?"

Abhiraka's eyes never left Puddapandyan, so he missed the looks of dismay on the others when he answered simply, "I have no idea."

Although the men cooped up on the ships of Caesar's fleet had learned the distance from Bharuch to Muziris, what Caesar had decided to keep from them, and had ordered Volusenus not to breathe a word even to Pollio or Hirtius, was the fact that the prevailing winds were from the south, which cut the daily distance to less than fifty miles. Another complication was due to what Volusenus had discovered, that there were relatively few places where a fleet the size of this one could either put into a natural harbor or even beach themselves. Life belowdecks was a misery, and fairly quickly, each ship that was transporting the men of the Legions was faced with a situation where angry rankers were demanding to be allowed out in the open air. This created a dangerous situation even without raw tempers, because having that many men higher up in the ship made it more likely to capsize. Two days after Volusenus' return, Caesar held an emergency meeting, where a system was worked out that allowed men to spend time on deck, but on a rotating schedule and in numbers that didn't threaten the stability of their ship. Unfortunately, not much could be done for the vessels carrying the animals, and many expired from the stifling heat, and it became a common sight to see men struggling to drag a carcass up on deck prior to dumping it overboard. In further recognition of the difficult conditions, men weren't required to wear their tunics, and very quickly, the sight of mostly naked men sprawled out over every available inch of the upper deck was a memory that every man would long remember. Pullus was just as miserable as his men, and while he tried to contain himself from lashing out because of the ill temper caused by the heat, he wasn't always successful.

As usual, it was left to Diocles to do whatever he could to keep his master and friend happy, yet he was also certain that there was something more than the heat that was causing Pullus' foul mood, but while he didn't know with any certainty, he also suspected that the reason for it had nothing to do with the weather, and was in fact back in Bharuch. The Greek desperately wanted to talk to someone about it, but while Balbus was aboard the same ship and was one of the two of Pullus' closest friends, the scarred Centurion simply didn't have it in him to understand why Pullus would be moping about a woman, and that was even if she was a queen. No, the only person he would definitely have confided in was Scribonius, although he also considered Gaius, given that he was aware of Gaius' own love affair with Amodini, but the Greek was also fairly certain that it would create an awkward situation given the familial connection between the two lovesick men. Scribonius, unfortunately, was on his own ship, although he did row over every couple of days, but there simply was no way to get him away to speak privately, even on a *quadrireme*. Diocles was also aware that, while he was most concerned about Pullus, neither he nor Gaius were as unique as it might have seemed. The Romans had been in Bharuch nine months by the time they actually departed, and as had happened in Susa, relationships had been formed that, while they had perhaps been entered into by the women of the city out of a sense of pragmatism and self-interest, had evolved into something else. When they had departed Susa, while it would have been a lie to say there was widespread weeping and gnashing of teeth, neither had the inhabitants of the city been particularly happy to see them go. And that, Diocles knew very well, as did most of the men attached to the Roman army, was due in large part to Caesar's strict orders, and the enforcement of those orders by his Primi Pili, who by this point in time had seen the wisdom of treating the civilians of a conquered city with clemency. When your conquerors actually treated you better, and actually offered protection under the law to a degree much higher than what had been the norm under the regime which they had replaced, it made controlling the populace even easier. What had taken place in Bharuch was somewhat different, mainly because of the actions of the men during the period starting the night Bharuch fell and in the ensuing week before some form of order was restored, so the mixing between Romans and all citizens of Bharuch remained strictly commercial for perhaps the next six months. The beginning of the canal project had marked a turning point, because not only did the Romans not simply drive the men of the city out and force them to work, those men were actually paid, while word was quietly spread that this was what they could expect from Rome in the future, provided they behaved. And, to their credit, the people of Bharuch had largely done so, but as every man attached to Caesar's army knew, the real test would come now that there were only three Legions and a few Cohorts of auxiliaries left behind.

"Master Diocles, do you think that we might spend the night ashore?"

Diocles was a patient man—he had to be serving Titus Pullus—yet he found it difficult not to snap at Barhinder to remind him that he wasn't anyone's master, and was in fact technically a slave. That he didn't do so was due to the fact that he simply found it impossible to stay more than momentarily angry at the Bharuch youth, if only because of the devotion Barhinder showed him.

Consequently, all Diocles did was heave a sigh that Barhinder had learned signaled the Greek's impatience, then replied, "I don't know, Barhinder. I wish I did." He offered the youth a grin. "I want to get off this ship just as much as you do." Then he pointed down to the scroll and wax tablet in Barhinder's lap and said sternly, "You need to finish your work, though. As soon as I learn anything, I will let you know."

The face Barhinder made momentarily reminded Diocles of his days as a tutor, back when he was not much older than Barhinder and teaching the children of the Roman Senator who had chosen to side with Pompeius Magnus and had fallen at Pharsalus, and through a series of events that found him hiding in a pile of corpses before emerging and being taken into captivity, then plucked out of the pen by Titus Pullus, for which he thanked his gods regularly. Although he hadn't given it a great deal of thought, Diocles was aware that this was at least part of why he felt a connection to Barhinder, although the youngster hadn't hidden in a pile of corpses of his own accord. There had been some resistance from Pullus, but he now viewed the budding relationship between the Greek who was so much more than a mere slave and Barhinder with a fair amount of indulgent amusement.

"I suppose," he had sighed, "everyone needs a pet." He had grinned at Diocles as he added, "But they usually have four legs, not two."

This was partially the reason for Barhinder sitting, crammed in a corner of the Primus Pilus' cabin, earnestly studying his lessons in Latin, because Diocles was determined that Barhinder would prove of some value to Pullus, and by extension, to Rome. It certainly helped that the boy had known Greek, not fluently, but he had a foundation, and had improved so rapidly that it caught Diocles by surprise. The boy was clever, but more importantly, for whatever reason, he had devoted himself to Diocles, and his fear of Pullus was slowly waning, although he still did his best to keep out of the Centurion's way. Which, as he had learned, was difficult aboard ship, and the chance to stretch his legs was only part of the reason why he had asked Diocles. As their ship plunged slowly but steadily south and Barhinder worked at learning his letters, the youth was happily unaware that it had been his brother whose sacrifice had set the events in motion that were a direct cause for what was now taking place.

Nedunj had thought that he would be, if not overjoyed, at least happy that with his father's absence, he was for all intents and purposes the ruler of Pandya, but it seemed as if every day brought a new concern that required another decision where the answer wasn't nearly as clear cut as he had thought when he had been watching Puddapandyan make them. What was even more surprising to him was how much he found he missed his wife Aarunya, who he had left back in Karoura. Here in Muziris, while he had availed himself of his father's concubines, it had been supremely unsatisfying, because once his fleshly needs were sated, there was nobody he could talk to and in whom he could confide. He had realized very quickly that there was more to Aarunya than just her beauty, and of course her bloodline; she was every bit the daughter of both Abhiraka and Hyppolita. Somewhat unusually, the King of Bharuch had actually been close with his daughter, which she ascribed to being the firstborn, and he had shared with her insights and guidance on the kind of things that a member of royalty should know, but to a higher degree than was customary for a female. However, as he also learned, it was her mother Hyppolita who had taught her the most, and Nedunj's young wife possessed a shrewd insight into the constantly shifting tides that came with a royal court, particularly where it concerned the men who advised first Puddapandyan, and now Nedunj. Naturally, some of the more important advisers had departed with the king, and there had been a fierce argument between father and son, Nedunj believing that it should be him who led Pandya's forces north with his father-in-law. His father, however, had refused to budge, insisting that as important as it was for a young prince to make his reputation in war, it was the task of governance that was actually more important, and more difficult. And, he ruefully admitted to himself, as usual, his father had been correct. It was the late afternoon, and he had spent almost the entire day in the palace, smaller than the one in the capital, but still a sumptuous residence, where he had been adjudicating matters between disputing parties, something that happened once a month and usually took two or three days. Once finished, he had walked to the western wall, climbing to the rampart to stare out at the seemingly endless expanse of water. It was one of his favorite spots and had been for as long as he could remember, spending long stretches of time just staring out at the sea and wondering what lay beyond the farthest edge of what he could see. Because of his status, he was much better educated than his subjects, so he knew in a general sense that, off to his right quarter, was where the country called Arabia was located, but that hadn't been enough for Nedunj. Almost directly south of him but far out of sight was the island that even his people referred to as Taprobane, and he had accompanied his father twice to visit the island, the first time ostensibly to meet the Greek traders there, but as his father told him later, their real purpose had been for Puddapandyan to get a better idea of the defenses.

"One day, it will be part of our kingdom," he had assured Nedunj, who had just turned twelve on their first excursion. "This was the first step in that."

But it was what was directly west, beyond Arabia, that fascinated Nedunj, and thanks to his Greek education, he knew of the existence of the land called Africa, but that was about all he knew, that it existed. When he had been young, he would vow to himself that one day, when he was king, he would sail across this huge expanse of water and claim Africa as part of his kingdom. The memory made him laugh, and he stood, reveling in the cool breeze that always blew here in Muziris, and while he understood the strategic reasons why the Kings of Pandya had chosen Karoura, this small city was much more pleasant as far as he was concerned. As he stood there, he saw the small craft, crewed by two or at most three men, with a triangular sail but also powered by oars, struggle back towards the city through slightly choppy surf, their day of fishing done. These were the only vessels that dared to risk the narrow mouth that had given the Greeks the idea for the name they called the river, although it was locally called the Periyar. Ships larger than these small fishing boats who were familiar with these waters knew that the real entrance to the river was a fair distance south, which meant that it was a fairly common sight to see ships go sailing past the walls of the city, only for the same vessels to reappear as they rowed upriver, either heading inland to Karoura or to the docks lining the southern bank outside Muziris. Not only was Muziris a more pleasant city, it was also larger and wealthier than Karoura, which was slightly unusual, but the city was the southernmost terminus of mainland India of the famed Silk Road, and while Bharuch was rich because of its hardwoods, cotton, and other commodities, the lands of the Pandya were perfect for the growing of all manner of spices and pepper that, particularly in the lands of the Han, were in huge demand, although a fair amount went West as well. To Nedunj, it had always been something of a puzzle why people from so many faraway places craved these things that had always been part of his diet, and he assumed it must be because they had no way to flavor their food. What couldn't be argued was the wealth that poured into his father's coffers; *his* coffers, he reminded himself, perhaps not today, but soon. It was a dream he nurtured, but because of his isolation, never dared to speak of, that somehow, his father wouldn't return from Bharuch; it would be quite some time, and much would happen in the meantime, before he would learn that his dream had just come true.

It had been at the suggestion of Papernus that the Romans who remained behind in Bharuch make a demonstration to whoever was watching the city.

"You know those bastards are out there somewhere," he had argued during a meeting of the three remaining Primi Pili with Ventidius. "I think that letting them know what's waiting for them will convince them they don't want to waste their fucking animals trying to retake this place."

Not only was it a sensible suggestion, but Papernus had no way of knowing that, despite his age and crusty exterior, Publius Ventidius wasn't afraid to try something unorthodox; he had been the man who experimented with the lead slingshot that had proven so devastatingly effective against the crown prince Pacorus of the Parthian Empire.

"What did you have in mind?" Ventidius asked.

"As I understand from my comrades here," Papernus indicated Batius and Aquilinus, "we have developed a way to use that naphtha as ammunition for our artillery, without it turning our *ballistae* into torches, and the *immunes* along with it."

"We have," Ventidius agreed. "Outside Ctesiphon and Seleucia, although it was only after we found out about that stuff the hard way."

Even now, more than three years later, the memory of seeing men turned into blazing torches, unable to get the sticky stuff with the consistency of honey off of their skin, made The Muleteer shudder, but it was nothing compared to Batius, who was actually just a handful of years younger than the *Praetor*, and as a result, the pair had a good relationship. He had seen the first time naphtha had been used against them, and the last time when the Romans had used it against Abhiraka's army.

"We have plenty in stores," Papernus continued. "So I think that we should use a few jars of the stuff by sending them outside the walls with our *ballistae*, and let those *cunni* know what to expect."

"You weren't here when we were down to our last jars," Batius interrupted. "And we sent almost all of what we had out with the 7th and 11th, and it didn't do any good, which means that they clearly didn't have enough to defeat however many elephants that bastard king to the south brought here." He shook his head, addressing Ventidius as he finished flatly, "It's a bad idea, sir. A very bad idea."

For Aquilinus, the objection was more practical.

"By doing as Papernus suggests, we also let them know exactly how far the range is of our artillery," he argued. "Isn't it better to keep them guessing?"

The fact was that Ventidius had already made up his mind to do as Papernus suggested, but he was aware that he had just arrived, although he knew both Batius and Aquilinus quite well from their time in Parthia, so he chose his words carefully.

"Actually, Papernus, I think this is a good idea, but I also think there is a way to make it more effective so that we can minimize the amount of naphtha we use."

And, once he was through, he was pleased, and relieved, to see that all three Centurions agreed.

Ventidius' decision was to not only wait a few days, and to not make a secret of what the Romans inside Bharuch had planned, but to make the demonstration at night and announce the date. His decision to wait was based in his certainty that, while there were undoubtedly men spying on the city from the outside, by this point in time, now that the Romans had allowed commercial activity to resume, albeit strictly controlled, there were eyes inside the walls, and he wanted to ensure that whoever they were heard. Then he wanted to give them the time to make their way out of the city to relay the information to whoever was watching outside, and while he knew this could have been accomplished within a day, he wanted to allow time for one of these scouts to ride to wherever Abhiraka and his army were lurking. In simple terms, Publius Ventidius knew from experience that receiving a report from an anonymous scout about an event wouldn't have the same impact on the commander of an army of any nation than if someone higher in the ranks saw it for themselves. For a brief period, he toyed with the idea of sending a small force out across the Narmada to lie in wait in the thick forest that was within sight of the southern wall, but quickly discarded it as a likely waste of men. No, he decided, it will be enough if this Abhiraka sends one of his commanders to see for himself; it was this thought that gave him the idea. The day of the demonstration, Ventidius presented himself at the palace in the morning, although this time, he wasn't wearing his uniform but one of the cotton tunics that he had learned very quickly were crucial to achieve even a modicum of comfort. It didn't keep the tunic from being soaked just in the short walk from the *Praetorium*, but this time, it was because of a rain shower, another thing for which the oldest Legate had to adjust when he arrived from Pattala. As expected, Ventidius was shown in, although unlike what had become a habit with Pullus, the elderly male attendant didn't lead him upstairs but left him waiting in the entrance area while he went to fetch Hyppolita. And, as Ventidius had anticipated, the Queen of Bharuch took her time in making her appearance, but despite expecting it, the wait put him in a foul mood, which was what he blamed for what was about to happen afterward.

"Praetor Ventidius, I apologize for the wait."

Ventidius had actually been examining a carved figurine that, to his eyes, appeared to be a woman with four arms, holding what was clearly some sort of musical instrument, and he spun about to see Hyppolita descending the stairs.

"While I accept your apology, Your Highness," Ventidius' bow was perfunctory, although it was the expression on his face that sent the most potent message, "I'm afraid I am rather busy, so I will be brief."

Hyppolita stopped, a foot hovering above the next step, the only sign that she was listening since she was veiled again.

"I understand, Praetor," she replied, "and again, I apologize. It is just that I was not expecting a visit, and it is our custom that the queen be…appropriately attired to receive a guest."

"Yes, yes." Ventidius made an impatient wave. "I understand, but the reason for me being here is to let you know in advance that your presence is requested tonight, just after dark."

Hyppolita resumed her descent, not speaking until she was standing in front of The Muleteer, and even with the veil, Ventidius heard the coolness in her voice as she asked, "May I ask what this is about? And," she added before he could reply, "why you are *requesting* my presence?"

"We are making a demonstration tonight that I want you to see with your own eyes," he answered bluntly, but when the queen's body went stiff, and he heard her gasp, he realized his error, and he held up a hand, turning somewhat apologetic as he assured her, "Your Highness, I assure you that this isn't some sort of punishment we are meting out to one of your subjects, nor will anyone be harmed. It's…" His voice trailed off as he realized that he didn't really know how to describe it, so he settled on, "…something that I believe you should see with your own eyes."

Hyppolita was silent for a heartbeat, then replied, "While I appreciate the invitation, Praetor, I must respectfully decline your kind offer."

Ventidius wasn't the most patient man under the best of circumstances, and there was no sign of it now as he snapped, "And I must respectfully insist that you join me tonight, Your Highness!"

"So, your request was not a request; it was a demand," she said coldly, the folds of her gown shifting slightly as she stiffened.

"Yes," Ventidius answered tersely. "It was an order." Pausing, Ventidius took a breath, realizing that this was going badly and, despite his ire, not wanting to exacerbate the situation, and he said more quietly, "Your Highness, I will be arriving at dusk with an escort. Please invite as many of your ladies who want to attend."

"May I at least inquire as to where we are going?" Hyppolita asked, still obviously angry, but it was a cool anger. "Or is that a secret? And," she finished pointedly, "will we be returning to the palace?"

This caused Ventidius to flush, and he answered defensively, "No, Your Highness, it's not a secret. And yes, you will be returning here to the palace."

"Very well, Praeto*r*." Hyppolita attempted to sound as if she was deciding of her own free will. "I will be ready, although I cannot say how many of my ladies will be coming. Unlike you," she couldn't resist adding bitterly, "I will not force them to attend something against their will."

Ventidius bit back the angry reply that was forming, forcing himself to sound gracious as he said, "Your Highness, I assure you that you will be perfectly safe, and it will not take very long."

"Oh, Praetor," Hyppolita sounded amused, "I know that I am safe. My subjects would not harm me, or any member of the royal court."

Before he could respond, Hyppolita turned and walked up the stairs, lifting the hem of her gown with one hand, her back straight, every inch a queen, and despite his irritation, Ventidius felt a grudging respect as he thought, At least she's not as bad as that bitch Cleopatra.

As he promised, Ventidius arrived just before dusk, but this time, he wasn't alone, Hyppolita immediately recognizing that the nine Romans accompanying him were either Centurions or officers, since they were all wearing their helmets, although, she noticed, that three of them bore white crests on their helmets that ran side to side, while the crests of the rest ran front to back and were black. Somewhat to her surprise, every one of her ladies, even Amodini, had been eager to accompany her, and it served as a reminder of the monotony and boredom that had been a part of their daily routine, which had been intensified in the days since Pullus had departed since they didn't even have their daily walk.

"Your Highness," Ventidius seemed in a better humor at least, although this time he was attired in his uniform like the Centurions, and he gestured in the direction of the southern gate, "if you will follow us."

He led her and her ladies across the compound, where she saw that just outside the gate, which was opened by a pair of Romans who had drawn the assignment of guarding the palace, which was now rotated among the three remaining Legions, there was a pair of coaches that she recognized. They were the conveyances used by Hyppolita and her husband for those times when they wanted to travel without exposing their identities; she loathed them with a passion because of how cramped, stuffy, and uncomfortable they were, although it did allow her to unveil herself and uncover her head if they were taking a trip out into the kingdom. Since this was a ride that only lasted a few moments, there was no opportunity to do so, but while the coach was enclosed, there were slits in the sides, which were made of canvas that allowed the passengers to look outside, and she instantly saw they were heading for the southern wall. However, they didn't exit the city, both coaches drawing to a halt just inside the walls, then the rear door was opened, and Ventidius was standing there, hand extended to help her out.

Once she and the ladies with her had unloaded, as did the other women who had been in the second, Ventidius said, "Please follow me, Your Highness, and watch your step."

She understood why when Ventidius walked to the stone stairway that led up to the rampart, which created the first small crisis, when several of her women balked. Despite them being attired as she was, Hyppolita immediately understood why the four women had come to a sudden halt, and who the women were.

"Praetor," she called out to Ventidius, who was already halfway up the stairs, "I'm afraid that some of my ladies are terrified of heights. Is it all right if they stay here?"

The light was fading quickly, but she saw the flash of irritation cross the Roman's face, although he didn't hesitate, giving a curt nod as he said, "Of course."

Leaning over slightly, Ventidius looked down at the rest of the Roman officers who would be following the women up and called to two of the men with the black crests on their helmets, ordering them to stay put. Hyppolita began ascending, and while she was nervous at the thought of climbing up a stairway that wasn't very wide nor had any kind of guard or railing on the side opposite from the wall, she held her gown up and tried to at least appear unafraid as she climbed the steps. Reaching the rampart, she was immediately greeted by a breeze, but it was the sight of the Narmada, the water catching the last rays of the sun, the green land beyond the river, and all the sights and smells that she had been missing for months that caused her to come to a stop, her eyes filling with tears. She longed to rip her veil and head covering off so that she could feel the breeze caress her cheek with warm air that carried with it the smell of earth, the smoke from the cooking fires that were streaming into the air above the city, all of the things that she didn't realize she had missed until they were suddenly there for her to savor. One by one, those ladies who were brave, or loyal enough to Hyppolita to follow their queen, reached the rampart, but rather than stay in place, Ventidius turned and began walking down the rampart. Every four or five paces, a Roman Legionary was standing, but the Praetor had obviously given them orders to stand facing south across the river, standing in a rigid pose that she had learned from Pullus the Romans called *intente*, and which had impressed her as far as the level of discipline that was required of their common soldiers. None of the men moved their heads, but there was still enough light to see that their eyes were anything but still, and she felt slightly uncomfortable under their gaze, although none of them made a sound. She was about to ask where Ventidius was leading them, but then he reached the corner, where the southern and eastern walls met, which was when she noticed for the first time that, unlike the southern rampart, this one seemed to be full of not just men, but machines. She recognized those machines, or at least she understood their purpose, although they were slightly different from the pieces that her husband had informed her were the artillery pieces that were placed on the rampart to defend Bharuch the one time he had escorted her onto the rampart. Obviously, her husband's version hadn't worked, but she was about to learn, in a visceral manner, that it had much less to do with the weapons than the ammunition. Once the ladies were gathered in the southeastern corner, Hyppolita watched for a moment, determining that, around each piece were four Romans, all of them wearing their armor and each of them with a specific task.

Turning to Ventidius, she asked, "Why did you bring us up here, Publius Ventidius?"

Ventidius finished shouting something in Latin before addressing Hyppolita, switching to Greek. "That is a very good question, Your Highness, and I am happy to explain." Pivoting slightly, Ventidius pointed back south at the river, now barely visible in the growing darkness. "Somewhere over there, across the river, are men who are commanded by your husband. They are undoubtedly watching, because I took steps for the word to be spread that we were planning this, and gave them enough time to come from wherever your husband's army is skulking about to see what we have planned." When he smiled at her, there was nothing pleasant in it, and Hyppolita would never think of Publius Ventidius as charming, nor would she ever trust him again. Turning in the direction of the eastern wall, he pointed downward as he explained, "We are using this side of the city because there isn't really much of anything between the wall and where the river and the canal split apart." Mention of the canal seemed to jog his memory. "Oh, and I am sure you are aware of the project to widen the canal." He waited for her to nod before continuing, "It's very close to completion, but not only would it be hard for whoever your husband sent to see what we have planned if we used the northern wall, there is still construction equipment and such that would be damaged." Then he pointed across the city towards the western wall as he explained, "The problem with the western side is one of our Legions is living there. And," he chuckled as he nodded towards the river, "of course we can't do what we have planned where the docks and our other camp is located. So," he returned his attention back to the large swathe of ground on the eastern side, "this is the best spot."

When he said nothing more, Hyppolita sensed that Ventidius actually was anticipating her to ask, so she did, "And what exactly is this demonstration going to be?"

Rather than respond to her directly, he actually turned his back to her, cupped his hands around his mouth, and bellowed something in Latin. Despite the darkness, and the fact that the mesh of her veil made it harder to see at night, Hyppolita caught a flurry of movement, but it was the sudden racket of a series of clicking sounds that arrested her attention. She watched intently as she saw that the two arms of the piece nearest to her seemed to inch backward with every click, but she was confused and intrigued when she noticed how one of the four men, who had walked a couple of paces where what appeared to be an ordinary wooden crate was sitting, extracted what seemed nothing more than a clay jar with a care that made him move in slow motion. It was when the third Roman made a violent motion that created a series of sparks, accompanied by the sound of iron striking flint that it registered in her mind that there were no torches anywhere along the eastern wall. After a couple of tries, the sparks flared into something more, and she now saw that a rag had been stuffed into the jar, the flicker of flame seeming quite bright. What was most interesting to her was how the men she surmised were trained to work with this particular piece went from slow, steady movements to placing the jar that was now plainly visible in the light from the rags with a haste that might have been comical, immediately leaping away from it as it lay nestled in what she could see from the gleam was an iron mesh basket. Then, even before her mind could register what had just happened, the fourth Roman who was standing at the rear of the piece but on the side opposite from her, moved his arm in a motion that told her he was yanking something. What happened next was too fast, but the crashing sound made her jump, while more than one of her ladies shrieked in surprise and a fair amount of fear. Naturally, now that the jar was lit, despite the distraction, her eye followed it as it went soaring out into the night, tumbling over and over, trailing small sparks from the rag, and she watched it arcing down towards the ground. When it hit, there was an explosion of a light so intense, it was actually painful, searing the image into her eyes and her memory as she realized what was happening. Her first instinct was to turn away, but with the self-control that came from her status, she stood and forced herself to watch, noticing how the flames looked similar to a pail of water that someone tossed, making an oblong pattern that pointed in the direction it had been traveling. Around the main point of impact, small globules of the substance she now realized was contained within the jar surrounded the larger fire with smaller ones, and she shuddered at the thought that this was how these invaders had bested her husband, forced him to flee and make her a virtual prisoner. Unfortunately for her and her ladies, and as she quickly learned, the demonstration wasn't confined to just one piece, and she realized that, while she had been so intent on watching the preparation by the nearest crew, the men of the other four pieces had been doing the same thing. One by one, they sent their deadly cargo streaking out into the night, so that before she could have counted to ten, there was now a raggedly uniform line of fire that was several paces in length in a line roughly parallel to the wall.

So fixated on the illuminated ground, the light bright enough now that she could see where the canal her husband had created intersected with the river, Hyppolita only became aware of the sound of sobbing from behind her during what turned out to be a brief lull as the five crews repeated the process. She spun about, and while her ladies' garb made them difficult to identify, even for Hyppolita, she immediately knew the identity of the lady who was stricken.

"Why is she crying?" Ventidius' voice sounded from behind her, and even if it hadn't been the tone, his words would have ignited her rage with the same volatility that was being demonstrated out beyond the wall.

His question arrested her moving to comfort the lady, and she spun about and walked in short but quick strides that had no gliding quality to it back to Ventidius.

"Because her husband and her son were burned to death by that...that...whatever that is, Praetor," she raged. "And she was required to identify their remains from among all of our people who were slain in this manner."

Ventidius didn't look sorrowful, necessarily, but he did appear acutely uncomfortable, and while he would never say as much, once more he was on his back foot with this queen, taken aback by the clear outrage in her voice.

Consequently, the best he could do was to clear his throat and say awkwardly, "Yes, well, that must have been very difficult for her. And," his voice softened a fraction, "if you will convey my sympathies to her, I would appreciate that, Your Highness."

"I have no doubt that she will be pleased to hear that, Praetor," Hyppolita shot back, not mollified in the least, her outrage just as strong as it was when it exploded. "However, I hope you will understand if I say that she would rather have her husband and son back," she finished acidly.

Then, in an obvious rebuke, Hyppolita turned and returned to her ladies, two of whom were trying to comfort their grieving companion. Speaking not in Greek, but in the local dialect, Ventidius only became aware of what she said when they all turned and began walking back along the southern wall.

"Your Highness!" Ventidius called out. "I am afraid the demonstration isn't over."

"It is for us," Hyppolita replied, but when Ventidius took a step in their direction, before he could signal to some of his men, she said, "Praetor, I recognize you may physically force us to remain here, but it is not in your power to make us watch. Unless," she added scornfully, "you intend to violate us by revealing our faces to you and your men and hold our faces so that we cannot look away."

Ventidius immediately realized that, as unpalatable as it was, Hyppolita was speaking the truth, so he didn't take another step.

Instead, he said flatly, "I will arrange for you to be transported back to the palace, Your Highness."

She, and her ladies, had already resumed moving, and he was left with the bitter taste that came from being thwarted by a woman. Maybe, he thought angrily, she's not better than Cleopatra.

Ventidius' gamble that Abhiraka would at the very least send men he trusted to watch what the Romans had planned paid off, as the king sent Bolon and Nahapana to take up a vantage point on the southern side of the river where the entirety of the eastern wall was in view, where they watched in grim silence as, by their count, the Romans sent five volleys of flaming naphtha, scorching the ground beyond the eastern wall out to what they agreed was well more than three hundred paces. As a further demonstration, the Romans had "walked" each volley outward from the wall, the last series of five jars landing the three hundred paces they estimated. Most importantly, it was barely more than a hundred paces to the riverbank.

"There is no way for us to move quickly enough if we used their method of attacking by ship," Bolon concluded glumly, to which Nahapana concurred with a grim nod.

"Now that they've widened the northern canal," Nahapana mused, "we'll have the same problem. And remember what Balas told us, that they widened it on the wall side, which means that anyone coming like they did will now be in range of that demon fire."

The mention of Balas, who was one of the handful of Bharuch men inside the walls who had remained loyal, and who was essentially doing the same job as Barhinder, but with the 5th, reminded Bolon to ask, "Did he find out where they store it?"

Nahapana replied with a hiss of frustration first, though not because Balas had failed.

"He said that they store it in different buildings, each building next to a wall."

This certainly wasn't good news, but while Bolon was dismayed, neither was he willing to give up on what had been taking shape as the plan to retake the city. At least, as it had been before Puddapandyan's sudden demise. The fact that the two men were still alive, let alone felt secure enough to leave their king with just Ranjeet and those royal bodyguards who remained alive, was a tribute to the cunning of Abhiraka. Rather than try to concoct a story about the Pandyan king suddenly disappearing, or as they discussed at some length, to fabricate a tale whereby Puddapandyan attempted an act of treachery, Abhiraka had confronted the problem squarely. Yes, he told an assembly of the officers of both armies, Puddapandyan was dead, but he hadn't been murdered, he had been executed, not by Abhiraka's order, but by those of his son-in-law Nedunj. It was a fantastic lie, but the one benefit of being afflicted with Puddapandyan's company was in how it had given Abhiraka a much clearer picture of the internal politics of Pandya. The one piece of crucial information was how the senior officers of the Pandyan army had been almost as unhappy that their king had accompanied them as Abhiraka, but it was the reason for their unhappiness at this that Abhiraka used. Nedunj had certainly been playing the part of the trustworthy son, but behind his father's back, he had essentially purchased the loyalty of the sub commanders of each arm of the Pandyan force. Apparently, Nedunj had been certain that his father would remain behind and he would lead the Pandyan part of the army, although it was unclear whether the crown prince had any intention of actually remaining on campaign with his father-in-law. What *was* clear was what Nedunj intended to do with his force when they returned to the Pandyan kingdom, and that was to essentially force his father from power. As far as Abhiraka was concerned, this was actually why Puddapandyan had insisted on accompanying the army, anticipating his son's actions and negating them by leaving Pandya with Abhiraka and taking the army with him. It was during the admittedly tense initial meeting with the Pandyan officers that Abhiraka learned why Puddapandyan's fear was valid; it was how he had seized power from his own father, although every Pandyan swore to Abhiraka that the crown prince only intended to depose his father and not murder him, which Puddapandyan had done to his father. Abhiraka had long heard the rumors to this effect but had dismissed them until these men confirmed it as fact. This forced Abhiraka to improvise; since the Pandyan officers had been assured by Nedunj he had no intention of murdering his father, the fact that Puddapandyan's body, along with those of his three most senior officers and about half of his royal bodyguards who refused to surrender were now growing bloated in his tent required an explanation. And, whether it was a stroke of good fortune, or a gift from the divine, which would be something that Bolon, Nahapana, and Ranjeet would debate for some time to come, the important thing was that Abhiraka claimed to have learned another piece of information, which he said came by secret courier sent by Nedunj directly to his father-in-law, that the Pandyan king had been in secret negotiations with the Chola, the only other kingdom in the southern part of India that rivaled his own, to enter into an alliance. While such agreements were common; after all, the reason the Pandyans were here in Bharuch was a result of such an arrangement, the Chola had been the bitterest foe of the Pandyans long before that dynasty came to power and the kingdom was called another name. As Abhiraka and his officers learned during that meeting, almost every single Pandyan had a personal story to tell whereby their fathers, grandfathers, and even more distant generations had suffered because of the neighboring kingdom. The mood, which had been understandably tense, almost instantly changed at that moment, but Abhiraka was far from out of danger, and he knew it. However, he possessed another piece of information that was even more crucial, and the fact that only he and his three most trusted officers knew it was thanks to Bolon's quick thinking in sending the scout who had brought the information about Caesar's direction of travel back out immediately, ordering that neither he nor any of the men in the scouting party who had witnessed the Roman fleet sailing south return to the army until summoned. Caesar's departure was known among the entire army, and Abhiraka was determined that the Pandyans remain ignorant of the fact that it appeared the Roman general had every intention on invading their kingdom instead of returning to Parthia as was widely assumed by every man in the combined army. Regardless of their ignorance, there was still a strong sentiment among the Pandyans that, with the death of Puddapandyan, their prince was essentially sending a signal to them to return, anticipating that the collapse of the supposed negotiations with the Chola would result in open hostilities. This was certainly plausible, since the Chola would undoubtedly be aware that such a substantial portion of the Pandyan army was now far to the north, but this was where Abhiraka was in a difficult position, since he knew that no such negotiations existed. It took a series of meetings, held over the next two days, before Abhiraka secured the agreement of the Pandyans to remain with Abhiraka long enough to retake Bharuch, whereupon they would be immediately released to return to their own kingdom. It was on the evening of reaching this decision that one of the men whose sole assignment was to keep Bharuch under constant observation arrived in camp with the news that Ventidius had wanted spread, which was the only reason why Abhiraka felt secure enough to send Bolon and Nahapana.

Bolon knew that Balas' news that the naphtha was stored in multiple buildings wasn't good, but he wasn't as despondent as Nahapana, and he said as much. "I actually think it won't be as hard to find as you think, Nahapana."

"How so?" his companion asked skeptically. "There are literally dozens of buildings across from each wall!"

"That's true," Bolon seemingly agreed, but then he added, "but how many of those buildings are made of stone?"

It took a moment for Nahapana to comprehend his friend's meaning, but Bolon was rewarded by Nahapana's gasp of realization.

"Of course!" Nahapana nodded vigorously. "They wouldn't put that stuff inside a wooden structure!" He paused as he tried to think, but finally said, "We'll need to talk to some others who live near each wall to find out where the stone buildings are, but I can think of two along the northern wall."

Bolon stood from where he had been kneeling in the dirt, peering through the branches of the outer fringe of the forest a hundred paces from the southern riverbank, and turned to where their horses were tied.

"I think we've seen what these dogs wanted us to see," he said over his shoulder. "Now we have to find out exactly how many places we're going to have to search when we go back inside the city."

"You know that the king isn't going to let either of us go," Nahapana pointed out. "Not after what happened to Gotra."

They had never been able to determine which of the charred corpses that surrounded the remnants of the naphtha wagon outside Kalliena belonged to Sagara Gotra, but it was obvious that he had sacrificed himself, since he hadn't been seen since. This was something that Bolon certainly couldn't argue, but he was more worried about the challenges that would be posed by a small party of men swimming across the river and using the secret entrance that they still didn't know with any certainty whether the Romans knew about, although Balas had insisted that he had passed by the building where the entrance inside the city was located, and it was not only still occupied by the same family, it was unguarded. Then they would have to be able to move across the city and search however many stone buildings there turned out to be before destroying the stocks of naphtha, and do it all undetected.

It was because of this that all Bolon said in response to Nahapana was a terse, "We'll see."

Then, they were at their horses, mounted and riding off a few heartbeats later, and while neither of them said as much, they both wondered if Abhiraka's ruse had been uncovered during their absence.

Chapter 7

When the storm came sweeping in from the west, afterward, most of the men of Caesar's army and fleet considered it a favor from the gods that when it struck, the scout ships of the fleet had located a protected natural harbor where a substantial sandbar had formed from silt from the mouth of a river. More importantly, there was also a town, larger than the southernmost Bharuch holding of Kalliena, which Caesar had invested with two Cohorts of Parthian auxiliaries after slaughtering the small garrison, while also leaving just enough ships for them to escape in the event that Abhiraka's army, whose precise whereabouts were still unknown to Caesar, marched back south from Bharuch. Caesar was gambling that, even if they turned away without assaulting Bharuch because of the Pandyan king's pressure, they would be too late in arriving at the city of Muziris, which was the Roman target. While Volusenus had done his usual thorough job of scouting the Pandyan coastal city, it had been from a distance, and he had learned long before that it wouldn't be until Caesar laid eyes on the city himself before he would have a comprehensive plan to assault it. Once they reached Muziris, they would see that there would be marked similarities between their temporary refuge and Muziris that would help the Roman cause. Not that this mattered in the moment, as every man; Legionaries, cavalrymen, the remaining auxiliaries, and even the experienced crews of every ship spent a tense period as men strained at the oars as their *navarch* struggled to keep the howling wind that was so strong that the rain came horizontally, from driving their vessels onto the shore, which in this stretch was lined with rocks, some of them extending more than a hundred paces out from shoreline.

Like every other man, Titus Pullus was miserable, both because of the relentless pitching and rolling, but more than anything, it was the sense of helplessness as he gripped the edge of his chair secured to the deck with both hands, trying to decide if he was better off sitting as he was or trying to stand while clinging to something solid. Diocles had managed to take a strap that normally was used to secure cargo and secure himself to one of the beams that supported the upper deck while he wrapped his arms tightly around Barhinder, who was managing to avoid moaning in fear, but had his eyes shut tightly. Balbus, who shared Pullus' quarters, had opted to go down below with his and Pullus' men, and Pullus did experience a pang of guilt he hadn't gone with his second in command, but by the time he had decided to join Balbus, it was too late to move. The shutters were fastened, although they didn't stop water from spraying all over the occupants, while the powerful wind forced through the gap between the shutters created a shrieking, moaning sound that, despite his general lack of superstition, made Pullus whisper a secret prayer against the evil *numeni* whose malevolent spirits might have been the cause of the sound. Despite the presence of the harbor, only the first part of the fleet reached the entrance with sufficient light to negotiate the entrance, and fortunately, Pullus' *quadrireme* was one of them, although by the time the ship was anchored it was dark, and while the ship no longer bucked and rolled, the wind was still howling. The part of the fleet who arrived after darkness were forced to drive their ships up onto the beach of the sandbar, but in a minor miracle, they managed to do so without incurring major damage to their vessels. Once his ship was anchored, Pullus ventured out onto the deck, but he didn't stay long, the rain still so heavy that he couldn't see the prow of his own ship, and the storm lasted most of the night. By dawn, while it was no longer raining so heavily, there was still a steady downpour, although the wind had died considerably, but Pullus simply couldn't stand being cooped up any longer, and he went out on deck, just in his cotton tunic, resigned to the idea of getting drenched. He wasn't alone; Balbus, along with Pullus' Optio Lutatius, and Balbus' Optio Servius Barbatus, replacing Tiberius Bestia, who had been one of the unfortunate Romans who were the first to experience the use of flaming naphtha by the Parthians, were like Pullus, deciding it was better to be wet but not cooped up belowdecks. They stood at the railing nearest to the low walls of the town, and while they were close enough to see that there were figures now lining the wall facing them, they were too far away to make out anything other than their presence.

"I wonder what they're thinking at all these ships suddenly showing up?" Lutatius mused.

"'We're fucked'," Balbus said immediately, prompting his comrades' laughter.

"*I* wonder what Caesar has in mind now?" Pullus pondered. "Are we going to just leave these people, because this certainly isn't Muziris?"

"I don't see how he can," Balbus replied. "If I was in charge over there, I would have already sent someone off to warn their king or whatever they call the bastard."

Before he could say anything more, there was movement that

caught their attention, and they turned to see one of the small *biremes* gliding across what they could now see was a fair-sized protected harbor, while the mouth of the river that fed into it was almost directly across from them. It didn't take long for them to determine that the ship was heading on a course that would place it at the river's mouth, directly across from the southwestern corner of the town.

"I think now that he has a better idea of the lay of the land, he's sending that *bireme* to intercept anyone who tries to get across the river," Pullus commented.

Because the town was situated on the northern bank, anyone who intended to warn whoever was in control south of them would have to cross the river, and while it wasn't as wide as the Narmada, it would still require a boat to get to the other side.

"Like I said, that's only if they haven't already done it," Balbus commented sourly.

This was certainly true, so Pullus didn't bother arguing, choosing instead to watch the *bireme* slow, then come to a stop, dead in the middle of the river, dropping their anchor.

"I wonder if Caesar sent them out there for something besides trying to stop anyone from getting across," Lutatius said. When Pullus turned to him in some surprise, he pointed up at the wall, where they could now see that the tiny figures who had been watching were now moving. "Maybe he's trying to draw their fire," the Optio ventured. "Trying to see whether they have any artillery and if they do, what the range is."

Pullus was impressed, and he nodded his agreement as he complimented his Optio. "That's a good thought, Lutatius, and I think you may be right."

Because their collective attention was on the town, they all saw that, as Lutatius predicted, a small object came arcing out from the wall, barely visible because of the rain, but they managed to track it with their eyes to watch it splash into the river well more than a hundred paces short of the *bireme*.

"You know what they just did?" The other three men looked to Pullus, who gave them a smile that they recognized, communicating a ferocious anticipation that served as a reminder that Titus Pullus was only truly happy with a *gladius* in his hand. "They just handed Caesar what he wanted. They loosed on us without provocation."

By the time Caesar had received reports from those *navarchae* who were responsible for what was in effect one of the squadrons of the fleet, he was pleased to learn that only a half-dozen ships had suffered damage, and all but one could be repaired within a day. The lone exception was a *trireme* that had been one of the last ships of the fleet to reach safety, but not before it had struck one of the rocky outcroppings that were no more than a mile north of the river, buckling several planks of the hull. While every available man worked feverishly to bail the water that was pouring into the ship, the oarsmen exhausted themselves bringing their crippled ship to a spot where their *navarch* could drive the ship up onto the sandbar. As soon as it was light enough, work had begun by dragging the ship up onto the strip of sand, although their efforts had been hampered by the rain. Caesar did wait for the downpour to stop before summoning his Primi Pili to the flagship, but this was all the time he would allow, and they had barely settled into their spots before he began.

"Before we resume our voyage, we're going to deal with this town," he began. "While they didn't do any damage, they launched an unprovoked attack on one of our ships without bothering to ascertain our intentions." Pullus experienced a pang of regret that he hadn't had the chance to inform at least Spurius about his prediction of this, viewing it as an opportunity lost. If Caesar noticed his smug smile, he made no comment as he continued, "Before we take decisive action, however, I'm sending a delegation under a flag of truce to at least attempt a peaceful surrender."

While there was a ripple of comment at this, it was left to Carfulenus to ask, "Do we know what these people use as a symbol of a truce, sir?"

It didn't last long, but Pullus was certain that he saw a look of chagrin flash across his general's features, although he answered quickly enough, "No, Carfulenus, not with any level of certainty, but I believe that they'll understand the intent just by the manner in which we'll be acting. Now," Caesar turned and gestured to the door that led up to the upper deck, "I've already dispatched Pollio and a party to attempt to initiate contact. We'll watch what transpires up on deck."

Naturally, they obeyed, filing out in a single line because of the width of the door, but Spurius lingered next to the ladder that led to the upper deck, waiting for Pullus, whispering to him, "What did Pollio do to make Caesar angry, do you wonder?"

Pullus shrugged. "Why do you think that's the case?"

"Oh," Spurius shot back, still keeping his voice down but raising it just enough for his friend to hear the sarcasm, "I don't know. Maybe it's because we have no fucking idea if waving a white flag means what we think it means, or if it's the signal they use to begin killing."

When put that way, Pullus could see Spurius' point, although he would never say as much, but then they were up on deck, finding a spot on the rail that faced the city to watch as Pollio, standing in the prow of a small boat that still required six men to row, was taken across the river. Standing behind him were two men; one of them, in armor and clearly a ranker, was holding a siege spear, longer than the standard javelin, upon which a large square of white cotton cloth was affixed. However, it was the other man that caught Pullus' eye.

"Isn't that the translator?" he asked of nobody in particular, but it was Caesar who answered, "Yes, Pullus. That is Achaemenes. Unfortunately, we still don't have anyone besides him who's fluent enough in the tongue of these people that I trust."

His comment caused Pullus to suddenly stand erect from where he had been leaning on the railing, the image of young Barhinder being tutored by Diocles, and how the Greek had commented on how quickly Barhinder was learning, but while he opened his mouth to say something, he didn't have the chance, because there was movement on the other side of the river. The double gates on the western side of the town opened, a paved road leading from the town down to the riverbank where a low wooden wharf lined the shore, although the only boats tied there were small vessels that they assumed were for fishing, while on the southern side along the river as it moved inland, there was a much larger one, with more than a dozen ships moored along the dock. As they watched, what they counted to be ten men appeared, walking very slowly down the road, and in the time it took them to reach the wooden dock, it gave the watching Romans the chance to examine them.

"They're a lot darker than those Bharuch bastards," Balbinus muttered.

"It looks like three of them are elders or members of the town council, and I suppose the rest are supposed to be their bodyguards."

There was a murmur of assent from the others to the comment by Flaminius, but it was Caesar who mattered, yet he seemed content to watch as the party reached the dock. Immediately, five of the men spread out, and while they didn't draw, they nocked the bows they were each carrying with an arrow, although they kept them pointed down at the wooden dock.

"They're not wearing hardly any armor," Pullus observed. Then he lifted his arm to point at the two men who remained standing behind the group of three, then thought better of it, indicating with his head. "It just looks like boiled leather cuirasses. Can you tell what their shields are made of? Wood? Or wicker?"

"Looks like wicker to me," Balbinus offered.

"They just have spears, no *gladius*," Pullus observed, but the talking ceased when Pollio suddenly made a gesture, holding both arms out.

They were much too far away to hear anything, relegated to trying to determine the tenor of the exchange just by the manner in which the two parties were behaving. And, as they would quickly learn, there were even more differences between these two people than they had learned about over the previous year.

"They're nodding their heads at least," Felix said, and Pullus saw this was true, that while the three men who were at least attired in a manner that indicated they were more prosperous, were the only ones making any gestures, it was obvious that one of the three was the leader of the delegation.

The first indication that something had changed came when, without any other visual clue, the five archers suddenly raised their bows and drew them back, pointing directly at the Romans standing in the boat. What happened next occurred so quickly that it was essentially over before it started as, from ships out of Pullus' immediate range of vision, the *immunes* manning the scorpions, of which every ship had at least one affixed to its deck, sent their bolts streaking across the space, and while not all of what Pullus estimated to be about twenty iron-tipped bolts hit their targets, before anyone could comment on it, the entire contingent from the town lay on the ground in a welter of blood and gore, although at least two men made some sort of weak gesture with an arm before going limp. Within five heartbeats of the archers drawing, there was no movement from one of the ten men who had exited the town.

"Pluto's *cock*," Pullus didn't even glance over at Spurius, who had uttered the words, although he certainly shared his friend's astonishment.

Instead, without ever taking his eyes off the small boat that was now being rowed with a frenetic speed that roiled the water around each oar, he commented, "I'm glad that Caesar was prepared."

Once Pollio and Achaemenes were safely aboard, the meeting was reconvened after Caesar had a brief talk in private with both men; only then were the Centurions invited back into the cabin. Pullus' first thought was that the Parthian interpreter, who he had come to regard almost as highly as Caesar did, was clearly shaken by the events. He was correct, but not in the way Pullus thought.

"Apparently," Caesar began, his face grim, "the dialect that the people of Honnavar speak, which is the name of this town, is sufficiently distinct that Achaemenes was uncertain that he was doing an adequate job of translating their words."

He turned to the young Parthian, who, although he looked uncomfortable, understood Caesar's nod, and it was left to him to explain, "While there are several words in common with the tongue of the people in Bharuch, what differences there are," he suddenly looked down at his feet as he finished, "are significant."

"It goes deeper than that, however," Caesar interjected, then gave Achaemenes a pat of encouragement, and he said quietly, "Go ahead, Achaemenes. Tell them."

"These people, who *are* part of the Pandyan kingdom," Achaemenes explained, "have not been influenced by the Greeks. In particular, they have not adopted the gestures that we have learned to interpret as meaning something."

Although Pullus thought that he understood in a general sense, this didn't explain the issue to everyone's satisfaction, and it was Torquatus who spoke up, "What exactly does that mean?"

Achaemenes opened his mouth, but then suddenly, something seemed to occur to him, and rather than answer the Primus Pilus of the 25th, he instead asked, "Would you ask me a question that you are certain that I will agree to, Primus Pilus Torquatus?"

This clearly flummoxed the Centurion, but he was far from alone; however, he shrugged then asked, "Do you miss Parthia? And your family?" Now it was Achaemenes' turn to appear surprised, although he immediately shook his head, which prompted Torquatus to snort, then say derisively, "I find that hard to believe!"

"Why, Primus Pilus?" Achaemenes asked, but while Pullus didn't know where the interpreter was going, he didn't miss the slight smile as he added, "Because I was agreeing with you. If," he held up a hand, "I was a native of Pandya."

There was a silence for no more than a couple of heartbeats, then it was broken as they all began to talk, or in Pullus' case, to groan aloud as he realized Achaemenes' meaning.

Over the noise, Achaemenes continued, "And if I did not, I would be doing this," whereupon he began to nod.

It was a seemingly odd moment; certainly, it was unusual, but it was one that Titus Pullus would have cause to remember, because it marked the beginning of the period where nothing that Caesar and his men would go on to encounter was within their realm of experience. All those things they took for granted, down to even innocuous gestures such as nodding one's head as a sign of agreement were now in abeyance, and as Caesar led his army eastward, this would become more obvious, almost with every mile. In the moment, however, it was something that at least partially explained things, as Pollio took up the tale of what had occurred during the encounter, explaining, "When we said that we had no intention of attacking the town and only requested a day to effect repairs, the elder..." He looked over to Achaemenes, who interpreted Pollio's gaze correctly, supplying, "Srinivas," and Pollio nodded, "...Yes, Srinivas was his name, nodded his head, but he also said something."

Achaemenes took up the recounting. "This was when I realized that there are substantial differences in their dialects, but what I did understand was that they were aware that their king, Puddapandyan, had marched north with his ally Abhiraka, and while Srinivas did not know specifically, he clearly suspected that we were the cause."

"That's when Srinivas gave the order to the archers," Pollio put in, but then he turned and gave Caesar a bow, finishing, "but thanks to Caesar, here we are, alive to tell the tale."

Although this certainly explained how and why the incident occurred, the next question was posed by Balbinus. "So now that they know we're not friendly, what are we going to do, sir?"

Caesar resumed his spot in front of the small desk that, like the chair, was secured to the deck to answer, "We are going to take this town Honnavar, Balbinus. That's what we're going to do."

This announcement was met with no surprise, and judging from the manner in which his fellow Primi Pili were behaving, Pullus believed that his comrades approved of Caesar's decision; he knew that he certainly did. What he would have been less happy about, although not particularly surprised, was the knowledge that there was already a party of horsemen, dispatched by the town elder Srinivas even before he walked out of the town gates, racing south to alert the crown prince that the Romans were coming.

As the crew of the *trireme*, along with help from other crews, worked on the repairs, Caesar wasted no time, performing a quick but thorough examination of all four walls of the town of Honnavar, just beyond the range of the missiles from the defenders. While it appeared that the only artillery capable of sending rock ammunition were arrayed on the western and southern walls, Caesar didn't exclude the possibility that the pieces were fixed in place. Armed parties were sent out into the countryside, not only to forage but to round up any natives who might prove to have valuable information about the defenses of the city. And, it was because one of those parties were men of the First Century of the First Cohort of the 10th that Pullus' hunch about Barhinder proved correct. As with many seemingly small events that turn out to have wider ramifications, it started innocently enough, when Diocles sent Barhinder ashore to bring Pullus something to eat. Although they hadn't constructed a camp yet, a makeshift headquarters had been set up north of the city directly across from the narrow entrance into the protected harbor, which included several canopies, one of which was where Pullus was standing. This was where Barhinder was hurrying to when the youth first spotted a group of men, marching in his general direction, and once he was within a few paces, he saw that they were surrounding a half-dozen people, all very dark, topless but wearing what was a little larger than a loincloth around their waists, and as filthy as they were, they were a stark contrast with the legs and torsos of what Barhinder recognized had to be local farmers. The Legionaries escorting them reached Pullus at about the same time as Barhinder, but from the opposite side, so the Centurion didn't see him as he was busy accepting and returning the salute of one of the Sergeants of his Century.

"We found these men hiding out in that bit of forest." The Sergeant turned and gestured to where a clump of trees stood out from the otherwise flat, open fields that surrounded the town on the north side.

"Did they try to run?" Pullus asked.

"No, Primus Pilus." The Sergeant shook his head. "They just huddled there like frightened rabbits." He gave a short laugh. "I think they hoped we wouldn't see them, but they were shaking so badly, it made the bushes they were hiding behind move."

This elicited a chuckle from Pullus, then he turned to where, under another canopy, Caesar was standing with the Legates, but it was Achaemenes he was looking for, and the Parthian happened to be looking in his direction. Barhinder wasn't willing to interrupt whatever Pullus was going to ask Achaemenes, correctly assuming that the Primus Pilus needed the Parthian's translation ability. He had only seen Achaemenes from a distance, but he was aware, from the other men of Bharuch now scattered among the army in roles similar to Barhinder, that he spoke their tongue quite well. When the Parthian arrived, while he was technically not a part of the army, he nevertheless saluted Pullus, and it ignited a queer feeling of pride in

Barhinder, who had set down the sack containing the food Diocles had packed, although he still held the jug of water he brought.

"I need you to question these men, Achaemenes," Pullus began, which the Parthian had guessed, and he nodded as he turned to address them.

Barhinder was fascinated, and since Pullus was unaware of his presence, he stood listening intently as Achaemenes began speaking to the group of men. Who, Barhinder could see, were only slightly less frightened of the tall Parthian who was at least of a darker hue, but within a matter of a few words, he understood that there was a problem.

"Primus Pilus, one of these men is saying that there are many war elephants in Honnavar," Achaemenes informed Pullus, understandably excited.

And, naturally, Pullus turned to call Caesar, but with his heart pounding, before he thought about it, Barhinder blurted out, "That is not what he said."

This stopped Pullus, who spun back to look at Barhinder, clearly surprised at seeing the youngster, which prompted him to ask more sharply than he intended, "And how do you know that?"

"Because these people use the Tamil tongue," Barhinder explained. "And what the people of Bharuch speak is Sanskrit, which is similar, but there are also many differences." Encouraged when Pullus simply nodded at him to continue, the Bharuch youth felt his confidence growing as he continued, "So the word we use for elephants who are trained for war and those trained to work are different, but there is no distinction in Tamil."

Pullus considered, but it was Achaemenes who, not particularly caring for the manner in which this youngster was exposing his deficiency, shot back, "That does not necessarily mean that they are not talking about war elephants, if they use the same term."

"Yes it does," Barhinder countered, not argumentatively but with a quiet confidence, and before either Achaemenes or Pullus could say more, he turned and asked the farmer who had spoken. A brief exchange took place, then with a smile, Barhinder turned back to explain, "You see, they do not call war elephants 'elephants,' they use another word for them that means…" He faltered for a moment as he tried to think of the proper term in Greek, "… 'creature.' That is how you can tell whether the animals they are referring to are made for war or not. And," he finished confidently, "while there are thirty such animals in the town, they are not war elephants."

It may have been grudging, but Achaemenes thanked

Barhinder, because he *was* grateful to have learned this distinction, even if it was not in the most flattering way possible, and when he resumed speaking to the farmer, he didn't mind all that much that Barhinder was next to him. Fortunately, there wasn't much more the farmers had to add, and in accordance with Caesar's orders, they were released, for the simple reason that, as Pullus and his men had learned during their first foray into the countryside, the range of the peasants of India was restricted by how far they could walk, making it unlikely that they would go racing away to summon reinforcements from whatever place that they probably had never visited before. As they went trotting away, Barhinder retrieved the sack, handing that and the jug to Pullus, who grunted in what the youth had learned was the Roman's way of thanking him, but he was totally unprepared for the moment when, once Pullus had taken a long swallow from the jug, he thrust it at Barhinder.

"Translating must be thirsty work," Pullus said this in Latin, recalling how Diocles had praised Barhinder's progress, and he was rewarded with a cheerful grin as Barhinder accepted it.

"Yes, it is," he answered, in Latin that, while heavily accented with an inflection that Pullus realized would take some getting used to, was still understandable.

On an impulse, Pullus said suddenly, "Come with me."

And, as was his habit, he didn't wait, expecting to be obeyed, which Barhinder did, but only after exchanging a glance with Achaemenes, who could only offer a shrug, which, as it turned out, seemed to be the one universal gesture understood by everyone. This forced Barhinder to sprint to catch up with Pullus before the Centurion turned around, so he was slightly out of breath already when, realizing where Pullus was taking him, he was suddenly certain that he would faint.

Caesar, seeing them coming, received Pullus' salute, whereupon the Primus Pilus related what they had just learned from the Pandyan farmers.

Then, he gestured at Barhinder, who had unconsciously stopped so that he was behind Pullus and hidden by the Roman's bulk, which caused Pullus to growl, "Get over here where we can see you, boy." Turning back to Caesar, Pullus said, "Sir, I think young Gotra here may be of some use to us."

Caesar, knowing that Pullus wouldn't be wasting his time, indicated for him to continue, and the Centurion offered a brief explanation about Barhinder, his circumstances, and most importantly, why Barhinder was valuable to the Roman cause.

Naturally, the youth was intensely interested, although they were speaking Latin, and with the rapidity that one would expect of native speakers. However, while he didn't catch every word, Barhinder caught enough to be relatively certain about one thing, that Pullus made no mention of *how* Barhinder found himself attached to the Centurion.

Once Pullus finished, Caesar didn't hesitate, saying, "Have him attached to my staff immediately."

Pullus' initial reaction was to stifle a groan as he cursed himself; of *course* that would be Caesar's first response, but this wasn't what Pullus had in mind.

Aloud, he said, "Actually, Caesar, the reason I brought him here was to make a suggestion."

"Oh? And what that might be?"

"There are others scattered through the army like Barhinder here. Although," he allowed, "I know that, according to Diocles, he's very bright and has picked things up quickly. What I would suggest is that we start out by finding the men who can at least speak Greek along with…" He turned to Barhinder to ask, "What did you call it? The tongue your people speak and what they speak here?"

"Sanskrit," Barhinder replied, staring at the ground so that he didn't glance up and meet Caesar's eyes; it was common knowledge with the others like Barhinder that the Roman general could kill men with a single look if he so chose, and while he felt reasonably certain that, given the matter at hand, Caesar wouldn't do that to him, he was still unwilling to take the risk. "My people speak Sanskrit. The Pandya speak Tamil."

"Right," Pullus turned back to Caesar, "that's it. Sanskrit and Tamil. If we can find a dozen men out of them who can communicate with the natives, they can each be attached to a Legion, which would leave Achaemenes free for your own use."

Caesar's first reaction was to argue, thinking that it was natural for Pullus to try and keep this youth, who he was amused to see refused to look anywhere near him. However, even as he was opening his mouth to tell Pullus to carry out his order, he thought it through and realized, with some chagrin, that Pullus was correct. He already had Achaemenes, and he had seen firsthand how worn down the young Parthian was when he had returned to Bharuch, forced to go out with every sortie out into the countryside. It had only been through the intervention of the gods that Achaemenes had been out scouting, or his corpse would be wherever those of Atartinus, Mus, and their men were moldering. Of all the challenges posed by this campaign, while the climate had proven to be the most difficult factor outside of actual combat, the strangeness of this land, which as Caesar and his army were learning seemed to increase with every mile farther away from the Greek and Macedonian influences, was proving to be as challenging in its own way as the environment. When he returned to his flagship, Caesar wasted no time in issuing orders to begin the process of combing through the small army of noncombatants for men like Barhinder. Only after this did he turn his attention to finalizing the plan for the assault of Honnavar, although it didn't take long, and the sun was setting when the Primi Pili were summoned. To the surprise of none of them, hanging over the larger map that was their guide on this voyage was a smaller sketch of the town and its immediate surroundings, and they all saw the dark lines outside the outline of the town.

"Does that mean what I think it means?" Pullus whispered to Spurius.

"If you think that…"

Before Spurius could finish, Caesar began and immediately answered Pullus' question by announcing, "I have decided that it will only take one Legion to assault this town, and that it won't require a protracted siege. And," he turned and indicated one of them, "Primus Pilus Crispus has asked for the task of assaulting the town."

When the others turned their attention on him, Crispus simply shrugged and said, "My boys got stuck in Susa while you lot had all the fun in Pattala and Bharuch. They're itching for a chance to get stuck in."

There wasn't any comment, nor was there much surprise that a town the size of Honnavar didn't require more than a Legion.

"I will be diverting some artillery for the use of Crispus and his Legion," Caesar said, "but I've already ordered the transfer to begin."

"Who's going to be losing artillery?"

If Balbinus' question irritated Caesar, and was the cause for his answer would never be known, although Pullus had a strong suspicion by the manner in which their general replied, "Yours, to begin with, Balbinus. Although," he held up a hand, "I am spreading it out. You and the other three Legions will only be giving up one *ballista* and two scorpions."

"What about naphtha?" Crispus asked. "How much will you leave us?"

"Although you shouldn't need it," Caesar answered, then

surprised Pullus by turning to indicate the large Primus Pilus, "thanks to a young man from Bharuch who informed us of a significant difference between the languages that turned out to be quite important, because the defenders don't have war elephants." Turning back to Crispus, he finished, "But I would suggest you be prepared and have two dozen or more crates near at hand. Also, in the event that somehow the Pandyan army with Abhiraka turns around and heads south, you'll be in their path, but between the walls and naphtha, you should be fine."

With this matter disposed of, Caesar then returned his attention to the larger army, informing them that the fleet would resume with the incoming tide, which was estimated to be shortly after midnight. And, as usual, this meant there wasn't much time for those Primi Pili, like Balbinus, to ensure that their one *ballista* and two scorpions were offloaded and rowed to shore. Pullus was just happy that he wasn't one of them, and he decided to return to his ship, mainly to inform Diocles of the change in Barhinder's fortunes. Which, he quickly learned, was unnecessary, as he entered his cabin to the youth talking excitedly, in Greek, to Diocles, while Balbus made no attempt to hide his boredom.

"They've been chattering away like this ever since the boy walked in," Balbus complained. He looked up from his seat accusingly at Pullus. "What did you do that makes him this excited?"

"He helped the army," Diocles switched to Latin without effort. "That's what he did." Then, switching back to Greek so Barhinder would understand, he said with undisguised pride, "I was just telling Barhinder how proud I am of him, and how blessed by Fortuna he is..."

"Yes," Balbus interjected, "he's lucky that Titus didn't kill him. Personally," he sniffed, lifting his cup to hide his version of a smile, "I just think he's getting soft in his old age."

Normally, talk of his near demise, which had been a topic of conversation before, aroused a number of emotions in Barhinder, including a fair amount of anger, because it inevitably led to thoughts of his friend Agathocles, yet this time seemed different somehow, which was why he said, "No, Master Titus is lucky that I tripped."

Whether it was his completely unexpected quip or the expression of shock on Pullus' face, both Diocles and Balbus roared with laughter, although for the span of a heartbeat, Barhinder was certain he had blundered as Pullus' expression seemed carved from stone.

Then, Barhinder saw the barest flicker of a smile, but all Pullus said was, "Oh, is that what happened." Then, his weathered features split into a grin, and he made a deep bow to the boy. "I thank the gods for saving me from you, Barhinder Gotra."

Before Barhinder could reply, Pullus reached over and cuffed the youth on the head, but to Barhinder, it was one of the best moments of his life as he finally felt accepted by Titus Pullus, and he smiled shyly up at the Roman, which even more surprisingly, Pullus returned.

"Now," Pullus said, "enough of this womanish behavior. I'm hungry!"

Abhiraka, Ranjeet, and the three remaining senior Pandyan commanders who had at least appeared to accept Abhiraka's fiction about their king and agreed to allow Abhiraka to continue leading the army approached Bharuch under the cover of darkness, using what by this point had become a regular spot for the army's scouts to observe. He had tried to prepare himself, but when the sun rose and, for the first time in months, he saw the walls of his city seeming to glow in the illumination from the morning light, he couldn't stop the tears from coursing down his cheeks and into his beard, which the others wisely ignored.

"It really doesn't look that different," he finally remarked.

Bolon, who was standing slightly behind his king, looked over at Nahapana who, understanding the signal, spoke up, "Your Highness, we've learned quite a bit about how these Romans are doing things inside the city."

The very manner in which Nahapana was speaking warned Abhiraka that he was unlikely to like what he was about to hear, but he had learned that it was unjust to punish men for telling him the truth, so he said, "Go ahead, Nahapana, tell me everything."

For the next few moments, Nahapana described how, after the initial period of turmoil and unrest, matters seemed to have settled down inside Bharuch to a point where the new conquerors had allowed the merchants of the city to resume their normal activities, albeit in a slow and methodical manner. What surprised Bolon and Nahapana was that what upset Abhiraka wasn't this but the news about the canal project, and how they had learned that Rome was actually paying the citizens for the work.

They understood why when Abhiraka said grimly, "I will wager that many of those laborers were men we used for the original project."

"Who," Bolon said almost to himself, "we didn't pay."

"No," the king agreed, "we did not."

"But, Your Highness," Ranjeet spoke up, "they also knew they were doing that for the defense of the city! They wouldn't hold it against you for that just because these Roman dogs are paying them!"

If this exchange had taken place a year earlier, Abhiraka would have agreed; the events of the intervening months had not only shaken him, they had opened his eyes to certain realities, and it was with these in mind that he shook his head and countered, "But we've never treated the peasants well, Ranjeet. No," he held up a hand, "don't deny it; we both know that we've never paid men for work when it came from the royal treasury. I," he sighed, "didn't want to spend money when I could just order men to obey me on pain of death." Pointing at the walls, "Now that my people have gotten a taste of this kind of treatment, are they truly going to be happy when I return?"

"They'll do their duty," Ranjeet snarled, "or I'll make them pay for it!"

Abhiraka looked up at his friend, then stood from his kneeling posture and patted Ranjeet on the shoulder, "One thing at a time, Ranjeet. One thing at a time." Returning his attention to the city, he was silent for a span of heartbeats, visualizing the plan that they had been working on for days. "So we're going to cross at the ford," naming the only spot, almost twenty miles upriver to the east, "at night. Then we must remain hidden for the entire day and begin moving just after dark to get into position. As we're doing that," now Abhiraka turned to Bolon and Nahapana, "one of you, along with your hand-picked men, will use the secret entrance to get inside the city. According to your man..."

"Balas, Your Highness," Bolon supplied, seeing that his king had forgotten the man's name.

"Yes, Balas," Abhiraka said, embarrassed enough to add, "and you must remind me to reward Balas when we retake our kingdom. So Balas is going to be there, along with three men that he trusts, and they'll take you and three of your men to the buildings that he's identified as the warehouse for the naphtha along each wall." He paused, studying each man's face, but they all nodded, and he continued, "While you're doing that, the other two men who are going with you, Bolon, are going to make their way to the eastern gate, where Balas will have two other men to meet them, and they'll wait for the signal to open the gates during the confusion caused by destroying their supplies of the demon fire." Abhiraka stopped to look at the walls of the city, noticing that the southern gate had been opened and already people were walking down to the docks, where he could see the group of Roman soldiers who were always posted there, day and night in the four watchtowers that lined the dock, two men to a tower. There was also a hut that hadn't been there that he had been informed served as the command post for the Romans on guard duty. Seeing the soldiers made him angry; seeing his subjects, going about their business, not knowing of the ordeal they would be facing at his hands, hit him with the force of a hammer, and it prompted him to speak in a manner none of them had ever heard from their king. "We are about to inflict a great deal of pain and suffering on our people, no matter whether we're victorious or not." He shifted his gaze to look at the other men, one at a time, before he asked, "Do you all understand this?" One by one, they all assured him with the same solemnity he was displaying that they did. Satisfied, Abhiraka returned to the final details by asking Ranjeet, "Are the rafts completed?"

"They're supposed to be finished by the end of today, Your Highness," Ranjeet assured him. "You'll see for yourself when we return to the army."

Abhiraka appeared to be anything but pleased, which he explained, "I had hoped that they'd be completed by now so that we could at least test them, Ranjeet. As it stands, we're going to have to begin moving them downstream at first light in order to be in position in time for our men to load on them."

That, Ranjeet realized, was true, prompting him to ask, "Should we delay a day, Your Highness?"

"We can't," Abhiraka countered, "not unless we're willing to move with moonlight."

This was true enough, but Ranjeet persisted, "Yes, that's true, but is there that much difference between a night with no moon, and a night with just a sliver of the moon?"

Abhiraka thought for a moment, then nodded slowly.

"You're right, as usual, Ranjeet," he acknowledged ruefully. "And if it means that we can ensure that the rafts are stable enough to carry as many men as needed, then yes, it is worth it."

Suddenly, he turned and began moving to where their horses were being held by one of the bodyguards who had accompanied them, but despite the three hurrying to join him, there were still matters to discuss, and once again, this particular topic had fallen on Ranjeet's shoulders.

He did wait until they were mounted and riding away before he asked carefully, "Have you reconsidered about telling our Pandyan allies what we intend to do?"

"Have I reconsidered, Ranjeet?" Abhiraka replied evasively, "Yes, I have."

When he didn't elaborate, while it essentially told Ranjeet and the two other men the answer, Ranjeet pressed, "And? May we know what you've decided?"

Abhiraka shot him a glance that was half-irritated and half-amused, grumbling, "You nag better than Hyppolita, do you know that, Ranjeet?"

This prompted a laugh from the other man, and Ranjeet said cheerfully, "Fortunately, that's the only talent I share with the Queen, but I do pride myself on being good at it."

As he hoped, this made Abhiraka laugh, although the king admitted, "But to answer your question, my friend, I've decided that they don't need to know." Anticipating the likely reaction, he continued, "My reasoning is this. By attempting this subterfuge first, and using only our men, we're actually sparing them what will almost undoubtedly be the high cost of storming the gates as we originally discussed. And, even if we aren't successful in taking the city, if we can destroy those supplies of the demons' fire, that will be better for all of us, will it not?"

That, Ranjeet instantly understood, was true, and he was not speaking lightly, or for the purpose of obsequiousness when he said, "And *that* is why you are king, Your Highness."

While this pleased Abhiraka, knowing that Ranjeet wasn't prone to flattery, he still answered wryly, "And here I thought it was because I was the firstborn son of a king."

If the others laughed more heartily than the jest deserved, Abhiraka was still a king, no matter how he ended up on his country's throne, so he didn't complain. The rest of the ride was spent discussing last moment details, so that before they realized it, they were already back with the army, just as the sun was going down. And, to Abhiraka's pleasure, the sight that greeted him were the twenty large rafts, floating in the river.

If Caesar had been apprised of Abhiraka's plan for the retaking of Bharuch, he would have instantly seen that, while it had merit, it was extremely complicated, and as he had learned through his own bitter experiences at Gergovia and Dyrrhachium, overly complex plans had the highest chance of going wrong. Granted, it was straightforward enough in its essence; a small, hand-picked band of men, using the secret entrance that, in fact, the Romans had yet to discover, would infiltrate the city, with two specific tasks. The most crucial, Caesar would have agreed, was the destruction of the naphtha, if only because it would hamper the defenders in a future assault should this attempt fail. However, if there was a fatal flaw in the Bharuch plan, it was in the reliance on using rafts to transport the surviving men of both the phalanx and the lighter infantry, which had been made necessary by the widening of the canal, the project being completed shortly after Caesar left with the bulk of the army, heading for Pandya. If it had been the original width, the rafts could have been used to create a makeshift bridge, although the Roman still hadn't determined the level of engineering skill of any of these new foes, and the rafts would have to have been secured and reinforced to handle the weight of armored elephants, which would take a fair amount of time even for Caesar's men. Destroying the naphtha, while crucial, wasn't the only task that had to be completed; the gates would have to be opened to allow the men transported by raft to immediately unload and rush through it to engage the men of the three Legions remaining behind. Then, everything depended on how quickly the elements of the Pandyan part of the army could cross the canal and enter the city. If one part of this plan failed, it seriously jeopardized the chances for success on the part of Abhiraka and the men of Bharuch.

His name was Maran, and while he hadn't been formally appointed, Abhiraka had treated him as the highest ranking commander of the Pandyan part of the army, probably because he now commanded the two hundred fifty armored elephants. It hadn't been a position he sought, having devolved to him with the deaths of not just Puddapandyan, but his immediate superior. Now he was aware he was treading a very narrow, dangerous path, because the other two men of Pandya who Abhiraka had appointed in the place of their predecessors had been pressing him to make a decision. The choice facing them was whether or not to continue going along with this fiction that what Abhiraka had done to their king had been at the direct command of his son Nedunj. While it would seem straightforward, the truth was that it was not, because while Maran was certain that no direct order had come from the crown prince, he was almost as sure that the demise of Puddapandyan wouldn't displease Nedunj. And, as Abhiraka had surmised, once he was asked directly, Maran had confirmed he had sworn loyalty to the son instead of the father. So had Vira; at least, that was his claim, but with every passing day, Maran's suspicion that Vira was the kind of man who told others what he thought they wanted to hear grew. It was only with Sundara, the third member of the command of the Pandyan element that Maran knew where he stood, because for Sundara, it was simple; whoever rewarded him the most handsomely would be the man who won his loyalty. And, while Abhiraka had taken Bolon, Nahapana, and Ranjeet with him to perform the last scout of Bharuch before moving into position for the attack, Maran had held his own meeting, well away from the army encampment, and after taking several precautions that ensured they could talk freely.

Maran hadn't been surprised when Sundara began by asking bluntly, "Well, what do you intend to do, Maran?"

Although he had been expecting it, Maran bristled at the tone as much as the question, snapping, "I intend to do my duty to Pandya, Sundara!" Pointing a finger at the other man, who was younger than his forty years, he asked belligerently, "What do *you* intend to do, eh?"

This did seem to unsettle Sundara, who replied stiffly, "The same thing as you, Maran."

The third man spoke for the first time, falling back into his usual role as mediator between the other two, "Then I suppose we need to decide what that means."

"Yes, Vira," Maran agreed, thankful as he usually was when Vira intervened, "we do."

Then, more calmly, the three men discussed their situation, and what their possible courses of action were. They had made it clear that before Abhiraka could count on their aid, men from Bharuch would have to infiltrate the city and destroy the deadly fire weapon. This had been non-negotiable, and the one thing that all three Pandyans agreed about without any dispute; the only way they were risking Pandya's precious elephants was if the substance that had immolated most of Abhiraka's elephants was destroyed, although certainly the men of their army were a consideration as well. Maran had noticed immediately that the Bharuch king hadn't argued, and while there had been some tension and the inevitable disputes between the Pandyan and Bharuch forces, by this point, there was sufficient trust and interaction between them that, when the men of Bharuch told their comrades of the horrors wrought by the Roman fire, they were believed. The question facing the Pandya commanders was whether or not this would be enough to justify risking their precious elephants, despite the knowledge that their late ruler had essentially extorted a literal king's ransom for their use from his rival. Now that Puddapandyan was dead, the challenge lay in trying to divine what their new king Nedunj would want them to do.

In answer to Maran's broaching of this subject, Vira pointed out, "Nedunj does love Aarunya a great deal."

"So?" Sundara scoffed. "What does that matter?"

Both Maran and Vira, who were married, had the same reaction, but it was Maran who pointed out, "If you have to ask that question, you don't know. Besides, she's not just his wife, she's the new queen. And," he finished quietly, "this is her father we're talking about."

Sundara seemed unconvinced, but he also realized this was not the battle to fight, and he turned to more practical objections by asking, "If we support Abhiraka, how many men and animals are we willing to lose? And remember," he reminded the pair, "our men don't have the advantage of that armor that they took from the dead Romans, so we're likely to suffer more losses than they are." Seeing that this had made an impression, he pressed, "Will Nedunj be pleased if we return with less than half of his army, even if it was to help his father-in-law recover what he couldn't hold?"

Secretly, Maran was impressed by Sundara's argument, but it wasn't enough to sway his mind, and he glanced over at Vira, who interpreted Maran's silent signal that, for once, he would actually be the tiebreaker.

Not surprisingly, he was clearly unhappy about this, but he accepted his role of the moment, and he understood that when it appeared that Sundara's ideas weren't at least seriously considered, it created even more friction. Consequently, he sat his horse, appearing to be deep in thought, although he had already made his decision, which was based in a simple enough premise; Puddapandyan represented the past, and Nedunj the future.

Finally, he turned to Sundara and said honestly, "You make a very good point, Sundara, especially about the armor. Which," he turned to Maran, "is something that we need to discuss with Abhiraka. It is unjust of him to refuse to give us armor because the men we have with us aren't accustomed to wearing it at this time." Maran nodded his agreement, his thoughts having run along the same lines, and he had secretly faulted Puddapandyan for not pressing Abhiraka more vigorously on the issue. Turning back to Sundara, Vira continued carefully, "At the same time, Sundara, I agree with Maran that Nedunj would want us to follow through on what his father promised Abhiraka, that we help him regain Bharuch."

The two men braced for what they viewed as the inevitable argument, but Sundara shrugged and said simply, "I understand." Seeing their surprise, he offered them a thin smile as he added, "And I agree. We should stay here and see this through."

Maran tried to hide his relief, but now that this was decided, he wheeled his mount around, heading back to the army encampment next to the Narmada, the other two following. It was late afternoon, and they had been informed that Abhiraka and his commanders were expected back before dusk, while the men laboring to construct the large rafts that would be required were busy finishing the last of the twenty. Just before they reached the outer edge of camp, a figure appeared from between the outermost line of tents, coming at a run in their direction. It didn't take them long to recognize the man as one of theirs, just by the Pandyan version of a uniform, but Maran didn't immediately place the man, which informed him that he was from the ranks, but not one of the archers or spearmen of the elephant corps.

Nevertheless, when Maran drew up as the man came to a panting halt, so did his companions, although when the ranker dropped to his knees, it was Sundara who spoke up, "I recognize him, he's one of my archers." Addressing the man, he asked coldly, "What is your name? And who is your commander?"

"Sibi, Lord. And my commander is Avani Nanmaran, Lord."

"And did he send you looking for us, Sibi?"

If Sundara was irritated that Maran had intervened, he hid it, but the archer surprised them all by nodding his head, demonstrating the trait that had confused Achaemenes when he first encountered it saying, "No, Lord Maran. I came on my own."

This was so singularly unusual, that a man from the ranks would directly approach one of the high-ranking commanders that all three officers reacted in the same way, exchanging surprised glances, but it was Sundara who recovered first.

"Then this had better be important. We're too busy to listen to complaining about rations," he said harshly.

As he intended, this clearly terrified the archer, but while he remained on his knees, he did look up at them for the first time as he answered shakily, "It *is* important, Lords! At least," suddenly, he seemed to reconsider, "I believe it is important."

This elicited a snarled curse from Sundara, who nudged his horse forward, raising the short whip he carried, but Maran stopped him by saying, "Then tell us what it is, Sibi, and we will decide."

"Yes, Lord," Sibi answered immediately, while he kept an eye on Sundara, who had drawn up just a couple of paces away. "I just overheard two of the Bharuch men talking. They're part of their phalanx troops, Lord. And they were saying something..." He stopped, clearly unsure how to proceed, but when Sundara raised his arm again, he apparently decided, because he blurted, "They were saying that the Roman general Caesar had left Bharuch."

"Yes, yes, we know that," Maran interrupted, now growing impatient himself. "They're clearly returning to Parthia."

"No, Lord," Sibi nodded emphatically. "They did not sail to Parthia. These two men said..." he had to swallow once before he could get the words out, "...they're sailing to Muziris, Lord. The Romans are heading for our lands."

Just that quickly, everything changed, not just for Maran and his counterparts, or for Pandya, but for Abhiraka.

Nedunj was roused from a peaceful sleep by the sharp rapping on the door, and he was still rubbing the sleep from his eyes when it was opened, and his chamberlain appeared in the doorway, holding a lamp that illuminated his face in a manner that, when Nedunj was a child, had always frightened him.

"Yes, Adi? What is it?"

The chamberlain bowed, but he wasted no more time on formalities. "Your Highness, a messenger has arrived from Honnavar, and he insists that it is extremely important, that Lord Dipaka sent him."

"Honnavar?" Nedunj frowned, although he was rising from his bed as he tried to think. "What could Dipaka want?"

Before Adi could respond, Nedunj was already pushing past him, having snatched up a light cotton robe; while he wasn't like his father, who insisted on being seen only in his full regalia as king, neither was Nedunj willing to appear before one of his subjects in just a loincloth. Descending the stairs, he saw the man who was clearly the courier, instantly recognizing that he was on the verge of collapse, weaving on his feet from exhaustion, which deepened his unease as he accepted that this indeed had to be more than important.

Nevertheless, the courier had the presence of mind to drop to his knees as he saw Nedunj approach, offering his obeisance in a voice hoarse with fatigue, which the prince waved off impatiently, "Yes, yes. Enough of that. Adi says that Lord Dipaka sent you? What happened?"

"Yes, Your Highness," the courier replied, then extended his hand that was holding the folded parchment he had carried with him but said nothing else.

Cursing, Nedunj snatched it from his hand, while Adi hurried to his side with the lamp. Breaking the seal, he opened it, read the message, reread it, then read it yet a third time before, with a strangled gasp, he staggered backward to collapse onto the stairway.

"Is...is Dipaka certain of this?" He finally managed, his voice suddenly a match for that of the courier's, whose answer was a shake of his head before he understood more was expected.

"Yes, Your Highness," he managed, then added, "I saw the ships with my own eyes. They arrived during a storm, and it was very dark, but Lord Dipaka sent me immediately. When I was being rowed across the river, I saw ships. Many, many ships," he concluded, every bit as distressed as his prince since he had left his family behind, huddled behind walls that, despite not being a military man, he knew wouldn't be enough to stop these demon Romans.

Nedunj, his mind reeling, was trying to cope with this devastating news, and for a brief moment a part of him said that perhaps it wasn't the Romans, but he almost instantly dismissed that, understanding that there would be no other force in the known world capable of a fleet this size. According to Dipaka's message, the headman of Honnavar, who was a longtime official of his father's kingdom, had counted more than five hundred vessels of varying sizes, but all of them clearly capable of carrying men.

To his credit, Nedunj's paralysis didn't last long. Standing back up, he turned to Adi and snapped, "Send someone to summon the commanders of the garrison. Then I want you to wake up Narayana and send him to me. I have a task for him."

Within an admirably short span of time, Nedunj had managed to dash upstairs to change into more appropriate attire, but not before he rewarded the courier and summoned a slave to attend to his needs, and most importantly, begun to form a plan, so that when he entered the large room that served as the throne room of this summer palace, every man he needed was present.

"Somehow, the Romans have managed to get past the army belonging to my father and Abhiraka by ship," he began. "And I was just informed that their fleet has already reached Honnavar." He was forced to wait for the inevitable uproar from his men to peak, an outburst for which he couldn't blame them because he felt the same way. But, he reminded himself, my father trusted me with our kingdom, and I can't indulge myself. Finally, he shouted for silence so that he could continue. "If everything we have heard about the size and power of these Romans is anywhere near true, then they will not be at Honnavar long, and even if they stop at Mangalaru (Mangalore)," he named the next coastal town that was less than two hundred miles north, "that will not take them much longer to reduce. Which means," he said grimly, "we don't have much time to prepare."

Before he could continue, the lord of the city and commander of the garrison, a grizzled veteran who had been in his father's service for long before Nedunj was born, used that status to interrupt, "With all respect, Your Highness, we can prepare all we like, but we don't have nearly enough men!"

"I understand Lord Subramanian," Nedunj agreed, with a patience he didn't feel. "Which is why I've already dispatched Lord Narayana to the capital, carrying my order to strip every available man to come to Muziris immediately, along with a royal order that every ship on the river be used for the purpose of transporting them."

If he had expected this to appease the old soldier, he was disappointed, as Subramanian interrupted, "There aren't any ships large enough that far upriver to transport the elephants, Your Highness! And don't forget that we only have fifty! The rest of them are with your father!"

Now Nedunj couldn't control himself, snapping, "I assure you, Lord Subramanian, that I am acutely aware of our current situation. However," he did pause to take a breath and get his emotions under control, "I don't believe that our elephants will make the difference in this battle, because I have an idea." Naturally, the assembled men clamored at the same time, asking what this idea was, but the crown prince refused to say anything more, other than, "Once we've been reinforced, only then will I inform all of you."

None of them liked it; Nedunj wasn't surprised that it was Subramanian who was the most vocal, but he refused to budge, and the men soon left to begin their respective tasks, while Nedunj was left alone, sitting on the edge of his father's throne, trying to think through the idea that had come to him, wondering if it would be enough.

With the delay provided by the extra day, Abhiraka was satisfied that the rafts were stable enough for their purposes, although they would be floated empty downriver that night under the cover of darkness, and would only be loaded with the men in the anticipation of the signal from Bolon inside the city. This was another facet of the plan that had worried Abhiraka, because the river ran straight for more than a mile before there was a bend that barred anyone from the walls viewing that section because of the thick stand of trees that grew all the way to the riverbank. With these details taken care of, there was nothing for any of them to do but wait, the day passing slowly, but Abhiraka was heartened to see how well his men were now getting along with their Pandyan comrades. Certainly, it had been tense for the first months, but their attack of the two Roman Legions had served to do more to cement the bond between these two forces than anything either king could have done. What surprised the Bharuch king was how, once the initial tension after the death of Puddapandyan, his chief lieutenants, and those bodyguards who refused to accept Maran's explanation that their king's death had been ordered by his son died down, the Pandyan rankers seemed to have come to an easier acceptance of the fiction than some of their higher ranking comrades. However, it had been Arshad, one of the few of Abhiraka's surviving royal bodyguards, who had been wounded in the fight for Bharuch and was from a lower class than his comrades like Bolon and Nahapana, who had informed his king why this was the case.

"Their lives haven't changed, Your Highness," he explained. "Their commanders are essentially the same man as before, giving them the same orders, and they're doing the same thing, eating the same food, and living the same life."

It had served to remind Abhiraka of something that he had been forced to recognize during his own travails, that for the common people, their lives didn't revolve around who sat on the throne, unless there was a dramatic change in their circumstances. And while Abhiraka had never asked Maran, Vira, or Sundara, he strongly suspected that they had made promises to their respective rankers that their circumstances would be improved with the ascent of Nedunj to the throne. As far as the three Pandyans, although they had seemed somewhat subdued when he had returned from his final scouting of the city, Abhiraka assumed that it was simply a case of pre-battle nerves, given this would be their first time as the top commander of their arms of the Pandyan army. As slowly as the day passed, it *did* do so, until it was time for the move into position for the various parts of this elaborate plan. Before Abhiraka departed with his infantry, instead of summoning the Pandyans, he walked to the tent that had been Puddapandyan's, which the three commanders were now sharing. Naturally, he was allowed entry, and again, he ascribed their reception to what lay ahead of them.

"You should begin moving into position at midnight," Abhiraka advised, something that he had mentioned several times, but Maran's response was proper, his demeanor respectful as always.

"You can count on us to do our duty, Your Highness," he assured Abhiraka, who missed the only clue that might have alerted him that something was amiss, distracted by other things.

"And you'll know it's time when you see the light from the fires in the sky," he reminded them. "Although the elephants may have to wait longer for the rafts to be secured to the point they can hold the weight and remain stable. But your spearmen, archers, and heavy infantry should cross first."

"We understand, Your Highness," Maran assured him, then in a seeming afterthought, asked, "Am I to assume that your elephants and their crews will remain with ours?"

Abhiraka's face communicated his chagrin that he had forgotten this minor yet somewhat important detail.

"Of course," he tried to behave as if this hadn't slipped his mind. "Although, I'll ride Darpashata with our part of the army, then leave him when I lead my men across the canal. His handler will bring him along with your animals as soon as it's safe to bring them across." He offered them a smile. "If all goes well, we won't need either your elephants or what's left of mine. I think that as long as things go according to our plan, the Romans inside my city will be begging for their lives before that happens."

"May Shiva make it so." Maran bowed, speaking for his two comrades, while Abhiraka acknowledged the blessing then moved to the entrance.

The three Pandyans watched the Bharuch king exit, but they were sure to wait until he was well out of earshot before Vira turned to Maran, "What are we going to do about them, Maran?"

While this was a problem, it wasn't an insurmountable one to Maran, who answered Vira by asking, "What, exactly, do you think they'll do when we move, Vira?"

"Try to stop us," Sundara interjected, but Maran refused to be drawn into another shouting match with the other man.

"You are correct, Sundara," he answered instead. "They *may* try to stop us."

"And we'll lose men and elephants when they do," Sundara was unwilling to concede the point that this was a possibility, not a certainty.

"Sundara," Maran felt his patience beginning to wear away, but he managed to keep this from showing, "how many men and animals do you think we're going to lose if we follow through with Abhiraka's plan, compared to the handful of their elephants and crews who will remain with us?" Deciding that it would be politic to soothe his counterpart, Maran continued, "Now, if he wasn't taking the rest of his army with him, I would absolutely agree that we couldn't risk losing the men and animals it would take to march back home. But," he shook his head, "they won't be there."

Much to his relief, he saw that this scored with Sundara, who, after a couple of heartbeats of time, said grudgingly, "You're right, Maran."

With this settled, the three men left the tent and walked to the edge of the camp to watch as the surviving men of Bharuch's army departed, surrounded by their Pandyan comrades, and it did cause in Maran a twinge of regret, seeing how men from his kingdom called out to a man in the ranks of Bharuch, having forged some sort of friendship. But, he thought grimly, their king lied to us about this Caesar, and there is no amount of gold that can compensate for the havoc that the Romans were almost certain to wreak on his homeland.

"Perhaps they won't need us," Sundara suggested as they watched the last men in the ranks disappear into the forest through which the road west ran. "If they're successful destroying that demon fire, the Romans will be too busy trying to keep it from spreading and being roasted alive to stop Abhiraka's men from retaking the city."

"Perhaps," Maran agreed, but not with much conviction. Then, in the tone he used to remind the other two men that he was senior, he said, "Let's make sure all of our animals are watered, and the men fed before we begin our march."

The other two acknowledged their agreement, and the trio headed to their respective commands, each of them knowing that the next span of time would be crucial to avoid tipping off their allies who remained behind that they were about to be betrayed.

While there was some debate among Caesar's officers, when they discovered that there was another, slightly larger town on the coast that was between them and their objective, Caesar decided not to devote another Legion to the task of reducing it.

He explained his reasoning. "Not only do I not want to reduce the size of the army without knowing what's waiting for us in Muziris, I also want to increase the distance that the Pandyan army is going to have to cover to reach us. Every day of delay in reaching Muziris works in their favor, not ours."

This certainly made sense, and the only point of contention was whether or not the Pandyans would actually turn back and abandon the Bharuch king, something that Caesar handled in his usual adroit manner, asking simply of Hirtius, who had raised the question, "If you were their general, what would you do? Would you honor your word to an allied king, but risk failing your own king and losing that kingdom in the process? Or would you risk the wrath of your ally and march south as quickly as you could?"

When put this way, it effectively ended the topic, and attention was returned to the task of taking Muziris itself, the plan for which was still in the formative stages because neither Caesar nor his officers with the exception of Volusenus had had the opportunity to see the city and its environs with their own eyes. It wasn't that Caesar mistrusted Volusenus; in matters such as this, the Legate was the most trusted officer under Caesar's command, but he had only gone ashore very briefly, and it had been at night, although he did determine that the ground immediately north of the city was extremely soft. Consequently, the fleet continued to beat southward, the crews having at least become accustomed to the almost constant fight against the wind, and at times, it seemed to Caesar and most of his men that their progress could be measured in paces. The slow progress, while wearing on the patience and nerves of the men, did yield some unexpected benefits, because it allowed time for Caesar and his Primi Pili to identify a number of men who, like Barhinder, could at least communicate in Greek to a degree that they were comprehensible, and in the process, the Romans learned more about the similarities and differences between the heavily Greek-influenced people of northern India and the Pandyans. To Pullus' chagrin, he realized he had never bothered to find out why Barhinder was able to speak Tamil with a reasonable degree of fluency.

"Because my mother's father came from Yeshwant," he explained, but quickly realized the name meant nothing to his audience, which consisted of Pullus, Balbus, Diocles, and in a rare visit, Scribonius, who had rowed over from his *quadrireme* to share the evening meal. "It is a village in the interior, north of Karoura," he elaborated. "It is part of the Pandyan holdings now, but it was not back when my grandfather was a boy. It was Puddapandyan's father who conquered and claimed it for Pandya."

"What brought your grandfather so far north?" Scribonius asked, and despite not having as much interaction with the

Centurion, Barhinder actually liked him a great deal, though he couldn't say why.

Barhinder shrugged. "Just that there was a bad drought and the wells dried up, so my grandfather and two of his brothers left Yeshwant because their father told them they must leave or the rest of the family would starve." Barhinder paused to sip from his cup as he tried to recall the stories his maternal grandfather had told him, but he had died when Barhinder was seven, so his memory was fuzzy. "I know that one brother died on their journey. He was bitten by a *Naja* as they were walking through a stretch of *jangla*." This induced a shudder from the youth, while the Romans gave each other uneasy glances, having learned about the deadly hooded serpents when they began making forays out into the countryside. Barhinder continued, "He and his surviving brother finally settled in Bharuch." A sudden smile creased his dark features as he remembered this story from his childhood. "My grandfather told me that he and his brother were only passing through, but then he went to the river to wash, and he said he saw the most beautiful girl he had ever seen. He told me he turned to his brother and said, 'I am not walking another step, brother. I have found the treasure I was looking for.'" Glancing up, he saw the smiles on the faces of his audience, and he added, "That was my grandmother."

"Yes," Pullus said dryly, but in a humorous way, "we gathered as much."

Both pleased and embarrassed, Barhinder shrugged and mumbled into his cup, which he had just lifted to his lips, "He lived with us until he died, and he is the one who taught me Tamil."

Pullus' smile faded, and he turned sober as he regarded the youth.

"Barhinder, you know that you are going to be with us when we land at Muziris."

"I do," Barhinder answered solemnly, and he looked Pullus in the eye to say, "and I have seen battle, Master Pullus. I know what to expect."

Although he gave no sign, Pullus was impressed at the frank manner of Barhinder, not seeing anything of the normally cheerful teenage boy that he had come to think of as Barhinder's normal demeanor.

"Good," Pullus answered.

They turned their attention to other, more mundane things, tacitly agreeing not to dwell any longer on what their immediate future held.

They waited for about a third of a Roman watch after it got dark before Bolon led his hand-picked party out from the thick undergrowth a mile west of the city. Moving in single file, each man carried nothing but a dagger, knowing that their only real defense was stealth; if they had to use their weapon, it in all likelihood spelled the failure of their part of the plan to retake the city. The party was dressed, somewhat unusually, in long-sleeved attire that had been dyed black, understanding that rubbing themselves with dirt, or even applying oil to their skin and using charcoal would be washed off when they swam across the canal. Similarly, they wore headcloths, also black, and when he made his inspection, Bolon had walked away a few paces and was pleased to see the men were nearly invisible. Certainly, it would have been better if it had been the night before, but even with a sliver of moon, it meant that Bolon could only see a couple paces ahead as he led the way. For the first half-mile, it was a direct line, and he walked as quickly as he dared, knowing that even the movement of several men would be impossible to see. To his dismay, however, he realized that the landmark he had chosen, which he thought would have been visible even in the dark wasn't, and he ended up stopping before he had planned. Consequently, he was almost knocked down by the man behind him, but he managed to keep his feet, and to refrain from hissing at the man for doing it, holding his hands out to press against the man's chest instead. Once stopped, they had dropped into a crouch, but now Bolon was forced to stand erect, feeling exposed in doing so, despite knowing there was no way he could be seen by the Romans standing in the wooden tower located just a few paces from the junction of the canal and the river on the eastern side. There was the barest glimmer on water from the sliver of moonlight that gave him the information he needed about how much farther they had to go, but he was finding it next to impossible to tell exactly where he was in relation to his landmark. He had chosen the path in daylight, and like with most things, it had been a compromise between the amount of distance they would have to cover to reach the secret entrance after swimming the canal, and the amount of cover that route would provide. Now that he was unable to spot the landmark that needed to be to his right, Bolon fought the surge of panic, worried that he would lead his men to a spot too close to the Roman watchtower. Finally, he murmured a plea for help from the divine, then resumed moving; it was within another twenty paces he almost exploded in a sigh of relief when he finally saw the bulk of the low shed where the tools for the canal project were kept. His confidence restored, he still took the precaution of dropping to his hands and knees, waiting long enough to sense as much as see that his men followed suit, then crept the remaining distance to the edge of the canal. Since the outer edge was part of the original created by Abhiraka, it was lined with pilings of a uniform height that abutted each other, and Bolon used them for purchase as he lowered himself carefully into the water. The spot Bolon had chosen to cross was more than two hundred paces away from the watchtower, but what he was worried about were the ripples that would be created by something like a man entering the water and how, even with as little light as there was, this was the kind of movement that would attract the eye. To that end, Bolon had been forced to choose his men carefully; not only did he have to trust them, they had to possess one skill in particular, the ability to swim underwater. They had practiced in the river, over and over, until Bolon was satisfied that the men he selected could cover close to a hundred paces before being forced to come up for breath. With the width of the canal now just a handful of paces more than two hundred, they should only have to surface once, or at most twice, and they had also practiced doing so slowly. Regardless of these precautions, almost from the heartbeat he lowered himself into the water, Bolon realized how unlikely it was that he would be able to replicate what had seemed so easy when practicing in the river. To begin with, despite having paused to catch his breath before entering the water, he was panting as if he had just sprinted a hundred paces, and the water seemed much colder than he would have thought.

"Remember," he whispered, hearing the slight clicking sound of his teeth chattering, ignoring it to remind his men, "count to one hundred before you get into the water. And," he warned, "the water is very cold."

He could just barely make out the heads of the men nearest to the edge nodding, and he turned, took a breath, went underwater, placed his feet against the pilings, and pushed. Even if there had been a full moon, it would have been impossible to see; this didn't make him feel any better when, certain that his lungs were about to burst, he pushed up to the surface. He was stopped from doing so and almost drowned, because his head struck something solid, something that was harder than his skull, causing a sudden explosion of thousands of lights inside his head. Before he could stop himself, his body reacted naturally, which meant that he opened his mouth to suck in air for a shout of pain, drawing in a mouthful of water, and then some. Suddenly, all thoughts of the need for quiet, and slow, steady movement were driven from Bolon's mind, and he broke the surface with a splash that even in his condition he heard, but it wasn't nearly as loud as the coughing, spluttering sound he made.

"What was that?"

Titus Glabius, a Gregarius of the First of the Seventh of the Alaudae turned to his comrade, close enough to see that the Legionary was staring off to their left, in the direction of the canal.

"What was what? I didn't hear anything, Norbanus."

"Shhh," Norbanus hissed. "Listen!"

Biting back a curse, Glabius did as Norbanus suggested, even untying his chin strap and lifting one ear flap. He was about to chide Norbanus for imagining things, but then he heard what sounded like a slight splashing sound. Unlike Norbanus, however, he wasn't alarmed.

"It's a fish," he scoffed. "That's all." When Norbanus didn't reply, he interpreted the silence as disagreement, arguing, "If it was a man, he would have made a lot more noise."

"I suppose," Norbanus finally answered, but Glabius could tell his comrade was unconvinced.

More to distract Norbanus than any real interest in holding a conversation, which was forbidden but ignored as long as it was held in whispers and the whereabouts of the Optio or Tesseraurius roaming about was known, Glabius asked, "Have you ever tried that whorehouse next to the eastern wall?"

He was rewarded by Norbanus turning away from his examination of the canal to ask, "The one across the street from the meat shop?"

"No." Glabius shook his head. "It's the one across from the temple with that statue of the woman who has the face of an elephant."

"Ah." Norbanus' tone told Glabius he was at least aware of the place. "No, not yet. Why?"

"When you go, ask for Sandhya," Glabius replied. "She does this thing with her…"

He was cut off by another noise, from the same general direction, but now closer to their side of the canal.

"Did…"

"Yes," Glabius cut Norbanus off tersely. "I heard it."

The two men stood, staring out into the darkness, straining both their eyes and ears, the tension growing with every heartbeat, but there was nothing more except for the sounds of the night that, even this close to the city, were essentially the same as if they had been in the middle of a forest in this part of the world, the only difference being the intensity.

Finally, Norbanus asked tentatively, "Should one of us go down and check? Or should we wait for Metellus to come back on his walking post?"

Glabius considered for a moment, then said, "Let's just keep listening for a bit longer. If we hear something more, we'll both get on the ground, and one of us will go check."

"All right," he agreed, then they returned their attention to the night, but they heard nothing else, and before much longer, it had become just one of those things that happened standing guard. Naturally, neither of them had any way of knowing that almost a year earlier, young Barhinder Gotra and his comrade Agathocles had been in an almost identical situation, with the difference being they had raised the alarm.

Bolon's head ached abominably, but he gritted his teeth and ignored the pain, although he did gingerly check his scalp as he waited for the first of his men, having determined that what he had hit was a large piece of wood that had presumably fallen into the canal and was drifting about. His hair was wet, so it made it a bit difficult, although after probing the lump on the top of his skull, he was relieved that the skin wasn't broken. He heard the first man, who normally served in the phalanx and was named Ashvath, break the surface of the water, but he didn't actually see him until his hand suddenly seemed to materialize from the dark water. Reacting quickly, Bolon reached out and grasped the hand to let Ashvath know he had arrived, then with a slowness that might have been comical under different circumstances, helped him up onto the pilings on the city side. This being the side that the Romans had widened by a hundred paces, matters had been made somewhat easier for Bolon and his men, since they had less distance of open ground to cover to get to their destination. One by one, each man made it across without any sign that they had been spotted, and while he knew it was far from over, Bolon did heave a sigh of relief. The final distance to where the entrance into the secret tunnel was located would be on their bellies, and Bolon actually tried to think of himself as a *Naja* as he slithered across the ground, pleased that he could barely hear the others doing the same thing. Still, it was an agonizing process, and Bolon knew that, just like him, they were all waiting for the shout that would change everything. Somehow, it never came, Bolon reaching the back of the otherwise nondescript shed, one of several that were used to store a variety of items for the men who worked down on the river docks a short distance away. This one was a shed that contained four small boats, lying on the dirt floor with their hulls up, used to help tow larger craft to different spots along the series of wharves that extended out into the river. Although he had faith in the man Balas, who had assured him that the hinges to the door were oiled, he still held his breath when, rising to a crouch, he worked the latch of the right hand of the double doors. When the door swung noiselessly open, only then did he feel it safe to breathe, but he wasted no time, scurrying inside to allow the other men to do the same, with the last one in shutting the door. The only sound now was the panting of several men, and it was completely dark, but Bolon had prepared, both himself and the men for this. Crawling slowly, he stopped when his groping hand touched what he determined was the bow of one of the boats, and using that as a reference point, he crawled over to what would be the second boat to the left of anyone entering. Only then did he whisper, calling Ashvath and one other man to his side, and with their help, they carefully tipped the small boat up on one side, exposing what to the observer would be a hardpacked dirt floor. In fact, it wasn't a dirt floor; it was a wooden floor with an inch thick layer of dirt over it, and now Bolon and the others went to work. Feeling for the telltale sign that marked the edge of the area they needed to work, his fingers grasped the piece of rope, pulling it up from the floor, and in the process loosening the dirt, which two of the other men began scooping out and away from what was a wooden hatch, set flush with the rest of the wooden part of the floor. Once they were done, Bolon ran his hand along the hatch, then found the rope handle and pulled the hatch open. Immediately, he and the others were assaulted by a foul smell, but Bolon had warned the others to expect it.

"Being this close to the river, the tunnel always has water in it," he had informed them. "When Nahapana and I escorted the king out of the city, the water was knee deep, and I think that there are probably rats and such that have drowned in there."

Bolon went first, feeling for the top of the wooden ladder that was fastened to one stone wall, and he began lowering himself into the hole, the others hearing the splash as he dropped off the last rung. The man who went next hadn't been involved in the work uncovering the tunnel, instead fumbling his way to the cloth sack tucked in one corner, so he was the next man down, and once he was down in the tunnel, he extracted the contents. Then, with Bolon holding one of the items from the sack, the man struck the iron and flint together, the tiny sparks seeming as bright as the sun, although it took three attempts before the oil-soaked rag that had been wrapped around and tied to the end of a stick caught. As slowly as they had gone to this point, things began moving very quickly, as Bolon, holding the torch, turned and waded through the filthy water, heading towards the city. One by one, the others dropped down into the tunnel, and while the last man made sure to shut the hatch, this was the one part of the plan that worried Bolon the most. Ideally, they would have left a man behind to replace the boat, making discovery even more difficult, but he was unwilling to spare a man, and leaving him behind would essentially be a death sentence. Underground as they were, there wasn't a need for silence, although they didn't speak much, the loudest noise the splashing as they hurried to get inside Bharuch. Bolon saw the ladder when he was still several paces away, and without thinking about it, he slowed his progress a bit, knowing that this was the most dangerous moment. Balas had been certain that the Romans hadn't discovered that, in a nondescript house directly across the street from the spot where the southern and eastern walls met, there was a similarly disguised hatch in the floor, but there was only one way to find out. He waited for the others to reach him, standing in a single line in the tunnel, then turned and handed the torch to one of them before he grasped a rung and, without any noticeable hesitation, began climbing. Bolon was three rungs up, when there was a scraping sound above him, but before he could react one way or another, the hatch was yanked open, and a shadowy face suddenly appeared, barely illuminated by the flickering torch below Bolon, which meant Bolon had no idea who it was.

"Lord Bolon?"

Hearing Balas' voice almost caused Bolon to relinquish his grip on the ladder as his entire body went limp with relief. Fortunately, he caught himself, and moving quickly, he ascended the rest of the way as Balas stepped aside to allow him to step into the room.

"Everything is ready, Lord," Balas whispered. "We have brought weapons, and there is a guide for each of you who knows where the demon fire is located."

Too overcome to speak, Bolon blindly reached out, groping for Balas' shoulder, giving it a squeeze as, one by one, his men appeared from the tunnel, although they did bring the stench with them. Just before the last man stepped onto the ladder, he dropped the torch into the water, returning the total darkness to the room, and Bolon had to go by sound to determine when he was out of the tunnel.

Once he was satisfied, he whispered, "Team up with one of Balas' men. They will tell you which wall they're going to take you to." He paused, realizing that the occasion called for something special, but all he could come up with was, "Let's take back our city and watch these Romans burn in the process."

Bolon, Balas, and their parties were in the same room for only the span of perhaps a hundred heartbeats, each pair slipping out into the night, leaving an empty house behind, the normal occupants warned to find another place for the night.

Hyppolita had been having trouble sleeping for the previous several days, and she often found herself up long after midnight, standing on the second floor balcony of the palace, although she had only been allowed to do this after a furious confrontation with Praetor Ventidius, when the pair of Legionaries from one of the three Legions who were on guard duty had blocked her path. She hadn't expected him to acquiesce, taking this as an opportunity to vent her pent-up anger at the changes in the circumstances for her and her ladies. As was often the case, Hyppolita hadn't realized how much she had come to depend on even short excursions out onto the grounds until they were gone, and this further restriction made matters worse. Much to her surprise, however, Ventidius had been what, for him, passed as apologetic, assuring her that she would no longer be barred from nocturnal wandering, inside the palace, of course. Which was why, on a night with just a sliver of moon, she was standing there, with only Amodini as her companion, enjoying the cool breeze. Her choice of Amodini hadn't been on a whim; the youngest of her attendants had been withdrawn as of late, and while Hyppolita had initially thought it was because her lover, young Gaius, had left with Caesar, she now suspected another cause that was somewhat related. Since Ventidius wouldn't go as far as allowing her to order the guards who stood post out of the main room, she and Hyppolita took great care to speak in Sanskrit, but at this moment, there wasn't any conversation. There was just the sight of her city that, while it hadn't altered much to the naked eye, had become foreign to her. One change was because of the Roman practice of insisting that lamps or torches be lit at certain intersections, something that had puzzled her at first until she realized that not only was it for illumination, it provided a map of sorts in the event the Legionaries had to go out into the city. There had only been some minor unrest after Caesar and the bulk of the army left, and while she had been frustrated in learning the cause of it, her instinct told her that it was connected in some way. Otherwise, the city was dark, and quiet, and Hyppolita stood, silently counting the heartbeats for her lady's silence to end.

"Your Highness?" Amodini's voice seemed unnaturally loud, although she was only whispering. "May I ask you a question?"

"Of course, Amodini *Kutta*," Hyppolita only used this term of endearment when the other ladies weren't present. "You may ask me anything."

"How…how does a woman know when she is with child?"

Hyppolita didn't answer immediately, suddenly torn about how to respond, despite the fact that she had been almost certain this was what weighed so heavily on Amodini's mind. But now, having her fears confirmed, what had seemed so straightforward a matter before was suddenly immensely complicated.

"Have you missed your flow?"

"Yes, Your Highness," Amodini answered, unable to look at her queen, even in the darkness, certain that she would see the disappointment and judgment in her queen's eyes that she knew she deserved.

"How many cycles of the moon?"

"Two, Your Highness."

"Has it happened before?"

"No, Your Highness, this is the first time."

Hyppolita sighed, and since Amodini wouldn't face her, she moved so that she stood in front of Amodini, her back to the sleeping city.

"Then," she wanted to sound severe, but she just couldn't do it, "I would say that is how a woman knows she is with child."

Amodini suddenly broke down, dropping her face into her hands, sobbing uncontrollably, and before she had conscious thought to do so, Hyppolita found herself with her arms wrapped around the younger woman.

"There, there, *Kutta*," she murmured. "This is not the end of the world, and you are not the first woman to find herself in this situation." This was certainly true, but Amodini wasn't just any woman, and the father of her baby was a man who, as far as Hyppolita's husband was concerned, was an enemy. Hating herself for what she was about to do, she decided to ask first, "Have you decided what you want to do with this child, Amodini?"

"No, Your Highness," Amodini's sobs had become slightly less forceful. "I wasn't sure until you just told me." She said nothing for a moment, then she tilted her face up, and despite the gloom, Hyppolita saw an expression in her lady's face she had never seen, but it was Amodini's words that were like a dagger to the queen's heart. "But, Your Highness, I know I cannot kill this child." Hearing her own voice seemed to fuel her resolve, as Hyppolita realized what her look meant, which Amodini confirmed, "I will not do anything to harm it, Your Highness. Not like the Lady Maira."

The mention of Maira, one of Hyppolita's attendants before Amodini's time, and who Amodini actually replaced, had the effect on Hyppolita similar to a slap in the face, her first thought being, How could she know about that? As quickly as the question came, it was answered; of course, Eurycleia, the worst gossip of all of her ladies, and one who enjoyed stirring things up. Hyppolita would have dismissed her long before, but she was the wife of Ranjeet, her husband's closest friend and commander of the royal bodyguard, or what was left of it.

When Hyppolita opened her mouth to speak, she wasn't sure what she would say, but before a word came, with no warning whatsoever, Amodini's face and body was suddenly illuminated in a manner that Hyppolita had never seen before, only knowing that the source must be coming from behind her back. She turned in time to see, in the area around the eastern gate, a roiling column of fire, burning so intensely that she had to shield her eyes as she watched in horror as the flames seemed to reach skyward, soaring above the height of the two-story buildings, and even the eastern wall directly across the street that was at least ten feet taller. The fire was still moving upward when the sound came rolling across the space, perhaps two heartbeats later, but it was a low, rumbling sound that she had never heard before.

"W-w-w..."

"I don't know what it is, Amodini," Hyppolita replied, surprised at how calm her voice sounded. "But I do know that it is not..."

The second eruption happened then, across the city at the western gate, but now she and Amodini weren't alone, the two Romans rushing out onto the balcony, both friend and foe temporarily united in shock, and more than a little fear now that day had come to Bharuch.

Abhiraka and the other men standing on the raft leading the procession down the river were in a perfect position to see the opening phase of the plan to retake Bharuch come to fruition in the form of the same towering column of fire that, unknown to him, his wife was witnessing at the same moment from their palace. While the current was helping, the men using the long poles to propel each raft weren't working quickly enough for the king, and he snapped an order to them to increase the pace. It wasn't just because of his understandable impatience; timing was crucial, and the destruction of the naphtha stores wasn't in a random sequence, with the cache at the eastern wall being the signal to the others, who would then, hopefully, ignite their cache in the agreed-upon order. By his estimate, they were still more than a quarter-mile to the entrance to the canal, and once they entered it, they still had to travel about the same distance to reach a spot where they could disembark the rafts then rush for the eastern gate, which should be opening soon, the pair of Bolon's men teaming up with however many men Balas managed to gather who were responsible for this task, waiting for their own signal. Because of the angle and bulk of the wall, the combustion of the western supply wasn't as obvious to Abhiraka, yet it was sufficient, and it did increase the ambient light. As it was, the easternmost guard tower was now not only visible, but there was enough light for the king to see two men standing in it, the sight eliciting a savage smile.

"Your day has come, you pigs," he muttered, only aware that he had spoken aloud when, from behind him, the other men on his raft growled their approval. This caused him to turn and give the men, Arshad among them, a savage smile, promising, "Tonight, we avenge ourselves, brothers! Tonight, we take back our city!"

As soon as the words were out, Abhiraka cursed himself, as his men forgot the admonition for quiet, roaring their approval.

Glabius and Norbanus were transfixed by the lurid glow above the rampart behind them, staring up in a mixture of confusion and dread, both of them immediately understanding the only thing that could create such an intense glow.

"Maybe," Glabius offered, though without much enthusiasm, "it was an accident."

Before Norbanus could respond, off to their left and also partially obscured by the wall since they were facing in that general direction, they both saw the very top of the flames boiling up into the sky. It vanished quickly, but both men knew it wasn't their imagination, if only because the light remained in the form of a flickering glow.

Norbanus turned to look at Glabius, knowing that his own

expression mirrored that of his comrade, which prompted him to say simply, "We're fucked."

"What should we do?" Glabius asked.

"Stand our post, I suppose," Norbanus answered grimly.

This was the moment when Abhiraka's men unleashed their roaring promise of revenge, causing both men to spin about. The glow from both conflagrations enabled them to see not just the leading raft, but the two behind it, and that they were loaded with armed men.

Swiveling his head, Norbanus cupped both hands to bellow, "Sound the alert! Armed force upriver! Sound the alarm!"

It was perhaps another heartbeat later when the *Cornicen* of their Century blew the notes that warned of an impending attack, but the pair of Legionaries were already scrambling down the ladder in preparation to join their comrades as they waited for orders. Neither of the men were officers, but they were veterans, understanding that it was a virtual certainty that at least one of these rafts would be disgorging its passengers to head straight for them, and they were quickly joined by their comrades from the other posts arrayed along the southern wall. Their Optio arrived, Fortuna having placed him at the farthest end of the outposts, but he quickly got the men arrayed, in their battle formation. He had just finished bellowing those orders when, from behind them, the southern cache was ignited, and within an eyeblink, they heard the shrill screams of their comrades, men of the Second of the Seventh standing watch on the rampart who were drenched in the globules of flaming naphtha that, contrary to the belief of the attackers, weren't contained by the walls of the stone buildings where they were stored, because the roofs were wooden, as were the shutters on the windows.

Abhiraka took it as a sign from the divinity that, just as his raft reached the entrance to the canal, the southern cache was ignited, exactly as had been planned. Knowing that there would be at least a Century of Romans arrayed outside the southern wall who would be in a position to rush around the southeast corner once they determined that this was where Abhiraka and his men were heading, the timing of the ignition of the cache on that side was imperative, and it happened exactly as planned. There was enough light now to see the entirety of the wall visible to Abhiraka outlined by a backdrop of raging flames, but it was also strong enough for him to see that the Romans were, as expected, forming up a short distance from the canal entrance on the opposite bank. When the southern cache went up, the additional light gave Abhiraka the ability to see how, without exception, the otherwise disciplined Roman Legionaries spun about to face back in the opposite direction. This was certainly a good sign, but it wasn't until he heard the sound of the Roman horn a second time and the purpose of which was made clear when, without hesitation, the enemy formation went running back towards the southern gate that Abhiraka knew the plan was working. Navigating the turn into the canal proved trickier than any of them would have imagined, given that none of the men tasked with guiding the raft had any experience with the unwieldy conveyance. The delay wasn't long, but it seemed an eternity, but quickly enough, they were gliding in the direction of the eastern gate, and the sight of it triggered in Abhiraka a somewhat odd thought, about how he had intended to build a bridge across the canal once the Roman threat to his kingdom had been ended. Well, after tonight, I can start having plans drawn up, he thought, but first, our streets will have to run red with blood. Despite the positive developments to this moment, Abhiraka was under no illusions that the cost for retaking the city wouldn't be high, and not just with his soldiers but his subjects. This recognition had been eating at him for days, but seeing the eastern gate now a matter of a couple hundred paces away, his impatience overcame him.

"This is close enough! Push us to the bank!"

Naturally, his men complied, but Abhiraka leapt onto the pilings while the raft was still a couple of paces away, and when his men followed him, it was inevitable that, even with the light from the blaze, one of the men misjudged the distance, dropping into the water with a huge splash, the iron chainmail armor taken from the Romans dragging him under immediately. Because the raft was still moving towards the pilings, even if his comrades had been disposed to help him, that was impossible when the raft collided into the wooden pilings. Abhiraka wasn't aware that he had just suffered one loss, already moving at close to a run and heading for the eastern gateway even as one of the two heavy doors was being pushed open. The two men who were struggling with the gate were starkly outlined by the flames, giving Abhiraka his first indication that, while this was part of the plan, it appeared as if they had significantly underestimated the intensity of the conflagration. This was confirmed when he reached the roadway that, before the canal had been built, led out from the city to the eastern part of Bharuch, the intense heat roiling out through the partially opened gateway with a force that reminded the king of a time he had once stood in front of an ironmonger's furnace as the workman described the process. It didn't stop Abhiraka, but he did slow to a walk, barely aware of the pounding footsteps of Arshad and the rest of his men from the first raft, although the other rafts behind his were already moving up the canal to unload directly next to the roadway. As he closed the distance, the other gate slowly swung open, and as soon as it was, the pair of men joined their two comrades in staggering towards their king. He initially thought that when they dropped to their knees it was to perform their obeisance, but he quickly saw that it was because all four men were scorched, and he could even see tendrils of smoke rising from their heads as their hair smoldered. Dropping down into a crouch, it took Abhiraka a moment to recognize one of Bolon's men, his face blackened from what he thought was soot to the point that the whites of his eyes seemed to leap out from it, and after a heartbeat, he remembered the man's name.

"You have done well, Ashvath," He reached out to touch his shoulder, and while the man recoiled, Abhiraka had touched him long enough for him to feel bare flesh instead of his tunic, informing him that the black was the man's flesh and not cloth, and he gasped, "I am sorry, Ashvath! I didn't mean to cause you pain."

"It…it is fine, Your Highness."

Acutely aware that every heartbeat was precious, Abhiraka told himself that this delay was only so more of his men could rally to him, but he felt compelled to offer this man, whose name he had never bothered to learn until just a day earlier, something that would convey his gratitude.

"You have performed your duty bravely, my friend," Abhiraka continued, "and I will not forget it. You will never have to labor for the rest of your days."

"T-thank you, Your Highness," Ashvath muttered, but then, surprising Abhiraka, he reached out and grabbed his king's arm, his voice edged with panic as he warned, "You can't go to the left once inside the walls, Your Highness. That demon fire doesn't just burn, it…" he stopped searching for the right words, coming up with, "…*leaps*, and it *flies*, Your Highness. I thought we were a safe distance away when I threw the torch through the door, and that the stone of the building would hold it, I swear it!"

Abhiraka was only partly listening, at least to the last part, thinking how he would have to lead his men into the city by another route now, but he knew he couldn't spend any more time with this man. He refrained from patting the man's shoulder now that he could see the charred flesh more clearly, although he did order Arshad to leave one man to attend to these four and provide what aid he could. Then, he was moving at a trot towards the gate, even as he was flinching from the extraordinary heat. It wasn't until he entered the gateway arch that he could hear screaming from within the walls, but the cries were so shrill that it was impossible to tell whether it was men or women who were in such mortal agony. Just before he exited the gateway into the city, he felt a hand grab him roughly from behind and jerk him backward to narrowly avoid colliding with the staggering figure fully aflame who passed across his intended path from his left. His attention had been to the right, looking to see if the crossing east/west street he would now be using was clear, so he hadn't seen the oncoming person, but Ranjeet, having just arrived from the second raft had, and it was he who saved Abhiraka from being badly burned. It was impossible to tell the sex of the victim, who only made it a few more steps before collapsing in a pile of sizzling meat, and the sight of it brought back the horrors that Abhiraka had witnessed when he was forced to flee from both the first battle outside Bharuch, and the night that the city had fallen. Swallowing the bile that came rushing up, the returning King of Bharuch forced the memories to the back of his mind, concentrating on what came next instead.

"Arshad, you know what you must do. Nahapana should be here any moment. Once he arrives, take your working party to string the rafts together, and Nahapana will hold the gate."

"Nahapana?" Ranjeet interjected, confused. "I thought that was my task."

"I changed my mind," Abhiraka answered. "You're coming with me to the palace. No matter what," he said grimly, "we're getting my queen and her ladies, and I need you with me."

It had been a source of argument, the one part of the plan where Abhiraka thought like a husband and not a king, but while he had seemingly acquiesced to the argument from his three faithful lieutenants, Ranjeet wasn't particularly surprised that this wasn't the case. Nor, he understood, was this the time to argue, despite the changed circumstances that forced them to take a longer route to the palace.

"I am with you, my King," Ranjeet heard himself say, then offering Abhiraka a grin, he added, "Besides, my wife is with yours. If she found out that I was here and didn't come see her, I'd never hear the end of it."

Chapter 8

Any man who achieved the Centurionate learned how to get by on less sleep, and to come awake quickly; when that man was a Primus Pilus, it was a matter of degree, so when the chief clerk of the First of the First of the Alaudae, who was also Batius' body slave, entered his master's private quarters, he knew exactly what he needed to do to rouse him.

Giving Batius a sharp rap on the bottom of one foot, the clerk, Perdiccas, was already speaking. "Master, we are under attack! Someone has managed to ignite the naphtha stores on the eastern..."

Before he even finished the sentence, and through the open windows of his quarters on the second floor of the Roman-built barracks inside the walls, a low rumbling sound, identical to what Hyppolita had heard from her balcony when the eastern cache had gone up, occurred a second time. Because of their location, both Perdiccas, and Batius, who had sat up immediately, although still blinking awake, were in a position to see the stores reserved for the defenders of the western wall suffer a similar fate.

"Pluto's thorny *cock*," Batius gasped, but to the credit of his clerk, Perdiccas had already begun moving, hurrying over to the stand where the Primus Pilus' armor was draped, lifting it up while Batius snatched up his cotton tunic, dropping it over his body and raising his arms just in time for Perdiccas to drop the armor over his head.

When Perdiccas turned away to grab Batius' *baltea*, the Centurion stopped him, snapping, "I'll do this. Go out and run next door to Valerius' quarters. Tell him to attend to me, then tell Centumalus to sound the alert. 'All Cohorts, camp under attack'!"

Batius was naturally impatient, but he found no cause to fault his clerk, who was out of the Primus Pilus' private quarters before the Centurion was even within reach of the rest of his gear. Through the open window, Batius heard the thin screams of men he knew belonged to him, the Seventh Cohort having the guard shift this night, and even as faintly audible as they were, they carried a quality that Batius remembered, just like Abhiraka, and while they would never know it, both men shared the same recurring dreams that centered on the horrors wrought by the terrible power of naphtha. By the time he exited his quarters, fully attired, the stores at the southern gate had gone up as well, and even with all of the buildings and distance, the light created by what were now three raging infernos whose flames towered above the walls was sufficient that he could read the facial expressions of his men as they came streaming out of their own quarters, the confusion, and yes, fear, plain for him to see.

"All right, you *cunni*," he bellowed, behaving as if this was nothing more than a regular day, "there's no time for gawking! Fall in on your standards!" Valerius, Batius' Optio, was still struggling with his *baltea* as he came running up to his Primus Pilus, the sounds of nine Cohorts of a Legion of Rome rushing to get into formation now drowning out all other noise. Lowering his voice, as only with his Optio would Batius voice his deep concern, he said, "I don't know what's going on any more than you do, Valerius, but we both know that this is more than just some locals making mischief. I'm not going to be surprised to find out that those Bharuch and Pandyan bastards that did for the 7th and 11th are either here or coming this way."

"What are your orders, Primus Pilus?" The fact that Valerius managed to use the same tone he would when it was a start to a normal day was something Batius would appreciate and remember, and he returned his Optio's salute.

"Stand ready for my orders, Valerius," Batius answered. "I'm going to try and find out more about what's happening. I'll tell Gemellus as well."

Vibius Gemellus was the Primus Pilus Posterior, the second in command of the Legion, and his Century, like the First, was already formed up. Batius stopped only long enough to essentially repeat himself, but it was Gemellus who called out to him, "Should you take Centumalus with you, Primus Pilus? In case something's happened at the *Praetorium*?"

Batius' grimace wasn't aimed at Gemellus, but at himself, and he bellowed for his *Cornicen*, who naturally came running, then the pair began heading down the street that led directly south to the center of the city, where the *Praetorium* was located. Before they covered a full block, the two Romans suddenly saw their shadows as the last of the stocks of naphtha were ignited at the northern gate.

The glow against the night sky was impossible to miss from where Maran, Vira, and Sundara were waiting, along with the rest of the Pandyan army and the Bharuch elephants, and it naturally created a stir among the men of both groups. The ranking officer from Bharuch, a man named Damisippos, had been standing next to his elephant, watching as the light intensified with each ignition. From where they were located, just inside the edge of the forest on the eastern side of the city, the walls were clearly outlined in the vicinity of where the caches were located, and once the right quarter of the city around the northern gate became visible with the last cache igniting, Damisippos gave the command to his animal, who knelt on its massive front legs, providing the step so the man could leap into the saddle to join the three men already in the basket. Since he was the nominal commander of Bharuch's remaining force of elephants, instead of two archers, he had one, the other a horn player who served the same purpose as the Roman *Cornicen*, and it was to this man Damisippos snapped his first order.

Using the sound of the horn as it played the three notes of the preparatory command, Vira spoke to Maran, calling up to him from his horse, "What do we do, Maran? Do we just refuse to move?"

"Follow my lead," Maran answered calmly, then using the Pandyan version of the goad, which was longer than that used by Bharuch, he tapped his animal on the head to get its attention.

With the first command sounded, the horn player paused, then sounded the one single but long note, and Damisippos put his animal in motion, as did Maran; the difference was that while Damisippos' elephant began moving towards the city, Maran's animal turned its massive head and began moving in the opposite direction.

Not surprisingly, this elicited a reaction from Damisippos, who jabbed his goad down into the tissue behind his animal's ear hard enough to not only stop the elephant, but to elicit a bellow of pain.

"What are you doing, Maran?" he shouted to the Pandyan. "Did you not hear my command?"

The fact that Maran actually halted his animal did come as a surprise to Vira, who had turned his horse about, but Maran called down to him, "Keep going, Vira. Give the command to your men and my elephants to turn about and have Sundara do the same." Without waiting for Vira to acknowledge his order, Maran returned his attention to Damisippos, answering calmly and just loudly enough for only the other man and his crew to hear, "I did, Damisippos. But this is no longer our fight."

Damisippos' reaction was to essentially not react at all, other than to stare at Maran. Finally, he repeated bewilderedly, "Not your fight?" The sound of his voice seemed to rouse him, his voice now raising. "How can you say this is no longer your fight, you...*dog*?" Jabbing a finger at Maran, he spat, "Your filthy king bankrupted our kingdom! What King Abhiraka paid would buy an army twice your size, and you know it!"

Rather than match the Bharuch commander's anger, Maran replied coolly, "That might have been true when this campaign began, but that is no longer the case."

For the first time, Damisippos' demeanor changed, and he asked suspiciously, "What makes you say this, Pandyan?"

Maran responded by asking bluntly, "Did you know that when Caesar left with his fleet, he didn't return to Parthia with his army but headed towards our lands?" He got his answer by the manner in which Damisippos recoiled, prompting Maran to shake his head. "I thought so."

"I swear, I just learned that this was the case!" Damisippos pleaded.

"I do not blame you, Damisippos," Maran assured him. "But that does not change anything. We are returning to Pandya, as quickly as we can."

Maran could read the desperation in his counterpart's expression, even in the relative darkness, so he wasn't surprised when Damisippos turned and snapped to the horn player, "Sound the halt! Then the signal to prepare to attack!" Thrusting his arm out, he shouted dramatically, "We will kill these traitors to our cause!"

Maran's initial instinct was to counter by having his own player sound the Pandyan version of that command, because he knew that, unlike the Bharuch forces, who had been lumbering past the pair as they closed on the city, his men were prepared to fight against their allies, having been forewarned. Not only that, every infantryman and archer belonging to Bharuch had already rushed towards the city, and were now more than a half-mile away, while his vastly numerically superior force was at hand.

However, he didn't do so, if only because he had a sliver of sympathy for the position Damisippos was in, so he raised a hand as a signal to the other man, prompting the Bharuch commander to wave at his horn player, then Maran pointed out reasonably, "To what end do you think turning your men around to fight us will achieve, Damisippos?" Pointing at the city, he continued, "Your king is going to need every man available to retake your city, and you know it." When Damisippos made no response, for the first time, Maran showed his anger, snapping, "And you know by how much we outnumber you, so you know that it will be to no purpose, other than ensuring Bharuch's final downfall!"

There was a long silence, one where the two men stared at each other, Damisippos' glare one of pure hatred, and Maran saw, impotent frustration.

Caesar Ascending - Pandya

Finally, Damisippos snarled, "Very well, Pandyan. Go! Skulk away like the cur that you are! But," he pointed again, "know this! We *will* be victorious! And then there will be a reckoning!"

For the first time, Maran smiled as he said amiably, "And when that day comes, I will look for you, Damisippos, just as you will look for me." He paused, then added quietly, "I wish that it could be another way, Damisippos, but your king lied to us. And we are of Pandya."

Then he touched his elephant, who immediately began moving to the south and away from Bharuch, leaving Damisippos to seethe with an impotent fury, but it was quickly replaced by the sense of dread as he realized that he would have to be the man to tell his king that the Pandyans weren't coming.

While Nedunj waited, both for the arrival of reinforcements and the dreaded Roman fleet, which he at least now had under observation by a relay system of mounted riders along the coast, he spent every spare moment walking the ground outside the walls of Muziris, usually alone. At this moment, there wasn't much for him to do; until the reinforcements arrived, along with every spare arrow, spear, and shield that could be spared while leaving the skeleton garrison sufficiently armed, his commanders were all busy making preparations with the garrison. Among his many concerns was the dearth of artillery, something that his father-in-law had stressed as being one of the contributing factors in his own failure to defend his city.

"If we had twice as many catapults on each wall, I wouldn't have been forced to send my elephants outside the walls. And," despite this being months after his flight, it still brought tears to Abhiraka's eyes, something that Nedunj pretended not to notice, "I wouldn't have had to watch them burn my beauties alive."

However, as Caesar and the Romans were learning, the nations of southern India practiced warfare in a decidedly different manner than those in the north, and despite his pleading, Nedunj had been unable to convince his father to invest the time and resources to manufacture more artillery pieces.

"Why should we need such things, when we're going to crush these Romans far to the north, in their kingdom and not mine?" Puddapandyan had said, the last time Nedunj had broached the subject. "And," the old man had given his son a sly smile, "if there is the kind of destruction that Abhiraka insists these Romans are capable of wreaking, the fact that it happens in Bharuch and not here is better for us. Especially," he had finished with a cackling laugh that, for as long as he could remember, set Nedunj's teeth on edge, "since he will be too poor to rebuild it now that we have most of his treasury."

This was the moment that Nedunj had decided what he must do, approach Abhiraka in secret, with an unusual request, the night before the combined army departed Karoura after the prince was informed that he wouldn't be leading the Pandyan element.

"I am asking that you leave at least one man behind from your army who has a knowledge of how to construct the artillery pieces you said you needed for Bharuch," he explained, to which Abhiraka's initial response was a raised eyebrow and a long silence.

Finally, the Bharuch king pursed his lips, then nodded slowly, although he warned, "I can only spare one man, but he is my best at this task." Eyeing Nedunj, he asked, "And why is this so important to you that you would go behind your father's back?"

"Because," Nedunj answered, without hesitation, "it is better to be prepared for these Romans in the event that you fail to stop them, Father Abhiraka."

For a brief moment, Nedunj thought that he had angered his father-in-law, but he learned that, in fact, it was the opposite, when Abhiraka nodded slowly.

"You," he said gravely, "are thinking like a king, now. But," he warned, "I still can't spare more than one man, but he is my best."

Nedunj hid his disappointment, offering his thanks to Abhiraka with as much sincerity as he could muster. He acknowledged to himself that he couldn't really blame Abhiraka for his seeming parsimony, especially since he felt somewhat certain that Abhiraka wasn't fooled in the slightest by Puddapandyan and what his father's ultimate goal was, the weakening of Bharuch, even while seeming to help. Nor was it either man's fault for not foreseeing this latest development that had a fleet of several hundred ships containing the largest army Nedunj had ever heard of being transported by this means heading in his direction. Nevertheless, it also meant that his efforts to bolster their paltry number of artillery pieces would fall woefully short; as of the day that he had learned that Caesar was approaching, only five pieces had been constructed, although the man Abhiraka left behind, a swarthy man in his forties named Demetrios, who was one of the few men of Bharuch who was still of pure Macedonian stock and whose father had served Abhiraka's father as chief of artillery, had assured him that the speed of production would increase.

"The hardest part," Demetrios had explained before the work began, "will be to train the men in how to construct each piece. The second hardest part will be to make sure that the wood for the pieces has been properly cured. Once those two problems are taken care of, we will be able to produce several pieces a week."

When Demetrios had told him this, Nedunj had been pleased, thinking that he would have months, even if his father and Abhiraka were unable to decisively defeat the Romans. Just that morning, however, he had received a dispatch from one of the men who were shadowing the Roman fleet along the coast, informing him that, contrary to what Nedunj had believed would occur, the Romans had sailed past Mangalaru without stopping as they had at Honnavar. Suddenly, with this piece of news, it was no longer a certainty that the reinforcements that he had sent for from Karoura a week earlier would be here in time. It was three hundred miles to Mangalaru, and as quickly as the messengers rode, the Roman ships would still have closed the distance between the two cities. These were the thoughts that consumed him as he stood, on the beach, racking his mind for something, anything, that might give him a decisive edge. He wouldn't have enough artillery, he was certain of that, and he recalled Abhiraka telling him how, if he had to do it over again, he would have defended his southern, eastern, and western walls in the same manner that he had with the northern side, with his men standing on a rampart immediately next to the newly constructed canal, and that he would have put his heaviest troops there, the phalanx infantry with their long spears that could keep the enemy at bay. It was as he was remembering this that it came to him, and he immediately turned and began running back to the city walls, knowing there was no time to lose.

Abhiraka led a thousand of his men at a brisk trot through the streets of Bharuch, but he guided them on a less direct route that avoided the center of the city where the *Praetorium* was located, having been indirectly informed by Balas that there were always Roman Legionaries in that area. He knew that it was inevitable that they would run into resistance, but he was determined to delay it as long as possible, to conserve his men, all of whom were from either the royal bodyguard or phalanx troops, the latter having discarded their bronze cuirasses for the Roman chainmail taken as spoils of war from the field. Down in the street, the illumination from the raging fires wasn't as strong, but he could see the dancing quality of the light on those buildings that were two or three stories, and he was worried that it seemed to be intensifying. Like Bolon and Nahapana, he had believed that the Romans selecting buildings made of stone to store the volatile substance would contain the conflagration when it was ignited, yet that didn't seem to be the case. Before long, he, the Roman defenders, and the citizens of Bharuch would learn just how woefully the forces of Bharuch had underestimated the destructive power of four buildings full of naphtha. At this moment, Abhiraka was more concerned with reaching the palace, and he rounded the last corner that blocked his view of the wall marking the southern boundary of the palace grounds to see Romans streaming out into the street, most of them still struggling to strap on their *balteae* or fumbling with their shields and javelins. While they were assembling quickly, Abhiraka saw that they were still confused, having been roused from sleep, and he understood this gave his men the advantage they needed.

Wheeling about, he spoke quickly and in a loud voice that might have carried to where the Romans were assembling, "We don't have time to get in a formation, so we're going straight to the sword! Drop your spears. We'll retrieve them once we're finished! Follow me!" Then, waiting just long enough to hear the clattering of wooden shafts dropping to the paving stones, Abhiraka, his own sword already out, bellowed, *"For Bharuch!"*

By the time he had run the length of the city block to the intersection with the cross street the Romans were using to assemble, Ranjeet was by his side, as were several other men, running essentially shoulder to shoulder across the street. The Romans directly in line with the oncoming king and his men, hearing the roaring voices of their enemies, had spun about, but Abhiraka saw the shock on the faces of his foes as, barely slowing, he slammed into a Roman Legionary, using his borrowed shield to send the man reeling. Before the Roman could recover, Abhiraka brought his sword down onto the man's helmet, cleaving it, along with his skull, the blow containing all the pent-up rage, frustration, and shame of the previous year, but the king was already moving, yanking the blade free to slash at another Legionary who had been staggered by Ranjeet. Between the fury of the Bharuch assault and the disorganized state of the defenders, any resistance by the Romans was shattered within a matter of heartbeats, all semblance of cohesion gone as each man began worrying about his own fate. Depending on where they were, the Romans, men of the 15th Legion who had moved into the buildings that had been appropriated for the 10th, fled in one of three directions. Most of them chose to run down the cross street, with perhaps a third of the men fleeing back towards the eastern wall, and the rest going in the opposite direction, leaving dozens of bodies littering the street. However, Abhiraka was initially dismayed to see that one Roman officer, obviously a Centurion since he was wearing a transverse crest, had gathered what appeared to be more than fifty men and was leading them to the gateway that served as the southern entrance into the palace compound. Before he could rally his own men, Abhiraka could only watch as they arrayed themselves in a line that filled the gateway, several ranks deep, clearly intent on fighting.

Suddenly, he felt a tap on his shoulder, seeing Ranjeet smiling, which caused him to snap, "I'm glad you find this amusing, Ranjeet! Now we have to fight our way into the palace. And," he turned and, while it was not with anxiety, he was clearly concerned as he pointed down the street in the direction the other Romans had fled, "it won't be long before these dogs regroup and come back!"

"The reason I'm smiling, my King," Ranjeet was completely unruffled, "is that you've obviously forgotten something."

"Oh?" Abhiraka scowled at him. "What? Spit it out, you're wasting time!"

In answer, Ranjeet turned and, since there was sufficient light from the fire at the northern wall beyond the palace, which was closest, only used his head to indicate an apparently blank section of wall.

Fortunately, he didn't need to elaborate. Abhiraka groaned, "Of *course*! The entrance to the garden." Thinking quickly, he ordered, "Take forty men and use the entrance. I'll lead the rest at these dogs to draw their attention."

Ranjeet didn't bother to render even a salute, turning and moving quickly, grabbing some of the men who were, predictably, more concerned with looting the bodies of the freshly killed Romans.

Meanwhile, Abhiraka bellowed, "These vipers want to keep your king from reuniting with his queen! Men of Bharuch, what do you intend to do about it?"

As he expected, his challenge was met with another roar, and more importantly, a sudden rush towards the gateway. The most eager of Abhiraka's men, however, were cut down by the hail of javelins, marking the first time that the Bharuch king actually witnessed the lethal Roman weapon that his surviving officers had commented about after the first battle against the invaders north of the city. Nevertheless, while it slowed the rush, it didn't stop it, Abhiraka's men leaping over their comrades writhing on the ground to slam into the Roman line blocking the gateway. This time, the king wasn't personally involved, standing to the side of the men doing the actual fighting, and just like the Centurion who was just out of his sight on the opposite side of the wall, exhorting his men to cut the dogs down. Just when Abhiraka began to wonder if there had been another force of Romans inside the compound to stop Ranjeet and his group from falling onto the rear of the men defending the gate, he heard several shrill screams, but more importantly, he could hear Ranjeet bellowing his personal war cry. As with the initial attack, the actual fighting was over quickly after that, and Abhiraka stepped over the bodies blocking the gate, barely noticing that the Centurion was wounded but alive, and was now kneeling as the blood dripped from a serious shoulder wound.

"Your Highness!"

That it was the voice of Arshad was the only reason Abhiraka stopped, and he turned in that direction to see his bodyguard standing behind the Roman, head bowed.

"What should we do with him, Your Highness? He is one of their officers, isn't he?"

Abhiraka was about to issue a peremptory order to kill the man, then thought better of it, "Keep him alive. He may be useful for us."

This was all the time he was willing to devote to this matter, and he began moving at a trot towards the palace, only one thing on his mind.

Once it became obvious that the destruction of the naphtha was part of a larger plan, the Legionaries on guard duty stopped behaving courteously, and while they weren't overtly hostile, nor did they strike Hyppolita or any of her ladies, they nonetheless forced them to gather together in the queen's audience room, where the pair of guards were reinforced by two more Legionaries. Downstairs, inside the palace, Hyppolita heard shouting in Latin, which Amodini interpreted in whispers, until one of the Legionaries heard and snarled at them in Greek to keep their mouths shut. The doors out to the balcony had been shut, the air quickly growing stale, but the order for silence had a benefit, allowing Hyppolita to listen intently to what noises did penetrate the windows and doors of the palace. Within a sixth part of a Roman watch, what the queen could hear informed her that there was a serious attack taking place, and the fighting was now within the city walls. Their guards clearly heard and interpreted things the same way, and she didn't need to know Latin to hear the strain and worry in their tone as they talked quietly to each other. It was the sudden roaring of male voices, originating in the general direction of the southern palace gate, which the audience room overlooked, that caused some of her women to gasp and others to begin moaning with fear.

This proved too much for one of the Legionaries, the one who spoke Greek, who wheeled about and stalked over to Hyppolita, thrusting a finger in her face as he snarled, "You better keep these whores' mouths shut, Your Highness, or they will be sorry!"

Hyppolita was certainly frightened; she was equally angry, both at the manner that this Roman cur had stuck a finger in her face, but at his slur against her ladies, and she answered coldly, "I will do what needs to be done, Gregarius," he seemed startled she knew his rank, which Pullus had taught her, "but there is no need for you to threaten us!"

He was obviously expecting something else, and his manner suddenly became uncertain.

"All right then," he finally muttered. "Just keep them quiet."

He turned and returned to the other three men who were now arrayed facing the doorway that was the most direct route from the first floor. It wasn't the only way, however, and Hyppolita found herself wondering just how thorough Titus Pullus had been in informing the 15th in the layout of this palace. Her thoughts were interrupted by another roar, once more of male voices, but now undoubtedly closer, and now she was certain that it came from the direction of the southern gate. Again, their captors clearly interpreted it the same way, because from downstairs, she heard a lone voice, shouting something.

"That is these men's Centurion, Your Highness," Amodini risked whispering. "He is calling them to come join the other men downstairs."

Hyppolita had no reason to doubt her lady, but the four men made no move to obey, and instead began holding what was clearly a very intense discussion that, despite the fact that none of the women could understand, or so they believed, they tried to conduct in a near whisper. Suddenly, the queen intuited that these Romans weren't trying to keep her and her ladies from overhearing, but the officer downstairs. Perhaps, she thought, they're hoping that the man downstairs will think they're not up here anymore and have already left. The Roman soldiers weren't the only ones whose attention was solely on their particular situation, because neither Hyppolita nor her ladies heard anything until, without any warning, the other door into this room burst open. Located as it was on the opposite side of the room from the main entrance, by the time Hyppolita whirled about, her ladies were shrieking in fear and, despite their bulky robes, doing an admirable job of scrambling out of the way of what she initially saw as just some armed men rushing into the room because of the dim illumination from the single lamp that was allowed to remain lit. It wasn't until they were halfway across the room, rushing at the four Legionaries who were now faced with a much more deadly question than whether to obey their Centurion, that Hyppolita recognized that at the head of what were a dozen men was her husband. Within a matter of a half-dozen heartbeats of her realization that her king had returned, the four Legionaries were dead, their blood mingling to form a large pool on the floor that was spreading more rapidly than she would have believed possible, and it arrested her attention as she watched it creep towards the elaborate carpet that had been a gift from Peithon, the King of Pattala, and she wondered whether she should grab the edge and pull it out of the way so it wouldn't be ruined.

"We will have to replace that carpet."

She knew that it was her voice, but it didn't seem like it, yet she couldn't seem to take her eyes off the sight.

"Is that any way to greet your husband and king?"

More than the words, it was the sound of her husband's voice that jerked her back to the moment, and she stared up at his smiling face, a torrent of emotions suddenly rushing through her that were so overpowering, and in conflict with each other that, despite knowing how unseemly it was, she couldn't stop herself from breaking down. Dropping her head, she covered her face with her hands as she began sobbing, so she only felt the arms around her, but it was the raw emotion in her husband's voice that she would remember for the rest of her days.

"I have dreamed for this moment every day I have been away from you, Hyppolita." The fact that he whispered this told her that, in this moment, he was Abhiraka the man and husband, and not the King of Bharuch. "It has been what has sustained me all these months. And," she heard the pain come, "there has been so much suffering, Hyppolita, and I'm afraid there will be more to come." Gently but firmly, he pulled her away from him, and she had no choice now but to look up into his eyes, yet while she did so, she also felt her heart start racing even harder than it had been as she worried if he would see the guilt somehow reflected in her gaze. And, for a moment, she was certain he had, because he suddenly frowned down at her, his eyes narrowing. "Hyppolita, did they harm you? Were you mistreated?"

It took a huge effort for her not to collapse in relief, but she answered quickly and firmly, "No, my King, they did not. I was treated honorably. Or," she felt compelled to amend, "honorably enough."

"What does that mean?"

She went on to explain the nature of her confinement, careful not to mention any Roman other than Caesar or Ventidius by name, implying but not directly saying that her escort had been a man from the ranks, knowing how he would react if she told the truth. Abhiraka listened intently, at least at first, but she quickly became aware that his attention was being torn away by the sounds outside the palace. Someone had thought to open the doors back up, and she realized that the light was even stronger now than it had been when the Romans had shut them.

"That's enough for now, my King," she stopped suddenly. Then, giving him a smile, she added, "You have more important matters to attend to than hearing your wife complain."

Abhiraka returned the smile, saying in a teasing tone, "I never thought I'd find myself missing hearing your complaints, my Queen. But," the smile vanished, and he looked at her in a way that she had almost forgotten, the way he had looked at her when they had been newly married, "I look forward to a lifetime of them. But you're correct, I must leave you." Turning, he found Ranjeet, who was similarly engaged with his wife Eurycleia, calling to him, "Ranjeet, how many men are left of your party?"

"All but two, my King," Ranjeet answered, "although I have five more wounded, but they aren't serious."

"Arshad," Abhiraka ordered, "you will take command of Lord Ranjeet's party, and you'll stay here at the palace to protect the Queen and her ladies. Ranjeet and I will take the rest of the men to meet with our reinforcements." He hesitated, and Hyppolita recognized that he was thinking. "By this time," he said finally, "the rafts should be strung across the canal and all but the elephants should at least be crossing by now. And," he added grimly, "the Romans won't be disorganized for much longer." Turning back to his queen, he was once more the King of Bharuch, and he offered her the same formal bow that he had when he escaped from the city. "My Queen, I must finish regaining our kingdom."

"I know that you will, my King," Hyppolita spoke loudly enough for the other occupants to hear, even as the sounds of fighting downstairs continued. "And your Queen will be here when you return...victorious."

Then Abhiraka and Ranjeet were gone, leaving her and her ladies, and a handful of guards who would be staying with them, while Arshad led the rest of the men out of the room to finish clearing the palace.

Like Batius, Publius Ventidius was a light sleeper, although it had as much to do with his age as his occupation, and he had even more help in readying himself for whatever was coming, which at this moment was still a confused mess of different reports. It wasn't until he left the *Praetorium* and was out in the middle of the large square, where his personal bodyguard was already assembled with men facing in each direction, that he saw the glow on three sides of the city. He was still trying to assess matters when the cache at the northern wall was ignited, and he was looking in that direction when one of his men shouted that Batius was approaching.

Despite the moment, they still exchanged salutes, and Batius reported, "I've sent men to each Century on the walls to find out what their situation is. But," his battered features turned even grimmer, "I'm certain that my Seventh has already taken losses, sir. There's no way that the men on the wall across the street from those supplies didn't get burned, probably to a crisp."

Ventidius didn't respond, mainly because there was no need, but he was also distracted, which was explained when he said suddenly, "Did you hear that? In the direction of the eastern gate?"

Both men turned in that direction, and after a couple heartbeats of silent listening, Batius nodded. "Yes, sir, I hear it. It sounds like someone is forcing the gate." Turning back to Ventidius, Batius asked, "What are your orders, sir?"

"Take your first and second line Cohorts to the eastern gate," Ventidius decided. "Send your third line here. This will be our rally point, and until I have a better idea of what's happening, I'm going to stay here." Pointing first in the direction of the western wall, where the lurid light from the blaze was only slightly less advanced than the eastern wall, then to the south, and finally the north, he said grimly, "We can't be certain that these bastards are going to come through just the eastern gate. Until we know more, I'm going to keep the 15th and 21st in reserve."

"Sir," Batius reminded Ventidius, "remember that the 21st is in the camp outside the walls on the western side." Indicating in that direction, he said, "He may not be able to get in through that gate at all, because the naphtha storehouse there was directly across from the gate."

Ventidius cursed bitterly, as much at himself for forgetting this as for the fact itself. Thinking for a moment, he turned and called to the German who commanded his bodyguard.

"Saddle up, take five men, and see if you can get out by the northern gate," he ordered. "If you can, go around to the 21st's camp and tell Primus Pilus Papernus to bring his Legion, at the double quick, into the town through the northern gate."

It was a sound order, and it would have worked, except that Ventidius was unaware that, by the time the German and his men had saddled their mounts, then made their way in the direction of the palace, which was between them and the northern gate, Abhiraka and his thousand men had already reached the palace. And, if it hadn't been for the actions of Maran and the Pandyans, this would have had catastrophic consequences, but just as Ventidius and Batius were unaware that the men the Praetor had sent would be intercepted, Abhiraka still had yet to learn that the vast majority of his army was now heading in the opposite direction from the fighting.

The same night that Abhiraka was attempting to retake Bharuch, Caesar's fleet finally made landfall at the mouth of a small river, twenty miles north of Muziris. It was the first time all of the men had walked on dry land in ten days, and even with the prospect of what lay ahead, the mood was almost festive, with a fair amount of horseplay and macabre humor, where men began haggling over a comrade's belongings while the man was standing there in the event the man fell in the coming battle. This didn't last long, as men of four Legions were put to work constructing a marching camp, complete with ditches and walls, while the Primi Pili were attending to Caesar, not on the flagship but on land, in the *praetorium*, always the first tent erected, even before the camp was completed. The map of the area around Muziris was still incomplete, although there was more detail than there had been the last time Pullus saw it.

Caesar opened the meeting by saying, "Since it's a certainty that we've been spotted, the element of surprise is gone, which is why we're going to take the time to perform a proper scouting of the city and the approaches." None of this was surprising to this point, but Caesar amended slightly, "However, although they know we're here, we can still surprise them." He pointed to the spot south of the town. "As Volusenus discovered, the real entrance to the harbor is almost twenty miles south of the city. If it's feasible, I intend to use that main entrance to bring at least two of the Legions to attack from the south, in a manner similar to what we did at Bharuch."

Before he could say anything more, Spurius raised his hand and said, "Caesar, if you mean you plan on having our ships run at full speed up onto their docks, I'd like to volunteer my boys...to do something else."

The room erupted in laughter, including Caesar, and once it quieted enough, he assured Spurius, "Duly noted, Spurius. And I'll make sure to keep that in mind."

Returning to the topic, the levity faded away as Caesar pointed to the completely empty space that marked the terrain upriver from Muziris.

"As you can imagine, we know next to nothing about what things look like on the far side of the city, but we do know that since it's much narrower than the Narmada all the way to where the river bends out of sight from the sea, which Volusenus estimates is a mile beyond their eastern wall, it's unlikely that it widens much more than that." Pausing to scan the faces, Caesar was satisfied that they were paying attention, and continued, "Therefore, depending on what we learn, I'm considering the idea of using the southern passage, but about three miles from the city, disembarking at least one Legion in light order, having them march out of sight of Muziris to a point upriver. If during their scouting of that area they find a ford suitable for the Legion to cross with assault ladders, that Legion will use the ford to attack the eastern wall." Moving his pointer, he indicated the northern wall. "This is the only part of the ground that Volusenus has been over, but he couldn't be thorough. However, if his initial impression is correct, we'll be unable to assault the north wall because it's essentially a bog. My fear is that it's likely this kind of ground extends inland and it may hamper our ability to assault the eastern wall as well as the northern."

He stopped, this time to take a sip from a cup, and there was a low buzz as the Primi Pili offered their comrades their opinion on what they had heard.

Pullus spoke up, "It sounds like it's a possibility that we may only be able to assault the western wall from the beach, and the southern wall from the river."

"That's correct, Pullus," Caesar replied succinctly. "That is my fear." Turning back to the map, knowing that he needed to offer something in the way of good news, he pointed to the space between the two lines that represented the beach and the western wall respectively. "There's substantial room between the city wall and the beach to accommodate more than one Legion, and even if we can assault from three sides, I intend to place at least two Legions on the western side." Placing the pointer on his desk as a signal that the meeting was over, he finished, "I'll be calling another meeting as soon as I'm satisfied that we've learned all we can." The men got up, not offering a salute, knowing that their general didn't bother with these formalities at moments like this, but as Pullus made his way to the flap that served as the door to the partition of Caesar's office, the general called to him. Ignoring Clustuminus' scowl and Spurius' smirk, Pullus returned to stand in front of Caesar's desk, wondering why the man did things like this. He could have just told me to stay and not wait until I was almost out of here, he thought sourly. Caesar was regarding him with an expression that always made Pullus uncomfortable, because it gave him the strong impression that the Dictator knew what was running through his mind. If he did this time, he made no comment, saying instead, "I suspect that I don't have to tell you this, but while I haven't decided on which Legions will be involved in the initial assault, I can tell you that you'll be leading the Equestrians against the western wall."

Caesar, as usual, had surmised correctly; this didn't surprise Pullus at all, and he knew that even if he wanted to argue the point, it would be useless to do so, recognizing in his general's expression that Caesar's mind was made up.

"When do you think is the earliest that we'll assault?" Pullus asked, and Caesar thought a moment before answering, "It all depends on tomorrow or the next day, Pullus. I'm going to be taking all of the cavalry with me, both for protection, and to see if I can provoke a response from the defenders. If I can make them sortie out from the city, that will give me an idea of the composition of their defenders. I know our information is that most of their elephants are north with their king and King Abhiraka, but I won't be caught by surprise again. Honestly," he admitted, "that's more important to me than having a chance to examine the ground."

"Well," Pullus grinned at him, "I'll make an offering to Fortuna that you get attacked tomorrow."

"Please do." Caesar laughed, then stood in a signal that their talk was over. "Every little bit helps."

This time, Pullus did salute, which Caesar returned, and the Primus Pilus pushed aside the leather flap, somewhat surprised that Spurius, Balbinus, or both men weren't still waiting out in the outer office, where the clerks and Tribunes were scurrying about, carrying in boxes of tablets and the various bits and pieces that made the headquarters of Caesar's army run as efficiently as it did. Pullus was actually thankful, because Caesar's mention of Abhiraka had immediately sent his thoughts on a completely unexpected, and given what was going on, unproductive train of thought that had nothing to do with what he needed to accomplish with his Legion. While he felt confident in the ability of his comrades in the three Legions who remained behind in Bharuch, Pullus couldn't lie to himself that there wasn't a nagging thought in the back of his mind where, somehow, the King of Bharuch and his army managed to retake the city. If that happened, he thought miserably, what will happen to her? So absorbed in his thoughts was he that, when he reached the spot of the huge camp where his Legion was always located, he didn't hear Scribonius calling to him.

That was why, when his friend grabbed his elbow, he spun around, his right hand bunching into a fist, which didn't faze Scribonius, who laughed, in the slightest. "What was your head in the clouds about? How you're going to be decorated by Caesar again after we take Muziris?"

It would have been simple enough for Pullus to laugh it off, but he was still sufficiently unsettled to be at least partially honest. "No, I was wondering about what's going on in Bharuch."

Scribonius' first reaction was to examine Pullus' face carefully, then ask, "Why? Did Caesar get word that something happened?"

"No," Pullus answered quickly, "nothing like that. It's just that we don't know exactly where that bastard king is at."

This, Scribonius knew was true; he was equally certain that, while Pullus' concern was valid, there was a more personal element to it than just the welfare of their comrades in the three Legions left behind to defend the city.

He had no idea why, but for the first time, Scribonius asked, "Titus, do you want to talk about it? I mean," he corrected himself, "talk about *her*?"

For an instant, Scribonius was certain that he had erred to the point where his best friend might strike him, as Pullus actually raised his fist, then drew it back partially, staring at his Pilus Prior through narrowed eyes with an expression in them that Scribonius had seen before, and which had never ended well for the object of his gaze. Then, with an explosive breath, Pullus sighed.

"How did you know?"

Once again, Scribonius had to refrain from his tendency to reply in a manner that was both flip and teasing, as he reminded his friend that Scribonius was more intelligent.

"Because I know you better than anyone else," he replied

instead.

Before he responded, Pullus glanced around, then with a gesture of his head, led Scribonius off a short distance away from where the slaves were putting their finishing touches on preparing the fires for the tent section for which they were responsible. Then, keeping his voice low, Pullus divulged everything to Scribonius, leaving nothing out, including the night before the army departed.

When he finished, Scribonius was silent for some time, and once more, he was struggling between saying what he wanted to say, that he was sorry that he had ever asked, and what he knew his friend needed to hear, finally settling on, "That is...quite a bit to take in, Titus. But," he frowned as he tried to analyze the situation rationally, "what is your concern, exactly?"

"That somehow that *cunnus* king will manage to take the city back, and when he does, somehow he'll find out that Hyppolita and I...about us," he finished lamely.

While this was what Scribonius suspected, he wasn't nearly as concerned about this possibility as his friend, and he pointed out, "We left Batius and the others with enough naphtha to roast a thousand elephants, Titus. And while we don't know exactly how the Pandyan army is made up, we do know that they rely on elephants, and I doubt that the Pandyan elephants are any more fireproof than the ones we put paid to last year. And," he finished, "that's not even counting the walls and the artillery on them."

This was something that Titus couldn't deny, and he had tried to tell himself this for days but hearing Scribonius confirm it did make him feel better.

"You're right," he sighed. "I know I'm worrying for nothing. And...thank you."

"Oh, that had to hurt," Scribonius could no longer restrain himself from having some fun, and he was rewarded by Pullus chuckling.

However, Titus Pullus was still Titus Pullus, and he smiled at Scribonius as he said pleasantly, "And you know that if you breathe a word of this, I'll pull your arms off."

"That," Scribonius answered dryly, "was never a doubt."

The pair parted to their respective Cohorts, neither of them, nor any man in Caesar's part of the army aware of the struggle taking place hundreds of miles to the north.

It was completely by accident that the men under Nahapana who were charged with securing the rafts in a makeshift bridge across the canal weren't required to do so, thanks to a pair of his men who, taking advantage of the inevitable confusion, wandered away from the eastern gateway, heading not towards the docks, but in the direction of the northern wall. And, at first, neither of them understood what they were looking at, which in the partial illumination from the recently ignited northern cache, seemed to be nothing more than a dozen boats, lined side to side, but nowhere near any of the partially constructed northern docks. More out of curiosity, and a desire to avoid work, the pair walked cautiously towards the boats, and when they got close enough, they saw something else.

"Why are they covered up with boards like that?" one of the men wondered, but his comrade couldn't supply an answer.

What it did do was encourage them to move even closer; it was the sight of the thick ropes that were threaded through large closed loops made of iron, which were driven into the wooden sides of each boat that gave them the answer. They went dashing back to their comrades, but it took precious time for them to spot Nahapana, who was standing on the wooden pilings of the bank, shouting orders to the men who were just in the process of aligning the rafts.

"Lord Nahapana! We found something!"

His first reaction was to snarl at both men not to disturb him, but thankfully, the bolder of the two refused to skulk away, choosing to stand his ground, although he did so with his head bowed. Seeing the man out of the corner of his vision, Nahapana cursed bitterly but strode over to them.

"You had better have a good reason, or I'll have you flayed," he said harshly, which seemed to come close to breaking the man's nerve.

Somehow, he managed to get out, "Lord, we've found a bridge."

This served to stop Nahapana just as he was opening his mouth to summon one of the other men to at least administer a beating, but while he was attentive, he wasn't convinced, demanding, "What do you mean you've found a bridge? Are you saying that there's a bridge across the canal that we can't see from here?"

"No, Lord." The man shook his head, hunching his shoulders in the expectation of a blow as he hurried on, "It isn't across the canal, but it's a bridge made of boats!" He did look up at Nahapana then, and seeing the doubt, said fervently, "I swear it, Lord! I am telling it true!"

"He is, Lord," the second man, after initially drifting away, certain that there was a beating in the offing, had sidled back, and was sufficiently encouraged to support his comrade. "Gajanan is telling it true!"

He turned to point, but Nahapana pushed past the pair, snapping, "Show me."

They moved at a brisk trot once again, except they didn't have to get as close the second time in order to convince their commander.

"Run back there. Tell Bhiman to stop with the rafts and come here immediately."

As both men ran to obey, Nahapana spent his time examining the boats. They weren't aligned directly across from the northern gate, but instead were much closer to the northeastern corner, and Nahapana wondered why this was so, not that it mattered in the moment. As he stood there, he sensed movement, although it was barely discernible in the darkness, and was in the direction of the far northwestern corner, opposite from where he was located. He stood watching for a span of time, but then the pounding footsteps of his men caused his attention to return to more immediate matters.

"Lord Nahapana, the rest of our men are approaching from the woods," Bhiman informed him. "It's hard to tell in the dark, but it looks like they're less than a half-mile away."

"Then we don't have time to waste."

Fortunately, Nahapana had been able to determine how the Roman bridge worked, and he pointed to two coils of thin rope, one end of each being attached to the larger cables.

"Two men need to swim across with these thin ropes," he ordered. "They're attached to the cables that will secure the boats that make up the bridge."

"Can two men pull that much weight?" Bhiman asked doubtfully, but Nahapana had thought of that, pointing in the direction the bodyguard had indicated.

"By the time they swim across with the guide ropes, there will be more than enough manpower available," he explained. Then, he thought to add, "Send one man across on the rafts to meet our men and lead them over here. They're not secured yet, but it won't be a problem for one man."

Bhiman turned and hurried away, while there was a brief delay as Nahapana had to find two men who could swim, but soon enough, they were into the water, the rope looped around their upper bodies and tied into a loose knot. Nahapana alternated between watching the pair and checking over his shoulder, just able to make out the man Bhiman had sent hopping nimbly from one raft to the next, until he made the leap up onto the opposite bank, barely breaking stride as he rushed towards the oncoming troops. His attention was drawn back to the pair of men when some of the men of the work party let out a cheer at the sight of the first man clambering up onto the opposite side before turning and helping the other man who, Nahapana could see, was swimming in only the loosest sense. The sight of him thrashing in the water caused him to take an anxious glance back up over his shoulder at the northern rampart, but to his surprise, he didn't see any sign of Roman soldiers, despite the fact that here at the northeastern corner, they were far enough away from the column of flame that Nahapana could see originated at a point on the western side of the northern gate. They must be busy trying to contain that fire, he thought, but then could give it no more attention as the first of the reinforcements arrived, giving Nahapana his first stirring of disquiet. Naturally, the first men to reach the pair of men on the opposite side were the mounted troops, but Nahapana instantly saw that there weren't nearly enough of them; in fact, he realized, there weren't more than a hundred, which was all that had remained of the Bharuch cavalry.

"Lord Nahapana, where are the rest of our mounted troops?"

Nahapana turned away to look at Bhiman, but all he could say was, "I don't know, Bhiman."

Their attention was returned by a shout from the men on the opposite bank, but it was the sight of movement beyond where the cavalrymen had begun dismounting, and the fact that it was significantly larger that gave Nahapana an idea of the identity.

"Is that Narinder bringing Darpashata?" Bhiman asked, but while that was the most logical explanation at the sight of what had materialized into an elephant moving at its version of a trot, Nahapana answered, "I don't think so, Bhiman. That animal isn't large enough to be Darpashata."

Fortunately, it was only a matter of a few more heartbeats before Nahapana could make a positive identification.

"That's Damisippos." He frowned as he added, "But he's acting strangely."

This Bhiman couldn't argue, because now that their comrade and his animal were within fifty paces of the men who had already arrived, they could see Damisippos was standing erect and waving his arms from the box atop the animal. When he finally reached the opposite bank, they could hear him bellowing something, but they couldn't make out the words, although the pair of men who had brought the guide ropes obviously explained what was needed. As they watched, Damisippos hopped down, and using his goad, got his animal turned around, while one of the men who swam across tossed the guide rope up to one of the men standing in the box. The second man's task was less straightforward, but Nahapana couldn't fault how quickly the men worked together, essentially harnessing three of the horses to compensate for the strength of one elephant. It was something that none of the men of Bharuch had ever even contemplated, let alone attempted, but even with all that was happening, and the sense of urgency knowing that with every passing heartbeat their king's numerically inferior force inside the walls was threatened, Nahapana's heart swelled with pride at how quickly and well these men tackled a task with which they had no familiarity. Whether it was by common consent or one of them had stressed the importance that the animals responsible for dragging the heavy cables across the canal had to move at the same pace in order to maintain an even tension, Nahapana never learned. And, even as smoothly as it went, the boats moved with an agonizing slowness, stretching out across the canal like a necklace whose pieces were so closely connected that there was less than a foot's gap between each. Since this bridge had obviously been used before, when the animals reached the two stout wooden posts the circumference of a man's torso that had been buried in the ground so that the exposed part was barely two feet above the ground, it was a straightforward task of dropping the huge loop that terminated each cable over the posts. Damisippos, however, hadn't waited for this last step; thankfully, he didn't bring his elephant, instead crossing on his own, although as he learned very quickly when he stepped onto the planked surface and tried to run that this wasn't a viable option. Forced to a quick walk, he nonetheless crossed rapidly, while behind him, the mounted troops began leading their animals onto the bridge, again without any specific orders being given to do so. Nahapana wouldn't have time to savor this moment, because when Damisippos was still fifty paces away on the bridge, Nahapana finally heard what the man had been shouting.

"We've been betrayed! Those Pandyan dogs have deserted us! We need to warn the King to retreat immediately!"

On Abhiraka's return to his force, while he wasn't surprised, he was dismayed to see that the Romans of the 15th Legion had managed to regroup, and now the Bharuch king was faced with a choice.

"They're expecting us to leave by the palace's southern gate," he said to Ranjeet, "which means they'll put most of their men there to stop us. So," he turned about and looked towards the north, the flames from the roaring cache illuminating his face so Ranjeet could see the lines etched into his king's face, "we're going to leave by the northern gate."

"Your Highness," Ranjeet warned. "Even if they're expecting us to leave by the southern gate, only a fool wouldn't send men to guard against that very thing. And," he added quietly, "nothing I've seen about these Romans makes me think they're led by fools."

"No," Abhiraka immediately agreed. "I know you're right, my friend. But," he glanced over at Ranjeet with a grim smile, "that doesn't mean they're going to have as many men guarding that gate than here." This was true, but Ranjeet still hesitated, which Abhiraka noticed, asking sharply, "What is it, Ranjeet?"

"Rather than fight our way back to the eastern gate to meet with our reinforcements, what if we waited here?" Ranjeet asked, but before Abhiraka could reply, he pointed to the wooden rampart that the Romans hadn't dismantled. "We could put men on the wall. And no, the gate won't hold if they bring a ram up, but we don't have to hold out for long." Shaking his head, he finished, "Going out there means we have no idea what we'll run into, my King. At least here, we have some control."

Even before Ranjeet had finished, Abhiraka realized this was prudent advice, yet at the same time, it wasn't without its own drawbacks. One of them was almost literally staring him in the face, since he was still facing to the north, and he pointed to the column of fire.

"That fire is spreading, Ranjeet. And," he pivoted to point at the eastern gate, "that looks like it's out of control, and it already blocked our most direct path here." Seeing this made up his mind for him, "If we stay here, then Nahapana and Maran will have to travel farther to join with us. Better that we at least make our way to the center of the city as we planned. If they arrive, and we aren't there, that only helps these dogs."

Ranjeet knew when Abhiraka had made up his mind, so he didn't press the issue, but he did point out, "Your Highness, I think the Romans are going to have to decide how many of their men they're willing to use trying to stop us and how many to stop these fires."

Once more, Abhiraka immediately saw the sense in this, but it actually bolstered his belief that the best solution was to fight their way back to the city center. If all went according to plan, the rest of his men, along with the Pandyans, would already be in the city.

"We'll still go out the northern gate," he decided. "Yes, we'll have to go around this compound to get to the center, but I'm certain the Romans don't have as many men waiting there, not this quickly with everything that's happening." Certainly, it was a gamble, yet Ranjeet didn't hesitate, but as he turned to go, Abhiraka stopped him. "We need to leave fifty men at the southern gate, Ranjeet, in the event that they do bring the gate down."

Understanding what Abhiraka was asking, Ranjeet bowed and said, "It will be done, Your Highness. And, I will lead these men."

"No, Ranjeet," Abhiraka replied immediately, slightly alarmed. "I need you with me by my side."

"Your Highness," Ranjeet's tone was, as always respectful but firm, "you'll need someone here who can make sure our men put up the kind of fight that will hold these dogs off long enough for you to join up with our reinforcements. Besides," he gave Abhiraka a grin, "Eurycleia just told me that if I leave her again, I'll be sleeping outside."

Despite himself, Abhiraka laughed, but while he didn't like the thought, he gave his permission. Ranjeet moved at a brisk trot back to where their men were standing, next to the gate that, while he hadn't ordered it, some quick-thinking man under his command had thought to drag the Roman bodies out of the gateway, shut both gates, and drop the locking bar in place. Abhiraka was quickly joined by the bulk of his men, Ranjeet obviously picking the men he wanted, and without saying anything, the king began hurrying towards the northern gate. *If our fortunes hold,* he thought, *I'll be right that even if there are Romans approaching from that side, the eight hundred plus men I still have will be enough to get to the city center.*

Like the other senior officers, Papernus had been jerked from his sleep in the wooden barracks that had been constructed on the western side outside the city walls. Because of the space restriction posed by the canal, the single Legion encampment not only didn't have a ditch and wall, but rather than huts for single sections, every building was three stories, each floor holding a Century, although the rooms were close to the same size as a section tent or hut, with two parallel wings connected by a covered walkway. There were ten of these structures spread evenly in two rows, with four Cohorts on the southern side of the western gate, and six on the other but while there was enough space between the Cohort buildings for the men to assemble, it was a tight fit. And, when matters were as confused as they were in that moment, it became clear that what had appeared to be a perfectly acceptable layout when sketched out on parchment was vastly different when disoriented men were roused from their slumber. This caused the first delay, but the second came quickly enough when the Legionaries from the Cohorts housed nearest to the gate reported that there was smoke roiling out from the inset gateway. Papernus, whose First Cohort was housed in the outer building on the southern side of the gate, had just had his *Cornicen* summon his Pili Priori, preparing to give the orders they were to enter through the western gate into the city, intending to do what both Batius and Aquilinus had done in seeking out Ventidius. It was from his Quintus Pilus Prior, who came rushing up at close to a full run that he learned that, because the cache of naphtha for the western wall was located in the only stone building along the row of buildings near the gate, which placed it on the righthand corner from the gate, and with only the width of the street running along the wall between them the ironbound wooden gates were now ablaze.

Understanding that this blocked the quickest access into the city, Papernus opened his mouth, fully intending to order his Legion to head for the southern gate instead, understandable since where they were currently standing put that gate closer, but what came out of his mouth was, "We're going to have to march to the northern gate, but we move at the double quick. And," he thought quickly, "in reverse order." Turning to his Decimus Pilus Prior, he commanded, "Your boys are going to lead the way, Atilius. I'm counting on you to set the pace. As soon as you're ready, have your *Cornicen* sound the call, and we'll move in column, reverse Cohort order, double quick."

If he had been asked at any point before this moment, Marcus Atilius would have insisted that he was the worst choice for the responsibility of leading a Cohort into the unknown, not because he didn't have faith in his abilities, but because he had replaced his predecessor, who had succumbed to a bilious fever, barely a month earlier. To his credit, his apprehension was nowhere in evidence as he saluted, and without waiting for further instruction, he went trotting off into the darkness that, heartbeat by heartbeat, was diminishing as the blaze inside the walls grew.

"The rest of you get to your Cohorts," Papernus ordered, although his eyes were on the flames that were now towering at least ten feet above the wall. "Wait for Atilius' signal."

The others departed, leaving Papernus to linger for just long enough to wonder about the fate of the men who had been posted on the western wall above the gate. However, they weren't men from his Legion, so it was no more than a passing thought before he was bellowing for his Cohort Centurions. Even before he was finished warning them of what was about to transpire, the notes from Atilius' *Cornicen* sounded, although there was an inevitable delay, despite the fact that every Century of every Cohort had been warned and had turned in the proper direction, waiting for the order. Under normal conditions, the officers wouldn't have tolerated the amount of chatter that was taking place, but even they were sufficiently distracted by the glowing sky that, depending on what Cohort they were in, was uncomfortably close to them, while those men nearest to the gateway were already feeling the intense heat as the wood of the gates became involved. Fortunately, they began moving, going immediately to the shuffling trot that was the double quick pace, holding their shields slightly to the side as they advanced.

Once the Roman-built pontoon bridge was secured, and the first of the reinforcements began moving, Nahapana commandeered a horse, leaping onto it to rush back into the city to warn his king. He returned to the gateway to find that the wooden building next to the stone structure holding the naphtha that had been four buildings down from the gateway had already collapsed into a blazing heap that blocked any access to the street heading to the southern gate. This would have required him to retrace the route Abhiraka had been forced to use to move into the city, but arrayed across his path in that direction, just in front of the intersecting street, was a Century of Romans, although he didn't know that was what it was called. What he could see was that both Romans and his men had drawn blood, evidenced by the bodies lying in the street just behind his men, some of whom were clearly wounded and trying to struggle back to their feet. It wasn't surprising; in fact, he understood perfectly well that, on this night, Abhiraka could expect to receive every last drop of energy and blood that his men had in their bodies, not because of their king, but because of their families who were presumably huddled within their homes around the city. He hadn't seen any of his civilian countrymen yet, but even over the sounds of the fighting now, he could hear feminine cries that, while inarticulate, clearly communicated their terror. The fact that this night it was at the hands of their own countrymen was something that Nahapana refused to think about, choosing to keep his attention on the action in front of him. And, as he hoped, the arrival of the first men across the bridge helped, although they quickly determined that they would have to leave their mounts outside the walls, the fire close enough to make controlling the animals next to impossible. Nahapana had already learned this, and he was back on foot, exhorting the men of the phalanx troops, packed more tightly than their foes, with the front rank aided by their long spears while their comrades in the second rank held their swords, waiting for an opportunity to strike.

"We have to push these dogs back beyond the cross street so that I can get to the King," Nahapana shouted in Ushabad's ear, and while the commander of the phalanx troops didn't reply verbally, he nodded, then shoved his way up through the rearmost ranks of Bharuch men.

He had no idea what Ushabad said, but Nahapana was pleased to see that, within a matter of heartbeats, their men seemed to find another burst of energy, learning this by the screams and curses in the Latin tongue. Most importantly, his men started shuffling forward, far too slowly for Nahapana's liking, but it was progress and he rushed to the rear of the formation. A glance over his shoulder enabled him to spot Bhiman, who was busy directing the flow of men into the city, pointing the men who were members of the lighter sword-wielding infantry towards one spot, and those phalanx troops who hadn't been part of the advance party in Nahapana's direction. The dismounted lancers who had been the first to rush into the city had consequently been the first to come into contact with the Romans, and most of the Bharuch casualties lying in the street now were those men, although they had certainly drawn blood, while the members of the mounted archers were essentially useless at this moment because the range to the Romans required a flat trajectory that would inevitably strike their comrades. It was proving difficult for not just Nahapana, but all of the men who weren't engaged, to maintain their attention on the fighting, all of them acutely aware of the flaming wreckage of the collapsed building that, while it did block any Roman attempt to fall on them from the rear, also appeared dangerously close to spreading to the next building, which was already beginning to smoke. Nahapana briefly considered ordering those men who weren't in the fight to turn their attention towards containing the fire, but while he was aware that there was a public well only one block deeper in the city, they would have to finish pushing the Romans back to the other side of the intersecting street before they could get to it. And, even then, while Nahapana wasn't close enough yet to even peek around the corner, he had to believe that there were Romans lurking there. The other alternative, sending them back out of the city to gather whatever buckets and fill from the canal would not only take too long, but deprive him of men he might need for a breakthrough. All that mattered, he reminded himself, was finding Abhiraka and informing their king that the day was lost, almost before it had really gotten started. His thoughts were suddenly interrupted by a small roar that seemed equally divided between men shouting in triumph and despair, and he saw that, finally, the collective will of their enemies had broken at least temporarily, although he was somewhat disappointed to see they were withdrawing north up the street paralleling the wall in good order. Regardless of this, Nahapana saw the perpendicular street leading into the city was now open and he wasted no time, shouting for the unengaged phalanx troops to attend to him. He did approach the corner cautiously, and it was a good thing that he did, because he had just peeked his head around the corner of the building when, from the deeper darkness provided by the buildings blocking the light from the fire next to the wall, he sensed more than saw several missiles streaking towards him. None of them hit anything other than the paving stones or in one case, the city wall because, reacting instinctively, he threw himself backward, and he would have fallen, but he was caught by the shield of one of his men, offering him a muttered thanks.

"We're going to have to be ready for more of those," he said loudly enough for all of them to hear, "so when we move into the street, keep your shields up!"

Taking a breath, he paused a heartbeat, then gave the command, which was instantly obeyed, the phalanx troops holding their shields a bit higher than they normally would as the bolder of them moved at a run to the far side of the perpendicular street, forming the right side of a line that would extend across the street. And, as Nahapana predicted, even more javelins came hurtling their direction, although the fact that they were coming out of the darkness made it more a matter of luck than anything when most of the men either blocked it with their shield, or leaned just enough for the missiles to go skittering across the paving stones in a shower of small sparks. Not all of them escaped, however, and Nahapana heard at least two men who were struck, one of them mortally, judging from the gurgling sound that lasted only a matter of a couple heartbeats before stopping. More crucially, those men who had blocked the javelins with their shields were quickly reminded of the devilishly ingenious design of the Roman javelin, which they had been unaware of just a bit more than a year earlier, and the next predominant noise came from them dropping their shields to the street, their comrades filling in the files behind them passing up their own protection to the men of the front rank who needed it.

"Remember these dogs only have two apiece! Once they're out, then we can close with them and cut them down!"

Nahapana turned in surprise; he had forgotten about Ushabad, and that he and these men had firsthand experience as part of the defense north of Bharuch against Pollio's part of the army, but he quickly realized that it was better for this man to give the commands, which he indicated by stepping aside and gesturing to the spot normally occupied by the commander. With a nod of understanding, Ushabad stepped into place, and within a matter of heartbeats, determined that the Romans, who were arrayed down the street about twenty paces away, had expended their supply. Ushabad bellowed the command that would begin this next part of the fight in earnest, the long spears of the men in the front rank, each of them with an undamaged shield, dropping into the horizontal position. Then, less than a heartbeat later, they began what would be considered a slow, almost stately advance towards their foes, the shouted challenges and insults hurled at each other that nobody understood bouncing off the walls of the buildings lining the street. Nahapana watched for a moment, then turned and ran the few paces back to the wall, finding Bhiman in command of those men who had been responsible for pushing the Romans away. To his surprise, when he looked towards the northern wall in the direction where the Romans had withdrawn, he saw the street was empty.

"They went around the corner two streets up," Bhiman explained. "Do you want us to pursue?"

"No," Nahapana answered immediately and without hesitation. Moving his gaze from the street, he looked Bhiman in the eye as he said, "You *must* keep this gate open at all costs, Bhiman. We have to get to the King so that we can retreat, and this is our only way out, as long as you and these men do your duty."

"We will, Lord," Bhiman assured him, then hesitated a fraction before asking, "May I have some of the swordsmen?"

"You can have a hundred, that's all," Nahapana agreed. "We may need them as replacements to get to King Abhiraka."

Then there was nothing more to be said, and Nahapana wasted no time, pausing just long enough to shout for all but a hundred of the light infantrymen to follow him. It wasn't lost on Nahapana that, because of the Pandyans' betrayal, the entirety of the army of Bharuch save the elephants was now contained within these walls, and it was not only possible, it was likely that those animals would be all their king had left. But, he thought grimly, if we lose him, all is lost anyway, and it was this thought that propelled him and the men with him forward.

Abhiraka and the eight hundred men with him didn't get more than two blocks from the southern boundary of the palace after brushing aside the lone Century that had been sent to the northern gate before they ran into resistance from two directions. Blocking their progress to the south towards the city center, Batius' 5th had moved past the square, searching for the enemy, while men of the First Cohort of the 15th fell on their right flank, using one of the streets that ran east/west. Very quickly, the king realized that Ranjeet had been right; he simply didn't have enough men to fight to where they needed to be. In some ways, it was fortunate that he would never learn that the three Centuries from the 5th, and the Cohort of the 15th were all the men that the two Primi Pili could spare to this effort, as they independently came to the same decision, that unless they devoted men to stopping the fires, the entire city and everyone in it was likely to burn to death. Nevertheless, to Abhiraka, standing in the middle of his city but still several blocks away from his goal, he didn't hesitate.

"We're falling back to the palace. Sound the call for a fighting withdrawal."

While the heavy spears wielded by phalanx troops were useful in keeping their foes at bay in the offense, they were even more valuable during the kind of withdrawal Abhiraka ordered, at least if the men were skilled enough, and as the Romans had learned when they faced the phalanx troops of Bharuch the first time, they were formidable foes. Now that they were wearing even better armor that, unlike the cuirass, offered more flexibility and allowed men to twist their torsos, the Romans facing them were frustrated in their attempts to close with their foes and inflict casualties, because on those rare occasions they managed to get past both shield and spear of their opponent, the Bharuch men simply twisted or ducked the thrust from the shorter Roman *gladius*. While the style was different, the withdrawal was performed in the same rhythmic manner used by the Romans. Rather than pushing off with their shields as the Romans did, they took advantage of the extra space because of their spears, launching a thrust in unison that occupied their enemies and allowed them to take a step backward. Similarly to the Romans, their commander shouted out a count, and it didn't take long for the Romans to recognize the resemblances, and more importantly, the futility of trying to stop them. When they reached the street paralleling the southern wall of the palace compound, to Abhiraka's relief, he saw that there were no Romans at the gate, which gave him another idea. Leaving the men to their slow but steady retreat, Abhiraka ran down the street, and one of the men Ranjeet had positioned standing on the makeshift rampart watching for a Roman attack saw and recognized him so that, before he reached the gateway, one side had been opened and Ranjeet hurried out to greet the king. In as few words as possible, Abhiraka let Ranjeet know that he had been right, but his subordinate knew there was nothing to be gained in showing any reaction, listening intently as the king explained his idea.

"You want to essentially do the same thing we did to get into the palace, but in reverse by using the secret door in the garden and hitting them from behind?" Ranjeet asked, trying not to let his skepticism show, yet he felt compelled to point out, "But if they let our men withdraw all the way back to the gate, why would we need to risk losing more men to inflict a few more casualties? Especially when we don't know if there will be more Romans coming that could do the same thing to us?"

Abhiraka's first reaction was to snap at Ranjeet, but he refrained, and the pause gave him time to consider. Realizing that Ranjeet was once again correct, that in a situation where they had to conserve men as they waited for the rest of the army to arrive, trading his own men's lives just to inflict a few more casualties on an enemy that would be outnumbered as soon as the rest of the army arrived wasn't the best use of resources.

Still, he only gave a curt nod, saying only, "Very well."

Then, they both turned to watch as men began to appear from the intersecting street, all of them at least in pairs, while a couple of men were carrying one of the more seriously wounded between them. It became obvious that the Romans had resigned themselves to the fact that the Bharuch force would withdraw with a minimum of more casualties, but they kept up the pressure, following the retreating enemy down the street back to the palace gate, albeit at a respectful distance. The only hectic moment came when the last rank of the phalanx troops reached the gateway, when the Centurion in command of the Century that was applying the pressure bellowed the command to rush the gate. Hampered as they were by the absence of any missile troops, those phalanx men standing on the wooden rampart next to the gate were faced with the choice of risking their own lives, leaning out to thrust their spears at the oncoming Romans to help the last of Abhiraka's beleaguered men, thereby delaying their enemies long enough for the single gate that had been opened to be slammed shut, or to refrain. None of those men hesitated, and it was a practical inevitability that a quick-thinking Roman first blocked the thrust from a spear with his shield, the point driving through the wood, then dropping his *gladius*, snatched at the shaft and gave a hard yank. Although the Bharuch man let go, it wasn't in time, and for a bare eyeblink, his upper body extended out and over the wall, but before his comrade next to him could grab the man and pull him to safety, he toppled over, landing heavily onto the paving stones at the base of the wall. His shout of alarm was quickly cut off as his comrades safe on the parapet were forced to watch as at least three *gladii* plunged into his body, but while the gate was closed and that was the only casualty, it still left a bitter taste in the mouths of the men forced to witness the end of one of theirs. In their enthusiasm, some of the Romans threw themselves at the gate in the instant before the locking bar was dropped into place, requiring the defenders to essentially do the same, hurling their bodies against the gate in the opposite direction, but after a brief struggle, they prevailed, the bar dropping. Even as this was taking place, Abhiraka sent a third of his men to the northern gate, preparing for what he viewed as the inevitable attempt by their enemies to force that entrance. Once this was done, Abhiraka turned to Ranjeet.

"Now," he said grimly, "we wait for the rest of our men and the Pandyans."

Ranjeet nodded, but while he couldn't actually say why, or pinpoint when the thought first came to him, he realized that a nagging suspicion had been growing in the back of his mind, and while outwardly he was engaged and speaking to Abhiraka, agreeing with his king's statement, internally he was struggling about whether he should utter this suspicion aloud to his friend. He knew from experience that things never went exactly as they were planned, and there were always delays, or one of the commanders showed up at the wrong place, or wrong time, and while he estimated that it had been just a bit more than a third of a Roman watch since the first naphtha cache had been ignited.

It was this thought that prompted Ranjeet to suddenly say, "I wonder what happened to Bolon."

Abhiraka glanced over at Ranjeet, his face grim, and Ranjeet noticed, unsurprised, which was explained when his king replied, "I was just thinking the same thing." Sighing, he said, "Hopefully, he's unhurt and just found a place to hide until it's safe to come out. And," while it was forced, Abhiraka smiled as he finished, "reap the rewards for what he did this night."

Then there was really not much to say, so the pair stood and silently watched the four separate fires, neither of them willing to point out that the fires on the southern and western walls seemed to be working their way towards each other.

When Pilus Prior Atilius led his Cohort around the northwest corner of the wall, he had no real idea what to expect, but the sight of what was clearly the tail end of a few thousand men in the process of crossing the pontoon bridge brought him to a dead stop.

He was about to order his *Cornicen* to issue the order for them to form up, but quickly realized the danger of this, and instead, while raising his voice, kept it from a full bellow as he ordered, "First Century form on me! Second Century align off the First!" Pausing, he moved a few paces so that he could get a better idea of how much space there was between the northern wall and the canal. "Third and Fourth Century in the first line! Stagger Fifth and Sixth in the second line and wait for my command to advance!"

What Atilius had immediately seen was that the manner in which the canal angled off of the river meant that there was less room at the corner of the wall, but within a matter of a hundred paces, there would be more space. It might have been more prudent to advance to the point where the Ninth Cohort could have aligned to his left, with both Cohorts in the more standard three Century front, but Atilius decided in the moment that speed was of the essence. While the fire did provide enough illumination for him to determine that there was movement across the bridge, that was all he could see with any clarity, and they were too far away for him to get any sense that he and his men had been spotted. As he stood and watched for a few moments, the one thing he could tell was that there were no elephants visible.

"They probably crossed first," he remarked, as much to himself as to his *Signifer*, but he wasn't prepared for the man's reaction.

"By the gods, I *hope* so," he shuddered. "I talked to my cousin in the 5th when we got here, and he said those fucking beasts are straight from Hades."

Although Atilius had certainly heard much the same thing from those Centurions who had encountered the animals, his first thought was to point out that there was a weapon that negated them, but while he hadn't been told, his assumption that the columns of fire that made the sky glow weren't a coincidence, and he was fairly certain what was fueling the blazes. This was part of the reason for his caution, but he also had the beginnings of an idea, and it began with his order to resume moving towards the northern gate to give them more room. However, once they reached a spot where he calculated at least one more Cohort would fit, he called the halt again, then turned and moved at close to a run back in the direction of the rest of the Legion, looking for his Primus Pilus. He almost missed Papernus because, while he was rushing to the rear along the wall, the Primus Pilus was heading the opposite direction but on the opposite side of the column. Fortunately, Atilius spotted the white crest, and cut across the ranks of men who were just now coming to a halt, realizing that the Tenth had stopped moving, sliding to a stop in front of his Primus Pilus.

"Why have you stopped?" Papernus snapped, then in a lower voice that only Atilius could hear, added menacingly, "You better have a good reason, Atilius."

"I think I do, Primus Pilus," Atilius forced himself to sound calm, then went on to explain, "We've gotten close enough to see that they're almost all on this side of the canal, but they're not stopping. They're clearly heading for the eastern gate. And," he paused, because this was the one thing that was pure guesswork on his part, "we haven't seen one elephant."

This gave Papernus pause, and he rubbed his chin as he said thoughtfully, "Probably because they would want those beasts to lead the way into the city. And," he glanced up at the glowing sky, "someone has set our supplies of naphtha to the torch on our side and here, so we have to assume that the eastern supply has gone up too. And," he finished grimly, "probably the southern as well."

"You brought the camp supply with the men of your Cohort, I assume?" Atilius tried to phrase it in a manner that impressed on Papernus that it was a formality, although he felt fairly certain he knew the answer, and that it wasn't the one Papernus would like giving.

"Pluto's balls," the Primus Pilus groaned. "No, I didn't." His chagrin was short-lived, and he turned and snapped to one of the rankers of what Atilius saw was the Eighth Cohort, "Go find Primus Hastatus Posterior Blaesus and tell him to take his Century back to the camp, grab every crate of naphtha there, and bring it to me immediately." Then, he ordered the first man's comrade next to him in the rank, "Go to Primus Pilus Posterior Cornuficius and tell him that I'm ordering him to bring the Cohort up to join the Tenth." Waiting until both men went dashing away into the darkness, and while he had no need to do so, Papernus felt sufficiently chastened at his oversight to explain to his Pilus Prior, "They're going to be the nearest to our camp. I'm going to bring the First up on your left flank, but we'll wait for the Sixth Century to get here with the naphtha before we move."

Atilius knew he was taking a risk, not just with his career but with his men; nevertheless, before he could talk himself out of it, he heard himself say, "Primus Pilus, I have an idea."

At first, he was certain Papernus would refuse him, but while he said nothing, he gave a curt nod that Atilius took as permission. "I'd like to lead my Cohort forward right now." He saw by Papernus' expression that he was about to be turned down, so he hurried on, "At least allow us to close with the enemy and engage those men who just crossed the bridge. If the elephants lead the way, and we come down on them from the rear, that will make whoever's commanding them turn them around, and they're already inside the city. Not only will that take time, it will keep the boys in the 5th and 15th from facing those beasts without the naphtha. If…"

"Do it," Papernus cut him off, having determined not only where Atilius was heading, but that his Pilus Prior was right. "Don't wait for us." He offered Atilius a savage smile, along with a clap on the shoulder as he said, "But save some of those *cunni* for us, eh?"

Exchanging salutes, Atilius turned, and this time, he went to an all-out sprint to rejoin his Cohort, wondering if he had just gotten his men killed.

"Your Highness! Lord Ranjeet!" The junior officer who had been placed in command of the men standing on the wooden rampart along the southern wall was facing inward, his hands cupped. "I hear fighting!"

The two men were standing among their soldiers who were being allowed to rest for whatever was coming, but it was Abhiraka who reacted first, rushing to where the officer was standing at the southeastern corner of the palace wall, this spot giving him the best vantage point. Since he was first, the king clambered up the ladder, but he waited for Ranjeet before the pair walked down the rampart, where the young officer was standing, along with a half-dozen men from the phalanx who were posted as the first line of defense. Even before he reached the man's side, Abhiraka heard the clashing sound of metal on metal, along with shouts and shrill cries of pain that every experienced fighting man recognized. And, as he stood listening intently, he was certain that the sound was increasing in volume, which could only mean that the fighting was coming closer to them and, most importantly, that relief was near. So sure was he that this was the case, in a most uncharacteristic act, Abhiraka turned to the officer and pounded him on the back with a huge smile on his face.

"They're almost here, Pradesh! And once they're here, the city is ours again!"

So flattered that a personage no less than King Abhiraka remembered his name, the young officer couldn't summon the proper words, so he just returned the king's smile with a grin of his own. It was left to Ranjeet, who, while he initially shared Abhiraka's joy, had actually continued listening, to disabuse them.

It took three times for Abhiraka to respond to having his name called, and he was clearly irritated with Ranjeet as he spun about, snapping, "What is it, Ranjeet?"

"Listen," Ranjeet replied, then said nothing more.

"I have been listening," Abhiraka shot back impatiently, but his friend saw the flicker of unease cross his face, and he asked more calmly, "What should I be listening for?"

"Does that sound like thousands of men, Your Highness?" Ranjeet said quietly, but then added, "And do you hear any elephants?"

The king spun back around to stare in the direction of the noise, seeing movement for the first time, and while he couldn't identify the meaning, by the location, he saw that it was originating at the corner of the street that ran along the southern wall of the palace compound and one of the perpendicular streets. Abhiraka watched and listened, his body suddenly going stiff in a manner that told Ranjeet that his king now understood the meaning.

Still, he wasn't quite ready to acknowledge this, and he said over his shoulder, "Maran probably didn't allow their elephants to lead the way, and their infantry is with ours."

"That's possible, Your Highness," Ranjeet seemingly agreed, but with a tone that Abhiraka recognized, that of one of his subordinates who didn't want to disagree publicly with his king.

Perhaps a half-dozen heartbeats later, the movement that Abhiraka had spotted became distinct enough for him to recognize men dragging other men, or men moving with a limp, but it was still the relative order in which they were moving that told him they were Romans. It was certainly heartening to see their enemy retreating, but Abhiraka understood that Ranjeet was not only right about the lack of sounds that were an inherent part of using elephants as weapons of war, the numbers of men he was seeing weren't sufficient to justify an attempt to stop an army of the size he was expecting. All that remained was to have his worst fears confirmed, and it occurred when the Romans, still retreating in good order, withdrew farther down the street paralleling the wall in the opposite direction from the palace, leaving the path open for the Bharuch attackers to move unmolested towards his position. Beyond his own men who were now moving as quickly in his direction as possible while still keeping their attention on the Romans, Abhiraka could dimly see that the Romans were reforming themselves, seemingly content to allow the Bharuch forces to withdraw to his own position, the most potent sign that they were unconcerned about it happening. There was a brief span of time as Abhiraka watched more men materialize out of the darkness as they reached the intersection with the perpendicular street where he hoped the stream wouldn't end, but once the last half-dozen men, who were moving in much the same manner as the last Romans who had retreated shortly before entered the street leading to the palace, either limping or aiding a comrade, he couldn't deny the reality.

"Open the gates!"

As the men on the ground scrambled to obey Ranjeet's order, Abhiraka stood watching what he was now beginning to understand was all that remained of his army when one of the men detached themselves and moved away from his comrades, heading directly for where Abhiraka was standing at a run.

It was Nahapana, who came to a stop just a few paces from the wall, and he dropped to his knees, refusing to look up at Abhiraka as he spoke just loudly enough for the king to hear, "Your Highness, I have failed you."

"The Pandyans aren't coming," Abhiraka replied, his tone flat and emotionless.

"No, Your Highness, they're not coming," Nahapana confirmed, yet despite trying to prepare himself, Abhiraka let out an explosive gasp, with enough force that made him so lightheaded he had to reach out and grab the top of the wall for support.

His mind reeling, Abhiraka struggled to maintain his focus, and it prompted him to ask, "Where is Damisippos and the elephants? Where is Darpashata?"

"Your Highness, it was Damisippos who came to warn me we had been betrayed," Nahapana explained. "And I told him that he should return to the rest of the elephants and stay on the other side of the canal, and Bhiman is with the rest of the men at the eastern gate. They are holding it open for us to return with you so that you can make your escape, but we must hurry!"

At first, Abhiraka was sure he had misheard Nahapana; it was Ranjeet who confirmed he had heard correctly when he said, "Nahapana is right, Your Highness. We have lost the day. Now all that matters is to get you out of here."

Abhiraka acted as if he hadn't heard, still staring down at Nahapana from the rampart, frowning as if he was thinking.

Just when Ranjeet opened his mouth to repeat himself, Abhiraka said suddenly, "No." Just the sound of his own voice seemed to strengthen his resolve, and he repeated more firmly, "No. I will not flee." He did turn his gaze from Nahapana to look Ranjeet directly in the eye as he said quietly, "I am done running, my friend. I've spent the last year of my life fleeing and behaving like a mangy cur. That is no way for a king to live."

Ranjeet was unable to immediately respond, staring at Abhiraka with his mouth open as he tried to summon the right words that would dissuade his king and his closest friend from this madness, yet Abhiraka's expression was one he had seen too many times to misinterpret, one that instead of an impassioned plea to reconsider, ended with him asking, "Are you certain, Abhiraka?"

"Yes, I am," the king replied. Then Abhiraka turned to face inward where the men who had come with Nahapana were celebrating a brief reunion with Abhiraka's force. "My soldiers!" he called out, his voice ringing with the same confident authority to which they had all become accustomed. "I know that those who arrived with Nahapana have probably informed you of the Pandyans' treachery, and that they have deserted us. And," his voice did waver a bit, "I don't have to tell you that, without them, we have no chance to retake our city." He paused, immediately seeing that the murmuring he was hearing wasn't that of men who were surprised, but who had already come to this realization. Now he had to swallow the hard, bitter lump as he continued, "At this moment, Bhiman and your comrades are holding the area around the eastern gate in order to give us a chance to escape. And this is what I am ordering…for you." Waiting for a heartbeat for the words to sink in, Abhiraka pointed in the direction of the bright orange glow to the east. "Go now, join Bhiman and the rest of your comrades while there is still time and escape with your lives! And know that," now he couldn't contain the raging grief, his voice suddenly breaking from the emotions surging through him, "you have served your king more strongly and more faithfully than any men in history! I have been truly blessed and fortunate to be your king."

"What are you going to do, Your Highness?"

The shout came from the men gathered around the rampart, and while Abhiraka didn't recognize the man's voice, he didn't hesitate.

"I am going to stay and fight and take as many of these Roman dogs with me as I can."

"We won't leave you! We are yours to the death!"

The only thing Abhiraka knew was that it wasn't the same voice, but even if he could have responded, he would have never been able to be heard over the sudden roar of voices as every man standing there added their own promise to not abandon their king, no matter what it meant.

Too overcome to speak, Abhiraka looked to Ranjeet, whose eyes were as filled as his own, but he did manage to make himself heard as he said, "If you think we'd leave you, my brother, you're truly mad."

Abhiraka allowed the demonstration to continue for a few more heartbeats before he raised his arms, and once it became quiet enough to be heard, he managed to say, "Your king has heard you, and he is honored by your decision. Now, let us prepare ourselves. We will make our families proud, and they will sing our names for the rest of time!"

Abhiraka was moving before he finished, clambering down the ladder, followed by Ranjeet and the rest of the men, while those soldiers standing on the ground immediately knelt, forming into two rough groups through which Abhiraka walked, touching each man's head as headed to the palace to say farewell to his queen.

Chapter 9

Nobody was more surprised at the complete absence of armored elephants than Decimus Pilus Prior Atilius, because he had been almost certain that, despite what he had said to Papernus, it was a virtual certainty that his men would have to face the huge beasts. His hope was that it wouldn't be for very long, that the First Cohort would arrive with their supply of naphtha to save his Cohort from heavy losses. By the time he returned to his Cohort and gotten them moving at the double quick along the northern wall, the entirety of the Bharuch forces had crossed the bridge and entered through the eastern gate. The absence of anybody outside the walls at the gate when Atilius halted his Cohort to move cautiously to the corner so that he could peek around it engendered another delay as he was forced to decide on the fly how he would carry out his attack. He had hoped that there would still be foes outside the wall, certain that the appearance of his Cohort would cause those men to warn their comrades who had already entered the city. In his envisioning the moment, Atilius had seen aligning his Cohort in a single line to face a similarly deployed foe, but with the complete absence of the enemy outside the walls, he understood that he would be forced to lead his men into the city. Leading his Century around the corner, he adjusted the width of his formation, preparing for entering through the narrow gateway, but while he hoped that the men of either the 5th or the 15th were in a position to meet this newly arrived force, he also correctly assumed that the fires would be at least an equal concern. Nevertheless, he was at the head of his Century as he led them at a run through the gateway, but he was completely unprepared to see nothing but the backs of their foes, already furiously engaged with what he would learn later was the 5th. It wasn't a battle as much as it was a slaughter, although the Bharuch men in the rear did manage to turn about after the first of their comrades were cut down from behind. Caught as they were between these two Roman forces, the end was inevitable; the fact that virtually no man in this trap begged for quarter was a topic of conversation for weeks to come, although in the moment it didn't really matter. They chose to die on their feet, and the Romans were happy to oblige them. In fact, the only Cohort of the 21st that faced the human enemy that night was the Tenth; the other foe, the raging fire, was not only as deadly, in terms of the potential to do damage, it presented a greater challenge than any men armed with spears, swords, and bows. The Tenth certainly didn't escape unscathed, Atilius' Century suffering several casualties, as did the Second, Third, and Fourth, while the Fifth and Sixth never had the chance to face the enemy. And, Atilius knew, his Cohort suffered more than one of the senior Cohorts would have because of the inexperience of his men, but he was equally certain that none of the surviving men would have accepted being replaced if they had been offered the opportunity. They were a Cohort of a Roman Legion, and this was what they had been paid to do, and of all the Tenth Cohorts in Caesar's army, from that day onward, the Tenth of the 21st was considered different by their comrades. None of which mattered in the moment, and none of this even occurred to Atilius until later when it was brought up by his fellow Pili Priores. All that did matter was sounding the relief at the right time, judging how his men were faring, adding the weight of his *gladius* where it was needed, and unlike any other battle he had participated in, keeping an eye on the fire raging behind them without doing it in such an obvious manner that his men were distracted. By the time the last clump of Bharuch men were finally cut down, the sky was already pinkening, while the fires were only beginning to be brought under control. Although most of the occupants of the threatened buildings had managed to flee within moments of the caches being destroyed, inevitably, those who were too elderly or infirm to find shelter deeper in the city perished, their charred remains turning up for days afterward. The casualties from burns weren't restricted to the civilian populace; men from all three Legions suffered burns of varying degrees as they worked feverishly to contain the fires, but by mid-morning, the work was mostly done. This was when Batius, Aquilinus, and Papernus made their way to the *Praetorium*, but it was Aquilinus who bore the news that the struggle wasn't over.

"They're holed up at the palace," he informed Ventidius and the two Centurions. "They're manning the walls, and they've got enough men at each gate that we're going to need more than a Century to force each one. Right now, all but my First Cohort is finishing with the fires."

When Ventidius turned to Batius, his answer was essentially the same, as was Papernus', although in his case, the identity of the Cohort engaged with the remnant out in the city was the Tenth.

"It's a long story," was all Papernus said when the other three men looked at him with some surprise. More to take the attention off of himself, he asked Aquilinus, "Have they said anything about what they want?"

"No." Aquilinus shook his head. "They're just standing there, clearly waiting for us to come get them."

As Ventidius listened, he was fighting the deep fatigue that came as much from not knowing exactly what was happening as the actual act of staying awake through the night and directing a battle, not against men but the raging fires.

"I suppose we should go find out what their intentions are," he said. "We'll go under a flag of truce and see what we can find out."

"Legate," Batius spoke up, "my suggestion is that you stay here. And," he glanced at the other two Primi Pili, "that only one of us go. These bastards may not know all that much about us, but I'm willing to wager that they know that the three of us wearing a white crest when the other Centurions wear different colors will mean something."

This was sensible, but neither Aquilinus nor Papernus were swayed, certain that Batius had an ulterior motive; such was the intense competition between the Primi Pili of Caesar's army, even when he wasn't present. Ventidius was the ultimate decision maker, however, and they all looked to him.

"I'm going," he said flatly. "First, I speak Greek. And second, I've been meeting with the Queen, and she may have some sort of influence over whoever's in there."

Knowing that they had been overruled, none of them tried to talk him out of it, although it was Aquilinus who said, "At least use some of my boys as a bodyguard in the event they have some treachery in mind."

Ventidius immediately saw the sense of this, and he agreed. Arrangements were quickly made, with a siege spear serving as the truce banner, with a section of Legionaries summoned to march with Ventidius the three blocks from the city center to the street along the southern wall.

Hyppolita had no idea how she knew, but when her husband reappeared, even without seeing his face, she understood it wasn't to inform her that the city was retaken, or that he would even be escorting her to safety elsewhere. Between the growing fires, and the sounds of fighting that, while distinct, remained muted and in essentially the same locations in the city instead of spreading as her husband had assured her would happen when the Pandyans arrived, this was what enabled her to correctly guess what had happened. Before her husband could speak, she crossed the room swiftly, grabbed him by the elbow, and ushered him from the room into her private chamber.

"They have abandoned us, haven't they?" she asked calmly, receiving the answer in his expression before he opened his mouth. Despite reading this in her demeanor, Abhiraka replied tersely, "Yes, my Queen. For reasons that I don't know, the Pandyans have decided to desert us."

"You haven't had a chance to speak to Puddapandyan?" she asked, making him realize that, as forthcoming as he had been when he first entered the palace, there was more that she didn't know than she did, but he made up his mind up at that moment to answer simply, "No, I haven't. But it doesn't matter now. Damisippos was waiting with our elephants for the signal, but when it came, they turned around and left."

"And this Damisippos didn't try to stop them?" Hyppolita's voice turned cold, and Abhiraka reached out to grasp her gently but firmly by the shoulders. "Hyppolita, even if Damisippos had tried, he and the remaining men would have been slaughtered. And," he chided gently, "I suspect that you know this to be true."

"I do." She dropped her head to break his gaze, almost overcome with a sense of loss and grief that felt like it was going to suffocate her. Forcing herself to take a deep breath, she lifted her head and asked, "What do you intend to do, my husband?"

"Why," he smiled at her, but it was one unlike any he had ever given her before, "we intend to fight, my Queen."

"Fight?" she echoed, slightly bewildered. "To what end, Abhiraka?"

"To make the Romans pay in blood for my kingdom," he didn't shout this, exactly, but it was with a vehemence that, like the smile, was something with which she was completely unfamiliar, and the thought that flashed through her mind was that his time in exile had done something to Abhiraka. Still, she attempted to reason with him. "But you cannot possibly win. And," she knew she was taking a terrible risk, but this was too important, "I have come to learn more about these Romans, husband. Yes, Caesar has come to conquer, but he's not a monster, nor is he unreasonable." She hesitated, and when the words came out, it was in a rush. "What if you could become a client king under Rome and keep your throne?"

At first, her fears that Abhiraka's mind had somehow been damaged seemed to be realized, because he stared down at her with an expression that registered a complete lack of understanding. Unfortunately, that look was swept away, his mouth suddenly twisting, and while he had kept his hands on her shoulders, his touch had been gentle. Now she gasped in pain from the increase in pressure as his hands began squeezing her flesh.

"How do you know this about Caesar?" While his tone was calm, she read the growing fury in his eyes, and she had just enough time to anticipate him asking, "Did you lay with that...that...Roman dog?"

"No," she replied, not loudly but with an emphatic tone. Then she challenged, "But what if I had? Do you have any doubt that if I had, it would be because I judged that it would help you regain your throne, husband?" Seeing the flicker of doubt, she pressed, "You think so little of me, Abhiraka? I am your *queen*, and I have been *here*, doing everything within my power to support you and work for this day!"

"That day has come, and I have lost," Abhiraka shot back bitterly. For the span of several heartbeats, she stared up at him, meeting his gaze while desperately hoping that he wouldn't pursue his line of questioning. Finally, he broke the silence by saying, "But, as you usually are, my Queen, you are right. I should have more faith in you, and know that, even if you had, it would have been because you saw no other way to help me."

She felt his grip relax, and she fought the urge to reach up and rub her shoulders, still aware that this was a dangerous moment, even if his suspicions had been assuaged, about Caesar.

"But, Abhiraka," she spoke carefully, "even if I had done as you suspected, it wouldn't change the situation in which we find ourselves. So, I must ask you again...what if you surrendered yourself and offered Caesar peace in exchange for allowing you to remain on the throne. And then?" She shrugged. "Who knows what the future holds, my husband? Nothing that these Romans have said to me makes me believe that they intend to stay."

"Then," Abhiraka asked, truly bewildered, "why did Caesar bring that army here, if it wasn't to conquer us?"

"I don't believe even Caesar truly knows," she answered instantly without thinking. Realizing that her words might return Abhiraka to a topic she wanted to keep in the past tense, she added, "Not that I've had more than one conversation with him personally, but I do know that one of his most senior and trusted officers believes that Caesar is obsessed with outdoing Alexander by reaching the Ganges, and once he does, he and his men will return home."

"Who told you that?" Abhiraka asked, genuinely curious.

"He was a Roman Centurion," she replied, hoping nothing gave her away. "Since he was with Caesar on the day the city fell, I insisted that he was the only Roman with whom I would have contact. He and the men under his command were my guards until Caesar took his Legion along with the rest of their army on their ships, and over the months, I had several conversations with him."

"Centurion?" Abhiraka frowned, then used his hand to mime the presence of a crest, "Those are the Romans who wear the crests like this?"

"Yes." Hyppolita nodded. "But this Centurion was in command of an entire Roman Legion." Suddenly, she remembered one nugget of information she had managed to glean, and she felt quite proud of herself for saying, "A Legion normally has less than five thousand men, but Caesar's Legions have six thousand. And," she added, "there were ten of them until Caesar returned, bringing one with him, then another arrived a few weeks later. Then he took nine and left three behind."

Abhiraka listened intently, yet he also knew that, ultimately, what Hyppolita was telling him no longer mattered. He was certain that, by the time the sun was fully in the sky, his concerns would be behind him. Still, he was proud of his wife, although there was something in her words that nagged at him.

"You said this Centurion was a senior officer to Caesar," he said once she stopped speaking. "But the information that we have is that even the Centurions are baseborn, from their peasant class. So," he asked what he thought was a logical question, "why would Caesar confide in or trust this Centurion who you talked to if they are of different classes?"

"That," she replied, again without thinking it through, "is something I don't know, but this Centurion was…different, husband. For one, he is *very* tall, but he is also very muscular. He is one of the largest men I have ever seen. And," she added, "he spoke Greek quite well." Hyppolita hesitated, then finished by saying, "And, he never lied to me, husband. So when he says that Caesar will probably leave, I believe him."

Hyppolita had no way to know that, for reasons she would never learn, her husband discerned that, although he would never know the specifics, while his fears about Caesar had been unfounded, there was something about this unnamed Centurion that he decided, in that moment, he would move into the afterlife never knowing. Of one thing he was certain, however; her description of this Roman matched the one in his own mind when he had been watching from the northern rampart as Memmon and some of his elephants were slaughtered. He couldn't see much, and certainly not to a level of detail, except for noticing that there was one Roman wearing that crest who towered over the others. Knowing himself, he shoved this knowledge into a corner of his mind, refusing to even think about it for however much time he had left.

Aloud, he replied firmly, "Be that as it may, even if the Romans do leave, what you're suggesting is that I surrender. And that," he finished, "is something I will not do."

"What about those men?" Hyppolita pointed in the general direction of the compound. "Don't they deserve a chance at life?"

"Those men," Abhiraka answered coldly, "are the ones who convinced me that surrender is not an option."

This was the moment she knew her husband wouldn't be swayed, and it ignited in her a feeling of such powerlessness that in her mind she was transported back to the moment when she watched two Romans, one of them covered in grime and blood that made her shudder to think from where it came, ascending the steps of the palace. What made this different was that, unlike the first time, there was no hope that her husband would return to rescue her and their kingdom from these conquerors, and it took every shred of her self-control not to break down, understanding that her husband's shame would be compounded.

They had been standing there in silence, then Hyppolita finally broke it by saying, "While I can't say that I agree with your decision because you're my husband, I understand it and will do all in my power to uphold the honor of this house, because you are my King."

Now it was Abhiraka's turn to be assaulted by a wave of emotions, one of which was a feeling of such gratitude towards his queen that, despite the fact that they were standing just inside her chamber with an open door, he took her in his arms and gave her the kind of kiss that, in other times, would have seemed most unkinglike.

"You," he whispered into her ear, "are a remarkable woman, Hyppolita, and I am a fortunate King to have such a Queen." Then, he stepped away from her, and spoke more loudly than needed if it was just for her ears, "And now I'll send Ranjeet to talk to Eurycleia before what comes next." He grinned down at her, winked and whispered, "We both know she's standing there listening."

Even through the tears, this made Hyppolita laugh, but she matched his whisper as she agreed, "Yes, she is. She's a terrible snoop."

Abhiraka turned away and walked out into the audience room then passed through it to the stairs, pausing for a moment to look at his surroundings, and to Hyppolita, it seemed as if he was actually seeing them for the first time. The murals that he had been so indifferent about when she had suggested they would enhance the palace, the walls painted with scenes that were from the history of Abhiraka's line seemed to attract his most intense attention. At the time, she had been infuriated that he barely seemed to notice, yet standing there, watching his eyes roam from one scene to the next, all she could feel was a terrible sense of loss. Then, he descended the stairs, and it wasn't lost on her that he refused to meet her gaze as he disappeared, the hard echoes of his boots marking his departure from her world.

Surrounded by a section of Legionaries, Publius Ventidius walked up the street that connected the center of the city to the palace, forced to make a weaving path around the bodies of the combatants who had fallen. While he was pleased to see that the only corpses belonged to the enemy, he was under no illusions that the Romans had suffered no losses, knowing that this was just another example of the efficiency that was a hallmark of the Legions, especially those who marched for Caesar. Although he allowed the escort, he insisted that the two men walking ahead of him not block his view, so that he was in effect between two columns of five men each, although the two rearmost Legionaries were walking side by side to protect his rear. It was light enough now that the glow from the fires was barely noticeable, but it was the smoke drifting across the city as the morning breeze from the south picked up that partially obscured his view, mainly because his eyes were beginning to burn, the tears following quickly. The Legionary to Ventidius' left was the man holding the spear aloft, the white square of cloth barely fluttering, and it was a sign of Ventidius' nerves that he snapped at the man to wave it back and forth so that it was more visible.

Finally, he reached a point where he was confident that he could be heard, acutely aware that it put him and the men with him within range of any archers, and before he began addressing the Bharuch defenders, he muttered, "Keep your attention on that wall, boys. If they have archers, they're probably down on the ground out of sight. I know that none of you want to get poked full of holes, and neither do I." He didn't bother to wait for a response, taking a breath and beginning, not fully bellowing, but powerfully enough he was sure he could be heard, in Greek, "My name is Publius Ventidius. I am a Legate, and the acting Praetor of this city, appointed to this post by Dictator for Life Gaius Julius Caesar, and I speak on behalf of him, and the Senate and People of Rome!" Stopping to take another breath, he continued, "Who is in command there?"

Now that they were close enough to make out facial features, Ventidius could tell which men lining the wall understood Greek and which did not, but at first, there was no response, and he could barely make out a buzzing noise that he knew meant they were talking amongst themselves. He was about to repeat himself when there was a stir, and two men on the wall directly across from him suddenly stepped aside, whereupon another figure appeared.

It was this man, who appeared to be in his early forties and spoke Greek with a barely detectable accent, who answered, "Abhiraka, second of his name and King of Bharuch is who commands here, Roman."

He said nothing more, causing Ventidius to experience a stab of irritation that he attributed later as the reason he didn't think to ask the obvious, saying instead, "My terms are for your King Abhiraka and him alone! Now will you summon him?"

This clearly amused the other man, and he replied, "I believe that we," he turned and indicated all of the men around him on either side, "should all hear what these terms are, Roman, before the King decides what his answer is."

"Very well!" Ventidius snapped, his annoyance now growing into something else, and his voice was as harsh and unyielding as he could make it, which he felt appropriate given the message. "Rome's terms are as follows. Your King, and all of the men with him inside the palace compound, will immediately throw down your weapons and surrender yourself to Rome! Once you do that, you will be subject to the mercy of the Dictator Gaius Julius Caesar, and it will be his decision and his alone as to your fate!"

"That," the man said mildly, yet Ventidius was certain he also heard anger, an emotion he actually understood, knowing that he would feel the same way, "does not sound like the kind of terms a King would agree to, Roman. In fact," the tone turned harder, as did the man's expression, "I strongly suspect that the King would reject these terms altogether, and simply say that you Romans are more than welcome to come and take our weapons from us."

While he didn't enjoy the idea, Ventidius also didn't hesitate, and he pointed in what might have been a dramatic gesture but was designed to be seen by all of the defenders, indicating the city around them as he answered harshly, "Then, not only will your King be responsible for getting you and all of your comrades with you slaughtered, but we will exact reprisals against the people of the city as well!" When he paused this time, it wasn't for breath, it was for effect, modulating his tone as he asked, "Haven't the people of this city suffered enough already? We," he indicated the men around him, "are not savages. In fact, most of our Legionaries haven't been fighting you, but the fire that was started by men who were commanded by your King!" Ventidius pointed directly at the man he was addressing, "Why don't you ask your King why he saw fit to endanger his own subjects in this manner? Does he *really* care about his people if he would do such a thing?"

"If it meant the King would regain what was taken from him, he is within his rights to do exactly as he did!"

Now Ventidius was certain that he had angered this man, but more importantly, he could see that those men who understood the exchange seemed to share his anger, some of them pointing their spears in his direction. Sensing that it would be wise to ease off the pressure at that moment, Ventidius held his hands out in a placating gesture.

"You are correct," he said. "If I were in your King's position, I would have undoubtedly done the same thing. But," he shook his head, "none of this changes the reality of your situation. Now may I speak to your King directly?"

Ventidius got a hint by the manner in which the other men he had seen understood Greek reacted, not with anger, but with smiles and some laughter, so he was not caught completely by surprise when the man replied with what was almost a cheerful tone, "Why, Publius Ventidius of Rome, you *have* been speaking to the King. And," all signs of humor vanished as Abhiraka pointed down at the Roman, "the King of Bharuch still rejects your…terms!" Abhiraka paused, and Ventidius saw how he not only took the time to glance to either side where the men lining the parapet began nodding, but then turned to face into the compound. Ventidius got the answer in the form of a roaring of male voices that was barely muffled by the compound wall, and when Abhiraka turned back to Ventidius, there was a smile that contained nothing but a promise of violence on the king's face.

"We are coming out, Roman," he called down. "The men of Bharuch are coming for you!"

Abhiraka's attempt to retake his city and his kingdom died with him, Ranjeet, and almost all of the men who remained as the last remnant of the army of Bharuch. The fighting was over less than a full Roman watch after Ventidius retreated back to the city center, leaving Batius and Aquilinus to lead the Centuries that had been tucked out of sight on the streets running parallel to the southern palace wall waiting for Abhiraka's decision out into the open. However, Ventidius overruled both Primi Pili, who intended to array their men so that they surrounded both southern and northern gate on three sides.

"If you do that, they'll just retreat into the palace compound, and make the palace and the other buildings their last stand. I don't know about you," he said grimly, "but I don't want to have to fight from room to room, especially when we don't know those buildings the way that bastard Abhiraka and his men do."

"What's to keep them from doing that anyway?" Batius asked, chagrined that he hadn't thought of this himself. "We're going to need to go in there after them anyway in that event. Better that we're in a position to move fast."

"No." Ventidius shook his head. "I don't think so. I think that if we back away and give Abhiraka and his men the opportunity, they'll leave the palace compound."

"Why would he do that?" Aquilinus asked, which Ventidius recognized was a perfectly reasonable question.

"Because he's king," Ventidius answered with more confidence than he actually felt. "And as king, he knows that if he did that, and we went in after them, we'd not only destroy the palace and every building they tried to defend, but his wife would definitely be raped and probably killed."

"Only if we let that happen!" Batius snorted, not liking the inference that he couldn't control his men. Ventidius didn't argue, at least directly, choosing instead to give Batius a long, level look that lasted several heartbeats before, finally, Batius grumbled, "But I see your point."

"Do you really think he's going to leave the only defensible position, sir?"

"There's only one way to find out, Aquilinus," Ventidius replied, then offered something of an olive branch. "But if he doesn't come out and you have to go in after him, I'll let you remind me I was wrong for the next month."

This did cause both men to chuckle, but Ventidius was quickly proven right. Once the Romans withdrew, retreating back to the large open area of the city center, Abhiraka didn't hesitate, the gates swinging open, although he did send out a small party of men who trotted to each of the streets that ran into the street paralleling the wall, all of whom signaled that there weren't any Romans within sight. Truthfully, once it was over, every man who participated in this moment would recall it as unusual, but it was an anonymous ranker who Batius overheard talking to a comrade that he had cause to remember.

"If there had been a crowd, this could have been one of those battles that Caesar staged for his triumphs!"

As soon as Batius heard this sentiment, he realized that this was what had struck him as well; the Romans had positioned themselves at the southern edge of the large square, while Abhiraka and his men had formed up along the northern edge. The silence had stretched out as each side watched the other, but it was Ventidius who was responsible for breaking it, turning and ordering his *Cornicen* to sound the advance, which triggered a corresponding roar from their foes. It was appropriate that, while the Romans didn't know it, Abhiraka led the charge with Ranjeet to his right and Nahapana to his left, although Nahapana was cut down by a javelin of the second volley hurled by the men of the Second Cohort of the 5th, who occupied the middle of the Roman line. Bhiman had just managed to reach Abhiraka's side to replace Nahapana when the two forces slammed into each other, and while the fight was furious and conducted at a frenzied pace, it didn't last long. Abhiraka, King of Bharuch acquitted himself in a manner that befitted his station, finally felled with four Romans he had personally dispatched at his feet, at the hands of the Secundus Pilus Posterior, Gnaeus Curso, although he was wounded by the king before Abhiraka succumbed with a third position thrust that penetrated his chest. Such was his valor that, when Ventidius ordered that Abhiraka's body not be looted or thrown into the mass grave, there was no grumbling from the men of the Second Century. In some ways, both Nahapana and Ranjeet were more fortunate because both of them were killed before their king, so in their last moments, they didn't have to endure the ultimate shame of failing to protect their sovereign. The Roman casualties were heavier than Ventidius and the Primi Pili cared for, although they weren't particularly surprised, given the desperate nature of this fight, this last gasp of the King of Bharuch.

"It's a shame," Aquilinus commented as he, Batius, and Ventidius stood together watching their men moving among the bodies, not one paving stone visible, either obscured by blood or by a corpse. "Those bastards were good fighters. We might have been able to use them as *tiros* after enough time passed."

This had run through Batius' mind as well, but he had dismissed it, saying, "Maybe if this had been last year, but not now. We," he indicated where Abhiraka's body had been lifted onto a door that was being used as a makeshift bier, "killed their king."

Aquilinus didn't argue; ultimately, it didn't matter, because not one of the men had even tried to surrender, each of them intent on fighting to the death rather than endure the shame of an ultimate defeat, while those who had been too seriously wounded to continue were dispatched by their victors.

Batius turned to Ventidius, "Do you want us to come with you, Legate?"

Ventidius thought a moment, then nodded. "I suppose it might be a good idea." He heaved a sigh, then admitted, "Gods know that I've been angry with the Queen more than once, but I still don't have any desire to cause her this kind of pain. But," he began walking towards the pair of men who were each holding one end of the door, "she needs to know."

Hyppolita had only watched as her husband led the men out of the compound, but she couldn't bear to witness whatever came next, so she retreated off the balcony and returned to her chair, seating herself as she was surrounded by her ladies. Eurycleia had been inconsolable, sobbing uncontrollably, and while she felt for Ranjeet's wife, she began to feel a mounting irritation, something that Amodini clearly sensed. To Hyppolita's deep surprise, it was the youngest member of her ladies who proved to be the most successful in calming Eurycleia, which she never would have guessed given their history. Regardless, at first she was deeply thankful for Amodini's actions, but the comparative quiet that ensued allowed her and the rest of her ladies to hear the sounds of fighting drifting through the open doors. Her initial thought was to order them closed, but she couldn't bring herself to do so, thinking that the least she owed her husband, and those subjects who were with him in what she understood would be his last moments, was to sit and listen as the kingdom of Bharuch lost its independence. Under normal circumstances, Hyppolita had an uncanny ability to track time, something that Abhiraka and her children had alternately marveled at and viewed more ruefully when they showed up tardy for something. When she thought about it later, however, she couldn't recall how much time had elapsed when she became aware that the noise had gradually died down and then was gone. She had been studying her hands, which she held in her lap, remembering how her mother had lectured her about how others could tell how much a young Hyppolita was agitated by how her hands behaved, which she tended to wave about or continually flex when she was under stress. "My Queen?" Hyppolita looked up at Darshwana. "It has gotten quiet. Have you noticed?"

Hyppolita rose to her feet, but she couldn't seem to force them to take her back to the doors that led onto the balcony.

"No," she admitted. "I hadn't."

"What do you think it means, my Queen?"

It took an effort for Hyppolita not to snap at Darshwana, but she heard the tension in her voice as she answered, "Nothing good for us, Lady Darshwana."

Finally, she did manage to make her way outside, and she was quickly joined by the other women, even Eurycleia, who was leaning heavily on Amodini, so much so that Hyppolita had to restrain herself from admonishing the older woman because of Amodini's condition, although she quickly thought better of it. They stood together watching as a small party of people came into sight up the street that led directly to the square. Before a half-dozen heartbeats, they could distinguish that there were five men, but it took a bit longer for Hyppolita to determine why two of the men were walking directly aligned, carrying something between them. Even when she recognized that they were carrying a body, her mind refused to acknowledge the most likely reason these men were approaching. Maybe, she thought, it's one of their Centurions, maybe they're heading for where they live outside the compound because he's wounded and that's where their physicians are located. Even as this ran through her mind, she knew it was a lie, and when they turned to the right once they reached the street paralleling the wall and obviously headed for the open gate, Hyppolita couldn't stop a choked sob from escaping her lips. Before her ladies could comfort her, she spun about and walked back into the room.

"Amodini, fetch my headscarf and veil," she ordered. "I will not receive these men without being properly attired."

This, she thought bitterly, *is one of the only times I'm thankful for that veil.* Amodini quickly returned, helping her queen fasten it and wrap her head covering, but when she turned to leave the room, her arm was caught. Turning, she saw that it was Eurycleia, who, she noticed, had fastened her own veil.

"Your Highness, my Queen," her voice was hoarse but understandable, and there was a strength there that Hyppolita immediately discerned, "may I go with you? I wish to serve you as my husband served yours."

"That," Hyppolita managed, although it was difficult to control her voice, "would be my honor, Lady Eurycleia."

Together, they walked to the exit, but when Eurycleia automatically hesitated a step so that she would be behind her queen as custom dictated, Hyppolita reached out and stopped her by threading her arm through the other woman's as she said, "We are two wives, Eurycleia. Two wives who must do their duty to their husbands."

Then they descended the staircase, and it was as if matters had been arranged in this manner beforehand, because the mute doorman, his face gleaming from the tears that he could only shed in silence, opened the door just as the three Roman officers reached the bottom of the stairs, coming to a stop as the two women glided out onto the large porch. So much, Hyppolita thought, has happened on this portico in the last year.

This time, when Publius Ventidius bowed, it was ungrudging, and she was surprised to see that the two Centurions, neither of them anywhere near the height or breadth of Titus Pullus but who were wearing the white crest that he had worn, bow as well, although theirs were offered somewhat awkwardly, as if it was an afterthought.

"Your Highness," Ventidius began, "I suspect that you know why we are here."

"Yes, Praetor." Hyppolita was determined to sound cool, but she couldn't stop herself from offering a jibe. "My husband's body borne by these two soldiers of yours is self-explanatory."

She was actually slightly disappointed that this didn't seem to unsettle Ventidius; if anything, he seemed even more sympathetic, and she had an insight that he recognized that her words were more of a defense than any intended insult.

"Yes," he continued. "I suppose it would be. However, I," he paused, then lifted his hands to indicate the other two men, "*we* have come bearing your husband's body out of the respect we hold for you. And," he hesitated again, "for your husband."

"Did he die well?" Hyppolita asked, although she was certain she knew the answer.

Rather than answer, Ventidius turned to one of the Centurions, a short, stocky Roman who appeared to be close in age to Ventidius himself, which clearly surprised the man.

"Ah." His voice sounded similar to Pullus', but with an even stronger gravelly quality that she deduced must be an occupational hazard for Centurions. "Ah," he repeated again, although it was because Batius was unaccustomed to speaking Greek; he understood it well enough, but he had to think before he finally answered, "Yes, Your Highness. He died like a king should. He..." he paused then, and she saw the sudden flash of what, despite not knowing the man, she was sure was pain, "...managed to slay several of my men before he fell. Your husband," he finished gravely, "was a brave and great warrior."

"Which is why we bring you his body, Your Highness," Ventidius resumed speaking. "We give him to you so that you may perform whatever funeral rituals your people practice, and he will be interred wherever you deem proper, with all the honors he has earned."

She knew she should feel angry, but Hyppolita was not, and in a strange way, she was moved by this gesture from her enemies. Suddenly, she wished desperately that Titus Pullus was still here, so he could explain to her if this was unusual, and it was really the honor Ventidius was claiming.

"I thank you, Publius Ventidius," she bowed her head as she spoke. Then her head came up and she said, "But I have another request of you."

"Oh?" Ventidius' expression became wary, which she could understand. "If it's in my power, I will do so."

"There is another man who fell," she explained, then turned to indicate Eurycleia, who had been a silent witness, as thankful as Hyppolita for the veil that obscured her face. "His name is Ranjeet Aristandros. He was the commander of my husband's royal bodyguard, and my husband's oldest and best friend. My lady Eurycleia is his wife. I request that you afford him the same honor that you do my husband."

"Of course," Ventidius agreed immediately, clearly relieved that it hadn't been something more. Then he seemed to think of something, which was explained when he said somewhat awkwardly, "Can your lady Eurycleia describe him? There are...many men from Bharuch who have fallen."

Hyppolita was happy that Eurycleia had always disdained learning the Greek tongue, so she was the one who provided the answer by asking, "Do you remember where my husband fell?" Ventidius nodded. "Then he is probably the man to my husband's right. However, if he isn't there..." She went on to offer a description.

"Thank you, Your Highness. We will retrieve him immediately. Now," he hesitated, "where would you like my men to take your husband so that you may prepare his body?"

This was really the last distinctive memory Hyppolita had; from this point forward and for the next few days, it would be nothing more than random snatches of moments that she would remember, with one exception. It was the next morning after her husband died that she was awakened, racked by nausea, and it would be the one constant feature of those days.

Five days after the death of King Abhiraka and the end to any threat of Bharuch not remaining in Roman hands, Caesar's fleet began putting out to sea again. It wasn't done all at once; one segment of the fleet, carrying three Legions, departed first, but rather than sail directly south and following the coast, they set a course out to sea. It had been agreed between the Primi Pili of those Legions, at Caesar's suggestion, that their men would remain unaware of this until it was literally too late to do anything about it, when the green line that represented land disappeared behind them. Consequently, every Centurion and Optio on these ships had their collective hands full to one degree or another as their men realized that they were going to be out in the depths where they all knew without a shred of doubt, even the officers, that huge sea monsters lurked, just waiting for the opportunity to devour entire ships. Fortunately, their westward course only lasted for a full watch, until the *navarchae* were certain that not even their mast tops would be visible from eyes on the shore no matter how high off the ground that observer was, then they turned south. These ships were heading for the main entrance to the river, which was almost forty miles from the anchorage, whereupon they would then essentially reverse their course, moving upstream the eighteen miles back towards Muziris, for a voyage of close to sixty miles. The ships carrying one Legion would stop three miles short, south of Muziris, where the men would disembark, and depending upon the terrain inland, would either haul their artillery with them to a fordable spot, again out of sight of the city, so that they could assault from the eastern side, or at a minimum carry assault ladders. The other two Legions would perform a repeat of the attack on Bharuch, running themselves up onto the docks along the southern wall, and as Spurius had requested, the 3rd Legion wasn't in that force. Instead, they would be one of the Legions who would be landing on the beach to the west, which of course included the 10th, as Caesar had warned Pullus. In the mark of an elite Legion, the reaction by the men was that this was no more than their due; in fact, Pullus and the other Centurions knew that if they had been excluded, the reaction would have been such that they would have had their collective hands full. While three Legions would be used for this phase of the assault, in a last moment decision, Caesar had decided to not keep one Legion in reserve and to instead land it a short distance to the north, but in a manner similar to the Legion crossing overland, to do the same in an attempt to find if there was solid ground that provided an approach to the northern wall. Finally, the cavalry under Prefect Silva was already riding inland, heading for Karoura, with the twin objectives of scouting and, if possible, intercepting any likely reinforcements coming from the capital. Like all of Caesar's plans, it was thorough, and for the men who were tasked with carrying it out, a daunting but not insurmountable task. And, as Pullus and the other Primi Pili had observed, with every major assault like this, not only did their men become more proficient, they became more confident in their ability to handle whatever came up. If that was at least partially due to the efforts of Pullus and his Centurions to circulate among their men reminding them of this reality, all that mattered to Pullus was that it worked.

"When they hit us with that naphtha at Ctesiphon and Seleucia, yes, we got hurt," he would say this, or a variation of it, at least once a night around a section fire, "but we took that fucking city. Then, when they tried the same trick at Susa, we were ready for it, with the vinegar. At Pattala, we were able to use Kamnaskires and his men to scale sheer walls *in the dark*!" This was usually when the men to whom he was speaking would begin expressing themselves more emphatically, going from the nods to exclamations of agreement, each of them drawing on their own memories of that moment. "Then," his voice would drop, not to a whisper, but close to it, "Bharuch. Bharuch and those fucking elephants." This was always the moment where he would begin to include the men, asking, "What happened then?" Using his intimate knowledge of the men of his Legion, and using the trick taught to him by Gaius Crastinus, where he had learned the name of at least one man in every section outside his own Cohort, he would turn and point, asking, "Do you remember, Glabius? Eh? You were there, weren't you? What happened?"

And, not only flattered to be remembered by Titus Pullus, but feeling the responsibility of telling the tale of the comrades of his section, which was the same yet unique in its own way, the ranker would respond. Some of them would rise to the occasion, telling what they had seen with enthusiasm and a gusto that had his comrades engaged, while others would stammer out the barest facts of that night, but what mattered most was that they spoke. It was in these small ways that Titus Pullus reinforced the luster and fame of

Caesar's 10th, the Equestrians, and every man who enlisted into the 10th learned very quickly of one salient fact; that for as long as the Legion had existed, Titus Pullus had been part of it, and most importantly, he was the only surviving man who was part of the episode that had earned the Legion its proudest nickname. He had been nineteen, nothing more than a Gregarius, just like them, the veterans would tell the new *Tirones*, when Caesar had accepted an invitation to meet with Ariovistus, a German chieftain. As part of the conditions, both parties had a bodyguard of ten men, but rather than trust the men of the cavalry, Caesar had personally selected ten men, all of them from his most trusted Legion, and Titus Pullus had been the only Gregarius of the group. He was already known to the men of his Legion, but that moment marked the beginning of the legend that was now walking from one fire to the next, alive, flesh and blood and breathing, a link to the most hallowed traditions of the 10th. Now, they were on their way to add another chapter, and while this was similar to their assault on both Bharuch and Pattala in that they would be borne to battle by ships, what differences there were carried great significance.

During his own briefing to his Pili Priores, Pullus explained, "Caesar is going to wait for low tide before we land, because then it will give us more room to form up. That means," he scanned the faces of his Centurions as he said, "we may stop and remain in place for a watch or more to wait until it happens, but we're trying to time it so that we won't have to do that."

"If we do, that just gives these Pandyans more time to prepare," Metellus of the Third muttered.

"They already know we're coming, Servius," Scribonius spoke up. "A watch isn't going to change much."

Metellus knew that he couldn't really argue this, so he didn't try, but he still was clearly unhappy with the idea of bobbing about motionless in the ocean, which Pullus realized was the real issue.

"Don't worry, Metellus," Pullus teased. "We won't make fun of you for puking your guts out while we're waiting."

"Oh, yes we will," Trebellius, the Quintus Pilus Prior interjected cheerfully. "We will *never* let him forget if he acts like a *tiro* on his first voyage."

Metellus twisted on his stool in Pullus' quarters and grabbed his crotch as he shot back, "And I'll never let you forget that favorite whore of yours in Susa who was carrying *this* instead of a *cunnus*!"

"That only happened one time!" Trebellius protested, although it was hard to hear him over the roaring laughter of the others.

Although Pullus was pleased to see this example of high spirits, he finally shouted for quiet so that he could continue.

"We're going to be landing in our order," he resumed, "with my Cohort on the right, and the Fourth anchoring the left in the first wave. The 3rd will be to our left, and the 25th is going to be on the other side. The faster we get to the city wall, the faster the second and third lines can unload."

Normally, it was the 10th, 3rd, and 12th who composed a three-Legion front when Caesar was in command, but the 12th would be leading the southern effort, something that Balbinus had claimed Spurius arranged. Pullus happened to know that the 3rd's Primus Pilus played no part in Caesar's decision, but he happily played along with Spurius, who, while not admitting it, simply gave Balbinus a grin whenever the topic came up.

"Whose boys are going to be the lucky bastards who get to slog through that muck to see if there's solid ground on the northern wall?" Gellius asked, which required Pullus to consult his wax tablet, then give a grunt of surprise.

When he looked up, he was grinning broadly, which his Centurions understood when he answered, "Why, Gellius, that honor goes to none other than Primus Pilus Clustuminus and the boys of his Legion."

Once again, Pullus' quarters rang with the roars of delight from his Pili Priores, each of them not only knowing of the antipathy between the two men, but having long before adopted that antagonism as their own, something that Pullus did nothing to dispel. Normally, Scribonius wasn't one for stoking the fires of antipathy between his 10th and other Legions, but he had been subjected to Clustuminus' surly resentment of the Equestrians enough that his voice was added to the shouts of happiness at the misfortune of their comrades.

"Hopefully, that bastard will step into quicksand and get swallowed up quicker than Pan," Metellus offered, but this earned Pullus a warning glance from Scribonius, and while he didn't want to, he also knew his friend was correct.

"All right, that's enough." Pullus held up a hand. "We don't wish for comrades to end up dead...even him."

The meeting broke up shortly thereafter, the men rowing back to their respective ships, except for Scribonius, who stayed and dined with Pullus and Balbus. While it had become something of a tradition that young Porcinus be included in the evening meal before an impending action, he had declined the invitation to row over with

Scribonius.

"He's still mooning over Amodini," Scribonius had explained, which reminded Pullus how futile a hope it had been that Gaius would have kept their affair a secret like Pullus made him promise the first night.

The fact that it was Scribonius was the only reason Pullus hadn't been livid, especially when Scribonius calmly pointed out that it had been Pullus who had blurted the secret to Balbus one night after too many cups of *sura*.

Without thinking, Pullus said, "Well, he better get over her because we're never going back to Bharuch again."

Even as the words came out, he realized that he had erred, as Scribonius, Balbus, and Diocles all froze in whatever stage of eating they were in, but it was Scribonius who reacted the quickest.

"How do you know that?" he demanded. "Did Caesar say that?"

"No." Pullus shook his head, but seeing they weren't convinced, he insisted, "He didn't say a word one way or another. But," he turned to Scribonius, "you and I have talked about this before, about why he's *really* here."

"Yes," Scribonius agreed, then pointed out, "but that would mean reaching the Ganges and Palibothra. Which," he had to orient himself before he pointed in a northerly direction, "is back that way. So it would make sense that we're going to return to the city where we've established a supply base."

This was all true, Pullus well knew, but it wasn't until he began to articulate his belief that it took a tangible enough form to explain.

"Yes," he seemingly agreed, "the Ganges is up north. But," on impulse, he got up and went to his small desk, automatically compensating for the rolling of the ship. After a moment of rummaging, he returned with a rolled parchment, which he unfurled and, using cups, lay flat on the table. On it was a map, not the detailed map of Muziris, but the map of India, at least as much as was known about it. Pointing to their approximate location, he began, "We're here, which is eight hundred miles south of Bharuch. So we would have to reverse course, sail back to Bharuch, and *then*," his thick finger traced a line that at first followed the Narmada, which had been scouted for more than fifty miles inland before moving his finger upward, "we're going to be marching northeast, across country that we've never seen." He paused to study his friends, and once he saw them nodding, he continued, "*Or*," he moved his finger back down to their position, "we sail southward to stop at Taprobane. Then, depending on the time of year, we sail back north...but up the eastern coast of India instead of retracing our route. That way," he finished, "we don't have to cross hundreds, or maybe more than a thousand miles through country we don't know, without being able to just get aboard the fleet and sail out of danger. If we get cut off and surrounded on dry land, we're fucked. If we run into trouble using this route, we can at least turn around and sail away." None of the other men said a word, and Pullus watched them as Scribonius looked at Balbus, who offered a barely perceptible shrug, but it was when Scribonius turned to Diocles that Pullus finally lost his patience, snapping, "Well? What do you think?"

"Have you talked to Caesar about this?" Scribonius asked, and Pullus shook his head. "Well, you need to. Because, Titus," Scribonius looked up at Pullus, and it was a moment Pullus would always remember, seeing the expression of respect in his friend's face as he said, "that is a brilliant plan, all things considered."

This flustered Pullus; Scribonius was sparing in his praise of his friend's intellect, so when he did so, Pullus knew he was being sincere, but he managed to mumble a thanks. Once their meal was finished, Scribonius departed, and Pullus followed him out onto the deck, where they stood side by side for a moment, looking at the single lamps that hung from the bow and stern of every ship that made it appear as if hundreds of stars had fallen from the sky to dance, just above the sea that shimmered below each pool of light.

"You know that he's going to finish that jug before you get back," Scribonius commented, and Pullus chuckled.

"Yes, I know," he admitted. "But he always fights better with a sore head and a sour stomach."

Now it was Scribonius' turn to laugh, because this was true, but when he spoke again, it was in a much quieter tone.

"If we never go back to Bharuch, would that be such a bad thing, Titus? I mean, for you?"

Pullus reacted by swiveling his head to pin Scribonius with a glare, but as always, his friend refused to flinch and just looked at him steadily.

Pullus gave a grunt, then turned to resume staring out over the water, and Scribonius thought that his friend would leave that as his answer, until he said softly, "No, it's probably not a bad thing, Sextus. And, I know that." Shaking his head, he added, "But it certainly doesn't *feel* right. It's just that I...worry. About her, I mean."

"Yes," Scribonius answered dryly, although he had returned his attention to the ships around them. "I gathered that's what you meant, Titus." Then, he straightened up and said, "Time for me to get back to my boys." Offering his arm, he said, "Since I won't see you until we're on the beach tomorrow...Mars and Bellona."

"Mars and Bellona," Pullus repeated, grasping his friend's arm. Suddenly, his face split into a grin as he said, "We'll be waiting for you tomorrow. Don't worry, my boys will make it safe for the Second."

"As if the First could wipe their asses if we weren't there to tell you how to do it," Scribonius scoffed as he swung a leg over the side to descend the rope ladder.

Pullus didn't reply, choosing to grin down at his friend as he was rowed far enough away his face couldn't be made out. Turning to return to his quarters, he thought, Sextus is right about one thing; I bet there are nothing but dregs in that fucking jug. And, as he quickly learned, this was the case, and Balbus was already in his hammock, snoring softly.

"I hope you puke your guts out in the morning," Pullus muttered as he followed Balbus' example, lowering himself into the hammock that, like everything involving him, had to be made larger than normal, and very quickly, he was asleep as well.

Unlike Pullus, Nedunj got no sleep that night, but it was only partially because of his nerves. If the Romans hadn't chosen to stop and make their camp twenty miles north, he was certain that the men defending Muziris wouldn't have had any chance of repelling the invaders. Now, it was still a daunting prospect, and he didn't have a great deal of confidence, but the outcome was no longer a foregone conclusion. Thanks to that delay, every available man that had been pulled from Karoura, bringing their own stocks of supplies, and most importantly to Nedunj's plans, sheaves and sheaves of arrows had arrived just the day before. As far as the plan went, he was aware that there were still detractors, particularly Subramanian, who, while not overtly rebelling, had certainly made his feelings known every step of the way, but despite his youth, Nedunj was certain he was doing the right thing. Now, according to the rider who came galloping into the city shortly after dawn, the Romans had begun departing in the night, starting with a portion that the scouts estimated to be not quite half of the entire fleet. The first problem was that, despite having men standing watch throughout the day, both on the walls but also at mile intervals up the coast, there had been no sighting of these ships, and there had been more than enough time for them to reach Muziris. It was shortly before midday when, as Nedunj was listening to his subordinate commanders offering their final reports on the readiness of their men, he sat suddenly upright from where he had been slumped in the throne.

Interrupting the officer talking, he exclaimed, "I know why we haven't seen that part of their fleet that left in the night!" Before any of the others could react, he leapt up and walked over to the table where a highly detailed map of Muziris' defenses lay on it. Pointing down, he ordered, "I want five of the pieces that we created as a reserve to be moved to our new fort across the river."

Predictably, it was Subramanian who objected, and while, as always, he used the correct title, there was no missing the smug condescension that seemed to be the only manner in which he could speak to the crown prince.

"Your Highness, surely you will reconsider! That will take several men to move them from the city, down to the docks, then load them on a ship. One of the ships which, I would point out," at this, he offered an unctuous smile as if to soften the blow, "you ordered would be sent upriver the moment the Roman ships are sighted."

"I know what I ordered, Lord Subramanian," Nedunj replied evenly, cautioning himself against losing his temper. "But I think I know what those ships that left in the night who we should have seen by now are going to do."

"And what is that?" the older man asked, still with the smile.

In answer, Nedunj pointed to a spot that wasn't actually on the map, but would have been to the south of the city as he said, "They've found the real entrance, and they're going to be sailing upriver to attack from the south, as well as trying to land on our western side. And the reason we haven't seen them is that they sailed out far enough so that they could pass the city without us seeing them."

For the barest instant, Nedunj saw not just the surprise on Subramanian's face, but the look of alarm, although he quickly recovered, the smile returning as he said, "That is an interesting possibility, my Prince." He paused, cocking his head as he asked gently, "And have we received any reports of ships sailing upriver from that direction?"

"No," Nedunj replied, but he reminded the older man, "but that doesn't mean that someone isn't riding this way at this moment."

Ignoring this, Subramanian persisted, "So you don't know that this is what's happening, do you?"

"No," Nedunj repeated. "But do you know that it's not?"

Before Subramanian could reply, Nedunj, having exhausted his patience indulging the old lord, turned and repeated his orders.

Only then did he return his attention to Subramanian and, offering him the same kind of false smile he had received, said, "And if I'm wrong, feel free to remind me of that."

"I just hope that we will be in a position to do so," Subramanian replied acidly.

In a deliberate insult, the older man turned and walked away, but while Nedunj was tempted to make an issue of this disrespect, he realized that, in the balance with everything else that was happening, this wasn't worthy of wasting his time. The rest of the day had passed in a blur, as the young prince tried to be everywhere at once, and while this wasn't part of his plan, his presence and relentless optimism did more than he would ever know to bolster the morale of not just his soldiers, but the people of the city who were understandably petrified. He should have been so exhausted that he collapsed into his bed, but despite trying, all he could do was toss and turn as he wondered what he was missing, the only certainty in his mind being that he *was* missing something. Finally, somewhere between midnight and dawn, he fell into a fitful doze, just deep enough that, when the high-pitched wailing horn began sounding, he was sure that he rose several feet off the bed before his feet touched the floor.

Adi was already in the room, holding his armor, and within a matter of heartbeats, he had helped his master prepare himself for the coming trial, but before he left, Nedunj grasped Adi by both shoulders and said sternly, "You need to find a place to hide in the event we can't stop these Romans, Adi. Do you understand? Save yourself."

"I will serve you until my last breath," Adi replied calmly, lifting his chin slightly to look Nedunj in the eye. "That is all I will promise, Master."

Rather than argue, Nedunj gave a curt nod, abruptly spinning about to stalk out of the room so that Adi, who had served him since his sixth birthday, when his father had given him a captive from one of Puddapandyan's raids, couldn't see the tears in his eyes.

Pullus was standing next to the high curved prow of his *quadrireme,* staring straight ahead at the walls of Muziris, which grew bigger and more distinct with every stroke of the oars. Not surprisingly, Balbus was standing next to him, while approximately half of the First and Second Century, all that would fit, were crowded on the deck, waiting for the moment when, at close to full speed, the oarsmen would guide their ship into what was essentially a collision with the sandy beach, the portion that was never covered by the tide looking impossibly white. It had taken longer to maneuver into position than Pullus had expected, because the entire fleet had to essentially row farther out to sea, then turn so that the bows of the ship were perpendicular to the beach, more of which was exposed because of the low tide. They had been fortunate that Caesar, or more accurately, his *Navarchae* had correctly calculated the amount of time it would take to reach the city without stopping to wait for the tide to go out, so there had been no pause in their progress. As Pullus tried to make out more detail, squinting against the glare of the sun off the water, he did wonder if the advantage of landing during low tide was negated by this light in their faces, but he also knew that it was useless to waste time speculating on this. Suddenly, Balbus spun about and leaned over the side of the ship, retching violently, which did cause Pullus to grin at his friend's back, although it was nowhere in evidence when Balbus straightened back up.

"The gods are punishing you for guzzling my share of the *sura*," he commented, keeping his eyes on surf crashing onto the darker sand that was only exposed during low tide. Balbus' lone reply was a moan, mainly because he had to repeat the process of a moment before, but when he returned this time, Pullus said simply, "You better not puke on my *caligae*, or I'll rip your balls off."

Even if Balbus was going to reply, other events took precedence, namely the shouted command by their *Navarch,* followed immediately by a cessation of the thumping drumbeat of the man who kept the rowers in their rhythm, and Pullus could feel the sudden slowing. Although the men crowding the deck reacted, it wasn't because they were surprised; this had been a preplanned pause to allow the ships of the first line to align with each other, which meant this was the last moment of relative peace.

"Remember, my boys go over on the right side, and yours over the other," Pullus reminded his second in command, who had sufficiently recovered to retort, "We'll be waiting for you."

Pullus laughed, clapped his friend on the shoulder, then turned to face his men.

"All right, boys, those of you who can, grab on to the side or something solid, the rest of you kneel on the deck! You know that we're going to be going full speed when we hit! And warn those still down below of what's coming!"

Pausing just long enough to see that his men obeyed, Pullus

glanced to his left, trying to judge whether the other ships of the 10th were properly aligned. There were no ships to his right, reinforcing that the 10th was the anchor of the Roman assault. The one point of contention had been whether some of the warships should beach themselves so that their artillery could be used, but this was one of the tradeoffs with assaulting at low tide, because it placed even the large *ballistae* out of range. Pullus knew that Caesar's flagship was somewhere behind him and to his left, placed roughly in the middle of the rows of ships carrying three assaulting Legions, but he didn't even try to find it. All that mattered was that the signal to begin would come from Caesar's flagship through two methods, with a blast from his *Cornicen* aboard the ship with the Dictator and the launching of a flaming missile aimed towards the beach. As they waited for the final ships to reach their assigned spot, for the hundredth time, Pullus scanned the area beyond the beach, but as he had every other time, he saw nothing but an expanse of grassy ground, with just a relative handful of small, stunted shrubs, which he guessed was all that would grow so near to salt water. He did think there was something different about a strip of that ground, a slight discoloration about two hundred paces from where the sand of the beach gave way to the vegetation, but it wasn't so obvious that it caused him anything other than a slight curiosity. Otherwise, there was nothing to impede their progress to Muziris, aside from whatever archers and artillery were arrayed on the western wall, but at this moment, they were too far away for him to even make out any figures standing on the rampart. Well, he thought, we'll find out soon enough what's waiting for us. Even as this thought crossed his mind, the relative quiet was broken by the sound of a long, single note coming from Caesar's flagship, which was cut off by the bellow of their *Navarch,* followed by the lurching created by the oarsmen shoving their oars into the water and making the first stroke towards the beach.

"Jupiter Optimus Maximus, protect this Legion, soldiers all!"

Pullus didn't recognize the man's voice, but he appreciated the sentiment, and he held on to the prow, watching as the beach drew nearer.

Unknown to Titus Pullus, Nedunj was standing on the western rampart, south of the gate that opened onto the beach, and was only used by a handful of the fishermen who couldn't afford to pay for a berth. It had been a hard choice to make for him, whether to place himself on the western wall or the southern, since he was certain that he was right about the likelihood of an assault from that direction. In something of a compromise, he had placed himself closer to the southwestern corner than in the middle of the western wall. It helped that the wall ran straight and true so that he could see the far end, slightly more than a mile away, but almost all of his attention was on that strip of ground that Pullus had noticed. It had been something of a battle for Nedunj to prevail with his idea, and it hadn't just been Subramanian who had balked.

"You're going to place a large number of defenders outside the wall," even his closest and most trusted adviser Alangudi expressed his reservations, "giving them minimal protection. And," he added, "they're the most lightly armed of our troops, Nedunj."

"They only need to buy enough time for the rest of the plan to work," Nedunj countered. "And I don't think these Romans will expect it."

"But you don't know that," Alangudi persisted, and it took all of Nedunj's self-control not to simply order him to shut his mouth. That, he thought, is something that my father would do. Instead, he acknowledged, "No, Alangudi, I do not. But it's still my decision, and it stands."

Now he stood there on the wall, barely conscious of the unusually strong breeze blowing in off the water, moments away from seeing whether his ploy would have any outcome on the battle. The one thing he hadn't expected was that the Romans would choose to land at low tide, which meant that the men outside the walls, who were essentially blind at this moment, would have to immediately close the range once they left their concealment. Although he wasn't alone on the rampart, there were only enough men spread along the wall that it wouldn't appear deserted to the Romans once they got closer. Their fleet, spread out in front of him, was a daunting sight, and Nedunj heard the muttering from the men around him as they all watched the enemy ships maneuvering into position. Despite the meaning, Nedunj couldn't deny the skill with which these ships, most of them with at least three banks of oars and many of them with four or more, which he had never seen before, were jockeyed so that, at last, they were in a more or less straight line that stretched from just off his left front quarter, all the way to a point where he could barely make them out, but clearly extending beyond the northwestern corner of the wall. They were too far away to hear the horn, but he had correctly deduced that the largest vessel, a behemoth with five banks of oars and more tellingly, flying a red pennant from the very top of the mast, was the one to watch. Suddenly, an object came streaking in his general direction, arcing up and over the masts of the ships arrayed in front of it, leaving a trail of greasy smoke behind it. He watched it descend, then smash into the ground, about a hundred paces beyond the fringe where the beach ended and scrub began, in a boiling explosion of fire that, unusually in Nedunj's experience, didn't seem to extinguish. This was all the attention he paid to it, however, because immediately the smooth surface of the gently rolling waves was obliterated by hundreds of large wooden oars that were thrust down into the water. Within a couple of heartbeats, the movement of the vessels was noticeable, albeit slowly at first, the smaller ships building speed more quickly. Despite the tension of the moment, Nedunj could only admire the precision on display, as the masters of each ship expertly maneuvered their craft so that the ships with three banks of oars didn't pull too far ahead of the larger, slower vessels. Once they did begin moving, the ships picked up speed more rapidly than he thought possible, so that before he realized it, they were already past the imaginary line he had picked to issue the preparatory command.

"Make ready but wait for my command!" he snapped, never taking his eyes off the oncoming fleet, but he did see the man holding the large horn lift it and place the mouthpiece to his lips.

Timing was everything; too soon and the Romans could conceivably change their tactics, but too late, and depending on how rapidly these warriors he had never seen moved, he would be forced to watch a substantial portion of his force be slaughtered, because in this respect, Alangudi was correct; they were unarmored and would be short work for men carrying swords or spears, and even if they managed to flee, Nedunj would never allow them back into the city, certain that once he opened the gate, it would never be shut in time to keep the Romans out. When the prows of the vessels hit the line where the surf began breaking was when Nedunj had originally planned to sound the signal, but for some reason, he suddenly decided to hold a couple of beats longer. Even from this distance, he was certain he could feel the impact when the Roman ships plowed into the sand of the beach, but it was the lurching movement from the men he saw on the decks of the nearest ships that gave him an idea of the power of the collision.

"Ready....ready..." Nedunj waited, then, when a Roman wearing a white crested helmet leapt down and over the side, he shouted, "...NOW!"

His horn player blew the note, instantly joined by the other trumpeters who had been arrayed down the rampart, all of them sounding one long call that unleashed the first surprise.

From Pullus' perspective, it was as if his landing on the hardpacked sand exposed by the low tide somehow triggered what took place about three hundred paces away. Even as he heard his *Aquilifer* Paterculus land next to him, ready to go to the spot Pullus sent him to serve as the reference point for the entire Roman effort with every *Signifer* aligning off of him, Pullus' eyes were drawn to a movement that essentially ran across his front, originating from a point off to his right front quarter that he estimated extended about a hundred paces beyond the southwestern corner of the city wall. If he had been forced to describe it, the best he could have done was that it appeared as if the ground opened up, to disgorge what he *could* see was hundreds of men rising up out of the earth. It was an extremely disorienting moment, and it served to stop the men of the First Century from vaulting over the side to join their Centurion and *Aquilifer*.

"What…where did they come from?"

Paterculus' question actually served to jerk Pullus out of his shock, and he snapped, "It doesn't fucking matter, does it?" Even as he said this, he had spun about to see his men, their feet on the edge of the ship but frozen with the same kind of shock Paterculus was experiencing, and he bellowed, "*Get off that fucking boat and form on your Centurion!*"

This served its purpose, and the first men dropped down onto the sand, while Pullus grabbed his *Aquilifer* and pulled him to where he wanted him to stand, so that he was about twenty paces in front of the prow of the ship, with the prow serving as the left border of the First Century. Only then did Pullus turn and give the scene in front of them more attention, and in that instant, he realized two things; that faintly discolored strip of land had been that way for a reason, because the Pandyans had obviously dug a trench designed to hold men in it, but it was the second thing that informed his decision.

"They're archers!" He shouted this, not aiming it at anyone, but he did glance over to his left to see that Balbus was standing, exactly where he should be, and while the damaged nerves to his face made it difficult to tell, Pullus was certain that his friend was as surprised as he was. Repeating himself, he forced his voice to sound as if this was the most natural thing in the world, using the power of his lungs to shout, "Nothing but a bunch of archers, boys! Nothing that we can't handle, but the quicker you get formed up, the better!"

More out of habit than anything, the men responded, rushing to their accustomed spot in the standard battle formation that Pullus had informed them they would be using before they began the rush towards the beach, and it was the men of the last five sections who were responsible for carrying the heavy assault ladders, which had been left on the upper deck for them to pick up as they swarmed up from below once their comrades had disembarked. No matter how well-trained, no matter how veteran a Legion was, even if they had practiced this, it would create a delay, but in the moment, Pullus realized that this was a maneuver for which Caesar and his Primi Pili hadn't anticipated, the smooth unloading of men on a hostile beach when the enemy wasn't content to let them do so. Nevertheless, Pullus couldn't fault the speed with which the men were moving, where a pair of men would heft the ladder up and over the side, dropping it down to another pair of men who began dragging it towards where the First was forming up. While the Romans were hurrying to get into their familiar formation, Pullus was consigned to watching as the Pandyans, all of them having emerged from their subterranean hideout, came dashing towards them, but stopping at a spot that Pullus was certain had been prearranged. From what Pullus could see, they were all archers, and he couldn't fault their speed, shaking out into what he thought was about a five rank deep formation, but spread out more loosely.

"Hurry, boys, hurry!" he shouted over his shoulder, never taking his eyes from the Pandyans. "We need to get into a *testudo* quicker than Pan!"

On the opposite side of the prow, which from the momentum of oarsmen who had been rowing at triple speed, had gouged a huge trough in the wet sand, only coming to a stop when the front third of the craft was out of the water, Pullus saw that Balbus was similarly occupied. It occurred to Pullus that the *navarch* may have been a bit too eager and driven what was, by any nation's standard, a large ship too far up onto the sand so that reversing oars with those oarsmen whose oars were in the water couldn't dislodge the craft. This was essential to the success of the plan; if the first wave of ships drove themselves too far up onto the beach to back away, this would prevent the ships carrying the second, and the third line of Cohorts from disgorging their passengers. Maybe, he thought with a certain amount of fatalistic humor, we'll have to wait for the tide to come in; he had no idea how right he would turn out to be.

Finally, Pullus heard Lutatius' whistle, sounding the signal that he'd been waiting for, and he didn't hesitate to bellow, "*Form testudo!*"

He had been watching the Pandyans the entire time, and he saw that it would be a race between how quickly his men could obey and how proficient the Pandyan archers were in raising, drawing, and loosing their bows. It was close; his men were still in the process of either sidestepping into position as, in a roughly coordinated movement, the three thousand Pandyan archers arrayed in front of the western wall sent their deadly missiles into the sky. Not until the arrows had reached the apex of their flight, and in that eyeblink of time seem to hover before plunging downward did Pullus realize that he hadn't drawn a shield from stores.

From where Nedunj stood, the opening phase of the battle couldn't have gone better. It was obvious that the Romans were surprised when, on his signal, the archers who had been sent in the night to the long entrenchment that ran the entire length of the western wall and overlapped each corner by a precisely measured hundred paces, suddenly appeared. The trench had been disguised by squares of sod that had been part of the grassy surface then laid across latticework frames that served as the cover, which were pushed up and off the trench at the sound of the horn. Just like Pullus, Nedunj couldn't fault how quickly his archers clambered up and out of the trench. There was the briefest of pauses as the commander of the archers, a veteran who had served his father but who Nedunj trusted, realized that the Romans had waited for low tide, which the crown prince hadn't anticipated, forcing them to move forward a hundred paces in front of the trench at a brisk trot, although he used this time to shake his men out into a formation that enabled each archer an unobstructed view of the enemy. The rearmost men were still trotting into their spot when Nedunj heard the thin wail of the single horn player with the archers, which triggered every man to raise their bows while simultaneously drawing an arrow from the quiver, then nocking it and drawing the string back in what to the observer appeared to be one smooth motion. There was only a brief pause, then on what Nedunj assumed was a verbal command he was too far away to hear, the archers of Pandya loosed what would be the first of what he hoped was a never-ending shower of arrows on the enemy.

So absorbed was Nedunj with what his men were doing that he missed the fact that the Romans were also busy, and as his eyes followed the first volley, they came naturally to a point where he saw that even as the missiles were in the air, the Romans were suddenly contracting their formation. It was Nedunj's first glimpse of the famed Roman *testudo*, but it didn't take one who was experienced with fighting Romans to see that, no matter what its name, it was the perfect response to an assault by missiles. As he watched in dismay, every group of Romans on the beach presented a seemingly impenetrable wall of shields, with the men within the ranks providing overhead cover, and the men on the outer edge using shields that he could see were quite a bit larger than what his men carried to protect themselves and their comrades and were slightly curved as well. His first reaction was to shout in dismay, and he heard his voice before he could stop himself, but in this, the men around him were similarly affected. Too far away to hear anything aside from the hissing of the surf as the waves broke, he did see the arrows plunge down to strike the seemingly impenetrable roof and walls of shields. Even as he was absorbing this sight, the archers had already drawn their second missile, nocked them, then, after a pause that was barely noticeable, sent them on their flight, the visual effect of which meant that to Nedunj, it appeared as if the Roman shields suddenly sprouted a fresh crop of arrows.

"Maybe they can't move when they're like that," he said this aloud, his anxiety lessening somewhat as he thought that, just perhaps, his strategy would work.

It was a feeling destined to last no longer than a couple more heartbeats because, despite the distance, he distinctly heard the sound of a horn that was much lower pitched than those used by the Pandyans, not realizing that it was that low pitch that made the sound carry farther. What mattered was that it was instantly repeated in a rippling manner all the way down the beach, where he had seen that every bunch of Romans, who seemed to be organized in such a way that there were two such units per ship, had contracted into the same formation. Then, although it wasn't with the kind of precision that every Primi Pili demanded from their men, those formations began moving. Slowly, no doubt; for the span of time Nedunj watched, he saw that even after ten heartbeats the Romans hadn't reached the portion of the beach that was never touched by the incoming tide, but they *were* moving.

"Sound the second command!" Nedunj ordered, and in a mimicry of the Romans shortly before, his personal horn player began the call that was picked up, not only by the other players on the wall, but down in the city, where the men who would be the next part of his plan awaited this signal.

The note was still hanging in the air as a flurry of movement down on the street that led out of the western gate occurred, beginning with the men charged with the task of opening the double gates, while, arrayed in neat rows of four men apiece, Nedunj's spearmen waited to emerge out from the city. Nedunj had instinctively turned his attention away from the beach to walk to the opposite side of the rampart, intending to watch as this second force prepared to move to the aid of their archer comrades, but quickly realized that his view was limited to just the area of the gate itself. When he hurried back, he was greeted by a surprise, one that for the first time brought the barely flickering flame of hope that his strategy would succeed back to life, in the form of the bodies of Romans who had been struck down, their prone figures lying behind the slow moving formations. Honestly, it wasn't much in terms of real damage; there were only two figures behind the tightly packed mass of the first Roman formation to his left, and only one behind the formation to their immediate left, but as he scanned the beach, he saw that almost every group within sight had taken losses. Suddenly, the Romans weren't nearly as invincible as they had seemed, and this was what formed Nedunj's next decision.

"Go ahead and sound the third signal," he told his horn player, and again, the man didn't hesitate.

Nedunj had to lean out slightly to get a better view, but he saw by the sudden appearance of the leading ranks of his spearmen that they had received their next order. He was throwing everything into his strategy that, despite stubborn resistance, he had insisted be implemented; he intended to at least stop these Romans coming from the sea on the beach and not let them even touch the western wall. Whether his plans for the attack from the south that he was certain was coming would yield similar results remained to be seen.

Aulus Hirtius stood next to Balbinus, both of them at the prow of the ship they were sharing at the moment, and while they were both looking in the same direction, it wasn't due north, where just the top of the wall and the handful of structures that peeked up above it were visible. Instead, they were looking more northwest, at a point on the narrow strip of land that separated this river from the sea for a distance of eighteen miles, and what they were watching for was the pair of men, the only two mounted scouts with this part of the army, who had been unloaded under the cover of darkness and sent north to a spot where they could see Caesar's part of the fleet. It certainly wasn't ideal, but it was the best solution that any of the Roman officers could come up with to achieve some sort of coordination, but both the Primus Pilus and the Legate standing next to him were acutely aware of all that could go wrong. Although it was certainly true that it would have been difficult for any Pandyans to sneak up on the scouts, given the fact that, even at its widest, the strip of land was no more than four hundred paces in this area, and there was only one stretch where a few stunted trees, permanently bent towards the east blocked their view, until they saw the pair with their own eyes, they refused to take anything for granted. They were at the spot, three miles south where there was enough of a bend in the river that men on the southern wall couldn't just look downriver to spot the Roman fleet, but they had been forced to pack themselves much more tightly than any of the *navarchae* liked, each of them concerned with the damage that would result when the ships collided with each other just from the gentle current of the river. Nevertheless, somehow they had managed, although they were aided by the ships that had deposited the 30th on the riverbank, moving downriver and out of the way. That Legion, selected by Caesar to be the one to march inland before turning north to search for a fordable spot along the river to the east of the city, had spent the night on land before moving at dawn, leaving Balbinus' 12th, Carfulenus' 28th, and Felix's 6th as the assault force that would assault the southern wall. Now all they had to wait for was the signal from those two scouts that Caesar's part of the army had begun their own assault, whereupon they would begin their move upstream, the time it would take for them to reach Muziris sufficient in Caesar's estimation to force the Pandyan defenders to commit to stopping what they believed to be the main assault from the sea.

  One consolation, at least in Balbinus' mind, was that because there was nothing to block it, there was a stiff breeze coming in off of the ocean, but he was still uncomfortably hot, and one glance at Hirtius and his face streaming with perspiration told him that he wasn't alone. Waiting, as any fighting man no matter the rank would agree, was the worst part, because it allowed the mind to roam freely over all the horrible things that could happen in the coming watches. For a Primus Pilus who had not only his own skin to worry about, while one never got accustomed to it, Balbinus, like Pullus and the others, had learned to accept that this was one of the hidden costs for any man who had the ambition to lead a Legion. None of that tension was in evidence, although it did occur to Balbinus that, if they waited much longer, the men who had been consigned to staying below deck might be struck down by the heat, even before an enemy arrow or spear could find them. He was seriously considering switching the men out and sending those men who were up with him and Hirtius down below to allow their comrades to recover, when he felt a hard jab in his ribs.

"I'm sorry to disrupt whatever you were dreaming about, Primus Pilus," Hirtius said with the heavy sarcasm that was a potent sign of the Legate's own distress, "but it appears that we're being hailed."

Balbinus hadn't realized that his gaze had shifted, but when he looked back at the spot, just as Hirtius said, he saw the two men, both mounted, waving their arms. As they had arranged, Balbinus responded by raising his *vitus* in acknowledgement, which signaled the scouts to reply with one of their own. Raising one hand, one of the scouts held it aloft long enough for the pair of officers to know this was a deliberate movement, then swept it down so that his hand was pointing directly north, towards Muziris. That marked the last moment of relative quiet, and very quickly, the word was passed from one ship to the other, the fact that they were so tightly arranged offering an unexpected benefit. Their proximity to each other also meant that pushing off from the riverbank and arranging themselves in a proper formation would take longer than any of the Romans aboard would have liked, but it was something that couldn't be helped. And Hirtius was experienced enough to know that, while Caesar prized rapidity of movement with his army, he also wanted that movement to occur without mishap, so the Legate felt confident he wouldn't be faulted by their general. Theirs was the first to begin moving, it taking two men with poles rushing up to take the spots from Balbinus and Hirtius to help shove the ship out of the mud, but one by one, this part of the Roman fleet floated back out into the river to a spot where, if there was an alert Pandyan still watching south, they would be seen. As long as Caesar's plan worked, however, it wasn't a huge concern, because by this moment, the Pandyans should be fully occupied by the sight of Roman Legions unloading and storming their western wall. What they had no way of knowing was the Pandyan strategy, one that would see the most veteran army under the most famous general of his age stuck on that beach, nowhere near the western wall.

From his vantage point on his *quinquereme*, and aided even further by the makeshift rostrum made of boxes that placed him even higher, Caesar saw Nedunj's plan unfolding, and realized that he had erred in using the low tide. So certain had he been that the defenders of Muziris would perform in the same manner as every defender they had faced, sheltering behind the walls that they hoped would break their attackers, it never occurred to him that his opponent might behave differently. It was another humbling moment for Caesar, although nobody around him could have told as he stood there, watching impassively as what he estimated to be at least three thousand archers seemingly appeared out of the ground.

His only comment was, "They must have been in a trench that they covered over with the sod."

Pollio was unsure whether a response was expected, so he just made a murmuring sound that he hoped would suffice, and it did appear that Caesar didn't even notice. Since he wasn't on the rostrum, Pollio's view was more limited, but he could see enough, especially how, even as some Centuries of the first Cohorts of the three assaulting Legions hadn't finished unloading, their comrades ashore were contracting into a *testudo*. Because there were so many of them, Pollio's attention was yanked from their men and to the sky, catching sight of hundreds of barely visible black streaks plummeting down. It would be the first of so many volleys that Pollio stopped counting at twenty, but it was Caesar who, once he saw the western gates open and the first Pandyan troops emerge, understood what was happening.

"They're going to try and stop us from putting one ladder against their wall," he did say this loudly enough so the others could hear. Then, realizing that he had the better view, he added, "They're sending out what looks like spearmen to support their archers. Although," his tone altered slightly, which Pollio recognized was the one Caesar used when he was musing aloud, "they're going to have to negotiate that trench if they intend to support their archers. That," he concluded, "will take some time. Not much, but perhaps it will be enough for Pullus and his men to close with the archers and destroy them."

Pollio immediately noticed that Caesar's mention was of Pullus alone, and not Spurius and Torquatus, but he was neither surprised nor did he intend to mention it to him later.

He did venture to ask, "How are we going to land the rest of their Legions if these Cohorts can't get off the beach, Caesar?"

"We don't," Caesar replied succinctly, while never taking his eyes off of the scene in front of him. After a heartbeat's silence, he concluded grimly, "It's all up to our men already on the beach. Unless they can get more room, they're going to be on their own."

Although Asinius Pollio hadn't been with Caesar when the then-Legate had taken two Legions across the narrow sea to

Britannia the first time, he had heard how close the Roman landing had come to being repulsed and driven back into the sea, and it had been because the Briton tribes had done the same thing that these Pandyans were doing, meeting the invaders on the beach. The Romans had prevailed that time, but after talking to many of the men who had been part of that effort, Pollio had determined that the consensus was that this had been more a case where Fortuna decided to smile on Caesar and his men than from any other single factor. I wonder, Pollio thought as he watched the struggle unfolding, if Fortuna is even watching us this far from home.

If it had been just a matter of absorbing the swarms of missiles that never seemed to end, while it would have been a hindrance, it wouldn't have been an insurmountable problem from Pullus' perspective. However, unknown to Caesar or anyone consigned to watching from a distance, Pullus and his comrades on the beach quickly learned that, for a reason that wouldn't become known until later, these Pandyans seemed to possess some arcane knowledge that made their missiles much more powerful than any they had ever encountered before. Starting with the first volley, where Pullus managed to avoid being struck by deliberately refusing to think, allowing his body to react so that the one arrow that might have struck him missed because he leaned over at the waist, while it missed him, it didn't miss Valerius, or his shield, more specifically. Pullus heard it strike even before he had straightened back up, but it was his *Aquilifer*'s startled yelp that might have undone the Primus Pilus, but he was too experienced to tear his eyes away from what was about to be the second volley.

"What is it? Are you all right?" he called over his shoulder, even as he was watching the missiles streaking into the sky again.

"Yes, but my shield must have started rotting!" Paterculus called out, and Pullus heard the alarm. "That fucking thing is more than halfway through it!"

Before Pullus could respond, the second volley showered down, but along with the tremendous racket that sounded like dozens of mallets striking blocks of wood at almost the same instant, this time, there were at least two shouts from within his Century's *testudo*, one similar to Paterculus', but the other was more a shriek of pain.

"Lutatius!" Pullus bellowed. "Find out who that is!"

However, even before his Optio could shout a reply, the third volley came plunging down, with almost identical results, except that this time, the sound from one of his men's throats had a gurgling quality that Pullus had heard far too often.

"You bastards keep those shields up and don't allow any space between them!" Pullus roared.

"We are, Primus Pilus! That's Percennius who's down and done, but that fucking arrow penetrated his shield, I swear it! It didn't come in between!"

Pullus instantly recognized and placed the fallen ranker, understanding that in Legion slang, "down and done" meant that he was either dead or out of the fight, but more importantly, he knew where Percennius would be, roughly in the middle of the formation, which was the hardest spot for archers to penetrate because of the angle.

While he knew this was something important, he also was aware that they had to start moving, so he shouted to his *Cornicen*, "Sound the advance!"

His *Cornicen*, standing just behind Pullus but to his left, while Paterculus was on his right, blew the note that alerted the men of the Cohort, paused long enough for it to be repeated by the other *Corniceni*, then sounded the next note. Pullus' Century, along with the other Centuries, obeyed, the front rank stepping off the instant the note ended, but rather than taking the full step they would in open formation, they took the half step that allowed the men behind them to keep their spacing. It had been quite some time, but Pullus would never forget what it was like to be a ranker in the middle of a *testudo*, in a dark, stinking, and cramped space, even more so for a man his size, unable to see anything other than what brief glimpse you could catch if you tilted your head and looked in between the helmets of your comrades ahead of you, and even then, only what might appear through the slight crack created by the men of the first rank who held their shields vertically, and their comrades in the second rank who held their shields up at an angle that wasn't completely horizontal, but was supposed to overlap the edge of the shield of the man in the front rank. Not only did you have to hold your shield above your head, which admittedly wasn't nearly the tiring chore for Gregarius Pullus as it had been for his comrades, you also had to remember to keep in step with the men around you, because if you didn't, it created enough of a bobble that a gap was inevitably created, one that a sharp-eyed, opportunistic archer or slinger could take advantage of. All in all, it was a miserable experience, and despite the fact that he was far more exposed in his current position, Pullus wouldn't have switched places for any amount of money. None of which mattered in the moment, just that he kept his eyes on the showering missiles and warned his men as they shuffled forward at an agonizingly slow pace. Unfortunately, after the first couple of volleys, either their commander had changed tactics or the natural difference in the speed of individual archers began to show, because by the time the Romans had managed to move another ten paces away from their starting point, the rain of arrows was nonstop. Twice more, Pullus heard men cry out above what was now a continuous racket of iron tips striking wood, or occasionally striking a metal boss. In fact, it was the latter that gave Pullus a better idea that, rather than Paterculus' shield having rotted, these Pandyans had some sort of unforeseen advantage, when there was a metallic clang that was instantly drowned out by a scream of agony that was so shrill that, before he could stop himself, Pullus turned towards the sound. It was something that he would never do normally, but this was one time that it saved his life, because as he did, he felt a puff of air and the hissing sound of an arrow that would have punched right through his face if he hadn't.

Now that he had turned his attention towards his Century, he first tried to determine which of the dozens of arrows now studding his men's shields might have caused the reaction, but when he couldn't, he shouted, "What happened?"

"It's Capito, Primus Pilus!" Pullus recognized the voice as belonging to the man himself, although it was shrill with pain, which he understood when Capito moaned, "My fucking hand is pinned to my shield, Primus Pilus! This fucking arrow punched through the boss and now I can't move it!"

This was so unusual that it caused Pullus to falter a step, but from within the *testudo*, he heard the voice of Dolabella, who he knew marched next to Capito, who assured him, "It's true, Primus Pilus! I'm looking at it now, and he's pinned!"

Pullus had never heard of anything like that happening; when an iron-tipped arrow struck an iron boss, the result had always been the arrow caroming off. Denting the boss, certainly; it had happened to him back when he was in the ranks, but he had never heard of a metal harder than iron, just that some iron was stronger than others. He was actually carrying proof of that, although it was still in the sheath, but not only had his *gladius* been created by a Gallic master smith, the iron to make it had come from Noricum, which was the source of the best iron in the known world. At least, until this moment.

Regardless of the importance of this discovery, in the moment, it was of limited value, and Pullus was forced to simply shout, "All right, Capito! I know it hurts like Dis, but you have to keep your shield up! Your comrades are depending on you!"

"Yes, Primus Pilus," Capito's voice still communicated the intense pain he was feeling, but Pullus heard the note of determination there as well. "You can count on me!"

This conversation had taken place even as the First was moving, but they were only now reaching the edge where the sand that was never covered with water met the darker hard-packed sand, and while Pullus had expected as much, now that he was close enough to see how loosely packed the whiter sand was, he cursed bitterly, knowing that this was yet another challenge. Such was his concentration on this, when he felt a tap on his hip, once more he almost forgot and turned around, but he managed to avoid doing so.

"Drop your *vitus* and stick your hand out," he heard Paterculus' voice close to his ear. "I've got a shield." Pullus did so, although there was a bit of fumbling as he felt for the handle, which Paterculus had turned in his direction. As he grasped it, Paterculus warned, "This was Percennius' so it's already got a couple holes in it, and…there's blood on it."

Pullus nodded but said nothing, now that he had firmly grasped the shield, bringing it up in front of him in one motion, which was when he saw that, if anything, Paterculus had understated the condition of the dead man's shield. Still, he knew that he couldn't be choosy, and even as he brought it up, he sensed as much as saw a black streak, moving the shield in front of his body to catch an arrow that hit with about the impact he would expect from this range, but to his shock, the point penetrated the wood to the point where about six inches of shaft protruded inside the shield, midway between his hand and the top.

"Pluto's *cock*!"

He recognized his own voice, but there was simply too much happening for him to examine the arrow's tip, despite it being just in front of his face, although in the moment, a part of his mind did notice that it seemed to be a slightly different color than the arrowheads he had seen before. Even as this was happening, the *testudo* was still moving forward, driven not by Pullus, but Lutatius, who had the advantage of being somewhat sheltered behind the formation, and the first two ranks of the Century were now in the soft sand, which almost immediately caused one of the men in that second rank to stumble. It wasn't much, but while he didn't pay the price, his comrade in the third rank directly behind him did, taking an arrow through the right eye, the point bursting out the back of the man's head, dropping him before he took another step.

"*Close up! Close up! Hurry, you bastards!*" Pullus roared, but his men were veterans, and they needed no encouragement, the Legionary in the fourth rank actually hopping with both feet over the corpse of his comrade to close the hole, while the men behind him moved as quickly.

It was this momentary distraction that meant Pullus wasn't the first to spot the rushing movement originating from behind the archers who, to this point, were standing their ground, aided by the slow pace required for a *testudo*.

"There are more men coming out of that gate!"

Because Pullus recognized Balbus' voice, he looked across his Century to his friend, noticing that he had a shield as well, which Balbus dropped slightly to point with his right hand towards the western wall. Despite the looser spacing of the enemy archers, it still was difficult for Pullus to see with any clarity, until his eye caught a glittering of points seemingly hovering above the heads of the Pandyans, in a regular enough pattern that gave him the answer.

"Spearmen! There's a column of spearmen heading towards us!" Pullus bellowed, both to let his own men know and in the event Balbus had been unable to tell.

And, that quickly, matters became infinitely more complicated for the Romans.

Caesar's comment about how the spearmen that he had been the first Roman to spot would be delayed by crossing the trench turned out to be incorrect. Instead of shaking out into a long line first, Caesar and the rest of his staff could only watch helplessly as leading ranks came moving at close to a run, seemingly intent on trying to leap the ditch. Instead, they barely slowed as they hopped down, but dropping only about a foot lower and crossed the ditch, Caesar only then realizing that whoever had engineered the trench hadn't dug a continuous line, but had left sections where they had dug out about a foot of soil, just enough that anyone from a distance couldn't see the difference, and the spearmen were using these sections as a bridge to get across the ditch.

"Those cunning bastards," Pollio murmured, but while Caesar didn't respond, he certainly agreed, mentally saluting his foe.

However, it was about to get worse, because after the first fifty ranks, the men exiting behind them, instead of following their comrades straight, took a right turn then ran parallel down the trench before, turning back to the beach to cross using another section of lowered dirt. Twenty ranks after them, the next Pandyans turned left, ran about the same distance as the second group, followed by a fourth who turned right, then a fifth who turned left, this pattern repeating itself several times. Although there was no way to really tell, Caesar was certain that this enabled the Pandyans to array themselves more quickly than if they had just crossed at one spot. Finally, the last of the spearmen emerged from the city, confirmed when the twin gates slammed shut.

"Did you get the count?" Caesar asked Pollio, having tasked the Legate with this task once it became clear that there was an order to what the Pandyans were doing.

"I counted seven thousand spearmen, Caesar," Pollio called out.

It took an effort for Caesar not to curse in a manner that would be more appropriate to a man of the ranks like Pullus. In sheer numbers, this wasn't all that much when compared to three Legions, but the Pandyans weren't facing three Legions, they were facing twelve Cohorts, most of whom were already understrength using Caesar's standard of one hundred instead of the eighty other Roman Legates had used in the past, Cohorts that even as they watched were being whittled down by the three thousand archers. What was even more distressing was the fact that, from appearances, his men were taking heavier casualties than would normally be expected from archers, but he could only watch as the number of men who were either able to move to the rear under their own power then cover themselves with their shields, or were dragged there through the *testudo* by their comrades, increased.

The situation was serious, but it wasn't dire yet. It was actually Teispes who noticed something from his spot slightly behind the rostrum, although he didn't say anything immediately, just staring at a particular spot for a long enough span of time to be sure. Finally, he was confident enough to call his general's name, and when Caesar turned, with an irritated expression, the Parthian knew he had to speak quickly.

Pointing, he said, "The tide is coming back in, Caesar."

Caesar had to lean over slightly to look past the high prow of his ship where Teispes was pointing, but the instant he did, he knew that the Parthian was correct. The *quadrireme* just off the left bow of his flagship, like Pullus' ship, had slammed into the beach with enough force that a full third of it was out of the water; now it was less than a quarter of the length. We're only thirty paces from the water and barely moving forward, he thought grimly; before he could even begin to think of what to do, there was a high, wailing sound which was quickly drowned out by the roar of male voices, and Caesar looked away from the tide line to see that the Pandyan infantry was now advancing towards his Cohorts, every Century of them still in *testudo*.

Sextus Scribonius and his First Century were a hundred paces from Pullus' First Century, and like his friend, he was struggling with the same challenges as his Primus Pilus; namely, he already had eight men down and out of the fight, and his Optio, Lucius Carbo, had informed him that three of the men were dead, and one was likely to expire. The only positive, at least in a personal sense, was that he was like every other Centurion participating in the assault and now equipped with a shield. Like Pullus, Spurius, Torquatus, and every other Roman wearing a transverse crest, he was waiting for the barrage of missiles to abate, certain that, at most, these archers had no more than fifty arrows apiece. It was just a quirk of fate that he happened to be glancing under the lower rim of his shield to see several bare-chested men moving in between the rearmost ranks of the archers and the trench, although it took him a moment to comprehend that while the men who were dashing back towards the city were emptyhanded, they quickly returned carrying wicker baskets, usually two at a time. The baskets, he saw, were stuffed with arrows, the feathered shafts sticking up.

Scribonius was not one given to cursing; he insisted that it was a waste of time, but Balbus was emphatic that it was because of his friend's background, coming from a wealthy equestrian family, which made him squeamish about using vulgarity, but this time, he couldn't stop himself from groaning, "Cerberus' hairy fucking balls!"

This was so unusual that his *Signifer* temporarily forgot the importance of keeping his shield up, but the gods were with him and he didn't pay the price.

"What is it, Pilus Prior?"

"They're bringing these *cunni* more arrows. They're lowering baskets of them down from the walls." Scribonius was careful to pitch his voice so that he could only be heard by his *Signifer*, who responded with a curse of his own, although he wisely matched his Centurion's tone.

Less than a heartbeat later, Scribonius' shield was almost jerked out of his hand as two missiles struck almost simultaneously, and while one hit above the boss and the other below, they were both on the left side, twisting the shield away from Scribonius' body. He recovered quickly, but in that moment, he got a better view of the area to his front.

"Spearmen! Spearmen coming, boys!" While he didn't have the capacity of his friend, Scribonius could still generate a respectable volume, and he used it now. "Front two ranks, javelins out and wait for my command!"

"Are we opening up?"

Scribonius recognized Carbo's voice, although it sounded as if he was now directly behind him instead of the opposite side, which told Scribonius his Optio had been helping a wounded man.

"We can't! Not yet!" he shouted back. "You hear me, boys? If we open up, they're going to skewer us like chickens on the spit! Hold tight and wait for my orders!"

As it turned out, the next order came from Pullus, in the form of his *Cornicen* sounding the command to halt their forward motion, as pitiful as it had been, and Scribonius understood that Pullus had seen the spearmen forming up behind the archers as well, but he disagreed with the command to halt. If anything, he thought it would be prudent to withdraw towards the surf line so that the Romans would be standing on the hardpacked sand while the spearmen who clearly intended to assault them would have to cope with the loose, shifting sand. And, for a brief moment, he considered giving that order himself, at least for his Century and for the Second to his left, where his Pilus Posterior Gnaeus Pacula had already been wounded in the thigh, but despite stopping the bleeding with his neckerchief, Scribonius saw how the blood had run all the way down Pacula's leg before he managed to do so. This was the moment when, for the first time since he could recall, Scribonius actually risked turning his head enough while stepping away from the shelter of his Century to look behind the formation to get a better idea of their casualties. But, while it was a grim sight; Scribonius counted ten men, at least three of whom were clearly dead, it was the fact that where there had been sand earlier, it was now covered with water that shook him. Not much, but it was enough to inform him that the tide was coming in already, although it didn't seem possible that they had been on this beach that long, but he also knew that didn't matter. Seeing this made Scribonius' decision, and he refrained from giving the order, returning his attention to the front in time to see the spearmen reach the rearmost ranks of the archers.

"They're going to be coming for us, boys! Are we going to be ready?"

The roar was muffled by the shields, but it was not only audible to Scribonius, he saw the archers nearest to them react in a manner that told him they had heard it as well, and while they were too far away, he offered them a grim smile.

"You think you can push us back into the sea? Then come and try!"

He hadn't meant to say this aloud, but it earned him another cheer, a more guttural promise that was even louder than the first, which made him feel better.

Nedunj could only watch helplessly as his plan unfolded, although to this point, it had gone better than he dared hope, but he also saw that time was running out for his archers and their ability to keep their enemy essentially pinned in their tight formation that, even from a distance, reminded the prince of huge porcupines, at least if the animals' quills were arrows. Now that his spearman had negotiated the trench, it took a few moments for them to rearrange themselves in the five ranks containing fifteen hundred men that enabled them to overlap the strip of beach that was now occupied by the Romans, and Nedunj acutely felt every passing heartbeat. Fortunately, it wasn't nearly as long as he thought before the Pandyan horn sounded across the distance that signaled the beginning of the infantry's advance. The archers were once again running low on arrows, but despite having another hundred wicker baskets of arrows that he had allocated for their use, Nedunj hadn't wanted to use them for the effort on the western side unless absolutely necessary, still uncertain about what to expect on the southern wall, the sentries on which, to this point, hadn't raised the alarm. Now, as Nedunj watched as the leading rank of spearmen came within shouting distance of their archer comrades, he was having second thoughts about his decision, but when he turned to Alangudi, intending to send him running down the wall to the gate and give the order for the men on the wall to lower more baskets, he stopped himself. This was partially caused by what he saw taking place out on the beach, as his spearmen moved more rapidly through the looser ranks of archers than he had expected. There was an inevitable lull in the shower of arrows as the exchange took place, and Nedunj naturally shifted his gaze to the line of ships and the Romans who were still in their tightly packed formation. What he saw made his heart race, a sudden rush of excitement at the sight animating him to the point that without warning, he gave Alangudi a playful shove.

"See, Alangudi? Do you see? They're retreating! They're almost back to the water's edge!"

However, while Nedunj had been understandably occupied with the entirety of the action taking place, Alangudi had kept his eyes on the Romans, and he replied, "No, my Prince. They haven't moved backward at all, but they did stop." Pointing, he continued, "I've been watching, and the tide is coming in. See? Some of their wounded are partially in the water already."

Nedunj instantly saw this was the case, and he also understood that Alangudi was correct; what it meant for their cause was something else entirely.

"If we can push…"

Nedunj never finished his thought, as there was an unexpected sound, another wailing cry from the horn player next to the commander of the spearmen, but it was what it meant that caught Nedunj completely by surprise. Whether the note ended or it was drowned out by the sudden roaring of thousands of men, Pandyan men, Nedunj would never know; it was the result that mattered, because rather than the ordered approach march to close within about fifty paces of their enemy, which was the usual manner of the Pandyan spearmen, all seven thousand five hundred men broke into a run, rushing at their Roman foes.

"What does he think he's doing?" Nedunj heard the tinge of hysteria in his voice, but he couldn't help it. "He wasn't supposed to…"

"He did it to catch them before they could move out of that formation they're using," Alangudi countered, his voice contrastingly calm, comparatively speaking at least.

And, just as he finished, the swiftest of Pandya's spearmen reached the soft, shifting sand of the beach, leading with their spears, which they used to slam into the shields of the Romans in the front rank. This was the moment when, from behind him on the southern wall, he heard several men shouting, although they were quickly drowned out by the sound of the same kind of horn.

"Roman ships! Roman ships are coming up the river!"

Nedunj froze for the span of a couple of heartbeats, unable to tear his eyes away at the sight of his lightly clad spearmen swarming around the tightly packed Romans on three sides, despite knowing that what was approaching was at least as potent a threat as the one already facing his people and his city. It was Alangudi who lightly but definitely pushed him, literally, from his trancelike state, in the direction of the southern wall. "You need to see for yourself, Your Highness. And there's nothing you can do here at the moment. I'll stay and watch the fight." This was enough for Nedunj, and he began running down the rampart, heading for the southern wall where, if all went as he hoped, these Romans would be receiving another surprise.

Chapter 10

Balbinus was in the same spot, standing at the prow, studying the southern wall of Muziris as it drew closer, but instead of Hirtius, it was his Primus Pilus Posterior beside him, Hirtius having briefly gone ashore to be picked up by one of the ships that wouldn't be participating in the first part of the assault.

"It's high, but not too high for our ladders," Balbinus commented, but then added to that bit of good news with some that wasn't, pointing with his *vitus*, "but we're about to be well within range of any *ballistae* or catapults, whatever they have."

"So we better move quickly," his second in command, Vibius Censorinus, said cheerfully, something he did because he knew it irritated his Primus Pilus.

Balbinus' only response was a scowl and obscene gesture, then his attention returned to the wall and the docks lining the riverbank. They had reached a point where he could now see where the river made a bend of almost ninety degrees to their right, while the left bank flared out to form what was almost a small bay so that the wharves and docks extended beyond the southwestern corner of the city wall. From Balbinus' perspective, it seemed to him that this enlarged area was manmade, but if so, it had been done long before, time and the elements erasing any signs of human intervention. As they advanced, they would have had a view of the western beach and his comrades in the 10th fighting their way towards the wall, except there was a line of what he assumed were small warehouses and sheds blocking his line of sight. That, he thought, would be a likely place to hide some men to fall on our flank when we land, and he reminded himself to send at least two sections to search them immediately after they landed. The fact that his attention was literally in the opposite direction from the right bank of the river and the small promontory at the "elbow" of the river meant that his first warning came with the shout of alarm from Censorinus. He reacted quickly, spinning about, but he didn't even see the hurtling missile that struck the other Centurion in the face, instantly decapitating him and, in one of the gruesome ironies of battle, saved Balbinus' life by serving to alter the rock's path just enough that it slashed past the Primus Pilus' head while spattering him in his comrade's gore. As disconcerting as this was, Balbinus both felt and heard the impact of other missiles, the ship shuddering under his feet as the screams of his tightly packed men on the upper deck filled the air, all while he was frantically pawing at his eyes, trying not to think about what that warm, sticky substance covering his face was. Above the cries of pain and alarm, he heard their ship's *navarch* bellowing orders, and he had enough presence of mind to brace himself when the large ship, with a speed and agility that always surprised him, suddenly heeled over, heading towards the right bank. It was the kind of maneuver that ran against the instincts, as the normal reaction of all animals was to flee from the source that was inflicting pain and damage, but Balbinus instantly understood what the *navarch* was doing, trying to get under the arcing rocks. With his vision sufficiently cleared, Balbinus got his first opportunity to survey the damage, and he felt the bile rushing up into his throat from the sight of at least two of his men who had been dismembered, the deck covered with their blood and viscera.

"*Face the bank! Shields up! Hurry, you bastards!*"

Events were happening so quickly that Balbinus had yet to try and locate where what he had at least identified as rocks hurled by some sort of artillery were originating, but even if he looked in the right direction and just happened to be looking at the exact spot, he would have missed it. As it was, his eye caught the blurred streak of a rock immediately after it had been launched a bare instant before his mind grasped what it was, and he could only watch helplessly as what he at least identified as a round stone slammed into the gunnel of his ship, smashing the wood into splinters before, barely slowing down, striking the shield of one of his rankers, snapping it into two pieces as it crushed the man's chest. The only blessing was that between the gunnel, shield, then his man's body, he was the only casualty, as his comrades were able to dive out of the path of the rock as it went bounding across the deck to the opposite side, striking that gunnel but not breaking through, yet with enough of an impact that Balbinus felt it up through his legs. Balbinus' *quadrireme* was still turning so that its bow was pointed at the right bank, but not before it was struck four more times, and it was the first two that crippled the vessel and the last that sealed its fate. The first rock didn't impact on the deck; in fact, Balbinus thought it had missed because of the tremendous column of water that fountained up about midway between the bow and stern, but then he felt another shuddering sensation through his legs, while the second struck slightly ahead of the first, just above the waterline. The first rock holed the hull, and within a matter of a couple heartbeats, Balbinus heard the shouts that water was now entering the stricken ship, but this was almost immediately drowned out by the carnage created by the second impact, which hit above the waterline but tore through the stout planks to eviscerate two oarsmen, while fragments of the shattered planks struck the pair whose station was immediately below the first. Finally, in an automatic and understandable reaction, their comrades on the two sets of benches below them momentarily forgot their duties, rising up from their spots to try and aid their dying shipmates, all of which coincided with the oarsmen on the opposite side, along with the uninjured oarsmen on their side pulling in the rhythm set by the beater. Because the force was unequal, with several oarsmen on the right side out of action, the ship lurched in that direction so violently that it sent the men still on their feet abovedeck careening into each other, an instant before the third and final rock arced down to sweep away both the *navarch* and the long handle attached to the tiller. With no one at the tiller, the wooden rudder suddenly swung, turning the stricken ship so that the holed side was upriver, and the *quadrireme* almost immediately came to a stop, still more than a hundred paces short of the riverbank; even worse, Balbinus felt the deck tilting under his feet with every heartbeat.

"Shed your armor! Shed your armor!" Balbinus began bellowing, even as he was staggering rearward, trying to ignore the smeared remnants of what had been men of his Century. "We're going down and you'll fucking drown quicker than Pan if you don't!"

The fact that he was shedding his own as he was shouting this, which his Optio Fibulenus was now repeating, gave his men the example they needed, and they hurried to comply, with men helping each other pull off their chainmail.

With Censorinus dead, Balbinus tried to pick out Censorinus' Optio out of the frenzied movement on the upper deck, but realized that he would have been below, so he turned and shouted for Fibulenus, "Go get the Second and bring them up on deck! Tell them the same thing!"

"There won't be any room, Primus Pilus!" Balbinus could barely make out his Optio over the tumult, but he did somehow.

"There will be!" he shouted back; then, he turned to see his *Aquilifer* Lucius Barbatus just as he shed his armor, while another ranker held the precious eagle standard before handing it back to Barbatus. "All right, Barbatus!" He turned and pointed to the water that, even in the span of perhaps ten heartbeats, was much closer to their feet. "Lead the way, and we'll follow!"

To his credit, the *Aquilifer* didn't hesitate, despite the fact that, while their general had decreed that every one of his Legionaries learn how to swim, he had never gotten around to it. Striding down the sloping deck, clutching the standard, Barbatus leapt into the water, and while he briefly disappeared under the brown water, he kept the eagle standard aloft, an image that would remain in the minds of all of his comrades who saw it, not just on the stricken ship but those on the other vessels who were consigned to do nothing but watch in horror.

"Follow the eagle, boys! Follow the eagle and follow me!"

Just before he threw himself into the water, Balbinus suddenly stopped, spun about, and scrambled up the sloping deck to retrieve his *baltea* and harness, shouting at his men to do the same as he did so. Only then did he follow Barbatus, while the survivors of the First and Century did the same, abandoning the ship, even as the enemy bombardment continued, but shifting to target other ships.

Hirtius was too far away to see the relatively small rocks, but he saw the effects on the *quadrireme* carrying Balbinus and two of his Centuries clearly enough. For seemingly no reason, the bow of the ship suddenly turned towards the riverbank near the spot where the river made the sharp bend, the water around the bow roiling at the abrupt change.

"What are they doing?" He said this aloud, although it wasn't aimed at anyone in particular. Before anyone could answer, the ship suddenly slowed dramatically, but it was its lurch even more to its right that gave Hirtius the first indication of the cause, and he gasped, "There must be artillery on that riverbank!"

Everything after that happened with a speed that was so astonishing that Hirtius almost convinced himself that he was in a dream, but the shouts and curses from the relatively small group of men standing behind him on the deck was proof that he was very much awake. Balbinus' *quadrireme* had come to a stop and was already listing noticeably, and while he couldn't make out details, Hirtius did see the kind of movement on the deck that betrayed the urgency of the moment. However, his attention was quickly drawn to another ship, also a *quadrireme*, that had been following Balbinus' but on the inside nearer to the right bank, watching helplessly as its *navarch* had to try and avoid the suddenly stopped vessel that was now turned perpendicular to the rest of the fleet's line of travel.

"I don't think there's enough room," Hirtius heard one of the Tribunes attached to him say.

"There may not be," he agreed grimly, "but this is his only

chance."

There was no more talking for the moment, as they all watched the large ship both veer to its right but also slow as the *navarch* ordered the oarsmen to reverse oars. It was a common enough command, although it was usually used when a ship was already moving slowly as it maneuvered its way to the dock. Unfortunately, at this moment, the ships of the Roman fleet carrying the men to attack the southern wall had been in the process of picking up their speed in anticipation with their collision with the southern docks, not slowing down. And, while the maneuver did slow the craft down, it wasn't enough. Before the *navarch* could use the tiller to swing his craft parallel to the riverbank, allowing it to slip past the crippled *quadrireme*, the momentum of the ship carried it into the shallow water, where the prow struck the riverbottom. From a distance, it looked to Hirtius as if the ship was stopped by magic; yes, it had been slowing, although it was still moving, and then it wasn't; he could only imagine what that jolt was like, certain that every man standing on deck would have been knocked off their feet. Now, there were two ships out of action, but it quickly became three. As Balbinus and the men with him had noticed, once Balbinus' ship was out of action, the hidden artillery had immediately switched their attention to the ship on the opposite side. Because of what was happening with the second vessel, Hirtius and the others were tardy in turning their attention to this ship. It was impossible to see what damage it had suffered, but what was clear to see was that this *navarch* had given the order to reverse course, although not by turning around. Aided by the current, it managed to come to a stop, then began moving back in Hirtius' direction quickly enough. What became clear later was that, in his panic, the *navarch* effectively exposed his ship to even more damage because of his decision, the Pandyan artillery concentrating every piece on it so that, before it had traveled a hundred paces back downstream, it was beginning to settle, and once it was low enough for the water to come pouring into the holes for the lowest bench of oarsmen, probably less than fifty heartbeats elapsed before it was effectively sunk. The Legionaries aboard had already begun abandoning ship, the water around the craft roiling from the thrashing of two Centuries of men now fighting for their lives.

"Sound the recall!" Hirtius finally found the words. "All ships. Reverse course!"

The *cornu* notes from his *Cornicen* began sounding even before he had finished, the most potent sign that he had waited too long, and the call was instantly picked up by the ships that had already passed by his ship near the seaward riverbank.

Suddenly, Hirtius spun about, scanning the faces of his staff, then he pointed to a Tribune of average height but a lean build.

"As I recall, you're quite a runner, Rufus."

Salvidienus Rufus looked apprehensive, but he answered cautiously, "I have won most of the races I've won, sir."

"Good," Hirtius nodded. Then he turned to the other Tribune assigned to him. "What about you, Bodroges? Can you run?"

"Run?" The Parthian looked wary. "I'm a better rider. But," he admitted, "yes, I can run."

"Because both of you are going ashore." Hirtius wasted no time. "You're going after Flaminius and the 30th, and you're to tell him that his orders have changed." He turned and pointed to the promontory as he continued, "He's to head as directly and as quickly as he can to where the river bends. Although we can't see them, there's clearly some Pandyan artillery hidden over there. And," he felt the bitterness rising, "you can see what they've done already. Unless we remove that threat, I'm afraid that the river will be blocked by sunken ships before we can even get to those docks."

In a manner eerily similar to Aulus Hirtius, Nedunj was standing on the southern wall, almost exactly the same distance from the action as his Roman foe, but he was sufficiently high enough to see the source of all the enemy's problems, and they were there because he had placed them. The promontory located at the bend of the river wasn't natural, it was manmade, but it had been created long before the Pandyans ruled this land. The best guess was that it had been a dirt wall that, over time, had overgrown to the point that, to the naked eye, it appeared natural. At its highest, it was barely ten feet above the riverbank, but it was the hollow created by this long-forgotten wall that gave Nedunj the idea, and he had assiduously checked that the height wasn't sufficient for anyone to see over the hump from the water. He hadn't stopped there, ordering that the hollow was actually deepened a bit more, then in a manner almost identical to the latticework covers for the western trench, frames were made and branches from the nearby trees and large fronded plants that grew so abundantly were woven in, so that even an enemy approaching from the south on land would have a difficult time seeing the five catapults aligned side by side. They were of what the Romans would call an ancient style, being copied from those used by the soldiers of Alexander, the design slowly migrating south over the years, but while the Roman weapons had a superior range, the version used by the Pandyan was sufficient to cover the river except for a span of perhaps a hundred fifty paces from the opposite bank. There had been discussion of placing artillery on that side, but it would have been impossible to conceal, so Nedunj had settled on leaving just that relatively narrow gap. It helped that barely a furlong beyond the promontory any ship was then within range of the artillery arrayed on the southern wall, so that the Romans would have to undergo a pounding as they rowed against the current, then once they were out of the range of the artillery on the promontory, they would then be subjected to the dozen pieces that Nedunj had gathered on just the southern wall. The only thing missing was the ability to hurl fire, which, after hearing Abhiraka describe the fiery destruction of his prized elephants and so many of his men, Nedunj had hoped to duplicate, if not with the natural substance of naphtha, then with what was called the Greek fire. But, like others who had tried, he had been singularly unsuccessful in trying to pry the secret from the Greek traders who made Muziris home. He had even dispatched Alangudi to Taprobane, filching a substantial amount of gold from his father-in-law's treasury that was now in the basement of the summer palace. Once it was clear he would be unsuccessful, he had resigned himself to using standard ammunition, but had required the men manning the pieces to establish the precise ranges to various points along the river. Using rafts, the crews had been drilled over and over, from dawn to dark, and a system had been developed using a series of rods painted different colors that were driven into the dirt of the promontory, but on the inner side so that they weren't visible from the river. It had taken quite a bit of practice, and there were already many smoothly rounded stones lying in the muddy bottom of the Pseudostoma, but Nedunj had essentially plundered the stores of not just arrows but artillery ammunition from Karoura, and he had commanded that the inhabitants of Muziris who were stonemasons turn their attention only to creating more, working with raw material that had been carted in from the mountains to the northeast. Now, he was watching the culmination of that work as, despite loosing blindly, his crews mercilessly pummeled two Roman ships, but never in his wildest dreams had he expected the level of success he was seeing. Although the river was not completely blocked, and in one way, his artillery had ensured that there would be no further danger to the Roman ships from the redoubt by forcing them to row as close to the opposite riverbank as they could without running aground, the respite from the pounding Nedunj intended to inflict before the first Roman ladder touched the walls of his city would be so brief that it hardly mattered. Despite this initial success, Nedunj also was aware that the danger was just beginning for his artillery and their crews on the opposite side of the river, watching as the Romans from the first ship began struggling out of the water. Even sodden, the cotton tunics were sufficiently lighter in color to alert Nedunj that these survivors weren't wearing their armor, which would make them even more vulnerable to what he had planned, and he turned to his personal horn player.

"Sound the signal."

While the horn used by the Romans was large and curved into close to a full circle, the Pandyans used a long, thin horn with a flared end that measured three feet long, and when the player lifted it to his lips, he pointed the flared end directly towards the promontory. It was a single note, played for perhaps ten heartbeats, but the response was, as Nedunj hoped, instantaneous, and the five hundred spearmen, supported by five men from Nedunj's personal guard, the only men who wore armor and used swords, each of them commanding a hundred of the men, leapt to their feet from their hiding spot in the hollow. Pushing one of the screens out of the way, they moved quickly to form up, while one of the guards climbed the small slope to the top of the promontory. It didn't take him long to locate exactly where Nedunj's signal was sending them, and he scampered back down, rejoining the others, whereupon they began moving towards the riverbank, ready to slaughter any of the Romans foolhardy or desperate enough to try to reach the riverbank. Satisfied that this small threat posed by half-drowned, unarmored survivors was contained, Nedunj returned his attention to the larger situation, and he couldn't restrain the shout of joy at seeing that every undamaged Roman ship had stopped, their oarsmen doing just enough to maintain their spot. No, the attack hadn't been repelled, but the fact that it had been temporarily stopped was good enough for Nedunj.

"Alert me when they start moving again," he ordered, but he was already moving back towards the western wall; it was time to see if his other gamble was paying off.

Because of their position outside the *testudo*, the seventy surviving Centurions of the twelve Cohorts on the beach saw the approaching spearmen suddenly go from their measured pace to an all-out run, but their reaction time varied widely. However, even those who immediately responded by shouting the order to open their formation to prepare for this assault, like Pullus, Balbus, and Scribonius were only partially successful. In Pullus' case, the First Century was still in the process of opening their ranks when the leading edge of the Pandyan spearmen reached the soft sand, and while they perceptibly slowed, it still wasn't enough time. While no longer in *testudo*, the men of Pullus' Century were spaced in a manner that they would have used on the march, where there was enough space for the men in the middle to lower their shields, but with barely two hands' width between their shield and the right arm of the comrade to their left. Not only did this hamper their ability to fight effectively, it also allowed the Pandyans to isolate each Century by flowing around the flanks; the only part not under threat was the Roman rear, but that was because of the incoming tide. Pullus didn't have the time to order it, but his men responded like the veterans they were, essentially splitting themselves so that half of what had been the files became ranks by facing out to their left, with the other half doing the same but facing the opposite direction. This worked for the rankers, but now Pullus, Paterculus, Lutatius, and the Legion *Cornicen* Gnaeus Valerius were outside the formation and exposed. This wasn't unusual, however, and both Paterculus and Valerius in particular had learned that the best place for them to be was behind and on either side of their Primus Pilus, protecting his flanks while allowing the giant Roman to do what he did better than any man they had ever seen. Pullus was always a natural target, both because of his white crest and his position next to the eagle, and because of his size and ferocity, becoming a tangible symbol to countless enemies who wanted to be the man to be able to tell his comrades later that he had slain a giant. This was clearly on the mind of the first spearman who, in his eagerness to reach this huge foe first, got just a couple paces ahead of his comrades, launching the thrust of his spear at what Pullus could see was the outer limit of his reach. Consequently, this made it relatively straightforward for Pullus to block with Percennius' shield, but in a repetition of what happened when the first Pandyan arrow struck, while the perceived impact told Pullus the truth that there wasn't much power behind the blow, he was shocked to see the spear point penetrate by at least three inches, far more than he had ever seen from the same force before. More strikingly, the noise from the impact as the other Pandyan spearmen began their attack on his Century was unlike anything he had ever heard, but he couldn't turn his attention away from the man who had penetrated his shield. With skin as dark as the mahogany wood that the Romans had encountered in India, the man was wearing nothing more than a vest that appeared to be lamellar armor, but instead of metal the overlapping pieces were leather, while his lower legs were protected by greaves made of the same material. He was also damnably quick, evading Pullus' counterthrust without bringing his shield up in front of him, and this was Pullus' only and last chance to dispatch this Pandyan, because his comrades had only been a pace behind. It also confirmed for Pullus the information that his ears had detected, that while these lightly armed men had indeed closed more quickly than any of the Romans on the beach anticipated, unlike their experience with all the other enemy spearmen they had encountered, their Pandyan foes didn't actually hurl themselves bodily at them. Instead, they slid to a stop, just out of reach of the Roman *gladii*, then used their longer spears to thrust at their opponent. While every man in the Roman ranks would attest that defeating a spearman in a one on one confrontation wasn't particularly challenging, that wasn't happening here, as Pullus quickly learned when the man to the right of his original foe and identically equipped took the step with his left foot that signaled the beginning of a spear thrust. Instinctively, Pullus moved his shield, not much, but enough to convince the Pandyan to the left of the first man to launch his own thrust with just the strength of his arm. What this Pandyan didn't know, nor would he live long enough to learn was that Pullus didn't need the warning shout from Paterculus, because moving his shield away from his body had been planned. Over the years, Titus Pullus had perfected the ability to use his peripheral vision, not only to keep track of movement but to gauge distance with the same accuracy as when he looked directly at an object.

From Paterculus' viewpoint, the thrust of the Pandyan came an instant before Pullus, moving his blade from the first position up in a sweeping blow, using his longer reach and the strength that had helped keep him alive through such moments to sever both spear and the lower portion of the man's arm, midway between elbow and wrist. It was left to Paterculus to dispatch the Pandyan who, while it was understandable, assured his own demise when he dropped his shield in an attempt to stem the spurting flow of blood, and he never saw the thrust that the *Aquilifer* aimed for his throat. Meanwhile, Pullus was in a perfect position to take the expected thrust from the Pandyan on the opposite side, catching it on his shield while tilting it slightly so that the spearpoint didn't strike square, and as he expected, this was the moment the original Pandyan who had struck the first blow chose to renew his assault. What Pullus hadn't anticipated was that, instead of a straightforward thrust, this Pandyan used his spear as a slashing weapon, swinging it in a wide arc but with unerring aim so that, if successful, the edge of the spearpoint would bite into the Roman's neck. It was only because of reflexes honed over years of training and countless battles that Pullus reacted in the same manner as when he was evading missile weapons, reacting without thinking by leaning backward to allow the broad leaf blade slash by just under his chin, nicking it in the process and eliciting a bellow of pain from him. Just like with all of Rome's enemies who favored a slashing attack, this Pandyan was temporarily vulnerable, both because of the position of his arm now placed his weapon out of position, and because when a man is counting on hitting his target and doesn't, it causes his weight to shift more dramatically. This Pandyan recovered, or attempted to quickly enough, but in what looked like a synchronized movement, Pullus used his upper body mass after it leaned back, whipping his torso forward, while using the shield as an extension of his arm, aiming the boss unerringly for his enemy's right cheek. If it had been one of his Legionaries instead of Pullus himself, the spearman would have reacted in much the same way Pullus had by simply leaning away from the blow so that it either missed him or hit him with negligible force. However, Pullus was one of the only men in Caesar's army, or any of the Legions of Rome, who could punch almost as quickly holding a heavy shield as he could with his bare fist, something that the Pandyan learned in the final lesson of his life. The shock of the impact ran up Pullus' arm, telling him that it was a solid blow, but the shield actually blocked his view until he recovered it to see his foe had already collapsed, the right side of his face crushed concave, his body twitching in a manner that was common with this kind of attack. There was a spearman immediately behind him, but while he moved into position, it wasn't with much enthusiasm, which allowed Pullus to glance around and take in the larger situation. A span of perhaps fifteen heartbeats had elapsed from the moment when the leading rank of Pandyans began their attempt to penetrate his Century formation, yet despite seeing there were perhaps a half-dozen bodies lying at the feet of the men on his side of the Century, he could also see that his men were tiring. The problem was that there was no way to sound a relief, both because of their collapsed spacing made it virtually impossible, but being surrounded on three sides made it infinitely more complicated. Using his height, he still had to stand on his tiptoes to see over the heads of his men to catch sight of Balbus and his Century, and while he couldn't see much, it was enough to know that his Second Century was in the same predicament as his own. And, until he could figure out a way to open his ranks and put his men closer to the Second as they did the same, he didn't like their chances of getting off this beach. Even as this thought struck him, he felt something at his feet, and he looked down just in time to see the wave of the incoming tide recede...and he was standing at the front of his Century.

It was Caesar who, because of his vantage point, determined what the Pandyan strategy was, and he instantly understood the danger.

"They're going to let the water do the work for them," he said grimly to Pollio, who had joined him on the rostrum at Caesar's command. "See?"

He pointed to where the men of the First Cohort of the 3rd Legion were in an almost identical position to Pullus and his men, and Pollio saw that the Legionaries at the rear of the formation were forced to do their best to keep the heads of their wounded comrades out of the water, prompting Pollio to take a moment to scan the other Centuries where his view wasn't blocked by the ships. Everywhere he looked, the situation was the same, the only difference being the degree of the distress each Century was under.

"Maybe..." Pollio actually had to swallow the lump that formed at the thought before he could continue. "...maybe we need to withdraw, Caesar."

To his surprise, Caesar didn't snap at him or even appear upset at the idea, but while he still shook his head, his objection was more practical in nature.

"And how can we load those men back up with those spearmen pressing them, Asinius?" A glance at his subordinate told Caesar that Pollio saw this was true. "But," he admitted, "we need to do something to break this deadlock. No, they're not pressing our men, and we've inflicted casualties while most of ours came from the archers. Which," he frowned, "I don't understand. I've never seen so many men fall from arrows before, have you?" Pollio didn't reply verbally, but the shake of his head was enough for Caesar to continue, "That's something for later, but right now, it's clear that those Pandyans are content to just keep us pinned down. We," he finished grimly, "need to come up with a way to break this deadlock because time is on their side."

Pollio said nothing immediately, watching the fighting, the sound from the clashing of metal on metal and the shouts of men from both sides slightly delayed by the distance. He was moving his head left to right, stopping when he reached the southwestern corner of the city wall, realizing that there might be something that could help.

"When are we expecting the signal from Hirtius and his Legions?"

"As soon as we begin the attack on the southern wall. They're going to loose a naphtha pot at a high angle so that we can see it," Caesar answered, although he kept his eyes on the nearest struggle, where it appeared that two of the Centuries that had shared a ship had managed to expand enough to be within just three or four paces between them, thereby squeezing the Pandyan spearmen who had inserted themselves between the two into a smaller and smaller space. In effect, the Pandyans were reaching the point that the Romans were facing in not having enough room to fight effectively, especially with a longer weapon like a spear, which was why Caesar still held out hope, albeit faint, that his Legions would prevail. But Pollio's mention of the attack on the southern wall did cause Caesar another pang of doubt; while it was impossible to tell with any precision, it did seem to him that the signal should have been sent by this point. He had Teispes and Gundomir tasked with that very thing, watching that quadrant of the sky, just above the line of buildings and the small trees that obscured their view of the Pseudostoma, so he was certain that they hadn't missed it. Something must have delayed them, just like the men in the twelve Cohorts of three Legions were still struggling to cross the sandy strip and reach the scrub grass beyond it. And now the strip of hardpacked sand was less than half its original size. If something didn't happen, many of his men would die, either by drowning if they stood, or being cut down as they sacrificed themselves to allow their comrades to get back aboard the ships. This would prove to be a seminal moment, not just for Caesar, but for the men of his Legions who would be following their general longer than any of them could possibly imagine, because as he was watching, Caesar experienced a sickening sensation. How, he wondered, are they going to get back aboard those ships? They had leapt over the side several feet down, but even if they attempted to reverse themselves and leap back up, how many of these men who were already exhausted, weighed down by their armor and weapons, and standing in rolling surf could actually make it back aboard?

Titus Pullus was contemplating that very thing, which was why he quickly discarded the idea. In strict terms, his Century was in relatively decent shape; most of the casualties they had absorbed to this point were from the archers, although he had lost two men because, very simply, they had become too tired to respond in time to a thrust from their Pandyan foe. Somehow, he had to create enough space so that these men who had been fighting now for what he estimated was almost a full sixth part of a watch, longer than he ever remembered going before without sounding the relief, could be replaced by their comrades behind them. After his dispatch of the three Pandyans, the spearmen around him had settled for occasionally offering a half-hearted jab, or a feinted attack, enough to keep him occupied, but not actually endangering themselves, something that he took a deep and savage satisfaction from, understanding that their reluctance was due to him, not that this helped with the more immediate problem.

Filling his lungs, Pullus bellowed with all the power he could muster, *"Boys, there's only one way off this beach, and that's to get to that fucking wall! And the only way to do that is open up so we can shift! Can I count on you?"* The answer was an unintelligible, guttural sound that, to Pullus' experienced ear, lacked something in enthusiasm, but he realized this wasn't the training ground; he also recognized that he had to set the example. He turned his head just enough to look over his shoulder without giving the Pandyans who continued to jab their spears in his direction the opening they had been seeking, and what he saw chilled his blood. He didn't think it was that long ago, but he was convinced that the last time he had checked on the wounded, those men were sitting in waist deep water, forcing their uninjured comrades at the rear to spend their energy on making sure that none of the men who were slumped at their feet went underwater. That at least five of his men were facedown in the water, and their prone bodies were almost completely covered by the surf fueled his desperate measures to rectify the situation.

"On my count, we're going to rush these *cunni*, do you understand? We'll go on three!"

It seemed straightforward enough to Pullus, but he realized he shouldn't have been surprised when he heard one of his men cry out, "But they'll know we're coming, Primus Pilus!"

Even in the moment, with all that was taking place, Pullus had to fight the grin that threatened to mar the immediacy of the moment, but he answered quickly enough, "Terentius, do you think these stupid bastards know how to speak Latin?"

He was rewarded by his men who laughed, and if it was forced, Pullus chose to ignore it, understanding how levity, feigned or not, at such a dire moment could surprise their enemies, and he saw by the suddenly puzzled, and anxious, expressions of their foes that this was such a moment.

"Now that we've settled that..." He held his *gladius* up. "One...two...*three!*"

He had already begun moving by the time he shouted the final number, having chosen the Pandyan he intended to slay next, while his men signaled their own readiness with a thunderous roar as they suddenly lunged forward, using their shields to physically press their enemy back, counting on the surprise to get past the enemy spears. Although Pullus could see that the Pandyans were startled, they reacted quickly, dropping into what he assumed was their defensive posture, and it was inevitable that Pullus heard men shrieking in pain in his tongue, but this wasn't the moment to worry about casualties, not if his Century, Cohort, and Legion was to survive. The Pandyan he had chosen had his fate sealed when the comrade protecting his weak side took a reflexive step backward at the sight of the huge Roman rushing in his general direction, while the targeted spearman instinctively reacted to the movement at the edge of his vision by turning his head, and Pullus saw it. He launched a high second position thrust that, if a *tiro* on the training ground had executed it, would have earned the ranker a swipe from Pullus' *vitus* because it relied on only the strength of the arm, but he did so with the supreme confidence that came from knowing he had the power to render a killing blow even at the farthest extension of his arm. And, just as he aimed it, the point of his *gladius* skimmed the top of the Pandyan's leather-covered wicker shield and under the man's chin, punching into the soft tissue before stopping when he felt the grating sensation as the point struck his spinal column, normally the signal to twist his wrist to finish the job by severing the large vessels in the neck. Instead, he kept his arm out straight and shoved the dying Pandyan backward, directly into the man who would have replaced him, using his weight and strength to create an open space behind him. By doing so, however, he placed himself in temporary jeopardy with his penetration so that he was now flanked on either side by the comrades of his first victim. Using his peripheral vision, he shot his shield out, this time not at an oblique angle but straight out from his side and without aiming it specifically, intending to simply distract the opponent to his left, counting on one of his men to fill in the spot he had just vacated to attack this Pandyan. Seeing that the spearman who he had shoved the first man's corpse into was still trying to untangle himself, Pullus was again moving, spinning on the ball of his right foot while still keeping his right arm extended, the blade ripping through the rest of the dead man's throat as he swung his *gladius* in a bloody arc. The Pandyan to his direct right had already been put in jeopardy because his reaction to Pullus' sudden move had been delayed, and a spear was the worst weapon for a close-quarter fight, while his shield was on the opposite side of his body. In the span of a perhaps two full heartbeats, Pullus had not only dispatched two more Pandyans, he had given his men room to separate. It wasn't enough, but it was better than it had been. Hearing as much as seeing that the Pandyan he had aimed his shield at was now under assault from one of his men, Pullus was certain that they were close to the moment, and he placed his bone whistle in his mouth. To his right, the men who would have normally been part of the first file but were now behaving as a rank because of being surrounded had managed to push the Pandyans back what Pullus judged was perhaps four paces, and a glance over his shoulder wasn't particularly informative, although he could see that the opposite side of his Century had expanded as well, meaning that Balbus' Century was now close enough that there was only a double line of Pandyans in between them, with two men facing his Century and the other two facing Balbus. That, he decided, would have to do, and he drew in a breath, then blew a long, single blast on his whistle.

Caesar's vantage point allowed him to see that, while his Centuries were finally making progress, it wasn't uniform; there were several spots where the collapsed formations still stood in roughly the same spot, particularly the Fourth of the 3rd, and the Second of the 25th but even with just those exceptions, he was still unhappy. With every passing heartbeat where there was no signal from Hirtius at the southern wall, his anxiety was growing, and with it, the recognition that he had to make a decision. And if there was anything that could be said about Gaius Julius Caesar, it was that when he made a decision, it was without hesitation, or even the appearance of doubt. Turning abruptly and without a word to Pollio, he hopped down and hurried to the rear of the *quinquereme*, leaving his second in command to wonder why, although he knew Caesar well enough to see in his general's face that he had come to some sort of decision. He got the answer when there was a sharp cry, followed by the men of the deck crew immediately scrambling into action, and in the ensuing uproar of men shouting to each other he didn't hear the command, not from the *Navarch*, but from the man responsible for maintaining the rhythm of the oarsmen, and he was almost knocked off his feet when the huge vessel began moving with a sudden lurch. He only regained his balance by dropping into a crouch and grabbing for the edge of one of the boxes making up the rostrum, and consequently, he didn't immediately spot Caesar returning from the stern. When he did identify the figure of his general among the scrambling crewmen, the fact that Caesar had snatched up a Legionary shield from somewhere didn't register immediately, but when Caesar stopped where both Teispes and Gundomir were standing and said something in a low tone, he didn't need to hear the words to know. Without thinking, he hopped off the rostrum, misjudging the increasing speed of the heavy warship, sending him stumbling once again as his feet hit the deck, the commotion causing Caesar to glance over his shoulder.

Standing back upright, Pollio, forgetting himself, demanded, "Are you doing what I think you're doing?"

Caesar actually smiled slightly, his voice sounding as if they were discussing something inconsequential.

"That depends on what you think I'm doing, Asinius."

"That you're going ashore!" Pollio snapped.

"Ah," Caesar answered lightly, "then yes, you are correct." Before Pollio could interject, he continued, all sign of levity gone, "It's either that or sound the withdrawal, Asinius. And I'm not willing to do that. The men seeing me with them will…"

Before he could continue, there was a shout of warning from one of the Tribunes who had managed to keep their attention on the rapidly approaching beach.

"At least wear a helmet," Pollio pleaded, but Caesar gave an abrupt shake of his head.

"It's in my cabin, and there's no time. Besides," he turned to where Teispes and Gundomir were standing, sharing the same expression that communicated their solidarity with Pollio, "Gundomir and Teispes will be with me. Now," Caesar turned and walked to the gunnel of the ship, raising his voice, "we're about to reach the beach."

"Brace for impact!"

Pollio didn't know who shouted it, but he was thankful because he managed to grab a support that braced the huge single mast and avoid the embarrassment of falling for a third time. Before Pollio fully recovered, Caesar was over the side, and the Legate only caught a glimpse of their general's red *paludamentum* streaming in the air, although he was in time to see first Gundomir then Teispes, both of them carrying shields, vault over the side.

Caesar had chosen his spot to reach the beach not with an eye towards his personal safety, but visibility, although he quickly learned he had misjudged the depth, landing in water that was nearly chest deep, and he almost lost his footing when a wave smashed into him from behind. Fortunately, a hand that felt like iron grabbed his arm, and he turned to see Gundomir glaring at him.

"You're not going to do anyone any good if you drown." The German had to raise his voice to be heard over the din of the fighting.

Caesar didn't reply, although he did give a nod, then began wading through the surf holding the borrowed shield above his head, sheltered by the towering sides of his flagship to his right, and the ship that had deposited the Fifth and Sixth Centuries of the Second of the 3rd to his left. It was a tight fit, but Caesar's *Navarch* had expertly guided the bow of the flagship into the space between the ships carrying the Third and Fourth Centuries and the Fifth and Sixth, but the *quinquereme* also served to obscure a wider view of the battle. He was still in knee deep water when he came upon the first bodies of the Fifth Century, an even half-dozen men who had been arrayed face up, but were still covered by the surf, their limbs moved by the waves in a gruesome parody of life.

"Their armor will keep them from being taken out."

This startled him, if only because Gundomir had closed the distance so that he could say this in his ear without being overheard by those rankers of the Fifth who, like their comrades, were out of the action but still living. That they were now sitting up, despite their wounds, was a function of these men leaning against discarded shields their unwounded comrades had shoved into the sand, and Caesar saw that they were being tended to not by some of their fellow Legionaries, but two section slaves who had left the safety of their ship and had either been trained as *medici* or were filling that role in an emergency. Most of these wounded men were conscious, and a couple of them even registered their recognition that it was their general wading past. Caesar ignored them, not out of indifference to their suffering but understanding that every heartbeat of time was crucial, although he did pause for a moment to turn and gesture to the two men with him.

"I want Gundomir to my right, and you to my left," Caesar addressed Teispes, and while the Parthian didn't hesitate, Caesar did notice that he seemed uncomfortable with the Legionary shield, which prompted Caesar to say with a grin, "That shield's not for you, Teispes. It's for me. I need you to keep me from being poked full of holes once those archers recognize what I'm doing."

He immediately saw this eased the Parthian's mind, and once the men were on either side of him, although they barely had room, he strode up the beach and into the small space of sand that was relatively clear, placing them directly on the left flank of those Pandyan spearmen who were still struggling to keep the two Centuries apart. It would be something to fill the watches for the foreseeable future, as men relived the moment when they saw their general, bareheaded but wielding a *gladius* like one of them, stride into that gap and, before the nearest Pandyan spearman could react, killed the man with a thrust to the neck, while his bearded German bodyguard dispatched the spearman who had been facing the Fifth Century to their right. It was a matter of heartbeats before the remainder of the Pandyans in between the Roman Centuries were cut down, although a couple spearmen nearest to their comrades facing the Roman front rank used the deaths of these Pandyans, managing to scamper to a safety that proved to be temporary. More importantly, the sudden juncture of the two Centuries allowed both to spread out into their normal spacing, and infused the Romans with a new energy when they understood that it was Caesar himself, and his two bodyguards, who were the cause. Caesar, his blade bloody, stood in what was now the normal spacing between the Fifth and Sixth Century, with the Secundus Hastatus Posterior, a swarthy Apulian named Lucius Terentius, watching as the Pandyans across from them, without any audible signal, began shuffling backward across the shifting sand, and while it was possible they were doing this to force their opponents to stand on the more treacherous footing, Caesar felt certain this wasn't the case.

"Where's your *Cornicen*, Terentius?" Caesar asked, demonstrating one facet of his leadership ability in the seemingly simple act of remembering the man's name.

"He's dead, sir," Terentius replied quickly enough, although even in the moment, he was imagining telling his fellow Centurions how their general called him by name.

Caesar muttered something unintelligible, then turned and ordered Gundomir, "Go to the Fifth and bring their *Cornicen* here." As Gundomir made his way between the now-open ranks, Caesar shouted, "*My comrades! I saw from my ship that you need my help, and Caesar has come to your aid just as I know you would come to mine!*" He didn't try to continue, allowing the men to roar their agreement, while he kept watch on the Pandyans, who had now retreated to a distance of perhaps fifteen paces, and although he couldn't hear anything over the din, he saw some of them looking behind them to where he assumed the commander of this section of men was located. Even as he was shouting, he saw Gundomir approaching, the Fifth's *Cornicen* trotting behind him as the German brought him back through the space between the second and third rank. Pointing with his *gladius*, he raised his voice to an even higher pitch, hoping that it would carry to the Centuries on either side of the two he was with. "*Now, who will follow me, my comrades? Can I count on you?*"

Once again, the men roared, but Caesar could tell by the volume that he had been heard by more than these two Centuries. Forced to shout the order, even so Caesar had to repeat it twice, but not because the *Cornicen* hadn't heard it. Nevertheless, he nodded, licked his lips, then began blowing the notes.

"That's Caesar's signal!"

This, or a variation of this was voiced across the entirety of the twelve battered Cohorts, the last ranks of all of them now standing in at least knee-deep surf, and every man not directly engaged turning towards the source of the *cornu* call. One of them who didn't, and in fact was barely aware of it was Pullus, who at that moment had finally gotten not just the First and Second Centuries finally into their proper spacing, but the entire First Cohort, the first Cohort of the twelve to do so. This was certainly a positive development, but they still hadn't made it off of the shifting sand and onto firmer ground, which he was in the process of addressing. His original intention had been to use the standard method of hurling javelins before dashing across the short distance the Pandyans now seemed content to allow as they fell back in a more defensive posture, but he quickly learned it wouldn't be with the potency he expected because his men had been forced to drop them during the Pandyans' initial attack, and most of them were now covered by the murky surf. They were never recovered, because before Pullus could order their retrieval, a second horn command sounded the notes that signaled the assault for all Centuries within hearing, which slightly startled Pullus because this was the first one that he heard quite clearly.

"Caesar must be ashore, Primus Pilus!" Paterculus shouted, "and he wants us to attack now! What are your orders?"

In answer, Pullus bellowed, "Straight to the *gladius*, boys! On my command!" If he had been going by the regulations, he would have had his own *Cornicen* sound the actual command, but instead, Pullus used the power of his lungs, knowing that he would be heard by all who mattered. "*Porro!*"

    Rufus and Bodroges finally caught up with Flaminius two miles inland, and once they regained their breath, relayed Hirtius' orders, which the Primus Pilus obeyed immediately, having his Legion simply change their facing, then after a series of relayed commands, moved from the column to a three line formation now marching on a northwesterly course. He was working off of slightly educated guesswork, aided by Volusenus' map that was mostly a sketch of what lay inland. His orders had been to search for a fordable spot inland while avoiding detection if possible and leaving it to the rest of the army to begin the assault on Muziris. Frankly, the news that the Legions under Hirtius' command needed help was a blessing as far as he was concerned, but he was also slightly worried that they would arrive too late, confident that the problem the Tribune had described would have been resolved without needing their help. Consequently, he set a pace that was probably faster than prudent, although when the leading Cohorts approached what appeared to be a manmade grove, he called a brief halt while sending a section for each lead Cohort out. A couple hundred heartbeats later, they resumed marching, sweating from the heat and the nerves of the moment, every man ready for what might be coming. It wasn't until they emerged from the shade of the grove that Flaminius learned two things; the first was that, either through skill or Fortuna smiling on the Primus Pilus and his Legion, he had clearly chosen the most direct path towards the bend in the river, and the city walls were now visible. The second was that, although the Pandyan commander had sent a force across the river to protect what he could now see was a cunningly disguised redoubt, they weren't between his men and their first objective. The sight of nothing but open ground, albeit with broad-leafed plants and some shrubbery that was no more than knee high, brought a grim smile to his lips, and he opened his mouth to give his *Cornicen* the command, then thought better of it.

    "No, we're going to get closer before we let them know we're here," he said conversationally, but both his *Aquilifer* and *Cornicen* were accustomed to Flaminius' habits and knew that no reply was expected.

    Like Pullus, he used his voice, confident that it wouldn't carry across the half-mile of open ground, and that the Second, Third, and Fourth Cohorts would follow the lead of his First quickly enough. As he expected, it wasn't forum perfect, but they hadn't covered fifty paces when, glancing to his left, he saw that the other three Cohorts were arrayed in a perfect line with his own. There was no real attempt at stealth, yet somehow, the leading Cohorts of the 30th managed to get within two hundred paces of the southeastern edge of the redoubt, close enough that he could see the latticework screens, without an alarm being raised. The approaching Romans could also see the blurring streaks created by the rocks hurled from the Pandyan artillery, arcing up and away from them as they presumably plunged down into their comrades in the 12th or perhaps the 6th, the second Legion in the line of ships. Well, he thought as he thrust his *vitus* in the air and called the halt, that's about to change, you fucking savages.

It had begun so well for Nedunj and his army, and it had lasted long enough for him to begin to believe that his plan would successfully repel these Romans. Even as he thought about it later, he wasn't sure exactly when things swung against him and his Pandyans to a decisive degree, although he suspected that he knew where the situation started to deteriorate, and it began with a runner dashing along the rampart from the southern wall.

"Your Highness, Lord Alangudi sent me to report that there are ships who are now using artillery on our position across the river!"

Before he left, Nedunj scanned the western beach, and while it was clear that the small Roman formations had managed to open themselves up, there were still spearmen in between each one. There was also a distressingly large number of prone figures, the difference between the two combatants making it easy for him to see how many of these casualties were his, and when he thought about it later, he recognized this was the first moment he experienced a stirring of unease.

"Send for me if something happens here," he ordered the runner, not missing the man's grateful glance at being allowed to stay put and not retrace his steps, but he was already moving at close to a run.

The men lining the rampart saw him coming, and they all leapt out of the way so that he reached Alangudi's side quickly but quite winded, and his aide dispensed with the formalities, pointing down at the river.

"See how they've arrayed those ships?" Nedunj still hadn't regained his wind, so he shook his head, and Alangudi continued grimly, "While they're out of range of our artillery; not," he allowed, "by much, the redoubt is within range of theirs. I can't tell with any certainty, but I've only seen four of our pieces launch anything since their first volley."

Nedunj had regained enough of his breath to say hopefully, "Maybe it just disabled the piece and they're repairing it."

"May Shiva make it so," Alangudi replied, a fervent note to his voice that told Nedunj he wasn't optimistic.

The news wasn't all bad, however; between the stranded ship and the two that had sunk, there was still only a very narrow passage for any vessel to navigate, but the Romans had clearly decided not to attempt it until they negated the Pandyan artillery at the redoubt. What they had no way of knowing was that, as precarious as matters were, the Romans had done their enemy the favor of deciding not to use their stores of naphtha, if only because the *navarchae* of all five ships who were now bombarding the redoubt flatly refused Hirtius' order. Not only would it require them to move within range of the Pandyan artillery, the masters and crews of every ship had been adamant in their refusal to even entertain the idea of using such a volatile substance on platforms made of nothing but wood, leather, and all sorts of other flammable material, particularly human flesh. It was natural that Nedunj's attention shift some, and he lowered his gaze to the spot where the grounded ship was, seeing that the deck was crammed full of men, but some of them were attired differently and he didn't know why.

Alangudi noticed and explained, "The men just in their tunics are from that ship." He pointed to the *quadrireme* that had carried Balbinus and his two Centuries, which had settled on the river bottom so that the deck was awash, while the bow was pointed at the eastern riverbank and the stern towards the western. Alangudi's finger moved to another spot, and for the first time, Nedunj noticed the corpses that were either lying on the riverbank or were at least partially in the water. "Our men cut these dogs down when they tried to come ashore."

This caused a pang of unease, and Nedunj asked, "Did they try to surrender?"

He got his answer in the manner in which Alangudi avoided his gaze as he shrugged. "I didn't really pay attention, Your Highness."

He didn't comment, choosing instead to ask, "So, where are our men now?"

"They're over there." Alangudi pointed to a spot between the redoubt and the riverbank, and Nedunj barely made out the crouching figures. "They're waiting to repel any attempt to try and land."

This eased Nedunj's mind, and he was just beginning to relax when something caught his eye, a flash of some sort, but in a spot well away from the redoubt and on the opposite side from the city. He stared for several long heartbeats, shading his eyes, before seeing the movement but not immediately understanding what it meant. Slowly, the movement that his eye had spotted resolved itself, yet it still took crucial moments for Nedunj to comprehend that it was a line of men, arranged in neat ranks and moving with a regularity that had never been part of the Pandyan way of waging war. He heard the strangled gasp, but barely recognized it as his own voice as he seized Alangudi's arm, hard, as he pointed.

"Those are Romans! *Romans!*" His fingers dug into his aide's arm as he physically turned him, wondering if the wide-eyed look of shock on Alangudi's face was the same as his own. "How? How did they get there? And," at this, he returned his attention back to the redoubt, "how are we going to warn our men? There's no way that they can see them coming! Not with the orchard in between them!"

Even in that moment, when it really made no difference, Nedunj couldn't smother the sudden rush of bitter anger, because this had been a source of contention between him and his father. Puddapandyan had never taken more than a passing interest in agricultural matters, so when the member of the royal household who was responsible for the maintenance of all the agrarian holdings of their house had come to complain, he had approached the prince. The orchard had become overgrown, he had informed Nedunj, and not only was it unsightly, it lowered the yield and overall efficiency of it. Nedunj in turn had broached the subject with his father, but Puddapandyan had flatly refused to address the issue, and was sufficiently irritated to inform his son that he would check to make sure that Nedunj hadn't wasted any of the treasury money to fix the issue. Well, Father, he thought angrily, your parsimony might see Muziris lost.

There was really nothing left for either of them to do but watch as helpless spectators. The Roman Legion briefly vanished in the orchard before, obviously aided by the undergrowth, they emerged without any sign that either the men in the redoubt, or the spearmen who were crouching on the river side, noticed the approach of the enemy force. Even with the horror he was feeling, Nedunj felt a grudging admiration at how, once they were back out in the open, his enemy paused, the distinct groups of men aligning themselves back into one long line composed of what he quickly counted were twelve smaller units, that were subdivided into four separate entities. There was a gap of what Nedunj judged was fifty paces, then there was another line composed of identically arranged units behind the first line, but there were only three of the larger ones. Despite the circumstances, the crown prince of the Pandyan was learning more about how the Romans waged war in these few moments than he had gleaned in all of his talks with his father-in-law.

"There are six small units in each large one," he commented. When the third line emerged, also spaced about fifty paces behind the second, and composed of three of the larger groups, he counted aloud, "So there are ten of the larger groups, and six of the smaller groups in each of the larger. That must be one of their Legions."

Alangudi tore his gaze away from the oncoming Romans, looking at his prince in alarm, not from what he said, but the flat, resigned tone in his voice, and he knew that, his relationship with Nedunj aside, he was about to commit a breach of protocol that could conceivably end in his death, but he was sufficiently worried to reach out and, just as Nedunj had done a moment earlier, grab his prince's arm and squeeze it hard.

"Your Highness," he kept his voice down so that only Nedunj could hear, "you *must* not despair! Not now! Not," Alangudi glanced around in a manner that Nedunj correctly interpreted, "in front of the men!"

Nedunj's first reaction to Alangudi's action was to glare at his aide; although he wasn't his father, he didn't appreciate a man who was still subservient to him grabbing him in this manner, despite their friendship.

Fortunately, for both of them, Nedunj shoved down the impulse to snap at the other man, giving a perfunctory shake of his head, saying tersely, "I understand." He hesitated, and Alangudi saw Nedunj's expression soften as he added, "And...thank you, Alangudi. You are correct."

They returned their attention to the scene, but fairly quickly, Nedunj was beginning to wish he hadn't, because the feeling of utter helplessness that overcame him as he watched this Roman Legion move at what seemed to be an obscenely leisurely pace towards the redoubt, where his men were still unaware of the danger. With the large screens obscuring his view, Nedunj had to rely on strictly what he *could* see, which was a figure darting out of the redoubt, dashing across to the force of spearmen who were still crouched, watching in essentially the wrong direction for a Roman attempt to climb the riverbank. He could tell that the Romans had been spotted by the manner in which the force of five hundred spearmen reacted, leaping to their feet and rushing in a disorganized manner back towards the redoubt. Regardless of this positive development, he felt nothing but sick to his stomach, knowing how paltry a force, both in numbers and in comparative armament, was about to face these Romans. The spearmen disappeared briefly behind the large screens, reappearing on the opposite side, where the Romans had temporarily stopped at a distance of what Nedunj estimated was about a hundred paces. There was a surreal quality to the scene, because it seemed as if the Romans were politely waiting for the heavily outnumbered spearmen to array themselves, and their commander was forced to form his men up in a pitifully thin line that was only two men deep to not be immediately enveloped by the Romans, who only began moving again once it was clear their enemy had finished their disposition. Neither the prince nor Alangudi said anything, and Nedunj noticed that it was deathly quiet along the wall, which caused him to take his eyes off the scene before him to glance at the men surrounding the pair, seeing that they were as transfixed as he was. Returning his attention to the redoubt, Nedunj was in time to see that, once again, the Romans suddenly stopped their march, but a heartbeat later, he saw a ripple of movement across the ranks that he guessed was preparation to launch some sort of missile, too far away to see precisely what they were, followed by the briefest of pauses. Because of their numbers, Nedunj and every other man on the rampart could sense the movement of these missiles that moved slower than arrows, helped by the sudden motion of more than a thousand arms, but there was no way for any of them to miss the horrible effect, the silence broken by gasps, moans, and curses as they were forced to watch what appeared to be well more than a third of the total Pandyan force struck down. It was as if an invisible giant hand swept across the entire length of the spearmen's lines, causing men to drop where they stood or stagger backwards into their comrades in the line behind them. Even with the horror, Nedunj noticed that some of the spearmen who remained standing did something that seemed to him as if they had gone mad, because while they appeared unhurt, they dropped their shields to the ground. And, knowing that the Pandyan version of armor were vests of boiled leather, this was tantamount to suicide on the part of these men, which Nedunj didn't understand.

 He learned he wasn't alone, hearing Alangudi gasp, "Why are those fools dropping their shields?"

 Before Nedunj could reply, although he had no more idea than Alangudi, he saw the same rippling motion, and he couldn't stop the moan from escaping his own lips as the nightmarish scene repeated itself. The way he learned that the Romans only carried two javelins was because, for the first time since he had been watching, when the Romans moved, it was not at the same slow, steady pace, but a sudden rush. And, also for the first time, he heard a sound that he knew came from across the river, in the form of more than two thousand men suddenly roaring their battle cry as they rushed at their foe. It was a small mercy that it was over quickly, although Nedunj certainly didn't feel that way, but he refused to look away as the Romans, barely stopping to cut down men who were already shattered and demoralized, swept into the redoubt. The first thing they did was to knock down the screens, which meant Nedunj was forced to watch as his essentially helpless artillery crews were butchered. However, it was Alangudi who noticed something.

"They're not destroying the artillery," he said this to Nedunj quietly so that only the prince could hear. "I think they intend to use it against us, Your Highness. You need to leave the wall before that happens."

Nedunj didn't seem to hear, but while he did, his attention was only partially on what Alangudi was saying, and he showed why by pointing downriver.

"They know there's no threat anymore," he said dully. "Look, the ships are moving again. And," he turned to look at Alangudi with an expression of what seemed to be apathetic resignation, "we probably won't be able to stop them from reaching the wall."

"That's why you need to leave here, Your Highness," Alangudi answered firmly. "Go to the western wall. If we can keep those dogs from reaching just one of the walls, we still have a chance, do we not?"

It took quite an effort, but this was the moment where Nedunj fully embraced being a king of his people, and all that came with it. The transformation was unmistakable as Nedunj suddenly straightened himself up and spoke more loudly than necessary, with a brisk tone that was designed to send a message.

"You are correct, Lord Alangudi. I'm going to go make sure these animals don't reach the other wall. You," his voice almost caught then, "stay here, keep me informed." In almost a whisper, he added, "And don't do anything to get yourself killed, my friend. I still need you."

Alangudi's answer was nothing more than a bow of his head, but Nedunj understood. Then, he spun about and went immediately to a trot, heading for the western wall to see if there was even a glimmer of hope for his people. Even before he rounded the southwestern corner, when he got his first glimpse of the western beach, he had his answer, seeing a bareheaded Roman in a flowing red cloak in front of the now-ordered lines that were almost identical to what Nedunj had seen with the Legion that was even now finishing the slaughter of his men at the redoubt. And, he saw with a sinking heart, the spearmen who remained standing were still facing the Romans, but moving backwards. The attempt to stop the Romans at the sea was failing.

With Caesar ashore, men who were certain they had no more energy to give were suddenly infused with a fresh supply, and their Centurions and Optios used that to drive the Pandyans back until the rearmost ranks were within fifty paces of the trench. Now that there was room, the *navarchae* of the ships bearing the first wave, aided by the rising tide, backed away from the beach far enough away that the vessels carrying the next three Cohorts of each Legion could take their place. However, before the first wave moved away from the beach the wounded and the dead were loaded aboard, although not without difficulty, which would be yet another thing for Caesar to correct in the future. Bolstered by their newly arrived comrades, it was Spurius' idea to have the fresh Centuries surrender a javelin apiece and pass them forward, but it was Caesar who ordered the Primus Pilus to wait until he had sent runners to Torquatus and to Pullus, commanding they do the same. The slight delay wasn't without cost, as the archers who had already retreated to the trench began resuming their volleys, but arcing them over the front-line Cohorts to rain down on the newly arrived reinforcements. This hampered the ability of the Cohorts of the 25th and 10th to accomplish what Spurius' 3rd had managed, costing even more time, but while Caesar chafed at this delay, he was not excessively worried, taking the opportunity to study their foes who now stood just in front of the entrenchment.

"They're making a grave mistake, Spurius," Caesar commented to the Primus Pilus while they waited, and the Centurion nodded in agreement.

"They should be on the other side of the trench. I wonder why whoever's commanding them hasn't done it," Spurius mused.

"Either he's dead or he's a fool," Caesar replied, but before Spurius could make the point, Caesar did it himself. "But given how they rushed us at the water, I don't think he's a fool. It," Caesar allowed, grudgingly, "was a good tactic, given the situation."

This was something that Spurius agreed with, though he didn't bother to say as much, and for the next few moments, they both stood watching as the arrows arced over their head on their way to shower the men of the second line Cohorts, of which the 3rd's had already contracted into *testudo*, and it was this thought that prompted Spurius to remember something.

"I don't know if their bows are stronger than even the Parthians, or they have some sort of special iron, but those arrows penetrate more than any I've ever seen, Caesar."

He was looking skyward, although he caught Caesar's head turning sharply to regard him, but before he could say anything in response, Torquatus signaled the readiness of the 25th with his *Cornicen*, which made Caesar temporarily forget what he knew was an important piece of news.

Instead, he grinned at Spurius as he said, "That means that you and Torquatus were ready faster than Pullus and the Equestrians. I suspect he's not going to be very happy."

This caused Spurius to laugh, inordinately pleased at the thought, and he heard both Gundomir and the one-eyed Parthian who were now standing behind Caesar chuckle.

"Those poor bastard Pandyans across from him are going to suffer," he agreed cheerfully, already planning on how he was going to needle his friend about the day that Pullus' Legion was the last one to be ready.

It wasn't much of a delay, as perhaps a half-dozen heartbeats elapsed before Pullus sent his own signal, whereupon Caesar wasted no more time, using Spurius' *Cornicen* to send the signal, "All Cohorts, ready javelins!" Knowing that every man was waiting for the command, Caesar didn't hesitate, watching the arms of the men in front him sweep back, then snapping, "Release!" Watching the Pandyans directly across from them as the men along the entire line hurled their missiles, nobody would ever know it, but Caesar actually felt sympathy for his foes when they were subjected to the onslaught from Roman javelins. This time was no exception, the screams of pain no less chilling because these men were crying out in a tongue he still couldn't understand.

With only one javelin, the next command he shouted out was, "Sound the charge!"

The last note was immediately drowned out by the roar of his men as they went from standing to an all-out sprint, shields held out to the side to allow them to pick up speed, but while he wasn't with the front rank when they slammed into the Pandyans, just Caesar's presence was more than enough. And, while it wasn't actually the case, the almost immediate collapse and rout of the Pandyan spearmen, along with their archer comrades would be attributed to Caesar simply being there, and it was something that Caesar, who almost immediately knew the true cause, wasn't inclined to dispel.

If he didn't know that he was awake, Nedunj would have sworn that he was having a nightmare, where he was forced to relive the same scene he had witnessed not long before, as the leading ranks of Romans, arrayed in an identical fashion, albeit with formations that were clearly smaller than with the Legion at the redoubt, hurled their javelins then went rushing at his men. This time, he was close enough to see exactly why some of the spearmen at the redoubt had behaved in such a seemingly bizarre fashion in discarding their shields, although he wasn't yet able to see exactly why having a Roman javelin pierce it was so much more damaging. He also noticed they only threw one before they went charging across the space between the two lines, although it didn't matter; he knew the outcome was already decided. Being closer also meant that he could almost feel the impact, and the fact that he had stopped a few paces from the southwestern corner meant that he was directly across from the last Roman formation in their line, so it was natural that his eyes were drawn to one man in particular, not only because he was the only Roman in that area wearing a white crest, but he was visibly larger than his fellow Romans. Nedunj would never know it, but the feeling he was experiencing as he watched this demon leading his men and actually reaching the spearmen of the front rank first was almost identical to that his father-in-law had experienced a year earlier. The only difference was the time of the day; otherwise, the feeling of rage and anguish that was exacerbated by the recognition that he was helpless to do anything about it was almost overwhelming, although it did give him a focal point for his hatred. Perhaps, he thought, just perhaps, I'll have a chance to strike that arrogant Roman down. He also understood that now wasn't the time to indulge in a fantasy, and he immediately realized he was in the wrong spot, breaking into as close to an all-out run as he could manage on the crowded rampart, ignoring the imploring looks of the men who would be facing the Romans next as he rushed past them, heading for the western gate. The battle for the beach was lost; now, all that remained was to try and save as many men as he could. Reaching where the ranking noble was standing, Nedunj ignored the blatant disrespect of Subramanian who refused to even bow his head, although the older man seemed content to just glare at his prince

without saying anything as Nedunj addressed the horn player.
"Sound...the...withdrawal," he managed to pant out.

This proved to be too much for Subramanian, but before he addressed his prince, he snapped at the horn player, "You will do no such thing!" Only then did he turn to address Nedunj, all signs of subservience missing, "Have you gone *mad*, boy?" Nedunj didn't respond immediately, still trying to catch his breath, and the nobleman took advantage, pressing, "If you open those gates, what's to stop those...*demons* from following our men into the city? They," he thrust his arm to point at where their men were struggling for their lives, "are expendable! And every one of those dogs they kill is one less for the rest of us to kill!"

Nedunj listened impassively, and when he saw that Subramanian was finished, he pointedly ignored the man to repeat his order to the horn player. What happened next occurred so quickly that not even Nedunj was sure the exact sequence of events, but it began when the horn player started to lift his horn to his lips. One of Subramanian's hands shot out, slapping at the horn with a snarled curse, but while he was reaching out with the other towards Nedunj, only his fingertips brushed the crown prince's left arm before it was suddenly withdrawn, going instead to his own throat in an ultimately vain attempt to stem the sudden spurting of bright red blood that the prince felt spatter his face. His attention, however, was on the dagger in his hand, regarding it with a bit of surprise as he tried to remember when he had drawn it, but he couldn't remember doing so. Subramanian tottered for perhaps another two heartbeats, his eyes wide in shock and disbelief as he stared at Nedunj, who lifted his head just in time for their eyes to meet before the older noble collapsed to his knees, his blood already pooled around him.

"Sound the withdrawal," Nedunj repeated for the third time, and there was no need for a fourth repetition, the horn player jerking the instrument back into position, sounding the notes just as Subramanian toppled facedown on the rampart.

Even as the notes were sounding, something caught Nedunj's eye, off to his far left, and while was too late to see the flaming pot of naphtha that was Hirtius' signal to Caesar that the assault on the southern wall was about to begin, he saw enough of the smoky trail before it was dissipated by the western breeze to know that whatever it meant, it wasn't to the advantage of Nedunj or his people.

Pullus was close to exhaustion, and he could see the same in his men, their faces drawn and gleaming with the perspiration that came with even the simplest of movements in this accursed place. They all heard the horn signal, the piercing high-pitched sound audible even over the thuds of iron striking wood, the grunts, and panting of hundreds of men desperately sucking in as much air as they could. Because of their position at the farthest end, Pullus could only see the western gateway arch, not the gates themselves, but it quickly became obvious what the signal meant when, with a haste that, to his eyes looked like an almost obscene eagerness, the archers who had placed themselves behind their entrenchment that had proven to be such a cunning disguise turned and went at the run towards the gateway.

"They're running, boys! Their archers are running!" Pullus didn't even recognize his own voice, having gone hoarse from what he would later learn was almost two full Roman watches since they began rowing towards shore. "Let's see what these spear-carrying bastards are going to do!"

They got their answer quickly enough, when first the rearmost rank, immediately followed by the second also went dashing away, slowed by the entrenchment, but while they were moving quickly, Pullus could see that they were retreating in relatively good order. This was how it began, at least; although it didn't start with the spearmen across from Pullus, the Pandyans of the first ranks who had the gate almost directly behind them clearly weren't willing to sacrifice themselves for their comrades. In simple terms, they turned and ran, the result a cascading effect in both directions along their long line as the last resistance attempting to keep the Romans from reaching the western wall dissolved, leaving behind foes who were, fortunately for them, too exhausted to immediately give chase. Later, when the men of Caesar's army relived this day, a running joke would develop that the one advantage their Pandyan spear-wielding foes with their light armor had was in their ability to run away. It would be a source of great amusement, although not on this day, and Caesar was initially furious that the men of the twelve Cohorts seemed content to allow so many men to escape, with only what he saw as a half-hearted effort to pursue them.

It was left to Spurius to tell him simply, "My boys are exhausted, sir. They're not chasing those *cunni* because they can't, not because they don't want to. And I'm guessing the boys in the 10th and 25th are in the same shape."

To his credit, Caesar instantly understood this, and there would be nothing more said about it, but neither was he willing to pass up the opportunity to inflict more punishment, so using Spurius'

Cornicen, he issued the command to send the second line Cohorts forward. They had opened back up when it became clear that the archers wouldn't be dropping arrows down on their heads any longer, and they responded immediately, moving through their comrades with a rapidity that bespoke of seemingly endless repetition, as the men in the first line ranks simply turned sideways, opening up the spaces between the files to allow their comrades to pass through. The most potent sign of their exhaustion came when there was virtually no talking done between the men being relieved and their comrades doing the relieving. Although this part occurred quickly enough, the ground between the relieving Cohorts and the entrenchment was littered with so many bodies, shields, and other detritus of battle that it was impossible to maintain any sort of formation, resulting in a delay that, while Caesar didn't appreciate it at the time, proved fortuitous for both sides. Just as had happened at places like Gergovia, the western gateway of Muziris was jammed with men bordering on the edge of panic, and even if they had done so in a more ordered fashion, there was an inevitable jam as so many men tried to pass through the gateway. However, whoever was commanding had retained the presence of mind to send his archers immediately up onto the ramparts, and fairly quickly, Caesar, and his Centurions, determined that trying to advance to inflict more casualties would prove costly. What puzzled Caesar and his officers was that the archers seemed content to launch only one volley as the relieving Cohorts quickly withdrew. No, it wouldn't have been many, but they could have inflicted more casualties, and while it was possible, Caesar was certain that it wasn't an exchange of courtesy for the Romans not rushing to slaughter the spearmen outside the walls.

They got their answer from an unlikely source, when one of the men in the ranks of the First of the Fifth Cohort of Spurius' Legion shouted, "Someone's waving a flag! Up on the rampart!"

Once alerted, it didn't take long for Caesar to spot it, and even less time for him to decide to accept it. That, however, wasn't as simple as it sounded, because like Nedunj, he had spotted the signal from Hirtius that, at last, his Legions were ready to assault the southern wall, and there simply wasn't time to send a man to Hirtius to relay Caesar's order to honor the request for truce.

Nevertheless, he didn't hesitate, saying loudly for the men around him to hear, "I need a square of white bandage and a javelin!" Then, he turned to the *Cornicen*. "Sound the call for the Primi Pili to attend to me. We have things to discuss."

The only reason that Aulus Hirtius independently decided to honor the Pandyans' truce request was because of the foresight of Nedunj, who had dispatched a man to run to Alangudi with the order to show a white banner, the crown prince not even knowing that this symbol of surrender was one of the few practices by the Greeks that had been adopted by the tribes of southern India, along with their more heavily influenced fellow tribes in the north. What mattered was that it worked, although in Hirtius' case, he welcomed the delay because it gave him time to reorganize, particularly with the First Cohort of the 12th, which had suffered heavy losses, not from blades, spears, or even arrows, but by the relentless pounding of rocks, and the river itself. The stranded *quadrireme* was now a hulk that, in Hirtius' inexpert opinion, was beyond salvage, but he had taken advantage of their own bombardment on the redoubt with the five artillery ships to send two smaller *triremes* to transfer the men, both of the 12th, and the surviving crew of the *quadrireme* to safety. Now he was relatively content to drop anchor in the river to await further developments, although he did worry slightly that Caesar wouldn't agree with his decision to honor this truce request, unaware that the same thing was happening on the western side. He had ordered a small boat to be made ready, in the event that the Pandyans sent someone out through the southern gate down to the docks, although he wasn't sure whether he would risk going himself in that event.

Meanwhile, the exhausted men of the 3rd, 10th, and 25th had retreated back to the edge of ground between the beach and the wall, where their Centurions allowed them to sit in place, while the *medici* of the reinforcing Cohorts were pressed into service to tend to the wounded of the front line Cohorts, their counterparts already occupied with the evacuated wounded back on the withdrawn ships. As the men guzzled down the contents of their canteens, this being their first real opportunity, and talked quietly among themselves, Caesar was conferring with the Primi Pili, standing a short distance away from the second line Cohorts, who had been ordered to remain standing and alert. The four men were understandably facing the city, but they were all pointedly ignoring the muttered complaints of the rankers, and Pullus couldn't help give Spurius a grin, knowing that since these were his men, his friend wasn't happy at the moment, although at the same time, Pullus was ignorant of his own impending comeuppance from his friend and fellow Primus Pilus.

"Do you think they're just trying to buy time?" Torquatus asked Caesar, and while he didn't dismiss it, the general's answer indicated he didn't think it likely.

"I think that they're coming to terms with the reality of their situation," Caesar answered. "And, whoever is in command has to make the decision about the fate of not just his men, but the people inside those walls. It," he finished quietly, "isn't a position I'd like to be in."

This surprised the others, although none of them said anything, and their attention was drawn by a flurry of movement on the wall immediately above the gateway. A moment later, one of the gates was opened just enough to allow a pair of men out, one of them holding a spear that had both a white piece of cloth, but also with what appeared to be some sort of branch with broad leaves wrapped around it. The other man was wearing armor, which was unusual in their limited experience with the Pandyans; it was the sudden glitter of a golden light around his head that gave the Romans at least a hint of the identity, something that Caesar intended to use. Once the pair was about a hundred paces from the gate, they came to a stop, clearly signaling their desire for Caesar to close the distance to them.

When he actually moved as if he was going to do that very thing, neither Spurius nor Torquatus even tried to object, leaving it to Pullus, who, as usual, blurted out, "Are you mad, Caesar? You can't go to them! Not that close!"

Caesar looked peeved, but he did stop, then after a heartbeat, nodded.

"You're correct, Pullus. However," he didn't point, but indicated the pair with their head, "it doesn't look like they're inclined to move any closer."

The impasse seemed destined to last for some time, but before Caesar could do anything to stop him, Pullus growled, "This is ridiculous, and it's too fucking hot to just stand here."

He was already walking towards the pair as he said this, and even if Caesar had been disposed to go after the huge Primus Pilus, his *dignitas* forbade such a thing; his men followed Caesar, Caesar didn't follow his men, even Titus Pullus. Caesar did open his mouth to call out instructions, then thought better of it, certain that Pullus knew what to do, but if he had known what was going through Pullus' mind, he wouldn't have been so sanguine.

"What the fuck have I done?" Pullus muttered to himself, his eyes going from the pair outside the walls to the men lining the rampart, the top part of their bows visible as they rested them on the stones, which he chose to take as a good sign. When he stopped, it was still a good distance away, but he relied on the power of his lungs as he came close to shouting, ignoring the pain in his throat from the effort, "Do you speak Greek?" For an instant, his heart dropped when the man who was obviously some sort of royalty didn't answer, which was exacerbated when he shook his head. Pullus was about to unleash a torrent of curses; then, he remembered Achaemenes and what he had learned with these people, so instead, he continued, in Greek, "My name is Titus Pullus. I am the Primus…" he stopped himself, knowing this would have no meaning, "…I am the Centurion who commands one of Rome's Legions. I speak on behalf of my commander Gaius Julius Caesar, Dictator for Life as appointed by the Senate and the People of Rome." While he knew that this noble wouldn't really know what a Dictator was any more than a Primus Pilus, Pullus was also taking a gamble that, being royalty, the longer the title, the more impressed the man would be. And the Pandyan did react, but he quickly learned the title had nothing to do with it.

"That," the Pandyan, who Pullus saw was young, giving him an idea who it might be, "is Caesar? Standing there behind you?" Pullus automatically began to nod, but then caught himself, verbally acknowledging this instead. The Pandyan countered, "Then why are you standing here, and not him?"

To Pullus, it was obvious, but this time, instead of using words, he felt confident that pointing up to the archers on the rampart would be sufficient to inform him, and he was rewarded by a look of chagrin on the young man's face.

"I understand," he said, and even with the distance between them, Pullus heard the rueful tone. "I will have them withdraw from the wall."

"That's not good enough," Pullus countered immediately. Then, on another impulse, he explained, "It was my Legion who your archers punished on the beach, so I know how skilled they are. Just because they are not on the wall does not remove the danger from my general."

The young Pandyan actually smiled slightly at this, giving Pullus the impression that he was pleased at the Roman's frank admission.

"What do you suggest, then?"

It was a sensible enough question, but Pullus immediately realized that he hadn't thought that far ahead, so it was his turn to feel embarrassed.

Finally, he replied, "How about we split the difference between us? You come another hundred paces, and my general will meet you there, because it's a hundred more paces from where he's at now?"

Suddenly, he had another idea, which he quickly explained, the young Pandyan listening intently. Then, surprising Pullus, he said, "That is acceptable. I will return."

Waiting just long enough for the pair to turn and walk back to the wall, Pullus spun about and trotted back to Caesar and the other two Primi Pili, while Caesar regarded him with a look of consternation.

"What did you say to them, Pullus? Why are they going back into the city?" he demanded, but he listened as Pullus answered, and by the time he was finished, Caesar was offering his Primus Pilus a slight smile.

"That's an excellent idea. So," he turned and began moving back towards the rest of their men, "let's get ready."

It wasn't quite a third of a Roman watch later when the gate opened again, except this time, the young Pandyan brought six men with him, while Caesar approached from the opposite direction, also accompanied by six men, his three Primi Pili and two other men who, while they wore the same transverse crest, was red compared to their comrades' white, while the last man of the party could hardly be called that, being in his teens. Between the two parties, at roughly the point Pullus had suggested, an awning had been erected, under which was a small table and chairs. The youngster was carrying a jug in one hand and balancing a tray with three cups with the other, announcing the role he was playing, yet despite the fact that none of the men on either side were armed, both parties slowed slightly as they approached this meeting place. Slowing, however, isn't the same as stopping, but then Caesar made a small gesture that stopped the men with him as he walked the rest of the way to stand under the awning.

He broke the awkward silence by saying, in Greek, "You are Crown Prince Nedunj, I assume, son of King Puddapandyan, ruler of what you call the Pandyan people?"

The young prince had been slowly walking towards the awning, having issued the same command to his companions, but he came to a stop, and despite being shocked that this Roman knew who he was, he managed to sound unruffled as he replied, "Yes. And you are Gaius Julius Caesar, Dictator for Life, as appointed..." He stopped suddenly, temporarily forgetting the rest of what the giant Roman, who he had instantly recognized as being the same man he had watched cutting his men down, had said in his introduction.

455

Fortunately for him, it was less than a heartbeat before he recalled, "...by the Senate and People of Rome." Then, before Caesar could respond, he asked pointedly, "Forgive my ignorance, Gaius Julius Caesar, but if I recall correctly from my lessons, Rome is very, very far from here, is it not?"

"It is, Your Highness," Caesar answered smoothly, more amused at the idea that this youngster thinking he could put him on the back foot. Deciding that two could play the game, he said in a cheerful tone, "But we Romans like to travel."

Nedunj smiled, but that was all he did, then apparently deciding to get to more important matters than trying to put his opponent off balance, saying, "Here are my five hostages. They are all high-born and play an important role in my father's administration. This," he pointed to the sixth man, "is Lord Alangudi, my chief councilor, who will attend to me while we talk."

Caesar nodded, then indicated his group. "These men are all officers under my command. The three wearing white crests are in command of one of my Legions, while the two with red command one of the units in those Legions."

"What about him?" Nedunj pointed at the youth who, he could clearly see, wasn't Roman, and if his guess was correct, was from Bharuch. "Is he going to be your councilor?"

He also noticed that the boy was trying to hide behind the large Roman, but it never occurred to Nedunj that there might be something other than the man's size and fierce countenance that was the reason for it.

Caesar actually laughed at this and answered readily enough, although it was a lie. "While I do not know his name, he is here simply to attend to our needs. He has brought refreshment, and he will be happy to fetch whatever you desire while we are talking."

Nedunj didn't really care, having deduced the boy's role; besides, he was more interested in the fact that this Caesar seemed determined to act alone, without an aide of any kind. It was curious, certainly, but it wasn't enough to keep Nedunj from turning, and in quiet Tamil, ordering the five men who were anything but high-ranking lords to go to the Romans. They did so readily enough, but two of the men were muttering to each other as they passed the Romans, completely ignoring the youth, who seemingly did the same, standing there with the blank expression worn by slaves and servants of every nation. Once the Pandyans were beyond the awning, the Roman hostages began walking past, although there wasn't a word exchanged, nor did they even bother looking at the prince and his companion. Nedunj's eyes were riveted on the huge Roman, the feeling of an almost smothering hatred so powerful that it took an effort for Nedunj not to at least snarl a curse at the Roman. Who, clearly sensing the eyes on him, turned to look Nedunj directly in the eye as he walked by, and when their eyes met, the hatred Nedunj felt was joined by an equally powerful, and in some ways more visceral fear. *Is this what Shiva looks like?* he wondered, then tore his gaze away as the Roman passed without a word. They were heading to where they would be within easy range of the Pandyan archers, the understanding implicit that, if things went badly, they would be cut down before they made it to safety.

"Please," Caesar extended a hand to the chairs on the wall side of the table, and as Nedunj took his seat, Caesar beckoned to the boy, saying in Greek, "Pour the crown prince, Lord Alangudi, and myself a cup of wine, boy."

"Yes, Master," the boy mumbled, also in Greek, but this didn't strike Nedunj, or Alangudi for that matter, as unusual, although it did confirm that the boy was from Bharuch.

He poured the dark liquid into each cup as the three men watched in silence, but when he stepped away from the table, neither Nedunj nor Alangudi made any move to pick up their cups. Rather than be offended, Caesar smiled slightly, then picked up his cup and took two long swallows before setting it down.

"I didn't realize how thirsty I was. I cannot imagine you feel any differently," he said, and despite himself, Nedunj was impressed not only by the Roman's flawless Greek, but how Caesar appeared completely unruffled to be sitting there, surrounded by the corpses of both Romans and Pandyans.

Somewhat reluctantly, Nedunj did pick up the cup and take his first sip of the wine, and as soon as it touched his tongue, he could tell that it was of a quality that was only used by his father for occasions of state and banquets with important lords because of the expense. And, he realized with some chagrin, Caesar was correct, he had been quite thirsty, so that before he could stop himself, he drained the cup. Alangudi seemed determined to hold out, but he correctly interpreted the glance his prince gave him, although when he drank, it was only a sip and nothing more. Immediately after Nedunj drained it, Caesar glanced over his shoulder at the youth, who quickly stepped forward and refilled the prince's cup, and when he stepped back again, the fact that he moved to a spot where he was behind the two Pandyans seemed a natural thing to do, which neither Nedunj or Alangudi noticed.

"What is it you wish to discuss, Prince Nedunj?" Caesar asked.

"How much will it cost for you and your army to leave our lands and never return?" Nedunj answered immediately.

Caesar didn't appear surprised, because he wasn't, suspecting something of this nature, but he countered, "Why would we do that, Your Highness?"

It was taking quite an effort for Nedunj to maintain the same cool demeanor as his foe, but he managed to sound dispassionate as he ticked off the reasons. "First, while I acknowledge that you *might* take this city, Caesar, the one thing I can promise you is that it will be at a terrible cost to your men." Pausing, he gauged the Roman's reaction, then, frustrated by what he saw, he went on, "The second reason is that taking Muziris and holding Muziris are not the same thing. And third, I am certain that you are aware that, while my wife's father King Abhiraka has the aid of a substantial portion of our army, which," he added, "I suspect is the reason you are here now, my father and our army will not be with the King forever. In fact," he spread his hands, "perhaps my father and his army are already on their way back."

Caesar listened silently, mainly because he was taking the measure of the young prince, and while his face didn't show it, he was quite impressed by the Pandyan. It is, he thought, a good assessment of the situation. When Nedunj finished, Caesar didn't reply immediately, his face revealing nothing as he sipped from his cup, appearing to consider the prince's words, and the silence dragged out.

"This dog is bluffing," Alangudi muttered to Nedunj, careful to use their common Tamil tongue. "There's no way he can hope to take the city and keep it."

Caesar certainly didn't understand what the prince's aide said, but Barhinder did, although he was careful not to move or even breathe loudly, having been forgotten by the two Pandyans. Suddenly, the Roman looked at him, but raised his cup as he did so, and the youth understood immediately, stepping forward to refill Caesar's cup.

"Thank you," Caesar said, in Latin. "Do they think I'm bluffing?"

At first, Barhinder was thrown, not by the words, which he understood, but by Caesar's inflection in posing the question as a statement, although he quickly recovered, answering, "Yes, Master."

Nedunj, not understanding a word of the exchange, was suspicious, although there wasn't anything tangible that he could point to for that feeling.

Finally, Caesar returned to Greek, starting by saying honestly, "That is a very astute observation, Your Highness." He paused, then added, "And you have given me much to think about. Essentially, your proposal is to offer up an amount that will be sufficient to convince me to load my men aboard my ships and leave, is that correct?" When Nedunj indicated that it was, Caesar asked, "And in what form would this wealth take? Gold? Silver?"

Slightly encouraged that the Roman seemed interested in talking details, Nedunj answered readily, "We have both, along with precious stones, pearls, valuable jewelry in large amounts." Using the only gesture that seemed to be universal, he finished with a shrug, "How you choose to receive it can be discussed."

"That sounds acceptable," Caesar replied. He paused to take another sip, but while Nedunj was certain this was a tactic, there was no way he could be prepared for what came out of the Roman's mouth. "However," Caesar began, "I am afraid that I must ask one…delicate question." For the first time, Caesar made it a point to look Nedunj directly in the eye, and while the Pandyan prince had heard that there were people with blue eyes, he realized that knowing it and having them staring at you was completely different, and he found it quite unsettling. "Are you proposing to use the funds from your treasury? Or from the portion that King Abhiraka's wife, Queen Hyppolita sent along with your wife's brother and Abhiraka's heir and other sister last year, before we arrived outside Bharuch?"

It was Alangudi's misfortune to have decided to finally take more than a sip from his own cup, and Caesar's question caused him a choking fit that was sufficient to alarm Nedunj, despite the prince being in the same state. Before Nedunj could react, Barhinder moved to the table from his spot to pound the Pandyan nobleman on his back, leaving the prince to grapple with this sudden shift on his own.

"How…how could he have known?" Alangudi managed this between coughs, in Tamil of course.

Nedunj was relatively certain that he knew the answer, but he managed to stop from blurting the name, choosing instead to reply softly, also in Tamil, "I think my mother-in-law might be the source."

"You are aware that the city and the kingdom of Bharuch are currently under Roman control," Caesar's tone, while not harsh, had changed sufficiently that Nedunj was aware that matters had shifted. "And by the rules of war that are recognized by every civilized nation, the funds from the Bharuch treasury now belong to Rome. In essence, you are attempting to bribe us with funds that rightfully belong to us already."

Nedunj's head was reeling, but he retained enough of his wits to snap, "You are assuming that King Abhiraka and my father have not driven you Romans from Bharuch."

"That is true," Caesar replied blandly. "I am assuming that very thing. However," he held up a hand in a placating gesture, "I bring this up not as a point of contention, but as an example of how there is much to think about. Which is why I am proposing that we extend this truce for a full day, when we will meet here at this spot again, and I will give you our answer. Is that acceptable?"

"Only if your army returns to their ships and waits offshore. Both of them," he added pointedly. "Including the one that found the real mouth of the river and is about to assail our southern wall."

Momentarily forgetting, Caesar shook his head, but he quickly realized his error by the look of surprise on the prince's face, prompting him to speak more harshly than he intended. "That is not happening, Your Highness. I will not surrender what ground we have gained." Suddenly, Caesar's expression changed, and he regarded Nedunj in a manner that the prince couldn't have identified, even if they had been better acquainted. "Who decided on the strategy you used, Your Highness? To fight us at the water instead of waiting for us to attack your walls?"

Nedunj didn't answer immediately, but after thinking it through, he didn't see how it could hurt, so he answered simply, "That was my idea."

"It was," Caesar said with the utmost sincerity, "a brilliant strategy, Your Highness, and I commend you for it. The only other time any of my men have faced that was many years ago, when we sailed to Britannia. In fact, only one of the Legions that landed today was present for that, but it gave us many problems then. Although," he added firmly, "we were successful in landing there as well. So no," Caesar finished firmly, "I will not give up this beach." Before Nedunj could reply one way or another, he added, "What I will agree to is to allow your men to carry your dead and tend to those wounded who are still alive back into the city. As you can see," he turned and indicated the area behind him, "we are already quite busy with that ourselves, and you have my word that we will not try anything. Provided, of course, that you do the same." For the first time, Caesar stood up and thrust his arm out. "Do we have an agreement?"

As Caesar stood with his officers, watching Nedunj, Alangudi, and their five hostages enter back into the city, before anyone could say anything, Caesar turned to address Pullus, but he was pointing at Barhinder.

"You need to thank young Gotra here that you and the others aren't spending the night inside those walls," he said, which unsurprisingly caused Barhinder to turn even darker as he flushed.

"Oh?" Pullus asked in surprise.

"I'll let him explain it," Caesar answered, and when Barhinder saw that he was the sole focus of attention, not just from Caesar, and Pullus, but the Primi Pili and the Legate Pollio, for a horrifying moment, Barhinder was certain he would vomit.

Somehow, he managed to answer quickly enough that it wasn't noticed, explaining, "When their hostages were walking by, two of them were talking in Tamil about how much Nedunj was paying them to pretend to be high ranking lords."

"Pluto's cock," Torquatus gasped. "Those devious bastards! That way, they could have chopped us, and they wouldn't have lost anything!"

"Which was why I told Nedunj that I was releasing them to return with the prince," Caesar explained. "And he was honor bound to do the same, although I know that he didn't like it. Which," he concluded, "tells me that they indeed had some plans for you."

Pullus could only stare at Barhinder for a moment, then he reached out, not to cuff him or tousle his hair, but as a Roman man, offering his arm as he said sincerely, "Thank you, Barhinder. You probably saved our lives, and I know I'll never forget it."

It took some effort to keep the ear to ear grin from his face, but Barhinder managed to look solemn as he imitated what he had seen the Romans do, immediately realizing two things; that his hand barely covered the inside of Pullus' massive forearm, and if he had been grasping a warm piece of iron the same size, he would have been unable to tell the difference. The moment was made more special as, one by one, Spurius, Torquatus, and the two Pili Priores did the same thing, while Caesar looked on. Then, he went on to explain the terms of the truce, finishing by turning to Pollio and ordering him to send a dispatch rider to find Hirtius, giving him instructions to remain in place, but aboard ships. He knew this wasn't going to be a popular decision, not so much because of being aboard, but because the city was so tantalizingly close, and he knew that his men had worked themselves up into a frenzy about the wealth that was stuffed inside the walls of that city, just waiting to be plucked. That this was actually true wasn't something he had any intention of sharing yet, although he was also fairly certain that Pullus knew this was where Abhiraka's treasury was located. By the time Caesar was finished issuing his instructions, the gates to the city had opened up, and men, all unarmed, began filing out, whereupon the general was persuaded that it would be prudent to withdraw a couple hundred paces back towards the beach. Now that the tide was fully in, the ships along the beach had to deploy their anchors, although the water under the bow wasn't more than a foot, while all along the beach, the section slaves and *medici* had begun streaming ashore. They would be out in the open for a night, but Caesar had been serious about refusing to give up the ground that had been won at such cost, although in the end he had agreed that the Romans would stay to the west of the entrenchment. There was naturally quite a bit of tension when the Pandyans first emerged, and the Centurions and Optios were placed along a line paralleling the entrenchment but well short of it, to stand in between their men and these Pandyans, with strict orders by Caesar that the men, many of whom had lost comrades and perhaps kin earlier on this day not be allowed to take matters into their own hands. And, for a brief span, Pullus and the others were worried that violence might erupt, because the Pandyans seemed equally disposed to resume the fighting. Fortunately, in the end, the two battered foes were more like dogs who had fought to a bloody draw and were content to snarl at each other but unwilling to resume the fight. As the sun began to set, a semblance of a camp was created, with fires built, although they had to be shared among several sections instead of just one, with men breaking out the rations brought ashore by the slaves. After some discussion by the Primi Pili and Pili Priores, the decision was made that those men who had either died on the beach or had succumbed to their wounds after being taken aboard one of the ships would be brought back to the beach so that their comrades could prepare their bodies for the funeral rites, although none of them had any idea how or even when they would be held. It was a macabre, but to many of the men still living, an appropriate site as men were wrapped in their *sagum* and placed on the beach in neat rows in rough approximation of their spot in the formation when they had landed, although they were all placed above the high tide line. To Pullus, it was also a gut-wrenching reminder of the cost of this battle, and while he had no doubt that, if Caesar and the Pandyan prince couldn't reach an accommodation, they could take this city, he had every intention of telling Caesar that his boys were out of that fight. Let those Legions who never landed bear the brunt of the fighting for this city, he thought with a fair amount of bitterness. It hadn't been until after the truce and Caesar's meeting before Pullus had time to go check on each of his Cohorts, but the fact that he went directly to the First Century of the Second was no accident, nor did it go unnoticed by others, although none of them would have made a comment about it. He found Scribonius, but while he was relieved to see that his friend only had a light slash right above his left greave, it wasn't until he saw the lean Gregarius who was almost his height before Pullus felt the tension leave his body. Porcinus' back was turned to him as he talked to the men from his section, and while the men facing him saw their Primus Pilus approaching, they obeyed his gesture, pretending to continue the conversation.

"You better have a good fucking reason to be standing there fucking off, Gregarius," Pullus growled, and as he hoped, Porcinus actually hopped in surprise, but with a yelp of pain that Pullus instantly heard.

Which, of course, his comrades thought was hilarious, but when Porcinus spun around, he was clearly favoring his side, causing Pullus to examine his nephew more closely, finally finding the slight rent in Porcinus' chain mail, directly under his right arm.

"What the fuck is that?" Pullus demanded, using anger to hide his anxiety.

"It's nothing," Porcinus insisted, but when Pullus suddenly grabbed his arm to lift it away from his body, he couldn't stop another groan from escaping.

Pullus, all humor gone, bent down to inspect the wound, but while he saw that it was in fact not serious, appearing to be a shallow cut that, while it managed to break some links, hadn't penetrated enough to drive the links into his nephew's body, he still wasn't happy.

"Have you seen the *medici*?" he demanded, getting his answer by Porcinus' expression, who protested, "Primus Pilus, it's really nothing. There are a lot more men hurt worse than I am."

"There are," Pullus seemingly agreed. "But they've all been seen to by now. So," he extended an arm, "go find a *medicus* and have him look at it. Now."

Knowing that, while this was his uncle expressing his concern, they were in the presence of others, Porcinus stiffened to *intente*, rendered a salute, albeit with a wince, then spun about and marched off. Once Pullus was certain that Porcinus wasn't just going to wander off, he walked over to where Scribonius was now seated on the ground, his helmet off, and talking to his Optio. When he saw

Pullus approaching, he made to get up, but Pullus waved him back down, although he didn't speak until, getting the hint, the Optio moved away, and Scribonius learned why when, in a low voice so he couldn't be overheard, Pullus explained what was happening.

Scribonius listened, then as Pullus hoped, he asked quietly, "Do you want to know what I think?" It was a sign of Pullus' fatigue that he simply nodded, and his friend noticed this but didn't comment on that, saying instead, "I think that Caesar's realized that he's bitten off more than we can chew, and he's trying to figure out a way to get out of this mess."

Although this was exactly what Pullus had deduced, it didn't make him feel any better that Scribonius agreed with him, and in fact, he had been hoping that his cerebral friend would have seen something else in Caesar's actions.

Heaving a sigh, Pullus didn't drop to the ground, but he did kneel down on one knee as he agreed, "That's what I think as well." They were silent for a moment, then Pullus added, "We're spread too thin, Sextus. And I know that he has the ultimate power, but at some point, those bastards in Rome like Cicero and what's left of his bunch are simply going to refuse to send more men."

"And they'd be right to," Scribonius replied, still keeping his voice down. "Titus, what are we doing here?"

Prior to this moment, Titus Pullus could be counted on to be Caesar's staunchest defender, finding justification for his actions that, while perhaps not accepted by his comrades and counterparts, at least made sense.

Consequently, Scribonius' surprise was second only to Pullus himself when, before he could stop himself, he admitted, "I have no idea, Sextus. I truly don't."

They fell silent then, which was what enabled them to hear, from behind them out on the water and over the hissing of the surf, the sound of a horn.

"That's not the change of watch," Scribonius frowned. "It sounded like the signal of something coming."

Both men came to their feet, shielding their eyes at the half-orb of the sun on the western horizon as they searched the part of the sea to the north that was empty of ships, and it was Scribonius who spotted it first.

"There! There's a sail!"

It took Pullus an extra heartbeat to spot it, which Scribonius was quick to hoot about, and as he knew it would, irritated Pullus, who hated being bested at anything; of course, this was why Scribonius reveled in the moment.

"It's probably just a fishing boat, or maybe a merchant vessel," Pullus said dismissively, and Scribonius didn't argue, knowing this was most likely, but they were both wrong.

Pullus was rolled up in his *sagum*, trying to catch some sleep, thankful that at least the breeze coming from the water was strong enough to keep the bugs away. Both Diocles and Barhinder were ashore, curled up on either side of him, but while he was dozing, Pullus felt as much as heard the pounding footsteps of someone running, causing him to sit upright. Out of the darkness, a figure materialized, and Pullus recognized that it was a ranker from the First of the Tenth of his Legion, who had been given guard duty since they hadn't been involved in the day's action.

"Primus Pilus," the man was panting, making it hard to understand him, "someone came ashore from the general's flagship. He's ordering you and all the Primi Pili to attend to him aboard the ship!"

Naturally, Pullus was on his feet in an instant, but when Diocles tried to get up to help, he assured him there was no need, and he only snatched up his *vitus* as he went trotting down the beach. Caesar's flagship was still in the same place the *Navarch* had guided it earlier in the day, but someone had placed one of the assault ladders against the side, which Pullus used. He saw that Spurius and Torquatus were already there, the deck lit by several lamps, and he joined them as they headed to the cabin at the rear of the ship.

"Any idea what this is about?" Pullus asked, but while Torquatus shook his head, Spurius replied, "I know that a Liburnian showed up just before dark. I'm guessing that it has something to do with that."

Entering, they saw that Pollio was present, but so was Clustuminus, and it took an effort on Pullus' part not to grin, having already heard that the 8th's task of trying to find a northern approach that wasn't across boggy ground had failed, and all the Legion had to show for it was being caked in mud and covered in bug bites, something that made Pullus inordinately happy. Caesar, somewhat unusually, wasn't present, and they passed the time by whispering to each other, but other than the knowledge that a ship had arrived, and that it belonged to Rome, nobody knew anything. When the door opened behind them, they all turned to see him stride in, looking slightly embarrassed.

"I apologize, especially to you three," Caesar began, indicating the three Centurions whose Legions had led the assault. "I know you're tired, but a short while ago, a Liburnian dispatched by Ventidius reached us, carrying some vital information that, frankly, changes everything." Naturally, every man present was suddenly paying close attention; while Caesar paused, this time it wasn't to build the drama but to reread a scroll on his desk, and to Pullus, it seemed as if their general was still struggling with what was contained there.

Finally, he was ready, and he began, saying bluntly, "The Pandyan king Puddapandyan is dead." Not surprisingly, this created a buzzing of conversation, but as they quickly learned, this was perhaps the least impactful news. "And," Caesar continued, "so is King Abhiraka. Bharuch no longer has a king."

Although this certainly was important to everyone, the news hit Pullus with the force of a punch to the gut; such was his distress that he didn't notice that Caesar was looking directly at him. Once the initial excitement died down, Caesar proceeded to explain what was known to the Romans at this moment, how Abhiraka's forces had managed to infiltrate the city, ignite the caches of naphtha that, not surprisingly, wrought a great deal of destruction to the four areas where they had been stored, and how the attack only failed because the Pandyans had refused to join their allies in attacking the city, effectively stranding Abhiraka and the remnants of the Bharuch forces, save for his armored elephants, within the walls. Ventidius had been very thorough in his report, describing for Caesar how they had come to learn about the death of the Pandyan king, from one badly burned prisoner who had been a member of Abhiraka's bodyguard, and, if his story was to be believed, had been one of the men who smuggled the king out of the city a year earlier. He also informed Caesar that it was by way of this secret tunnel that this man and one other companion had smuggled Abhiraka out of the city that they managed to sneak back inside the walls, and with the help of parties still unknown to Ventidius, had located the stores of naphtha placed at each of the four walls. Caesar didn't deem this crucial information, leaving it out as he explained to his Primi Pili that this had substantially changed the situation. Exactly *how* it changed things, Caesar didn't say, something that, despite his distraction, Pullus noticed, although his thoughts were consumed with the knowledge that Hyppolita was a widow.

"How does this effect the situation with this prince?" Spurius asked.

"That," Caesar acknowledged, "is a good question. Does it help us? Or does it hurt us? That's what we need to determine."

"One thing it means," Torquatus offered, "is that we've got a large army that, if our information is correct, hasn't suffered any losses."

"You're right," Caesar acknowledged. "The question there is..." He turned to the large map hanging on the wall. "...where are they now? And how soon can they get here?"

Chapter 11

Maran knew how much he was hated at this moment, but it didn't stop him from pushing Pandya's army ruthlessly, and it wasn't restricted to the animals. Men who fell behind on the march were given one chance, and only one; if they straggled a second time, the only thing they had to look forward to when they rejoined the army was a painful death. To his surprise, both Vira and Sundara fully supported him, the three of them clamping an iron discipline on their men, but part of the cause for the discontent among the two-legged members of this force was that every resource that might have gone to them was spent on the four-legged animals, as long as they were part of the corps of elephants. The reason for that was simple enough; although all three Pandyans had heard from Abhiraka, Damisippos, and almost every man of the rank and file from the Bharuch forces about the horrific weapon the Romans used that rendered the most powerful force in the known world to nothing more than flaming, sizzling pieces of meat, they had no other choice. The result was that the army of the Pandyan kingdom moved as quickly as it was possible for them to move, where the period of rest was regulated not by the men but the elephants. In an effort to speed up their progress, Maran took a calculated risk by allowing the elephants to march unencumbered, which forced the army to commandeer every cart and wagon they came across, although this wasn't a large concern as long as they took these things from the people of Bharuch. It didn't take long for it to become more than wagons, as some of the animals inevitably broke down because of the pace and replacements were needed. Then, their food supplies began running low, since both kings had calculated that by taking Bharuch, the needs of the Pandyans for their return would be sufficiently served by stores from the city. This was when Abhiraka's decision to lay waste to his own kingdom came back to haunt the Pandyans, and Maran was forced to take harsh measures to force the villagers in their path to reveal the secret caches of food that every noble knew peasants maintained against times where the harvest was bad. Abhiraka had known this as well, but he had steadfastly refused to go to that extreme, contenting himself with destroying this year's crop. While Maran took no pleasure in their actions, neither did he hesitate, and the result was that the army continued to move at a pace that, frankly, he would have never believed was possible until circumstances forced them to do that very thing. The only obstacle was the town of Kalliena, when the Pandyans had been surprised at the presence of well-armed and well-equipped men who, while not Roman, had clearly declared their loyalty to Rome. Vira had been certain that these men were from Parthia, something that his counterparts found difficult to believe, but Vira had actually been to Parthia when he was a young man, accompanying his father on a diplomatic mission sent by Puddapandyan, where a trade deal was negotiated. The manner in which the Pandyans discovered that the town wasn't defenseless like it had been the first time, while not particularly costly, stung nevertheless, as they lost more than fifty men of the party who had been sent to the town. When the survivors returned to the army, Sundara had insisted that they avenge the deaths of their men, but in this he was overruled by Maran, with the support of Vira. It wasn't until they had crossed into the northern reaches of the Pandyan kingdom when they ran into the first tangible bit of news after they stopped a small merchant caravan, heading north to Kalliena, part of the everyday commerce between the two kingdoms that the Romans had, after a brief cessation, allowed to resume. Maran, Vira, and Sundara were using the shade of a banyan tree when four men were brought to them, and while they were anxious, seeing the three officers and recognizing them as Pandyans put them more at ease. And, Maran in particular took great care to treat them cordially, even taking the time to offer them refreshments before beginning their questioning.

"Our scouts who stopped you did so because you're coming from the south," Maran began. "And, since we're returning after a long absence, we simply wanted to talk to you about how things are in our kingdom."

As he suspected would be the case, there was one man to whom the other three immediately looked, and he was the one who answered, "Things are...unsettled, Lord." Pausing to stroke his beard, Maran could see he was choosing his words carefully, and he heard Sundara, who was seated next to him, mutter irritably, but before the impatient nobleman could interject, the merchant continued, "While we haven't seen it with our own eyes, Lord, we have run into too many people to count who say the same thing."

Once again, he fell silent, and now it was Maran who grew impatient, but he managed to keep this veiled, asking, "And what are all of these people saying?"

"That those Roman demons landed at Honnavar and attacked without provocation." For the first time, the merchant looked nervous, and Maran noticed that his eyes kept flitting to Sundara. "And," he actually closed his eyes as he added, "they captured the city."

This brought all three Pandyan officers to their feet, which in turn caused the four merchants to begin shifting nervously, and it took an effort on Maran's part to assure them, "We're not angry with any of you, and you won't be punished just for telling us this news." Returning his attention to the first man, he asked, "What else do you know?"

This time, the merchant made no secret that he was worried more about Sundara than either Maran or Vira, and when Maran glanced at his counterpart, he saw that Sundara's hand was actually on his sword, and while Maran knew this was likely an unconscious reaction, he couldn't rule it out completely that Sundara was considering slaughtering these men. Consequently, even as he knew it ran the risk of exacerbating the situation, Maran reached out and placed a hand on Sundara's arm. Fortunately, this not only startled the other officer, it seemed to make him realize what he had done, and he dropped his hand from his hilt.

Only then did Maran turn back to the merchants, and there was no mistaking the relief on their faces, although their leader was still clearly nervous, but he said readily enough, "We heard that the Romans put every man, woman, and child in Honnavar to the sword, my Lord. But," he held up a hand, "we only heard that from two men traveling together, and not from anyone else."

Although Maran understood why it made the merchant nervous to relay this piece of information, he actually didn't believe it, and he saw that neither did Sundara or Vira, simply because of what they had witnessed while with Abhiraka and how the Romans had treated his people.

"They didn't do that," Maran assured the men. "We were in King Abhiraka's kingdom, and while we didn't enter Bharuch, we learned from the villagers and men like yourselves that this isn't how the Romans do things."

While he could see that this eased their minds, Maran inadvertently created another small crisis with his mention of the monarch of Bharuch.

Encouraged by the manner in which they had been treated, the merchant asked, "Speaking of kings, is King Puddapandyan nearby? We," he turned and indicated the other three, "would be most honored to pay our respects to our own king."

Maran heard Vira's sharp indrawn breath, while on his other

side, Sundara shifted, and although he couldn't see his own face, he was certain that it displayed something that caught the attention of the merchant, who looked to Vira, then Sundara.

"Is there something wrong?" the merchant asked cautiously. "Is the king ill?"

"Yes!" Vira spoke up, shaking his head vigorously and adopting a grave expression as he repeated, "Yes. I am afraid that is true. He's very ill and is being carried in one of our wagons."

"We're trying to get him home," Maran put in, thankful for Vira's quick thinking. "Before…" His voice trailed off, but he saw that the four men understood.

"We'll give offerings for his recovery, then," the merchant said, and with this small crisis averted, Maran returned to the subject of the Romans.

"And the Romans are still at Honnavar then?" he asked, and the merchant agreed this was the case, at least as far as he knew. "How long ago did you run into these people who told you this?"

The merchant thought for a moment, then glanced over his shoulder, and it was one of his companions who supplied the answer, "Four days ago, my Lord."

Satisfied that they had learned all that they could from this group, Maran thanked them and offered them a piece of advice.

"Kalliena is also occupied by troops who fight for Rome, but they're not Roman," he told them. Indicating Vira, he explained, "Lord Vira is certain that they're Parthians, but Parthians who are now part of the Roman army. I can't guarantee that they'll behave the same way as the actual Romans do when you reach Kalliena."

Bowing, the merchants offered their own thanks and were escorted back to their wagons and the other people with it, leaving the three officers to talk, although it was a short conversation.

"We," Maran said grimly, "are going to Honnavar first."

At the same time the next day, the gates of Muziris opened, and when Nedunj and Alangudi reappeared, they were accompanied by the same man who bore the flag of truce the day before, but as Caesar and his officers stood on the opposite side of the awning, which had remained standing, they saw that nobody else was accompanying them out of the gate.

"I suppose they decided that trying a ruse with hostages a second time wasn't in their best interest," Pollio commented wryly, and the other Primi Pili chuckled, all of them secretly relieved that they wouldn't have to worry about this.

The other difference on this occasion was that it was all of the Primi Pili, and Aulus Hirtius as well, who were present for this, the officers of the southern arm of the assault taking advantage of the truce, and the high tide, to be rowed through the narrow passage that gave the river its name, at least to the Greeks. Caesar had informed them beforehand that he was going to base his actions on how the Pandyans behaved, and the first sign that matters weren't quite as tense as they had been the day before was the absence of hostages.

"I won't be needing any of you as hostages, and I'll be meeting with them in the same manner I did yesterday."

He turned and was beckoning to Barhinder, who Caesar had expressly commanded to be present again, so it was Pollio who cleared his throat in a manner that got their general's attention.

"It appears that they have other ideas about who'll be serving refreshments this time, Caesar," Pollio pointed to where a slight figure, darker even than Barhinder was hurrying to catch up, but that wasn't the only difference; this was clearly a female, carrying a tray balanced on her head in a manner that betrayed almost a lifetime of practice, steadying it with one hand while in another, she carried a jug that was quite a bit larger than the one Barhinder had brought the day before.

Caesar was irritated, but he was also amused, and he gave Barhinder a smile as he said, "Well, young Gotra, it appears that you won't be spying for me today."

"Y-yes, Lord," the boy stammered, but his composure wasn't helped when he heard a growl behind him that he had long before learned belonged to Titus Pullus, and he knew why, so he attempted to correct himself, "I mean, yes, sir. And, I am sorry, sir." Seeing Caesar's expression, he mistook it, and felt compelled to explain, not in Latin but Greek, not wanting to make another error. "I obviously was not careful enough for them to have discovered this."

"It's not your fault, young Gotra," Caesar assured him; this was all the time he would devote to this topic, seeing that the prince and his councilor were now about the same distance away from the canopy as he and his officers. "I suggest that you go wait in the shade. This may take a while."

He didn't bother looking back to see if he was obeyed, striding towards the table, eager to get under the shade himself since he had decided to continue wearing his armor. It wasn't that he thought it necessary, but his officers had protested so strongly he decided that it wasn't worth the trouble, and now he could feel how his tunic, cotton as it was, was now saturated with sweat. He had surreptitiously mopped his face with a cloth just after Nedunj had emerged, but he could already feel the beads forming on his forehead, which caused him to quicken his stride a bit, wanting to avoid the appearance that he suffered in this climate. This seeming imperviousness to things that bothered other men was such an integral part of being Caesar that he had long since stopped thinking about, or even being aware of these small acts he carried out to perpetuate the idea that he wasn't like other men, mortal men. It wouldn't be much longer after this that the whispers would begin among the men of the ranks, now salted with other nations, that Caesar *was* different, that perhaps he *was* a god. At this moment, however, he was a Roman, Dictator for Life, and he was about to negotiate what might be the most important agreement of his life in terms of his larger ambition.

"Your Highness, I see that you have decided to bring the refreshment this time. And," for the first time, Caesar actually examined the servant, instantly noticing that she wasn't wearing cotton, but a silk garment that was dyed more colors than he had ever seen before, yet as striking as her clothing was, it didn't detract from her beauty, which Caesar noted, "I will confess that she is much more attractive than the young man yesterday."

Nedunj, who seemed, if not more relaxed, a bit refreshed, actually smiled as he countered, "And while she speaks Tamil, she doesn't understand Greek. Or," he added cheerfully, "perhaps she does. It is so hard to remember."

Caesar understood what Nedunj was doing, and he laughed heartily at the subtle manner in which the prince was informing him that he knew Barhinder had served another role, but he also was an expert in exchanges of this sort.

"Well, yesterday, you tried to fool us by dressing up men of your lower class as members of your nobility," Caesar replied, careful to maintain the same bantering tone. "So I suppose that makes us even, does it not?"

"It does," Nedunj agreed; only then did he take his seat, Alangudi following suit. Once Caesar took his own, Nedunj turned and beckoned to the girl, in Tamil, and as she approached, asked Caesar, "May I offer you some refreshment of our own making, Caesar? It is not wine, but I believe you will find it pleasing."

"As long as it's not *sura*," Caesar answered, and now it was Nedunj's turn to laugh, while even Alangudi chuckled.

"Ah, I see you have experienced *sura*," Nedunj said genially, and Caesar, remembering not to nod, admitted ruefully, "Yes.

Once."

"This is not *sura*," Nedunj assured him, then paused as they watched the girl who, Caesar could see, was aware that the three men's eyes were on her and, if he was any judge, was accustomed to such attention. The liquid was light in color, although it wasn't clear, and Nedunj explained, "This is actually a mixture of the juice of some of the fruits that grow here in our kingdom, but we serve it fresh, not fermented."

Once the cups were filled, they all reached for theirs, except that, while Nedunj was prepared to do as Caesar had the day before, the Roman made sure that he lifted it to his lips first and drank deeply, while looking the prince in the eye. The message was unmistakable, and just as Caesar had been the day before with the young prince, this act had a similar impact on Nedunj, which he signified with a slight lift of his cup and a nod before he drank.

Normally, Caesar was indifferent to food and drink, but his eyes widened slightly as he tasted the beverage, and when he set the cup down, he exclaimed, "By the gods! That is truly one of the best drinks I have ever tasted. Not even Cleopatra ever offered anything like this."

"I am happy that you are pleased," Nedunj responded, and he meant it. However, he was also here for another reason, and he turned to it, asking, "Now that you have had time to consider our offer, have you come to a decision?"

"I have," Caesar replied calmly. "I am afraid that I cannot in good conscience accept these terms." This brought both Nedunj and Alangudi to their feet, but Caesar held up a hand and, his tone not modulating at all, added, "However, I do have a counterproposal that I think you might be interested in."

Nedunj took his time sitting back down, and he was forced to grab Alangudi's sleeve and yank him back down to his seat, muttering something in Tamil to his aide, but Caesar immediately turned to the girl, who was hovering in almost the exact spot Barhinder had been in the day before, so while he didn't know exactly what was said, he could tell by her expression it was something that was unusual.

Gathering himself, Nedunj said, "Very well. We will listen. But," his voice hardened, "please understand that we will never surrender our freedom to you, Caesar."

"Actually," Caesar answered immediately, "that is exactly what I'm offering you."

Although it took two more days of negotiations, by the time Nedunj stood and, copying the Roman fashion, which he had seen them do in the days previous, offered his arm in acceptance of the final terms, he was certain that he was living in a dream, and the changes to his fortunes, both personally and for his kingdom, were almost physically dizzying. He had learned on the second day that he was no longer the crown prince of Pandya, he was King Nedunj, and while Alangudi had argued vehemently that this Roman was lying, somehow he was certain that Caesar was speaking the truth, although he had verbally stated that he needed independent confirmation. That, however, was just the beginning of it, because Caesar, acting in his office of Dictator for Life, had bestowed Friend and Ally status of Rome and all that came with it, which began with a trade agreement for Pandya's most profitable export of spices, with terms that were very favorable; indeed, they were quite generous compared to any other agreement Pandya had with the other nations, even the equally distant Han Empire. In exchange for that, Nedunj would surrender the contents of Bharuch's treasury, which as Caesar had surmised, was what Nedunj was planning to use as the bribe to send the Romans away. This wasn't something that would cause the young king much trouble with his remaining nobles, especially now that Subramanian was dead. Nor would the annual tribute payment that he would pay to Rome damage his kingdom's economy, because the one sticking point had been about when that payment was due. During the back and forth, which grew even tenser than when Caesar seemingly rejected Nedunj's proposal, this was one area where Alangudi's advice had held sway.

"He wants us to pay first, before we see any return from our spice trade," he argued the night before.

"But with the terms he's offering, our tribute payment will be less than what we're going to make!" Nedunj protested, but Alangudi was unmoved, pointing out, "And what if that payment never comes? We'll have already given up money, and we'll have nothing in return."

This, Nedunj had realized was true, and while Caesar clearly didn't like it, or at least appeared not to, he had agreed that the first Pandyan tribute payment wouldn't be due for one year, and it was contingent on receiving the first payment from Rome for the spices that would be traveling the thousands of miles to the most powerful city in the known world. What neither Pandyan knew was that this payment would be coming much earlier than they could have anticipated, because the money wouldn't be coming from Rome, but from one of two sources, which was the only thing Caesar had yet to decide, whether it would be Egypt or Parthia's treasury that supplied the money. This was also something of a test of the young king and whether he could be relied on to honor his part of the agreement, although in one sense it was the other major piece that Caesar was most concerned about. At the end of the second day, Caesar didn't inform his officers of the proposal he had offered, saying only that negotiations were ongoing, but when they were dismissed, Caesar called Pullus back, and the Primus Pilus suspected that he knew the subject, certain that it had been building for some time.

And, as Pullus acknowledged to himself afterward, Caesar was full of surprises, because what he asked was, "What's your opinion on the qualities of the men of Pandya in terms of their fighting abilities?"

It actually took Pullus a couple of heartbeats to mentally switch his train of thought, and a few more to consider the question.

Finally, he offered, "The Bharuch men were better trained, I'll say that. And," he acknowledged, "they were better equipped and it's certainly more similar to us than the Pandyans. Although," his mouth turned down into a frown as he thought more about it, "I'll say that the Pandyans put up more of a fight. The Bharuch men..." He finished by shrugging, "I think that they were counting on those fuc...those elephants to save them. And once they saw them go up in flames, it took much of the fight out of them."

Although Caesar agreed in general terms, he also felt compelled to point out, "Couldn't it have been the way we destroyed the animals that did it?"

This, Pullus acknowledged was true enough, and the Pandyans hadn't been subjected to the powerful weapon two days earlier, which made him think a little more about Caesar's question.

Deciding to take a measure of small revenge, Pullus posed a question to Caesar, "Did you notice that none of their spearmen wore anything more than boiled leather vests for armor? And they only carried spears?"

"Why, yes I did, Pullus," Caesar replied, slightly nettled that Pullus could think that he would miss something like that. As soon as the thought came, he realized that the Primus Pilus was repaying him in his own coin, which he signaled with a slight smile and nod, then actually thought about the question, understanding there was a point to it. "Perhaps," he mused aloud, "they're not sturdy enough to wear armor? Is that what you're suggesting?"

"Something like that," Pullus nodded. "Although it could have as much to do with the climate as anything. The gods know that we've had a rough time of it. Before the other day, I've had more men down from the heat than anything else since we took Bharuch."

"Why do you think the men of Bharuch bear up better?" Caesar countered, genuinely curious what Pullus thought, because when it came to the practical matters of leading men under arms, while he would never say as much, Caesar respected the opinion of his giant Primus Pilus more than any other man in the army, including his Legates.

Since Pullus had thought about it, he offered, "I suppose it's because ever since Alexander, they've been accustomed to wearing armor from the first day, even if it is bronze, but clearly, these Pandyans don't use it because they don't need it." He paused for a moment then added, "Although, it's even worse here with the heat and wet than it is even in Bharuch."

"So," Caesar mused, "you think it's just a case of getting these Pandyans accustomed to wearing our type of armor, is that what you're saying?"

"They're about the same size as we are," Pullus agreed, then colored slightly at Caesar's snort, "or, most Romans are, and they're certainly not physically weaker." Then, unable to restrain himself any longer, Pullus asked bluntly, "Are you thinking of doing what we did with the Parthians, Caesar?"

"No," Caesar replied immediately, "I'm not thinking about it. I've made the decision already."

"Which means," Pullus said almost to himself, "you have no intention of stopping."

Caesar regarded Pullus a long moment, his expression inscrutable as he intended, before he finally answered quietly, "No, Pullus. No, I don't."

"Then, if we're going to be calling a *dilectus*," Pullus said, completely unsurprised, "I'd rather have to train the men of Bharuch than these Pandyans."

It was something in the manner in which Caesar reacted that warned Pullus that there was something he was missing, and the feeling intensified when Caesar suddenly looked away, seeming to prefer studying his feet. Nevertheless, he spoke readily enough, in a flat and emotionless tone.

"If that was possible, I'd agree, Pullus, but it's not possible." When Pullus didn't respond, he glanced up to see that the Centurion didn't understand. "Pullus, when Abhiraka made his last stand, his men chose to stand with him, and they were cut down to the last man.

And the men we captured last year that we used to man the fleet I'm not willing to free, at least not yet." Shaking his head, Caesar concluded, "There's not enough men to fill our ranks from Bharuch. Otherwise, I'd do it."

Pullus remained silent for a moment, finally understanding, and he ruthlessly forced himself to keep from thinking of Hyppolita, and all the people in Bharuch who would be sharing in her grief at losing a loved one.

Suddenly, Pullus heard Scribonius' voice inside his head, reminding him of something, which prompted him to ask, "Caesar, may I offer you an idea?"

"It depends," Caesar answered bluntly. "If that idea is how I take this army back to Parthia on the way back to Rome, then no, you may not."

This caused Pullus to grin, certain now that Caesar had no idea of what he was about to propose. And, within a matter of heartbeats, he was rewarded by the look of complete surprise on Caesar's face, which quickly transformed into intense interest.

Finally, when Pullus was finished, Caesar was smiling, and he said with utmost sincerity, "Pullus, that may be the best idea you've ever had."

Once the details had been finalized, Caesar again summoned the officers, and while he didn't show it, he had a case of nerves, understanding that the first few moments would create the most uproar, but he was certain that once he explained everything, his Primi Pili would be satisfied in every sense.

"The cause for the delay in the negotiations," Caesar began, "was in working out the details of the agreement that I've concluded, in the name of Rome." While seemingly straightforward, Caesar was acutely aware of what many of his men, of all ranks, thought. "And this will be very profitable…for all of you."

Unsurprisingly, this aroused the interest of both the Centurions, and Pollio and Hirtius, and Caesar proceeded to explain the details. When he announced that he was offering Pandya the status of Friend and Ally, while it wasn't an uproar, it was close, and it was Clustuminus who thrust up a hand first, which Caesar had anticipated, both that this would be the moment, and who the most likely to object would be.

"How are we supposed to tell our boys that the bastards who slaughtered the 7th and 11th are now our friends?"

"We'll start by reminding them that, while the Pandyans were involved, it was at the direction of King Abhiraka, who was slain trying to retake Bharuch. Unsuccessfully," Caesar added.

"That won't be enough," Clustuminus interjected flatly, and while Caesar was irritated at the interruption, he also noticed that the heads of the other Primi Pili were moving in the same direction.

"I am aware of that, Clustuminus," Caesar's tone was cold. "Which brings me to the second point." He paused, exacting a small revenge by making them wait. "I've decided that I will turn over the contents of Bharuch's treasury that was moved here to Muziris last year, to the army here in India, just as I promised them last year."

The astonished silence was supremely satisfying to Caesar, but it wasn't long before Balbinus asked, "How much will that work out to per man, Caesar?"

"That," Caesar answered truthfully, "I don't know with any certainty. However, based on the figures that I was given by Prince..." He caught himself, "...King Nedunj, if they turn out to be accurate, my estimate is that it will be around five thousand *drachmae* per Gregarius. Naturally, the sums will increase for the officers."

The assembled Centurions weren't as silent at this, although the reaction was essentially nonverbal as they alternately gasped in shock, muttered something to themselves or to the man sitting next to them, all of them trying to grasp what was a staggering sum. For men who were paid three hundred *denarii* per year and given that a *drachma* was roughly equivalent to that Roman currency, this would be more money than most of these men had ever dared dream about, at least in one lump sum. Certainly, they had enriched themselves in Parthia, and after the fall of Pattala and Bharuch, but in the manner of most soldiers, the majority of the rankers had managed to gamble, drink, and whore a substantial portion of that away. This, they all understood, was on a scale that only those men like Pullus, who had been with Caesar in Gaul, could truly appreciate.

"Where are our men supposed to spend all this money?"

It was Spurius who posed the question, loudly enough to cut through the chatter and, as quickly as the noise had erupted, it died down, almost as if Caesar had commanded it.

Caesar had been expecting this, but it was still a serious and potentially explosive question, which he answered by saying quietly, "Here, Spurius."

"So," Felix spoke up, not disguising his bitterness, "is this your way of telling us that we're going to be stuck in this place for..." He spread out his hands, "...how long, Caesar? How long are we going to be stuck in this *ca*chole?"

"For as long as your general commands it," Caesar didn't raise his voice, but every man present recognized the tone, that this was Caesar at his most dangerous, when he felt as if his authority was being threatened, "and for as long as men's enlistments are still valid."

It was at this moment that Titus Pullus truly began to wonder whether Caesar had ever intended to be satisfied with just subduing Parthia, because shortly before their departure from Brundisium, now close to four years earlier, Caesar had taken the unusual step of ensuring that none of the Legions had less than ten years remaining on their sixteen-year enlistment. At the time, it had just struck Pullus, and the other Primi Pili, as an example of Caesar's peculiar obsession with details that seemed unimportant. Now, as he sat in the gently rocking cabin witnessing this tense exchange, Pullus had a sick feeling in his stomach, and he wanted the meeting to end so that he could go talk to Scribonius and Balbus.

Felix clearly realized that he had pushed their general as far as he dared, and he was the one to break eye contact with Caesar, who waited briefly before resuming, "I'm also going to offer the men something in exchange for money." This refocused the attention of his listeners, and he went on, "I'll give them the option of taking a portion of their bonus in goods and not in cash."

"Goods?" Flaminius spoke up, clearly puzzled. "What kind of goods? And what would they do with them?"

Caesar explained, and while not everyone was convinced, they were all clearly intrigued at the idea of investing in something exotic, and they all knew how much wealthy Romans and wealthy people across the known world were willing to pay for spices and silk.

With this matter disposed of, temporarily, Caesar moved on to different matters that were actually more pressing.

"King Nedunj has agreed to house our men in the two major cities, here in Muziris, and upriver at Karoura. But," his expression altered subtly, "before I'm willing to disperse, the King's chief councilor is going to be traveling north, looking for the Pandyan army, which we know abandoned Abhiraka to return here. As soon as Silva and the cavalry return from their scouting around Karoura, which should be tomorrow, they'll have a day to rest and refit, then they'll be accompanying the King's councilor and," he turned and indicated Hirtius, "the Legate to find the army, inform them that hostilities have ceased, and they're to return to Karoura. In the meantime, we'll set up the army on the southern side of the city across the river and on the eastern side, which I had Volusenus and his men survey and measure today."

The meeting concluded shortly after that, and while Caesar had been as thorough as always, Pullus was certain that their general was still withholding important information. That, he thought as he was rowed back to his own ship, is something for Diocles to find out.

The Legates stayed behind after the meeting, and while they knew more than the Primi Pili, they still weren't fully informed of all that Caesar had planned. This changed after Caesar refreshed himself from the jug of the juice mixture that Nedunj had given him as a gift.

"I want to tell you what I've decided to do with Pattala and Bharuch," he began, and the three men exchanged a glance, none of them missing the wording that indicated they weren't being asked for advice.

"We're stretched too thin," Caesar said bluntly. "And I'm not going to be sending for any more Legions. In fact, I've sent orders to Rome that Antonius is to hold a *dilectus* for two more Legions, one in Syria and one in Italia. But," he shook his head, "even with twelve Legions total, thirteen counting the *Crassoi*, there's simply too much territory to cover. Not," he seemingly added this as an afterthought, "with what I have planned." None of them were fooled at Caesar's casualness, but neither were they willing to be the one to address this. Caesar turned to the wall behind his desk and picked up a large, rolled map made up of several pieces of vellum stitched together, and hung it in place of the map of Muziris and its environs. The sight of this map elicited a gasp from the Legates, because it was something they hadn't seen before. "As you can see," Caesar indulged in a bit of dry understatement, "our men have been quite busy these last few years." While it wasn't a full map of Parthia, with the twin cities of Ctesiphon and Seleucia placed on the far left and closer to the top, it still gave an accurate and impressive representation. Picking up a pointer, Caesar indicated Ecbatana first, explaining, "While I believe that he already intends to, I ordered Octavian to winter at Ecbatana with the 14th once they take the city. Which," he added, "I'm almost certain they already have. Then, as soon as the weather changed, they were to return to Susa, where there will always be a Legion. And," he admitted, "I realize that I took a risk in ordering the 21st not to wait in Susa for Octavian and the 14th to return, but I have confidence that the auxiliaries from King Polemon and King Herod who I transferred from Ctesiphon will be sufficient for a few months." This came as no surprise to them, and seeing this, Caesar went on, "I'm going to have the 14th transferred here to India, although I haven't yet decided which Legion I'm going to send back to Susa, but it will most likely be one of the Legions in Bharuch." Moving the pointer, for the first time, Caesar sounded, if not unhappy, then troubled, "Which brings us to Pattala. Before Ventidius left to go to Bharuch, I had him inform their King Peithon that I was conferring on them Friend and Ally status as I have with the Pandya, in recognition of his upholding his end of the agreement I made with him after we took the city. Honestly," he shook his head, "Pattala isn't as important as I thought it might be, given its location on the trade route. But now that we've seen Bharuch, while it's farther south and makes it more inconvenient for the silk trade, it more than makes up for that with its access to the cotton, hardwoods, and the spices from the south. And, as long as we maintain control of Harmozeia and Barbaricum, Pattala is too far up the Indus to have any value as a resupply station. Which," Caesar moved the pointer down, "brings us to Bharuch. And," for the first time, when Caesar turned to face his most trusted subordinates, "I still don't know what to do about Bharuch." He set the pointer down, moved around to sit on his desk and asked, "What are your thoughts?" He turned to Pollio first. "Asinius? I know that you didn't have as much to do with Queen Hyppolita as our favorite Primus Pilus, but you had to deal with her for several months. What can you tell me?"

The question caused Pollio to shift uncomfortably, sensing that Caesar was asking about more than just the queen, which prompted him to ask, "What do you mean, Caesar? Tell you about what?"

"Whether Pullus fucked her," Caesar answered bluntly, the use of the vulgarity flustering Pollio exactly as he intended.

"I...I don't know, Caesar. Not," he added, "with any certainty. But," he allowed, "I know that they had become...close. He spent almost every day with her for months."

This was something that Caesar hadn't known, and his eyes narrowed as he asked sharply, "What do you mean?"

Pollio went on to explain how, about a month after Bharuch fell, Pullus had approached him about allowing the queen and her ladies to take a stroll inside the palace grounds. At the time, Pollio's main concern was that it did not create a burden for himself, which was why he granted the request. It was only a few weeks later that Pollio began to wonder whether this had been a wise choice, given that it was only Pullus who now had access to the queen. However, there had been no attempt on her part to make mischief or attempt to escape; if Pollio had been aware of the secret entrance, he would have indeed had serious second thoughts. Caesar listened, and finally, he held up a hand.

"It's clear that I have to talk to Pullus before I make the decision."

"And what would that decision be, Caesar?" Hirtius asked.

"Whether or not I appoint a Praetor and keep Queen Hyppolita confined, or whether she can be trusted to rule Bharuch in a manner that benefits us."

"But she's a woman," Hirtius protested, not seeing Pollio wince.

"So is Cleopatra," Caesar replied dryly.

He dismissed them shortly afterward, but while he considered summoning Pullus, he decided that it could wait a day or two. First, they had to determine whether or not the young King of Pandya had the kind of control over his generals that he claimed.

The work of constructing the marching camps, the corner of the southern one actually on the site of the redoubt, began the next morning, but instead of the normal grumbling, the men, while not eager, didn't mind the work because they passed the time discussing exactly how much money would be coming to them. And, as Caesar had understood, the fact that the money was coming from the Bharuch treasury was almost as important as the sum...almost.

"It took him awhile, but Caesar did live up to his promise."

This, and variations on this, were the most common theme among the men of every Legion, which was no accident; Caesar knew the value of judiciously placed silver in the right hands. As part of the process of settling in, the portion of the fleet anchored along the western wall sailed south to the real mouth of the river, returning upriver. Once the camps were constructed, the transfer of everything took another full day, yet despite the new treaty, Caesar bowed to the demands of the Primi Pili in constructing true marching camps, with ditch and wall. This offended King Nedunj, but neither could he argue since he couldn't guarantee that his returning army would honor the terms. As Caesar had said, the cavalry returned to Muziris, but their mounts weren't in good shape, and would require more than a day to recover. After some negotiations, Nedunj reluctantly offered up his available mounts, although it wasn't enough to equip the entire cavalry. Rather than wait, Caesar ordered that a reduced force ride with Hirtius and Alangudi, and he included a small, select party that he trusted with another task, something that Pullus in particular didn't care for at all.

Along with the extra artillery, Primus Pilus Crispus and his Legion had been given one *turma* of cavalry, which was the only reason he and the men of the 22nd had advance warning of a large force approaching from the north. The fight for Honnavar hadn't taken long, and while they had suffered losses, Crispus was happy overall with the condition of his Legion, although like all of his men, he was anxious to return to the greater security of the larger army. With a population of just under ten thousand, in Crispus' judgment, the town could be held with five Cohorts as long as they were provided with enough artillery, along with some defensive improvements, and of course, a sizable supply of naphtha. The garrison of Honnavar only had five war elephants, but one of them had to be killed by its handler, while the other four were now chained and secured in the large pen next to the barracks that housed the troops, never actually seeing battle before the garrison commander surrendered the town. As far as the assault itself, Crispus and his men, like their comrades outside Muziris, suffered more heavily from the Pandyan archers than they ever did against the Parthians, although the spearmen put up a stiff fight as well, and as the Romans knew, spears were the most effective weapon in the defense, particularly when defending a wall. Nevertheless, it took no more than two full watches before the surrender was offered and which Crispus accepted, despite some sentiment from his Centurions to slaughter the defenders, both two- and four-legged. And, under Caesar's strict orders, Crispus had limited the amount of looting his men were allowed to do, understanding that trying to prevent them from doing anything at all would have resulted in serious repercussions; besides, while he and his Legion hadn't been present in Bharuch, he had heard more than enough from his counterparts about all that had transpired. Consequently, he allowed his men one night to slake their desires, and aside from one isolated fire, he had been pleased with the behavior of his Legion. Now, three weeks later, the *turma* returned to the town; more accurately, the survivors returned after clashing with the leading elements of a huge force that could only be the Pandyan army, marching from Bharuch. Fortunately, Crispus had been forewarned that this was even a possibility, although it had only been the day before when a Liburnian rowed into the small harbor that was strikingly similar to that of Muziris, carrying a dispatch from Caesar, informing him of the situation in Bharuch and to be alert for the return of the Pandyans.

And, while he didn't go into details why, Caesar warned that this force would be at full strength, which was substantiated by the acting Decurion who had replaced the man who had fallen during what, to Crispus, sounded very much like an ambush. However, it wasn't his place, nor was he particularly interested in ascertaining the particulars of the matter; what mattered was that, according to the report, this force seemed to be heading directly for Honnavar, and there was a substantial number of elephants as part of it.

"The one strange thing," the acting Decurion, Gnaeus Vorenus, who had been Duplicarius, informed Crispus, "none of the elephants we saw were wearing armor, so maybe they aren't war elephants."

"Were they carrying or hauling anything?" Crispus asked, and he got his answer in the sheepish expression of the cavalryman, who replied, "No, Primus Pilus, they weren't."

"Then they're war elephants," Crispus assured him.

"We have enough of that naphtha *cac*, don't we?" Vorenus asked, not bothering to hide his concern.

"We have five hundred jars," Crispus assured him, but internally, he was already worrying about the prospect of facing the animals, which he kept from the cavalrymen, who he dismissed, then sent for his Pili Priores.

When they arrived, he wasted no time, explaining the dilemma they were facing.

"We have extra artillery, and we have naphtha," he informed his Centurions. "But what we don't have is a platform to put our artillery on. Not inside the town, at least."

There was no need for him to explain any further, since they all understood the problem immediately because they had confronted it when they scaled the walls of the town. The parapet of Honnavar hadn't been built to accommodate anything more than a line of men to stand there, with just enough room for men to pass behind them, and it was made of wood, as was the wall. At most, the rampart could accommodate a scorpion, but not with enough room for the crew to move behind it, which was required to operate it. The *ballistae* would have to be placed at a spot inside the walls where they could fling the naphtha at a high enough angle that there was no danger of one of the flaming pots striking the wooden wall, while the scorpions would be useless because of their flat trajectory, and the *ballistae* would be loosing blindly, relying on men on the wall to locate targets.

Finally, the silence was broken by the Secundus Pilus Prior, who only spoke up after being physically prodded by his counterparts on either side, saying, "We have the ships anchored here, Primus Pilus."

Crispus had been staring down at his desk, frowning in concentration at the message from Caesar, searching in the neatly incised lines for some sort of instruction, and now he looked up to glare at the Centurion.

"What are you suggesting, Libo? That we abandon the town?"

When put this way, it caused Libo to shift uncomfortably, but before he could reply, the Tertius Pilus Prior, Gaius Furnius argued, "If we don't have a way to fight those beasts off without burning this fucking town down around our ears, why would we want to try and hold it, Primus Pilus?" Crispus didn't reply immediately, and Furnius finished, "Besides, it's not like we're supposed to spend the winter here."

This, Crispus knew, was true, because Caesar himself had stressed that taking the town was an expedient measure while the rest of the army assaulted Muziris. As far as Muziris was concerned, Crispus had relayed what he knew to his Centurions, but this was an example where Caesar's brevity in passing on information came into play, because while they knew whatever happened at Muziris had resulted in some form of victory for the army, they had no idea exactly how it happened, or what it meant. Despite his irritation with his Pili Priores, once the idea was planted, Crispus couldn't force it from his mind. His initial idea had been to entrench around the town, creating a ditch and dirt rampart from which the artillery could be used with impunity, but with just a Legion and this Pandyan force arriving in as little as a day or two, he quickly discarded it.

Finally, he stood and announced, "We're going to withdraw to the ships, starting immediately."

Barhinder Gotra was terrified, exhilarated, and sorer than he had been since his first days of training as a swordsman for Bharuch. The terror stemmed from two causes; this was his first time on horseback, although with every mile, the fear slowly eased, but the second was the main cause for his distress. He had been ordered by Caesar himself to accompany the mounted party from Muziris to serve as a backup interpreter, along with Achaemenes, who rode beside him in the column and who, despite his earlier ambivalence, clearly liked Barhinder a great deal. In fact, everyone who came in contact with the youth did, with one glaring exception, and that was the Lord Alangudi who, apparently, hadn't forgiven him for his translation of the overheard conversation with the five "noble" hostages, and Barhinder would feel eyes on him, look up and see the Pandyan lord staring at him with a hatred that needed no interpreter. It was so blatantly obvious that, before the end of the first day, Barhinder had gained another protector, although the youth was almost as scared of this man as he was of Alangudi. Part of it, he understood, was for reasons the man couldn't really help; missing an eye that he refused to wear a patch over, so the scarred, empty socket was visible, would make any man look formidable. And, he was almost as large as Master Titus, but Teispes was a Parthian, which added to his air of menace. It wasn't until their third day, when Barhinder was literally weaving in the saddle and he felt a gentle but firm hand grasping his arm to keep him astride his horse, and he offered Teispes a smile of thanks, that Barhinder sensed there was more to the man.

Up to that point, Barhinder hadn't heard Teispes speak Latin, and had barely heard him utter two words in Greek, but now the Parthian said, in the Roman tongue, "By the time I was your age, I had spent more time in the saddle than walking."

Both surprised, and pleased, to have a chance to practice his Latin, Barhinder asked him why this was the case. For the next several miles, Teispes talked about Parthia, although in Greek, and he was quickly joined by Achaemenes riding on the opposite side, telling Barhinder about their homeland, and how, despite its desolation, it was a place they loved. As he listened, two things occurred; Barhinder forgot about his fatigue and sore muscles, and he felt a connection to these two men, one a decade older, the other more than two, because he felt the same way about leaving Bharuch as they did about leaving Parthia. The three of them, he realized with some surprise, were the same; yes, they loved their homeland, but they also saw in Rome, in the form of Gaius Julius Caesar, an opportunity to see more of the world, and to do things that few men would ever do. They were brothers in this regard, men who recognized that the future was ahead of them, even as they missed their past.

It was the next day that Barhinder finally worked up the nerve to ask Teispes, "Why did Caesar send you too, Teispes?"

Barhinder had learned that the Parthian never answered immediately, preferring to think before he spoke, but he also sensed that there was more involved this time, and he regretted asking, certain that he was forcing Teispes to possibly betray a confidence. Although he was partially correct, Teispes wasn't worried about Barhinder, or Achaemenes. He had perfected the ability to use his one good eye to its maximum extent, so while he appeared to be looking straight ahead, he could see that, just ahead of them at the head of the column, riding next to Legate Hirtius, Lord Alangudi had been trying to listen in on their conversation. Then Hirtius turned to say something to the Pandyan, and Alangudi soon became engaged in his own conversation.

"Caesar," he said softly, "has some concerns about our new ally."

Achaemenes leaned forward slightly to look past Barhinder, slightly alarmed, and asked in a whisper, "He's worried about King Nedunj?"

Teispes shook his head, then in a deliberate move, nodded it in the direction of Alangudi as he explained, "Our general thinks that he has some ambitions of his own." Suddenly, he turned to look not at Achaemenes, but at Barhinder. "That is why you're with us, Barhinder. Since you speak Tamil, he wants you to listen for anything that Alangudi says to whoever is leading their army." Seeing Barhinder's dark features go a shade paler, Teispes assured him, "That is why I am here, Barhinder. I will protect you, I swear it."

Suddenly, all the sense of adventure went out of this for Barhinder, but what replaced it was a resolve that he wouldn't fail Caesar or Master Titus. How exactly he was going to do what was expected of him, he had no idea. Hopefully, he would know what to do when the moment came.

Maran put the army in camp within sight of the walls of Honnavar, making no attempt to hide their presence. This was deliberate on his part, because he was now aware that the Romans occupying Honnavar consisted of only one of their Legions, which he had learned from a scouting party who had counted the ships in the harbor of the town. As often happened, the clash between the Pandyan version of the cavalry and their Roman foes was an accident; Crispus' suspicion that it was an ambush was only partially correct, since both forces essentially blundered into each other, although the Pandyans came out with lighter losses. It did serve to alert Maran that what the merchants had told them was true, since this was less than ten miles from Honnavar, and he sent a smaller scouting party to examine the town. Knowing that he outnumbered the enemy was why Maran made camp two miles from the town's eastern wall, with nothing but open fields between them. While his men were busy constructing their version of a camp, which didn't include defenses, nor did it have the organization of a Roman marching camp, he, Vira, and Sundara rode closer to the town, choosing to ride horses, drawing up far enough away that they were out of bow range, completely unaware that the Romans had artillery that could have conceivably ended their lives. Approaching from the east, their view of the harbor was blocked by the walls of the town, and after a brief discussion they rode south, towards the river which, unlike the Pseudostoma, emptied directly into the sea after running due west. They were close enough to see that they were observed by men wearing helmets standing on the town walls, and while the elite troops of Pandya did wear helmets, as did the officers like Maran and his counterparts, they knew that men stationed in a garrison of a normally somewhat sleepy town like Honnavar wouldn't. When they reached the point where they could see the harbor, they drew up, none of them willing to speak first because, while this was only a fraction of Caesar's fleet, the number of ships required to carry a Legion of Rome and its baggage was substantial enough to give them pause, all of them realizing that hearing how many ships and seeing them were two different things.

"Are you certain that there is only one of their Legions there?" Vira asked Maran, who didn't immediately acknowledge the other man.

Finally, he admitted, "No." Then he turned and gave both of his companions a level look as he responded in a challenging tone, "But does it really matter? We're going to attack them before we continue on. Or," he asked pointedly, "do you want to leave these dogs in our rear?"

As he expected, neither man thought this was a good idea, and it was Sundara who asked the practical question, "How are we going to take the town?"

"That," Maran acknowledged, "is a good question, my friend. But," he turned his horse, "I've seen enough to know that we're going to have to scale the walls. Which means we need to build ladders."

Returning to the camp at a trot, they arrived to a scene of excitement and turmoil, with men dashing about in a clearly agitated manner, but Maran didn't get the sense that it was from a threat. It wasn't until they dismounted and were walking to their tent when one of their subordinates, who had been left in temporary command came rushing up.

"Lord Maran! There is a mounted party approaching from the south! They are about five miles from here!"

Maran was already moving before the man was finished, heading for the rope enclosure where the elephants were held, and he got perhaps fifty paces away before Vira, after calling his name repeatedly, got him to stop. Stalking back to where the other two were standing with the junior officer, snarling, "What is it?"

Faced with the senior commander clearly angry, the junior officer hesitated, but Vira nudged him.

"Go ahead, tell him."

"One of the scouts who spotted these riders is Azhakan, Lord," the officer explained. "He was part of Lord Alangudi's household guard…"

"I don't care about some scout's connection to Prince Nedunj's friend," Maran cut him off, but Vira reached out and touched Maran's arm.

"You need to hear this, Maran."

Maran returned his attention to the young officer, who, bolstered by Vira's silent encouragement explained, "These horsemen aren't Pandyan, at least not completely, but Azhakan saw Lord Alangudi, and he is riding at the head of this force, Lord."

For a long span of heartbeats, Maran said nothing, staring at the young officer, then, before he made his decision, he asked, "How far are they?"

"When Azhakan sent one of his men back, they were five miles south," the officer answered.

"And how many men were there?" Vira asked, then, realizing he needed to clarify, "How many of them were Pandyan?"

"Half, Lord," the officer answered. "That's what the man Azhakan sent said. As far as how many?" Of this he was less certain, although he relayed, "Azhakan said five thousand men, but all on horseback."

Turning to Vira, Maran commanded, "Ready half of your men, Vira. Same for you, Sundara," he told the other man. "We don't have time to armor the elephants, but I'll have them prepared while we go see what this is about."

"Why," Sundara asked, "would Alangudi be with these Romans?"

"That's a good question," Maran allowed. "Which is why we're going to go find out, but with enough men that if we're walking into a trap, we can fight our way out."

Barhinder was alerted by Teispes, although not by what the Parthian said, but how he suddenly stiffened in the saddle, sitting up a bit straighter as he stared ahead and slightly off their left front quarter.

"There are men watching us," he said calmly, remembering to speak in Greek, but then nudged his horse into a trot to ride up the column next to Silva, who was on end of the rank of horsemen leading the way.

Meanwhile, Barhinder used one hand to shade his eyes, staring until they began to water before, finally, seeing some movement just at the base of a treeline.

Achaemenes was unable to see from his spot on the other side of the column, and he finally lost patience, demanding, "Well? What do you see, Barhinder?"

Part of Barhinder noticed that Achaemenes asked in Sanskrit, so he replied in the same tongue, "It looks like about twenty men on horseback."

Even as he finished, Silva, who had been given operational command by Caesar for moments such as this, suddenly called a halt, alerting the rest of the party that something was happening, and Barhinder turned his attention to where Hirtius was conversing with Alangudi. There was a fair amount of gesturing, and to Barhinder, it appeared as if tensions were growing, but after a discussion, the column resumed, while Teispes waited to fall in beside Barhinder and Achaemenes.

When, as was his habit, the Parthian said nothing, Barhinder, emboldened by his recognition that Teispes liked him, demanded, "Well? Did you tell them?"

Teispes glanced over at the youth, although his face gave nothing away.

"I did."

Then he fell silent again; if Barhinder had bothered to glance to his right, he would have seen Achaemenes grinning broadly, aware that Teispes was having some fun.

Finally, after more than a dozen heartbeats of silence, Barhinder couldn't take it any longer.

"What did Prefect Silva say?"

Teispes shrugged. "That it is up to the gods whether we die today."

"Die?" Barhinder squawked, suddenly alarmed. "Who said anything about dying?"

Now the Parthian turned to regard him for a moment, but while Barhinder had gotten to know Teispes, he was still coming to grips with the man's mordant sense of humor, and Teispes asked, "Why do you think those men are watching us, Barhinder? To inquire about our health?"

When put that way, Barhinder understood immediately; those men were clearly scouts and probably for the Pandyan force, watching them approaching. And, he realized in something of a revelation, there was nothing he could do about it, so worrying about what might happen was essentially pointless. Regardless, he was still unsettled, but he also resigned himself to finding out what lay in his future when it happened; it was another lesson for Barhinder Gotra in his new life.

They didn't stop, nor did they slow, but maintained the same steady pace for the next couple of miles. Barhinder had finally begun to relax when suddenly, without any kind of reason he could see, Prefect Silva suddenly called the halt, and despite his relative inexperience, he understood something was happening. Because of his position near the front, Barhinder could see both Hirtius and Alangudi, provided he leaned over slightly, but he was a bit too far away to make out exactly what was said, although he could tell by the cadence of their speech that they were conversing in Greek. He did see the Pandyan pointing ahead, which caused Alangudi to shift his attention to farther in front; what he saw made him gasp aloud.

"That is..."

Teispes finished for him, "...the Pandyan army that we are looking for. At least," he allowed, "part of it."

It quickly became obvious that Hirtius had prepared for this moment, because seemingly from nowhere, a spear materialized, upon the point of which was affixed a large square of white cloth, which was then handed to Silva, who took it without hesitation.

Only as the Prefect raised the spear did Barhinder hear Hirtius shout, in Greek, "Everyone stay here. Lord Alangudi and the Prefect are going forward. We will wait here for their return!"

"If he *does* return," Barhinder heard Achaemenes mutter, and he glanced in some surprise at his fellow translator.

"Why do you say that?" he asked in a mixture of curiosity and concern.

Achaemenes looked at him with some amusement, but he answered Barhinder directly, "Never underestimate other men's dishonesty, Barhinder. Or," he added, "their disloyalty. Like Caesar said," he reminded the youth, "Alangudi may have plans of his own."

Although Barhinder appreciated the honesty, he wasn't particularly happy about it, muttering, "Now I have something else to worry about."

Caesar Ascending - Pandya

Fortunately, for Barhinder and the mounted party sent by Caesar, Alangudi didn't have any deceit planned, at least for this meeting with Maran, Vira, and Sundara, all three of whom he knew, although he knew Maran better than the other two men.

Regardless of the seemingly peaceful atmosphere, the three Pandyans were clearly suspicious of their counterpart, their eyes shifting to Silva who, frankly, was certain that this would end badly. Once it became clear that the Roman and Pandyan had detached themselves from the other horsemen, only then did Maran acquiesce and nudge his own mount forward. Consequently, they met more than a hundred paces from their comrades, but once they were across from each other, Maran refused to be the first man to speak, which he had warned the other two would be the case.

"Lord Maran," Alangudi called out, once he realized this was the situation, and hiding his irritation. "I bring you greetings from King Nedunj."

This caused Maran and the other two men to visibly start, sitting more erectly in their saddles; how did Alangudi know about Puddapandyan? Unless, Maran thought with some unease, Nedunj *did* have his father murdered?

Instantly seeing and interpreting their reaction, Alangudi continued, "Yes, we know about King Puddapandyan's death. And," Alangudi was gambling now, "that this was already ordained to happen." Deciding to leave it to the vagaries of the divine, Alangudi continued, "What matters is that he is no longer king, and his son, *our* Lord Nedunj, is now King of Pandya."

Maran didn't turn his gaze away from Alangudi, but he was intently watching the reaction of Vira and Sundara out of the corners of his vision. When they both turned to look at him, Maran recognized that the decision was his, and his alone.

"It sounds," he said finally, "as if we have much to discuss."

"We do," Alangudi agreed, then looked up at the broiling sun. "But perhaps we should do it in a more comfortable setting."

Maran thought for a moment, then said, "Of course, Lord Alangudi. But," he pointed, not directly at Silva, but the column behind him, "I'm not sure that I'm willing to have that many Roman...Romans," he decided to forego the epithet most commonly used in association with them, "coming to our camp. Especially," he finished pointedly, "since you haven't explained why you're with them."

"That is certainly understandable," Alangudi agreed, appearing unruffled by this jibe. He turned to regard Silva for a moment, then gave a glance over his shoulder. "Only the Prefect here, Legate Hirtius, who speaks for Rome, the translators that came with us who can speak their tongue and ours, and," he seemed to consider, "twenty men, ten Roman and ten of ours, will accompany us to wherever you're camped. Is this acceptable?"

Maran thought for a moment before agreeing, and things proceeded quickly from that point forward. Trotting back to the column, Silva explained the situation, Hirtius allowing him to choose the ten men he wanted to go with him, which of course included Teispes, then made arrangements for the rest of the force. They would rest in the shade of the nearby forest, which unknown to them, screened their view of the Pandyan camp, while Hirtius, Silva, Alangudi, and their respective parties proceeded to the camp.

Barhinder was close enough to hear and had enough Latin to pick up when Silva said to the ranking Decurion, another Roman, "We may not be back for some time. Get the men settled, but I want you to be alert for any trouble. If we come back to you, we may be moving quickly. Fifty percent alert, and keep the horses saddled."

The Decurion saluted, then Silva returned to Hirtius and Alangudi's side. The smaller party resumed, and Teispes, taking pity on Barhinder, didn't take the opportunity for more fun, riding in silence, none of the other men seemingly interested in conversation. Because of their approach, they passed within sight of the walls of Honnavar, but while their view of the small harbor was obscured, Silva suddenly drew up, thrusting a hand into the air as he stared in that direction. Barhinder followed the Prefect's gaze, but he didn't immediately understand why even Teispes seemed, if not agitated, then suddenly alert to the point his hand dropped to his sword. Barhinder looked back to see the Roman engaged in what was clearly a tense conversation, and he turned to Teispes.

"What is it, Teispes?"

"No ships," Teispes replied readily enough, although this didn't particularly enlighten the youth, but before he could press the issue, Hirtius called out, "I need Achaemenes up here!" The young Parthian instantly moved his mount, but then the Roman added, "Bring the boy too!"

Like Achaemenes, he didn't hesitate, but Barhinder's heart was pounding so rapidly that he thought he might actually faint; fortunately, that idea was so mortifying that he managed to gather himself.

They were just approaching when Hirtius, addressing Alangudi but clearly asking the Pandyan named Maran, "What happened to the Legion that was here?"

If Lord Alangudi had any thought to engage his counterparts in Tamil, he was precluded from it by the presence of Barhinder, and judging from the poisonous glance he gave the youth, Barhinder was almost certain that he had planned on some sort of exchange he didn't want the Roman to understand.

It didn't help when, after a brief exchange, Alangudi explained, "There was one of your Legions here, but they departed at dawn," and Hirtius immediately turned to Barhinder.

"Is that what they said?"

"Yes, Legate," Barhinder answered, trying to ignore Alangudi's hiss of anger at this sign of distrust.

Hirtius considered for a long moment, seemingly oblivious to the tension as the four Pandyans stared at him.

Finally, he shrugged and said loudly enough to be heard, "If Crispus and his men left, they had a good reason for it."

Turning his horse, he resumed heading for the camp; after a brief pause, the Pandyans followed, going to a trot to draw even, the journey resuming, and they reached the camp a short time later. Whatever tension had been eased soon returned at the sight of what Barhinder guessed was several thousand men, standing on either side of the track that bisected the camp, watching in silence as the party reached the outer row of tents. Barhinder's experience with a Roman camp was limited, and the layout of the Pandyan camp was more familiar to him, although he did know that the largest tent would belong to the commander, located in the rough center of the camp. Reaching the large tent, which had two sides rolled up so it wasn't so stifling inside, the Pandyans dismounted first, while for the first time, Hirtius seemed uncertain what to do, and there was a short, muttered conversation with Alangudi, and while they were speaking Greek, Barhinder was unable to make out what was being said. What was impossible to miss was how Hirtius suddenly stiffened, then shook his head, which made both Barhinder and Achaemenes wince, knowing that the Prefect was inadvertently weakening whatever argument he was making. However, Alangudi was equally adamant, and even Teispes was so absorbed in whatever was taking place that he failed to notice that the Pandyan rankers who had watched them enter the camp had followed behind their party and were now surrounding them on three sides. Thankfully, Hirtius noticed this as well before he turned to address the Roman contingent.

"Dismount and go find some shade, but don't get out of

earshot," he spoke calmly enough, but Barhinder wasn't fooled; this was a tense moment, where behaving cautiously was the requirement. As Hirtius swung out of the saddle, he added, "Right now, Lord Alangudi is insisting on speaking to these men alone." He had said this in Greek, but then switching to Latin, he added, "He *says* that they'll be calling me in shortly, but these *cunni* are up to something. Which means," he maintained the same tone, as if he was issuing orders, "I'm going to need one of you who can understand these dogs to figure out a way to hear what they're saying." Switching back to Greek, Hirtius finished by addressing Alangudi, who was clearly furious, "We'll be waiting here...Lord."

Barhinder could see that Alangudi wasn't just angry, he was concerned, but while this gave the youth a deep satisfaction, he was also acutely aware that when Hirtius had issued the orders for someone to eavesdrop, it wasn't meant for Achaemenes, it was meant for him and him alone. Fortunately, he had had the presence of mind not to acknowledge that in any way when the Legate had issued his orders, although it didn't keep the Pandyan lord from giving both him and Achaemenes a suspicious scowl before he entered the tent behind his three countrymen. Nobody in the party was surprised when the first thing that happened was the two sides that had been furled were dropped into place.

"How," Barhinder spoke in Latin, trying to ignore the openly hostile stares of the Pandyans who, whether on orders or on their own initiative, had closed in around the dismounted party, "am I supposed to...?"

He didn't finish, and there was no need to, because, also in Latin, Teispes said calmly, "Leave that to me."

Then, without any warning, he turned, and leading his horse by the reins, he shoved one of the Pandyans out of the way with enough force to send him careening into two of his comrades, and the relative quiet evaporated into chaos.

"The Roman told his men to rest their horses in the shade," Alangudi informed Maran and the others as they returned to the tent after quelling the near riot. "And that large Parthian dog shoved some of our men who wouldn't move out of the way."

Maran had gathered that the one-eyed Parthian had something to do with it, but his Greek was scanty, so he had been forced to ask Alangudi what had resulted from the heated exchange with the Parthian cavalry officer who was fighting for Rome.

"That wasn't our men's fault!" Sundara exclaimed angrily.

"How were they supposed to know when those savages make their noise that sound like the babbling of infants?"

"I don't disagree, Lord Sundara," Alangudi replied, holding up a placating hand, "but these kinds of things are to be expected when we don't understand each other, wouldn't you agree?"

It was Maran who instantly sensed that there was more to Alangudi's words than what appeared on the surface, so he was the one who answered, "Yes, Lord Alangudi, we would." Shooting a warning glance at Sundara who, for once, indicated with a shake of his head he understood, Maran indicated the cushions upon which they sat for their meals and for discussions as he said, "So perhaps you could explain to us exactly what's happening, so there is no misunderstanding."

Alangudi sat down, but when Vira beckoned to the servant for refreshment, he said quickly, "While I appreciate the hospitality, lords, I'm afraid that the Roman outside isn't going to be willing to wait very long, and what I have to say is very important."

Then, without waiting for the other three to sit down, he explained the situation, about how their King had entered into an agreement with the Roman Caesar that, on its face, seemed to allow Pandya to retain some sort of autonomy, and in fact, if the Roman was to be believed, actually increase Pandya's power, at least in economic terms. The others listened intently, while to this point, Alangudi was being straightforward in his description of the terms and the situation facing Nedunj.

When he paused, Maran asked Alangudi, "How did Nedunj learn about his father's death?"

"From the Roman," Alangudi answered, then laid his first stone in the game of tables he was playing. He gave an elaborate shrug. "Now how else would this Roman know unless he arranged it himself?"

"Abhiraka told us that it was on the order of Nedunj," Vira interjected.

"Abhiraka is dead," Alangudi replied flatly. "He was killed in Bharuch...by the Romans."

"Because we abandoned him," Maran said quietly, but when his two companions began to protest, he added quickly, "and it was the right decision, obviously, given that this Caesar is outside Muziris." Returning his attention to Alangudi, he pointed out, "Clearly, you think those two things are somehow connected, Lord Alangudi."

"Isn't it obvious?" Alangudi countered. "Caesar arranged it somehow!" Seeing they were unconvinced, he allowed, "While I don't know exactly how he did it, this Roman made contact with the Prince and promised to make him king! And," he argued, "perhaps he persuaded Abhiraka to do the actual deed, in exchange for a promise that he would return Bharuch to him."

Maran held up a hand and interrupted, "That's not true, Lord. At least the last part. The Romans had every intention of defending Bharuch. And," for the first time, Maran betrayed his true feelings, his tone turning bitter, "we betrayed him when he needed us." Nodding, he finished, "So, while I can't dispute what you say about the possibility of Caesar somehow making contact with Prince Nedunj, it doesn't make sense that Caesar had an agreement with Abhiraka. Besides," he finished, "we were with him, up until the very last moment, and he expected the Romans to put up a fight. And they did."

Maran nor his two counterparts had any way of knowing that, while Alangudi was disappointed, he hadn't placed much hope in this first gambit, and he signaled his acceptance with a bow of his head.

"You're obviously correct, Maran. But that doesn't explain Nedunj's puzzling actions with these Romans."

"Puzzling?" Maran asked with a frown. "What do you mean by that?"

"Because," Alangudi lied, "we had defeated these Romans at Muziris and forced them back onto their ships." He leaned forward, understanding that everything relied on his ability to persuade these three men, and said, "We had *defeated* them, Maran! They were beaten! So," he sat back up and held his hands out, "why would Nedunj enter into an agreement like this? One where we agree to give up men to fight for these Romans, and *one hundred* of our armored elephants? For what?" He finished contemptuously, "A promise of more gold and silver? And that's only if this Caesar is good to his word!"

He stopped then, while Maran exchanged troubled glances with his comrades sitting on either side.

"So, Lord Alangudi," Maran asked after a silence. "What are you proposing? Exactly."

The three officers understandably listened intently as Alangudi made his attempt to seize the throne of the Pandyan kingdom; however, Barhinder didn't wait to hear their answer.

It wasn't much of a challenge for Barhinder to lose himself in the furor and chaos started by Teispes, then slip around to the opposite side of the tent, dropping down into a crouch and using some conveniently placed sacks and a barrel that servants had placed for easy access to serve the occupants, squeezing in between them. At first, it was difficult for him to hear because of the uproar, but he was unknowingly aided by Alangudi's intervention, the tumult dying down as Teispes, Silva, and the other men of the Roman party were allowed to take their mounts away, although it left him feeling quite exposed. Before long, he quickly forgot his danger, completely engrossed in what he was hearing, all of it in Tamil, as Alangudi essentially solicited the commanders of the majority of the Pandyan army to overthrow their new king. The fact that the youngster had the presence of mind to realize that, while it would be good to know how Maran and the other two men responded, the most crucial piece of information was that the councilor entrusted by Nedunj to convince these men to return and accept the new order would be something that not just Caesar would want to know, but the newly crowned King. None of this was in his mind at the moment; all he knew was that he needed to find Teispes and Silva, counting on them to know what to do. Where they and the others were wasn't hard for him to figure out once he stood erect and moved away from the tent; getting there was another matter, but after thinking about it a moment, he chose to take a more indirect route, actually moving in the opposite direction first, seemingly wandering among the tents. He didn't try to be furtive, using his youth and non-threatening demeanor to blend in with the other men, and he found it useful to pretend that he was simply one of the noncombatants who performed the same functions as the slaves and freedmen of the Roman army. Only once did he worry, when he felt a pair of eyes on him, watching as he crossed what was essentially the main street of the camp as he finished his journey to the clump of banyan trees at the outer edge of the Pandyan camp, but no command to halt came. It was Achaemenes who spotted him first when he happened to glance over his shoulder, and he immediately touched Teispes to alert the Parthian. Barhinder wasted no time, explaining what he had heard, but also that he hadn't waited to hear how the Pandyans responded.

"It might have been better to wait," Silva suggested, but Teispes shook his head.

"No." He was already moving to where the horses had been allowed to drink from a meandering stream that passed through the small copse of trees. "Because he needs to start riding, now." He paused, examining the horses, but Barhinder wasn't prepared for the Parthian to actually select his own mount and lead him over to the youth, handing him the reins. "You need to ride back to Muziris and alert Caesar and the King what Alangudi is attempting. Take Ninurta here; he will not fail you. And, Barhinder," he put both hands on the youth's shoulders, "I know that you can do this, or I would not have chosen you, I would have chosen one of the Romans."

Barhinder was frightened, but that wasn't why he protested, "What about the Prefect? Or Achaemenes? He's Parthian," he pointed out, needlessly, but his point was practical. "I've just begun riding! He is born to the saddle, remember? That is what you two told me when we were coming here!"

Teispes did look slightly embarrassed, but he shook his head. "Both the Prefect and Achaemenes will be missed immediately, Barhinder."

Swallowing the lump that threatened to come roaring up and out of his mouth, Barhinder tried to sound resolute. "Very well, Teispes. I will go."

Teispes helped Barhinder into the saddle, while Achaemenes hurried off, and the Parthian spoke, in Latin, "You will need to ride hard, Barhinder, but trust Ninurta, he will not let you down, and as long as you head south, he will go directly to Muziris."

Despite his trepidation, this intrigued Barhinder.

"How can he know how to get back?"

Teispes shrugged and admitted, "I do not know, but he has never failed." Patting the roan stallion's neck, he said fondly, "Even when I thought I was wrong, he would yank the reins out of my hands, and once I learned to trust him, I discovered he was always right. And," he added, "as long as you don't have to run him to escape trouble, he doesn't need as much rest as other horses. If you don't have any problems, you won't have to stop more than twice to rest him. Just make sure he has water and some grazing."

Achaemenes came back at a trot, with two water skins draped around his neck, and a small sack, which he handed up to Barhinder, who gratefully accepted it. Then, Achaemenes unstrapped his sword, his face solemn as he said, "Here. It is better that you have it and not need it."

Barhinder took the weapon, and if the other three men noticed his hand was shaking, they made no comment, then Silva gave the youth a grave nod, and without another word, smacked the horse on the rump, sending Barhinder on his way to deliver what might be the most important message of his life.

Hirtius came to find them perhaps a third of a watch later to report that Alangudi had supposedly convinced Maran, Vira and Sundara to return to Muziris with them, under the flag of truce, to receive their new orders directly from King Nedunj.

Silva, Teispes, Achaemenes, and the other men of the Roman contingent listened, but by silent assent, they actually let the Prefect among them ask, "And do you trust him, sir?"

"No," Hirtius answered flatly. "I can't explain it, but I know they're up to something."

"We can," Teispes assured him, then informed Hirtius of what Barhinder had overheard, which prompted the Legate to suddenly realize the youth was absent, becoming clearly concerned, but Silva assured him, "He's a few miles from here already, on his way to Muziris." Turning his attention to the more immediate situation, the Prefect asked Hirtius, "What's next, for us?"

"We're going to be their...guests tonight," Hirtius answered, then made a face that communicated how he felt about it.

"All of us?" Decurion Pindarus asked, one of the Galatians in what was still the most polyglot arm of Caesar's army.

"Yes," Hirtius replied sourly. "I tried to keep it to just us, but Lord Alangudi made it clear that since half of our bunch are Pandyans that he would take it is an insult and sign that I don't trust him if I kept them away."

"But we don't trust them," Pindarus objected, "and we have reason not to now given what young Gotra heard them saying!"

"I know that!" Hirtius snapped, then took a breath to say in a calmer voice, "But our hands are tied. So," he told Pindarus, "you're going to go get them and bring them back."

Waiting for the Decurion to salute, Hirtius watched the man mount then leave the shade of the trees before turning back to Teispes to ask, "Am I correct in assuming that we need to keep Lord Alangudi from noticing we're missing a translator as long as possible?"

"Yes, Legate," Teispes agreed. "We do."

It took some doing, but Hirtius, Silva, Teispes, and Achaemenes managed to provide Alangudi with a plausible reason on the occasions that the Pandyan lord asked why he hadn't seen Barhinder, and despite their concern, the night passed uneventfully, even if nobody slept particularly well. Their cause was aided by the uproar and tumult of an army preparing to break camp the next morning, but finally, when the Pandyans were formed up, there was no way for Alangudi to miss that Barhinder was absent. However, when he accosted Hirtius, the Legate could honestly say that, since he had been involved in the discussions the day before, he hadn't noticed. The Pandyan then kicked his horse and guided it to where the two Parthians were sitting their mounts, but while Alangudi took care to approach from Achaemenes' side, his eyes went not to Teispes, but his animal.

"That is not the mount you rode here," Alangudi said with a frown; he was obviously suspicious, but Teispes could see he didn't know exactly why.

"You have a good eye, Lord Alangudi," Teispes spoke in Greek. "And yes, you are correct. This is not my horse; I had to borrow it."

"Borrow it?" Alangudi echoed, clearly confused. "Why? Did your horse come up lame?"

"No." Teispes forgot and shook his head, realizing the error by Alangudi's initial reaction. "I seem to have...misplaced him."

Suddenly, a look of dawning understanding came over the Pandyan's face, and while he kept his voice low, the fury was there to hear.

"Misplaced?" he demanded. "Or stolen? By that...that *minion* from Bharuch?"

"My Greek is clearly not as fluent as yours, Lord," Teispes replied blandly. "So I must apologize. I do not know what a minion is." Suddenly, he turned to Achaemenes, his demeanor unchanged as he said, "Your Greek is better than mine, Achaemenes. Do you know what this word means?"

Achaemenes, understanding, barely managed to maintain his composure as he replied, "Yes, I do. It means..." He used the Parthian word, and Teispes' one eye widened slightly.

"Lord Alangudi, I can assure you that I know nothing about Gotra's...proclivities."

"*Where did he go?*"

Alangudi shouted this, his face contorted in rage, but his temper wasn't helped when Teispes offered a shrug and said simply, "Perhaps he missed his mother and took Ninurta and returned to Bharuch."

For a brief moment, a very brief moment, Teispes, Achaemenes, and Silva, who was watching, thought that Alangudi would do something that, depending on how Maran and the other two officers reacted, might have solved their problems or gotten them all killed. More than anything, it was Teispes who convinced Alangudi that striking down the Parthian would be easier said than done, simply by the manner in which he sat his horse, gazing calmly at the Pandyan, whose hand had dropped to his sword. Finally, Alangudi released an explosive breath, then savagely yanked the head of his mount around, and without a word, returned to his spot next to Silva. The thin wail of the Pandyan horn sounded, and the new allies began their return to Muziris.

Chapter 12

Teispes had proven good to his word about Ninurta, because Barhinder had no real memory of the last thirty miles of his ride. The reason for this was that, much to his surprise, he learned that it was possible to sleep while in the saddle, lulled by the swaying of the steady walk of the mount under him. He stopped two times, as Teispes had advised, taking care to stay out of sight, where he gave all of one water skin to Ninurta each time, while he consumed some of the food that Achaemenes had managed to scrounge for him, then sat down, leaned against a tree, and was asleep within a matter of heartbeats. Somehow, he managed to wake himself perhaps two-thirds of a Roman watch later, both times to see Ninurta cropping tender shoots of plants that sprouted underneath the larger, broad-leafed vegetation, but the first time, when he tried to get up, he let out such a loud groan that he worried it could be heard by some predator, although he was more concerned with the two-legged variety. It took him two tries to vault into the saddle, but he didn't even need to kick Ninurta, the horse immediately beginning to move, and in their same direction of travel, despite the fact that it was now the middle of the night. He tried to use the stars as his guide, but he quickly gave up, deciding to trust Teispes' mount, and at the second stop, he had learned his lesson and used a stump to get into the saddle. He was rewarded when, in the late afternoon of the second day, he was awakened by the sudden cessation of movement. Once he rubbed his eyes, he was shocked to see, no more than two miles distant and off to his right quarter, the walls of what he recognized was Muziris; he had done it! Immediately on the heels of that thought, the voice Barhinder heard in his head was his, but somehow older, and sterner. *No, you have not done it, not yet. Not until you warn Caesar and the Pandyan king, only then can you congratulate yourself.* That, he reminded himself, was what Master Titus would do. This time, he did have to nudge Ninurta to get him moving, but Barhinder's time alone wasn't long, getting no more than a half-mile when he saw the group of riders coming at the canter. Fortunately, it was the German Barvistus who was leading the contingent of Caesar's bodyguard, and he immediately recognized not just the Bharuch youth but Teispes' horse.

While he wasn't as close to the Parthian as his older brother, he was still concerned enough to demand from Barhinder, "What happened to Teispes? Why are you riding his horse?"

A greeting would have been nice, Barhinder thought, but kept that within his skull as he gave Barvistus a brief explanation of the events that found him traveling almost without rest to reach Caesar. To his credit, the German was listening as they rode back to the Roman camp on the eastern side of the city, following the road that bypassed the stretch of marshy ground that meant there wasn't even a gate on the northern wall, and which Caesar had used as the *Via Principalis* for the second camp. Waved through immediately, Barhinder didn't really have a chance to prepare himself for the idea that he would be in the presence of Caesar before he was escorted by Barvistus into the *praetorium*, whereupon he was taken by Apollodorus directly into Caesar's private office. Ultimately, it worked out for Barhinder, since he didn't have a chance to get nervous, telling the general why he was there and what he had heard between Alangudi and the three Pandyan officers.

The fact that Caesar didn't look surprised informed Barhinder that he had expected this or something like it, but he wasn't prepared for Caesar to suddenly stand and say, "Come with me, Gotra."

Naturally, he followed, although he was forced to almost run to keep up with Caesar and his longer legs. Barvistus was already outside, and whether or not he anticipated what his commander would need, or Apollodorus had hurried out to warn him, Barhinder saw that the horse named Toes was saddled and ready, but instead of Ninurta, there was another horse waiting.

"I had him sent to the stables to be rubbed down and given some oats and water," Barvistus explained, handing Barhinder the reins. "This is a spare."

Caesar waited only long enough for Barvistus to swing into his saddle, while the youth noticed for the first time the other men had never dismounted, then they were moving, except up the *Via Praetoria* to the *Porta Praetoria,* which was directly aligned with the eastern gate a bit less than a mile away. They went immediately to the canter outside of the camp, forcing Barhinder to grab on to his saddle, but when they arrived at the eastern gate, he was surprised to see them swing open, although he took this is a good sign. If he hadn't been near exhaustion, the youth would have been intensely interested in seeing the city for the first time, but he was surprised that the Pandyans didn't seem overtly hostile. They did look nervous, which he could understand, and once he did glance over his shoulder at a man who was attired in the rich robes of a merchant, and the look he was giving to the Romans behind their backs was decidedly different than the carefully neutral expression he had been wearing as they rode past. Pulling up in front of the palace, Caesar dropped down with an ease that Barhinder wondered if he would ever demonstrate when he dismounted a horse, because he had determined that, while it still made him nervous, he loved riding. Maybe, he thought as he slid out of his saddle to land clumsily on the street, Caesar will allow me to join Teispes as a bodyguard, quickly subduing the thought as he hurried behind Caesar. Once again, while there were two Pandyans standing at the double doors, they were attired differently than those spearmen and archers Barhinder had seen, actually wearing armor that appeared to be rectangles made of iron sewn to a leather vest, along with helmets that were more conical in shape than the Roman version, and they wore swords, although their primary weapon were the same kind of spears. And, as had occurred at the gate, they opened the doors, although Caesar did give them a nod of acknowledgement as he strode past with Barhinder walking as closely behind as he could manage, sensing that the guards were more curious about him than anything. There were a pair of men standing in the middle of the large reception room, dressed in the same kind of richly decorated but lightweight robes that Barhinder recognized as the material silk, which his mother had always looked longingly at when she walked by the bolts of the shiny fabric in the cloth merchant's section of the Bharuch market, but only wealthy people could afford it, and Barhinder's family was decidedly not.

"I need to speak to King Nedunj immediately," Caesar said, although he did return the bow the pair of men offered, and Barhinder saw the men exchange a glance, but while he could tell that one of them muttered in Tamil, he couldn't hear what was said.

To Caesar, one of the courtiers, with an expression of regret that was clearly counterfeit, answered in Greek that was barely understandable, "I am afraid that our King is currently occupied, Lord Caesar. He has issued instructions that he is not to be disturbed for any reason." He paused, then asked, "Is there a message I may relay to him?"

Barhinder hadn't learned to read Caesar well, yet he didn't need to, seeing the sudden narrowing of the Roman's eyes and knowing what it meant, but he was unprepared for Caesar to suddenly resume walking, pushing the pair of men aside, the second man who hadn't spoken shouting for the guards in Tamil.

Whether Caesar understood or not, he said over his shoulder to Barvistus, "Kill them only if you must, Barvistus."

He ascended the stairs without looking back, and it took Barhinder a moment to realize that he was expected to follow, and he had to take the stairs two at a time to reach Caesar's side when they reached the top. Nedunj was emerging from a room that was at the far end of a long hallway, drawn by the sounds, but to Barhinder, he didn't look as if he had been sleeping or engaged in something that precluded him meeting with Caesar.

"Your Highness," Caesar called out, not breaking his stride, "there's something you need to know, and it cannot wait!"

Nedunj regarded Caesar warily enough, but he didn't seem alarmed to Barhinder, and he stepped back to the door, opened it, and walked back into the room, clearly expecting Caesar to follow him. And, Barhinder understood, for Barhinder to follow Caesar, which he did, the odd thought crossing his mind of how his parents would feel if they could see him at that moment, talking to a king!

When he entered the room behind Caesar, Nedunj had already resumed his seat, but it wasn't a throne, and Barhinder noted that this clearly wasn't the audience room, which he did find somewhat disappointing. In fact, it looked like a normal room where someone might perform their work, provided that work involved writing, given the desk placed in the middle.

Caesar's version of a bow was to incline his head, which Nedunj was still getting accustomed to, yet he listened attentively as the Roman began, "Your Highness, young Gotra here," he indicated Barhinder, "has ridden nonstop from where Lord Alangudi and Legate Hirtius met with the officers commanding your army."

Before he could continue, Nedunj interrupted to ask, "Did you learn the name or names of these men?"

An expression that could have been chagrin flashed across Caesar's face, but he turned to Barhinder, who was happy that he knew the answer, "Lord Maran, Lord Vira, and Lord Sundara, Your Highness. But," he thought to add, "Lord Vira and Lord Sundara clearly defer to Lord Maran."

Nedunj listened, his face giving nothing away, then he finally said, "Maran is a good man, and while he was loyal to my father, he is loyal to our kingdom first. Vira?" He held out a hand and rocked it back and forth. "He goes with whichever wind blows the strongest, and Sundara is only concerned with how things impact him, so…"

Now it was Caesar who interrupted by asking Nedunj, "And what about Lord Alangudi?"

"What about him?" Nedunj replied, clearly disturbed, but now it was Barhinder's turn, Caesar turning to him, and he didn't hesitate to tell the young king of the conversation he had overheard. Nedunj was clearly attentive, and there was no mistaking the look of growing concern on his face, but Barhinder was certain that the king was unconvinced. When Barhinder, who had been speaking in Greek, paused, Nedunj asked in Tamil, "Why are you saying this?"

Caesar looked over at Barhinder sharply, unhappy at what sounded like a question in a tongue he didn't understand, while the youth actually paused before answering, suspecting that what Nedunj was asking had a deeper meaning.

Consequently, when he answered, he did so in Tamil. "Because, Your Highness, it is true. Every word I said was spoken by Lord Alangudi and Lord Maran. But," he hurried on before Nedunj could stop him, "am I correct in assuming that you are not just asking about that? That you are asking why I am standing here, with Caesar and Rome?"

Nedunj shifted in his chair, looking at the Bharuch youth with what might have been respect, and he shook his head, in the Pandyan manner. "Yes, that is what I am asking."

"What are you two saying? Why are you speaking in Tamil?" Caesar didn't say it loudly, but Barhinder's knees suddenly went weak, recognizing the menace there.

He wasn't sure how he managed, but Barhinder's voice sounded calm and collected as he answered, not in Greek but in Latin, so that Nedunj wouldn't understand, "Master Caesar, I am asking you to trust me. And I will tell you everything, later."

He held his breath, but he made certain to meet Caesar's gaze, feeling the cool appraisal that seemed to last forever before he gave an abrupt nod, and Barhinder was suddenly struck with a thought that was amusing later when he recalled it, how much of a catastrophe it could be if he got confused between the Bharuch and Roman custom and the Pandyan of nodding the head.

Barhinder returned his attention to Nedunj and resumed in Tamil, "I have seen what Rome can do, Your Highness. I watched their Legions destroy King Abhiraka's elephants, and it was horrible to see." This wasn't technically true, since Barhinder was unconscious for this part of the fight, but he felt no compunction in this tiny untruth. "No creature should suffer the way those animals did, and I happen to know that these Romans have even more of this substance that comes from Parthia than they had when they took my city." As Barhinder spoke, he was surprised at the sudden rush of bitter, helpless anger as he relived what was still the worst night of his life, but he forced this to the back of his mind. "And, Your

Highness," he continued, "while they did terrible things to my people in the first week, I learned that it was because of...internal matters, and is not how they normally treat the people they conquer. They are strict, but they are very fair." Barhinder paused once again, understanding that he was about to say something that might, at the very least, irritate the young king, yet as he had with Caesar, he looked Nedunj in the eye as he explained, "And they treat us better than we were treated by King Abhiraka, and I have learned enough about Rome that, while this is unusual, it is because of this man here. And," he concluded simply, "I do not believe his army can be defeated as long as he is alive."

Nedunj stared at Barhinder for a long moment, but when he spoke, it was to Caesar, in Greek, "Your translator has made a very persuasive case why I should trust you, Caesar." He stood up suddenly, and now his agitation was clear to see as he asked, "So what is your suggestion in how to deal with Alangudi and his treachery?"

Understanding this for what it was, Caesar didn't belabor the point, saying only, "I have a suggestion, Your Highness."

The tension felt by every man, both Pandyan and Roman, who was part of the returning army seemed increase with every mile. Hirtius, Silva, Teispes, and Achaemenes knew that they were in grave danger, especially once Alangudi came the first night on the march and abruptly informed them that they wouldn't be riding at the head of the army any longer, but roughly in the middle, just ahead of the elephants and behind the mounted archers. He had also broached the idea of disarming Silva and his men, but the Prefect bluntly informed him that the Pandyan would have to be willing to accept losing a fair number of men, and Alangudi, clearly angry, stalked away, but leaving them armed. From that moment forward, when Teispes and the translator spoke privately, they did so in their native tongue, while with Hirtius and Silva, they conversed in Latin. The topic of conversation was almost always the same; how they could manage to escape should the need arise, but the result was invariably the same.

"Some of us will get away, but with those archers, we'll be lucky if we don't lose more than half of us," Hirtius concluded glumly.

At midday on the fourth day, a halt was called, which wasn't unusual, but what was out of the ordinary was what happened next, because rather than rest, there was a sudden flurry of activity, starting with the elephants behind Silva and his men. In strict terms, it was both interesting and informative to watch as the line of wagons that was part of the "tail" of the Pandyan army were brought forward, and the process of armoring the animals began. It was, the Romans saw, a labor-intensive process, but the Pandyans clearly had much practice, as men from the infantry were involved in carrying the heavy blankets that took four men to carry, while other men were involved in the other major task, assembling the boxes in which the crew rode. As the Romans watched from under the shade of the ubiquitous banyan trees, they observed how the only men who actually approached each animal were the men who rode that particular elephant, yet even so, they could see that, much like humans, the elephants weren't uniform in their acceptance of the flurry of activity around them.

"I wonder how often some of those beasts decide they've had enough?" Silva mused as they sat together, leaning against one of the trees.

"I think," Teispes commented, pointing to one of the animals, "we are about to find out."

And, as they watched, one of the elephants began swinging its trunk, using it to swat one of the men who was trying to place the bronze cap on one of its tusks, sending the cap flying as the Pandyan staggered but kept his feet. This was the beginning of the trouble with this elephant, who was issuing a deep-throated noise that sounded like a human groan, seemingly ignoring the man they assumed was the one responsible for handling the animal, who was trying to soothe it by stroking the side of its massive head. Although this seemed to help, it proved to be temporary, as the Pandyan who had the job of capping its tusks approached again, and this time it wasn't just with its trunk that the elephant swatted the man, swinging his entire head so that its right tusk struck the man across his body, sending the Pandyan flying into the air and hurling him several paces away, where he landed heavily on his back.

"Maybe," Silva observed wryly, "it's not the elephant that's the problem. Maybe it's him."

This elicited some chuckles from his comrades, until the elephant, displaying an astonishing agility for a beast its size, suddenly spun about and, raising its trunk almost directly above its head, broke into a lumbering run, sending the men around him scrambling and shouting a warning that needed no translation. It was with a combination of fascination, concern, and a fair amount of horror that Silva, Teispes, and Achaemenes who, like the other

Romans in the area, leapt to their feet to watch as the elephant clearly targeted the Pandyan who had aroused his ire. The Pandyan, shouting in terror, obviously lost his head because he ran from the elephant in a straight line, not attempting to outmaneuver the animal, which meant that within a matter of fifty paces, the beast was on him. Lowering its head, the elephant used the flat plane of its skull to slam into the man, sending him flying to land, facedown in the dirt, then before he could react, the elephant lifted one huge foot, and with an unimaginable amount of force, brought it down in the center of the Pandyan's back. The impact was so tremendous that it instantly drove all the air from the man's lungs so that he couldn't even scream in protest at his death, and despite the distance from where they were standing, they clearly heard the wet, crunching sound of the bones in the Pandyan's body snapping as if they were a handful of twigs. Then, just as suddenly, it was over; the elephant made one trumpeting cry, which was instantly met by similar sounds from his fellow animals, then more slowly, it spun about and lumbered back to where its handler and the remaining crew were standing. The fact that, while there was certainly some excited chatter among the Pandyans, they didn't seem to be overly concerned that one of their comrades was now a bloody ruin indicated to Silva that this wasn't an uncommon occurrence.

"It acted like we do when we stomp on an insect," Achaemenes broke the silence, his tone one of an uncomfortable awe.

Teispes was no less disturbed, but he hid it better, commenting, "Apparently, the beast held a grudge against that man. Maybe," he shrugged as he sat back down against the tree, "the elephant saw a chance to get even."

Following the Parthian's lead, they settled back down to watch, and while there were some other incidents where one of the animals balked at what was clearly a tedious process for them, nothing nearly as dramatic occurred. The Romans also learned that preparing the elephants, culminating with the animals kneeling on their front legs to allow the crew and handler to mount, took a full Roman watch to achieve. Finally, when all was ready, before they resumed, there was a further shuffling, as the entire column made way for the elephants as the animals were sent to the front of the column. Standing next to their mounts, Hirtius, Silva, and the other two men watched in silence, each of them with their own grim thoughts at this sign that Alangudi was prepared for some sort of confrontation. Through a series of gestures, they were informed by the Pandyan they had deduced was one of the commanders of the horse archers that they were to fall into their spot in the column, but when they mounted and guided their animals to the position they had previously occupied, they saw that instead of the elephants behind them, the archers had divided into two separate groups, placing the Romans directly in the middle.

"So we're fucked no matter which way we go," Silva muttered, while Hirtius actually hesitated for a moment, feeling the eyes of the men under his command watching him, waiting for his command. It didn't take the Legate long to make the decision, and he said loudly enough in Latin for his men to hear, "Now's not the time, men! But be ready!"

Then he nudged his horse and guided him to fall in to their spot in the now moving column, with the Prefect, Teispes, Achaemenes, and the Decurion Pindarus pulling alongside him.

Emerging out into the bright sunlight, they finally realized where they were, barely a mile farther away from Muziris than where Barhinder had awoken a handful of days earlier. Because of their position in the column, they couldn't see that in their absence, Caesar had constructed a camp astride the road, and when they halted again, signaled by a horn call from the front of the column, they were prevented from moving from behind the obscuring elephants, infantry and archers as the group of Pandyans behind them immediately spread out around them. It was clearly a preplanned move, yet despite the fact that they couldn't see the actual encampment, Hirtius and the others immediately knew the cause, which the Legate summed up succinctly.

"Caesar is waiting."

Nedunj was standing next to Caesar on the dirt rampart of the eastern camp, watching as Alangudi, with Maran next to him, rode the two elephants leading the approaching column.

"Now," Caesar murmured to him, "we'll see what Lord Alangudi intends."

Caesar didn't elaborate, because there was no need; they had discussed the possibilities at length, and in the process, both men had learned a great deal about their new ally, particularly when it came to waging war. Although, Caesar reflected as they watched the column come to a halt well out of artillery range, he had been expecting that, like many tribal people, if Alangudi was intent on seizing the throne, it would likely begin with a direct challenge to Nedunj in one-on-one combat. However, Nedunj had been confident in his answer.

"While that is certainly our custom, Alangudi would never do that," he assured Caesar, and when Caesar asked why, the young king replied flatly, "Because he would be dead before he could count to ten. And," he looked Caesar in the eye, "he knows that."

This led to a lengthy discussion about what tactic Alangudi might employ, narrowing it down to one of three possibilities, and now both men were waiting to see if they were right with any of them. This was particularly important because they had agreed on a response for each of them, and they were different, ranging from the subtle to a display of the raw, naked power of the Roman Legions, particularly as it pertained to their ability to defeat the Pandyans' most potent weapon. Standing with the pair was every senior officer of Caesar's army; Pollio, Volusenus, and every Primus Pilus save Crispus, he and his Legion not arriving from Honnavar yet. Actually, as far as Nedunj knew, that town was still occupied by the Romans, which was something he had intended to broach, but this matter with the possibility of treachery by Alangudi had taken precedence. The fact that, standing no more than a dozen paces from the young king was the huge Roman who he had wanted a chance to kill not long before was still something that Nedunj was getting used to, although, while he would only admit it to himself, once he was in closer proximity to this Roman he now knew was named Titus Pullus, he wondered what he had been thinking, understanding that, as skilled as he may have been, he would have stood no chance against the man. Forcing himself to think like a king, Nedunj had been reminded of the Bharuch youth Gotra, when he had explained why he had chosen to stand with Rome, and despite some deeply rooted feelings about the situation in which he found himself, he had come to the same conclusion; it was better to stand with Caesar, and Rome, than against him, at least for this moment and the immediate future. Like every other monarch in India before the arrival of Rome in his kingdom, Nedunj had certainly heard about this man Caesar, and his supposedly invincible Legions, but just as Peithon of Pattala, then Abhiraka of Bharuch, Nedunj now understood that there was a vast difference between an abstract reality and a tangible one, in the form of these Romans who had stormed ashore and absorbed as much punishment as Nedunj could devise, yet still kept coming. He was proud of how his men had fought, and while Caesar had never said as much, Nedunj was certain that one reason why Caesar proposed this alliance was in recognition of that fact. And now, he had to decide what to do about Alangudi, but it was up to the man who had been his closest adviser, and his friend, to make the first move.

Which, it seemed for an increasingly long and tense stretch of time, was to simply sit there, still in their column, but too far away for Nedunj to determine exactly what was going on. As far as he could tell, there was no gesticulating or anything that would indicate that Maran and Alangudi were in some sort of discussion or dispute, besides which Nedunj felt certain that whatever they had planned would have been agreed upon before this moment. Or, he wondered, is Maran having second thoughts? It was possible, he realized, that it might actually be Alangudi who was rethinking whatever action he had intended to take, but he didn't believe that; it simply wasn't in Alangudi's nature to reconsider matters once he had made a decision.

Caesar broke the silence, echoing Nedunj's thoughts by saying, "It appears that Lord Alangudi is reconsidering."

"I doubt it," Nedunj replied. "If that's happening, it's because of Maran, not Alangudi."

Even as he was finishing, at last there was some movement, and within a span of perhaps a dozen heartbeats, both Caesar and Nedunj, along with the rest of the Romans who were in position to see, learned what Alangudi intended. At least, Nedunj thought as the elephants arrayed behind the two Pandyan lords began fanning out in a long line on either side, what he wants us to think he intends. As the animals lumbered into what would become a triple line, from behind them, men on foot came running to array themselves across the road a short distance in front of the leading line of elephants. These men were identical in their equipment as the spearmen who had come close to stopping the Romans on the beach, but now that Nedunj had seen the Roman Legionaries up close, he had no illusions that it was just their armor that made them superior, but their training and discipline. The one thing that he had persuaded Caesar to share with him was the mystery of the Roman javelin, and while he was clearly reluctant, the Roman had brought one to show him. It was, Nedunj had to acknowledge, an ingenious design, one where even if it didn't strike a man down, it rendered his protection useless because of the soft metal shaft and the wooden pin that was actually designed to shear off, something that Nedunj had never even heard of before. And, if Alangudi went ahead with this madness, those spearmen would be slaughtered, but it was the elephants he was most concerned about, especially given his agreement with Caesar.

Nedunj suddenly noticed something, asking aloud, "Where are the mounted archers? Using the formation that Alangudi is using, they should be on each wing."

"If I had to guess, Your Highness," Caesar replied, his eyes never leaving the Pandyan host, "they are probably in a position where they can cut down Legate Hirtius, Prefect Silva, and our men who accompanied your Lord."

As soon as Caesar said it, Nedunj was certain this was the case, but before he could comment on it, finally, there was movement in the direction of the camp, which prompted Caesar to turn to the young king.

"Your Highness, it's time for our demonstration." Nedunj had expected this, but he was completely unprepared for Caesar to say, "Would you give the command, Your Highness?"

Startled, Nedunj replied, "I do not know Latin, Caesar!"

"You may give it in Greek," Caesar assured him. "My men will understand."

What Caesar didn't tell Nedunj was that he had planned this beforehand, and alerted the *immunes* manning the scorpions arrayed on the rampart, the only rankers visible to the Pandyans across from them, that the moment Nedunj said anything loud enough for them to hear, they were to take it as the command to begin. As far as what the demonstration actually was, it had actually indirectly come from Pullus when, in the aftermath of the fall of Bharuch, the Primus Pilus had described how his men had used scorpion bolts wrapped in rags soaked in naphtha, loosing them at a series of jars that they had placed, creating a line of fire that enabled the Equestrians to funnel the elephants sent out by Abhiraka and led by Memmon into a more manageable area where they could be assaulted from more than one side. Caesar had no desire to hurt these animals now, nor the men of the Pandyan forces, although he was less concerned with them than the elephants.

Nedunj hesitated, looking embarrassed, but it was Caesar who was chagrined, realizing that the king would have no idea what to say, and he added quickly, "Just say, 'prepare to loose'. Then, when they are ready, they will look this way, and you say, 'Loose.' The rest," he finished, "will be done by them."

Nedunj actually caught himself, remembering to nod, which felt decidedly odd to him, but he turned and, just short of a full bellow, commanded in Greek, "Prepare to loose!"

What happened then was both fascinating to the Pandyan king, and it was also another stark reminder of just how foolish it was for anyone, no matter what size of their army, to think that they could easily defeat these people. As a precaution, the strips of cloth that had already been soaked in naphtha were laid out on the inner edge of the rampart, and Nedunj watched as one Roman carefully wrapped the strip around what looked to him like a large arrow, but with leather fletching instead of one made with feathers. Then, surprisingly to Nedunj, the first Roman handed the arrow to a second man, who walked quickly across to what the Pandyan now knew were called scorpions, dropping the arrow into the groove cut in the body of the weapon but rather than stand there, the second Roman then moved quickly back across the rampart.

Caesar, seeing Nedunj's interest, explained, "We learned the hard way that naphtha is so volatile that, when a spark is struck anywhere around it, the substance can ignite. We believe it's because of the fumes that it gives off. And," he finished grimly, "we lost many men who had done what those two did, wrapping the bolt and putting it on the scorpion because the naphtha had gotten on their hands and arms."

Even as Caesar was speaking, the third *immune* of what was for this demonstration a four-man crew instead of the normal three, struck the flint, although because of the daylight it wasn't visible. What was impossible to miss was what happened next; an eruption of flame that Nedunj's eye barely registered when the fourth man, and the chief of the crew, pulled, not yanked, the cord that released the torsion rope. Faster than his eye could track, the first bolt shot out and away from the rampart, followed in quick succession by a second, third, fourth, and ending with a fifth from each scorpion arrayed down the rampart. And, as with everything Caesar prepared, these crews had practiced enough that one after another, the pots of naphtha that were hidden from the view of anyone approaching from the north exploded along a line that would block the center of the Pandyan line. Even before the fifth and final pot exploded in a burst of roiling flame and black smoke, the elephants bearing Alangudi and Maran, along with a half-dozen others had already reacted, most of them trumpeting in alarm, and despite being more than a hundred paces away from the flames, every animal began backing away, while the elephant on Maran's side opposite from Alangudi reared onto its two massive legs, sending the occupants of the box flying into the air.

"It would have been better at night," Caesar commented as if they were speaking on the weather, but his eyes never left the scene before them, watching the handlers struggle to get their animals under control. Then, as the elephants subsided somewhat, willing to at least stand their ground, although their ears were flapping back and forth, which even the Romans had learned was a sign of their agitation, Caesar asked Nedunj, "Do you think we need to offer another demonstration, Your Highness?" When Nedunj looked up at him quizzically, Caesar turned inward, and indicated the line of *ballistae* that had been placed deeper in the camp than normal. "With these, we can hurl pots of naphtha that will land fifty paces closer to where they're standing right now."

Nedunj turned back to face outward, and he relaxed slightly, pointing as he said, "I do not believe that is necessary, Caesar."

Caesar paused to signal to the *immune* standing next to the first *ballista* to stand down, then faced back around to see Alangudi thrusting a large square of cloth affixed to a spear up above his head, waving it back and forth.

"At least they came prepared to offer a truce," Caesar commented, nodding to Pollio, who picked up the siege spear with the white bandage they had ready, then thrust it aloft and imitated Alangudi's gesture.

Nedunj was certainly relieved, but he also knew that this wasn't settled, and he said as much. "Now I want to hear what Alangudi has to say in his defense."

Seeing the Roman response, the elephants bearing Alangudi and Maran knelt, the two Pandyan lords hopped down, and there was a slight delay, which was explained when two men appeared leading a pair of horses. Once they were mounted, the pair approached at a walk, and there was a further delay when Alangudi's horse balked as it approached the flaming patches of ground, from which issued the thick black smoke that was a feature of burning naphtha.

Guiding their animals the long way around, they returned to the road, but when they got within a hundred paces, before Nedunj could say anything, Caesar shouted in Greek, "That is far enough for the moment!"

The pair stopped, glancing at each other, but it was Alangudi who shouted back, "Why are you stopping us this far away, Roman? Do you expect us to shout at each other?"

"No," Caesar assured them. Then he cupped his hands to make sure there was no misunderstanding, "I am giving you to the count of one hundred to release my men and allow them to return to their comrades!"

Nedunj spun to stare at Caesar; the Roman hadn't said anything about this being a condition for a truce, but while he was angry, it was more at himself. Of course, he thought bitterly, I should have foreseen that, because it's something I'd do. He turned back without saying anything to watch Maran and Alangudi apparently arguing about what to do.

"If you do not comply," Caesar called out, still using his hands to amplify his voice, "then there is no truce! And," somehow, he managed to harden his tone, "we will consider you a hostile force, and both of you will be cut down before you get a hundred paces!"

"Are you willing to accept this, Prince Nedunj?" Alangudi shouted back, clearly enraged. "You will let this foreigner, this *Roman,* threaten me and Lord Maran?"

And, just that quickly, Nedunj fully believed what he had been told, because of one word, and in his anger, Alangudi almost certainly sealed his fate.

It was with an effort, but Nedunj kept his voice controlled as he shouted back, "Do as Caesar says, Alangudi! Only then will we continue this talk!"

Alangudi didn't respond, nor did he move for several heartbeats, then with an abrupt and savage yank on his horse's head, he spun around and went at the gallop back to where the Pandyan host was waiting. Meanwhile, Nedunj studied Maran intently, wishing that he was closer to the man to read his face, but there was nothing in his demeanor that betrayed his thoughts one way or another. While it took longer than the count to one hundred that Caesar had demanded, they saw the movement beyond the spearmen and elephants first, materializing into a column of mounted men, moving at the canter with Alangudi at its head, although he drew to a stop next to Maran as Hirtius, with Silva, Teispes and Achaemenes in the first rank, the Romans returned to their comrades, entering through the gate, with Decurion Pindarus taking command of the rest of the men while Hirtius and Silva turned to draw up behind the part of the rampart occupied by Caesar and the king. The Legate and Prefect strode up the dirt rampart and saluted Caesar, while Teispes paused to talk with Gundomir, leaving Achaemenes momentarily to his own devices. This didn't last long, as the Parthian translator heard someone call his name and turned to see Barhinder, a broad smile on his face, trotting from the direction of the *praetorium.*

"I heard you were coming in," Barhinder spoke in Sanskrit, knowing that Achaemenes was more comfortable with that than Tamil, although it had improved. "I'm happy to see you and Teispes made it back!"

"I was not sure for a bit," Achaemenes admitted honestly. "They had us surrounded with their archers, and I was worried that they would turn us into a pincushion!"

This made Barhinder laugh, and he clapped his companion on

the shoulder, then by unspoken consent, they turned their attention to what was taking place up on the rampart.

"What do you think?" Barhinder asked in a low voice. "Do you think the king believed what I told him?"

"You would know better than I would," Achaemenes countered. Then, realizing how his words might be interpreted, he grinned at Barhinder and said, "But we're about to find out."

They both learned quickly that this was truer than they realized when Caesar, glancing over his shoulder, saw the pair, and he called to them both.

"Both of you come up here. You may be needed."

Pullus understood that what was taking place was important; indeed, it was crucial for not just Caesar's plans, but for the army as well, yet it didn't change the fact that he was hot and he was bored. Standing on the rampart like a statue, only there to provide this Pandyan traitor with a visible representation of his Legion, he was flanked by Spurius and Balbinus, who was still angry about what had occurred with his Legion at the hands of the young king. Privately, Pullus had some concerns about Balbinus, who, while he wasn't as close to the 12th's Primus Pilus as he was to Spurius, he still considered a friend. He certainly sympathized; there was probably no worse fate for a Centurion, particularly a Primus Pilus to be forced to watch the men under his command take punishment without being able to retaliate, and while he hadn't gone into detail about it, Pullus had gleaned that Balbinus felt some guilt about his decision to order his men into the water, unaware that the Pandyan king had spearmen posted across the river at the bend to support the hidden artillery. And now, here he was, just paces away from the man he knew was the architect of that event but who was also supposedly now an ally. Pullus and Spurius had only had a moment to hold a muttered conversation out of their friend's earshot, but the Primus Pilus of the 3rd shared the same opinion, that Balbinus was secretly hoping this new agreement would fall apart. Judging from the tension at this moment, Pullus thought it was certainly a possibility, but like his counterparts, he was consigned to just witnessing what was taking place. Once Silva and his men had been released, as Nedunj had expected, the mounted archers, still in two groups, had arrayed themselves out on the wings, another reason Pullus felt pessimistic that this would be resolved peacefully. Not that he was worried if it came to combat, because for once, his Equestrians were safely out of the fight, in the camp on the southern bank of the river, where they had been occupied in the previous days with the inevitable reshuffling and promotions that were required after suffering heavy losses. This day, it would fall on the shoulders of the 8th, the 6th, the 28th, and the 30th, who were in the eastern camp, should matters reach that point. Alangudi and the other Pandyan whose name Pullus didn't know, were now allowed to approach so that the exchange didn't have to be shouted, but while he couldn't understand Nedunj since he was speaking in Tamil, there was no mistaking the cold anger in his voice. Nedunj showed a flicker of irritation at the appearance of Barhinder and Achaemenes, but he wasn't surprised, and he ignored their presence as he called down, not to Alangudi, but to Maran.

"Lord Maran, what did Lord Alangudi tell you? What did he say my message was?"

Maran's face didn't change expression, and he answered readily, "That you have reached an agreement with these…Romans, and that we were to return home, my King."

Nedunj was actually watching Alangudi more closely than Maran, and he saw the flicker of surprise cross his councilor's face when Maran called him "king" and not "prince," as Alangudi had. At the time, he had wondered if this was simply a slip of the tongue on Alangudi's part; he hadn't been king long, after all, so it was conceivable, but the councilor's reaction told Nedunj differently.

"And?" Nedunj pressed. "Was there anything else that he said, Lord Maran? Something that your *king* should know?"

Although Maran's expression didn't change, he did shift in his saddle a bit, twisting slightly to glance over at Alangudi. There was perhaps a heartbeat of silence, then in a subtle but unmistakable manner, Maran turned back, away from Alangudi as he answered, "That you had successfully repelled these Romans, yet you chose to enter into a pact with them anyway."

Because Barhinder was whispering to Caesar, Nedunj found it difficult to concentrate on what Maran was saying, yet even so, there was nothing overtly objectionable in what Maran claimed Alangudi had said. It was, he conceded, essentially the truth, although in his bones, he knew that while he had slowed the Romans, he hadn't stopped them.

"Who do you serve, Maran?" he asked suddenly, completely on an impulse, clearly surprising the other man.

"I serve Pandya, my King," Maran said cautiously, forcing Nedunj to mask his disappointment, realizing that he had been hoping for an open declaration of loyalty to him, not to Pandya.

"And how do I know what that means, Maran?" Nedunj countered. Before he could respond, Nedunj shifted his attention away from Maran to address Alangudi. "What do you have to say for yourself, Alangudi? Why did you come here and array *my* army as if you intended to attack?"

"I was simply being cautious, my King!" Alangudi protested. "I had nothing else in mind, I swear it!" Pointing up to Caesar, he insisted, "We do *not* know if he can be trusted!"

Nedunj actually waited, wanting Gotra to translate his councilor's words, but once he did, contrary to his expectation, Caesar clearly wasn't offended, and in fact, turned to Nedunj and said in Greek, "Lord Alangudi is correct, Your Highness. We have not known each other long, and I can certainly understand why he would be suspicious." His voice altered a fraction, but it wasn't lost on Nedunj as he added, "But Alangudi is not King of Pandya. You are. And you must decide who to trust."

This was obviously true, yet it didn't make Nedunj feel better, and not for the first time, he experienced what he swore was an almost overwhelming burden that was so intense, it actually felt as if an invisible force was pressing down on his shoulders.

Turning back to Maran, Nedunj asked, "What say you, Lord Maran? Who should I trust?"

"My King," Maran replied, unknowingly echoing Caesar, "I cannot tell you who can trust." He paused, then added, "But I *can* tell you who you *cannot* trust."

Nobody, not Nedunj, Caesar, or even Pullus saw it coming, although he had idly noticed that as the Pandyans were jabbering at each other, the horse of Alangudi's counterpart had sidestepped perhaps a pace closer to the king's councilor, but this sort of thing happened all the time, especially when tensions were running high and the animal felt that tension from their rider. He, and everyone watching, only learned this had been intentional on Maran's part when, with one smooth, continuous motion, the Pandyan drew his sword, brought it up above his horse's head and swung his arm in a backhand stroke that struck Alangudi right in the middle of the lump all men have in their throat, the blade barely slowing as it severed through muscle and bone, sending Alangudi's head tumbling up and forward into the air in a shower of blood before falling to strike his horse on its head, causing it to react, undoubtedly further disturbed by the smell of blood. Rearing, it sent Alangudi's corpse flying, still spurting blood from the stump of his neck, to land with a dull, meaty thud, limbs flailing during its short trip to the hard-packed dirt as the horse, four hooves now on the ground, bolted by executing a tight turn to go galloping back towards where the rest of the army was waiting. For a long span of heartbeats, the only sound was the drumming hoofbeats, every witness shocked to their core, even men like Pullus who were accustomed to scenes of sudden, violent death, and when he glanced over at Caesar, the Primus Pilus was rewarded with a sight that was rarely if ever seen, his general standing as open-mouthed and in shock as everyone else.

The only man who didn't seem to be frozen in place was Maran, who calmly used a corner of his cloak to wipe his blade clean, then looked up at Nedunj and said calmly, "You could not trust Alangudi, my King. He would have been a danger to you as long as he lived." Then, he dismounted and walked to the edge of the ditch, directly in front of Nedunj, knelt, and offered his now-clean blade up in two hands as he said, "But I am loyal to Pandya, which means I am loyal to my King, King Nedunj."

Crispus and the 22nd Legion arrived at Muziris the next day, but on foot and not by ship, and it was learned that Caesar, having received word of his Primus Pilus' decision to vacate Honnavar by Liburnian, had sent that ship back to intercept the small fleet, ordering them to heave to and remain in place until Alangudi and the Pandyan army had passed. Once the *turma* sent ashore reported this had happened, the Legion unloaded and marched the short distance inland to the road leading south to Muziris, shadowing the Pandyans. It never occurred to Alangudi, or Maran for that matter, to set a rearguard, and it was just an example of how Caesar seemingly thought of everything. Now, with the army that had departed Bharuch back together, it was time for Caesar to discuss what came next.

"We're going to be wintering in two locations this year," he informed the officers the next night, in the *praetorium* in the eastern camp. Behind him was a new map, but one that was focused on a section of the Pseudostoma, where Muziris was on the left side of the map, and another city was on the opposite side and slightly above the first. "Obviously, one of those spots will be here, but," he pointed to the city to the west, also on the river, "the other will be Karoura, which is the Pandyan capital, and where King Nedunj will be returning." Returning his attention to the men, he continued, "I've decided that those Legions who suffered the highest casualties will be with me in Karoura, where a *dilectus* will be held as part of the agreement with King Nedunj." Since the Primi Pili had already been forewarned by their respective spies in the *praetorium*, there was virtually no reaction to this, which Caesar ignored, despite how much it irritated him. Let's see, he thought with some amusement, if their little birds told them this. "For the Legions who remain here in Muziris, for those of you who are thinking that you'll have a slack winter, put that out of your mind." As he hoped, the smug grins on the faces of men like Flaminius, Clustuminus, and Felix vanished as they exchanged uneasy glances, while Caesar continued, "You'll have two main tasks to keep your men busy. The first will be to help fix those ships that can be repaired, replace those that we've either lost, or are deemed unsalvageable, and building a new type of vessel that will serve us in the future."

Pullus was the only Primus Pilus who, thanks to Diocles, knew what was coming, and while it had been difficult, he had kept it to himself, but now he couldn't fight his own grin spreading across his face, which caused the others to scowl at him suspiciously, each of them knowing how adept Pullus' Greek was at extracting information.

"Well, Pullus," Caesar said cuttingly, "you seem very pleased with yourself. Would you care to explain why?"

"No, Caesar," Pullus answered cheerfully. "I'll let you do it."

What Pullus didn't know was that Caesar had entertained that very idea, allowing Pullus to break the news that he knew would cause an uproar, and he realized ruefully that his Primus Pilus had been aware of that.

I owe you one, Pullus, he thought as he said aloud, "The reason that you'll be constructing a ship based on a new design is related to the second task I have for you." Taking a breath, he said, "The 6th, 8th, 28th, and 30th Legions will be training to work with the armored elephants of Pandya that King Nedunj will be loaning us."

That was the last quiet moment of the meeting, one that was destined to last for another watch, making Pullus even happier that he had avoided allowing Caesar to drop him in the *cac*, especially since he had some sympathy for his fellow Primi Pili. Obviously, Batius and his boys in the 5th would have been a better choice, but they were still in Bharuch, and he had no idea when and if those three Legions would be reunited with the army. Since he wasn't directly involved, Pullus tried to shut out the argument raging inside Caesar's office by thinking about Bharuch, wondering how Hyppolita was, and whether she was mourning the death of her husband. So absorbed was he in his thoughts that he barely noticed that, at last, Caesar called the meeting to an end by simply declaring that his decision was final, although when the others came to their feet, he did the same.

"Pullus, stay behind. We need to talk."

Again? Pullus just managed to contain his groan and to control his expression when he walked back to where Caesar was leaning against his desk. Unusually, instead of holding their conversation there, Caesar walked over to the small round table, telling Pullus to drag one of the stools over to join him. Bemused, Pullus naturally complied, but then he saw Apollodorus appear carrying a jug and two cups, and his suspicion grew that, whatever this was about, he wouldn't care for it. Then, when he accepted the cup from Caesar's secretary, tasted that it was wine and immediately identified it as a Falernian, which had to be worth its weight in gold this far from home, Pullus was certain he knew what was coming.

"I," Caesar began, "have a decision to make, Pullus, and I need your help in making it."

Just as quickly as he had been certain, Pullus was suddenly confused, but he answered honestly, "I'll do what I can to help, Caesar."

"I know you will," Caesar answered. Then, he paused to take a sip, then said, "It has to do with Bharuch."

Pullus immediately was back where he started, although he had been expecting to hear Hyppolita's name, so he asked cautiously, "What about Bharuch?"

"Can I trust Queen Hyppolita?" Caesar asked frankly. "If I make the same arrangement with her that I've made with King Nedunj and King Peithon, will she be content with that? Or will she use our absence to make mischief?"

"Make mischief?" Pullus repeated with a frown. "Make mischief about what, exactly? There's three Legions there, Caesar. Even if she wanted to, she's too clever to try anything like that."

"And," Caesar asked quietly, "if the Legions weren't there?"

This caused Pullus to think for a moment, but he could only shrug.

Deciding to try something different, Caesar got up and went to his desk, picking up a furled map that he brought back and spread out, and Pullus saw that it was essentially a miniature version of the large map of all that Caesar had conquered, thanks to the strong right arms of Titus Pullus and his comrades.

"Here, it might make it easier to see this way," Caesar explained. Starting at the new port of Caesarea, he pointed to the row of dots that were spaced evenly along the curving coast that eventually joined India with Rome's newest province, "As you can see, we've created supply ports, all of them located at strategic points, along the coast and down to Harmozeia. Pattala is next to useless for our purposes; it's too far inland and, frankly, it wasn't nearly as prosperous as I expected. But," he moved his finger down to the dot that was, on a map of this scale, less than a small finger's width from the line designating the western coast of India, "Bharuch is only twenty miles inland, and it's also at an important junction of the trade routes that are part of the Silk Road, but more than that, it serves as a conduit to the spices that are the main source of wealth here in Pandya." Shaking his head, Caesar said emphatically, "We must keep Bharuch under our control, Pullus, but we're already spread thin. At most, I'd keep a Legion there, although ideally, I'd like to be able to have auxiliaries serve as the garrison."

"Auxiliaries from where?" Pullus asked. "Haven't you already allocated those Parthians you returned with to other duties?"

"Yes, I have," Caesar admitted. "But I still would rather have auxiliaries there than giving up a Legion, but I'll only consider that *if* I can trust your Queen."

"*My* Queen?" Pullus protested. "Why do you call her my Queen?"

Pullus didn't realize it, but he had handed Caesar the opening he needed, and he didn't hesitate.

"I think you know why I call her that, Pullus."

Feeling the sudden stirring of anger, Pullus also understood that this was precisely what Caesar was looking for, a sign that he was emotionally attached to the Queen of Bharuch, and he managed to keep his tone controlled.

"No, Caesar," Pullus answered coldly, looking Caesar in the eye as he subtly but unmistakably drew his shoulders back, having long before learned that, no matter who it was he was facing, he was an imposing figure when he emphasized his size. "Explain to me why you refer to her that way."

As Pullus hoped, Caesar was uneasy, yet he was determined not to show it, and for a long moment the pair glared at each other, neither looking away until, exhaling slightly, Caesar said, "Pollio told me that you escorted her around the palace grounds once a day. Which," he held up a hand, "was a good thing you did, Pullus. I only had that one conversation with her before I…left, but I'm afraid she would have been a bit much for Pollio to handle, or Hirtius for that matter. However," his tone altered slightly as he admonished, "please don't play me for a fool, Pullus. There is no way that you spent that much time together without developing a...bond with the woman. The truth is that you know her better than any other Roman." This, Pullus knew, was something he couldn't argue, so he set aside the swirl of feelings, and thought about it for a long moment before he answered, "She's devoted to her husband, Caesar. Or," he amended, surprised at the stab of pain at his own words, "she was. But she also is pragmatic, and more than anything, she wants her subjects to be happy with their lot. It took her completely by surprise to see how, once things calmed down, we treated her people. And," he allowed, "I think it also made her think about how her husband had been treating them before." Pullus paused, then, hating himself for what he was about to do, he said, "And as long as you have control of her children? She can be trusted."